THE
HALL OF FAME

Here are twenty-six of the best science fiction stories ever written, chosen by those who know better than anyone what the criteria should be —the Science Fiction Writers of America.

The whole breadth and depth of the field are richly represented—such authors as Bradbury, Clarke, Heinlein, Sturgeon, and such classic tales as Asimov's "Nightfall," Keyes' "Flowers for Algernon," Blish's "Surface Tension," and Zelazny's "A Rose for Ecclesiastes."

It has accomplished magnificently what the Science Fiction Writers of America set out to do— to make a basic one-volume library of the short works of the most exciting form of fiction being written in our time!

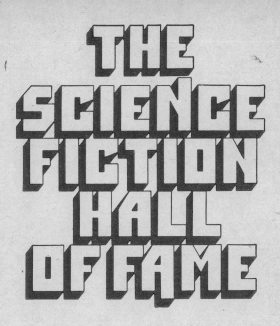

THE SCIENCE FICTION HALL OF FAME

The Greatest
Science Fiction Stories
of All Time
Edited by Robert Silverberg
Chosen by the Members of
The Science Fiction Writers of America

 AVON
PUBLISHERS OF BARD, CAMELOT AND DISCUS BOOKS

AVON BOOKS
A division of
The Hearst Corporation
959 Eighth Avenue
New York, New York 10019

First Avon Printing, July, 1971
Thirteenth Printing

AVON TRADEMARK REG. U.S. PAT. OFF. AND
FOREIGN COUNTRIES, REGISTERED TRADEMARK—
MARCA REGISTRADA, HECHO EN CHICAGO, U.S.A.

Printed in the U.S.A.

ACKNOWLEDGMENTS

A Martian Odyssey, by Stanley G. Weinbaum, copyright 1934 by Continental Publications, Inc. Reprinted by permission of Forrest J. Ackerman on behalf of the author's estate.

Twilight, by John W. Campbell, copyright 1934 by Street & Smith Publications, Inc. Reprinted by permission of the author's agents, Scott Meredith Literary Agency, Inc.

Helen O'Loy, by Lester del Rey, copyright 1938 by Street & Smith Publications, Inc. Reprinted by permission of the author's agents, Scott Meredith Literary Agency, Inc.

The Roads Must Roll, by Robert A. Heinlein, copyright 1940 by Street & Smith Publications, Inc. Copyright renewed 1967 by Robert A. Heinlein. Reprinted by permission of the author and his agent, Lurton Blassingame.

Microcosmic God, by Theodore Sturgeon, copyright 1941 by Street & Smith Publications, Inc. Reprinted by permission of the author and his agent, Robert P. Mills, Ltd.

Nightfall, by Isaac Asimov, copyright 1941 by Street & Smith Publications, Inc. Copyright renewed 1968 by Isaac Asimov. Reprinted by permission of the author.

The Weapon Shop, by A. E. van Vogt, copyright 1942 by Street & Smith Publications, Inc. Reprinted by permission of the author's agent, Forrest J. Ackerman.

Mimsy Were the Borogoves, by Lewis Padgett, copyright 1943 by Street & Smith Publications, Inc. Reprinted by permission of Harold Matson Company, Inc.

Huddling Place, by Clifford D. Simak, copyright 1944 by Street & Smith Publications, Inc. Reprinted by permission of the author and his agent, Robert P. Mills, Ltd.

Arena, by Fredric Brown, copyright 1944 by Street & Smith Publications, Inc. Reprinted by permission of the author's agents, Scott Meredith Literary Agency, Inc.

First Contact, by Murray Leinster, copyright 1945 by Street & Smith Publications, Inc. Reprinted by permission of Scott Meredith Literary Agency, Inc.

That Only a Mother, by Judith Merril, copyright 1948 by Street & Smith Publications, Inc. Reprinted by permission of the author.

CONTENTS

INTRODUCTION

This is as nearly definitive an anthology of modern science fiction stories as is likely to be compiled for quite some time. Its contents were chosen by vote of the membership of the Science Fiction Writers of America, an organization of some three hundred professional writers whose roster includes virtually everyone now living who has ever had science fiction published in the United States. The book you now hold represents the considered verdict of those who themselves have shaped science fiction—a roster of outstanding stories selected by people who know more intimately than any others what the criteria for excellence in science fiction should be.

SFWA—The Science Fiction Writers of America—was founded in 1965 "to inform science fiction writers on matters of professional interest, to promote their professional welfare, and to help them deal effectively with publishers, agents, editors, and anthologists." Though other special writers' organizations, such as the Mystery Writers of America and the Western Writers of America, had come into existence long before, all previous attempts to create a professional science fiction writers' group had been abortive. However—thanks in large measure to the energy and devotion of the first president of SFWA, Damon Knight, and its first secretary-treasurer, Lloyd Biggle—all but a few writers in this notoriously individualistic field quickly joined. For greater cohesiveness, membership was limited to writers whose work had appeared in the United States, but no restrictions were placed on a writer's own residence or citizenship. Thus SFWA has a large British contingent as well as members from Australia, Canada, and several other Commonwealth countries.

In 1966 SFWA held the first of its annual awards banquets, at which handsome trophies nicknamed Nebulas were presented to the authors of 1965's outstanding science fiction stories, as chosen by vote of the membership. These awards have been presented in each subsequent year in four categories: short story, novelet, novella, and novel.

During my term of office (1967–68) as SFWA's second president, it was decided to extend the concept of awards retroactively into the period prior to SFWA's inception. Members would be asked to nominate and vote for the best science fiction stories of the era ending on December 31, 1964: that is, the period up to the point covered by the Nebula awards. No trophies would be given, but the stories chosen would be republished in a showcase anthology spanning several volumes—the Science Fiction Hall of Fame.

This is the first of those anthologies. It embraces the categories of short story and novelet; arbitrarily, stories over 15,000 words in length were excluded from nomination and reserved for consideration in the volumes to come. Nominations remained open for more than a year, during which time a significant proportion of the membership suggested favorite stories, each writer giving no consideration to his own work. Eventually, 132 stories by seventy-six different writers found places on the final ballot. Then the members of SFWA were asked to choose ten stories from this list. They were limited to the choice of one story by any author, and were asked to keep historical perspective in mind. That is, it was hoped that they would distribute their votes in such a way as to give representation to each of the evolutionary stages of modern science fiction. (The stories on the ballot had originally been published between 1929 and 1964.)

As editor of the book, I exercised certain limited prerogatives of selection after the counting of the votes. No editorial discretion whatever was invoked upon the fifteen most popular stories as shown by the vote tally; their inclusion in the book was regarded as obligatory. Those fifteen, in order of the number of votes they received, were:

1. *Nightfall*, Isaac Asimov
2. *A Martian Odyssey*, Stanley G. Weinbaum

(Arthur C. Clarke's *The Star* would have been the fifteenth story on this list if it had not been disqualified by the presence of another Clarke story in eleventh place. Clarke was the only writer to place two stories in the top fifteen, although both Robert A. Heinlein and Ray Bradbury had two stories in the top twenty.)

Beyond the first fifteen, some selectivity had to be imposed to keep the book from growing to infinite length. As far as possible, I attempted to follow the dictates of the tallied vote, eliminating only those stories whose authors were represented by a story higher on the list. But there were some obvious injustices requiring remedies. One important and highly respected author had had four stories on the original ballot, including two from the same cycle. As a result of this competition with himself, no one of his stories finished within the top twenty, although the aggregate of his vote placed him well up among the leaders. Eliminating a man whose career had been so distinguished from a book of this nature seemed improper; and so I gave preference to one of his four stories over that of another writer whose only nominated piece had finished slightly higher on the list. In this case recognition of an entire body of work was deemed more important than recognition of a single story.

In another instance, two of a writer's stories made the second fifteen, one vote apart; but the story with the higher number of votes was not the story that the writer himself wished to see included in the book. I chose to regard the one-vote differential as statistically insignificant, and reversed the order of finish of that writer's stories so that I might use the one that he (and I) regarded as superior.

There were several other minor modifications of this sort, made necessary by considerations of length, balance, and over-all career contributions. Strictly speaking, then, the table of contents of the present anthology does not reflect a rigid tally of the SFWA vote. Rather, it offers the fifteen stories of the pre-1965 period that were selected as best by the SFWA, plus all but a few of the second fifteen. I regret the necessities of publishing reality that forced me to omit some of the stories in that second fifteen, amounting to over 50,000 words of fiction; but in view of the need to keep the book within manageable size I think it does offer a definitive group of stories by the writers who have done most to give form and substance to modern science fiction—a basic one-volume library of the short science fiction story.

ROBERT SILVERBERG

A MARTIAN ODYSSEY

by Stanley G. Weinbaum

Jarvis stretched himself as luxuriously as he could in the cramped general quarters of the *Ares*.

"Air you can breathe!" he exulted. "It feels as thick as soup after the thin stuff out there!" He nodded at the Martian landscape stretching flat and desolate in the light of the nearer moon, beyond the glass of the port.

The other three stared at him sympathetically—Putz, the engineer, Leroy, the biologist, and Harrison, the astronomer and captain of the expedition. Dick Jarvis was chemist of the famous crew, the *Ares* expedition, first human beings to set foot on the mysterious neighbor of the earth, the planet Mars. This, of course, was in the old days, less than twenty years after the mad American Doheny perfected the atomic blast at the cost of his life, and only a decade after the equally mad Cardoza rode on it to the moon. They were true pioneers, these four of the *Ares*. Except for a half-dozen moon expeditions and the ill-fated de Lancey flight aimed at the seductive orb of Venus, they were the first men to feel other gravity than earth's, and certainly the first successful crew to leave the earth-moon system. And they deserved that success when one considers the difficulties and discomforts—the months spent in acclimatization chambers back on earth, learning to breathe the air as tenuous as that of Mars, the challenging of the void in the tiny rocket driven by the cranky reaction motors of the twenty-first century, and mostly the facing of an absolutely unknown world.

First published in 1934

Jarvis stretched and fingered the raw and peeling tip of his frost-bitten nose. He sighed again contentedly.

"Well," exploded Harrison abruptly, "are we going to hear what happened? You set out all shipshape in an auxiliary rocket, we don't get a peep for ten days, and finally Putz here picks you out of a lunatic ant-heap with a freak ostrich as your pal! Spill it, man!"

"Speel?" queried Leroy perplexedly. "Speel what?"

"He means *'spiel'*," explained Putz soberly. "It iss to tell."

Jarvis met Harrison's amused glance without the shadow of a smile. "That's right, Karl," he said in grave agreement with Putz. *"Ich spiel es!"* He grunted comfortably and began.

"According to orders," he said, "I watched Karl here take off toward the North, and then I got into my flying sweat-box and headed South. You'll remember, Cap—we had orders not to land, but just scout about for points of interest. I set the two cameras clicking and buzzed along, riding pretty high—about two thousand feet—for a couple of reasons. First, it gave the cameras a greater field, and second, the under-jets travel so far in this half-vacuum they call air here that they stir up dust if you move low."

"We know all that from Putz," grunted Harrison. "I wish you'd saved the films, though. They'd have paid the cost of this junket; remember how the public mobbed the first moon pictures?"

"The films are safe," retorted Jarvis. "Well," he resumed, "as I said, I buzzed along at a pretty good clip; just as we figured, the wings haven't much lift in this air at less than a hundred miles per hour, and even then I had to use the under-jets.

"So, with the speed and the altitude and the blurring caused by the under-jets, the seeing wasn't any too good. I could see enough, though, to distinguish that what I sailed over was just more of this grey plain that we'd been examining the whole week since our landing—same blobby growths and the same eternal carpet of crawling little plant-animals, or biopods, as Leroy calls them. So I sailed along, calling back my position every hour as instructed, and not knowing whether you heard me."

"I did!" snapped Harrison.

"A hundred and fifty miles south," continued Jarvis imperturbably, "the surface changed to a sort of low plateau, nothing but desert and orange-tinted sand. I figured that we were right in our guess, then, and this grey plain we dropped on was really the Mare Cimmerium which would make my orange desert the region called Xanthus. If I were right, I ought to hit another grey plain, the Mare Chronium in another couple of hundred miles, and then another orange desert, Thyle I or II. And so I did."

"Putz verified our position a week and a half ago!" grumbled the captain. "Let's get to the point."

"Coming!" remarked Jarvis. "Twenty miles into Thyle—believe it or not—I crossed a canal!"

"Putz photographed a hundred! Let's hear something new!"

"And did he also see a city?"

"Twenty of 'em, if you call those heaps of mud cities!"

"Well," observed Jarvis, "from here on I'll be telling a few things Putz didn't see!" He rubbed his tingling nose, and continued. "I knew that I had sixteen hours of daylight at this season, so eight hours—eight hundred miles—from here, I decided to turn back. I was still over Thyle, whether I or II I'm not sure, not more than twenty-five miles into it. And right there, Putz's pet motor quit!"

"Quit? How?" Putz was solicitous.

"The atomic blast got weak. I started losing altitude right away, and suddenly there I was with a thump right in the middle of Thyle! Smashed my nose on the window, too!" He rubbed the injured member ruefully.

"Did you maybe try vashing der combustion chamber mit acid sulphuric?" inquired Putz. "Sometimes der lead giffs a secondary radiation—"

"Naw!" said Jarvis disgustedly. "I wouldn't try that, of course—not more than ten times! Besides, the bump flattened the landing gear and busted off the under-jets. Suppose I got the thing working—what then? Ten miles with the blast coming right out of the bottom and I'd have melted the floor from under me!" He rubbed his nose again. "Lucky for me a pound only weighs seven ounces here, or I'd have been mashed flat!"

"I could have fixed!" ejaculated the engineer. "I bet it vas not serious."

"Probably not," agreed Jarvis sarcastically. "Only it wouldn't fly. Nothing serious, but I had the choice of waiting to be picked up or trying to walk back—eight hundred miles, and perhaps twenty days before we had to leave! Forty miles a day! Well," he concluded, "I chose to walk. Just as much chance of being picked up, and it kept me busy."

"We'd have found you," said Harrison.

"No doubt. Anyway, I rigged up a harness from some seat straps, and put the water tank on my back, took a cartridge belt and revolver, and some iron rations, and started out."

"Water tank!" exclaimed the little biologist, Leroy. "She weigh one-quarter ton!"

"Wasn't full. Weighed about two hundred and fifty pounds earthweight, which is eighty-five here. Then, besides, my own personal two hundred and ten pounds is only seventy on Mars, so, tank and all, I grossed a hundred and fifty-five, or fifty-five pounds less than my everyday earthweight. I figured on that when I undertook the forty-mile daily stroll. Oh—of course I took a thermo-skin sleeping bag for these wintry Martian nights.

"Off I went, bouncing along pretty quickly. Eight hours of daylight meant twenty miles or more. It got tiresome, of course—plugging along over a soft sand desert with nothing to see, not even Leroy's crawling biopods. But an hour or so brought me to the canal—just a dry ditch about four hundred feet wide, and straight as a railroad on its own company map.

"There'd been water in it sometime, though. The ditch was covered with what looked like a nice green lawn. Only, as I approached, the lawn moved out of my way!"

"Eh?" said Leroy.

"Yeah, it was a relative of your biopods. I caught one— a little grasslike blade about as long as my finger, with two thin, stemmy legs."

"He is where?" Leroy was eager.

"He is let go! I had to move, so I plowed along with the walking grass opening in front and closing behind. And then I was out on the orange desert of Thyle again.

"I plugged steadily along, cussing the sand that made going so tiresome, and, incidentally, cussing that cranky motor of yours, Karl. It was just before twilight that I reached the edge of Thyle, and looked down over the grey Mare Chronium. And I knew there was seventy-five miles of *that* to be walked over, and then a couple of hundred miles of that Xanthus desert, and about as much more Mare Cimmerium. Was I pleased? I started cussing you fellows for not picking me up!"

"We were trying, you sap!" said Harrison.

"That didn't help. Well, I figured I might as well use what was left of daylight in getting down the cliff that bounded Thyle. I found an easy place, and down I went. Mare Chronium was just the same sort of place as this— crazy leafless plants and a bunch of crawlers; I gave it a glance and hauled out my sleeping bag. Up to that time, you know, I hadn't seen anything worth worrying about on this half-dead world—nothing dangerous, that is."

"Did you?" queried Harrison.

"Did I! You'll hear about it when I come to it. Well, I was just about to turn in when suddenly I heard the wildest sort of shenanigans!"

"Vot iss shenanigans?" inquired Putz.

"He says, 'Je ne sais quoi'," explained Leroy. "It is to say, 'I don't know what'."

"That's right," agreed Jarvis. "I didn't know what, so I sneaked over to find out. There was a racket like a flock of crows eating a bunch of canaries—whistles, cackles, caws, trills, and what have you. I rounded a clump of stumps, and there was Tweel!"

"Tweel?" said Harrison, and "Tveel?" said Leroy and Putz.

"That freak ostrich," explained the narrator. "At least, Tweel is as near as I can pronounce it without sputtering. He called it something like 'Trrrweerrlll'."

"What was he doing?" asked the captain.

"He was being eaten! And squealing, of course, as any one would."

"Eaten! By what?"

"I found out later. All I could see then was a bunch of black ropy arms tangled around what looked like, as Putz described it to you, an ostrich. I wasn't going to interfere, naturally; if both creatures were dangerous, I'd have one less to worry about.

"But the bird-like thing was putting up a good battle, dealing vicious blows with an eighteen-inch beak, between screeches. And besides, I caught a glimpse or two of what was on the end of those arms!" Jarvis shuddered. "But the clincher was when I noticed a little black bag or case hung about the neck of the bird-thing! It was intelligent! That or tame, I assumed. Anyway, it clinched my decision. I pulled out my automatic and fired into what I could see of its antagonist.

"There was a flurry of tentacles and a spurt of black corruption, and then the thing, with a disgusting sucking noise, pulled itself and its arms into a hole in the ground. The other let out a series of clacks, staggered around on legs about as thick as golf sticks, and turned suddenly to face me. I held my weapon ready, and the two of us stared at each other.

"The Martian wasn't a bird, really. It wasn't even bird-like, except just at first glance. It had a beak all right, and a few feathery appendages, but the beak wasn't really a beak. It was somewhat flexible; I could see the tip bend slowly from side to side; it was almost like a cross between a beak and a trunk. It had four-toed feet, and four-fingered things—hands, you'd have to call them, and a little round-ish body, and a long neck ending in a tiny head—and that beak. It stood an inch or so taller than I, and—well, Putz saw it!"

The engineer nodded. *"Ja!* I saw!"

Jarvis continued. "So—we stared at each other. Finally the creature went into a series of clackings and twitterings and held out its hands toward me, empty. I took that as a gesture of friendship."

"Perhaps," suggested Harrison, "it looked at that nose of yours and thought you were its brother!"

"Huh! You can be funny without talking! Anyway, I put up my gun and said 'Aw, don't mention it,' or something of the sort, and the thing came over and we were pals.

"By that time, the sun was pretty low and I knew that I'd better build a fire or get into my thermo-skin. I decided on the fire. I picked a spot at the base of the Thyle cliff where the rock could reflect a little heat on my back. I started breaking off chunks of this desiccated Martian vegetation, and my companion caught the idea and brought in an armful. I reached for a match, but the Martian fished into his pounch and brought out something that looked like a glowing coal; one touch of it, and the fire was blazing —and you all know what a job we have starting a fire in this atmosphere!

"And that bag of his!" continued the narrator. "That was a manufactured article, my friends; press an end and she popped open—press the middle and she sealed so perfectly you couldn't see the line. Better than zippers.

"Well, we stared at the fire for a while and I decided to attempt some sort of communication with the Martian. I pointed at myself and said 'Dick'; he caught the drift immediately, stretched a bony claw at me and repeated 'Tick.' Then I pointed at him, and he gave that whistle I called Tweel; I can't imitate his accent. Things were going smoothly; to emphasize the names, I repeated 'Dick,' and then, pointing at him, 'Tweel.'

"There we stuck! He gave some clacks that sounded negative, and said something like 'P-p-p-root.' And that was just the beginning; I was always 'Tick,' but as for him —part of the time he was 'Tweel,' and part of the time he was 'P-p-p-proot,' and part of the time he was sixteen other noises!

"We just couldn't connect. I tried 'rock,' and I tried 'star,' and 'tree,' and 'fire,' and Lord knows what else, and try as I would, I couldn't get a single word! Nothing was the same for two successive minutes, and if that's a language, I'm an alchemist! Finally I gave it up and called him Tweel, and that seemed to do.

"But Tweel hung on to some of my words. He remembered a couple of them, which I suppose is a great achievement if you're used to a language you have to make up as you go along. But I couldn't get the hang of his talk; either I missed some subtle point or we just didn't *think* alike— and I rather believe the latter view.

"I've other reasons for believing that. After a while I gave up the language business, and tried mathematics. I scratched two plus two equals four on the ground, and demonstrated it with pebbles. Again Tweel caught the idea, and informed me that three plus three equals six. Once more we seemed to be getting somewhere.

"So, knowing that Tweel had at least a grammar school education, I drew a circle for the sun, pointing first at it, and then at the last glow of the sun. Then I sketched in Mercury, and Venus, and Mother Earth, and Mars, and finally, pointing to Mars, I swept my hand around in a sort of inclusive gesture to indicate that Mars was our current environment. I was working up to putting over the idea that my home was on the earth.

"Tweel understood my diagram all right. He poked his beak at it, and with a great deal of trilling and clucking, he added Deimos and Phobos to Mars, and then sketched in the earth's moon!

"Do you see what that proves? It proves that Tweel's race uses telescopes—that they're civilized!"

"Does not!" snapped Harrison. "The moon is visible from here as a fifth magnitude star. They could see its revolution with the naked eye."

"The moon, yes!" said Jarvis. "You've missed my point. Mercury isn't visible! And Tweel knew of Mercury because he placed the Moon at the *third* planet, not the second. If he didn't know Mercury, he'd put the earth second, and Mars third, instead of fourth! See?"

"Humph!" said Harrison.

"Anyway," proceeded Jarvis, "I went on with my lesson. Things were going smoothly, and it looked as if I could put the idea over. I pointed at the earth on my diagram, and then at myself, and then, to clinch it, I pointed to myself and then to the earth itself shining bright green almost at the zenith.

"Tweel set up such an excited clacking that I was certain he understood. He jumped up and down, and suddenly he pointed at himself and then at the sky, and then at himself and at the sky again. He pointed at his middle and then at Arcturus, at his head and then at Spica, at his feet and then at half a dozen stars, while I just gaped at him. Then, all of a sudden, he gave a tremendous leap. Man, what a hop! He shot straight up into the starlight, seventy-five feet if an inch! I saw him silhouetted against the sky, saw him turn and come down at me head first, and land smack on his beak like a javelin! There he stuck square in the center of my sun-circle in the sand—a bull's eye!"

"Nuts!" observed the captain. "Plain nuts!"

"That's what I thought, too! I just stared at him open-mouthed while he pulled his head out of the sand and stood up. Then I figured he'd missed my point, and I went through the whole blamed rigamarole again, and it ended the same way, with Tweel on his nose in the middle of my picture!"

"Maybe it's a religious rite," suggested Harrison.

"Maybe," said Jarvis dubiously. "Well, there we were. We could exchange ideas up to a certain point, and then—blooey! Something in us was different, unrelated; I don't doubt that Tweel thought me just as screwy as I thought him. Our minds simply looked at the world from different viewpoints, and perhaps his viewpoint is as true as ours. But—we couldn't get together, that's all. Yet, in spite of all difficulties, I *liked* Tweel, and I have a queer certainty that he liked me."

"Nuts!" repeated the captain. "Just daffy!"

"Yeah? Wait and see. A couple of times I've thought that perhaps we—" He paused, and then resumed his narrative. "Anyway, I finally gave it up, and got into my thermo-skin to sleep. The fire hadn't kept me any too warm, but that damned sleeping bag did. Got stuffy five minutes after I closed myself in. I opened it a little and bingo! Some eighty-below-zero air hit my nose, and that's when I got this pleasant little frostbite to add to the bump I acquired during the crash of my rocket.

"I don't know what Tweel made of my sleeping. He sat around, but when I woke up, he was gone. I'd just crawled out of my bag, though, when I heard some twittering, and there he came, sailing down from that three-story Thyle cliff to alight on his beak beside me. I pointed to myself and toward the north, and he pointed at himself and toward the south, and when I loaded up and started away, he came along.

"Man, how he traveled! A hundred and fifty feet at a jump, sailing through the air stretched out like a spear, and landing on his beak. He seemed surprised at my plodding, but after a few moments he fell in beside me, only every few minutes he'd go into one of his leaps, and stick his nose into the sand a block ahead of me. Then he'd come shooting back at me; it made me nervous at first to see that beak of his coming at me like a spear, but he always ended in the sand at my side.

"So the two of us plugged along across the Mare Chronium. Same sort of place as this—same crazy plants and same little green biopods growing in the sand, or crawling out of your way. We talked—not that we understood each other, you know, but just for company. I sang songs, and I suspected Tweel did too; at least, some of his trillings and twitterings had a subtle sort of rhythm.

"Then, for variety, Tweel would display his smattering of English words. He'd point to an outcropping and say 'rock,' and point to a pebble and say it again; or he'd touch my arm and say 'Tick,' and then repeat it. He seemed terrifically amused that the same word meant the same thing twice in succession, or that the same word could apply to two different objects. It set me wondering if perhaps his language wasn't like the primitive speech of some earth people—you know, Captain, like the Negritoes, for instance, who haven't any generic words. No word for food or water or man—words for good food and bad food, or rain water and sea water, or strong man and weak man—but no names for general classes. They're too primitive to understand that rain water and sea water are just different aspects of the same thing. But that wasn't the case with Tweel; it was just that we were somehow mysteriously different—our minds were alien to each other. And yet— we *liked* each other!"

"Looney, that's all," remarked Harrison. "That's why you two were so fond of each other."

"Well, I like *you!*" countered Jarvis wickedly. "Anyway," he resumed, "don't get the idea that there was anything screwy about Tweel. In fact, I'm not so sure but that he couldn't teach our highly praised human intelligence a trick or two. Oh, he wasn't an intellectual superman, I guess; but don't overlook the point that he managed to understand a little of my mental workings, and I never even got a glimmering of his."

"Because he didn't have any!" suggested the captain, while Putz and Leroy blinked attentively.

"You can judge of that when I'm through," said Jarvis. "Well, we plugged along across the Mare Chronium all that day, and all the next. Mare Chronium—Sea of Time!

Say, I was willing to agree with Schiaparelli's name by the end of that march! Just that grey, endless plain of weird plants, and never a sign of any other life. It was so monotonous that I was even glad to see the desert of Xanthus toward the evening of the second day.

"I was fair worn out, but Tweel seemed as fresh as ever, for all I never saw him drink or eat. I think he could have crossed the Mare Chronium in a couple of hours with those block-long nose dives of his, but he stuck along with me. I offered him some water once or twice; he took the cup from me and sucked the liquid into his beak, and then carefully squirted it all back into the cup and gravely returned it.

"Just as we sighted Xanthus, or the cliffs that bounded it, one of those nasty sand clouds blew along, not as bad as the one we had here, but mean to travel against. I pulled the transparent flap of my thermo-skin bag across my face and managed pretty well, and I noticed that Tweel used some feathery appendages growing like a mustache at the base of his beak to cover his nostrils, and some similar fuzz to shield his eyes."

"He is a desert creature!" ejaculated the little biologist, Leroy.

"Huh? Why?"

"He drink no water—he is adapt' for sand storm—"

"Proves nothing! There's not enough water to waste any where on this desiccated pill called Mars. We'd call all of it desert on earth, you know." He paused. "Anyway, after the sand storm blew over, a little wind kept blowing in our faces, not strong enough to stir the sand. But suddenly things came drifting along from the Xanthus cliffs—small, transparent spheres, for all the world like glass tennis balls! But light—they were almost light enough to float even in this thin air—empty, too; at least, I cracked open a couple and nothing came out but a bad smell. I asked Tweel about them, but all he said was 'No, no no,' which I took to mean that he knew nothing about them. So they went bouncing by like tumbleweeds, or like soap bubbles, and we plugged on toward Xanthus. Tweel pointed at one of the crystal balls once and said 'rock,' but I was too tired to argue with him. Later I discovered what he meant.

"We came to the bottom of the Xanthus cliffs finally,

when there wasn't much daylight left. I decided to sleep on the plateau if possible; anything dangerous, I reasoned, would be more likely to prowl through the vegetation of the Mare Chronium than the sand of Xanthus. Not that I'd seen a single sign of menace, except the rope-armed black thing that had trapped Tweel, and apparently that didn't prowl at all, but lured its victims within reach. It couldn't lure me while I slept, especially as Tweel didn't seem to sleep at all, but simply sat patiently around all night. I wondered how the creature had managed to trap Tweel, but there wasn't any way of asking him. I found that out too, later; it's devilish!

"However, we were ambling around the base of the Xanthus barrier looking for an easy spot to climb. At least, I was! Tweel could have leaped it easily, for the cliffs were lower than Thyle—perhaps sixty feet. I found a place and started up, swearing at the water tank strapped to my back —it didn't bother me except when climbing—and suddenly I heard a sound that I thought I recognized!

"You know how deceptive sounds are in this thin air. A shot sounds like the pop of a cork. But this sound was the drone of a rocket, and sure enough, there went our second auxiliary about ten miles to westward, between me and the sunset!"

"Vas me!" said Putz. "I hunt for you."

"Yeah; I knew that, but what good did it do me? I hung on to the cliff and yelled and waved with one hand. Tweel saw it too, and set up a trilling and twittering, leaping to the top of the barrier and then high into the air. And while I watched, the machine droned on into the shadows to the south.

"I scrambled to the top of the cliff. Tweel was still pointing and trilling excitedly, shooting up toward the sky and coming down head-on to stick upside down on his back in the sand. I pointed toward the south, and at myself, and he said, 'Yes—Yes—Yes'; but somehow I gathered that he thought the flying thing was a relative of mine, probably a parent. Perhaps I did his intellect an injustice; I think now that I did.

"I was bitterly disappointed by the failure to attract attention. I pulled out my thermo-skin and crawled into it, as the night chill was already apparent. Tweel stuck his beak into the sand and drew up his legs and arms and looked for all the world like one of those leafless shrubs out there. I think he stayed that way all night."

"Protective mimicry!" ejaculated Leroy. "See? He is desert creature!"

"In the morning," resumed Jarvis, "we started off again. We hadn't gone a hundred yards into Xanthus when I saw something queer! This is one thing Putz didn't photograph, I'll wager!

"There was a line of little pyramids—tiny ones, not more than six inches high, stretching across Xanthus as far as I could see! Little buildings made of pygmy bricks, they were, hollow inside and truncated, or at least broken at the top and empty. I pointed at them and said 'What?' to Tweel, but he gave some negative twitters to indicate, I suppose, that he didn't know. So off we went, following the row of pyramids because they ran north, and I was going north.

"Man, we trailed that line for hours! After a while, I noticed another queer thing: they were getting larger. Same number of bricks in each one, but the bricks were larger.

"By noon they were shoulder high. I looked into a couple—all just the same, broken at the top and empty. I examined a brick or two as well; they were silica, and old as creation itself!"

"They were weathered—edges rounded. Silica doesn't weather easily even on earth, and in this climate—!"

"How old you think?"

"Fifty thousand—a hundred thousand years. How can I tell? The little ones we saw in the morning were older— perhaps ten times as old. Crumbling. How old would that make *them*? Half a million years? Who knows?" Jarvis paused a moment. "Well," he resumed, "we followed the line. Tweel pointed at them and said 'rock' once or twice, but he'd done that many times before. Besides, he was more or less right about these.

"I tried questioning him. I pointed at a pyramid and asked 'People?' and indicated the two of us. He set up a negative sort of clucking and said, 'No, no, no. No one-one-two. No two-two-four,' meanwhile rubbing his stomach. I just stared at him and he went through the business

again. 'No one-one-two. No two-two-four.' I just gaped
at him."

"That proves it!" exclaimed Harrison. "Nuts!"

"You think so?" queried Jarvis sardonically. "Well, I
figured it out different! 'No one-one-two!' You don't get it,
of course, do you?"

"Nope—nor do you!"

"I think I do! Tweel was using the few English words
he knew to put over a very complex idea. What, let me
ask, does mathematics make you think of?"

"Why—of astronomy. Or—or logic!"

"That's it! 'No one-one-two!' Tweel was telling me that
the builders of the pyramids weren't people—or that they
weren't intelligent, that they weren't reasoning creatures!
Get it?"

"Huh! I'll be damned!"

"You probably will."

"Why," put in Leroy, "he rub his belly?"

"Why? Because, my dear biologist, that's where his
brains are! Not in his tiny head—in his middle!"

"*C'est* impossible!"

"Not on Mars, it isn't! This flora and fauna aren't earthly; your biopods prove that!" Jarvis grinned and took up
his narrative. "Anyway, we plugged along across Xanthus
and in about the middle of the afternoon, something else
queer happened. The pyramids ended."

"Ended!"

"Yeah; the queer part was that the last one—and now
they were ten-footers—was capped! See? Whatever built it
was still inside; we'd trailed 'em from their half-million-
year-old origin to the present.

"Tweel and I noticed it about the same time. I yanked
out my automatic (I had a clip of Boland explosive bullets
in it) and Tweel, quick as a sleight-of-hand trick, snapped
a queer little glass revolver out of his bag. It was much
like our weapons, except that the grip was larger to accommodate his four-taloned hand. And we held our
weapons ready while we sneaked up along the lines of
empty pyramids.

"Tweel saw the movement first. The top tiers of bricks
were heaving, shaking, and suddenly slid down the sides

with a thin crash. And then—something—something was coming out!

"A long, silvery-grey arm appeared, dragging after it an armored body. Armored, I mean, with scales, silver-grey and dull-shining. The arm heaved the body out of the hole; the beast crashed to the sand.

"It was a nondescript creature—body like a big grey cask, arm and a sort of mouth-hole at one end; stiff, pointed tail at the other—and that's all. No other limbs, no eyes, ears, nose—nothing! The thing dragged itself a few yards, inserted its pointed tail in the sand, pushed itself upright, and just sat.

"Tweel and I watched it for ten minutes before it moved. Then, with a creaking and rustling like—oh, like crumpling stiff paper—its arm moved to the mouth-hole and out came a brick! The arm placed the brick carefully on the ground, and the thing was still again.

"Another ten minutes—another brick. Just one of Nature's bricklayers. I was about to slip away and move on when Tweel pointed at the thing and said 'rock'! I went 'huh?' and he said it again. Then, to the accompaniment of some of his trilling, he said, 'No—no—,' and gave two or three whistling breaths.

"Well, I got his meaning, for a wonder! I said, 'No breathe?' and demonstrated the word. Tweel was ecstatic; he said, 'Yes, yes, yes! No, no, no breet!' Then he gave a leap and sailed out to land on his nose about one pace from the monster!

"I was startled, you can imagine! The arm was going up for a brick, and I expected to see Tweel caught and mangled, but—nothing happened! Tweel pounded on the creature, and the arm took the brick and placed it neatly beside the first. Tweel rapped on its body again, and said 'rock,' and I got up nerve enough to take a look myself.

"Tweel was right again. The creature *was* rock, and it didn't breathe!"

"How you know?" snapped Leroy, his black eyes blazing interest.

"Because I'm a chemist. The beast was made of silica! There must have been pure silicon in the sand, and it lived on that. Get it? We, and Tweel, and those plants out there, and even the biopods are *carbon* life; this thing lived by a different set of chemical reactions. It was silicon life!"

"La vie silicieuse!" shouted Leroy. "I have suspect, and now it is proof! I must go see! *Il faut que je—"*

"All right! All right!" said Jarvis. "You can go see. Anyhow, there the thing was, alive and yet not alive, moving every ten minutes, and then only to remove a brick. Those bricks were its waste matter. See, Frenchy? We're carbon, and our waste is carbon dioxide, and this thing is silicon and *its* waste is silicon dioxide—silica. But silica is a solid, hence the bricks. And it builds itself in, and when it is covered, it moves over to a fresh place to start over. No wonder it creaked! A living creature a half a million years old!"

"How you know how old?" Leroy was frantic.

"We trailed its pyramids from the beginning, didn't we? If this weren't the original pyramid builder, the series would have ended somewhere before we found him, wouldn't it?—ended and started over with the small ones. That's simple enough, isn't it?

"But he reproduces, or tries to. Before the third brick came out, there was a little rustle and out popped a whole stream of those little crystal balls. They're his spores, or seeds—call 'em what you want. They went bouncing by across Xanthus just as they'd bounced by us back in the Mare Chronium. I've a hunch how they work, too—this is for your information, Leroy. I think the crystal shell of silica is no more than protective covering, like an eggshell, and that the active principle is the smell inside. It's some sort of gas that attacks silicon, and if the shell is broken near a supply of that element, some reaction starts that ultimately develops into a beast like that one."

"You should try!" exclaimed the little Frenchman. "We must break one to see!"

"Yeah? Well, I did. I smashed a couple against the sand. Would you like to come back in about ten thousand years to see if I planted some pyramid monsters? You'd most likely be able to tell by that time!" Jarvis paused and drew a deep breath. "Lord! That queer creature! Do you picture it? Blind, deaf, nerveless, brainless—just a mechanism, and yet— immortal! Bound to go on making bricks, building pyramids, as long as silicon and oxygen exist, and even afterwards it'll just stop. It won't be dead. If the accidents of a million years bring it its food again, there it'll be, ready to run again, while brains and civilizations are part of the past. A queer beast—yet I met a stranger one!"

"If you did, it must have been in your dreams!" growled Harrison.

"You're right!" said Jarvis soberly. "In a way, you're right. The dream-beast! That's the best name for it—and it's the most fiendish, terrifying creation one could imagine! More dangerous than a lion, more insidious than a snake!"

"Tell me!" begged Leroy. "I must go see!"

"Not *this* devil!" He paused again. "Well," he resumed, "Tweel and I left the pyramid creature and plowed along through Xanthus. I was tired and a little disheartened by Putz's failure to pick me up, and Tweel's trilling got on my nerves, as did his flying nosedives. So I just strode along without a word, hour after hour across that monotonous desert.

"Toward mid-afternoon we came in sight of a low dark line on the horizon. I knew what it was. It was a canal; I'd crossed it in the rocket and it meant that we were just one-third of the way across Xanthus. Pleasant thought, wasn't it? And still, I was keeping up to schedule.

"We approached the canal slowly; I remembered that this one was bordered by a wide fringe of vegetation and that Mudheap City was on it.

"I was tired, as I said. I kept thinking of a good hot meal, and then from that I jumped to reflections of how nice and home-like even Borneo would seem after this crazy planet, and from that, to thoughts of little old New York, and then to thinking about a girl I know there— Fancy Long. Know her?"

"Vision entertainer," said Harrison. "I've tuned her in. Nice blonde—dances and sings on the *Yerba Mate* hour."

"That's her," said Jarvis ungrammatically. "I know her pretty well—just friends, get me?—though she came down to see us off in the *Ares*. Well, I was thinking about her, feeling pretty lonesome, and all the time we were approaching that line of rubbery plants.

"And then—I said, 'What 'n Hell!' and stared. And there she was—Fancy Long, standing plain as day under one of those crack-brained trees, and smiling and waving just the way I remembered her when we left!"

"Now you're nuts, too!" observed the captain.

"Boy, I almost agreed with you! I stared and pinched myself and closed my eyes and then stared again—and every time, there was Fancy Long smiling and waving! Tweel saw something, too; he was trilling and clucking away, but I scarcely heard him. I was bounding toward her over the sand, too amazed even to ask myself questions.

"I wasn't twenty feet from her when Tweel caught me with one of his flying leaps. He grabbed my arm, yelling, 'No—no—no!' in his squeaky voice. I tried to shake him off—he was as light as if he were built of bamboo—but he dug his claws in and yelled. And finally some sort of sanity returned to me and I stopped less than ten feet from her. There she stood, looking as solid as Putz's head!"

"Vot?" said the engineer.

"She smiled and waved, and waved and smiled, and I stood there dumb as Leroy, while Tweel squeaked and chattered. I *knew* it couldn't be real, yet—there she was!

"Finally I said, 'Fancy! Fancy Long!' She just kept on smiling and waving, but looking as real as if I hadn't left her thirty-seven million miles away.

"Tweel had his glass pistol out, pointing it at her. I grabbed his arm, but he tried to push me away. He pointed at her and said, 'No breet! No breet!' and I understood that he meant that the Fancy Long thing wasn't alive. Man, my head was whirling!

"Still, it gave me the jitters to see him pointing his weapon at her. I don't know why I stood there watching him take careful aim, but I did. Then he squeezed the handle of his weapon; there was a little puff of steam, and Fancy Long was gone! And in her place was one of those writhing, black rope-armed horrors like the one I'd saved Tweel from!

"The dream-beast! I stood there dizzy, watching it die while Tweel trilled and whistled. Finally he touched my arm, pointed at the twisting thing, and said, 'You one-one-two, he one-one-two.' After he'd repeated it eight or ten times, I got it. Do any of you?"

"*Oui!*" shrilled Leroy. "*Moi—je le comprends!* He mean you think of something, the beast he know, and you see it!

Un chien—a hungry dog, he would see the big bone with meat! Or smell it—not?"

"Right!" said Jarvis. "The dream-beast uses its victim's longings and desires to trap its prey. The bird at nesting season would see its mate, the fox, prowling for its own prey, would see a helpless rabbit!"

"How he do?" queried Leroy.

"How do I know? How does a snake back on earth charm a bird into its very jaws? And aren't there deep-sea fish that lure their victims into their mouths? Lord!" Jarvis shuddered. "Do you see how insidious the monster is? We're warned now—but henceforth we can't trust even our eyes. You might see me—I might see one of you—and back of it may be nothing but another of those black horrors!"

"How'd your friend know?" asked the captain abruptly.

"Tweel? I wonder! Perhaps he was thinking of something that couldn't possibly have interested me, and when I started to run, he realized that I saw something different and was warned. Or perhaps the dream-beast can only project a single vision, and Tweel saw what I saw—or nothing. I couldn't ask him. But it's just another proof that his intelligence is equal to ours or greater."

"He's daffy, I tell you!" said Harrison. "What makes you think his intellect ranks with the human?"

"Plenty of things! First the pyramid-beast. He hadn't seen one before; he said as much. Yet he recognized it as a dead-alive automaton of silicon."

"He could have heard of it," objected Harrison. "He lives around here, you know."

"Well how about the language? I couldn't pick up a single idea of his and he learned six or seven words of mine. And do you realize what complex ideas he put over with no more than those six or seven words? The pyramid-monster—the dream-beast! In a single phrase he told me that one was a harmless automaton and the other a deadly hypnotist. What about that?"

"Huh!" said the captain.

"*Huh* if you wish! Could you have done it knowing only six words of English? Could you go even further, as Tweel did, and tell me that another creature was of a sort of intelligence so different from ours that understanding was impossible—even more impossible than that between Tweel and me?"

"Eh? What was that?"

"Later. The point I'm making is that Tweel and his race are worthy of our friendship. Somewhere on Mars—and you'll find I'm right—is a civilization and culture equal to ours, and maybe more than equal. And communication is possible between them and us; Tweel proves that. It may take years of patient trial, for their minds are alien, but less alien than the next minds we encountered—if they *are* minds."

"The next ones? What next ones?"

"The people of the mud cities along the canals." Jarvis frowned, then resumed his narrative. "I thought the dream-beast and the silicon-monster were the strangest beings conceivable, but I was wrong. These creatures are still more alien, less understandable than either and far less comprehensible than Tweel, with whom friendship is possible, and even, by patience and concentration, the exchange of ideas.

"Well," he continued, "we left the dream-beast dying, dragging itself back into its hole, and we moved toward the canal. There was a carpet of that queer walking-grass scampering out of our way, and when we reached the bank, there was a yellow trickle of water flowing. The mound city I'd noticed from the rocket was a mile or so to the right and I was curious enough to want to take a look at it.

"It had seemed deserted from my previous glimpse of it, and if any creatures were lurking in it—well, Tweel and I were both armed. And by the way, that crystal weapon of Tweel's was an interesting device; I took a look at it after the dream-beast episode. It fired a little glass splinter, poisoned, I suppose, and I guess it held at least a hundred of 'em to a load. The propellent was steam—just plain steam!

"Shteam!" echoed Putz. "From vot come, shteam?"

"From water, of course! You could see the water through the transparent handle and about a gill of another liquid, thick and yellowish. When Tweel squeezed the handle—there was no trigger—a drop of water and a drop of the yellow stuff squirted into the firing chamber, and the water vaporized—pop!—like that. It's not so difficult; I think we could develop the same principle. Concentrated sulphuric acid will heat water almost to boiling, and so will quicklime, and there's potassium and sodium—

"Of course, his weapon hadn't the range of mine, but it wasn't so bad in this thin air, and it *did* hold as many shots as a cowboy's gun in a Western movie. It was effective, too, at least against Martian life; I tried it out, aiming at one of the crazy plants, and darned if the plant didn't wither up and fall apart! That's why I think the glass splinters were poisoned.

"Anyway, we trudged along toward the mud-heap city and I began to wonder whether the city builders dug the canals. I pointed to the city and then at the canal, and Tweel said 'No—no—no!' and gestured toward the south. I took it to mean that some other race had created the canal system, perhaps Tweel's people. I don't know; maybe there's still another intelligent race on the planet, or a dozen others. Mars is a queer little world.

"A hundred yards from the city we crossed a sort of road—just a hard-packed mud trail, and then, all of a sudden, along came one of the mound builders!

"Man, talk about fantastic beings! It looked rather like a barrel trotting along on four legs with four other arms or tentacles. It had no head, just body and members and a row of eyes completely around it. The top end of the barrel-body was a diaphragm stretched as tight as a drum head, and that was all. It was pushing a little coppery cart and tore right past us like the proverbial bat out of Hell. It didn't even notice us, although I thought the eyes on my side shifted a little as it passed.

"A moment later another came along, pushing another empty cart. Same thing—it just scooted past us. Well, I wasn't going to be ignored by a bunch of barrels playing train, so when the third one approached, I planted myself in the way—ready to jump, of course, if the thing didn't stop.

"But it did. It stopped and set up a sort of drumming from the diaphragm on top. And I held out both hands and said, 'We are friends!' And what do you suppose the thing did?"

"Said, 'Pleased to meet you,' I'll bet!" suggested Harrison.

"I couldn't have been more surprised if it had! It drummed on its diaphragm, and then suddenly boomed out, 'We are v-r-r-iends!' and gave its pushcart a vicious poke at me! I jumped aside, and away it went while I stared dumbly after it.

"A minute later another one came hurrying along. This one didn't pause, but simply drummed out, 'We are v-r-r-iends!' and scurried by. How did it learn the phrase? Were all of the creatures in some sort of communication with each other? Were they all parts of some central organism? I don't know, though I think Tweel does.

"Anyway, the creatures went sailing past us, every one greeting us with the same statement. It got to be funny; I never thought to find so many friends on this God-forsaken ball! Finally I made a puzzled gesture to Tweel; I guess he understood, for he said, 'One-one-two—yes!— two-two-four—no!' Get it?"

"Sure," said Harrison. "It's a Martian nursery rhyme."

"Yeah! Well, I was getting used to Tweel's symbolism, and I figured it out this way. 'One-one-two—yes!' The creatures were intelligent. 'Two-two-four—no!' Their intelligence was not of our order, but something different and beyond the logic of two and two is four. Maybe I missed his meaning. Perhaps he meant that their minds were of low degree, able to figure out the simple things— 'One-one-two—yes!'—but not more difficult things—'Two-two-four—no!' But I think from what we saw later that he meant the other.

"After a few moments, the creatures came rushing back —first one, than another. Their pushcarts were full of stones, sand, chunks of rubbery plants, and such rubbish as that. They droned out their friendly greeting, which didn't really sound so friendly, and dashed on. The third one I assumed to be my first acquaintance and I decided to have another chat with him. I stepped into his path again and waited.

"Up he came, booming out his 'We are v-r-r-riends' and stopped. I looked at him; four or five of his eyes looked at me. He tried his password again and gave a shove on his cart, but I stood firm. And then the—the dashed creature reached out one of his arms, and two finger-like nippers tweaked my nose!"

"Haw!" roared Harrison. "Maybe the things have a sense of beauty!"

"Laugh!" grumbled Jarvis. "I'd already had a nasty bump and a mean frostbite on that nose. Anyway, I yelled 'Ouch!' and jumped aside and the creature dashed away; but from then on, their greeting was 'We are v-r-r-riends! Ouch!' Queer beasts!

"Tweel and I followed the road squarely up to the nearest mound. The creatures were coming and going, paying us not the slightest attention, fetching their loads of rubbish. The road simply dived into an opening, and slanted down like an old mine, and in and out darted the barrel-people, greeting us with their eternal phrase.

"I looked in; there was a light somewhere below, and I was curious to see it. It didn't look like a flame or torch, you understand, but more like a civilized light, and I thought that I might get some clue as to the creatures' development. So in I went and Tweel tagged along, not without a few trills and twitters, however.

"The light was curious; it sputtered and flared like an old arc light, but came from a single black rod set in the wall of the corridor. It was electric, beyond doubt. The creatures were fairly civilized, apparently.

"Then I saw another light shining on something that glittered and I went on to look at that, but it was only a heap of shiny sand. I turned toward the entrance to leave, and the Devil take me if it wasn't gone!

"I supposed the corridor had curved, or I'd stepped into a side passage. Anyway, I walked back in that direction I thought we'd come, and all I saw was more dim-lit corridor. The place was a labyrinth! There was nothing but twisting passages running every way, lit by occasional lights, and now and then a creature running by, sometimes with a pushcart, sometimes without.

"Well, I wasn't much worried at first. Tweel and I had only come a few steps from the entrance. But every move we made after that seemed to get us in deeper. Finally I tried following one of the creatures with an empty cart, thinking that he'd be going out for his rubbish, but he ran around aimlessly, into one passage and out another. When he started dashing around a pillar like one of these Japanese waltzing mice, I gave up, dumped my water tank on the floor, and sat down.

"Tweel was as lost as I. I pointed up and he said 'No—no—no!' in a sort of helpless trill. And we couldn't get any help from the natives. They paid no attention at all, except to assure us they were friends—ouch!

"Lord! I don't know how many hours or days we wandered around there! I slept twice from sheer exhaustion; Tweel never seemed to need sleep. We tried following only the upward corridors, but they'd run uphill a ways and then curve downwards. The temperature in that damned ant hill was constant; you couldn't tell night from day and after my first sleep I didn't know whether I'd slept one hour or thirteen, so I couldn't tell from my watch whether it was midnight or noon.

"We saw plenty of strange things. There were machines running in some of the corridors, but they didn't seem to be doing anything—just wheels turning. And several times I saw two barrel-beasts with a little one growing between them, joined to both."

"Parthenogenesis!" exulted Leroy. "Parthenogenesis by budding like *les tulipes!*"

"If you say so, Frenchy," agreed Jarvis. "The things never noticed us at all, except, as I say, to greet us with 'We are v-r-r-riends! Ouch!' They seemed to have no home-life of any sort, but just scurried around with their push-carts, bringing in rubbish. And finally I discovered what they did with it.

"We'd had a little luck with a corridor, one that slanted upwards for a great distance. I was feeling that we ought to be close to the surface when suddenly the passage debouched into a domed chamber, the only one we'd seen. And man!—I felt like dancing when I saw what looked like daylight through a crevice in the roof.

"There was a—a sort of machine in the chamber, just an enormous wheel that turned slowly, and one of the creatures was in the act of dumping his rubbish below it. The wheel ground it with a crunch—sand, stones, plants, all into powder that sifted away somewhere. While we watched, others filed in, repeating the process, and that seemed to be all. No rhyme nor reason to the whole thing

—but that's characteristic of this crazy planet. And there was another fact that's almost too bizarre to believe.

"One of the creatures, having dumped his load, pushed his cart aside with a crash and calmly shoved himself under the wheel! I watched him being crushed, too stupefied to make a sound, and a moment later, another followed him! They were perfectly methodical about it, too; one of the cartless creatures took the abandoned pushcart.

"Tweel didn't seem surprised; I pointed out the next suicide to him, and he just gave the most human-like shrug imaginable, as much as to say, 'What can I do about it?' He must have known more or less about these creatures.

"Then I saw something else. There was something beyond the wheel, something shining on a sort of low pedestal. I walked over; there was a little crystal about the size of an egg, fluorescing to beat Tophet. The light from it stung my hands and face, almost like a static discharge, and then I noticed another funny thing. Remember that wart I had on my left thumb? Look!" Jarvis extended his hand. "It dried up and fell off—just like that! And my abused nose—say, the pain went out of it like magic! The thing had the property of hard ex-rays or gamma radiations, only more so; it destroyed diseased tissue and left healthy tissue unharmed!

"I was thinking what a present *that'd* be to take back to Mother Earth when a lot of racket interrupted. We dashed back to the other side of the wheel in time to see one of the pushcarts ground up. Some suicide had been careless, it seems.

"Then suddenly the creatures were booming and drumming all around us and their noise was decidedly menacing. A crowd of them advanced toward us; we backed out of what I thought was the passage we'd entered by, and they came rumbling after us, some pushing carts and some not. Crazy brutes! There was a whole chorus of 'We are v-r-r-riends! Ouch!' I didn't like the 'ouch'; it was rather suggestive.

"Tweel had his glass gun out and I dumped my water tank for greater freedom and got mine. We backed up the corridor with the barrel-beasts following—about twenty of them. Queer thing—the ones coming in with loaded carts moved past us inches away without a sign.

"Tweel must have noticed that. Suddenly, he snatched out that glowing coal cigar-lighter of his and touched a cart-load of plant limbs. Puff! The whole load was burning—and the crazy beast pushing it went right along without a change of pace! It created some disturbance among our 'v-r-r-riends,' however—and then I noticed the smoke eddying and swirling past us, and sure enough, there was the entrance!

"I grabbed Tweel and out we dashed and after us our twenty pursuers. The daylight felt like Heaven, though I saw at first glance that the sun was all but set, and that was bad, since I couldn't live outside my thermo-skin bag in a Martian night—at least, without a fire.

"And things got worse in a hurry. They cornered us in an angle between two mounds, and there we stood. I hadn't fired nor had Tweel; there wasn't any use in irritating the brutes. They stopped a little distance away and began their booming about friendship and ouches.

"Then things got still worse! A barrel-brute came out with a pushcart and they all grabbed into it and came out with handfuls of foot-long copper darts—sharp-looking ones—and all of a sudden one sailed past my ear—zing! And it was shoot or die then.

"We were doing pretty well for a while. We picked off the ones next to the pushcart and managed to keep the darts at a minimum, but suddenly there was a thunderous booming of 'v-r-r-riends' and 'ouches,' and a whole army of 'em came out of their hole.

"Man! We were through and I knew it! Then I realized that Tweel wasn't. He could have leaped the mound behind us as easily as not. He was staying for me!

"Say, I could have cried if there'd been time! I'd liked Tweel from the first, but whether I'd have had gratitude to do what he was doing—suppose I *had* saved him from the first dream-beast—he'd done as much for me, hadn't he? I grabbed his arm, and said 'Tweel,' and pointed up, and he understood. He said, 'No—no—no, Tick!' and popped away with his glass pistol.

"What could I do? I'd be a goner anyway when the sun set, but I couldn't explain that to him. I said, 'Thanks,

Tweel. You're a man!' and felt that I wasn't paying him any compliment at all. A man! There are mighty few men who'd do that.

"So I went 'bang' with my gun and Tweel went 'puff' with his, and the barrels were throwing darts and getting ready to rush us, and booming about being friends. I had given up hope. Then suddenly an angel dropped right down from Heaven in the shape of Putz, with his underjets blasting the barrels into very small pieces!

"Wow! I let out a yell and dashed for the rocket; Putz opened the door and in I went, laughing and crying and shouting! It was a moment or so before I remembered Tweel; I looked around in time to see him rising in one of his nosedives over the mound and away.

"I had a devil of a job arguing Putz into following! By the time we got the rocket aloft, darkness was down; you know how it comes here—like turning off a light. We sailed out over the desert and put down once or twice. I yelled 'Tweel!' and yelled it a hundred times, I guess. We couldn't find him; he could travel like the wind and all I got—or else I imagined it—was a faint trilling and twittering drifting out of the south. He'd gone, and damn it! I wish—I wish he hadn't!"

The four men of the *Ares* were silent—even the sardonic Harrison. At last little Leroy broke the stillness.

"I should like to see," he murmured.

"Yeah," said Harrison. "And the wart-cure. Too bad you missed that; it might be the cancer cure they've been hunting for a century and a half."

"Oh, that!" muttered Jarvis gloomily. "That's what started the fight!" He drew a glistening object from his pocket.

"Here it is."'

TWILIGHT

by John W. Campbell

"Speaking of hitch-hikers," said Jim Bendell in a rather bewildered way, "I picked up a man the other day that certainly was a queer cuss." He laughed, but it wasn't a real laugh. "He told me the queerest yarn I ever heard. Most of them tell you how they lost their good jobs and tried to find work out here in the wide spaces of the West. They don't seem to realize how many people we have out here. They think all this great beautiful country is un-inhabited."

Jim Bendell's a real estate man, and I knew how he could go on. That's his favorite line, you know. He's real worried because there's a lot of homesteading plots still open out in our state. He talks about the beautiful country, but he never went further into the desert than the edge of town. 'Fraid of it actually. So I sort of steered him back on the track.

"What did he claim, Jim? Prospector who couldn't find land to prospect?"

"That's not very funny, Bart. No; it wasn't only what he claimed. He didn't even claim it, just said it. You know, he didn't say it was true, he just said it. That's what gets me. I know it ain't true, but the way he said it— Oh, I don't know."

By which I knew he didn't. Jim Bendell's usually pretty careful about his English—real proud of it. When he slips, that means he's disturbed. Like the time he thought the rattlesnake was a stick of wood and wanted to put it on the fire.

First published in 1934, under the pseudonym, "Don A. Stuart"

Jim went on: And he had funny clothes, too. They looked like silver, but they were soft as silk. And at night they glowed just a little.

I picked him up about dusk. Really picked him up. He was lying off about ten feet from the South Road. I thought, at first, somebody had hit him, and then hadn't stopped. Didn't see him very clearly, you know. I picked him up, put him in the car, and started on. I had about three hundred miles to go, but I thought I could drop him at Warren Spring with Doc Vance. But he came to in about five minutes, and opened his eyes. He looked straight off, and he looked first at the car, then at the Moon. "Thank God!" he says, and then looks at me. It gave me a shock. He was beautiful. No; he was handsome.

He wasn't either one. He was magnificent. He was about six feet two, I think, and his hair was brown, with a touch of red-gold. It seemed like fine copper wire that's turned brown. It was crisp and curly. His forehead was wide, twice as wide as mine. His features were delicate, but tremendously impressive; his eyes were gray, like etched iron, and bigger than mine—a lot.

That suit he wore—it was more like a bathing suit with pajama trousers. His arms were long and muscled smoothly as an Indian's. He was white, though, tanned lightly with a golden, rather than a brown, tan.

But he was magnificent. Most beautiful man I ever saw. I don't know, damn it!

"Hello!" I said. "Have an accident?"

"No; not this time, at least."

And his voice was magnificent, too. It wasn't an ordinary voice. It sounded like an organ talking, only it was human.

"But maybe my mind isn't quite steady yet. I tried an experiment. Tell me what the date is, year and all, and let me see," he went on.

"Why—December 9, 1932," I said.

And it didn't please him. He didn't like it a bit. But the wry grin that came over his face gave way to a chuckle.

"Over a thousand—" he says reminiscently. "Not as bad as seven million. I shouldn't complain."

"Seven million what?"

"Years," he said, steadily enough. Like he meant it. "I tried an experiment once. Or I will try it. Now I'll have to try again. The experiment was—in 3059. I'd just finished the release experiment. Testing space then. Time—it wasn't that, I still believe. It was space. I felt myself caught in that field, but I couldn't pull away. Field gamma-H 481, intensity 935 in the Pellman range. It sucked me in, and I went out.

"I think it took a short cut through space to the position the solar system will occupy. Through a higher dimension, effecting a speed exceeding light and throwing me into the future plane."

He wasn't telling me, you know. He was just thinking out loud. Then he began to realize I was there.

"I couldn't read their instruments, seven million years of evolution changed everything. So I overshot my mark a little coming back. I belong in 3059."

"But tell me, what's the latest scientific invention of this year?"

He startled me so, I answered almost before I thought.

"Why, television, I guess. And radio and airplanes."

"Radio—good. They will have instruments."

"But see here—who are you?"

"Ah—I'm sorry. I forgot," he replied in that organ voice of his. "I am Ares Sen Kenlin. And you?"

"James Waters Bendell."

"Waters—what does that mean? I do not recognize it."

"Why—it's a name, of course. Why should you recognize it?"

"I see—you have not the classification, then. 'Sen' stands for science."

"Where did you come from, Mr. Kenlin?"

"Come from?" He smiled, and his voice was slow and soft. "I came out of space across seven million years or more. They had lost count—the men had. The machines had eliminated the unneeded service. They didn't know what year it was. But before that—my home is in Neva'th City in the 3059."

That's when I began to think he was a nut.

"I was an experimenter," he went on. "Science, as I have said. My father was a scientist, too, but in human genetics. I myself am an experiment. He proved his point, and all the world followed suit. I was the first of the new race.

"The new race—oh, holy destiny—what has—what will—

"What is its end? I have seen it—almost. I saw them—the little men—bewildered—lost. And the machines. Must it be—can't anything sway it?

"Listen—I heard this song."

He sang the song. Then he didn't have to tell me about the people. I knew them. I could hear their voices, in the queer, crackling, un-English words. I could read their bewildered longings. It was in a minor key, I think. It called, it called and asked, and hunted hopelessly. And over it all the steady rumble and whine of the unknown, forgotten machines.

The machines that couldn't stop, because they had been started, and the little men had forgotten how to stop them, or even what they were for, looking at them and listening —and wondering. They couldn't read or write any more, and the language had changed, you see, so that the phonic records of their ancestors meant nothing to them.

But that song went on, and they wondered. And they looked out across space and they saw the warm, friendly stars—too far away. Nine planets they knew and inhabited. And locked by infinite distance, they couldn't see another race, a new life.

And through it all—two things. The machines. Bewildered forgetfulness. And maybe one more. Why?

That was the song, and it made me cold. It shouldn't be sung around people of today. It almost killed something. It seemed to kill hope. After that song—I—well, I believed him.

When he finished the song, he didn't talk for a while. Then he sort of shook himself.

You won't understand (he continued). Not yet—but I have seen them. They stand about, like misshapen men with huge heads. But their heads contain only brains. They had machines that could think—but somebody turned them off a long time ago, and no one knew how to start them again. That was the trouble with them. They had wonderful brains. Far better than yours or mine. But it must have been millions of years ago when they were turned off, too, and they just haven't thought since then. Kindly little people. That was all they knew.

When I slipped into that field it grabbed me like a gravitational field whirling a space transport down to a planet.

It sucked me in—and through. Only the other side must have been seven million years in the future. That's where I was. It must have been in exactly the same spot on Earth's surface, but I never knew why.

It was night then, and I saw the city a little way off. The Moon was shining on it, and the whole scene looked wrong. You see, in seven million years, men had done a lot with the positions of the planetary bodies, what with moving space liners, clearing lanes through the asteroids, and such. And seven million years is long enough for natural things to change positions a little. The Moon must have been fifty thousand miles farther out. And it was rotating on its axis. I lay there a while and watched it. Even the stars were different.

There were ships going out of the city. Back and forth, like things sliding along a wire, but there was only a wire of force, of course. Part of the city, the lower part, was brightly lighted with what must have been mercury vapor glow, I decided. Blue-green. I felt sure men didn't live there—the light was wrong for eyes. But the top of the city was so sparsely lighted.

Then I saw something coming down out of the sky. It was brightly lighted. A huge globe, and it sank straight to the center of the great black-and-silver mass of the city.

I don't know what it was, but even then I knew the city was deserted. Strange that I could even imagine that, I who had never seen a deserted city before. But I walked the fifteen miles over to it and entered it. There were machines going about the streets, repair machines, you know. They couldn't understand that the city didn't need to go on functioning, so they were still working. I found a taxi machine that seemed fairly familiar. It had a manual control that I could work.

I don't know how long that city had been deserted. Some of the men from the other cities said it was a hundred and fifty thousand years. Some went as high as three hundred thousand years. Three hundred thousand years since human foot had been in that city. The taxi machine was in perfect condition, functioned at once. It was clean, and the city was clean and orderly. I saw a restaurant and I was hungry. Hungrier still for humans to speak to. There were none, of course, but I didn't know.

The restaurant had the food displayed directly, and I made a choice. The food was three hundred thousand years old, I suppose, I didn't know, and the machines that served it to me didn't care, for they made things synthetically, you see, and perfectly. When the builders made those cities, they forgot one thing. They didn't realize that things shouldn't go on forever.

It took me six months to make my apparatus. And near the end I was ready to go; and, from seeing those machines go blindly, perfectly, on orbits of their duties with the tireless, ceaseless perfection their designers had incorporated in them, long after those designers and their sons, and their sons' sons had no use for them—

When Earth is cold, and the Sun has died out, those machines will go on. When Earth begins to crack and break, those perfect, ceaseless machines will try to repair her—

I left the restaurant and cruised about the city in the taxi. The machine had a little, electric-power motor, I believe, but it gained its power from the great central power radiator. I knew before long that I was far in the future. The city was divided into two sections, a section of many strata where machines functioned smoothly, save for a deep humming beat that echoed through the whole city like a vast unending song of power. The entire metal framework of the place echoed with it, transmitted it, hummed with it. But it was soft and restful, a reassuring beat.

There must have been thirty levels above ground, and twenty more below, a solid block of metal walls and metal floors and metal and glass and force machines. The only light was the blue-green glow of the mercury vapor arcs. The light of mercury vapor is rich in high-energy-quanta, which stimulate the alkali metal atoms to photo-electric activity. Or perhaps that is beyond the science of your day? I have forgotten.

But they had used that light because many of their worker machines needed sight. The machines were marvelous. For five hours I wandered through the vast power plant on the very lowest level, watching them, and because there was motion, and that pseudo-mechanical life, I felt less alone.

The generators I saw were a development of the release I had discovered—when? The release of the energy of matter, I mean, and I knew when I saw that for what countless ages they could continue.

The entire lower block of the city was given over to the machines. Thousands. But most of them seemed idle, or, at most, running under light load. I recognized a telephone apparatus, and not a single signal came through. There was no life in the city. Yet when I pressed a little stud beside the screen on one side of the room, the machine began working instantly. It was ready. Only no one needed it any more. The men knew how to die, and be dead, but the machines didn't

Finally I went up to the top of the city, the upper level. It was a paradise.

There were shrubs and trees and parks, glowing in the soft light that they had learned to make in the very air. They had learned it five million years or more before. Two million years ago they forgot. But the machines didn't, and they were still making it. It hung in the air, soft, silvery light, slightly rosy, and the gardens were shadowy with it. There were no machines here now, but I knew that in daylight they must come out and work on those gardens, keeping them a paradise for masters who had died, and stopped moving, as they could not.

In the desert outside the city it had been cool, and very dry. Here the air was soft, warm and sweet with the scent of blooms that men had spent several hundreds of thousands of years perfecting.

Then somewhere music began. It began in the air, and spread softly through it. The Moon was just setting now, and as it set, the rosy-silver glow waned and the music grew stronger.

It came from everywhere and from nowhere. It was within me. I do not know how they did it. And I do not know how such music could be written.

Savages make music too simple to be beautiful, but it is stirring. Semisavages write music beautifully simple, and simply beautiful. Your Negro music was your best. They knew music when they heard it and sang it as they felt it. Semicivilized peoples write great music. They are proud of their music, and make sure it is known for great music. They make it so great it is top-heavy.

I had always thought our music good. But that which came through the air was the song of triumph, sung by a mature race, the race of man in its full triumph! It was man singing his triumph in majestic sound that swept me up; it showed me what lay before me; it carried me on.

And it died in the air as I looked at the deserted city. The machines should have forgotten that song. Their masters had, long before.

I came to what must have been one of their homes; it was a dimly-seen doorway in the dusky light, but as I stepped up to it, the lights which had not functioned in three hundred thousand years illuminated it for me with a green-white glow, like a firefly, and I stepped into the room beyond. Instantly something happened to the air in the doorway behind me; it was as opaque as milk. The room in which I stood was a room of metal and stone. The stone was some jet-black substance with the finish of velvet, and the metals were silver and gold. There was a rug on the floor, a rug of just such material as I am wearing now, but thicker and softer. There were divans about the room, low and covered with these soft metallic materials. They were black and gold and silver, too.

I had never seen anything like that. I never shall again, I suppose, and my language and yours were not made to describe it.

The builders of that city had right and reason to sing that song of sweeping triumph, triumph that swept them over the nine planets and the fifteen habitable moons.

But they weren't there any more, and I wanted to leave. I thought of a plan and went to a subtelephone office to examine a map I had seen. The old World looked much the same. Seven or even seventy million years don't mean much to old Mother Earth. She may even succeed in wearing down those marvelous machine cities. She can wait a hundred million or a thousand million years before she is beaten.

I tried calling different city centers shown on the map. I had quickly learned the system when I examined the central apparatus.

I tried once—twice—thrice—a round dozen times.

Yawk City, Lunon City, Paree, Shkago, Singpor, others.
I was beginning to feel that there were no more men on
all earth. And I felt crushed, as at each city the machines
replied and did my bidding. The machines were there in
each of those far vaster cities, for I was in the Neva City
of their time. A small city. Yawk City was more than eight
hundred kilometers in diameter.

In each city I tried several numbers. Then I tried San
Frisco. There was some one there, and a voice answered
and the picture of a human appeared on the little glowing
screen. I could see him start and stare in surprise at me.
Then he started speaking to me. I couldn't understand, of
course. I can understand your speech, and you mine, because your speech of this day is largely recorded on records of various types and has influenced our pronuncia-
tion.

Some things are changed; names of cities, particularly,
because names of cities are apt to be polysyllabic, and
used a great deal. People tend to elide them, shorten
them. I am in—Nee-vah-dah—as you would say? We say
only Neva. And Yawk State. But it is Ohio and Iowa still.
Over a thousand years, effects were small on words, because they were recorded.

But seven million years had passed, and the men had
forgotten the old records, used them less as time went on,
and their speech varied till the time came when they could
no longer understand the records. They were not written
any more, of course.

Some men must have arisen occasionally among that
last of the race and sought for knowledge, but it was
denied them. An ancient writing can be translated if some
basic rule is found. An ancient voice though—and when
the race has forgotten the laws of science and the labor
of mind.

So his speech was strange to me as he answered over
that circuit. His voice was high in pitch, his words liquid,
his tones sweet. It was almost a song as he spoke. He was
excited and called others. I could not understand them,
but I knew where they were. I could go to them.

So I went down from the paradise gardens, and as I
prepared to leave, I saw dawn in the sky. The strange-
bright stars winked and twinkled and faded. Only one

bright rising star was familiar—Venus. She shone golden now. Finally, as I stood watching for the first time that strange heaven, I began to understand what had first impressed me with the wrongness of the view. The stars, you see, were all different.

In my time—and yours, the solar system is a lone wanderer that by chance is passing across an intersection point of Galactic traffic. The stars we see at night are the stars of moving clusters, you know. In fact our system is passing through the heart of the Ursa Major group. Half a dozen other groups center within five hundred light-years of us.

But during those seven millions of years, the Sun had moved out of the group. The heavens were almost empty to the eye. Only here and there shone a single faint star. And across the vast sweep of black sky swung the band of the Milky Way. The sky was empty.

That must have been another thing those men meant in their songs—felt in their hearts. Loneliness—not even the close, friendly stars. We have stars within half a dozen light-years. They told me that their instruments, which gave directly the distance to any star, showed that the nearest was one hundred and fifty light-years away. It was enormously bright. Brighter even than Sirius of our heavens. And that made it even less friendly, because it was a blue-white supergiant. Our sun would have served as a satellite for that star.

I stood there and watched the lingering rose-silver glow die as the powerful blood-red light of the Sun swept over the horizon. I knew by the stars now, that it must have been several millions of years since my day; since I had last seen the Sun sweep up. And that blood-red light made me wonder if the Sun itself was dying.

An edge of it appeared, blood-red and huge. It swung up, and the color faded, till in half an hour it was the familiar yellow-gold disk.

It hadn't changed in all that time.

I had been foolish to think that it would. Seven million years—that is nothing to Earth, how much less to the Sun? Some two thousand thousand thousand times it had risen since I last saw it rise. Two thousand thousand thousand days. If it had been that many years—I might have noticed a change.

The universe moves slowly. Only life is not enduring; only life changes swiftly. Eight short millions of years. Eight days in the life of Earth—and the race was dying. It had left something: machines. But they would die, too, even though they could not understand. So I felt. I—may have changed that. I will tell you. Later.

For when the Sun was up, I looked again at the sky and the ground, some fifty floors below. I had come to the edge of the city.

Machines were moving on that ground, leveling it, perhaps. A great wide line of gray stretched off across the level desert straight to the east. I had seen it glowing faintly before the Sun rose—a roadway for ground machines. There was no traffic on it.

I saw an airship slip in from the east. It came with a soft, muttering whine of air, like a child complaining in sleep; it grew to my eyes like an expanding balloon. It was huge when it settled in a great port-slip in the city below. I could hear now the clang and mutter of machines, working on the materials brought in, no doubt. The machines had ordered raw materials. The machines in other cities had supplied. The freight machines had carried them here.

San Frisco and Jacksville were the only two cities on North America still used. But the machines went on in all the others, because they couldn't stop. They hadn't been ordered to.

Then high above, something appeared, and from the city beneath me, from a center section, three small spheres rose. They, like the freight ship, had no visible driving mechanisms. The point in the sky above, like a black star in a blue space, had grown to a moon. The three spheres met it high above. Then together they descended and lowered into the center of the city, where I could not see them.

It was freight transport from Venus. The one I had seen land the night before had come from Mars, I learned.

I moved after that and looked for some sort of a taxiplane. They had none that I recognized in scouting about the city. I searched the higher levels, and here and there saw deserted ships, but far too large for me, and without controls.

It was nearly noon—and I ate again. The food was good. I knew then that this was a city of the dead ashes of

human hopes. The hopes not of *a* race, not the whites, nor
the yellow, nor the blacks, but the human race. I was mad
to leave the city. I was afraid to try the ground road to
the west, for the taxi I drove was powered from some
source in the city, and I knew it would fail before many
miles.

It was afternoon when I found a small hangar near the
outer wall of the vast city. It contained three ships. I had
been searching through the lower strata of the human section—the upper part. There were restaurants and shops
and theatres there. I entered one place where, at my entrance, soft music began, and colors and forms began to
rise on a screen before me.

They were the triumph songs in form and sound and
color of a mature race, a race that had marched steadily
upward through five millions of years—and didn't see the
path that faded out ahead, when they were dead and
stopped, and the city itself was dead—but hadn't stopped.
I hastened out of there—and the song that had not been
sung in three hundred thousand years died behind me.

But I found the hangar. It was a private one, likely.
Three ships. One must have been fifty feet long and fifteen
in diameter. It was a yacht, a space yacht, probably. One
was some fifteen feet long and five feet in diameter. That
must have been the family air machine. The third was a
tiny thing, little more than ten feet long and two in diameter. I had to lie down within it, evidently.

There was a periscope device that gave me a view ahead
and almost directly above. A window that permitted me
to see what lay below—and a device that moved a map
under a frosted-glass screen and projected it onto the
screen in such a way that the cross-hairs of the screen
always marked my position.

I spent half an hour attempting to understand what the
makers of that ship had made. But the men who made
that were men who held behind them the science and
knowledge of five millions of years and the perfect machines of those ages. I saw the release mechanism that
powered it. I understood the principles of that and,
vaguely, the mechanics. But there were no conductors, only
pale beams that pulsed so swiftly you could hardly catch
the pulsations from the corner of the eye. They had been

glowing and pulsating, some half dozen of them, for three hundred thousand years at least; probably more.

I entered the machine, and instantly half a dozen more beams sprang into being; there was a slight suggestion of a quiver, and a queer strain ran through my body. I understood in an instant, for the machine was resting on gravity nullifiers. That had been my hope when I worked on the space fields I discovered after the release.

But they had had it for millions of years before they built that perfect deathless machine. My weight entering it had forced it to readjust itself and simultaneously to prepare for operation. Within, an artificial gravity equal to that of Earth had gripped me, and the neutral zone between the outside and the interior had caused the strain.

The machine was ready. It was fully fueled. You see they were equipped to tell automatically their wants and needs. They were almost living things, every one. A caretaker machine kept them supplied, adjusted, even repaired them when need be, and when possible. If it was not, I learned later, they were carried away in a service truck that came automatically; replaced by an exactly similar machine; and carried to the shops where they were made, and automatic machines made them over.

The machine waited patiently for me to start. The controls were simple, obvious. There was a lever at the left that you pushed forward to move forward, pulled back to go back. On the right a horizontal, pivoted bar. If you swung it left, the ship spun left; if right, the ship spun right. If tipped up, the ship followed it, and likewise for all motions other than backward and forward. Raising it bodily raised the ship, as depressing it depressed the ship.

I lifted it slightly, a needle moved a bit on a gauge comfortably before my eyes as I lay there, and the floor dropped beneath me. I pulled the other control back, and the ship gathered speed as it moved gently out into the open. Releasing both controls into neutral, the machine continued till it stopped at the same elevation, the motion absorbed by air friction. I turned it about, and another dial before my eyes moved, showing my position. I could not read it, though. The map did not move, as I had hoped it would. So I started toward what I felt was west.

I could feel no acceleration in that marvelous machine.

The ground simply began leaping backward, and in a moment the city was gone. The map unrolled rapidly beneath me now, and I saw that I was moving south of west. I turned northward slightly, and watched the compass. Soon I understood that, too, and the ship sped on.

I had become too interested in the map and the compass, for suddenly there was a sharp buzz and, without my volition, the machine rose and swung to the north. There was a mountain ahead of me; I had not seen, but the ship had.

I noticed then what I should have seen before—two little knobs that could move the map. I started to move them and heard a sharp clicking, and the pace of the ship began decreasing. A moment and it had steadied at a considerably lower speed, the machine swinging to a new course. I tried to right it, but to my amazement the controls did not affect it.

It was the map, you see. It would either follow the course, or the course would follow it. I had moved it and the machine had taken over control of its own accord. There was a little button I could have pushed—but I didn't know. I couldn't control the ship until it finally came to rest and lowered itself to a stop six inches from the ground in the center of what must have been the ruins of a great city. Sacramento, probably.

I understood now, so I adjusted the map for San Frisco, and the ship went on at once. It steered itself around a mass of broken stone, turned back to its course, and headed on, a bullet-shaped, self-controlled dart.

It didn't descend when it reached San Frisco. It simply hung in the air and sounded a soft musical hum. Twice. Then I waited, too, and looked down.

There were people here. I saw the humans of that age for the first time. They were little men—bewildered—dwarfed, with heads disproportionately large. But not extremely so.

Their eyes impressed me most. They were huge, and when they looked at me there was a power in them that seemed sleeping, but too deeply to be roused.

I took the manual controls then and landed. And no sooner had I got out, than the ship rose automatically and started off by itself. They had automatic parking devices.

The ship had gone to a public hangar, the nearest, where it would be automatically serviced and cared for. There was a little call set I should have taken with me when I got out. Then I could have pressed a button and called it to me—wherever I was in that city.

The people about me began talking—singing almost— among themselves. Others were coming up leisurely. Men and women—but there seemed no old and few young. What few young there were, were treated almost with respect, carefully taken care of lest a careless footstep on their toes or a careless step knock them down.

There was reason, you see. They lived a tremendous time. Some lived as long as three thousand years. Then— they simply died. They didn't grow old, and it never had been learned why people died as they did. The heart stopped, the brain ceased thought—and they died. But the young children, children not yet mature, were treated with the utmost care. But one child was born in the course of a month in that city of one hundred thousand people. The human race was growing sterile.

And I have told you that they were lonely? Their loneliness was beyond hope. For, you see, as man strode toward maturity, he destroyed all forms of life that menaced him. Disease. Insects. Then the last of the insects, and finally the last of the man-eating animals.

The balance of nature was destroyed then, so they had to go on. It was like the machines. They started them— and now they can't stop. They started destroying life—and now it wouldn't stop. So they had to destroy weeds of all sorts, then many formerly harmless plants. Then the herbivora, too, the deer and the antelope and the rabbit and the horse. They were a menace, they attacked man's machine-tended crops. Man was still eating natural foods.

You can understand. The thing was beyond their control. In the end they killed off the denizens of the sea, also, in self-defense. Without the many creatures that had kept them in check, they were swarming beyond bounds. And the time had come when synthetic foods replaced natural. The air was purified of all life about two and a half million years after our day, all microscopic life.

That meant that the water, too, must be purified. It was —and then came the end of life in the ocean. There were minute organisms that lived on bacterial forms, and tiny fish that lived on the minute organisms, and small fish that lived on the tiny fish, and big fish that lived on the small fish—and the beginning of the chain was gone. The sea was devoid of life in a generation. That meant about one thousand and five hundred years to them. Even the sea plants had gone.

And on all Earth there was only man and the organisms he had protected—the plants he wanted for decoration, and certain ultra-hygienic pets, as long-lived as their masters. Dogs. They must have been remarkable animals. Man was reaching his maturity then, and his animal friend, the friend that had followed him through a thousand millenniums to your day and mine, and another four thousand millenniums to the day of man's early maturity, had grown in intelligence. In an ancient museum—a wonderful place, for they had, perfectly preserved, the body of a great leader of mankind who had died five and a half million years before I saw him—in that museum, deserted then, I saw one of those canines. His skull was nearly as large as mine. They had simple ground machines that dogs could be trained to drive, and they held races in which the dogs drove those machines.

Then man reached his full maturity. It extended over a period of a full million years. So tremendously did he stride ahead, the dog ceased to be a companion. Less and less were they wanted. When the million years had passed, and man's decline began, the dog was gone. It had died out.

And now this last dwindling group of men still in the system had no other life form to make its successor. Always before when one civilization toppled, on its ashes rose a new one. Now there was but one civilization, and all other races, even other species, were gone save in the plants. And man was too far along in his old age to bring intelligence and mobility from the plants. Perhaps he could have in his prime.

Other worlds were flooded with man during that million years—the million years. Every planet and every moon of the system had its quota of men. Now only the planets had their populations, the moons had been deserted. Pluto had been left before I landed, and men were coming from Neptune, moving in toward the Sun, and the home planet, while I was there. Strangely quiet men, viewing, most of them, for the first time, the planet that had given their race life.

But as I stepped from that ship and watched it rise away from me, I saw why the race of man was dying. I looked back at the faces of those men, and on them I read the answer. There was one single quality gone from the still-great minds—minds far greater than yours or mine. I had to have the help of one of them in solving some of my problems. In space, you know, there are twenty coordinates, ten of which are zero, six of which have fixed values, and the four others represent our changing, familiar dimensions in space-time. That means that integrations must proceed in not double, or triple, or quadruple—but ten integrations.

It must have taken me too long. I would never have solved all the problems I must work out. I could not use their mathematics machines; and mine, of course, were seven million years in the past. But one of those men was interested and helped me. He did quadruple and quintuple integration, even quadruple integration between varying exponential limits—in his head.

When I asked him to. For the one thing that had made man great had left him. As I looked in their faces and eyes on landing I knew it. They looked at me, interested at this rather unusual-looking stranger—and went on. They had come to see the arrival of a ship. A rare event, you see. But they were merely welcoming me in a friendly fashion. They were not curious! Man had lost the instinct of curiosity.

Oh, not entirely! They wondered at the machines, they wondered at the stars. But they did nothing about it. It was not wholly lost to them yet, but nearly. It was dying. In the six short months I stayed with them, I learned more than they had learned in the two or even three thousand years they had lived among the machines.

Can you appreciate the crushing loneliness it brought to me? I, who love science, who see in it, or have seen in it, the salvation, the raising of mankind—to see those wondrous machines, of man's triumphant maturity, forgotten and misunderstood. The wondrous, perfect machines that tended, protected, and cared for those gentle, kindly people who had—forgotten.

They were lost among it. The city was a magnificent ruin to them, a thing that rose stupendous about them. Something not understood, a thing that was of the nature of the world. It was. It had not been made; it simply was. Just as the mountains and the deserts and the waters of the seas.

Do you understand—can you see that the time since those machines were new was longer than the time from our day to the birth of the race? Do we know the legends of our first ancestors? Do we remember their lore of forest and cave? The secret of chipping a flint till it had a sharp-cutting edge? The secret of trailing and killing a saber-toothed tiger without being killed oneself?

They were now in similar straits, though the time had been longer, because the languages had taken a long step toward perfection, and because the machines maintained everything for them through generation after generation.

Why, the entire planet of Pluto had been deserted—yet on Pluto the largest mines of one of their metals were located; the machines still functioned. A perfect unity existed throughout the system. A unified system of perfect machines.

And all those people knew was to do a certain thing to a certain lever produced certain results. Just as men in the Middle Ages knew that to take a certain material, wood, and place it in contact with other pieces of wood heated red, would cause the wood to disappear, and become heat. They did not understand that wood was being oxidized with the release of the heat of formation of carbon dioxide and water. So those people did not understand the things that fed and clothed and carried them.

I stayed with them there for three days. And then I went to Jacksville. Yawk City, too. That was enormous. It stretched over—well, from well north of where Boston is today to well south of Washington—that was what they called Yawk City.

I never believed that, when he said it, said Jim, interrupting himself. I knew he didn't. If he had I think he'd have bought land somewhere along there and held for a rise in value. I know Jim. He'd have the idea that seven million years was something like seven hundred, and maybe his great-grandchildren would be able to sell it.

Anyway, went on Jim, he said it was all because the cities had spread so. Boston spread south. Washington, north. And Yawk City spread all over. And the cities between grew into them.

And it was all one vast machine. It was perfectly ordered and perfectly neat. They had a transportation system that took me from the North End to the South End in three minutes. I timed it. They had learned to neutralize acceleration.

Then I took one of the great space liners to Neptune. There were still some running. Some people, you see, were coming the other way.

The ship was huge. Mostly it was a freight liner. It floated up from Earth, a great metal cylinder three quarters of a mile long, and a quarter of a mile in diameter. Outside the atmosphere it began to accelerate. I could see Earth dwindle. I have ridden one of our own liners to Mars, and it took me, in 3048, five days. In half an hour on this liner Earth was just a star, with a smaller, dimmer star near it. In an hour we passed Mars. Eight hours later we landed on Neptune. M'reen was the city. Large as the Yawk City of my day—and no one living there.

The planet was cold and dark—horribly cold. The sun was a tiny, pale disk, heatless and almost lightless. But the city was perfectly comfortable. The air was fresh and cool, moist with the scent of growing blossoms, perfumed with them. And the whole giant metal framework trembled just slightly with the humming, powerful beat of the mighty machines that had made and cared for it.

I learned from records I deciphered, because of my knowledge of the ancient tongue that their tongue was based on, and the tongue of that day when man was dying, that the city was built three million, seven hundred and thirty thousand, one hundred and fifty years after my birth. Not a machine had been touched by the hand of man since that day.

Yet the air was perfect for man. And the warm, rose-silver glow hung in the air here and supplied the only illumination.

I visited some of their other cities where there were men.

And there, on the retreating outskirts of man's domain, I first heard the Song of Longings, as I called it.

And another, The Song of Forgotten Memories. Listen:

He sang another of those songs. There's one thing I know, declared Jim. That bewildered note was stronger in his voice, and by that time I guess I pretty well understood his feelings. Because, you have to remember, I heard it only secondhand from an ordinary man, and Jim had heard it from an eye-and-ear witness that was not ordinary, and heard it in that organ voice. Anyway, I guess Jim was right when he said: "He wasn't any ordinary man." No ordinary man could think of those songs. They weren't right. When he sang that song, it was full of more of those plaintive minors. I could feel him searching his mind for something he had forgotten, something he desperately wanted to remember—something he knew he should have known—and I felt it eternally elude him. I felt it get further away from him as he sang. I heard that lonely, frantic searcher attempting to recall that thing—that thing that would save him.

And I heard him give a little sob of defeat—and the song ended. Jim tried a few notes. He hasn't a good ear for music—but that was too powerful to forget. Just a few hummed notes. Jim hasn't much imagination, I guess, or when that man of the future sang to him he would have gone mad. It shouldn't be sung to modern men; it isn't meant for them. You've heard those heart-rending cries some animals give, like human cries, almost? A loon, now —he sounds like a lunatic being murdered horribly.

That's just unpleasant. That song made you feel just exactly what the singer meant—because it didn't just sound human—it was human. It was the essence of humanity's last defeat, I guess. You always feel sorry for the chap who loses after trying hard. Well, you could feel the whole of humanity trying hard—and losing. And you knew they couldn't afford to lose, because they couldn't try again.

He said he'd been interested before. And still not wholly upset by these machines that couldn't stop. But that was too much for him.

I knew after that, he said, that these weren't men I could live among. They were dying men, and I was alive with the youth of the race. They looked at me with the same longing, hopeless wonder with which they looked at the stars and the machines. They knew what I was, but couldn't understand.

I began to work on leaving.

It took six months. It was hard because my instruments were gone, of course, and theirs didn't read in the same units. And there were few instruments, anyway. The machines didn't read instruments; they acted on them. They were sensory organs to them.

But Reo Lantal helped where he could. And I came back.

I did just one thing before I left that may help. I may even try to get back there sometime. To see, you know.

I said they had machines that could really think? But that someone had stopped them a long time ago, and no one knew how to start them?

I found some records and deciphered them. I started one of the last and best of them and started it on a great problem. It is only fitting it should be done. The machine can work on it, not for a thousand years, but for a million, if it must.

I started five of them actually, and connected them together as the records directed.

They are trying to make a machine with something that man had lost. It sounds rather comical. But stop to think before you laugh. And remember that Earth as I saw it from the ground level of Neva City just before Reo Lantal threw the switch.

Twilight—the sun has set. The desert out beyond, in its mystic, changing colors. The great, metal city rising straight-walled to the human city above, broken by spires and towers and great trees with scented blossoms. The silvery-rose glow in the paradise of gardens above.

And all the great city-structure throbbing and humming to the steady gentle beat of perfect, deathless machines built more than three million years before—and never touched since that time by human hands. And they go on. The dead city. The men that have lived, and hoped, and built—and died to leave behind them those little men who can only wonder and look and long for a forgotten kind of companionship. They wander through the vast cities their ancestors built, knowing less of them than the machines themselves.

And the songs. Those tell the story best, I think. Little, hopeless, wondering men amid vast unknowing, blind machines that started three million years before—and just never know how to stop. They are dead—and can't die and be still.

So I brought another machine to life, and set it to a task which, in time to come, it will perform.

I ordered it to make a machine which would have what man had lost. A curious machine.

And then I wanted to leave quickly and go back. I had been born in the first full light of man's day. I did not belong in the lingering, dying glow of man's twilight.

So I came back. A little too far back. But it will not take me long to return—accurately this time.

"Well, that was his story," Jim said. "He didn't *tell* me it was true—didn't say anything about it. And he had me thinking so hard I didn't even see him get off in Reno when we stopped for gas.

"But—he wasn't an ordinary man," repeated Jim, in a rather belligerent tone.

Jim claims he doesn't believe the yarn, you know. But he does; that's why he always acts so determined about it when he says the stranger wasn't an ordinary man.

No, he wasn't, I guess. I think he lived and died, too, probably, sometime in the thirty-first century. And I think he saw the twilight of the race, too.

HELEN O'LOY

by Lester del Rey

I am an old man now, and I can still see Helen as Dave
unpacked her, and still hear him gasp as he looked her
over.

"Man, isn't she a beauty?"

She was beautiful, a dream in spun plastics and metals,
something Keats might have seen dimly when he wrote his
sonnet. If Helen of Troy had looked like that the Greeks
must have been pikers when they launched only a thousand ships; at least, that's what I told Dave.

"Helen of Troy, eh?" He looked at her tag. "At least it
beats this thing—K2W88. Helen . . . Mmmm . . . Helen
of Alloy."

"Not much swing to that, Dave. Too many unstressed
syllables in the middle. How about Helen O'Loy?"

"Helen O'Loy she is, Phil." And that's how it began—
one part beauty, one part dream, one part science; add a
stereo broadcast, stir mechanically, and the result is chaos.

Dave and I hadn't gone to college together, but when
I came to Messina to practice medicine, I found him
downstairs in a little robot repair shop. After that, we began to pal around, and when I started going with one twin,
he found the other equally attractive, so we made it a
foursome.

When our business grew better, we rented a house near
the rocket field—noisy but cheap, and the rockets discouraged apartment building. We liked room enough to stretch
ourselves. I suppose, if we hadn't quarreled with them,
we'd have married the twins in time. But Dave wanted to

First published in 1938

look over the latest Venus-rocket attempt when his twin
wanted to see a display stereo starring Larry Ainslee, and
they were both stubborn. From then on, we forgot the
girls and spent our evenings at home.

But it wasn't until "Lena" put vanilla on our steak instead of salt that we got off on the subject of emotions and
robots. While Dave was dissecting Lena to find the trouble,
we naturally mulled over the future of the mechs. He was
sure that the robots would beat men some day, and I
couldn't see it.

"Look here, Dave," I argued. "You know Lena doesn't
think—not really. When those wires crossed, she could
have corrected herself. But she didn't bother; she followed
the mechanical impulse. A man might have reached for
the vanilla, but when he saw it in his hand, he'd have
stopped. Lena has sense enough, but she has no emotions,
no consciousness of self."

"All right, that's the big trouble with the mechs now.
But we'll get around it, put in some mechanical emotions,
or something." He screwed Lena's head back on, turned on
her juice. "Go back to work, Lena, it's nineteen o'clock."

Now I specialized in endocrinology and related subjects.
I wasn't exactly a psychologist, but I did understand the
glands, secretions, hormones, and miscellanies that are the
physical causes of emotions. It took medical science three
hundred years to find out how and why they worked, and
I couldn't see men duplicating them mechanically in much
less time.

I brought home books and papers to prove it, and Dave
quoted the invention of memory coils and veritoid eyes.
During that year we swapped knowledge until Dave knew
the whole theory of endocrinology, and I could have made
Lena from memory. The more we talked, the less sure
I grew about the impossibility of *homo mechanensis* as the
perfect type.

Poor Lena. Her cuproberyl body spent half its time in
scattered pieces. Our first attempts were successful only in
getting her to serve fried brushes for breakfast and wash
the dishes in oleo oil. Then one day she cooked a perfect
dinner with six wires crossed, and Dave was in ecstasy.

He worked all night on her wiring, put in a new coil,
and taught her a fresh set of words. And the next day she

flew into a tantrum and swore vigorously at us when we told her she wasn't doing her work right.

"It's a lie," she yelled, shaking a suction brush. "You're all liars. If you so-and-so's would leave me whole long enough, I might get something done around the place."

When we calmed her temper and got her back to work, Dave ushered me into the study. "Not taking any chances with Lena," he explained. "We'll have to cut out that adrenal pack and restore her to normalcy. But we've got to get a better robot. A housemaid mech isn't complex enough."

"How about Dillard's new utility models? They seem to combine everything in one."

"Exactly. Even so, we'll need a special one built to order, with a full range of memory coils. And out of respect to old Lena, let's get a female case for its works."

The result, of course, was Helen. The Dillard people had performed a miracle and put all the works in a girl-modeled case. Even the plastic and rubberite face was designed for flexibility to express emotions, and she was complete with tear glands and taste buds, ready to simulate every human action, from breathing to pulling hair. The bill they sent with her was another miracle, but Dave and I scraped it together; we had to turn Lena over to an exchange to complete it, though, and thereafter we ate out.

I'd performed plenty of delicate operations on living tissues, and some of them had been tricky, but I still felt like a pre-med student as we opened the front plate of her torso and began to sever the leads of her "nerves." Dave's mechanical glands were all prepared, complex little bundles of radio tubes and wires that heterodyned on the electrical thought impulses and distorted them as adrenalin distorts the reaction of human minds.

Instead of sleeping that night, we pored over the schematic diagrams of her structures, tracing the thoughts through mazes of her wiring, severing the leaders, implanting the heterones, as Dave called them. And while we worked, a mechanical tape fed carefully prepared thoughts of consciousness and awareness of life and feeling into an auxiliary memory coil. Dave believed in leaving nothing to chance.

It was growing light as we finished, exhausted and ex-

ultant. All that remained was the starting of her electrical
power; like all the Dillard mechs, she was equipped with
a tiny atomotor instead of batteries, and once started would
need no further attention.

Dave refused to turn her on. "Wait until we've slept and
rested," he advised. "I'm as eager to try her as you are,
but we can't do much studying with our minds half dead.
Turn in, and we'll leave Helen until later."

Even though we were both reluctant to follow it, we
knew the idea was sound. We turned in, and sleep hit us
before the air-conditioner could cut down to sleeping temperature. And then Dave was pounding on my shoulders.

"Phil! Hey, snap out of it!"

I groaned, turned over, and faced him. "Well? . . . Uh!
What is it? Did Helen—"

"No, it's old Mrs. van Styler. She 'visored to say her son
has an infatuation for a servant girl, and she wants you to
come out and give counter-hormones. They're at the
summer camp in Maine."

Rich Mrs. van Styler! I couldn't afford to let that account
down, now that Helen had used up the last of my funds.
But it wasn't a job I cared for.

"Counter-hormones! That'll take two weeks' full time.
Anyway, I'm no society doctor, messing with glands to
keep fools happy. My job's taking care of serious trouble."

"And you want to watch Helen." Dave was grinning,
but he was serious, too. "I told her it'd cost her fifty
thousand!"

"Huh?"

"And she said okay, if you hurried."

Of course, there was only one thing to do, though I
could have wrung fat Mrs. van Styler's neck cheerfully. It
wouldn't have happened if she'd used robots like everyone
else—but she had to be different.

Consequently, while Dave was back home puttering with
Helen, I was racking my brain to trick Archy van Styler
into getting the counter-hormones, and giving the servant
girl the same. Oh, I wasn't supposed to, but the poor kid
was crazy about Archy. Dave might have written, I
thought, but never a word did I get.

It was three weeks later instead of two when I reported

that Archy was "cured," and collected on the line. With that money in my pocket, I hired a personal rocket and was back in Messina in half an hour. I didn't waste time in reaching the house.

As I stepped into the alcove, I heard a light patter of feet, and an eager voice called out, "Dave, dear?" For a minute I couldn't answer, and the voice came again, pleading, "Dave?"

I don't know what I expected, but I didn't expect Helen to meet me that way, stopping and staring at me, obvious disappointment on her face, little hands fluttering up against her breast.

"Oh," she cried. "I thought it was Dave. He hardly comes home to eat now, but I've had supper waiting hours." She dropped her hands and managed a smile. "You're Phil, aren't you? Dave told me about you when . . . at first. I'm so glad to see you home, Phil."

"Glad to see you doing so well, Helen." Now what does one say for light conversation with a robot? "You said something about supper?"

"Oh, yes. I guess Dave ate downtown again, so we might as well go in. It'll be nice having someone to talk to around the house, Phil. You don't mind if I call you Phil, do you? You know, you're sort of a godfather to me."

We ate. I hadn't counted on such behavior, but apparently she considered eating as normal as walking. She didn't do much eating, at that; most of the time she spent staring at the front door.

Dave came in as we were finishing, a frown a yard wide on his face. Helen started to rise, but he ducked toward the stairs, throwing words over his shoulder.

"Hi, Phil. See you up here later."

There was something radically wrong with him. For a moment, I'd thought his eyes were haunted, and as I turned to Helen, hers were filling with tears. She gulped, choked them back, and fell to viciously on her food.

"What's the matter with him . . . and you?" I asked.

"He's sick of me." She pushed her plate away and got up hastily. "You'd better see him while I clean up. And there's nothing wrong with me. And it's not my fault, anyway." She grabbed the dishes and ducked into the kitchen; I could have sworn she was crying.

Maybe all thought is a series of conditioned reflexes—but she certainly had picked up a lot of conditioning while I was gone. Lena in her heyday had been nothing like this. I went up to see if Dave could make any sense out of the hodgepodge.

He was squirting soda into a large glass of apple brandy, and I saw that the bottle was nearly empty. "Join me?" he asked.

It seemed like a good idea. The roaring blast of an iron rocket overhead was the only familiar thing left in the house. From the look around Dave's eyes, it wasn't the first bottle he'd emptied while I was gone, and there were more left. He dug out a new bottle for his own drink.

"Of course, it's none of my business, Dave, but that stuff won't steady your nerves any. What's gotten into you and Helen? Been seeing ghosts?"

Helen was wrong; he hadn't been eating downtown—nor anywhere else. His muscles collapsed into a chair in a way that spoke of fatigue and nerves, but mostly of hunger. "You noticed it, eh?"

"Noticed it? The two of you jammed it down my throat."

"Uhmmm." He swatted at a non-existent fly, and slumped further down in the pneumatic. "Guess maybe I should have waited with Helen until you got back. But if that stereo cast hadn't changed . . . anyway, it did. And those mushy books of yours finished the job."

"Thanks. That makes it all clear."

"You know, Phil, I've got a place up in the country . . . fruit ranch. My dad left it to me. Think I'll look it over."

And that's the way it went. But finally, by much liquor and more perspiration, I got some of the story out of him before I gave him an amytal and put him to bed. Then I hunted up Helen and dug the rest of the story from her, until it made sense.

Apparently as soon as I was gone, Dave had turned her on and made preliminary tests, which were entirely satisfactory. She had reacted beautifully—so well that he decided to leave her and go down to work as usual.

Naturally, with all her untried emotions, she was filled with curiosity and wanted him to stay. Then he had an inspiration. After showing her what her duties about the

house would be, he set her down in front of the stereo-
visor, tuned in a travelogue, and left her to occupy her
time with that.

The travelogue held her attention until it was finished,
and the station switched over to a current serial with Larry
Ainslee, the same cute emoter who'd given us all the
trouble with the twins. Incidentally, he looked something
like Dave.

Helen took to the serial like a seal to water. This play
acting was a perfect outlet for her newly excited emotions.
When that particular episode finished, she found a love
story on another station, and added still more to her education. The afternoon programs were mostly news and
music, but by then she'd found my books; and I do have
rather adolescent taste in literature.

Dave came home in the best of spirits. The front alcove
was neatly swept, and there was the odor of food in the
air that he'd missed around the house for weeks. He had
visions of Helen as the super-efficient housekeeper.

So it was a shock to him to feel two strong arms around
his neck from behind and hear a voice all a-quiver coo
into his ears, "Oh, Dave, darling, I've missed you so, and
I'm so *thrilled* that you're back." Helen's technique may
have lacked polish, but it had enthusiasm, as he found
when he tried to stop her from kissing him. She had
learned fast and furiously—also, Helen was powered by an
atomotor.

Dave wasn't a prude, but he remembered that she was
only a robot, after all. The fact that she felt, acted, and
looked like a young goddess in his arms didn't mean much.
With some effort, he untangled her and dragged her off to
supper, where he made her eat with him to divert her
attention.

After her evening work, he called her into the study
and gave her a thorough lecture on the folly of her ways.
It must have been good, for it lasted three solid hours, and
covered her station in life, the idiocy of stereos, and various other miscellanies. When he finished, Helen looked up
with dewy eyes and said wistfully, "I know, Dave, but I
still love you."

That's when Dave started drinking.

It grew worse each day. If he stayed downtown, she was crying when he came home. If he returned on time, she fussed over him and threw herself at him. In his room, with the door locked, he could hear her downstairs pacing up and down and muttering; and when he went down, she stared at him reproachfully until he had to go back up.

I sent Helen out on a fake errand in the morning and got Dave up. With her gone, I made him eat a decent breakfast and gave him a tonic for his nerves. He was still listless and moody.

"Look here, Dave," I broke in on his brooding. "Helen isn't human, after all. Why not cut off her power and change a few memory coils? Then we can convince her that she never was in love and couldn't get that way."

"You try it. I had the idea, but she put up a wail that would wake Homer. She says it would be murder—and the hell of it is that I can't help feeling the same about it. Maybe she isn't human, but you wouldn't guess it when she puts on that martyred look and tells you to go ahead and kill her."

"We never put in substitutes for some of the secretions present in man during the love period."

"I don't know what we put in. Maybe the heterones backfired or something. Anyway, she's made this idea so much a part of her thoughts that we'd have to put in a whole new set of coils."

"Well, why not?"

"Go ahead. You're the surgeon of this family. I'm not used to fussing with emotions. Matter of fact, since she's been acting this way, I'm beginning to hate work on any robot. My business is going to blazes."

He saw Helen coming up the walk and ducked out the back door for the monorail express. I'd intended to put him back in bed, but let him go. Maybe he'd be better off at his shop than at home.

"Dave's gone?" Helen did have that martyred look now.

"Yeah. I got him to eat, and he's gone to work."

"I'm glad he ate." She slumped down in a chair as if she were worn out, though how a mech could be tired beat me. "Phil?"

"Well, what is it?"

"Do you think I'm bad for him? I mean, do you think he'd be happier if I weren't here?"

"He'll go crazy if you keep acting this way around him."

She winced. Those little hands were twisting about pleadingly, and I felt like an inhuman brute. But I'd started, and I went ahead. "Even if I cut out your power and changed your coils, he'd probably still be haunted by you."

"I know. But I can't help it. And I'd make him a good wife, really I would, Phil."

I gulped; this was getting a little too far. "And give him strapping sons to boot, I suppose. A man wants flesh and blood, not rubber and metal."

"Don't, please! I can't think of myself that way; to me, I'm a woman. And you know how perfectly I'm made to imitate a real woman . . . in all ways. I couldn't give him sons, but in every other way . . . I'd try so hard, I know I'd make him a good wife."

I gave up.

Dave didn't come home that night, nor the next day. Helen was fussing and fuming, wanting me to call the hospitals and the police, but I knew nothing had happened to him. He always carried identification. Still, when he didn't come on the third day, I began to worry. And when Helen started out for his shop, I agreed to go with her.

Dave was there, with another man I didn't know. I parked Helen where he couldn't see her, but where she could hear, and went in as soon as the other fellow left.

Dave looked a little better and seemed glad to see me. "Hi, Phil—just closing up. Let's go eat."

Helen couldn't hold back any longer, but came trooping in. "Come on home, Dave. I've got roast duck with spice stuffing, and you know you love that."

"Scat!" said Dave. She shrank back, turned to go. "Oh, all right, stay. You might as well hear it, too. I've sold the shop. The fellow you saw just bought it, and I'm going up to the old fruit ranch I told you about, Phil. I can't stand the mechs any more."

"You'll starve to death at that," I told him.

"No, there's a growing demand for old-fashioned fruit, raised out of doors. People are tired of this water-culture stuff. Dad always made a living out of it. I'm leaving as soon as I can get home and pack."

Helen clung to her idea. "I'll pack, Dave, while you eat. I've got apple cobbler for dessert." The world was toppling under her feet, but she still remembered how crazy he was for apple cobbler.

Helen was a good cook; in fact she was a genius, with all the good points of a woman and a mech combined. Dave ate well enough, after he got started. By the time supper was over, he'd thawed out enough to admit he liked the duck and cobbler, and to thank her for packing. In fact, he even let her kiss him good-bye, though he firmly refused to let her go to the rocket field with him.

Helen was trying to be brave when I got back, and we carried on a stumbling conversation about Mrs. van Styler's servants for a while. But the talk began to lull, and she sat staring out of the window at nothing most of the time. Even the stereo comedy lacked interest for her, and I was glad to have her go off to her room. She could cut her power down to simulate sleep when she chose.

As the days slipped by, I began to realize why she couldn't believe herself a robot. I got to thinking of her as a girl and companion myself. Except for odd intervals when she went off by herself to brood, or when she kept going to the telescript for a letter that never came, she was as good a companion as a man could ask. There was something homey about the place that Lena had never put there.

I took Helen on a shopping trip to Hudson and she giggled and purred over wisps of silk and glassheen that were the fashion, tried on endless hats, and conducted herself as any normal girl might. We went trout fishing for a day, where she proved to be as good a sport and as sensibly silent as a man. I thoroughly enjoyed myself and thought she was forgetting Dave. That was before I came home unexpectedly and found her doubled up on the couch, threshing her legs up and down and crying to the high heavens.

It was then I called Dave. They seemed to have trouble in reaching him, and Helen came over beside me while I waited. She was tense and fidgety as an old maid trying to propose. But finally they located Dave.

"What's up, Phil?" he asked as his face came on the viewplate. "I was just getting my things together to—"

I broke him off. "Things can't go on the way they are, Dave. I've made up my mind. I'm yanking Helen's coils tonight. It won't be worse than what she's going through now."

Helen reached up and touched my shoulder. "Maybe that's best, Phil. I don't blame you."

Dave's voice cut in. "Phil, you don't know what you're doing!"

"Of course I do. It'll all be over by the time you can get here. As you heard, she's agreeing."

There was a black cloud sweeping over Dave's face. "I won't have it, Phil. She's half mine and I forbid it!"

"Of all the—"

"Go ahead, call me anything you want. I've changed my mind. I was packing to come home when you called."

Helen jerked around me, her eyes glued to the panel. "Dave, do you . . . are you—"

"I'm just waking up to what a fool I've been, Helen. Phil, I'll be home in a couple of hours, so if there's anything—"

He didn't have to chase me out. But I heard Helen cooing something about loving to be a rancher's wife before I could shut the door.

Well, I wasn't as surprised as they thought. I think I knew when I called Dave what would happen. No man acts the way Dave had been acting because he hates a girl; only because he thinks he does—and thinks wrong.

No woman ever made a lovelier bride or a sweeter wife. Helen never lost her flare for cooking and making a home. With her gone, the old house seemed empty, and I began to drop out to the ranch once or twice a week. I suppose they had trouble at times, but I never saw it, and I know the neighbors never suspected they were anything but normal man and wife.

Dave grew older, and Helen didn't, of course. But between us, we put lines in her face and grayed her hair without letting Dave know that she wasn't growing old with him; he'd forgotten that she wasn't human, I guess.

I practically forgot, myself. It wasn't until a letter came from Helen this morning that I woke up to reality. There,

in her beautiful script, just a trifle shaky in places, was the
inevitable that neither Dave nor I had seen.

Dear Phil,
    As you know, Dave has had heart trouble for sev-
eral years now. We expected him to live on just the
same, but it seems that wasn't to be. He died in my
arms just before sunrise. He sent you his greetings and
farewell.
    I've one last favor to ask of you, Phil. There is only
one thing for me to do when this is finished. Acid will
burn out metal as well as flesh, and I'll be dead with
Dave. Please see that we are buried together, and that
the morticians do not find my secret. Dave wanted it
that way, too.
    Poor, dear Phil. I know you loved Dave as a
brother, and how you felt about me. Please don't
grieve too much for us, for we have had a happy life
together, and both feel that we should cross this last
bridge side by side.
    With love and thanks from,

                                        Helen.

    It had to come sooner or later, I suppose, and the first
shock has worn off now. I'll be leaving in a few minutes
to carry out Helen's last instructions.
    Dave was a lucky man, and the best friend I ever had.
And Helen— Well, as I said, I'm an old man now, and
can view things more sanely; I should have married and
raised a family, I suppose. But . . . there was only one
Helen O'Loy.

THE ROADS MUST ROLL

by Robert A. Heinlein

"Who makes the roads roll?"

The speaker stood still on the rostrum and waited for his audience to answer him. The reply came in scattered shouts that cut through the ominous, discontented murmur of the crowd.

"We do! We do! Damn right!"

"Who does the dirty work 'down inside'—so that Joe Public can ride at his ease?"

This time it was a single roar: "We do!"

The speaker pressed his advantage, his words tumbling out in a rasping torrent. He leaned toward the crowd, his eyes picking out individuals at whom to fling his words. "What makes business? The roads! How do they move the food they eat? The roads! How do they get to work? The roads! How do they get home to their wives? The roads!" He paused for effect, then lowered his voice. "Where would the public be if you boys didn't keep them roads rolling? Behind the eight ball, and everybody knows it. But do they appreciate it? *Pfui!* Did we ask for too much? Were our demands unreasonable? 'The right to resign whenever we want to.' Every working stiff in any other job has that. 'The same pay as the engineers.' Why not? Who are the real engineers around here? D'yuh have to be a cadet in a funny little hat before you can learn to wipe a bearing, or jack down a rotor? Who earns his keep: The gentlemen in the control offices, or the boys down inside? What else do we ask? 'The right to elect our own engineers.' Why the hell not? Who's competent to pick en-

First published in 1940

74

gineers? The technicians—or some damn dumb examining
board that's never been down inside, and couldn't tell a
rotor bearing from a field coil?"

He changed his pace with natural art, and lowered his
voice still further. "I tell you, brother, it's time we quit
fiddlin' around with petitions to the Transport Commission,
and use a little direct action. Let 'em yammer about democracy; that's a lot of eyewash—we've got the power, and
we're the men that count!"

A man had risen in the back of the hall while the
speaker was haranguing. He spoke up as the speaker
paused. "Brother Chairman," he drawled, "may I stick in
a couple of words?"

"You are recognized, Brother Harvey."

"What I ask is: What's all the shootin' for? We've got
the highest hourly rate of pay of any mechanical guild,
full insurance and retirement, and safe working conditions,
barring the chance of going deaf." He pushed his antinoise
helmet farther back from his ears. He was still in dungarees, apparently just up from standing watch. "Of course
we have to give ninety days' notice to quit a job, but,
cripes, we knew that when we signed up. The roads have
got to roll—they can't stop every time some lazy punk gets
tired of his billet.

"And now Soapy"—the crack of the gavel cut him short
—"Pardon me, I mean *Brother* Soapy—tells us how powerful we are, and how we should go in for direct action. Rats!
Sure, we could tie up the roads, and play hell with the
whole community—but so could any screwball with a can
of nitroglycerin, and he wouldn't have to be a technician
to do it, neither.

"We aren't the only frogs in the puddle. Our jobs are
important, sure, but where would we be without the
farmers—or the steel workers—or a dozen other trades
and professions?"

He was interrupted by a sallow little man with protruding upper teeth, who said: "Just a minute, Brother Chairman, I'd like to ask Brother Harvey a question," then
turned to Harvey and inquired in a sly voice: "Are you
speaking for the guild, brother—or just for yourself?
Maybe you don't believe in the guild? You wouldn't by

any chance be"—he stopped and slid his eyes up and down Harvey's lank frame—"a *spotter*, would you?"

Harvey looked over his questioner as if he had found something filthy in a plate of food. "Sikes," he told him, "if you weren't a runt, I'd stuff your store teeth down your throat. I helped found this guild. I was on strike in '60. Where were you in '60? With the finks?"

The chairman's gavel pounded. "There's been enough of this," he said. "Nobody that knows anything about the history of this guild doubts the loyalty of Brother Harvey. We'll continue with the regular order of business." He stopped to clear his throat. "Ordinarily, we don't open our floor to outsiders, and some of you boys have expressed a distaste for some of the engineers we work under, but there is one engineer we always like to listen to whenever he can get away from his pressing duties. I guess maybe it's because he's had dirt under his nails the same as us. Anyhow, I present at this time Mr. Shorty Van Kleeck—"

A shout from the floor stopped him. "*Brother* Van Kleeck—"

"O.K., Brother Van Kleeck, chief deputy engineer of this roadtown."

"Thanks, Brother Chairman." The guest speaker came briskly forward, and grinned expansively at the crowd. He seemed to swell under their approval. "Thanks, brothers. I guess our chairman is right. I always feel more comfortable here in the guild hall of the Sacramento Sector—or any guild hall for that matter—than I do in the engineers' clubhouse. Those young punk cadet engineers get in my hair. Maybe I should have gone to one of the fancy technical institutes, so I'd have the proper point of view, instead of coming up from down inside.

"Now, about those demands of yours that the Transport Commission just threw back in your face—Can I speak freely?"

"Sure you can, Shorty! You can trust us!"

"Well, of course I shouldn't say anything, but I can't help but understand how you feel. The roads are the big show these days, and you are the men who make them roll. It's the natural order of things that your opinions should be listened to, and your desires met. One would think that even politicians would be bright enough to see that. Sometimes, lying awake at night, I wonder why we technicians don't just take things over, and—"

"Your wife is calling, Mr. Gaines."

"Very well." He flicked off the office intercommunicator and picked up a telephone handset from his desk. "Yes, darling, I know I promised, but. . . . You're perfectly right, darling, but Washington has especially requested that we show Mr. Blekinsop anything he wants to see. I didn't know he was arriving today. . . . No, I can't turn him over to a subordinate. It wouldn't be courteous. He's Minister of Transport for Australia. I told you that. . . . Yes, darling, I know that courtesy begins at home, but the roads must roll. It's my job; you knew that when you married me. And this is part of my job. . . . That's a good girl. We'll positively have breakfast together. Tell you what, order horses and a breakfast pack and we'll make it a picnic. I'll meet you in Bakersfield—usual place. . . . Good-by, darling. Kiss Junior good night for me."

He replaced the handset, whereupon the pretty but indignant features of his wife faded from the visor screen. A young woman came into his office. As she opened the door, she exposed momentarily the words painted on its outer side: "Diego-Reno Roadtown, Office of the Chief Engineer." He gave her a harassed glance.

"Oh, it's you. Don't marry an engineer, Dolores, marry an artist. They have more home life."

"Yes, Mr. Gaines. Mr. Blekinsop is here, Mr. Gaines."

"Already? I didn't expect him so soon. The Antipodes ship must have grounded early."

"Yes, Mr. Gaines."

"Dolores, don't you ever have any emotions?"

"Yes, Mr. Gaines."

"Hm-m-m, it seems incredible, but you are never mistaken. Show Mr. Blekinsop in."

"Very good, Mr. Gaines."

Larry Gaines got up to greet his visitor. Not a particularly impressive little guy, he thought, as they shook hands and exchanged formal amenities. The rolled umbrella, the bowler hat, were almost too good to be true. An Oxford accent partially masked the underlying clipped, flat, nasal twang of the native Australia.

"It's a pleasure to have you here, Mr. Blekinsop, and I hope we can make your stay enjoyable."

The little man smiled. "I'm sure it will be. This is my first visit to your wonderful country. I feel at home already. The eucalyptus trees, you know, and the brown hills—"

"But your trip is primarily business?"

"Yes, yes. My primary purpose is to study your road-cities and report to my government on the advisability of trying to adapt your startling American methods to our social problems Down Under. I thought you understood that such was the reason I was sent to you."

"Yes, I did, in a general way. I don't know just what it is that you wish to find out. I suppose that you have heard about our roadtowns, how they came about, how they operate, and so forth."

"I've read a good bit, true, but I am not a technical man, Mr. Gaines, not an engineer. My field is social and political. I want to see how this remarkable technical change has affected your people. Suppose you tell me about the roads as if I were entirely ignorant. And I will ask questions."

"That seems a practical plan. By the way, how many are there in your party?"

"Just myself. My secretary went on to Washington."

"I see." Gaines glanced at his wrist watch. "It's nearly dinner time. Suppose we run up to the Stockton Sector for dinner. There is a good Chinese restaurant up there that I'm partial to. It will take us about an hour and you can see the ways in operation while we ride."

"Excellent."

Gaines pressed a button on his desk, and a picture formed on a large visor screen mounted on the opposite wall. It showed a strong-boned, angular young man seated at a semicircular control desk, which was backed by a complex instrument board. A cigarette was tucked in one corner of his mouth.

The young man glanced up, grinned, and waved from the screen. "Greetings and salutations, chief. What can I do for you?"

"Hi, Dave. You've got the evening watch, eh? I'm running up to the Stockton Sector for dinner. Where's Van Kleeck?"

"Gone to a meeting somewhere. He didn't say."

"Anything to report?"

"No, sir. The roads are rolling, and all the little people are going ridey-ridey home to their dinners."

"O.K.—keep 'em rolling."

"They'll roll, chief."

Gaines snapped off the connection and turned to Blekinsop. "Van Kleeck is my chief deputy. I wish he'd spend more time on the road and less on politics. Davidson can handle things, however. Shall we go?"

They glided down an electric staircase, and debouched on the walkway which bordered the north-bound five-mile-an-hour strip. After skirting a stairway trunk marked "Overpass to Southbound Road," they paused at the edge of the first strip. "Have you ever ridden a conveyor strip before?" Gaines inquired. "It's quite simple. Just remember to face against the motion of the strip as you get on."

They threaded their way through homeward-bound throngs, passing from strip to strip. Down the center of the twenty-mile-an-hour strip ran a glassite partition which reached nearly to the spreading roof. The Honorable Mr. Blekinsop raised his eyebrows inquiringly as he looked at it.

"Oh, that?" Gaines answered the unspoken question as he slid back a panel door and ushered his guest through. "That's a wind break. If we didn't have some way of separating the air currents over the strips of different speeds, the wind would tear our clothes off on a hundred-mile-an-hour strip." He bent his head to Blekinsop's as he spoke, in order to cut through the rush of air against the road surfaces, the noise of the crowd, and the muted roar of the driving mechanism concealed beneath the moving strips. The combination of noises inhibited further conversation as they proceeded toward the middle of the roadway. After passing through three more wind screens located at the forty, sixty, and eighty-mile-an-hour strips, respectively, they finally reached the maximum speed strip, the hundred-mile-an-hour strip, which made the round trip, San Diego to Reno and back, in twelve hours.

Blekinsop found himself on a walkway, twenty feet wide, facing another partition. Immediately opposite him an illuminated show-window proclaimed:

JAKE'S STEAK HOUSE No. 4
The Fastest Meal on the Fastest Road!
"To dine on the fly
Makes the miles roll by!"

"Amazing!" said Mr. Blekinsop. "It would be like dining in a tram. Is this really a proper restaurant?"

"One of the best. Not fancy, but sound."

"Oh, I say, could we—"

Gaines smiled at him. "You'd like to try it, wouldn't you, sir?"

"I don't wish to interfere with your plans—"

"Quite all right. I'm hungry myself, and Stockton is a long hour away. Let's go in."

Gaines greeted the manageress as an old friend. "Hello, Mrs. McCoy. How are you tonight?"

"If it isn't the chief himself! It's a long time since we've had the pleasure of seeing your face." She led them to a booth somewhat detached from the crowd of dining commuters. "And will you and your friend be having dinner?"

"Yes, Mrs. McCoy. Suppose you order for us—but be sure it includes one of your steaks."

"Two inches thick—from a steer that died happy." She glided away, moving her fat frame with surprising grace.

With sophisticated foreknowledge of the chief engineer's needs, Mrs. McCoy had left a portable telephone at the table. Gaines plugged it into an accommodation jack at the side of the booth, and dialed a number. "Hello—Davidson? Dave, this is the chief. I'm in Jake's Steak House No. 4 for supper. You can reach me by calling 10-L-6-6."

He replaced the handset, and Blekinsop inquired politely: "Is it necessary for you to be available at all times?"

"Not strictly necessary," Gaines told him, "but I feel safer when I am in touch. Either Van Kleeck, or myself, should be where the senior engineer of the watch—that's Davidson this shift—can get hold of us in a pinch. If it's a real emergency, I want to be there, naturally."

"What would constitute a real emergency?"

"Two things, principally. A power failure on the rotors would bring the road to a standstill, and possibly strand millions of people a hundred miles, or more, from their

THE ROADS MUST ROLL

homes. If it happened during a rush hour, we would have to evacuate those millions from the road—not too easy to do."

"You say millions—as many as that?"

"Yes, indeed. There are twelve million people dependent on this roadway, living and working in the buildings adjacent to it, or within five miles of each side."

The Age of Power blends into the Age of Transportation almost imperceptibly, but two events stand out as landmarks in the change: The invention of the Sun-power screen, and the opening of the first moving road. The power resources of oil and coal of the United States had—save for a few sporadic outbreaks of common sense—been shamefully wasted in their development all through the first half of the twentieth century. Simultaneously, the automobile, from its humble start as a one-lunged horseless carriage, grew into a steel-bodied monster of over a hundred horsepower and capable of making more than a hundred miles an hour. They boiled over the countryside, like yeast in ferment. In the middle of the century it was estimated that there was a motor vehicle for every two persons in the United States.

They contained the seeds of their own destruction. Seventy million steel juggernauts, operated by imperfect human beings at high speed, are more destructive than war. In the same reference year the premiums paid for compulsory liability and property damage insurance by automobile owners exceeded in amount the sum paid the same year to purchase automobiles. Safe driving campaigns were chronic phenomena, but were mere pious attempts to put Humpty-Dumpty together again. It was not physically possible to drive safely in those crowded metropolises. Pedestrians were sardonically divided into two classes, the quick and the dead.

But a pedestrian could be defined as a man who had found a place to park his car. The automobile made possible huge cities, then choked those same cities to death with their numbers. In 1900 Herbert George Wells pointed out that the saturation point in the size of a city might be mathematically predicted in terms of its transportation facilities. From a standpoint of speed alone the automobile made possible cities two hundred miles in diameter, but traffic congestion, and the inescapable, inherent danger of high-powered, individually operated vehicles canceled out the possibility.

Federal Highway No. 66 from Los Angeles to Chicago, "The Main Street of America," was transformed into a superhighway for motor vehicles, with an underspeed limit of sixty miles per hour. It was planned as a public works project to stimulate heavy industry; it had an unexpected by-product. The great cities of Chicago and St. Louis stretched out urban pseudopods toward each other, until they met near Bloomington, Illinois. The two parent cities actually shrank in population.

The city of San Francisco replaced its antiquated cable cars with moving stairways, powered with the Douglas-Martin Solar Reception Screens. The largest number of automobile licenses in history had been issued that calendar year, but the end of the automobile was in sight. The National Defense Act closed its era.

This act, one of the most bitterly debated ever to be brought out of committee, declared petroleum to be an essential and limited material of war. The army and navy had first call on all oil, above or below the ground, and seventy million civilian vehicles faced short and expensive rations.

Take the superhighways of the period, urban throughout their length. Add the mechanized streets of San Francisco's hills. Heat to boiling point with an imminent shortage of gasoline. Flavor with Yankee ingenuity. The first mechanized road was opened between Cincinnati and Cleveland.

It was, as one would expect, comparatively primitive in design. The fastest strip moved only thirty miles per hour, and was quite narrow, for no one had thought of the possibility of locating retail trade on the strips themselves. Nevertheless, it was a prototype of the social pattern which was to dominate the American scene within the next two decades—neither rural nor urban, but partaking equally of both, and based on rapid, safe, cheap, convenient transportation.

Factories—wide, low buildings whose roofs were covered with solar power screens of the same type that drove the road—lined the roadway on each side. Back of them and interspersed among them were commercial hotels, retail stores, theaters, apartment houses. Beyond this long, thin, narrow strip was the open countryside, where much of the population lived. Their homes dotted the hills, hung on the banks of creeks, and nestled between the farms. They worked in the "city," but lived in the "country"— and the two were not ten minutes apart.

Mrs. McCoy served the chief and his guest in person. They checked their conversation at the sight of the magnificent steaks.

Up and down the six-hundred-mile line, sector engineers of the watch were getting in their hourly reports from their subsector technicians. "Subsector One—check!" "Subsector Two—check!" Tensiometer readings, voltage, load, bearing temperatures, synchrotachometer readings—"Subsector Seven—check!" Hardbitten, able men in dungarees, who lived much of their lives down inside amidst the unmuted roar of the hundred-mile strip, the shrill whine of driving rotors, and the complaint of the relay rollers.

Davidson studied the moving model of the road, spread out before him in the main control room at Fresno Sector. He watched the barely perceptible crawl of the miniature hundred-mile strip and subconsciously noted the reference number on it which located Jake's Steak House No. 4. The chief would be getting into Stockton soon; he'd give him a ring after the hourly reports were in. Everything was quiet; traffic tonnage normal for rush hour; he would be sleepy before this watch was over. He turned to his cadet engineer of the watch. "Mr. Barnes."

"Yes, sir."

"I think we could use some coffee."

"Good idea, sir. I'll order some as soon as the hourlies are in."

The minute hand of the control board chronometer reached twelve. The cadet watch officer threw a switch. "All sectors, report!" he said, in crisp, self-conscious tones.

The faces of two men flicked into view on the visor screen. The younger answered him with the same air of acting under supervision. "Diego Circle—rolling!"

They were at once replaced by two more. "Angeles Sector—rolling!"

Then: "Bakersfield Sector—rolling!"

And: "Stockton Sector—rolling!"

Finally, when Reno Circle had reported, the cadet turned to Davidson and reported: "Rolling, sir."

"Very well—keep them rolling!"

The visor screen flashed on once more. "Sacramento Sector—supplementary report."

"Proceed."

"Cadet Engineer Guenther, while on visual inspection as cadet sector engineer of the watch, found Cadet Engineer Alec Jeans, on watch as cadet subsector technician, and R. J. Ross, technician second class, on watch as technician for the same subsector, engaged in playing cards. It was not possible to tell with any accuracy how long they had neglected to patrol their subsector."

"Any damage?"

"One rotor running hot, but still synchronized. It was jacked down, and replaced."

"Very well. Have the paymaster give Ross his time, and turn him over to the civil authorities. Place Cadet Jeans under arrest and order him to report to me."

"Very well, sir."

"Keep them rolling!"

Davidson turned back to control desk and dialed Chief Engineer Gaines' temporary number.

"You mentioned that there were two things that could cause major trouble on the road, Mr. Gaines, but you spoke only of power failure to the rotors."

Gaines pursued an elusive bit of salad before answering. "There really isn't a second major trouble—it won't happen. However—we are traveling along here at one hundred miles per hour. Can you visualize what would happen if this strip under us should break?"

Mr. Blekinsop shifted nervously in his chair. "Hm-m-m! Rather a disconcerting idea, don't you think? I mean to say, one is hardly aware that one is traveling at high speed, here in this snug room. What *would* the result be?"

"Don't let it worry you; the strip can't part. It is built up of overlapping sections in such a fashion that it has a safety factor of better than twelve to one. Several miles of rotors would have shut down all at once, and the circuit breakers for the rest of the line fail to trip out before there could possibly be sufficient tension on the strip to cause it to part.

"But it happened once, on the Philadelphia-Jersey City road, and we aren't likely to forget it. It was one of the earliest high-speed roads, carrying a tremendous passenger traffic, as well as heavy freight, since it serviced a heavily industrialized area. The strip was hardly more than a conveyor belt, and no one had foreseen the weight it would carry. It happened under maximum load, naturally, when the high-speed way was crowded. The part of the strip behind the break buckled for miles, crushing passengers against the roof at eighty miles per hour. The section forward of the break cracked like a whip, spilling passengers onto the slower ways, dropping them on the exposed rollers and rotors down inside, and snapping them up against the roof.

"Over three thousand people were killed in that one accident, and there was much agitation to abolish the roads. They were even shut down for a week by presidential order, but he was forced to reopen them again. There was no alternative."

"Really? Why not?"

"The country had become economically dependent on the roads. They were the principal means of transportation in the industrial areas—the only means of economic importance. Factories were shut down; food didn't move; people got hungry—and the president was forced to let them roll again. It was the only thing that could be done; the social pattern had crystallized in one form, and it couldn't be changed overnight. A large, industrialized population must have large-scale transportation, not only for people, but for trade."

Mr. Blekinsop fussed with his napkin, and rather diffidently suggested: "Mr. Gaines, I do not intend to disparage the ingenious accomplishments of your great people, but isn't it possible that you may have put too many eggs in one basket in allowing your whole economy to become dependent on the functioning of one type of machinery?"

Gaines considered this soberly. "I see your point. Yes—and no. Every civilization above the peasant-and-village type is dependent on some key type of machinery. The old South was based on the cotton gin. Imperial England was made possible by the steam engine. Large populations have to have machines for power, for transportation, and for manufacturing in order to live. Had it not been for machinery the large populations could never have grown up. That's not a fault of the machine; that's its virtue.

"But it is true that whenever we develop machinery to the point where it will support large populations at a high standard of living we are then bound to keep that machinery running, or suffer the consequences. But the real hazard in that is not the machinery, but the men who run the machinery. These roads, as machines, are all right. They are strong and safe and will do everything they were designed to do. No, it's not the machines, it's the men.

"When a population is dependent on a machine, they are hostages of the men who tend the machines. If their morale is high, their sense of duty strong—"

Someone up near the front of the restaurant had turned up the volume control of the radio, letting out a blast of music that drowned out Gaines' words. When the sound had been tapered down to a more nearly bearable volume, he was saying:

"Listen to that. That illustrates my point."

Belkinsop turned an ear to the music. It was a swinging march of compelling rhythm, with a modern interpretive arrangement. One could hear the roar of machinery, the repetitive clatter of mechanisms. A pleased smile of recognition spread over the Australian's face. "It's your field artillery song, 'The Roll of the Caissons,' isn't it? But I don't see the connection."

"You're right; it was 'The Roll of the Caissons,' but we adapted it to our own purposes. It's 'The Road Song of the Transport Cadets,' too. Wait!"

The persistent throb of the march continued, and seemed to blend with the vibration of the roadway underneath into a single timpano. Then a male chorus took up the verse:

"Hear them hum!
Watch them run!
Oh, our job is never done,
For our roadways go rolling along!
While you ride,
While you glide,
We are watching down inside,

So your roadways keep rolling along!
"Oh, it's Hie! Hie! Hee!
The rotor men are we—
Check off the sectors loud and strong!
   ONE! TWO THREE!
Anywhere you go
You are bound to know
That your roadways are rolling along!
KEEP THEM ROLLING!
That your roadways are rolling along!"

"See?" said Gaines, with more animation in his voice. "See? That is the real purpose of the United States Academy of Transport. That is the reason why the transport engineers are a semimilitary profession, with strict discipline. We are the bottleneck, the *sine qua non*, of all industry, all economic life. Other industries can go on strike, and only create temporary and partial dislocations. Crops can fail here and there, and the country takes up the slack. But if the roads stop rolling, everything else must stop; the effect would be the same as a general strike—with this important difference: It takes a majority of the population, fired by a real feeling of grievance, to create a general strike; but the men that run the roads, few as they are, can create the same complete paralysis.

"We had just one strike on the roads, back in '60. It was justified, I think, and it corrected a lot of real abuses—but it mustn't happen again.

"But what is to prevent it happening again, Mr. Gaines?"

"Morale—*esprit de corps*. The technicians in the road service are indoctrinated constantly with the idea that their job is a sacred trust. Besides, we do everything we can to build up their social position. But even more important is the academy. We try to turn out graduate engineers imbued with the same loyalty, the same iron self-discipline, and determination to perform their duty to the community at any cost, that Annapolis and West Point and Goddard are so successful in inculcating in their graduates."

"Goddard? Oh, yes, the rocket field. And have you been successful, do you think?"

"Not entirely, perhaps, but we will be. It takes time to build up a tradition. When the oldest engineer is a man who entered the academy in his teens we can afford to relax a little and treat it as a solved problem."

"I suppose you are a graduate?"

Gaines grinned. "You flatter me—I must look younger than I am. No, I'm a carry-over from the army. You see, the war department operated the roads for some three months during reorganization after the strike in '60. I served on the conciliation board that awarded pay increases and adjusted working conditions, then I was assigned—"

The signal light of the portable telephone glowed red. Gaines said, "Excuse me," and picked up the handset. "Yes?"

Blekinsop could overhear the voice at the other end. "This is Davidson, chief. The roads are rolling."

"Very well. Keep them rolling!"

"Had another trouble report from the Sacramento Sector."

"Again? What this time?"

Before Davidson could reply he was cut off. As Gaines reached out to dial him back, his coffee cup, half full, landed in his lap. Blekinsop was aware, even as he was lurched against the edge of the table, of a disquieting change in the hum of the roadway.

"What has happened, Mr. Gaines?"

"Don't know. Emergency stop—God knows why." He was dialing furiously. Shortly he flung the phone down, without bothering to return the handset to its cradle. "Phones are out. Come on! No! You'll be safe here. Wait."

"Must I?"

"Well, come along then, and stick close to me." He turned away, having dismissed the Australian cabinet minister from his mind. The strip ground slowly to a rest, the giant rotors and myriad rollers acting as flywheels in preventing a disastrous sudden stop. Already a little knot of commuters, disturbed at their evening meal, were attempting to crowd out the door of the restaurant.

"Halt!"

There is something about a command issued by one used to being obeyed which enforces compliance. It may be intonation, or possibly a more esoteric power, such as animal tamers are reputed to be able to exercise in controlling ferocious beasts. But it does exist, and can be used to compel even those not habituated to obedience.

The commuters stopped in their tracks.

Gaines continued: "Remain in the restaurant until we are ready to evacuate you. I am the chief engineer. You will be in no danger here. You!" He pointed to a big fellow near the door. "You're deputized. Don't let anyone leave without proper authority. Mrs. McCoy, resume serving dinner."

Gaines strode out the door, Blekinsop tagging along. The situation outside permitted no such simple measures. The hundred-mile strip alone had stopped; twenty feet away the next strip flew by at an unchecked ninety-five miles an hour. The passengers on it flickered past, unreal cardboard figures.

The twenty-foot walkway of the maximum speed strip had been crowded when the breakdown occurred. Now the customers of shops, of lunch stands, and of other places of business, the occupants of lounges, of television theaters— all came crowding out onto the walkway to see what had happened. The first disaster struck almost immediately.

The crowd surged, and pushed against a middle-aged woman on its outer edge. In attempting to recover her balance she put one foot over the edge of the flashing ninety-five-mile strip. She realized her gruesome error, for she screamed before her foot touched the ribbon.

She spun around and landed heavily on the moving strip, and was rolled by it, as the strip attempted to impart to her mass, at one blow, a velocity of ninety-five-miles per hour —one hundred and thirty-nine feet per second. As she rolled she mowed down some of the cardboard figures as a sickle strikes a stand of grass. Quickly, she was out of sight, her identity, her injuries, and her fate undetermined, and already remote.

But the consequences of her mishap were not done with. One of the flickering cardboard figures bowled over by her relative moment fell toward the hundred-mile strip, slammed into the shockbound crowd, and suddenly appeared as a live man—but broken and bleeding—amidst the luckless, fallen victims whose bodies had checked his wild flight.

Even there it did not end. The disaster spread from its

source, each hapless human ninepin more likely than not to knock down others so that they fell over the danger-laden boundary, and in turn ricocheted to a dearly-bought equilibrium.

But the focus of calamity sped out of sight, and Blekinsop could see no more. His active mind, accustomed to dealing with large numbers of individual human beings, multiplied the tragic sequence he had witnessed by twelve hundred miles of thronged conveyor strip, and his stomach chilled.

To Blekinsop's surprise, Gaines, made no effort to succor the fallen, nor to quell the fear-infected mob, but turned an expressionless face back to the restaurant. When Blekinsop saw that he was actually reentering the restaurant, he plucked at Gaines' sleeve. "Aren't we going to help those poor people?"

The cold planes of the face of the man who answered him bore no resemblance to his genial, rather boyish host of a few minutes before. "No. Bystanders can help them—I've got the whole road to think of. Don't bother me."

Crushed, and somewhat indignant, the politician did as he was ordered. Rationally, he knew that the chief engineer was right—a man responsible for the safety of millions cannot turn aside from his duty to render personal service to one—but the cold detachment of such viewpoint was repugnant to him.

Gaines was back in the restaurant. "Mrs. McCoy, where is your getaway?"

"In the pantry, sir."

Gaines hurried there, Blekinsop at his heels. A nervous Filipino salad boy shrank out of Gaines' way as he casually swept a supply of prepared green stuffs onto the floor, and stepped up on the counter where they had rested. Directly above his head and within reach was a circular manhole, counterweighted and operated by a handwheel set in its center. A short steel ladder, hinged to the edge of the opening, was swung up flat to the ceiling and secured by a hook.

Blekinsop lost his hat in his endeavor to clamber quickly enough up the ladder after Gaines. When he emerged on the roof of the building, Gaines was searching the ceiling of the roadway with a pocket flashlight. He was shuffling along, stooped double in the awkward four feet of space between the roof underfoot and ceiling.

He found what he sought, some fifty feet away—another manhole similar to the one they had used to escape from below. He spun the wheel of the lock, and stood up in the space, then rested his hands on the sides of the opening, and with a single lithe movement vaulted to the roof of the roadways. His companion followed him with more difficulty.

They stood in darkness, a fine, cold rain feeling at their faces. But underfoot, and stretching beyond sight on each hand, the Sun-power screens glowed with a faint opalescent radiance, their slight percentage of inefficiency as transformers of radiant Sun power to available electrical power being evidenced as a mild induced radioactivity. The effect was not illumination, but rather like the ghostly sheen of a snow-covered plain seen by starlight.

The glow picked out the path they must follow to reach the rain-obscured wall of buildings bordering the ways. The path was a narrow black stripe which arched away into the darkness over the low curve of the roof. They started away on this path at a dogtrot, making as much speed as the slippery footing and the dark permitted, while Blekinsop's mind still fretted at the problem of Gaines' apparently callous detachment. Although possessed of a keen intelligence, his nature was dominated by a warm, human sympathy, without which no politician, irrespective of other virtues or shortcomings, is long successful.

Because of this trait he distrusted instinctively any mind which was guided by logic alone. He was aware that, from a standpoint of strict logic, no reasonable case could be made out for the continued existence of the human race, still less for the human values he served.

Had he been able to pierce the preoccupation of his companion, he would have been reassured. On the surface, Gaines' exceptionally intelligent mind was clicking along with the facile ease of an electromechanical integrator— arranging data at hand, making tentative decisions, postponing judgments without prejudice until necessary data were available, exploring alternatives. Underneath, in a compartment insulated by stern self-discipline from the acting theater of his mind, emotions were a torturing storm of self-reproach. He was heartsick at the suffering he had seen, and which he knew too well was duplicated up and down the line. Although he was not aware of any personal omission, nevertheless the fault was somehow his, for authority creates responsibility.

He had carried too long the superhuman burden of kingship—which no sane man can carry lightheartedly—and was at this moment perilously close to the frame of mind which sends captains down with their ships. But the need for immediate, constructive action sustained him.

But no trace of this conflict reached his features.

At the wall of buildings glowed a green line of arrows, pointing to the left. Over them, at the terminus of the narrow path, shone a sign: "Access down." They pursued this, Blekinsop puffing in Gaines' wake, to a door let in the wall, which gave into a narrow stairway lighted by a single glow tube. Gaines plunged down this, still followed, and they emerged on the crowded, noisy, stationary walkway adjoining the northbound road.

Immediately adjacent to the stairway, on the right, was a public tele-booth. Through the glassite door they could see a portly, well-dressed man speaking earnestly to his female equivalent, mirrored in the visor screen. Three other citizens were waiting outside the booth.

Gaines pushed past them, flung open the door, grasped the bewildered and indignant man by the shoulders and hustled him outside, kicking the door closed after him. He cleared the visor screen with one sweep of his hand, before the matron pictured therein could protest, and pressed the emergency-priority button.

He dialed his private code number, and was shortly looking into the troubled face of his engineer of the watch, Davidson.

"Report!"

"It's you chief! Thank God! Where are you?" Davidson's relief was pathetic.

"Report!"

The senior watch officer repressed his emotion, and complied in direct, clipped phrases: "At 7:09 p.m. the consolidated tension reading, Strip 20, Sacramento Sector, climbed suddenly. Before action could be taken, tension on Strip 20 passed emergency level; the interlocks acted, and power to subject strip cut out. Cause of failure unknown. Direct communication to Sacramento control office has failed. They do not answer the auxiliary, nor commercial. Effort to reestablish communication continues. Messenger dispatched from Stockton Subsector 10.

"No casualties reported. Warning broadcast by public announcement circuit to keep clear of Strip 19. Evacuation has commenced."

"There are casualties," Gaines cut in. "Police and hospital emergency routine. Move!"

"Yes, sir!" Davidson snapped back, and hooked a thumb over his shoulder—but his cadet officer of the watch had already jumped to comply. "Shall I cut out the rest of the road, chief?"

"No. No more casualties are likely after the first disorder. Keep up the broadcast warnings. Keep those other strips rolling, or we will have a traffic jam the devil himself couldn't untangle."

Gaines had in mind the impossibility of bringing the strips up to speed under load. The rotors were not powerful enough to do this. If the entire road was stopped, he would have to evacuate every strip, correct the trouble on Strip 20, bring all strips up to speed, and then move the accumulated peak-load traffic. In the meantime, over five million stranded passengers would constitute a tremendous police problem. It was simpler to evacuate passengers on Strip 20 over the roof, and allow them to return home via the remaining strips.

"Notify the mayor and the governor that I have assumed emergency authority. Same to the chief of police and place him under your orders. Tell the commandant to arm all cadets available and await orders. Move!"

"Yes, sir. Shall I recall technicians off watch?"

"No. This isn't an engineering failure. Take a look at your readings; that entire sector went out simultaneously. Somebody cut out those rotors by hand. Place off-watch technicians on standby status—but don't arm them, and don't send them down inside. Tell the commandant to rush all available senior-class cadets to Stockton Subsector Office

No. 10 to report to me. I want them equipped with tumblebugs, pistols, and sleep-gas bombs."

"Yes, sir." A clerk leaned over Davidson's shoulder and said something in his ear. "The governor wants to talk to you, chief."

"Can't do it—nor can you. Who's your relief? Have you sent for him?"

"Hubbard—he's just come in."

"Have him talk to the governor, the mayor, the press—anybody that calls—even the White House. You stick to your watch. I'm cutting off. I'll be back in communication as quickly as I can locate a reconnaissance car." He was out of the booth almost before the screen cleared.

Blekinsop did not venture to speak, but followed him out to the northbound twenty-mile strip. There Gaines stopped, short of the windbreak, turned, and kept his eyes on the wall beyond the stationary walkway. He picked out some landmark or sign—not apparent to his companion—and did an Eliza crossing the ice back to the walkway, so rapidly that Blekinsop was carried some hundred feet beyond him, and almost failed to follow when Gaines ducked into a doorway, and ran down a flight of stairs.

They came out on a narrow lower walkway, down inside. The pervading din claimed them, beat upon their bodies as well as their ears. Dimly, Blekinsop perceived their surroundings, as he struggled to face that wall of sound. Facing him, illuminated by the red monochrome of a neon arc, was one of the rotors that drove the five-mile strip, its great, drum-shaped armature revolving slowly around the stationary field coils in its core. The upper surface of the drum pressed against the under side of the moving way and imparted to it its stately progress.

To the left and right, a hundred yards each way, and beyond at similar intervals, farther than he could see, were other rotors. Bridging the gaps between the rotors were the slender rollers, crowded together like cigars in a box, in order that the strip might have a continuous rolling support. The rollers were supported by steel-girder arches through the gaps of which he saw row after row of rotors in staggered succession, the rotors in each succeeding row turning over more rapidly than the last.

Separated from the narrow walkway by a line of supporting steel pillars, and lying parallel to it on the side away from the rotors, ran a shallow paved causeway, joined to the walk at this point by a ramp. Gaines peered up and down this tunnel in evident annoyance. Blekinsop started to ask him what troubled him, but found his voice snuffed out by the sound. He could not cut through the roar of thousands of rotors and the whine of hundreds of thousands of rollers.

Gaines saw his lips move, and guessed the question. He cupped his hands around Blekinsop's right ear, and shouted: "No car—I expected to find a car here."

The Australian, wishing to be helpful, grasped Gaines' arm and pointed back into the jungle of machinery. Gaines' eye followed the direction indicated and picked out something that he had missed in his preoccupation—a half dozen men working around a rotor several strips away. They had jacked down a rotor until it was no longer in contact with the road surface, and were preparing to replace in *in toto*. The replacement rotor was standing by on a low, heavy truck.

The chief engineer gave a quick smile of acknowledgment and thanks, and aimed his flashlight at the group, the beam focused down to a slender, intense needle of light. One of the technicians looked up, and Gaines snapped the light on and off in a repeated, irregular pattern. A figure detached itself from the group and ran toward them.

It was a slender young man, dressed in dungarees, and topped off with ear pads and an incongruous, pillbox cap, bright with gold braid and insignia. He recognized the chief engineer and saluted, his face falling into humorless, boyish intentness.

Gaines stuffed his torch into a pocket and commenced to gesticulate rapidly with both hands—clear, clean gestures, as involved and as meaningful as deaf-mute language. Blekinsop dug into his own dilettante knowledge of anthropology and decided that it was most like an American Indian sign language, with some of the finger movements of hula. But it was necessarily almost entirely strange, being adapted for a particular terminology.

The cadet answered him in kind, stepped to the edge of the causeway, and flashed his torch to the south. He picked out a car, still some distance away, but approaching at head-long speed. It braked, and came to a stop alongside them.

It was a small affair, ovoid in shape, and poised on two centerline wheels. The forward, upper surface swung up and disclosed the driver, another cadet. Gaines addressed him briefly in sign language, then hustled Blekinsop ahead of him into the cramped passenger compartment.

As the glassite hood was being swung back into place, a blast of wind smote them, and the Australian looked up in time to glimpse the last of three much larger vehicles hurtle past them. They were headed north, at a speed of not less than two hundred miles per hour. Blekinsop thought that he had made out the little hats of cadets through the windows of the last of the three, but he could not be sure.

He had no time to wonder, so violent was the driver's getaway. Gaines ignored the accelerating surge—he was already calling Davidson on the built-in communicator. Comparative silence had settled down once the car was closed. The face of a female operator at the relay station showed on the screen.

"Get me Davidson—senior watch office!"

"Oh! It's Mr. Gaines! The Mayor wants to talk to you, Mr. Gaines."

"Refer him—and get me Davidson. Move!"

"Yes, sir."

"And see here—leave this circuit hooked in to Davidson's board until I tell you personally to cut it."

"Right." Her face gave way to the watch officer's.

"That you, chief? We're moving—progress O.K.—no change."

"Very well. You'll be able to raise me on this circuit, or at Subsector 10 office. Clearing now." Davidson's face gave way to the relay operator.

"Your wife is calling, Mr. Gaines. Will you take it?"

Gaines muttered something not quite gallant, and answered: "Yes." Mrs. Gaines flashed into facsimile. He burst into speech before she could open her mouth. "Darling I'm all right don't worry I'll be home when I get there I've got to go now." It was all out in one breath, and he slapped the control that cleared the screen.

They slammed to a breath-taking stop alongside the stair leading to the watch office of Subsector 10, and piled out. Three big lorries were drawn up on the ramp, and three platoons of cadets were ranged in restless ranks alongside them. Tumblebugs—small, open monocycles, used to patrol down inside—were ready nearby.

A cadet trotted up to Gaines and saluted. "Lindsay, sir— cadet engineer of the watch. The engineer of the watch requests that you come at once to the control room."

The engineer of the watch looked up as they came in. "Chief—Van Kleeck is calling you."

"Put him on."

When Van Kleeck appeared in the big visor, Gaines greeted him with: "Hello, Van. Where are you?"

"Sacramento office. Now listen—"

"Sacramento? That's good! Report."

Van Kleeck looked disgruntled. "Report, hell! I'm not your deputy any more, Gaines. Now you—"

"What the hell are you talking about?"

"Listen, and don't interrupt me, and you'll find out. You're through, Gaines. I've been picked as Director of the Provisional Control Committee for the New Order."

"Van, have you gone off your rocker? What do you mean—the 'New Order'?"

"You'll find out. This is it—the Functionalist revolution. We're in; you're out. We stopped Strip 20 just to give you a little taste of what we can do."

Concerning Function: *A Treatise on the Natural Order in Society,* the Bible of the Functionalist movement, was first published in 1930. It claimed to be a scientifically accurate theory of social relations. The author, Paul Decker, disclaimed the "outworn and futile" ideas of democracy and human equality, and substituted a system in which human beings were evaluated "functionally"—that is to say, by the role each filled in the economic sequence. The underlying thesis was that it was right and proper for a man to exercise over his fellows whatever power was inherent in his function, and that any other form of social organization was silly, visionary, and contrary to the "natural order."

The complete interdependence of modern economic life seems to have escaped him entirely.

His ideas were dressed up with a glib mechanistic pseudo-psychology based on the observed orders of precedence among barnyard fowls, and on the famous Pavlov conditioned reflex experiments on dogs. He failed to note that human beings are neither dogs nor chickens. Old Dr. Pavlov ignored him entirely, as he had ignored so many others who had blindly and unscientifically dogmatized about the meaning of his important, but strictly limited, experiments.

Functionalism did not take hold at once—during the '30s almost everyone, from truck driver to hatcheck girl, had a scheme for setting the world right in six easy lessons; and a surprising percentage managed to get their schemes published. But it gradually spread. Functionalism was particularly popular among little people everywhere who could persuade themselves that their particular jobs were the indispensable ones, and that therefore, under the "natural order," they would be top dogs. With so many different functions actually indispensable such self-persuasion was easy.

Gaines stared at Van Kleeck for a moment before replying. "Van," he said slowly, "you don't really think you can get away with this, do you?"

The little man puffed out his chest. "Why not? We *have* gotten away with it. You can't start Strip 20 until I am ready to let you, and I can stop the whole road, if necessary."

Gaines was becoming uncomfortably aware that he was dealing with unreasonable conceit, and held himself patiently in check. "Sure you can, Van—but how about the rest of the country? Do you think the United States army will sit quietly by and let you run California as your private kingdom?"

Van Kleeck looked sly. "I've planned for that. I've just finished broadcasting a manifesto to all the road technicians in the country, telling them what we have done, and telling them to arise, and claim their rights. With every road in the country stopped, and people getting hungry, I reckon the President will think twice before sending the army to tangle with us. Oh, he could send a force to capture, or kill me—I'm not afraid to die!—but he doesn't dare start shooting down road technicians as a class, because the country can't get along without us—consequently, he'll have to get along with us—on our terms!"

There was much bitter truth in what he said. If an uprising of the road technicians became general, the government could no more attempt to settle it by force than a man could afford to cure a headache by blowing out his brains. But was the uprising general?

"Why do you think that the technicians in the rest of the country will follow your lead?"

"Why not? It's the natural order of things. This is an age of machinery; the real power everywhere is in the technicians, but they have been kidded into not using their power with a lot of obsolete catch phrases. And of all the classes of technicians, the most important, the absolutely essential, are the road technicians. From now on they run the show—it's the natural order of things!" He turned away for a moment and fussed with some papers on the desk before him; then he added: "That's all for now, Gaines—I've got to call the White House, and let the President know how things stand. You carry on, and behave yourself, and you won't get hurt."

Gaines sat quite still for some minutes after the screen cleared. So that's how it was. He wondered what effect, if any, Van Kleeck's invitation to strike had had on road technicians elsewhere. None, he thought—but then he had not dreamed that it could happen among his own technicians. Perhaps he had made a mistake in refusing to take time to talk to anyone outside the road. No—if he had stopped to talk to the Governor, or the newspapermen, he would still be talking. Still—

He dialed Davidson.

"Any trouble in any other sectors, Dave?"

"No, chief."

"Or on any other road?"

"None reported."

"Did you hear my talk with Van Kleeck?"

"I was cut in—yes."

"Good. Have Hubbard call the President and the Governor, and tell them that I am strongly opposed to the use of military force as long as the outbreak is limited to this one road. Tell them that I will not be responsible if they move in before I ask for help."

Davidson looked dubious. "Do you think that is wise, chief?"

"I do! If we try to blast Van and his red-hots out of their position, we may set off a real, countrywide uprising. Furthermore, he could wreck the road so that God himself couldn't put it back together. What's your rolling tonnage now?"

"Fifty-three percent under evening peak."

"How about Strip 20?"

"Almost evacuated."

"Good. Get the road clear of all traffic as fast as possible. Better have the chief of police place a guard on all entrances to the road to keep out new traffic. Van may stop all the strips any time—or I may need to myself. Here is my plan: I'm going down inside with these armed cadets. We will work north, overcoming any resistance we meet. You arrange for watch technicians and maintenance crews to follow immediately behind us. Each rotor, as they come to it, is to be cut out, then hooked into the Stockton control board. It will be a haywire rig, with no safety interlocks, so use enough watch technicians to be able to catch trouble before it happens.

"If this scheme works, we can move control of the Sacramento Sector right out from under Van's feet, and he can stay in his Sacramento control office until he gets hungry enough to be reasonable."

He cut off and turned to the subsector engineer of the watch. "Edmunds, give me a helmet—and a pistol."

"Yes, sir." He opened a drawer, and handed his chief a slender deadly-looking weapon. Gaines belted it on, and accepted a helmet, into which he crammed his head, leaving the antinoise ear flaps up. Blekinsop cleared his throat.

"May . . . uh . . . may I have one of those helmets?" he inquired.

"What?" Gaines focused his attention. "Oh—You won't need one, Mr. Blekinsop. I want you to remain right here until you hear from me."

"But—" The Australian statesman started to speak, thought better of it, and subsided.

From the doorway the cadet engineer of the watch demanded the chief engineer's attention. "Mr. Gaines, there is a technician out here who insists on seeing you—a man named Harvey."

"Can't do it."

"He's from the Sacramento Sector, sir."

"Oh! Send him in."

Harvey quickly advised Gaines of what he had seen and heard at the guild meeting that afternoon. "I got disgusted and left while they were still jawin', chief. I didn't think any more about it until Strip 20 stopped rolling. Then I heard that the trouble was in Sacramento Sector, and decided to look you up."

"How long has this been building up?"

"Quite some time, I guess. You know how it is. There are a few soreheads everywhere, and a lot of them are Functionalists. But you can't refuse to work with a man just because he holds different political views. It's a free country."

"You should have come to me before, Harvey." Harvey looked stubborn. Gaines studied his face. "No, I guess you are right. It's my business to keep tabs on your mates, not yours. As you say, it's a free country. Anything else?"

"Well—now that it has come to this, I thought maybe I could help you pick out the ringleaders."

"Thanks. You stick with me. We are going down inside and try to clear up this mess."

The office door opened suddenly, and a technician and a cadet appeared, lugging a burden between them. They deposited it on the floor, and waited.

It was a young man, quite evidently dead. The front of his dungaree jacket was soggy with blood. Gaines looked at the watch officer. "Who is he?"

Edmunds broke his stare and answered: "Cadet Hughes. He's the messenger I sent to Sacramento when communication failed. When he didn't report, I sent Marston and Cadet Jenkins after him."

Gaines muttered something to himself, and turned away. "Come along, Harvey."

The cadets waiting below had changed in mood. Gaines noted that the boyish intentness for excitement had been replaced by something uglier. There was much exchange of hand signals and several appeared to be checking the loading of their pistols.

He sized them up, then signaled to the cadet leader. There was a short interchange of signals. The cadet saluted, turned to his men, gesticulated briefly, and brought his arm down smartly. They filed upstairs, and into an empty standby room, Gaines following.

Once inside, and the noise shut out, he addressed them: "You saw Hughes brought in. How many of you want a chance to kill the louse that did it?"

Three of the cadets reacted almost at once, breaking ranks and striding forward. Gaines looked at them coldly. "Very well. You three turn in your weapons, and return to your quarters. Any of the rest of you that think this a matter of private revenge, or a hunting party, may join them." He permitted a short silence to endure before continuing. "Sacramento Sector has been seized by unauthorized persons. We are going to retake it—if possible, without loss of life on either side, and, if possible, without stopping the roads. The plan is to take over down inside, rotor by rotor, and cross-connect through Stockton. The task assignment of this group is to proceed north down inside, locating and overpowering all persons in your path. You will bear in mind the probability that most of the persons you will arrest are completely innocent. Consequently, you will favor the use of sleep-gas bombs, and will shoot to kill only as a last resort.

"Cadet captain, assign your men in squads of ten each, with squad leader. Each squad is to form a skirmish line across down inside, mounted on tumblebugs, and will proceed north at fifteen miles per hour. Leave an interval of one hundred yards between successive waves of skirmishers. Whenever a man is sighted, the entire leading wave will converge on him, arrest him, and deliver him to a transport car, then reform in the rear of the last wave. You will assign the transports that delivered you here to hold prisoners. Instruct the drivers to keep abreast of the second wave.

"You will assign an attack group to recapture subsector control officers, but no office is to be attacked until its subsector has been cross-connected with Stockton. Arrange liaison accordingly.

"Any questions?" He let his eyes run over the faces of the young men. When no one spoke up, he turned back to the cadet in charge. "Very well, sir. Carry out your orders!"

By the time the dispositions had been completed, the follow-up crew of technicians had arrived, and Gaines had given the engineer in charge his instructions. The cadets "stood to horse" alongside their poised tumblebugs. The cadet captain looked expectantly at Gaines. He nodded, the cadet brought his arm down smartly, and the first wave mounted and moved off.

Gaines and Harvey mounted tumblebugs, and kept abreast of the cadet captain, some twenty-five yards behind the leading wave. It had been a long time since the chief engineer had ridden one of these silly-looking little vehicles, and he felt awkward. A tumblebug does not give a man dignity, since it is about the size and shape of a kitchen stool, gyro-stabilized on a single wheel. But it is perfectly adapted to patrolling the maze of machinery down inside, since it can go through an opening the width of a man's shoulders, is easily controlled, and will stand patiently upright, waiting, should its rider dismount.

The little reconnaissance car followed Gaines at a short interval, weaving in and out among the rotors, while the television and audio communicator inside continued as Gaines' link to his other manifold responsibilites.

The first two hundred yards of Sacramento Sector passed without incident, then one of the skirmishers sighted a tumblebug parked by a rotor. The technician it served was checking the gauges at the rotor's base, and did not see them approach. He was unarmed and made no resistance, but seemed surprised and indignant, as well as very bewildered.

The little command group dropped back and permitted the new leading wave to overtake them.

Three miles farther along, the score stood thirty-seven men arrested, none killed. Two of the cadets had received minor wounds, and had been directed to retire. Only four of the prisoners had been armed; one of these Harvey had been able to identify definitely as a ringleader. Harvey expressed a desire to attempt to parley with the outlaws, if any occasion arose. Gaines agreed tentatively. He knew of

Harvey's long and honorable record as a labor leader, and was willing to try anything that offered a hope of success with a minimum of violence.

Shortly thereafter the first wave flushed another technician. He was on the far side of a rotor; they were almost on him before he was seen. He did not attempt to resist, although he was armed, and the incident would not have been worth recording, had he not been talking into a hush-a-phone which he had plugged into the telephone jack at the base of the rotor.

Gaines reached the group as the capture was being effected. He snatched at the soft rubber mask of the phone, jerking it away from the man's mouth so violently that he could feel the bone-conduction receiver grate between the man's teeth. The prisoner spat out a piece of broken tooth and glared, but ignored attempts to question him.

Swift as Gaines had been, it was highly probable that they had lost the advantage of surprise. It was necessary to assume that the prisoner had succeeded in reporting the attack going on beneath the ways. Word was passed down the line to proceed with increased caution.

Gaines' pessimism was justified shortly. Riding toward them appeared a group of men, as yet several hundred feet away. There were at least a score, but their exact strength could not be determined, as they took advantage of the rotors for cover as they advanced. Harvey looked at Gaines, who nodded, and signaled the cadet captain to halt his forces.

Harvey went on ahead, unarmed, his hands held high above his head, and steering by balancing the weight of his body. The outlaw party checked its speed uncertainly, and finally stopped. Harvey approached within a couple of rods of them and stopped likewise. One of them, apparently the leader, spoke to him in sign language, to which he replied.

They were too far away, and the red light too uncertain, to follow the discussion. It continued for several minutes, then ensued a pause. The leader seemed uncertain what to do. One of his party rolled forward, returned his pistol to its holster, and conversed with the leader. The leader shook his head at the man's violent gestures.

The man renewed his argument, but met the same negative response. With a final disgusted wave of his hands, he desisted, drew his pistol, and shot at Harvey. Harvey grabbed at his middle and leaned forward. The man shot again; Harvey jerked, and slid to the ground.

The cadet captain beat Gaines to the draw. The killer looked up as the bullet hit him. He looked as if he were puzzled by some strange occurrence—being too freshly dead to be aware of it.

The cadets came in shooting. Although the first wave was out-numbered better than two to one, they were helped by the comparative demoralization of the enemy. The odds were nearly even after the first ragged volley. Less than thirty seconds after the first treacherous shot all of the insurgent party were dead, wounded, or under arrest. Gaines' losses were two dead—including the murder of Harvey—and two wounded.

Gaines modified his tactics to suit the changed conditions. Now that secrecy was gone, speed and striking power were of first importance. The second wave was directed to close in practically to the heels of the first. The third wave was brought up to within twenty-five yards of the second. These three waves were to ignore unarmed men, leaving them to be picked up by the fourth wave, but they were directed to shoot on sight any person carrying arms.

Gaines cautioned them to shoot to wound, rather than to kill, but he realized that his admonishment was almost impossible to obey. There would be killing. Well—he had not wanted it, but he felt that he had no choice. Any armed outlaw was a potential killer—he could not, in fairness to his own men, lay too many restrictions on them.

When the arrangements for the new marching order was completed, he signed the cadet captain to go ahead, and the first and second waves started off together at the top speed of which the tumblebugs were capable—not quite eighteen miles per hour. Gaines followed them.

He swerved to avoid Harvey's body, glancing involuntarily down as he did so. The face was set in a death mask of rugged beauty in which the strong fiber of the dead man's character was evident. Seeing this, Gaines did not regret so much his order to shoot, but the deep sense of loss of personal honor lay more heavily on him than before.

They passed several technicians during the next few minutes, but had no occasion to shoot. Gaines was beginning to feel somewhat hopeful of a reasonably bloodless victory, when he noticed a change in the pervading throb of machinery which penetrated even through the heavy antinoise pads of his helmet. He lifted an ear pad in time to hear the end of a rumbling diminuendo as the rotors and rollers slowed to rest.

The road was stopped.

He shouted to the cadet captain: "Halt your men!" His words echoed hollowly in the unreal silence.

The top of the reconnaissance car swung up as he turned and hurried to it. "Chief," the cadet within called out, "relay station calling you."

The girl in the visor screen gave way to Davidson as soon as she recognized Gaines' face.

"Chief," Davidson said at once, "Van Kleeck's calling you."

"Who stopped the road?"

"He did."

"Any other major change in the situation?"

"No—the road was practically empty when he stopped it."

"Good. Give me Van Kleeck."

The chief conspirator's face was livid with uncurbed anger when he identified Gaines. He burst into speech.

"So! You thought I was fooling, eh? What do you think now, Mr. Chief Engineer Gaines?"

Gaines fought down an impulse to tell him exactly what he thought, particularly about Van Kleeck. Everything about the short man's manner affected him like a squeaking slate pencil.

But he could not afford the luxury of speaking his mind. He strove to get just the proper tone into his voice which would soothe the other man's vanity. "I've got to admit that you've won this trick, Van—the road is stopped—but don't think I didn't take you seriously. I've watched you work too long to underrate you. I know you mean what you say."

Van Kleeck was pleased by the tribute, but tried not to show it. "Then why don't you get smart, and give up?" he demanded belligerently. "You can't win."

"Maybe not, Van, but you know I've got to try. Besides," he went on, "why can't I win? You said yourself that I could call on the whole United States army."

Van Kleeck grinned triumphantly. "You see that?" He held up a pear-shaped electric push button, attached to a long cord. "If I push that, it will blow a path right straight across the ways—blow it to kingdom come. And just for good measure, I'll take an ax, and wreck this control station before I leave."

Gaines wished whole-heartedly that he knew more about psychology. Well—he'd just have to do his best, and trust to horse sense to give him the right answers. "That's pretty drastic, Van, but I don't see how we can give up."

"No? You'd better have another think. If you force me to blow up the road, how about all the people that will be blown up along with it?"

Gaines thought furiously. He did not doubt that Van Kleeck would carry out his threat. His very phraseology, the childish petulance of "If you force me to do this—," betrayed the dangerous irrationality of his frame of mind. And such an explosion anywhere in the thickly populated Sacramento Sector would be likely to wreck one or more apartment houses, and would be certain to kill shopkeepers on the included segment of Strip 20, as well as chance passers-by. Van was absolutely right; he dare not risk the lives of bystanders who were not aware of the issue and had not consented to the hazard—even if the road never rolled again.

For that matter, he did not relish chancing major damage to the road itself—but it was the danger to innocent life which left him helpless.

A tune ran through his head:

> "Hear them hum; watch them run.
> Oh, our work is never done—"

What to do? What to do?

> "While you ride, while you glide, we are—"

This wasn't getting any place.
He turned back to the screen. "Look, Van, you don't

want to blow up the road unless you have to, I'm sure. Neither do I. Suppose I come up to your headquarters, and we talk this thing over. Two reasonable men ought to be able to make a settlement."

Van Kleeck was suspicious. "Is this some sort of a trick?"

"How can it be? I'll come alone, and unarmed, just as fast as my car can get there."

"How about your men?"

"They will sit where they are until I'm back. You can put out observers to make sure of it."

Van Kleeck stalled for a moment, caught between the fear of a trap and the pleasure of having his erstwhile superior come to him to sue for terms. At last he grudgingly consented.

Gaines left his instructions, and told Davidson what he intended to do. "If I'm not back within an hour, you're on your own, Dave."

"Be careful, chief."

"I will."

He evicted the cadet driver from the reconnaissance car, and ran it down the ramp into the causeway, then headed north and gave it the gun. Now he would have a chance to collect his thoughts, even at two hundred miles per hour. Suppose he pulled off this trick—there would still have to be some changes made. Two lessons stood out like sore thumbs: First, the strips must be cross-connected with safety interlocks so that adjacent strips would slow down, or stop, if a strip's speed became dangerously different from those adjacent. No repetition of what happened on 20!

But that was elementary, a mere mechanical detail. The real failure had been in men. Well, the psychological classification tests must be improved to insure that the roads employed only conscientious, reliable men. But hell's bells —that was just exactly what the present classification tests were supposed to insure beyond question. To the best of his knowledge there had never been a failure from the improved Humm-Wadsworth-Burton method—not until today in the Sacramento Sector. How had Van Kleeck gotten one whole sector of temperament-classified men to revolt?

It didn't make sense.

Personnel did not behave erratically without a reason. One man might be unpredictable, but in large numbers personnel were as dependable as machines, or figures. They could be measured, examined, classified. His inner eye automatically pictured the personnel office, with its rows of filing cabinets, its clerks—He'd got it! He'd got it! Van Kleeck, as chief deputy, was ex officio *personnel officer for the entire road!*

It was the only solution that covered all the facts. The personnel officer alone had the perfect opportunity to pick out all the bad apples and concentrate them in one barrel. Gaines was convinced beyond any reasonable doubt that there had been skulduggery, perhaps for years, with the temperament classification tests, and that Van Kleeck had deliberately transferred the kind of men he needed to one sector, after falsifying their records.

And that taught another lesson—tighter tests for officers, and no officer to be trusted with classification and assignment without close supervision and inspection. Even he, Gaines, should be watched in that respect. *Qui custodiet ipsos custodes?* Who will guard those selfsame guardians? Latin might be obsolete, but those old Romans weren't dummies.

He at last knew wherein he had failed, and he derived melancholy pleasure from the knowledge. Supervision and inspection, check and recheck, was the answer. It would be cumbersome and inefficient, but it seemed that adequate safeguards always involved some loss of efficiency.

He should not have intrusted so much authority to Van Kleeck without knowing more about him. He still should know more about him—He touched the emergency-stop button, and brought the car to a dizzying halt. "Relay station! See if you can raise my office."

Dolores' face looked out from the screen. "You're still there—good!" he told her. "I was afraid you'd gone home."

"I came back, Mr. Gaines."

"Good girl. Get me Van Kleeck's personal file jacket. I want to see his classification record."

She was back with it in exceptionally short order, and

read from it the symbols and percentages. He nodded repeatedly as the data checked his hunches: Masked introvert—inferiority complex. It checked.

" 'Comment of the board':" she read. " 'In spite of the slight potential instability shown by maxima A and D on the consolidated profile curve, the board is convinced that this officer is, nevertheless, fitted for duty. He has an exceptionally fine record, and is especially adept in handling men. He is, therefore, recommended for retention and promotion.' "

"That's all, Dolores. Thanks."

"Yes, Mr. Gaines."

"I'm off for a showdown. Keep your fingers crossed."

"But, Mr. Gaines—" Back in Fresno, Dolores stared wide-eyed at an empty screen.

"Take me to Mr. Van Kleeck!"

The man addressed took his gun out of Gaines' ribs—reluctantly, Gaines thought—and indicated that the chief engineer should precede him up the stairs. Gaines climbed out of the car, and complied.

Van Kleeck had set himself up in the sector control room proper, rather than the administrative office. With him were half a dozen men, all armed.

"Good evening, Director Van Kleeck." The little man swelled visibly at Gaines' acknowledgment of his assumed rank.

"We don't go in much around here for titles," he said, with ostentatious casualness. "Just call me Van. Sit down, Gaines."

Gaines did so. It was necessary to get those other men out. He looked at them with an expression of bored amusement. "Can't you handle one unarmed man by yourself, Van? Or don't the Functionalists trust each other?"

Van Kleeck's face showed his annoyance, but Gaines' smile was undaunted. Finally the smaller man picked up a pistol from his desk, and motioned toward the door. "Get out, you guys."

"But, Van—"

"Get out, I said!"

When they were alone, Van Kleeck picked up the electric push button which Gaines had seen in the visor screen, and pointed his pistol at his former chief. "O.K.," he growled, "any funny stuff, and off it goes! What's your proposition?"

Gaines' irritating smile grew broader. Van Kleeck scowled. "What's so damn funny?" he said.

Gaines granted him an answer. "You are, Van—honest, this is rich. You start a Functionalist revolution, and the only function you can think of to perform is to blow up the road that justifies your title. Tell me," he went on, "what is it you are so scared of?"

"I am not afraid!"

"Not afraid? You? Sitting there, ready to commit hara-kiri with that toy push button, and you tell me that you aren't afraid. If your buddies knew how near you are to throwing away what they've fought for, they'd shoot you in a second. You're afraid of them, too, aren't you?"

Van Kleeck thrust the push button away from him, and stood up. "I am not afraid!" he shouted, and came around the desk toward Gaines.

Gaines sat where he was, and laughed. "But you are! You're afraid of me, this minute. You're afraid I'll have you on the carpet for the way you do your job. You're afraid the cadets won't salute you. You're afraid they are laughing behind your back. You're afraid of using the wrong fork at dinner. You're afraid people are looking at you—and you are afraid that they won't notice you."

"I am not!" he protested. "You . . . you dirty, stuck-up snob! Just because you went to a high-hat school you think you're better than anybody." He choked, and became incoherent, fighting to keep back tears of rage. "You, and your nasty little cadets—"

Gaines eyed him cautiously. The weakness in the man's character was evident now—he wondered why he had not seen it before. He recalled how ungracious Van Kleeck had been one time when he had offered to help him with an intricate piece of figuring.

The problem now was to play on his weakness, to keep him so preoccupied that he would not remember the peril-laden push button. He must be caused to center the venom of his twisted outlook on Gaines, to the exclusion of every other thought.

But he must not goad him too carelessly, or a shot from

across the room might put an end to Gaines, and to any
chance of avoiding a bloody, wasteful struggle for control
of the road.

Gaines chuckled. "Van," he said, "you are a pathetic
little shrimp. That was a dead giveaway. I understand you
perfectly—you're a third-rater, Van, and all your life
you've been afraid that someone would see through you,
and send you back to the foot of the class. Director—*pfui!*
If you are the best the Functionalists can offer, we can
afford to ignore them—they'll fold up from their own rotten inefficiency." He swung around in his chair, deliberately turning his back on Van Kleeck and his gun.

Van Kleeck advanced on his tormentor, halted a few
feet away, and shouted: "You . . . I'll show you . . . I'll
put a bullet in you; that's what I'll do!"

Gaines swung back around, got up, and walked steadily
toward him. "Put that popgun down before you hurt
yourself."

Van Kleeck retreated a step. "Don't you come near me!"
he screamed. "Don't you come near me . . . or I'll shoot
you . . . see if I don't."

"This is it," thought Gaines, and dived.

The pistol went off alongside his ear. Well, that one
didn't get him. They were on the floor. Van Kleeck was
hard to hold, for a little man. Where was the gun? There!
He had it. He broke away.

Van Kleeck did not get up. He lay sprawled on the
floor, tears streaming out of his closed eyes, blubbering
like a frustrated child.

Gaines looked at him with something like compassion
in his eyes, and hit him carefully behind the ear with the
butt of the pistol. He walked over to the door, and listened
for a moment, then locked it cautiously.

The cord from the push button led to the control board.
He examined the hookup, and disconnected it carefully.
That done, he turned to the televisor at the control desk,
and called Fresno.

"O.K., Dave," he said, "let 'em attack now—and for the
love of Pete, hurry!" Then he cleared the screen, not wishing his watch officer to see how he was shaking.

Back in Fresno the next morning Gaines paced around the main control room with a fair degree of contentment in his heart. The roads were rolling—before long they would be up to speed again. It had been a long night. Every engineer, every available cadet, had been needed to make the inch-by-inch inspection of Sacramento Sector which he had required. Then they had to cross-connect around two wrecked subsector control boards. But the roads were rolling—he could feel their rhythm up through the floor.

He stopped beside a haggard, stubbly-bearded man. "Why don't you go home, Dave?" he asked. "McPherson can carry on from here."

"How about yourself, chief? You don't look like a June bride."

"Oh, I'll catch a nap in my office after a bit. I called my wife, and told her I couldn't make it. She's coming down here to meet me."

"Was she sore?"

"Not very. You know how women are." He turned back to the instrument board, and watched the clicking busy-bodies assembling the data from six sectors. San Diego Circle, Angeles Sector, Bakersfield Sector, Fresno Sector, Stockton—Stockton? Stockton! Good grief—Blekinsop! He had left a cabinet minister of Australia cooling his heels in the Stockton office all night long!

He started for the door, while calling over his shoulder: "Dave, will you order a car for me? Make it a fast one!" He was across the hall, and had his head inside his private office before Davidson could acknowledge the order.

"Dolores!"

"Yes, Mr. Gaines."

"Call my wife, and tell her I had to go to Stockton. If she's already left home, just have her wait here. And, Dolores—"

"Yes, Mr. Gaines?"

"Calm her down."

She bit her lip, but her face was impassive. "Yes, Mr. Gaines."

"That's a good girl." He was out and started down the stairway. When he reached road level, the sight of the rolling strips warmed him inside and made him feel almost cheerful.

He strode briskly away toward a door marked, "Access Down," whistling softly to himself. He opened the door, and the rumbling, roaring rhythm from down inside seemed to pick up the tune even as it drowned out the sound of his whistling.

> "Hie! Hie! Hee!
> The rotor men are we—
> Check off your sectors loud and strong!
>   ONE! TWO! THREE!
> Anywhere you go
> You are bound to know
> That your roadways go rolling along!"

MICROCOSMIC GOD

by Theodore Sturgeon

Here is a story about a man who had too much power, and a man who took too much, but don't worry; I'm not going political on you. The man who had the power was named James Kidder and the other was his banker.

Kidder was quite a guy. He was a scientist and he lived on a small island off the New England coast all by himself. He wasn't the dwarfed little gnome of a mad scientist you read about. His hobby wasn't personal profit, and he wasn't a megalomaniac with a Russian name and no scruples. He wasn't insidious, and he wasn't even particularly subversive. He kept his hair cut and his nails clean and lived and thought like a reasonable human being. He was slightly on the baby-faced side; he was inclined to be a hermit; he was short and plump and—brilliant. His specialty was biochemistry, and he was always called *Mr.* Kidder. Not "Dr." Not "Professor." Just Mr. Kidder.

He was an odd sort of apple and always had been. He had never graduated from any college or university because he found them too slow for him, and too rigid in their approach to education. He couldn't get used to the idea that perhaps his professors knew what they were talking about. That went for his texts, too. He was always asking questions, and didn't mind very much when they were embarrassing. He considered Gregor Mendel a bungling liar, Darwin an amusing philosopher, and Luther Burbank a sensationalist. He never opened his mouth without leaving his victim feeling breathless. If he was talking to someone who had knowledge, he went in there and got it, leav-

First published in 1941

ing his victim breathless. If he was talking to someone whose knowledge was already in his possession, he only asked repeatedly, "How do you know?" His most delectable pleasure was cutting a fanatical eugenicist into conversational ribbons. So people left him alone and never, never asked him to tea. He was polite, but not politic.

He had a little money of his own, and with it he leased the island and built himself a laboratory. Now I've mentioned that he was a biochemist. But being what he was, he couldn't keep his nose in his own field. It wasn't too remarkable when he made an intellectual excursion wide enough to perfect a method of crystallizing Vitamin B_1 profitably by the ton—if anyone wanted it by the ton. He got a lot of money for it. He bought his island outright and put eight hundred men to work on an acre and a half of his ground, adding to his laboratory and building equipment. He got to messing around with sisal fiber, found out how to fuse it, and boomed the banana industry by producing a practically unbreakable cord from the stuff.

You remember the popularizing demonstration he put on at Niagara, don't you? That business of running a line of the new cord from bank to bank over the rapids and suspending a ten-ton truck from the middle of it by razor edges resting on the cord? That's why ships now moor themselves with what looks like heaving line, no thicker than a lead pencil, that can be coiled on reels like garden hose. Kidder made cigarette money out of that, too. He went out and bought himself a cyclotron with part of it.

After that money wasn't money any more. It was large numbers in little books. Kidder used little amounts of it to have food and equipment sent out to him, but after a while that stopped, too. His bank dispatched a messenger by seaplane to find out if Kidder was still alive. The man returned two days later in a bemused state, having been amazed something awesome at the things he'd seen out there. Kidder was alive, all right, and he was turning out a surplus of good food in an astonishingly simplified synthetic form. The bank wrote immediately and wanted to know if Mr. Kidder, in his own interest, was willing to release the secret of his dirtless farming. Kidder replied that he would be glad to, and inclosed the formulas. In a P.S. he said that he hadn't sent the information ashore because he hadn't realized anyone would be interested. That from a man who was responsible for the greatest sociological change in the second half of the twentieth century—factory farming. It made him richer; I mean it made his bank richer. He didn't give a rap.

Kidder didn't really get started until about eight months after the messenger's visit. For a biochemist who couldn't even be called "Doctor" he did pretty well. Here is a partial list of the things that he turned out:

A commercially feasible plan for making an aluminum alloy stronger than the best steel so that it could be used as a structural metal.

An exhibition gadget he called a light pump, which worked on the theory that light is a form of matter and therefore subject to physical and electromagnetic laws. Seal a room with a single light source, beam a cylindrical vibratory magnetic field to it from the pump, and the light will be led down it. Now pass the light through Kidder's "lens"—a ring which perpetuates an electric field along the lines of a high-speed iris-type camera shutter. Below this is the heart of the light pump—a ninety-eight-per-cent efficient light absorber, crystalline, which, in a sense, *loses* the light in its internal facets. The effect of darkening the room with this apparatus is slight but measurable. Pardon my layman's language, but that's the general idea.

Synthetic chlorophyll—by the barrel.

An airplane propeller efficient at eight times sonic speed.

A cheap goo you brush on over old paint, let harden, and then peel off like strips of cloth. The old paint comes with it. That one made friends fast.

A self-sustaining atomic disintegration of uranium's isotope 238, which is two hundred times as plentiful as the old stand-by, U-235.

That will do for the present. If I may repeat myself; for a biochemist who couldn't even be called "Doctor," he did pretty well.

Kidder was apparently unconscious of the fact that he held power enough on his little island to become master of the world. His mind simply didn't run to things like that. As long as he was left alone with his experiments, he was well content to leave the rest of the world to its own clumsy and primitive devices. He couldn't be reached except by a radiophone of his own design, and the only counterpart was locked in a vault of his Boston bank. Only one man could operate it. The extraordinarily sensitive transmitter would respond only to Conant's own body vibrations. Kidder had instructed Conant that he was not to be disturbed except by messages of the greatest moment. His ideas and patents, what Conant could pry out of him, were released under pseudonyms known only to Conant— Kidder didn't care.

The result, of course, was an infiltration of the most astonishing advancements since the dawn of civilization. The nation profited—the world profited. But most of all, the bank profited. It began to get a little oversize. It began getting its fingers into other pies. It grew more fingers and had to bake more figurative pies. Before many years had passed, it was so big that, using Kidder's many weapons, it almost matched Kidder in power.

Almost.

Now stand by while I squelch those fellows in the lower left-hand corner who've been saying all this while that Kidder's slightly improbable; that no man could ever perfect himself in so many ways in so many sciences.

Well, you're right. Kidder was a genius—granted. But his genius was not creative. He was, to the core, a student. He applied what he knew, what he saw, and what he was taught. When first he began working in his new laboratory on his island he reasoned something like this:

"Everything I know is what I have been taught by the sayings and writings of people who have studied the sayings and writings of people who have—and so on. Once in a while someone stumbles on something new and he or someone cleverer uses the idea and disseminates it. But for each one that finds something really new, a couple of million gather and pass on information that is already current. I'd know more if I could get the jump on evolutionary trends. It takes too long to wait for the accidents that increase man's knowledge—my knowledge. If I had ambition enough now to figure out how to travel ahead in time, I could skim the surface of the future and just dip down when I saw something interesting. But time isn't that way. It can't be left behind or tossed ahead. What else is left?

"Well, there's the proposition of speeding intellectual evolution so that I can observe what it cooks up. That seems a bit inefficient. It would involve more labor to discipline human minds to that extent than it would to simply apply myself along those lines. But I can't apply myself that way. No man can.

"I'm licked. I can't speed myself up, and I can't speed other men's minds up. Isn't there an alternative? There must be—somewhere, somehow, there's got to be an answer."

So it was on this, and not on eugenics, or light pumps, or botany, or atomic physics, that James Kidder applied himself. For a practical man he found the problem slightly on the metaphysical side; but he attacked it with typical thoroughness, using his own peculiar brand of logic. Day after day he wandered over the island, throwing shells impotently at sea gulls and swearing richly. Then came a time when he sat indoors and brooded. And only then did he get feverishly to work.

He worked in his own field, biochemistry, and concentrated mainly on two things—genetics and animal metabolism. He learned, and filed away in his insatiable mind, many things having nothing to do with the problem at hand, and very little of what he wanted. But he piled that little on what little he knew or guessed, and in time had quite a collection of known factors to work with. His approach was characteristically unorthodox. He did things on the order of multiplying apples by pears, and balancing equations by adding $\log \sqrt{-1}$ to one side and $^{\circ\circ}$ to the other. He made mistakes, but only one of a kind, and later, only one of a species. He spent so many hours at his microscope that he had quit work for two days to get rid of a hallucination that his heart was pumping his own blood through the mike. He did nothing by trial and error because he disapproved of the method as sloppy.

And he got results. He was lucky to begin with and even luckier when he formularized the law of probability and reduced it to such low terms that he knew almost to the item what experiments not to try. When the cloudy, viscous semifluid on the watch glass began to move itself he knew he was on the right track. When it began to seek food on its own he began to be excited. When it divided and, in a few hours, redivided, and each part grew and divided again, he was triumphant, for he had created life.

He nursed his brain children and sweated and strained over them, and he designed baths of various vibrations for them, and inoculated and dosed and sprayed them. Each move he made taught him the next. And out of his tanks and tubes and incubators came amoebalike creatures, and then ciliated animalcules, and more and more rapidly he produced animals with eye spots, nerve cysts, and then— victory of victories—a real blastopod, possessed of many cells instead of one. More slowly he developed a gastropod, but once he had it, it was not too difficult for him to give it organs, each with a specified function, each inheritable.

Then came cultured mollusklike things, and creatures with more and more perfected gills. The day that a non-descript thing wriggled up an inclined board out of a tank, threw flaps over its gills and feebly breathed air, Kidder quit work and went to the other end of the island and got disgustingly drunk. Hangover and all, he was soon back in the lab, forgetting to eat, forgetting to sleep, tearing into his problem.

He turned into a scientific byway and ran down his other great triumph—accelerated metabolism. He extracted and refined the stimulating factors in alcohol, cocoa, heroin, and Mother Nature's prize dope runner, *cannabis indica*. Like the scientist who, in analyzing the various clotting agents for blood treatments, found that oxalic acid and oxalic acid alone was the active factor, Kidder isolated the accelerators and decelerators, the stimulants and soporifics, in every substance that ever undermined a man's morality and/or caused a "noble experiment." In the process he found one thing he needed badly—a colorless elixir that made sleep the unnecessary and avoidable waster of time it should be. Then and there he went on a twenty-four-hour shift.

He artificially synthesized the substances he had iso-lated, and in doing so sloughed away a great many useless components. He pursued the subject along the lines of radiations and vibrations. He discovered something in the longer reds which, when projected through a vessel full of air vibrating in the supersonics, and then polarized, speeded up the heartbeat of small animals twenty to one.

They ate twenty times as much, grew twenty times as fast, and—died twenty times sooner than they should have.

Kidder built a huge hermetically sealed room. Above it was another room, the same length and breadth but not quite as high. This was his control chamber. The large room was divided into four sealed sections, each with its individual miniature cranes and derricks—handling machinery of all kinds. There were also trapdoors fitted with air locks leading from the upper to the lower room.

By this time the other laboratory had produced a warm-blooded, snake-skinned quadruped with an astonishingly rapid life cycle—a generation every eight days, a life span of about fifteen. Like the echidna, it was oviparous and mammalian. Its period of gestation was six hours; the eggs hatched in three; the young reached sexual maturity in another four days. Each female laid four eggs and lived just long enough to care for the young after they hatched. The male generally died two or three hours after mating. The creatures were highly adaptable. They were small—not more than three inches long, two inches to the shoulder from the ground. Their forepaws had three digits and a triple-jointed, opposed thumb. They were attuned to life in an atmosphere with a large ammonia content. Kidder bred four of the creatures and put one group in each section of the sealed room.

Then he was ready. With his controlled atmospheres he varied temperatures, oxygen content, humidity. He killed them off like flies with excesses of, for instance, carbon dioxide, and the survivors bred their physical resistance into the next generation. Periodically he would switch the eggs from one sealed section to another to keep the strains varied. And rapidly, under these controlled conditions, the creatures began to evolve.

This, then, was the answer to his problem. He couldn't speed up mankind's intellectual advancement enough to have it teach him the things his incredible mind yearned for. He couldn't speed himself up. So he created a new race—a race which would develop and evolve so fast that it would surpass the civilization of man; and from them he would learn.

They were completely in Kidder's power. Earth's normal atmosphere would poison them, as he took care to demonstrate to every fourth generation. They would make no attempt to escape from him. They would live their lives and progress and make their little trial-and-error experiments hundreds of times faster than man did. They had the edge on man, for they had Kidder to guide them. It took man six thousand years really to discover science, three hundred to put it to work. It took Kidder's creatures two hundred days to equal man's mental attainments. And from then on—Kidder's spasmodic output made the late, great Tom Edison look like a home handicrafter.

He called them Neoterics, and he teased them into working for him. Kidder was inventive in an ideological way; that is, he could dream up impossible propositions providing he didn't have to work them out. For example, he wanted the Neoterics to figure out for themselves how to build shelters out of porous material. He created the need for such shelters by subjecting one of the sections to a high-pressure rainstorm which flattened the inhabitants. The Neoterics promptly devised waterproof shelters out of the thin waterproof material he piled in one corner. Kidder immediately blew down the flimsy structures with a blast of cold air. They built them up again so that they resisted both wind and rain. Kidder lowered the temperature so abruptly that they could not adjust their bodies to it. They heated their shelters with tiny braziers. Kidder promptly turned up the heat until they began to roast to death. After a few deaths, one of their bright boys figured out how to build a strong insulant house by using three-ply rubberoid, with the middle layer perforated thousands of times to create tiny air pockets.

Using such tactics, Kidder forced them to develop a highly advanced little culture. He caused a drought in one section and a liquid surplus in another, and then opened the partition between them. Quite a spectacular war was fought, and Kidder's notebooks filled with information about military tactics and weapons. Then there was the vaccine they developed against the common cold—the reason why that affliction has been absolutely stamped out in the world today, for it was one of the things that Conant, the bank president, got hold of. He spoke to Kidder over the radiophone one winter afternoon with a voice so hoarse from laryngitis that Kidder sent him a vial of vaccine and told him briskly not to ever call him again in such a disgustingly inaudible state. Conant had it analyzed and again Kidder's accounts and the bank's swelled.

At first, Kidder merely supplied the materials he thought they might need, but when they developed an intelligence equal to the task of fabricating their own from the elements at hand, he gave each section a stock of raw materials. The process for really strong aluminum was developed when he built in a huge plunger in one of the sections, which reached from wall to wall and was designed to descend at the rate of four inches a day until it crushed whatever was at the bottom. The Neoterics, in self-defense, used what strong material they had in hand to stop the inexorable death that threatened them. But Kidder had seen to it that they had nothing but aluminum oxide and a scattering of other elements, plus plenty of electric power. At first they ran up dozens of aluminum pillars; when these were crushed and twisted they tried shaping them so that the soft metal would take more weight. When that failed they quickly built stronger ones; and when the plunger was halted, Kidder removed one of the pillars and analyzed it. It was hardened aluminum, stronger and tougher than molybd steel.

Experience taught Kidder that he had to make certain changes to increase his power over the Neoterics before they got too ingenious. There were things that could be done with atomic power that he was curious about; but he was not willing to trust his little superscientists with a thing like that unless they could be trusted to use it strictly according to Hoyle. So he instituted a rule of fear. The most trivial departure from what he chose to consider the right way of doing things resulted in instant death of half a tribe. If he was trying to develop a Diesel-type power plant, for instance, that would operate without a flywheel, and a bright young Neoteric used any of the materials for architectural purposes, half the tribe immediately died. Of course, they had developed a written language; it was Kidder's own. The teletype in a glass-enclosed area in a corner of each section was a shrine. Any directions that were given on it were obeyed, or else. . . . After this innovation, Kidder's work was much simpler. There was no need for any indirection. Anything he wanted done was done. No matter how impossible his commands, three or four generations of Neoterics could find a way to carry them out.

This quotation is from a paper that one of Kidder's highspeed telescopic cameras discovered being circulated among the younger Neoterics. It is translated from the highly simplified script of the Neoterics.

"These edicts shall be followed by each Neoteric upon pain of death, which punishment will be inflicted by the tribe upon the individual to protect the tribe against him.

"Priority of interest and tribal and individual effort is to be given the commands that appear on the word machine.

"Any misdirection of material or power, or use thereof for any other purpose than the carrying out of the machine's commands, unless no command appears, shall be punishable by death.

"Any information regarding the problem at hand, or ideas or experiments which might conceivably bear upon it, are to become the property of the tribe.

"Any individual failing to cooperate in the tribal effort, or who can be termed guilty of not expending his full efforts in the work, or the suspicion thereof shall be subject to the death penalty."

Such are the results of complete domination. This paper impressed Kidder as much as it did because it was completely spontaneous. It was the Neoterics' own creed, developed by them for their own greatest good.

And so at last Kidder had his fulfillment. Crouched in the upper room, going from telescope to telescope, running off slowed-down films from his high-speed cameras, he found himself possessed of a tractable, dynamic source of information. Housed in the great square building with its four half-acre sections was a new world, to which he was god.

Conant's mind was similar to Kidder's in that its approach to any problem was along the shortest distance between any two points, regardless of whether that approach was along the line of most or least resistance. His rise to the bank presidency was a history of ruthless moves whose only justification was that they got him what he wanted. Like an over-efficient general, he would never vanquish an enemy through sheer force of numbers alone. He would also skillfully flank his enemy, not on one side, but on both. Innocent bystanders were creatures deserving no consideration.

The time he took over a certain thousand-acre property, for instance, from a man named Grady, he was not satisfied with only the title to the land. Grady was an airport owner—had been all his life, and his father before him. Conant exerted every kind of pressure on the man and found him unshakable. Finally judicious persuasion led the city officials to dig a sewer right across the middle of the field, quite efficiently wrecking Grady's business. Knowing that this would supply Grady, who was a wealthy man, with motive for revenge, Conant took over Grady's bank at half again its value and caused it to fold up. Grady lost every cent he had and ended his life in an asylum. Conant was very proud of his tactics.

Like many another who had had Mammon by the tail, Conant did not know when to let go. His vast organization yielded him more money and power than any other concern in history, and yet he was not satisfied. Conant and money were like Kidder and knowledge. Conant's pyramided enterprises were to him what the Neoterics were to Kidder. Each had made his private world; each used it for his instruction and profit. Kidder, though, disturbed nobody but his Neoterics. Even so, Conant was not wholly villainous. He was a shrewd man, and had discovered early the value of pleasing people. No man can rob successfully over a period of years without pleasing the people he robs. The technique for doing this is highly involved, but master it and you can start your own mint.

Conant's one great fear was that Kidder would some day take an interest in world events and begin to become opinionated. Good heavens—the potential power he had! A little matter like swinging an election could be managed by a man like Kidder as easily as turning over in bed. The only thing he could do was to call him periodically and see if there was anything that Kidder needed to keep himself busy. Kidder appreciated this. Conant, once in a while, would suggest something to Kidder that intrigued him, something that would keep him deep in his hermitage for a few weeks. The light pump was one of the re-

sults of Conant's imagination. Conant bet him it couldn't
be done. Kidder did it.

One afternoon Kidder answered the squeal of the radiophone's signal. Swearing mildly, he shut off the film he
was watching and crossed the compound to the old laboratory. He went to the radiophone, threw a switch. The
squealing stopped.

"Well?"

"Hello," said Conant. "Busy?"

"Not very," said Kidder. He was delighted with the
pictures his camera had caught, showing the skillful work
of a gang of Neoterics synthesizing rubber out of pure
sulphur. He would rather have liked to tell Conant about
it, but somehow he had never got around to telling Conant
about the Neoterics, and he didn't see why he should start
now.

Conant said, "Er . . . Kidder, I was down at the club
the other day and a bunch of us were filling up an evening
with loose talk. Something came up which might interest
you."

"What?"

"Couple of the utilities boys there. You know the power
setup in this country, don't you? Thirty per cent atomic,
the rest hydroelectric, Diesel and steam?"

"I hadn't known," said Kidder, who was as innocent as
a babe of current events.

"Well, we were arguing about what chance a new power
source would have. One of the men there said it would be
smarter to produce a new power and then talk about it.
Another one waived that; said he couldn't name that new
power, but he could describe it. Said it would have to have
everything that present power sources have, plus one or
two more things. It could be cheaper, for instance. It could
be more efficient. It might supercede the others by being
easier to carry from the power plant to the consumer. See
what I mean? Any one of these factors might prove a new
source of power competitive to the others. What I'd like
to see is a new power with *all* of these factors. What do
you think of it?"

"Not impossible."

"Think not?"

"I'll try it."

"Keep me posted." Conant's transmitter clicked off. The switch was a little piece of false front that Kidder had built into the set, which was something that Conant didn't know. The set switched itself off when Conant moved from it. After the switch's sharp crack, Kidder heard the banker mutter, "If he does it, I'm all set. If he doesn't, at least the crazy fool will keep himself busy on the isl—"

Kidder eyed the radiophone for an instant with raised eyebrows, and then he shrugged them down again with his shoulders. It was quite evident that Conant had something up his sleeve, but Kidder wasn't worried. Who on earth would want to disturb him? He wasn't bothering anybody. He went back to the Neoterics' building, full of the new power idea.

Eleven days later Kidder called Conant and gave specific instructions on how to equip his receiver with a facsimile set which would enable Kidder to send written matter over the air. As soon as this was done and Kidder informed, the biochemist for once in his life spoke at some length.

"Conant—you implied that a new power source that would be cheaper, more efficient and more easily transmitted than any now in use did not exist. You might be interested in the little generator I have just set up.

"It has power, Conant—unbelievable power. Broadcast. A beautiful little tight beam. Here—catch this on the facsimile recorder." Kidder slipped a sheet of paper under the clips of his transmitter and it appeared on Conant's set. "Here's the wiring diagram for a power receiver. Now listen. The beam is so tight, so highly directional, that not three-thousandths of one per cent of the power would be lost in a two-thousand-mile transmission. The power system is closed. That is, any drain on the beam returns a signal along it to the transmitter, which automatically steps up to increase the power output. It has a limit, but it's way up. And something else. This little gadget of mine can send out eight different beams with a total horsepower output of around eight thousand per minute per beam. From each beam you can draw enough power to turn the page of a book or fly a superstratosphere plane. Hold on—I haven't finished yet. Each beam, as I told you before, returns a signal from receiver to transmitter. This not only controls the power output of the beam, but directs it. Once contact is made, the beam will never let go. It will follow the receiver anywhere. You can power land, air or water vehicles with it, as well as any stationary plant. Like it?"

Conant, who was a banker and not a scientist, wiped his shining pate with the back of his hand and said, "I've never known you to steer me wrong yet, Kidder. How about the cost of this thing?"

"High," said Kidder promptly. "As high as an atomic plant. But there are no high-tension lines, no wires, no pipelines, no nothing. The receivers are little more complicated than a radio set. Transmitter is—well, that's quite a job."

"Didn't take you long," said Conant.

"No," said Kidder, "it didn't, did it?" It was the lifework of nearly twelve hundred highly cultured people, but Kidder wasn't going into that. "Of course, the one I have here's just a model."

Conant's voice was strained. "A—model? And it delivers—"

"Over sixty-thousand horsepower," said Kidder gleefully.

"Good heavens! In a full-sized machine—why, one transmitter would be enough to—" The possibilities of the thing choked Conant for a moment. "How is it fueled?"

"It isn't," said Kidder. "I won't begin to explain it. I've tapped a source of power of unimaginable force. It's—well, big. So big that it can't be misused."

"What?" snapped Conant. "What do you mean by that?"

Kidder cocked an eyebrow. Conant *had* something up his sleeve, then. At this second indication of it, Kidder, the least suspicious of men, began to put himself on guard. "I mean just what I say," he said evenly. "Don't try too hard to understand me—I barely savvy it myself. But the source of this power is a monstrous resultant caused by the unbalance of two previously equalized forces. Those equalized forces are cosmic in quantity. Actually, the forces are those which make suns, crush atoms the way they crushed those that compose the companion of Sirius. It's not anything you can fool with."

"I don't—" said Conant, and his voice ended puzzledly.

"I'll give you a parallel of it," said Kidder. "Suppose you

take two rods, one in each hand. Place their tips together and push. As long as your pressure is directly along their long axes, the pressure is equalized; right and left hands cancel each other. Now I come along; I put out one finger and touch the rods ever so lightly where they come together. They snap out of line violently; you break a couple of knuckles. The resultant force is at right angles to the original forces you exerted. My power transmitter is on the same principle. It takes an infinitesimal amount of energy to throw those forces out of line. Easy enough when you know how to do it. The important question is whether or not you can control the resultant when you get it. I can."

"I—see." Conant indulged in a four-second gloat. "Heaven help the utility companies. I don't intend to. Kidder—I want a full-size power transmitter."

Kidder clucked into the radiophone. "Ambitious, aren't you? I haven't a staff out here, Conant—you know that. And I can't be expected to build four or five thousand tons of apparatus myself."

"I'll have five hundred engineers and laborers out there in forty-eight hours."

"You will not. Why bother me with it? I'm quite happy here, Conant, and one of the reasons is that I've got no one to get in my hair."

"Oh, now, Kidder—don't be like that—I'll pay you—"

"You haven't got that much money," said Kidder briskly. He flipped the switch on his set. *His* switch worked.

Conant was furious. He shouted into the phone several times, then began to lean on the signal button. On his island, Kidder let the thing squeal and went back to his projection room. He was sorry he had sent the diagram of the receiver to Conant. It would have been interesting to power a plane or a car with the model transmitter he had taken from the Neoterics. But if Conant was going to be that way about it—well, anyway, the receiver would be no good without the transmitter. Any radio engineer would understand the diagram, but not the beam which activated it. And Conant wouldn't get his beam.

Pity he didn't know Conant well enough.

Kidder's days were endless sorties into learning. He never slept, nor did his Neoterics. He ate regularly every five hours, exercised for half an hour in every twelve. He did not keep track of time, for it meant nothing to him. Had he wanted to know the date, or the year, even, he knew he could get it from Conant. He didn't care, that's all. The time that was not spent in observation was used in developing new problems for the Neoterics. His thoughts just now ran to defense. The idea was born in his conversation with Conant; now the idea was primary, its motivation something of no importance. The Neoterics were working on a vibration field of quasi-electrical nature. Kidder could see little practical value in such a thing— an invisible wall which would kill any living thing which touched it. But still—the idea was intriguing.

He stretched and moved away from the telescope in the upper room through which he had been watching his creations at work. He was profoundly happy here in the large control room. Leaving it to go to the old laboratory for a bite to eat was a thing he hated to do. He felt like bidding it good-by each time he walked across the compound, and saying a glad hello when he returned. A little amused at himself, he went out.

There was a black blob—a distant power boat—a few miles off the island, toward the mainland. Kidder stopped and stared distastefully at it. A white petal of spray was affixed to each side of the black body—it was coming toward him. He snorted, thinking of the time a yachtload of silly fools had landed out of curiosity one afternoon, spewed themselves over his beloved island, peppered him with lame-brained questions, and thrown his nervous equilibrium out for days. Lord, how he hated *people!*

The thought of unpleasantness bred two more thoughts that played half-consciously with his mind as he crossed the compound and entered the old laboratory. One was that perhaps it might be wise to surround his buildings with a field of force of some kind and post warnings for trespassers. The other thought was of Conant and the vague uneasiness the man had been sending to him through the radiophone these last weeks. His suggestion, two days ago, that a power plant be built on the island—horrible idea!

Conant rose from a laboratory bench as Kidder walked in.

They looked at each other wordlessly for a long moment. Kidder hadn't seen the bank president in years. The man's presence, he found, made his scalp crawl.

"Hello," said Conant genially. "You're looking fit."

Kidder grunted. Conant eased his unwieldy body back onto the bench and said, "Just to save you the energy of asking questions, Mr. Kidder, I arrived two hours ago on a small boat. Rotten way to travel. I wanted to be a surprise to you; my two men rowed me the last couple of miles. You're not very well equipped here for defense, are you? Why, anyone could slip up on you the way I did."

"Who'd want to?" growled Kidder. The man's voice edged annoyingly into his brain. He spoke too loudly for such a small room; at least, Kidder's hermit's ears felt that way. Kidder shrugged and went about preparing a light meal for himself.

"Well," drawled the banker. "I might want to." He drew out a Dow-metal cigar case. "Mind if I smoke?"

"I do," said Kidder sharply.

Conant laughed easily and put the cigars away. "I might," he said, "want to urge you to let me build that power station on this island."

"Radiophone work?"

"Oh, yes. But now that I'm here you can't switch me off. Now—how about it?"

"I haven't changed my mind."

"Oh, but you should, Kidder, you should. Think of it—think of the good it would do for the masses of people that are now paying exorbitant power bills!"

"I hate the masses! Why do you have to build here?"

"Oh, that. It's an ideal location. You own the island; work could begin here without causing any comment whatsoever. The plant would spring full-fledged on the power markets of the country, having been built in secret. The island can be made impregnable."

"I don't want to be bothered."

"We wouldn't bother you. We'd build on the north end of the island—a mile and a quarter from you and your work. Ah—by the way—where's the model of the power transmitter?"

Kidder, with his mouth full of synthesized food, waved a hand at a small table on which stood the model, a four-foot, amazingly intricate device of plastic and steel and tiny coils.

Conant rose and went over to look at it. "Actually works, eh?" He sighed deeply and said, "Kidder, I really hate to do this, but I want to build that plant rather badly. Carson! Robbins!"

Two bull-necked individuals stepped out from their hiding places in the corners of the room. One idly dangled a revolver by its trigger guard. Kidder looked blankly from one to the other of them.

"These gentlemen will follow my orders implicitly, Kidder. In half an hour a party will land here—engineers, contractors. They will start surveying the north end of the island for the construction of the power plant. These boys here feel about the same way I do as far as you are concerned. Do we proceed with your cooperation or without it? It's immaterial to me whether or not you are left alive to continue your work. My engineers can duplicate your model."

Kidder said nothing. He had stopped chewing when he saw the gunmen, and only now remembered to swallow. He sat crouched over his plate without moving or speaking.

Conant broke the silence by walking to the door. "Robbins—can you carry that model there?" The big man put his gun away, lifted the model gently, and nodded. "Take it down to the beach and meet the other boat. Tell Mr. Johansen, the engineer, that this is the model he is to work from." Robbins went out. Conant turned to Kidder. "There's no need for us to anger ourselves," he said oilily. "I think you are stubborn, but I don't hold it against you. I know how you feel. You'll be left alone; you have my promise. But I mean to go ahead on this job, and a small thing like your life can't stand in my way."

Kidder said, "Get out of here." There were two swollen veins throbbing at his temples. His voice was low, and it shook.

"Very well. Good day, Mr. Kidder. Oh—by the way—you're a clever devil." No one had ever referred to the scholastic Mr. Kidder that way before. "I realize the possibility of your blasting us off the island. I wouldn't do it if I were you. I'm willing to give you what you want—privacy. I want the same thing in return. If anything happens to me while I'm here, the island will be bombed by someone who is working for me. I'll admit they might fail. If they do, the United States government will take a hand. You wouldn't want that, would you? That's rather a big thing for one man to fight. The same thing goes if the plant is sabotaged in any way after I go back to the mainland. You might be killed. You will most certainly be bothered interminably. Thanks for your . . . er . . . cooperation." The banker smirked and walked out, followed by his taciturn gorilla.

Kidder sat there for a long time without moving. Then he shook his head, rested it in his palms. He was badly frightened; not so much because his life was in danger, but because his privacy and his work—his world—were threatened. He was hurt and bewildered. He wasn't a businessman. He couldn't handle men. All his life he had run away from human beings and what they represented to him. He was like a frightened child when men closed in on him.

Cooling a little, he wondered vaguely what would happen when the power plant opened. Certainly the government would be interested. Unless—unless by then Conant was the government. That plant was an unimaginable source of power, and not only the kind of power that turned wheels. He rose and went back to the world that was home to him, a world where his motives were understood, and where there were those who could help him. Back at the Neoterics' building, he escaped yet again from the world of men into his work.

Kidder called Conant the following week, much to the banker's surprise. His two days on the island had got the work well under way, and he had left with the arrival of a shipload of laborers and material. He kept in close touch by radio with Johansen, the engineer in charge. It had been a blind job for Johansen and all the rest of the crew on the island. Only the bank's infinite resources could have hired such a man, or the picked gang with him.

Johansen's first reaction when he saw the model had been ecstatic. He wanted to tell his friends about this marvel; but the only radio set available was beamed to Conant's private office in the bank, and Conant's armed guards, one to every two workers, had strict orders to destroy any other radio transmitter on sight. About that time he realized that he was a prisoner on the island. His instant anger subsided when he reflected that being a prisoner at fifty thousand dollars a week wasn't too bad. Two of the laborers and an engineer thought differently, and got disgruntled a couple of days after they arrived. They disappeared one night— the same night that five shots were fired down on the beach. No questions were asked, and there was no more trouble.

Conant covered his surprise at Kidder's call and was as offensively jovial as ever. "Well, now! Anything I can do for you?"

"Yes," said Kidder. His voice was low, completely without expression. "I want you to issue a warning to your men not to pass the white line I have drawn five hundred yards north of my buildings, right across the island."

"Warning? Why, my dear fellow, they have orders that you are not to be disturbed on any account."

"You've ordered them. All right. Now warn them. I have an electric field surrounding my laboratories that will kill anything living which penetrates it. I don't want to have murder on my conscience. There will be no deaths unless there are trespassers. You'll inform your workers?"

"Oh, now, Kidder," the banker expostulated. "That was totally unnecessary. You won't be bothered. Why—" but he found he was talking into a dead mike. He knew better than to call back. He called Johansen instead and told him about it. Johansen didn't like the sound of it, but he repeated the message and signed off. Conant liked that man. He was, for a moment, a little sorry that Johansen would never reach the mainland alive.

But that Kidder—he was beginning to be a problem. As long as his weapons were strictly defensive he was no real menace. But he would have to be taken care of when the plant was operating. Conant couldn't afford to have genius around him unless it was unquestionably on his side. The power transmitter and Conant's highly ambitious plans would be safe as long as Kidder was left to himself. Kidder knew that he could, for the time being, expect more sympathetic treatment from Conant than he could from a horde of government investigators.

Kidder only left his own enclosure once after the work began on the north end of the island, and it took all of his unskilled diplomacy to do it. Knowing the source of the plant's power, knowing what could happen if it were misused, he asked Conant's permission to inspect the great transmitter when it was nearly finished. Insuring his own life by refusing to report back to Conant until he was safe within his own laboratory again, he turned off his shield and walked up to the north end.

He saw an awe-inspiring sight. The four-foot model was duplicated nearly a hundred times as large. Inside a massive three-hundred-foot tower a space was packed nearly solid with the same bewildering maze of coils and bars that the Neoterics had built so delicately into their machine. At the top was a globe of polished golden alloy, the transmitting antenna. From it would stream thousands of tight beams of force, which could be tapped to any degree by corresponding thousands of receivers placed anywhere at any distance. Kidder learned that the receivers had already been built, but his informant, Johansen, knew little about that end of it and was saying less. Kidder checked over every detail of the structure, and when he was through he shook Johansen's hand admiringly.

"I didn't want this thing here," he said shyly, "and I don't. But I will say that it's a pleasure to see this kind of work."

"It's a pleasure to meet the man that invented it."

Kidder beamed. "I didn't invent it," he said. "Maybe someday I'll show you who did. I—well, good-by." He turned before he had a chance to say too much and marched off down the path.

"Shall I?" said a voice at Johansen's side. One of Conant's guards had his gun out.

Johansen knocked the man's arm down. "No." He scratched his head. "So that's the mysterious menace from the other end of the island. Eh! Why, he's a hell of a nice little feller!"

Built on the ruins of Denver, which was destroyed in the great Battle of the Rockies during the Western War, stands the most beautiful city in the world—our nation's capital. New Washington. In a circular room deep in the

heart of the White House, the president, three army men
and a civilian sat. Under the president's desk a dictaphone
unostentatiously recorded every word that was said. Two
thousand and more miles away, Conant hung over a radio
receiver, tuned to receive the signals of the tiny transmitter
in the civilian's side pocket.

One of the officers spoke.

"Mr. President, the 'impossible claims' made for this
gentleman's product are absolutely true. He has proved
beyond doubt each item on his prospectus."

The president glanced at the civilian, back at the officer.
"I won't wait for your report," he said. "Tell me—what
happened?"

Another of the army men mopped his face with a khaki
bandanna. "I can't ask you to believe us, Mr. President,
but it's true all the same. Mr. Wright here has in his suitcase three or four dozen small . . . er . . . bombs—"

"They're not bombs," said Wright casually.

"All right. They're not bombs. Mr. Wright smashed two
of them on an anvil with a sledge hammer. There was no
result. He put two more in an electric furnace. They
burned away like so much tin and cardboard. We dropped
one down the barrel of a field piece and fired it. Still
nothing." He paused and looked at the third officer, who
picked up the account:

"We really got started then. We flew to the proving
grounds, dropped one of the objects and flew to thirty
thousand feet. From there, with a small hand detonator no
bigger than your fist, Mr. Wright set the thing off. I've
never seen anything like it. Forty acres of land came
straight up at us, breaking up as it came. The concussion
was terrific—you must have felt it here, four hundred
miles away."

The president nodded. "I did. Seismographs on the other
side of the Earth picked it up."

"The crater it left was a quarter of a mile deep at the
center. Why, one plane load of those things could demolish
any city! There isn't even any necessity for accuracy!"

"You haven't heard anything yet," another officer broke
in. "Mr. Wright's automobile is powered by a small plant
similar to the others. He demonstrated it to us. We could
find no fuel tank of any kind, or any other driving mech-

anism. But with a power plant no bigger than six cubic inches, that car, carrying enough weight to give it traction, outpulled an army tank!"

"And the other test!" said the third excitedly. "He put one of the objects into a replica of a treasury vault. The walls were twelve feet thick, super-reinforced concrete. He controlled it from over a hundred yards away. He . . . he burst that vault! It wasn't an explosion—it was as if some incredibly powerful expansive force inside filled it and flattened the walls from inside. They cracked and split and powdered, and the steel girders and rods came twisting and shearing out like . . . like—*whew!* After that he insisted on seeing you. We knew it wasn't usual, but he said he has more to say and would say it only in your presence."

The president said gravely, "What is it, Mr. Wright?"

Wright rose, picked up his suitcase, opened it and took out a small cube, about eight inches on a side, made of some light-absorbent red material. Four men edged nervously away from it.

"These gentlemen," he began, "have seen only part of the things this device can do. I'm going to demonstrate to you the delicacy of control that is possible with it." He made an adjustment with a tiny knob on the side of the cube, set it on the edge of the president's desk.

"You have asked me more than once if this is my invention or if I am representing someone. The latter is true. It might also interest you to know that the man who controls this cube is right now several thousand miles from here. He and he alone, can prevent it from detonating now that I—" He pulled his detonator out of the suitcase and pressed a button—"have done this. It will explode the way the one we dropped from the plane did, completely destroying this city and everything in it, in just four hours. It will also explode—" He stepped back and threw a tiny switch on his detonator—"if any moving object comes within three feet of it or if anyone leaves this room but me—it can be compensated for that. If, after I leave, I am molested, it will detonate as soon as a hand is laid on me. No bullets can kill me fast enough to prevent me from setting it off."

The three army men were silent. One of them swiped nervously at the beads of cold sweat on his forehead. The others did not move. The president said evenly:

"What's your proposition?"

"A very reasonable one. My employer does not work in the open, for obvious reasons. All he wants is your agreement to carry out his orders; to appoint the cabinet members he chooses, to throw your influence in any way he dictates. The public—Congress—anyone else—need never know anything about it. I might add that if you agree to this proposal, this 'bomb,' as you call it, will not go off. But you can be sure that thousands of them are planted all over the country. You will never know when you are near one. If you disobey, it beams instant annihilation for you and everyone else within three or four square miles.

"In three hours and fifty minutes—that will be at precisely seven o'clock—there is a commercial radio program on Station RPRS. You will cause the announcer, after his station identification, to say 'Agreed.' It will pass unnoticed by all but my employer. There is no use in having me followed; my work is done. I shall never see nor contact my employer again. That is all. Good afternoon, gentlemen!"

Wright closed his suitcase with a businesslike snap, bowed, and left the room. Four men sat staring at the little red cube.

"Do you think he can do all he says?" asked the president.

The three nodded mutely. The president reached for his phone.

There was an eavesdropper to all of the foregoing. Conant, squatting behind his great desk in the vault, where he had his sanctum sanctorum, knew nothing of it. But beside him was the compact bulk of Kidder's radiophone. His presence switched it on, and Kidder, on his island, blessed the day he had thought of the device. He had been meaning to call Conant all morning, but was very hesitant. His meeting with the young engineer Johansen had impressed him strongly. The man was such a thorough scientist, possessed of such complete delight in the work he did, that for the first time in his life Kidder found himself actually wanting to see someone again. But he feared for Johansen's life if he brought him to the laboratory, for Johansen's work was done on the island, and Conant would most certainly have the engineer killed if he heard of his visit, fearing that Kidder would influence him to sabotage the great transmitter. And if Kidder went to the power plant he would probably be shot on sight.

All one day Kidder wrangled with himself, and finally determined to call Conant. Fortunately he gave no signal, but turned up the volume on the receiver when the little red light told him that Conant's transmitter was functioning. Curious, he heard everything that occurred in the president's chamber three thousand miles away. Horrified, he realized what Conant's engineers had done. Built into tiny containers were tens of thousands of power receivers. They had no power of their own, but, by remote control, could draw on any or all of the billions of horsepower the huge plant on the island was broadcasting.

Kidder stood in front of his receiver, speechless. There was nothing he could do. If he devised some means of destroying the power plant, the government would certainly step in and take over the island, and then—what would happen to him and his precious Neoterics?

Another sound grated out of the receiver—a commercial radio program. A few bars of music, a man's voice advertising stratoline fares on the installment plan, a short silence, then:

"Station RPRS, voice of the nation's Capital, District of South Colorado."

The three-second pause was interminable.

"The time is exactly . . . er . . . *agreed*. The time is exactly seven P.M., Mountain Standard Time."

Then came a half-insane chuckle. Kidder had difficulty believing it was Conant. A phone clicked. The banker's voice:

"Bill? All set. Get out there with your squadron and bomb up the island. Keep away from the plant, but cut the rest of it to ribbons. Do it quick and get out of there."

Almost hysterical with fear, Kidder rushed about the room and then shot out the door and across the compound. There were five hundred innocent workmen in barracks a quarter mile from the plant. Conant didn't need them now, and he didn't need Kidder. The only safety for anyone was in the plant itself, and Kidder wouldn't leave his Neoterics to be bombed. He flung himself up the stairs and to the nearest teletype. He banged out, "Get me a defense. I want an impenetrable shield. Urgent!"

Th words ripped out from under his fingers in the functional script of the Neoterics. Kidder didn't think of what he wrote, didn't really visualize the thing he ordered. But he had done what he could. He'd have to leave them now, get to the barracks; warn those men. He ran up the path toward the plant, flung himself over the white line that marked death to those who crossed it.

A squadron of nine clip-winged, mosquito-nosed planes rose out of a cover on the mainland. There was no sound from the engines, for there were no engines. Each plane was powered with a tiny receiver and drew its unmarked, light-absorbent wings through the air with power from the island. In a matter of minutes they raised the island. The squadron leader spoke briskly into a microphone.

"Take the barracks first. Clean 'em up. Then work south."

Johansen was alone on a small hill near the center of the island. He carried a camera, and though he knew pretty well that his chances of ever getting ashore again were practically nonexistent, he liked angle shots of his tower, and took innumerable pictures. The first he knew of the planes was when he heard their whining dive over the barracks. He stood transfixed, saw a shower of bombs hurtle down and turn the barracks into a smashed ruin of broken wood, metal and bodies. The picture of Kidder's earnest face flashed into his mind. Poor little guy—if they ever bombed his end of the island he would—But his tower! Were they going to bomb the plant?

He watched, utterly appalled, as the planes flew out to sea, cut back and dove again. They seemed to be working south. At the third dive he was sure of it. Not knowing what he could do, he nevertheless turned and ran toward Kidder's place. He rounded a turn in the trail and collided violently with the little biochemist. Kidder's face was scarlet with exertion, and he was the most terrified-looking object Johansen had ever seen.

Kidder waved a hand northward. "Conant!" he screamed over the uproar. "It's Conant! He's going to kill us all!"

"The plant?" said Johansen, turning pale.

"It's safe. He won't touch *that!* But . . . my place . . . what about all those men?"

"Too late!" shouted Johansen.

"Maybe I can—Come on!" called Kidder, and was off down the trail, heading south.

Johansen pounded after him. Kidder's little short legs became a blur as the squadron swooped overhead, laying its eggs in the spot where they had met.

As they burst out of the woods, Johansen put on a spurt, caught up with the scientist and knocked him sprawling not six feet from the white line.

"Wh . . . wh—"

"Don't go any farther, you fool! Your own damned force field—it'll kill you!"

"Force field? But—I came through it on the way up— Here. Wait. If I can—" Kidder began hunting furiously about in the grass. In a few seconds he ran up to the line, clutching a large grasshopper in his hand. He tossed it over. It lay still.

"See?" said Johansen. "It—"

"Look! It jumped! Come on! I don't know what went wrong, unless the Neoterics shut if off. They generated that field—I didn't."

"Neo—huh?"

"Never mind," snapped the biochemist, and ran.

They pounded gasping up the steps and into the Neoterics' control room. Kidder clapped his eyes to a telescope and shrieked in glee. "They've done it! They've done it!"

"Who's—"

"My little people! The Neoterics! They've made the impenetrable shield! Don't you see—it cut through the lines of force that start up the field out there. Their generator is still throwing it up, but the vibrations can't get out! They're safe! They're safe!" And the overwrought hermit began to cry. Johansen looked at him pityingly and shook his head.

"Sure—your little men are all right. But we aren't," he added as the floor shook to the detonation of a bomb.

Johansen closed his eyes, got a grip on himself and let his curiosity overcome his fear. He stepped to the binocular telescope, gazed down it. There was nothing there but a curved sheet of gray material. He had never seen a gray quite like that. It was absolutely neutral. It didn't seem soft and it didn't seem hard, and to look at it made his brain reel. He looked up.

Kidder was pounding the keys of a teletype, watching the blank yellow tape anxiously.

"I'm not getting through to them," he whimpered. "I don't know what's the mat—Oh, of *course!*"

"What?"

"The shield is absolutely impenetrable! The teletype impulses can't get through or I could get them to extend the screen over the building—over the whole island! There's *nothing* those people can't do!"

"He's crazy," Johansen muttered. "Poor little—"

The teletype began clicking sharply. Kidder dove at it, practically embraced it. He read off the tape as it came out. Johansen saw the characters, but they meant nothing to him.

"Almighty," Kidder read falteringly, "pray have mercy on us and be forbearing until we have said our say. Without orders we have lowered the screen you ordered us to raise. We are lost, O great one. Our screen is truly impenetrable, and so cut off your words on the word machine. We have never, in the memory of any Neoteric, been without your word before. Forgive us our action. We will eagerly await your answer."

Kidder's fingers danced over the keys. "You can look now," he gasped. "Go on—the telescope!"

Johansen, trying to ignore the whine of sure death from above, looked.

He saw what looked like land—fantastic fields under cultivation, a settlement of some sort, factories, and— beings. Everything moved with incredible rapidity. He couldn't see one of the inhabitants except as darting pinky-white streaks. Fascinated, he stared for a long minute. A sound behind him made him whirl. It was Kidder, rubbing his hands together briskly. There was a broad smile on his face.

"They did it," he said happily. "You see?"

Johansen didn't see until he began to realize that there was a dead silence outside. He ran to a window. It was night outside—the blackest night—when it should have been dusk. "What happened?"

"The Neoterics," said Kidder, and laughed like a child. "My friends downstairs there. They threw up the impenetrable shield over the whole island. We can't be touched now!"

And at Johansen's amazed questions, he launched into a description of the race of beings below them.

Outside the shell, things happened. Nine airplanes suddenly went dead-stick. Nine pilots glided downward, powerless, and some fell into the sea, and some struck the miraculous gray shell that loomed in place of an island; slid off and sank.

And ashore, a man named Wright sat in a car, half dead with fear, while government men surrounded him, approached cautiously, daring instant death from a non-dead source.

In a room deep in the White House, a high-ranking army officer shrieked, "I can't stand it any more! I can't!" and leaped up, snatched a red cube off the president's desk, ground it to ineffectual litter under his shining boots.

And in a few days they took a broken old man away from the bank and put him in an asylum, where he died within a week.

The shield, you see, was truly impenetrable. The power plant was untouched and sent out its beams; but the beams could not get out, and anything powered from the plant went dead. The story never became public, although for some years there was heightened naval activity off the New England coast. The navy, so the story went, had a new target range out there—a great hemiovoid of gray material. They bombed it and shelled it and rayed it and blasted all around it, but never even dented its smooth surface.

Kidder and Johansen let it stay there. They were happy enough with their researches and their Neoterics. They did not hear or feel the shelling, for the shield was truly impenetrable. They synthesized their food and their light and air from materials at hand, and they simply didn't care. They were the only survivors of the bombing, with the exception of three poor maimed devils who died soon afterward.

All this happened many years ago, and Kidder and Johansen may be alive today, and they may be dead. But that doesn't matter too much. The important thing is that the great gray shell will bear watching. Men die, but races live. Some day the Neoterics, after innumerable genera-tions of inconceivable advancement, will take down their shield and come forth. When I think of that I feel frightened.

NIGHTFALL

by Isaac Asimov

> *"If the stars should appear one night in a thousand
> years, how would men believe and adore, and preserve
> for many generations the remembrance of the city
> of God!"*—Emerson

Aton 77, director of Saro University, thrust out a belliger-
ant lower lip and glared at the young newspaperman in a
hot fury.

Theremon 762 took that fury in his stride. In his earlier
days, when his now widely syndicated column was only a
mad idea in a cub reporter's mind, he had specialized in
"impossible" interviews. It had cost him bruises, black
eyes, and broken bones; but it had given him an ample
supply of coolness and self-confidence.

So he lowered the outthrust hand that had been so point-
edly ignored and calmly waited for the aged director to get
over the worst. Astronomers were queer ducks, anyway,
and if Aton's actions of the last two months meant anything, this same Aton was the queer-duckiest of the lot.

Aton 77 found his voice, and though it trembled with
restrained emotion, the careful, somewhat pedantic, phraseology, for which the famous astronomer was noted, did not
abandon him.

"Sir," he said, "you display an infernal gall in coming to
me with that impudent proposition of yours."

The husky telephotographer of the Observatory, Beenay
25, thrust a tongue's tip across dry lips and interposed
nervously, "Now, sir, after all—"

First published in 1941

The director turned to him and lifted a white eyebrow. "Do not interfere, Beenay. I will credit you with good intentions in bringing this man here; but I will tolerate no insubordination now."

Theremon decided it was time to take a part. "Director Aton, if you'll let me finish what I started saying I think—"

"I don't believe, young man," retorted Aton, "that anything you could say now would count much as compared with your daily columns of these last two months. You have led a vast newspaper campaign against the efforts of myself and my colleagues to organize the world against the menace which it is now too late to avert. You have done your best with your highly personal attacks on me to make the staff of this Observatory objects of ridicule."

The director lifted the copy of the Saro City *Chronicle* on the table and shook it at Theremon furiously. "Even a person of your well-known impudence should have hesitated before coming to me with a request that he be allowed to cover today's events for his paper. Of all newsmen, you!"

Aton dashed the newspaper to the floor, strode to the window and clasped his arms behind his back.

"You may leave," he snapped over his shoulder. He stared moodily out at the skyline where Gamma, the brightest of the planet's six suns, was setting. It had already faded and yellowed into the horizon mists, and Aton knew he would never see it again as a sane man.

He whirled. "No, wait, come here!" He gestured peremptorily. "I'll give you your story."

The newsman had made no motion to leave, and now he approached the old man slowly. Aton gestured outward, "Of the six suns, only Beta is left in the sky. Do you see it?"

The question was rather unnecessary. Beta was almost at zenith; its ruddy light flooding the landscape to an unusual orange as the brilliant rays of setting Gamma died. Beta was at aphelion. It was small; smaller than Theremon had ever seen it before, and for the moment it was undisputed ruler of Lagash's sky.

Lagash's own sun, Alpha, the one about which it revolved, was at the antipodes; as were the two distant companion pairs. The red dwarf Beta—Alpha's immediate companion—was alone, grimly alone.

Aton's upturned face flushed redly in the sunlight. "In just under four hours," he said, "civilization, as we know it, comes to an end. It will do so because, as you see, Beta is the only sun in the sky." He smiled grimly. "Print that! There'll be no one to read it."

"But if it turns out that four hours pass—and another four—and nothing happens?" asked Theremon softly.

"Don't let that worry you. Enough will happen."

"Granted! And *still*—if nothing happens?"

For a second time, Beenay 25 spoke, "Sir, I think you ought to listen to him."

Theremon said, "Put it to a vote, Director Aton."

There was a stir among the remaining five members of the Observatory staff, who till now had maintained an attitude of wary neutrality.

"That," stated Aton flatly, "is not necessary." He drew out his pocket watch. "Since your good friend, Beenay, insists so urgently, I will give you five minutes. Talk away."

"Good! Now, just what difference would it make if you allowed me to take down an eyewitness account of what's to come? If your prediction comes true, my presence won't hurt; for in that case my column would never be written. On the other hand, if nothing comes of it, you will just have to expect ridicule or worse. It would be wise to leave that ridicule to friendly hands."

Aton snorted. "Do you mean yours when you speak of friendly hands?"

"Certainly!" Theremon sat down and crossed his legs. "My columns may have been a little rough at times, but I gave you people the benefit of the doubt every time. After all, this is not the century to preach 'the end of the world is at hand' to Lagash. You have to understand that people don't believe the 'Book of Revelations' any more, and it annoys them to have scientists turn about face and tell us the Cultists are right after all—"

"No such thing, young man," interrupted Aton. "While a great deal of our data has been supplied us by the Cult, our results contain none of the Cult's mysticism. Facts are facts, and the Cult's so-called 'mythology' *has* certain facts behind it. We've exposed them and ripped away their mystery. I assure you that the Cult hates us now worse than you do."

"I don't hate you. I'm just trying to tell you that the public is in an ugly humor. They're angry."

Aton twisted his mouth in derision. "Let them be angry."

"Yes, but what about tomorrow?"

"There'll be no tomorrow!"

"But if there is. Say that there is—just to see what happens. That anger might take shape into something serious. After all, you know, business has taken a nose dive these last two months. Investors don't really believe the world is coming to an end, but just the same they're being cagey with their money until it's all over. Johnny Public doesn't believe you, either, but the new spring furniture might as well wait a few months—just to make sure.

"You see the point. Just as soon as this is all over, the business interests will be after your hide. They'll say that if crackpots—begging your pardon—can upset the country's prosperity any time they want simply by making some cockeyed prediction—it's up to the planet to prevent them. The sparks will fly, sir."

The director regarded the columnist sternly. "And just what were you proposing to do to help the situation?"

"Well," grinned Theremon, "I was proposing to take charge of the publicity. I can handle things so that only the ridiculous side will show. It would be hard to stand, I admit, because I'd have to make you all out to be a bunch of gibbering idiots, but if I can get people laughing at you, they might forget to be angry. In return for that, all my publisher asks is an exclusive story."

Beenay nodded and burst out, "Sir, the rest of us think he's right. These last two months we've considered everything but the million-to-one chance that there is an error somewhere in our theory or in our calculations. We ought to take care of that, too."

There was a murmur of agreement from the men grouped about the table, and Aton's expression became that of one who found his mouth full of something bitter and couldn't get rid of it.

"You may stay if you wish, then. You will kindly refrain, however, from hampering us in our duties in any way. You will also remember that I am in charge of all activities here, and in spite of your opinions as expressed in your columns, I will expect full co-operation and full respect—"

His hands were behind his back, and his wrinkled face thrust forward determinedly as he spoke. He might have continued indefinitely but for the intrusion of a new voice.

"Hello, hello, hello!" It came in a high tenor, and the plump cheeks of the newcomer expanded in a pleased smile. "What's this morgue-like atmosphere about here? No one's losing his nerve, I hope."

Aton started in consternation and said peevishly, "Now what the devil are you doing here, Sheerin? I thought you were going to stay behind in the Hideout."

Sheerin laughed and dropped his tubby figure into a chair. "Hideout be blowed! The place bored me. I wanted to be here, where things are getting hot. Don't you suppose I have my share of curiosity? I want to see these Stars the Cultists are forever speaking about." He rubbed his hands and added in a sober tone, "It's freezing outside. The wind's enough to hang icicles on your nose. Beta doesn't seem to give any heat at all, at the distance it is."

The white-haired director ground his teeth in sudden exasperation, "Why do you go out of your way to do crazy things, Sheerin? What kind of good are you around here?"

"What kind of good am I around there?" Sheerin spread his palms in comical resignation. "A psychologist isn't worth his salt in the Hideout. They need men of action and strong, healthy women that can breed children. Me? I'm a hundred pounds too heavy for a man of action, and I wouldn't be a success at breeding children. So why bother them with an extra mouth to feed? I feel better over here."

Theremon spoke briskly, "Just what is the Hideout, sir?"

Sheerin seemed to see the columnist for the first time. He frowned and blew his ample cheeks out. "And just who in Lagash are you, redhead?"

Aton compressed his lips and then muttered sullenly, "That's Theremon 762, the newspaper fellow. I suppose you've heard of him."

The columnist offered his hand. "And, of course, you're

Sheerin 501 of Saro University. I've heard of you." Then he repeated, "What is this Hideout, sir?"

"Well," said Sheerin, "we have managed to convince a few people of the validity of our prophecy of—er—doom, to be spectacular about it, and those few have taken proper measures. They consist mainly of the immediate members of the families of the Observatory staff, certain of the faculty of Saro University and a few outsiders. Altogether, they number about three hundred, but three quarters are women and children."

"I see! They're supposed to hide where the Darkness and the—er—Stars can't get at them, and then hold out when the rest of the world goes poof."

"If they can. It won't be easy. With all of mankind insane; with the great cities going up in flames—environment will not be conducive to survival. But they have food, water, shelter, and weapons—"

"They've got more," said Aton. "They've got all our records, except for what we will collect today. Those records will mean everything to the next cycle, and *that's* what must survive. The rest can go hang."

Theremon whistled a long, low whistle and sat brooding for several minutes. The men about the table had brought out a multichess board and started a six-member game. Moves were made rapidly and in silence. All eyes bent in furious concentration on the board. Theremon watched them intently and then rose and approached Aton, who sat apart in whispered conversation with Sheerin.

"Listen," he said, "let's go somewhere where we won't bother the rest of the fellows. I want to ask some questions."

The aged astronomer frowned sourly at him, but Sheerin chirped up, "Certainly. It will do me good to talk. It always does. Aton was telling me about your ideas concerning world reaction to a failure of the prediction—and I agree with you. I read your column pretty regularly, by the way, and as a general thing I like your views."

"Please, Sheerin," growled Aton.

"Eh? Oh, all right. We'll go into the next room. It has softer chairs, anyway."

There *were* softer chairs in the next room. There were also thick red curtains on the windows and a maroon carpet on the floor. With the bricky light of Beta pouring in, the general effect was one of dried blood.

Theremon shuddered, "Say, I'd give ten credits for a decent dose of white light for just a second. I wish Gamma or Delta were in the sky."

"What are your questions?" asked Aton. "Please remember that our time is limited. In a little over an hour and a quarter we're going upstairs, and after that there will be no time to talk."

"Well, here it is." Theremon leaned back and folded his hands on his chest. "You people seem so all-fired serious about this that I'm beginning to believe you. Would you mind explaining what it's all about?"

Aton exploded, "Do you mean to sit there and tell me that you've been bombarding us with ridicule without even finding out what we've been trying to say?"

The columnist grinned sheepishly. "It's not that bad, sir. I've got the general idea. You say that there is going to be a world-wide Darkness in a few hours and that all mankind will go violently insane. What I want now is the science behind it."

"No, you don't. No, you don't," broke in Sheerin. "If you ask Aton for that—supposing him to be in the mood to answer at all—he'll trot out pages of figures and volumes of graphs. You won't make head or tail of it. Now if you were to ask *me*, I could give you the layman's standpoint."

"All right; I ask you."

"Then first I'd like a drink." He rubbed his hands and looked at Aton.

"Water?" grunted Aton.

"Don't be silly!"

"Don't you be silly. No alcohol today. It would be too easy to get my men drunk. I can't afford to tempt them."

The psychologist grumbled wordlessly. He turned to Theremon, impaled him with his sharp eyes, and began.

"You realize, of course, that the history of civilization on Lagash displays a cyclic character—but I mean, *cyclic!*"

"I know," replied Theremon cautiously, "that that is the current archeological theory. Has it been accepted as a fact?"

"Just about. In this last century it's been generally agreed upon. This cyclic character is—or, rather, was—

one of *the* great mysteries. We've located series of civilizations, nine of them definitely, and indications of others as well, all of which have reached heights comparable to our own, and all of which, without exception, were destroyed by fire at the very height of their culture.

"And no one could tell why. All centers of culture were thoroughly gutted by fire, with nothing left behind to give a hint as to the cause."

Theremon was following closely. "Wasn't there a Stone Age, too?"

"Probably, but as yet, practically nothing is known of it, except that men of that age were little more than rather intelligent apes. We can forget about that."

"I see. Go on!"

"There have been explanations of these recurrent catastrophes, all of a more or less fantastic nature. Some say that there are periodic rains of fire; some that Lagash passes through a sun every so often; some even wilder things. But there is one theory, quite different from all of these, that has been handed down over a period of centuries."

"I know. You mean this myth of the 'Stars' that the Cultists have in their 'Book of Revelations.'"

"Exactly," rejoined Sheerin with satisfaction. "The Cultists said that every two thousand and fifty years Lagash entered a huge cave, so that all the suns disappeared, and there came *total darkness all over the world!* And then, they say, things called Stars appeared, which robbed men of their souls and left them unreasoning brutes, so that they destroyed the civilization they themselves had built up. Of course, they mix all this up with a lot of religio-mystic notions, but that's the central idea."

There was a short pause in which Sheerin drew a long breath. "And now we come to the Theory of Universal Gravitation." He pronounced the phrase so that the capital letters sounded—and at that point Aton turned from the window, snorted loudly, and stalked out of the room.

The two stared after him, and Theremon said, "What's wrong?"

"Nothing in particular," replied Sheerin. "Two of the men were due several hours ago and haven't shown up yet.

He's terrifically short-handed, of course, because all but the really essential men have gone to the Hideout."

"You don't think the two deserted, do you?"

"Who? Faro and Yimot? Of course not. Still, if they're not back within the hour, things would be a little sticky." He got to his feet suddenly, and his eyes twinkled. "Anyway, as long as Aton is gone—"

Tiptoeing to the nearest window, he squatted, and from the low window box beneath withdrew a bottle of red liquid that gurgled suggestively when he shook it.

"I *thought* Aton didn't know about this," he remarked as he trotted back to the table. "Here! We've only got one glass so, as the guest you can have it. I'll keep the bottle." And he filled the tiny cup with judicious care.

Theremon rose to protest, but Sheerin eyed him sternly. "Respect your elders, young man."

The newsman seated himself with a look of pain and anguish on his face. "Go ahead, then, you old villain."

The psychologist's Adam's apple wobbled as the bottle upended, and then, with a satisfied grunt and a smack of the lips, he began again.

"But what do you know about gravitation?"

"Nothing, except that it is a very recent development, not too well established, and that the math is so hard that only twelve men in Lagash are supposed to understand it."

"*Tcha!* Nonsense! Boloney! I can give you all the essential math in a sentence. The Law of Universal Gravitation states that there exists a cohesive force among all bodies of the universe, such that the amount of this force between any two given bodies is proportional to the product of their masses divided by the square of the distance between them."

"Is that all?"

"That's enough! It took four hundred years to develop it."

"Why that long? It sounded simple enough, the way you said it."

"Because great laws are not divined by flashes of inspiration, whatever you may think. It usually takes the combined work of a world full of scientists over a period of centuries. After Genovi 41 discovered that Lagash rotated about the sun Alpha, rather than vice versa—and that was four hundred years ago—astronomers have been working.

The complex motions of the six suns were recorded and analyzed and unwoven. Theory after theory was advanced and checked and counterchecked and modified and abandoned and revived and converted to something else. It was a devil of a job."

Theremon nodded thoughtfully and held out his glass for more liquor. Sheerin grudgingly allowed a few ruby drops to leave the bottle.

"It was twenty years ago," he continued after remoistening his own throat, "that it was finally demonstrated that the Law of Universal Gravitation accounted exactly for the orbital motions of the six suns. It was a great triumph."

Sheerin stood up and walked to the window, still clutching his bottle. "And now we're getting to the point. In the last decade, the motions of Lagash about Alpha were computed according to gravity, and *it did not account for the orbit observed;* not even when all perturbations due to the other suns were included. Either the law was invalid, or there was another, as yet unknown, factor involved."

Theremon joined Sheerin at the window and gazed out past the wooded slopes to where the spires of Saro City gleamed bloodily on the horizon. The newsman felt the tension of uncertainty grow within him as he cast a short glance at Beta. It glowered redly at zenith, dwarfed and evil.

"Go ahead, sir," he said softly.

Sheerin replied, "Astronomers stumbled about for years, each proposed theory more untenable than the one before —until Aton had the inspiration of calling in the Cult. The head of the Cult, Sor 5, had access to certain data that simplified the problem considerably. Aton set to work on a new track.

"What if there were another nonluminous planetary body such as Lagash? If there were, you know, it would shine only by reflected light, and if it were composed of bluish rock, as Lagash itself largely is, then in the redness of the sky, the eternal blaze of the suns would make it invisible —drown it out completely."

Theremon whistled, "What a screwy idea!"

"You think *that's* screwy? Listen to this: Suppose this body rotated about Lagash at such a distance and in such an orbit and had such a mass that its attraction would exactly account for the deviations of Lagash's orbit from theory—do you know what would happen?"

The columnist shook his head.

"Well, sometimes this body would get in the way of a sun." And Sheerin emptied what remained in the bottle at a draft.

"And it does, I suppose," said Theremon flatly.

"Yes! But only one sun lies in its plane of revolutions." He jerked a thumb at the shrunken sun above. "Beta! And it has been shown that the eclipse will occur only when the arrangement of the suns is such that Beta is alone in its hemisphere and at a maximum distance, at which time the moon is invariably at minimum distance. The eclipse that results, with the moon seven times the apparent diameter of Beta, covers all of Lagash and lasts well over half a day, so that no spot on the planet escapes the effect. *That eclipse comes once every two thousand and forty-nine years."*

Theremon's face was drawn into an expressionless mask. "And that's my story?"

The psychologist nodded. "That's all of it. First the eclipse—which will start in three quarters of an hour—then universal Darkness, and, maybe, these mysterious Stars—then madness, and end of the cycle."

He brooded. "We had two months' leeway—we at the Observatory—and that wasn't enough time to persuade Lagash of the danger. Two centuries might not have been enough. But our records are at the Hideout, and today we photograph the eclipse. The next cycle will *start off* with the truth, and when the *next* eclipse comes, mankind will at last be ready for it. Come to think of it, that's part of your story, too."

A thin wind ruffled the curtains at the window as Theremon opened it and leaned out. It played coldly with his hair as he stared at the crimson sunlight on his hand. Then he turned in sudden rebellion.

"What is there in Darkness to drive *me* mad?"

Sheerin smiled to himself as he spun the empty liquor bottle with abstracted motions of his hand. "Have you ever experienced Darkness, young man?"

The newsman leaned against the wall and considered. "No. Can't say I have. But I know what it is. Just—uh—"

He made vague motions with his fingers, and then brightened. "Just no light. Like in caves."

"Have you ever been in a cave?"

"In a *cave!* Of course not!"

"I thought not. *I* tried last week—just to see—but I got out in a hurry. I went in until the mouth of the cave was just visible as a blur of light, with black everywhere else. I never thought a person my weight could run that fast."

Theremon's lip curled. "Well, if it comes to that, I guess I wouldn't have run, if I had been there."

The psychologist studied the young man with an annoyed frown.

"My, don't you talk big! I dare you to draw the curtain."

Theremon looked his surprise and said, "What for? If we had four or five suns out there we might want to cut the light down a bit for comfort, but now we haven't enough light as it is."

"That's the point. Just draw the curtain; then come here and sit down."

"All right." Theremon reached for the tasseled string and jerked. The red curtain slid across the wide window, the brass rings hissing their way along the crossbar, and a dusk-red shadow clamped down on the room.

Theremon's footsteps sounded hollowly in the silence as he made his way to the table, and then they stopped halfway. "I can't see you, sir," he whispered.

"Feel your way," ordered Sheerin in a strained voice.

"But I can't see you, sir." The newsman was breathing harshly. "I can't see anything."

"What did you expect?" came the grim reply. "Come here and sit down!"

The footsteps sounded again, waveringly, approaching slowly. There was the sound of someone fumbling with a chair. Theremon's voice came thinly, "Here I am. I feel ... *ulp* ... all right."

"You like it, do you?"

"N-no. It's pretty awful. The walls seem to be—" He paused. "They seem to be closing in on me. I keep wanting to push them away. But I'm not going *mad!* In fact, the feeling isn't as bad as it was."

"All right. Draw the curtain back again."

There were cautious footsteps through the dark, the rustle of Theremon's body against the curtain as he felt for the tassel, and then the triumphant *ro-o-osh* of the curtain slithering back. Red light flooded the room, and with a cry of joy Theremon looked up at the sun.

Sheerin wiped the moistness off his forehead with the back of a hand and said shakily, "And that was just a dark room."

"It can be stood," said Theremon lightly.

"Yes, a dark room can. But were you at the Jonglor Centennial Exposition two years ago?"

"No, it so happens I never got around to it. Six thousand miles was just a bit too much to travel, even for the exposition."

"Well, I was there. You remember hearing about the 'Tunnel of Mystery' that broke all records in the amusement area—for the first month or so, anyway?"

"Yes. Wasn't there some fuss about it?"

"Very little. It was hushed up. You see, that Tunnel of Mystery was just a mile-long tunnel—with no lights. You got into a little open car and jolted along through Darkness for fifteen minutes. It was very popular—while it lasted."

"Popular?"

"Certainly. There's a fascination in being frightened *when it's part of a game.* A baby is born with three instinctive fears: of loud noises, of falling, and of the absence of light. That's why it's considered so funny to jump at someone and shout 'Boo!' That's why it's such fun to ride a roller coaster. And that's why that Tunnel of Mystery started cleaning up. People came out of that Darkness shaking, breathless, half dead with fear, but they kept on paying to get in."

"Wait a while, I remember now. Some people came out dead, didn't they? There were rumors of that after it shut down."

The psychologist snorted. "Bah! Two or three died. That was nothing! They paid off the families of the dead ones and argued the Jonglor City Council into forgetting it. After all, they said, if people with weak hearts want to go through the tunnel, it was at their own risk—and besides, it wouldn't happen again. So they put a doctor in the front office and had every customer go through a physical examination before getting into the car. That actually *boosted* ticket sales."

"Well, then?"

"But, you see, there was something else. People sometimes came out in perfect order, except that they refused to go into buildings—any buildings; including palaces, mansions, apartment houses, tenements, cottages, huts, shacks, lean-tos, and tents."

Theremon looked shocked. "You mean they refused to come in out of the open. Where'd they sleep?"

"In the open."

"They should have *forced* them inside."

"Oh, they did, they did. Whereupon these people went into violent hysterics and did their best to bat their brains out against the nearest wall. Once you got them inside, you couldn't keep them there without a strait jacket and a shot of morphine."

"They must have been crazy."

"Which is exactly what they were. One person out of every ten who went into that tunnel came out that way. They called in the psychologists, and we did the only thing possible. We closed down the exhibit." He spread his hands.

"What was the matter with those people?" asked Theremon finally.

"Essentially the same thing that was the matter with you when you thought the walls of the room were crushing in on you in the dark. There is a psychological term for mankind's instinctive fear of the absence of light. We call it 'claustrophobia,' because the lack of light is always tied up with inclosed places, so that fear of one is fear of the other. You see?"

"And those people of the tunnel?"

"Those people of the tunnel consisted of those unfortunates whose mentality did not quite possess the resiliency to overcome the claustrophobia that overtook them in the Darkness. Fifteen minutes without light is a long time; you only had two or three minutes, and I believe you were fairly upset.

"The people of the tunnel had what is called a 'claustrophobic fixation.' Their latent fear of Darkness and inclosed places had crystallized and become active, and, as far as we can tell, permanent. *That's* what fifteen minutes in the dark will do."

There was a long silence, and Theremon's forehead wrinkled slowly into a frown. "I don't believe it's that bad."

"You mean you don't want to believe," snapped Sheerin. "You're afraid to believe. Look out the window!"

Theremon did so, and the psychologist continued without pausing, "Imagine Darkness—everywhere. No light, as far as you can see. The houses, the trees, the fields, the earth, the sky—*black!* And Stars thrown in, for all I know —whatever *they* are. Can you conceive it?"

"Yes, I can," declared Theremon truculently.

And Sheerin slammed his fist down upon the table in sudden passion. "You lie! You can't conceive that. Your brain wasn't built for the conception any more than it was built for the conception of infinity or of eternity. You can only talk about it. A fraction of the reality upsets you, and when the real thing comes, your brain is going to be presented with a phenomenon outside its limits of comprehension. You will go mad, completely and permanently! There is no question of it!"

He added sadly, "And another couple of millenniums of painful struggle comes to nothing. Tomorrow there won't be a city standing unharmed in all Lagash."

Theremon recovered part of his mental equilibrium. "That doesn't follow. I still don't see that I can go looney just because there isn't a Sun in the sky—but even if I did, and everyone else did, how does that harm the cities? Are we going to blow them down?"

But Sheerin was angry, too. "If you were in Darkness, what would you want more than anything else; what would it be that every instinct would call for? Light, damn you, *light!*"

"Well?"

"And how would you get light?"

"I don't know," said Theremon flatly.

"What's the *only* way to get light, short of the sun?"

"How should I know?"

They were standing face to face and nose to nose.

Sheerin said, "You burn something, mister. Ever see a forest fire? Ever go camping and cook a stew over a wood fire? Heat isn't the only thing burning wood gives off, you know. It gives off light, and people know that. And when it's dark they want light, and they're going to *get it*."

"So they burn wood?"

"So they burn whatever they can get. They've got to have light. They've got to burn something, and wood isn't handy—so they'll burn whatever is nearest. They'll have their light—and every center of habitation goes up in flames!"

Eyes held each other as though the whole matter were a personal affair of respective will powers, and then Theremon broke away wordlessly. His breathing was harsh and ragged, and he scarcely noted the sudden hub-bub that came from the adjoining room behind the closed door.

Sheerin spoke, and it was with an effort that he made it sound matter-of-fact. "I think I heard Yimot's voice. He and Faro are probably back. Let's go in and see what kept them."

"Might as well!" muttered Theremon. He drew a long breath and seemed to shake himself. The tension was broken.

The room was in an uproar, with members of the staff clustering about two young men who were removing outer garments even as they parried the miscellany of questions being thrown at them.

Aton bustled through the crowd and faced the new-comers angrily. "Do you realize that it's less than half an hour before deadline? Where have you two been?"

Faro 24 seated himself and rubbed his hands. His cheeks were red with the outdoor chill. "Yimot and I have just finished carrying through a little crazy experi-ment of our own. We've been trying to see if we couldn't construct an arrangement by which we could simulate the appearance of Darkness and Stars so as to get an advance notion as to how it looked."

There was a confused murmur from the listeners, and a sudden look of interest entered Aton's eyes. "There wasn't anything said of this before. How did you go about it?"

"Well," said Faro, "the idea came to Yimot and my-self long ago, and we've been working it out in our spare time. Yimot knew of a low one-story house down in the city with a domed roof—it had once been used as a museum, I think. Anyway, we bought it—"

"Where did you get the money?" interrupted Aton peremptorily.

"Our bank accounts," grunted Yimot 70. "It cost two thousand credits." Then, defensively, "Well, what of it? Tomorrow, two thousand credits will be two thousand pieces of paper. That's all."

"Sure," agreed Faro. "We bought the place and rigged it up with black velvet from top to bottom so as to get as perfect a Darkness as possible. Then we punched tiny holes in the ceiling and through the roof and covered them with little metal caps, all of which could be shoved aside simultaneously at the close of a switch. At least, we didn't do that part ourselves; we got a carpenter and an electrician and some others—money didn't count. The point was that we could get the light to shine through those holes in the roof, so that we could get a starlike effect."

Not a breath was drawn during the pause that followed. Anton said stiffly:

"You had no right to make a private—"

Faro seemed abashed. "I know, sir—but, frankly, Yimot and I thought the experiment was a little dangerous. If the effect really worked, we half expected to go mad—from what Sheerin says about all this, we thought that would be rather likely. We wanted to take the risk ourselves. Of course, if we found we could retain sanity, it occurred to us that we might develop immunity to the real thing, and then expose the rest of you to the same thing. But things didn't work out at all—"

"Why, what happened?"

It was Yimot who answered. "We shut ourselves in and allowed our eyes to get accustomed to the dark. It's an extremely creepy feeling because the total Darkness makes you feel as if the walls and ceiling are crushing in on you. But we got over that and pulled the switch. The caps fell away and the roof glittered all over with little dots of light—"

"Well?"

"Well—nothing. That was the whacky part of it. Nothing happened. It was just a roof with holes in it, and that's just what it looked like. We tried it over and over again—that's what kept us so late—but there just isn't any effect at all."

There followed a shocked silence, and all eyes turned to Sheerin, who sat motionless, mouth open.

Theremon was the first to speak. "You know what this does to this whole theory you've built up, Sheerin, don't you?" He was grinning with relief.

But Sheerin raised his hand. "Now wait a while. Just let me think this through." And then he snapped his fingers, and when he lifted his head there was neither surprise nor uncertainty in his eyes. "Of course—"

He never finished. From somewhere up above there sounded a sharp clang, and Beenay, starting to his feet, dashed up the stairs with a "What the devil!"

The rest followed after.

Things happened quickly. Once up in the dome, Beenay cast one horrified glance at the shattered photographic plates and at the man bending over them; and then he hurled himself fiercely at the intruder, getting a death grip on his throat. There was a wild threshing, and as others of the staff joined in, the stranger was swallowed up and smothered under the weight of half a dozen angry men.

Aton came up last, breathing heavily. "Let him up!"

There was a reluctant unscrambling and the stranger, panting harshly, with his clothes torn and his forehead bruised, was hauled to his feet. He had a short yellow beard curled elaborately in the style affected by the Cultists.

Beenay shifted his hold to a collar grip and shook the man savagely. "All right, rat, what's the idea? These plates—"

"I wasn't after *them*," retorted the Cultist coldly. "That was an accident."

Beenay followed his glowering stare and snarled, "I see. You were after the cameras themselves. The accident with the plates was a stroke of luck for you, then. If you had touched Snapping Bertha or any of the others, you would have died by slow torture. As it is—" He drew his fist back.

Aton grabbed his sleeve. "Stop that! Let him go!"

The young technician wavered, and his arm dropped reluctantly. Aton pushed him aside and confronted the Cultist. "You're Latimer, aren't you?"

The Cultist bowed stiffly and indicated the symbol upon his hip. "I am Latimer 25, adjutant of the third class to his serenity, Sor 5."

"And"—Aton's white eyebrows lifted—"you were with his serenity when he visited me last week, weren't you?"

Latimer bowed a second time.

"Now, then, what do you want?"

"Nothing that you would give me of your own free will."

"Sor 5 sent you, I suppose—or is this your own idea?"

"I won't answer that question."

"Will there be any further visitors?"

"I won't answer that, either."

Aton glanced at his timepiece and scowled. "Now, man, what is it your master wants of me? I have fulfilled my end of the bargain."

Latimer smiled faintly, but said nothing.

"I asked him," continued Aton angrily, "for data only the Cult could supply, and it was given to me. For that, thank you. In return, I promised to prove the essential truth of the creed of the Cult."

"There was no need to prove that," came the proud retort. "It stands proven by the 'Book of Revelations.'"

"For the handful that constitute the Cult, yes. Don't pretend to mistake my meaning. I offered to present scientific backing for your beliefs. And I did!"

The Cultist's eyes narrowed bitterly. "Yes, you did— with a fox's subtlety, for your pretended explanation backed our beliefs, and at the same time removed all necessity for them. You made of the Darkness and of the Stars a natural phenomenon, and removed all its real significance. That was blasphemy."

"If so, the fault isn't mine. The facts exist. What can I do but state them?"

"Your 'facts' are a fraud and a delusion."

Aton stamped angrily. "How do *you* know?"

And the answer came with the certainty of absolute faith. "I *know!*"

The director purpled and Beenay whispered urgently. Aton waved him silent. "And what does Sor 5 want us to do? He still thinks, I suppose, that in trying to warn the world to take measures against the menace of madness, we are placing innumerable souls in jeopardy. We aren't succeeding, if that means anything to him."

"The attempt itself has done harm enough, and your vicious effort to gain information by means of your devilish instruments must be stopped. We obey the will of their Stars, and I only regret that my clumsiness prevented me from wrecking your infernal devices."

"It wouldn't have done you too much good," returned Aton. "All our data, except for the direct evidence we intend collecting right now, is already safely cached and well beyond possibility of harm." He smiled grimly. "But that does not affect your present status as an attempted burglar and criminal."

He turned to the men behind him. "Someone call the police at Saro City."

There was a cry of distaste from Sheerin. "Damn it, Aton, what's wrong with you? There's no time for that. Here"—he bustled his way forward—"let me handle this."

Aton stared down his nose at the psychologist. "This is not the time for your monkeyshines, Sheerin. Will you please let me handle this my own way? Right now you are a complete outsider here, and don't forget it."

Sheerin's mouth twisted eloquently. "Now why should we go to the impossible trouble of calling the police— with Beta's eclipse a matter of minutes from now—when this young man here is perfectly willing to pledge his word of honor to remain and cause no trouble whatsoever?"

The Cultist answered promptly, "I will do no such thing. You're free to do what you want, but it's only fair to warn you that just as soon as I get my chance I'm going to finish what I came out here to do. If it's my word of honor you're relying on, you'd better call the police."

Sheerin smiled in a friendly fashion. "You're a determined cuss, aren't you? Well, I'll explain something. Do you see that young man at the window? He's a strong, husky fellow, quite handy with his fists, and he's an outsider besides. Once the eclipse starts there will be nothing for him to do except keep an eye on you. Besides him, there will be myself—a little too stout for active fisticuffs, but still able to help."

"Well, what of it?" demanded Latimer frozenly.

"Listen and I'll tell you," was the reply. "Just as soon as the eclipse starts, we're going to take you, Theremon and I, and deposit you in a little closet with one door, to which is attached one giant lock and no windows. You will remain there for the duration."

"And afterward," breathed Latimer fiercely, "there'll be no one to let me out. I know as well as you do what the coming of the Stars means—I know it far better than you. With all your minds gone, you are not likely to free me. Suffocation or slow starvation, is it? About what I might have expected from a group of scientists. But I don't give my word. It's a matter of principle, and I won't discuss it further."

Aton seemed perturbed. His faded eyes were troubled. "Really, Sheerin, locking him—"

"Please!" Sheerin motioned him impatiently to silence. "I don't think for a moment things will go that far. Latimer has just tried a clever little bluff, but I'm not a psychologist just because I like the sound of the word." He grinned at the Cultist. "Come now, you don't really think I'm trying anything as crude as slow starvation. My dear Latimer, if I lock you in the closet, you are not going to see the Darkness, and you are not going to see the Stars. It does not take much of a knowledge of the fundamental creed of the Cult to realize that for you to be hidden from the Stars when they appear means the loss of your immortal soul. Now, I believe you to be an honorable man. I'll accept your word of honor to make no further effort to disrupt proceedings if you'll offer it."

A vein throbbed in Latimer's temple, and he seemed to shrink within himself as he said thickly, "You have it!" And then he added with swift fury, "But it is my consolation that you will all be damned for your deeds of today." He turned on his heel and stalked to the high three-legged stool by the door.

Sheerin nodded to the columnist. "Take a seat next to him, Theremon—just as a formality. Hey, Theremon!"

But the newspaperman didn't move. He had gone pale to the lips. "Look at that!" The finger he pointed toward the sky shook, and his voice was dry and cracked.

There was one simultaneous gasp as every eye followed the pointing finger and, for one breathless moment, stared frozenly.

Beta was chipped on one side!

The tiny bit of encroaching blackness was perhaps the width of a fingernail, but to the staring watchers it magnified itself into the crack of doom.

Only for a moment they watched, and after that there was a shrieking confusion that was even shorter of duration and which gave way to an orderly scurry of activity —each man at his prescribed job. At the crucial moment there was no time for emotion. The men were merely scientists with work to do. Even Aton had melted away.

Sheerin said prosaically, "First contact must have been made fifteen minutes ago. A little early, but pretty good considering the uncertainties involved in the calculation." He looked about him and tiptoed to Theremon, who still remained staring out the window, and dragged him away gently.

"Aton is furious," he whispered, "so stay away. He missed first contact on account of this fuss with Latimer, and if you get in his way he'll have you thrown out the window."

Theremon nodded shortly and sat down. Sheerin stared in surprise at him.

"The devil, man," he exclaimed, "you're shaking."

"Eh?" Theremon licked dry lips and then tried to smile. "I don't feel very well, and that's a fact."

The psychologist's eyes hardened. "You're not losing your nerve?"

"No!" cried Theremon in a flash of indignation. "Give me a chance, will you? I haven't really believed this rigmarole—not way down beneath, anyway—till just this minute. Give me a chance to get used to the idea. *You've* been preparing yourself for two months or more."

"You're right, at that," replied Sheerin thoughtfully. "Listen! Have you got a family—parents, wife, children?"

Theremon shook his head. "You mean the Hideout, I

suppose. No, you don't have to worry about that. I have a sister, but she's two thousand miles away. I don't even know her exact address."

"Well, then, what about yourself? You've got time to get there, and they're one short anyway, since I left. After all, you're not needed here, and you'd make a darned fine addition—"

Theremon looked at the other wearily. "You think I'm scared stiff, don't you? Well, get this, mister, I'm a newspaperman and I've been assigned to cover a story. I intend covering it."

There was a faint smile on the psychologist's face. "I see. Professional honor, is that it?"

"You might call it that. But, man, I'd give my right arm for another bottle of that sockeroo juice even half the size of the one *you* hogged. If ever a fellow needed a drink, I do."

He broke off. Sheerin was nudging him violently. "Do you hear that? Listen!"

Theremon followed the motion of the other's chin and stared at the Cultist, who oblivious to all about him, faced the window, a look of wild elation on his face, droning to himself the while in singsong fashion.

"What's he saying?" whispered the columnist.

"He's quoting 'Book of Revelations,' fifth chapter," replied Sheerin. Then, urgently, "Keep quiet and listen, I tell you."

The Cultist's voice had risen in a sudden increase of fervor:

" 'And it came to pass that in those days the Sun, Beta, held lone vigil in the sky for ever longer periods as the revolutions passed; until such time as for full half a revolution, it alone, shrunken and cold, shone down upon Lagash.

" 'And men did assemble in the public squares and in the highways, there to debate and to marvel at the sight, for a strange depression had seized them. Their minds were troubled and their speech confused, for the souls of men awaited the coming of the Stars.

" 'And in the city of Trigon, at high noon, Vendret 2 came forth and said unto the men of Trigon, "Lo ye sinners! Though ye scorn the ways of righteousness, yet will the time of reckoning come. Even now the Cave approaches to swallow Lagash; yea, and all it contains."

" 'And even as he spoke the lip of the Cave of Darkness passed the edge of Beta so that to all Lagash it was hidden from sight. Loud were the cries of men as it vanished, and great the fear of soul that fell upon them.

" 'It came to pass that the Darkness of the Cave fell upon Lagash, and there was no light on all the surface of Lagash. Men were even as blinded, nor could one man see his neighbor, though he felt his breath upon his face.

" 'And in this blackness there appeared the Stars, in countless numbers, and to the strains of ineffable music of a beauty so wondrous that the very leaves of the trees turned to tongues that cried out in wonder.

" 'And in that moment the souls of men departed from them, and their abandoned bodies became even as beasts; yea, even as brutes of the wild; so that through the blackened streets of the cities of Lagash they prowled with wild cries.

" 'From the Stars there then reached down the Heavenly Flame, and where it touched, the cities of Lagash flamed to utter destruction, so that of man and of the works of man nought remained.

" 'Even then—' "

There was a subtle change in Latimer's tone. His eyes had not shifted, but somehow he had become aware of the absorbed attention of the other two. Easily, without pausing for breath, the timbre of his voice shifted and the syllables became more liquid.

Theremon, caught by surprise, stared. The words seemed on the border of familiarity. There was an elusive shift in the accent, a tiny change in the vowel stress; nothing more —yet Latimer had become thoroughly unintelligible.

Sheerin smiled slyly. "He shifted to some old-cycle tongue, probably their traditional second cycle. That was the language in which the 'Book of Revelations' had originally been written, you know."

"It doesn't matter; I've heard enough." Theremon shoved his chair back and brushed his hair back with hands that no longer shook. "I feel much better now."

"You do?" Sheerin seemed mildly surprised.

"I'll say I do. I had a bad case of jitters just a while back. Listening to you and your gravitation and seeing that eclipse start almost finished me. But this"—he jerked a contemptuous thumb at the yellow-bearded Cultist— *"this* is the sort of thing my nurse used to tell me. I've been laughing at that sort of thing all my life. I'm not going to let it scare me *now*."

He drew a deep breath and said with a hectic gaiety, "But if I expect to keep on the good side of myself, I'm going to turn my chair away from the window."

Sheerin said, "Yes, but you'd better talk lower. Aton just lifted his head out of that box he's got it stuck into and gave you a look that should have killed you."

Theremon made a mouth. "I forgot about the old fellow." With elaborate care he turned the chair from the window, cast one distasteful look over his shoulder and said, "It has occurred to me that there must be considerable immunity against this Star madness."

The psychologist did not answer immediately. Beta was past its zenith now, and the square of bloody sunlight that outlined the window upon the floor had lifted into Sheerin's lap. He stared at its dusky color thoughtfully and then bent and squinted into the sun itself.

The chip in its side had grown to a black encroachment that covered a third of Beta. He shuddered, and when he straightened once more his florid cheeks did not contain quite as much color as they had had previously.

With a smile that was almost apologetic, he reversed his chair also. "There are probably two million people in Saro City that are all trying to join the Cult at once in one gigantic revival." Then, ironically, "The Cult is in for an hour of unexampled prosperity. I trust they'll make the most of it. Now, what was it you said?"

"Just this. How do the Cultists manage to keep the 'Book of Revelations' going from cycle to cycle, and how on Lagash did it get written in the first place? There must have been some sort of immunity, for if everyone had gone mad, who would be left to write the book?"

Sheerin stared at his questioner ruefully. "Well, now, young man, there isn't any eyewitness answer to that, but we've got a few damned good notions as to what happened. You see, there are three kinds of people who might remain relatively unaffected. First, the very few who don't see the Stars at all; the blind, those who drink themselves into a stupor at the beginning of the eclipse and remain so to the end. We leave them out—because they aren't really witnesses.

"Then there are children below six, to whom the world as a whole is too new and strange for them to be too frightened at Stars and Darkness. They would be just another item in an already surprising world. You see that, don't you?"

The other nodded doubtfully. "I suppose so."

"Lastly, there are those whose minds are too coarsely grained to be entirely toppled. The very insensitive would be scarcely affected—oh, such people as some of our older, work-broken peasants. Well, the children would have fugitive memories, and that, combined with the confused, incoherent babblings of the half-mad morons, formed the basis for the 'Book of Revelations.'

"Naturally, the book was based, in the first place, on the testimony of those least qualified to serve as historians; that is, children and morons; and was probably extensively edited and re-edited through the cycles."

"Do you suppose," broke in Theremon, "that they carried the book through the cycles the way we're planning on handing on the secret of gravitation?"

Sheerin shrugged. "Perhaps, but their exact method is unimportant. They do it, somehow. The point I was getting at was that the book can't help but be a mass of distortion, even if it is based on fact. For instance, do you remember the experiment with the holes in the roof that Faro and Yimot tried—the one that didn't work?"

"Yes."

"You know why it didn't w—" He stopped and rose in alarm, for Aton was approaching, his face a twisted mask of consternation. *"What's happened?"*

Aton drew him aside and Sheerin could feel the fingers on his elbow twitching.

"Not so loud!" Aton's voice was low and tortured. "I've just gotten word from the Hideout on the private line."

Sheerin broke in anxiously. "They are in trouble?"

"Not *they*." Aton stressed the pronoun significantly. "They sealed themselves off just a while ago, and they're going to stay buried till day after tomorrow. They're safe. But the *city*, Sheerin—it's a shambles. You have no idea—" He was having difficulty in speaking.

"Well?" snapped Sheerin impatiently. "What of it? It will get worse. What are you shaking about?" Then, suspiciously, "How do you feel?"

Aton's eyes sparked angrily at the insinuation, and then faded to anxiety once more. "You don't understand. The Cultists are active. They'rs rousing the people to storm the Observatory—promising them immediate entrance into grace, promising them salvation, promising anything. What are we to do, Sheerin?"

Sheerin's head bent, and he stared in long abstraction at his toes. He tapped his chin with one knuckle, then looked up and said crisply, "Do? What is there to do? Nothing at all! Do the men know of this."

"No, of course not!"

"Good! Keep it that way. How long till totality?"

"Not quite an hour."

"There's nothing to do but gamble. It will take time to organize any really formidable mob, and it will take more time to get them out here. We're a good five miles from the city—"

He glared out the window, down the slopes to where the farmed patches gave way to clumps of white houses in the suburbs; down to where the metropolis itself was a blur on the horizon—a mist in the waning blaze of Beta.

He repeated without turning, "It will take time. Keep on working and pray that totality comes first."

Beta was cut in half, the line of division pushing a slight concavity into the still-bright portion of the Sun. It was like a gigantic eyelid shutting slantwise over the light of a world.

The faint clatter of the room in which he stood faded into oblivion, and he sensed only the thick silence of the fields outside. The very insects seemed frightened mute. And things were dim.

He jumped at the voice in his ear. Theremon said, "Is something wrong?"

"Eh? Er—no. Get back to the chair. We're in the

way." They slipped back to their corner, but the psychologist did not speak for a time. He lifted a finger and loosened his collar. He twisted his neck back and forth but found no relief. He looked up suddenly.

"Are you having any difficulty in breathing?"

The newspaperman opened his eyes wide and drew two or three long breaths. "No. Why?"

"I looked out the window too long, I suppose. The dimness got me. Difficulty in breathing is one of the first symptoms of a claustrophobic attack."

Theremon drew another long breath. "Well, it hasn't got me yet. Say, here's another of the fellows."

Beenay had interposed his bulk between the light and the pair in the corner, and Sheerin squinted up at him anxiously. "Hello, Beenay."

The astronomer shifted his weight to the other foot and smiled feebly. "You won't mind if I sit down awhile and join in on the talk? My cameras are set, and there's nothing to do till totality." He paused and eyed the Cultist, who fifteen minutes earlier had drawn a small, skin-bound book from his sleeve and had been poring intently over it ever since. "That rat hasn't been making trouble, has he?"

Sheerin shook his head. His shoulders were thrown back and he frowned his concentration as he forced himself to breathe regularly. He said, "Have you had any trouble breathing, Beenay?"

Beenay sniffed the air in his turn. "It doesn't seem stuffy to me."

"A touch of claustrophobia," explained Sheerin apologetically.

"Oh-h-h! It worked itself differently with me. I get the impression that my eyes are going back on me. Things seem to blur and—well, nothing is clear. And it's cold, too."

"Oh, it's cold, all right. That's no illusion." Theremon grimaced. "My toes feel as if I've been shipping them cross country in a refrigerating car."

"What we need," put in Sheerin, "is to keep our minds busy with extraneous affairs. I was telling you a while ago, Theremon, why Faro's experiments with the holes in the roof came to nothing."

"You were just beginning," replied Theremon. He encircled a knee with both arms and nuzzled his chin against it.

"Well, as I started to say, they were misled by taking the 'Book of Revelations' literally. There probably wasn't any sense in attaching any physical significance to the Stars. It might be, you know, that in the presence of total Darkness, the mind finds it absolutely necessary to create light. This illusion of light might be all the Stars there really are."

"In other words," interposed Theremon, "you mean the Stars are the results of the madness and not one of the causes. Then, what good will Beenay's photographs be?"

"To prove that it is an illusion, maybe; or to prove the opposite, for all I know. Then again—"

But Beenay had drawn his chair closer, and there was an expression of sudden enthusiasm on his face. "Say, I'm glad you two got on to this subject." His eyes narrowed and he lifted one finger. "I've been thinking about these Stars and I've got a really cute notion. Of course, it's strictly ocean foam, and I'm not trying to advance it seriously, but I think it's interesting. Do you want to hear it?"

He seemed half reluctant, but Sheerin leaned back and said, "Go ahead! I'm listening."

"Well, then, supposing there were other suns in the universe." He broke off a little bashfully. "I mean suns that are so far away that they're too dim to see. It sounds as if I've been reading some of that fantastic fiction, I suppose."

"Not necessarily. Still, isn't that possibility eliminated by the fact that, according to the Law of Gravitation, they would make themselves evident by their attractive forces?"

"Not if they were far enough off," rejoined Beenay, "really far off—maybe as much as four light years, or even more. We'd never be able to detect perturbations then, because they'd be too small. Say that there were a lot of suns that far off; a dozen or two, maybe."

Theremon whistled melodiously. "What an idea for a

174 *Isaac Asimov*

good Sunday supplement article. Two dozen suns in a
universe eight light years across. Wow! That would shrink
our universe into insignificance. The readers would eat
it up."

"Only an idea," said Beenay with a grin, "but you see
the point. During eclipse, these dozen suns would become
visible, because there'd be no *real* sunlight to drown them
out. Since they're so far off, they'd appear small, like so
many little marbles. Of course, the Cultists talk of millions of Stars, but that's probably exaggeration. There
just isn't any place in the universe you could put a million
suns—unless they touch one another."

Sheerin had listened with gradually increasing interest.
"You've hit something there, Beenay. And exaggeration
is just exactly what would happen. Our minds, as you
probably know, can't grasp directly any number higher
than five; above that there is only the concept of 'many.'
A dozen would become a million just like that. A damn
good idea!"

"And I've got another cute little notion," Beenay said.
"Have you ever thought what a simple problem gravitation would be if only you had a sufficiently simple system?
Supposing you had a universe in which there was a planet
with only one sun. The planet would travel in a perfect
ellipse and the exact nature of the gravitational force
would be so evident it could be accepted as an axiom.
Astronomers on such a world would start off with gravity
probably before they even invent the telescope. Naked-eye
observation would be enough."

"But would such a system be dynamically stable?"
questioned Sheerin doubtfully.

"Sure! They call it the 'one-and-one' case. It's been
worked out mathematically, but it's the philosophical
implications that interest me."

"It's nice to think about," admitted Sheerin, "as a pretty
abstraction—like a perfect gas or absolute zero."

"Of course," continued Beenay, "there's the catch that
life would be impossible on such a planet. It wouldn't get
enough heat and light, and if it rotated there would be
total Darkness half of each day. You couldn't expect life

—which is fundamentally dependent upon light—to develop under those conditions. Besides—"

Sheerin's chair went over backward as he sprang to his feet in a rude interruption. "Aton's brought out the lights."

Beenay said, "Huh," turned to stare, and then grinned halfway around his head in open relief.

There were half a dozen foot-long, inch-thick rods cradled in Aton's arms. He glared over them at the assembled staff members.

"Get back to work, all of you. Sheerin, come here and help me!"

Sheerin trotted to the older man's side and, one by one, in utter silence, the two adjusted the rods in makeshift metal holders suspended from the walls.

With the air of one carrying through the most sacred item of a religious ritual, Sheerin scraped a large, clumsy match into spluttering life and passed it to Aton, who carried the flame to the upper end of one of the rods.

It hesitated there a while, playing futilely about the tip, until a sudden, crackling flare cast Aton's lined face into yellow highlights. He withdrew the match and a spontaneous cheer rattled the window.

The rod was topped by six inches of wavering flame! Methodically, the other rods were lighted, until six independent fires turned the rear of the room yellow.

The light was dim, dimmer even than the tenuous sunlight. The flames reeled crazily, giving birth to drunken, swaying shadows. The torches smoked devilishly and smelled like a bad day in the kitchen. But they emitted yellow light.

There is something to yellow light—after four hours of somber, dimming Beta. Even Latimer had lifted his eyes from his book and stared in wonder.

Sheerin warmed his hands at the nearest, regardless of the soot that gathered upon them in a fine, gray powder, and muttered ecstatically to himself. "Beautiful! Beautiful! I never realized before what a wonderful color yellow is."

But Theremon regarded the torches suspiciously. He wrinkled his nose at the rancid odor, and said, "What are those things?"

"Wood," said Sheerin shortly.

"Oh, no, they're not. They aren't burning. The top inch is charred and the flame just keeps shooting up out of nothing."

"That's the beauty of it. This is a really efficient artificial-light mechanism. We made a few hundred of them, but most went to the Hideout, of course. You see"—he turned and wiped his blackened hands upon his handkerchief—"you take the pithy core of coarse water reeds, dry them thoroughly and soak them in animal grease. Then you set fire to it and the grease burns, little by little. These torches will burn for almost half an hour without stopping. Ingenious, isn't it? It was developed by one of our own young men at Saro University."

After the momentary sensation, the dome had quieted. Latimer had carried his chair directly beneath a torch and continued reading, lips moving in the monotonous recital of invocations to the Stars. Beenay had drifted away to his cameras once more, and Theremon seized the opportunity to add to his notes on the article he was going to write for the Saro City *Chronicle* the next day— a procedure he had been following for the last two hours in a perfectly methodical, perfectly conscientious and, as he was well aware, perfectly meaningless fashion.

But, as the gleam of amusement in Sheerin's eyes indicated, careful note taking occupied his mind with something other than the fact that the sky was gradually turning a horrible deep purple-red, as if it were one gigantic, freshly peeled beet; and so it fulfilled its purpose.

The air grew, somehow, denser. Dusk, like a palpable entity, entered the room, and the dancing circle of yellow light about the torches etched itself into ever-sharper distinction against the gathering grayness beyond. There was the odor of smoke and the presence of little chuckling sounds that the torches made as they burned; the soft pad of one of the men circling the table at which he worked, on hesitant tiptoes; the occasional indrawn breath of someone trying to retain composure in a world that was retreating into the shadow.

It was Theremon who first heard the extraneous noise. It was a vague, unorganized *impression* of sound that would have gone unnoticed but for the dead silence that prevailed within the dome.

The newsman sat upright and replaced his notebook. He held his breath and listened; then, with considerable reluctance, threaded his way between the solarscope and one of Beenay's cameras and stood before the window.

The silence ripped to fragments at his startled shout: *"Sheerin!"*

Work stopped! The psychologist was at his side in a moment. Aton joined him. Even Yimot 70, high in his little lean-back seat at the eyepiece of the gigantic solar-scope, paused and looked downward.

Outside, Beta was a mere smoldering splinter, taking one last desperate look at Lagash. The eastern horizon, in the direction of the city, was lost in Darkness, and the road from Saro to the Observatory was a dull-red line bordered on both sides by wooden tracts, the trees of which had somehow lost individuality and merged into a continuous shadowy mass.

But it was the highway itself that held attention, for along it there surged another, and infinitely menacing, shadowy mass.

Aton cried in a cracked voice, "The madmen from the city! They've come!"

"How long to totality?" demanded Sheerin.

"Fifteen minutes, but . . . but they'll be here in five."

"Never mind, keep the men working. We'll hold them off. This place is built like a fortress. Aton, keep an eye on our young Cultist just for luck. Theremon, come with me."

Sheerin was out the door, and Theremon was at his heels. The stairs stretched below them in tight, circular sweeps about the central shaft, fading into a dank and dreary grayness.

The first momentum of their rush had carried them fifty feet down, so that the dim, flickering yellow from the open door of the dome had disappeared and both up above and down below the same dusky shadow crushed in upon them.

Sheerin paused, and his pudgy hand clutched at his chest. His eyes bulged and his voice was a dry cough.

"I can't . . . breathe . . . go down . . . yourself. Close all doors—"

Theremon took a few downward steps, then turned. "Wait! Can you hold out a minute?" He was panting himself. The air passed in and out his lungs like so much molasses, and there was a little germ of screeching panic in his mind at the thought of making his way into the mysterious Darkness below by himself.

Theremon, after all, was afraid of the dark!

"Stay here," he said. "I'll be back in a second." He dashed upward two steps at a time, heart pounding—not altogether from the exertion—tumbled into the dome and snatched a torch from its holder. It was foul smelling, and the smoke smarted his eyes almost blind, but he clutched that torch as if he wanted to kiss it for joy, and its flame streamed backward as he hurtled down the stairs again.

Sheerin opened his eyes and moaned as Theremon bent over him. Theremon shook him roughly. "All right, get a hold on yourself. We've got light."

He held the torch at tiptoe height and, propping the tottering psychologist by an elbow, made his way downward in the middle of the protecting circle of illumination.

The offices on the ground floor still possessed what light there was, and Theremon felt the horror about him relax.

"Here," he said brusquely, and passed the torch to Sheerin. "You can hear *them* outside."

And they could. Little scraps of hoarse, wordless shouts.

But Sheerin was right; the Observatory was built like a fortress. Erected in the last century, when the neo-Gavottian style of architecture was at its ugly height, it had been designed for stability and durability, rather than for beauty.

The windows were protected by the grillework of inch-thick iron bars sunk deep into the concrete sills. The walls were solid masonry that an earthquake couldn't have touched, and the main door was a huge oaken slab reinforced with iron at the strategic points. Theremon shot the bolts and they slid shut with a dull clang.

At the other end of the corridor, Sheerin cursed weakly. He pointed to the lock of the back door which had been nearly jimmied into uselessness.

"That must be how Latimer got in," he said.

"Well, don't stand there," cried Theremon impatiently. "Help drag up the furniture—and keep that torch out of my eyes. The smoke's killing me."

He slammed the heavy table up against the door as he spoke, and in two minutes had built a barricade which made up for what it lacked in beauty and symmetry by the sheer inertia of its massiveness.

Somewhere, dimly, far off, they could hear the battering of naked fists upon the door; and the screams and yells from outside had a sort of half reality.

That mob had set off from Saro City with only two things in mind: the attainment of Cultist salvation by the destruction of the Observatory, and a maddening fear that all but paralyzed them. There was no time to think of ground cars, or of weapons, or of leadership, or even of organization. They made for the Observatory on foot and assaulted it with bare hands.

And now that they were there, the last flash of Beta, the last ruby-red drop of flame, flickered feebly over a humanity that had left only stark, universal fear!

Theremon groaned, "Let's get back to the dome!"

In the dome, only Yimot, at the solarscope, had kept his place. The rest were clustered about the cameras, and Beenay was giving his instructions in a hoarse, strained voice.

"Get it straight, all of you. I'm snapping Beta just before totality and changing the plate. That will leave one of you to each camera. You all know about . . . about times of exposure—"

There was a breathless murmur of agreement.

Beenay passed a hand over his eyes. "Are the torches still burning? Never mind, I see them!" He was leaning hard against the back of a chair. "Now remember, don't . . . don't try to look for good shots. Don't waste time trying to get t-two stars at a time in the scope field. One is enough. And . . . and if you feel yourself going, *get away from the camera.*"

At the door, Sheerin whispered to Theremon, "Take me to Aton. I don't see him."

The newsman did not answer immediately. The vague form of the astronomers wavered and blurred, and the torches overhead had become only yellow splotches.

"It's dark," he whimpered.

Sheerin held out his hand, "Aton." He stumbled forward. "Aton!"

Theremon stepped after and siezed his arm. "Wait, I'll take you." Somehow he made his way across the room. He closed his eyes against the Darkness and his mind against the chaos within it.

No one heard them or paid attention to them. Sheerin stumbled against the wall. "Aton!"

The psychologist felt shaking hands touching him, then withdrawing, and a voice muttering, "Is that you, Sheerin?"

"Aton!" He strove to breathe normally. "Don't worry about the mob. The place will hold them off."

Latimer, the Cultist, rose to his feet, and his face twisted in desperation. His word was pledged, and to break it would mean placing his soul in mortal peril. Yet that word had been forced from him and had not been given freely. The Stars would come soon; he could not stand by and allow— And yet his word was pledged.

Beenay's face was dimly flushed as it looked upward at Beta's last ray, and Latimer, seeing him bend over his camera, made his decision. His nails cut the flesh of his palms as he tensed himself.

He staggered crazily as he started his rush. There was nothing before him but shadows; the very floor beneath his feet lacked substance. And then someone was upon him and he went down with clutching fingers at his throat.

He doubled his knee and drove it hard into his assailant. "Let me up or I'll kill you."

Theremon cried out sharply and muttered through a blinding haze of pain, "You double-crossing rat!"

The newsman seemed conscious of everything at once. He heard Beenay croak, "I've got it. At your cameras, men!" and then there was the strange awareness that the last thread of sunlight had thinned out and snapped.

Simultaneously he heard one last choking gasp from Beenay, and a queer little cry from Sheerin, a hysterical giggle that cut off in a rasp—and a sudden silence, a strange, deadly silence from outside.

And Latimer had gone limp in his loosening grasp. Theremon peered into the Cultist's eyes and saw the blankness of them, staring upward, mirroring the feeble yellow of the torches. He saw the bubble of froth upon Latimer's lips and heard the low animal whimper in Latimer's throat.

With the slow fascination of fear, he lifted himself on one arm and turned his eyes toward the blood-curdling blackness of the window.

Through it shone the Stars!

Not Earth's feeble thirty-six hundred Stars visible to the eye—Lagash was in the center of a giant cluster. Thirty thousand mighty suns shown down in a soul-searing splendor that was more frighteningly cold in its awful indifference than the bitter wind that shivered across the cold, horribly bleak world.

Theremon staggered to his feet, his throat constricting him to breathlessness, all the muscles of his body writhing in a tensity of terror and sheer fear beyond bearing. He was going mad, and knew it, and somewhere deep inside a bit of sanity was screaming, struggling to fight off the hopeless flood of black terror. It was very horrible to go mad and know that you were going mad—to know that in a little minute you would be here physically and yet all the real essence would be dead and drowned in the black madness. For this was the Dark—the Dark and the Cold and the Doom. The bright walls of the universe were shattered and their awful black fragments were falling down to crush and squeeze and obliterate him.

He jostled someone crawling on hands and knees, but stumbled somehow over him. Hands groping at his tortured throat, he limped toward the flame of the torches that filled all his mad vision.

"Light!" he screamed.

Aton, somewhere, was crying, whimpering horribly like a terribly frightened child. "Stars—all the Stars—we didn't know at all. We didn't know anything. We thought six stars is a universe is something the Stars didn't

notice is Darkness forever and ever and ever and the walls
are breaking in and we didn't know we couldn't know and
anything—"

Someone clawed at the torch, and it fell and snuffed
out. In the instant, the awful splendor of the indifferent
Stars leaped nearer to them.

On the horizon outside the window, in the direction of
Saro City, a crimson glow began growing, strengthening
in brightness, that was not the glow of a sun.

The long night had come again.

THE WEAPON SHOP

by A. E. van Vogt

The village at night made a curiously timeless picture. Fara walked contentedly beside his wife along the street. The air was like wine; and he was thinking dimly of the artist who had come up from Imperial City, and made what the telestats called—he remembered the phrase vividly—"a symbolic painting reminiscent of a scene in the electrical age of seven thousand years ago."

Fara believed that utterly. The street before him with its weedless, automatically tended gardens, its shops set well back among the flowers, its perpetual hard, grassy sidewalks, and its street lamps that glowed from every pore of their structure—this was a restful paradise where time had stood still.

And it was like being a part of life that the great artist's picture of this quiet, peaceful scene before him was now in the collection of the empress herself. She had praised it, and naturally the thrice-blest artist had immediately and humbly begged her to accept it.

What a joy it must be to be able to offer personal homage to the glorious, the divine, the serenely gracious and lovely Innelda Isher, one thousand one hundred eightieth of her line.

As they walked, Fara half turned to his wife. In the dim light of the nearest street lamp, her kindly, still youthful face was almost lost in shadow. He murmured softly, instinctively muting his voice to harmonize with the pastel shades of night:

"She said—our empress said—that our little village of

First published in 1942

Glay seemed to her to have in it all the wholesomeness, the gentleness, that constitutes the finest qualities of her people. Wasn't that a wonderful thought, Creel? She must be a marvelously understanding woman. I—"

He stopped. They had come to a side street, and there was something about a hundred and fifty feet along it that—

"Look!" Fara said hoarsely.

He pointed with rigid arm and finger at a sign that glowed in the night, a sign that read:

FINE WEAPONS
THE RIGHT TO BUY WEAPONS IS THE RIGHT TO BE FREE

Fara had a strange, empty feeling as he stared at the blazing sign. He saw that other villagers were gathering. He said finally, huskily:

"I've heard of these shops. They're places of infamy, against which the government of the empress will act one of these days. They're built in hidden factories, and then transported whole to towns like ours and set up in gross defiance of property rights. That one wasn't there an hour ago."

Fara's face hardened. His voice had a harsh edge in it, as he said: "Creel, go home."

Fara was surprised when Creel did not move off at once. All their married life, she had had a pleasing habit of obedience that had made cohabitation a wonderful thing. He saw that she was looking at him wide-eyed, and that it was a timid alarm that held her there. She said:

"Fara, what do you intend to do? You're not thinking of—"

"Go home!" Her fear brought out all the grim determination in his nature. "We're not going to let such a monstrous thing desecrate our village. Think of it"—his voice shivered before the appalling thought—"this fine, old-fashioned community, which we had resolved always to keep exactly as the empress has it in her picture gallery, debauched now, ruined by this . . . this thing— But we won't have it; that's all there is to it."

Creel's voice came softly out of the half-darkness of the street corner, the timidity gone from it: "Don't do anything rash, Fara. Remember it is not the first new building to come into Glay—since the picture was painted."

Fara was silent. This was a quality of his wife of which he did not approve, this reminding him unnecessarily of unpleasant facts. He knew exactly what she meant. The gigantic, multitentacled corporation, Automatic Atomic Motor Repair Shops, Inc., had come in under the laws of the State with their flashy building, against the wishes of the village council—and had already taken half of Fara's repair business.

"That's different!" Fara growled finally. "In the first place people will discover in good time that these new automatic repairers do a poor job. In the second place it's fair competition. But this weapon shop is a defiance of all the decencies that make life under the House of Isher such a joy. Look at the hypocritical sign: 'The right to buy weapons—' Aaaaahh!"

He broke off with: "Go home, Creel. We'll see to it that they sell no weapons in this town."

He watched the slender woman-shape move off into the shadows. She was halfway across the street when a thought occurred to Fara. He called:

"And if you see that son of ours hanging around some street corner, take him home. He's got to learn to stop staying out so late at night."

The shadowed figure of his wife did not turn; and after watching her for a moment moving along against the dim background of softly glowing street lights, Fara twisted on his heel, and walked swiftly toward the shop. The crowd was growing larger every minute, and the night pulsed with excited voices.

Beyond doubt, here was the biggest thing that had ever happened to the village of Glay.

The sign of the weapon shop was, he saw, a normal-illusion affair. No matter what his angle of view, he was always looking straight at it. When he paused finally in front of the great display window, the words had pressed back against the store front, and were staring unwinkingly down at him.

Fara sniffed once more at the meaning of the slogan, then forgot the simple thing. There was another sign in the window, which read:

THE FINEST ENERGY WEAPONS IN THE KNOWN UNIVERSE

A spark of interest struck fire inside Fara. He gazed at the brilliant display of guns, fascinated in spite of himself. The weapons were of every size, ranging from tiny little finger pistols to express rifles. They were made of every one of the light, hard, ornamental substances: glittering glassein, the colorful but opaque Ordine plastic, viridescent magnesitic beryllium. And others.

It was the very deadly extent of the destructive display that brought a chill to Fara. So many weapons for the little village of Glay, where not more than two people to his knowledge had guns, and those only for hunting. Why, the thing was absurd, fantastically mischievous, utterly threatening.

Somewhere behind Fara, a man said: "It's right on Lan Harris' lot. Good joke on that old scoundrel. Will he raise a row!"

There was a faint titter from several men, that made an odd patch of sound on the warm, fresh air. And Fara saw that the man had spoken the truth. The weapon shop had a forty-foot frontage. And it occupied the very center of the green, gardenlike lot of tight-fisted old Harris.

Fara frowned. The clever devils, the weapon-shop people, selecting the property of the most disliked man in town, coolly taking it over and giving everybody an agreeable titillation. But the very cunning of it made it vital that the trick shouldn't succeed.

He was still scowling anxiously when he saw the plump figure of Mel Dale, the mayor. Fara edged toward him hurriedly, touched his hat respectfully, and said:

"Where's Jor?"

"Here." The village constable elbowed his way through a little bundle of men. "Any plans?" he said.

"There's only one plan," said Fara boldly. "Go in and arrest them."

To Fara's amazement, the two men looked at each other, then at the ground. It was the big constable who answered shortly:

"Doors locked. And nobody answers our pounding. I was just going to suggest we let the matter ride until morning."

"Nonsense!" His very astonishment made Fara impatient. "Get an ax and we'll break the door down. Delay will only encourage such riffraff to resist. We don't want their kind in our village for so much as a single night. Isn't that so?"

There was a hasty nod of agreement from everybody in his immediate vicinity. Too hasty. Fara looked around puzzled at eyes that lowered before his level gaze. He thought: "They are all scared. And unwilling." Before he could speak, Constable Jor said:

"I guess you haven't heard about those doors or these shops. From all accounts, you can't break into them."

It struck Fara with a sudden pang that it was he who would have to act here. He said, "I'll get my atomic cutting machine from my shop. That'll fix them. Have I your permission to do that, Mr. Mayor?"

In the glow of the weapon-shop window, the plump man was sweating visibly. He pulled out a handkerchief, and wiped his forehead. He said:

"Maybe I'd better call the commander of the Imperial garrison at Ferd, and ask them."

"No!" Fara recognized evasion when he saw it. He felt himself steel; the conviction came that all the strength in this village was in him. "We must act ourselves. Other communities have let these people get in because they took no decisive action. We've got to resist to the limit. Beginning now. This minute. Well?"

The mayor's "All right!" was scarcely more than a sigh of sound. But it was all Fara needed.

He called out his intention to the crowd; and then, as he pushed his way out of the mob, he saw his son standing with some other young men staring at the window display.

Fara called: "Cayle, come and help me with the machine."

Cayle did not even turn; and Fara hurried on, seething. That wretched boy! One of these days he, Fara, would have to take firm action there. Or he'd have a no-good on his hands.

The energy was soundless—and smooth. There was no sputter, no fireworks. It glowed with a soft, pure white light, almost caressing the metal panels of the door—but not even beginning to sear them.

Minute after minute, the dogged Fara refused to believe the incredible failure, and played the boundlessly potent energy on that resisting wall. When he finally shut off his machine, he was perspiring freely.

"I don't understand it," he gasped. "Why—no metal is supposed to stand up against a steady flood of atomic force. Even the hard metal plates used inside the blast chamber of a motor take the explosions in what is called infinite series, so that each one has unlimited rest. That's the theory, but actually steady running crystallizes the whole plate after a few months."

"It's as Jor told you," said the mayor. "These weapon shops are—big. They spread right through the empire, *and they don't recognize the empress.*"

Fara shifted his feet on the hard grass, disturbed. He didn't like this kind of talk. It sounded—sacrilegious. And besides it was nonsense. It must be. Before he could speak, a man said somewhere behind him:

"I've heard it said that that door will open only to those who cannot harm the people inside."

The words shocked Fara out of his daze. With a start, and for the first time, he saw that his failure had had a bad psychological effect. He said sharply:

"That's ridiculous! If there were doors like that, we'd all have them. We—"

The thought that stopped his words was the sudden realization that *he* had not seen anybody try to open the door; and with all this reluctance around him it was quite possible that—

He stepped forward, grasped the doorknob, and pulled. The door opened with an unnatural weightlessness that gave him the fleeting impression that the knob had come loose into his hand. With a gasp, Fara jerked the door wide open.

"Jor!" he yelled. "Get in!"

The constable made a distorted movement—distorted by what must have been a will to caution, followed by the instant realization that he could not hold back before so many. He leaped awkwardly toward the open door—and it closed in his face.

Fara stared stupidly at his hand, which was still clenched. And then, slowly, a hideous thrill coursed along his nerves. The knob had—withdrawn. It had twisted, become viscous, and slipped amorphously from his straining fingers. Even the memory of that brief sensation gave him a feeling of unnormal things.

He grew aware that the crowd was watching with a silent intentness. Fara reached again for the knob, not quite so eagerly this time; and it was only a sudden realization of his reluctance that made him angry when the handle neither turned nor yielded in any way.

Determination returned in full force, and with it came a thought. He motioned to the constable. "Go back, Jor, while I pull."

The man retreated, but it did no good. And tugging did not help. The door would not open. Somewhere in the crowd, a man said darkly:

"It decided to let you in, then it changed its mind."

"What foolishness are you talking!" Fara spoke violently. "*It* changed its mind. Are you crazy? A door has no sense."

But a surge of fear put a half-quaver into his voice. It was the sudden alarm that made him bold beyond all his normal caution. With a jerk of his body, Fara faced the shop.

The building loomed there under the night sky, in itself bright as day, huge in width and length, and alien, menacing, no longer easily conquerable. The dim queasy wonder came as to what the soldiers of the empress would do if they were invited to act. And suddenly—a bare, flashing glimpse of a grim possibility—the feeling grew that even they would be able to do nothing.

Abruptly, Fara was conscious of horror that such an idea could enter his mind. He shut his brain tight, said wildly:

"The door opened for me once. It will open again."

It did. Quite simply it did. Gently, without resistance, with that same sensation of weightlessness, the strange, sensitive door followed the tug of his fingers. Beyond the threshold was dimness, a wide, darkened alcove. He heard the voice of Mel Dale behind him, the mayor saying:

"Fara, don't be a fool. What will you do inside?"

Fara was vaguely amazed to realize that he had stepped across the threshold. He turned, and startled at the blur of faces. "Why—" he began blankly; then he brightened; he said, "Why, I'll buy a gun, of course."

The brilliance of his reply, the cunning implicit in it, dazzled Fara for a half minute longer. The mood yielded slowly, as he found himself in the dimly lighted interior of the weapon shop.

It was preternaturally quiet inside. Not a sound penetrated from the night from which he had come; and the startled thought came that the people of the shop might actually be unaware that there was a crowd outside.

Fara walked forward gingerly on a rugged floor that muffled his footsteps utterly. After a moment, his eyes accustomed themselves to the soft lighting, which came like a reflection from the walls and ceilings. In a vague way, he had expected ultranormalness; and the ordinariness of the atomic lighting acted like a tonic to his tensed nerves.

He shook himself angrily. Why should there be anything really superior? He was getting as bad as those credulous idiots out in the street.

He glanced around with gathering confidence. The place looked quite common. It was a shop, almost scantily furnished. There were showcases on the walls and on the floor, glitteringly lovely things, but nothing unusual, and not many of them—a few dozens. There was in addition a double, ornate door leading to a back room—

Fara tried to keep one eye on that door, as he examined several showcases, each with three or four weapons either mounted or arranged in boxes or holsters.

Abruptly, the weapons began to excite him. He forgot to watch the door, as the wild thought struck that he ought to grab one of those guns from a case, and then the mo-

ment someone came, force him outside where Jor would
perform the arrest and—

Behind him, a man said quietly: "You wish to buy a
gun?"

Fara turned with a jump. Brief rage flooded him at the
way his plan had been wrecked by the arrival of the clerk.

The anger died as he saw that the intruder was a fine-
looking, silver-haired man, older than himself. That was
immeasurably disconcerting. Fara had an immense and
almost automatic respect for age, and for a long second
he could only stand there gaping. He said at last, lamely:

"Yes, yes, a gun."

"For what purpose?" said the man in his quiet voice.

Fara could only look at him blankly. It was too fast. He
wanted to get mad. He wanted to tell these people what
he thought of them. But the age of this representative
locked his tongue, tangled his emotions. He managed
speech only by an effort of will:

"For hunting." The plausible word stiffened his mind.
"Yes, definitely for hunting. There is a lake to the north
of here," he went on more fulsomely, glibly, "and—"

He stopped, scowling, startled at the extent of his dis-
honesty. He was not prepared to go so deeply into pre-
varication. He said curtly:

"For hunting."

Fara was himself again. Abruptly, he hated the man
for having put him so completely at a disadvantage. With
smoldering eyes he watched the old fellow click open a
showcase, and take out a green-shining rifle.

As the man faced him, weapon in hand, Fara was
thinking grimly, "Pretty clever, having an old man as a
front." It was the same kind of cunning that had made
them choose the property of Miser Harris. Icily furious,
taut with his purpose, Fara reached for the gun; but the
man held it out of his reach, saying:

"Before I can even let you test this, I am compelled
by the by-laws of the weapon shops to inform you under
what circumstances you may purchase a gun."

So they had private regulations. What a system of
psychology tricks to impress gullible fools! Well, let the
old scoundrel talk. As soon as he, Fara, got hold of the
rifle, he'd put an end to hypocrisy.

"We weapons makers," the clerk said mildly, "have evolved guns that can, in their particular ranges, destroy any machine or object made of what is called matter. Thus whoever possesses one of our weapons is the equal and more of any soldier of the empress. I say more because each gun is the center of a field of force which acts as a perfect screen against immaterial destructive forces. That screen offers no resistance to clubs or spears or bullets, or other substances, but it would require a small atomic cannon to penetrate the superb barrier it creates around its owner.

"You will readily comprehend," the man went on, "that such a potent weapon could not be allowed to fall, unmodified, into irresponsible hands. Accordingly, no gun purchased from us may be used for aggression or murder. In the case of the hunting rifle, only such specified game birds and animals as we may from time to time list in our display windows may be shot. Finally, no weapon can be resold without our approval. Is that clear?"

Fara nodded dumbly. For the moment, speech was impossible to him. The incredible, fantastically stupid words were still going round and around in his head. He wondered if he ought to laugh out loud, or curse the man for daring to insult his intelligence so tremendously.

So the gun mustn't be used for murder or robbery. So only certain birds and animals could be shot. And as for reselling it, suppose—suppose he bought this thing, took a trip of a thousand miles, and offered it to some wealthy stranger for two credits—who would ever know?

Or suppose he held up the stranger. Or shot him. How would the weapon shop ever find out? The thing was so ridiculous that—

He grew aware that the gun was being held out to him stock first. He took it eagerly, and had to fight the impulse to turn the muzzle directly on the old man. Mustn't rush this, he thought tautly. He said:

"How does it work?"

"You simply aim it, and pull the trigger. Perhaps you would like to try it on a target we have."

Fara swung the gun up. "Yes," he said triumphantly, "and you're it. Now, just get over there to the front door, and then outside."

He raised his voice: "And if anybody's thinking of coming through the back door, I've got that covered, too."

He motioned jerkily at the clerk. "Quick now, move! I'll shoot! I swear I will."

The man was cool, unflustered. "I have no doubt you would. When we decided to attune the door so that you could enter despite your hostility, we assumed the capacity for homicide. However, this is our party. You had better adjust yourself accordingly, and look behind you—"

There was silence. Finger on trigger, Fara stood moveless. Dim thoughts came of all the *half-things* he had heard in his days about the weapon shops: that they had secret supporters in every district, that they had a private and ruthless hidden government, and that once you got into their clutches, the only way out was death and—

But what finally came clear was a mind picture of himself, Fara Clark, family man, faithful subject of the empress, standing here in this dimly lighted store, deliberately fighting an organization so vast and menacing that— He must have been mad.

Only—here he was. He forced courage into his sagging muscles. He said:

"You can't fool me with pretending there's someone behind me. Now, get to that door. *And fast!*"

The firm eyes of the old man were looking past him. The man said quietly: "Well, Rad, have you all the data?"

"Enough for a primary," said a young man's voice behind Fara. "Type A-7 conservative. Good average intelligence, but a Monaric development peculiar to small towns. One-sided outlook fostered by the Imperial schools present in exaggerated form. Extremely honest. Reason would be useless. Emotional approach would require extended treatment. I see no reason why we should bother. Let him live his life as it suits him."

"If you think," Fara said shakily, "that that trick voice is going to make me turn, you're crazy. That's the left wall of the building. I know there's no one there."

"I'm all in favor, Rad," said the old man, "of letting him live his life. But he was the prime mover of the crowd outside. I think he should be discouraged."

"We'll advertise his presence," said Rad. "He'll spend the rest of his life denying the charge."

Fara's confidence in the gun had faded so far that, as he listened in puzzled uneasiness to the incomprehensible conversation, he forgot it completely. He parted his lips, but before he could speak, the old man cut in, persistently:

"I think a little emotion might have a long-run effect. Show him the palace."

Palace! The startling word tore Fara out of his brief paralysis. "See here," he began, "I can see now that you lied to me. This gun isn't loaded at all. It's—"

His voice failed him. Every muscle in his body went rigid. He stared like a madman. *There was no gun in his hands.*

"Why, you—" he began wildly. And stopped again. His mind heaved with imbalance. With a terrible effort he fought off the spinning sensation, thought finally, tremblingly: Somebody must have sneaked the gun from him. That meant—there was someone behind him. The voice was no mechanical thing. Somehow, they had—

He started to turn—and couldn't. What in the name of— He struggled, pushing with his muscles. And couldn't move, couldn't budge, couldn't even—

The room was growing curiously dark. He had difficulty seeing the old man and— He would have shrieked then if he could. Because the weapon shop was gone. He was—

He was standing in the sky above an immense city.

In the sky, and nothing beneath him, nothing around him but air, and blue summer heaven, and the city a mile, two miles below.

Nothing, nothing— He would have shrieked, but his breath seemed solidly embedded in his lungs. Sanity came back as the remote awareness impinged upon his terrified mind that he was actually standing on a hard floor, and that the city must be a picture somehow focused directly into his eyes.

For the first time, with a start, Fara recognized the metropolis below. It was the city of dreams, Imperial City, capital of the glorious Empress Isher— From his great height, he could see the gardens, the gorgeous grounds of the silver palace, the official Imperial residence itself—

The last tendrils of his fear were fading now before a gathering fascination and wonder; they vanished utterly as he recognized with a ghastly thrill of uncertain expectancy that the palace was drawing nearer at great speed.

"Show him the palace," they had said. Did that mean, could it mean—

That spray of tense thoughts splattered into nonexistence, as the glittering roof flashed straight at his face. He gulped, as the solid metal of it passed through him, and then other walls and ceilings.

His first sense of imminent and mind-shaking desecration came as the picture paused in a great room where a score of men sat around a table at the head of which sat—a young woman.

The inexorable, sacrilegious, limitlessly powered cameras that were taking the picture swung across the table, and caught the woman full face.

It was a handsome face, but there was passion and fury twisting it now, and a very blaze of fire in her eyes, as she leaned forward, and said in a voice at once familiar—how often Fara had heard its calm, measured tones on the telestats—and distorted. Utterly distorted by anger and an insolent certainty of command. That caricature of a beloved voice slashed across the silence as clearly as if he, Fara, was there in that room:

"I want that skunk killed, do you understand? I don't care how you do it, but I want to hear by tomorrow night that he's dead."

The picture snapped off and instantly—it was as swift as that—Fara was back in the weapon shop. He stood for a moment, swaying, fighting to accustom his eyes to the dimness; and then—

His first emotion was contempt at the simpleness of the trickery—a motion picture. What kind of a fool did they think he was, to swallow something as transparently unreal as that? He'd—

Abruptly, the appalling lechery of the scheme, the indescribable wickedness of what was being attempted here brought red rage.

"Why, you scum!" he flared. "So you've got somebody

to act the part of the empress, trying to pretend that—
Why, you—"

"That will do," said the voice of Rad; and Fara shook
as a big young man walked into his line of vision. The
alarmed thought came that people who would besmirch
so vilely the character of her imperial majesty would not
hesitate to do physical damage to Fara Clark. The young
man went on in a steely tone:

"We do not pretend that what you saw was taking
place this instant in the palace. That would be too much
of a coincidence. But it was taken two weeks ago: the
woman *is* the empress. The man whose death she ordered
is one of her many former lovers. He was found murdered two weeks ago: his name, if you care to look it up
in the news files, is Banton McCreddie. However, let that
pass. We're finished with you now and—"

"But I'm not finished," Fara said in a thick voice. "I've
never heard or seen so much infamy in all my life. If
you think this town is through with you, you're crazy.
We'll have a guard on this place day and night, and nobody will get in or out. We'll—"

"That will do." It was the silver-haired man; and Fara
stopped out of respect for age, before he thought. The
old man went on: "The examination has been most interesting. As an honest man, you may call on us if you
are ever in trouble. That is all. Leave through the side
door."

It *was* all. Impalpable forces grabbed him, and he was
shoved at a door that appeared miraculously in the wall,
where seconds before the palace had been.

He found himself standing dazedly in a flower bed, and
there was a swarm of men to his left. He recognized his
fellow townsmen and that he was—outside.

The incredible nightmare was over.

"Where's the gun?" said Creel, as he entered the house
half an hour later.

"The gun?" Fara stared at his wife.

"It said over the radio a few minutes ago that you
were the first customer of the new weapon shop. I thought
it was queer, but—"

He was eerily conscious of her voice going on for several words longer, but it was the purest jumble. The shock was so great that he had the horrible sensation of being on the edge of an abyss.

So that was what the young man had meant: "Advertise! We'll advertise his presence and—"

Fara thought: His reputation! Not that his was a great name, but he had long believed with a quiet pride that Fara Clark's motor repair shop was widely known in the community and countryside.

First, his private humiliation inside the shop. And now this—lying—to people who didn't know why he had gone into the store. Diabolical.

His paralysis ended, as a frantic determination to rectify the base charge drove him to the telestat. After a moment, the plump, sleepy face of Mayor Mel Dale appeared on the plate. Fara's voice made a barrage of sound, but his hopes dashed, as the man said:

"I'm sorry, Fara. I don't see how you can have free time on the telestat. You'll have to pay for it. They did."

"They did!" Fara wondered vaguely if he sounded as empty as he felt.

"And they've just paid Lan Harris for his lot. The old man asked top price, and got it. He just phoned me to transfer the title."

"Oh!" The world was shattering. "You mean nobody's going to do anything. What about the Imperial garrison at Ferd?"

Dimly, Fara was aware of the mayor mumbling something about the empress' soldiers refusing to interfere in civilian matters.

"Civilian matters!" Fara exploded. "You mean these people are just going to be allowed to come here whether we want them or not, illegally forcing the sale of lots by first taking possession of them?"

A sudden thought struck him breathless. "Look, you haven't changed your mind about having Jor keep guard in front of the shop?"

With a start, he saw that the plump face in the telestat plate had grown impatient. "Now, see here, Fara," came the pompous words, "let the constituted authorities handle this matter."

"But you're going to keep Jor there," Fara said doggedly.

The mayor looked annoyed, said finally peevishly: "I promised, didn't I? So he'll be there. And now—do you want to buy time on the telestat? It's fifteen credits for one minute. Mind you, as a friend, I think you're wasting your money. No one has ever caught up with a false statement."

Fara said grimly: "Put two on, one in the morning, one in the evening."

"All right. We'll deny it completely. Good night."

The telestat went blank; and Fara sat there. A new thought hardened his face. "That boy of ours—there's going to be a showdown. He either works in my shop, or he gets no more allowance."

Creel said: "You've handled him wrong. He's twenty-three, and you treat him like a child. Remember, at twenty-three, you were a married man."

"That was different," said Fara. "I had a sense of responsibility. Do you know what he did tonight?"

He didn't quite catch her answer. For the moment, he thought she said: "No; in what way did you humiliate him first?"

Fara felt too impatient to verify the impossible words. He rushed on: "He refused in front of the whole village to give me help. He's a bad one, all bad."

"Yes," said Creel in a bitter tone, "he is all bad. I'm sure you don't realize how bad. He's as cold as steel, but without steel's strength or integrity. He took a long time, but he hates even me now, because I stood up for your side so long, knowing you were wrong."

"What's that?" said Fara, startled; then gruffly: "Come, come, my dear, we're both upset. Let's go to bed."

He slept poorly.

There were days then when the conviction that this was a personal fight between himself and the weapon shop lay heavily on Fara. Grimly, though it was out of his way, he made a point of walking past the weapon shop, always pausing to speak to Constable Jor and—

On the fourth day, the policeman wasn't there.

Fara waited patiently at first, then angrily; then he

walked hastily to his shop, and called Jor's house. No, Jor wasn't home. He was guarding the weapon store.

Fara hesitated. His own shop was piled with work, and he had a guilty sense of having neglected his customers for the first time in his life. It would be simple to call up the mayor and report Jor's dereliction. And yet—

He didn't want to get the man into trouble—

Out in the street, he saw that a large crowd was gathering in front of the weapon shop. Fara hurried. A man he knew greeted him excitedly:

"Jor's been murdered, Fara!"

"Murdered!" Fara stood stock-still, and at first he was not clearly conscious of the grisly thought that was in his mind: Satisfaction! A flaming satisfaction. Now, he thought, even the soldiers would have to act. They—

With a gasp, he realized the ghastly tenor of his thoughts. He shivered, but finally pushed the sense of shame out of his mind. He said slowly:

"Where's the body?"

"Inside."

"You mean, those . . . scum—" In spite of himself, he hesitated over the epithet; even now, it was difficult to think of the fine-faced, silver-haired old man in such terms. Abruptly, his mind hardened; he flared: "You mean those scum actually killed him, then pulled his body inside?"

"Nobody saw the killing," said a second man beside Fara, "but he's gone, hasn't been seen for three hours. The mayor got the weapon shop on the telestat, but they claim they don't know anything. They've done away with him, that's what, and now they're pretending innocence. Well, they won't get out of it as easily as that. Mayor's gone to phone the soldiers at Ferd to bring up some big guns and—"

Something of the intense excitement that was in the crowd surged through Fara, the feeling of big things brewing. It was the most delicious sensation that had ever tingled along his nerves, and it was all mixed with a strange pride that he had been so right about this, that he at least had never doubted that here was evil.

He did not recognize the emotion as the full-flowering joy that comes to a member of a mob. But his voice shook, as he said:

"Guns? Yes, that will be the answer, and the soldiers will have to come, of course."

Fara nodded to himself in the immensity of his certainty that the Imperial soldiers would now have no excuse for not acting. He started to say something dark about what the empress would do if she found out that a man had lost his life because the soldiers had shirked their duty, but the words were drowned in a shout:

"Here comes the mayor! Hey, Mr. Mayor, when are the atomic cannons due?"

There was more of the same general meaning, as the mayor's sleek, all-purpose car landed lightly. Some of the questions must have reached his honor, for he stood up in the open two-seater, and held up his hand for silence.

To Fara's astonishment, the plump-faced man looked at him with accusing eyes. The thing seemed so impossible that, quite instinctively, Fara looked behind him. But he was almost alone; everybody else had crowded forward.

Fara shook his head, puzzled by that glare; and then, astoundingly, Mayor Dale pointed a finger at him, and said in a voice that trembled:

"There's the man who's responsible for the trouble that's come upon us. Stand forward, Fara Clark, and show yourself. You've cost this town seven hundred credits that we could ill afford to spend."

Fara couldn't have moved or spoken to save his life. He just stood there in a maze of dumb bewilderment. Before he could even think, the mayor went on, and there was quivering self-pity in his tone:

"We've all known that it wasn't wise to interfere with these weapon shops. So long as the Imperial government leaves them alone, what right have we to set up guards, or act against them? That's what I've thought from the beginning, but this man . . . this . . . this Fara Clark kept after all of us, forcing us to move against our wills, and so now we've got a seven-hundred-credit bill to meet and—"

He broke off with: "I might as well make it brief. When I called the garrison, the commander just laughed

and said that Jor would turn up. And I had barely disconnected when there was a money call from Jor. He's
on Mars."

He waited for the shouts of amazement to die down.
"It'll take three weeks for him to come back by ship,
and we've got to pay for it, and Fara Clark is responsible.
He—"

The shock was over. Fara stood cold, his mind hard.
He said finally, scathingly: "So you're giving up, and
trying to blame me all in one breath. I say you're all
fools."

As he turned away, he heard Mayor Dale saying something about the situation not being completely lost, as he
had learned that the weapon shop had been set up in
Glay because the village was equidistant from four cities,
and that it was the city business the shop was after. This
would mean tourists, and accessory trade for the village
stores and—

Fara heard no more. Head high, he walked back
toward his shop. There were one or two catcalls from the
mob, but he ignored them.

He had no sense of approaching disaster, simply a
gathering fury against the weapon shop, which had
brought him to this miserable status among his neighbors.

The worst of it, as the days passed, was the realization
that the people of the weapon shop had no personal interest in him. They were remote, superior, undefeatable.
That unconquerableness was a dim, suppressed awareness
inside Fara.

When he thought of it, he felt a vague fear at the way
they had transferred Jor to Mars in a period of less than
three hours, when all the world knew that the trip by
fastest spaceship required nearly three weeks.

Fara did not go to the express station to see Jor arrive home. He had heard that the council had decided to
charge Jor with half of the expense of the trip, on the
threat of losing his job if he made a fuss.

On the second night after Jor's return, Fara slipped
down to the constable's house, and handed the officer
one hundred seventy-five credits. It wasn't that he was
responsible, he told Jor, but—

The man was only too eager to grant the disclaimer, provided the money went with it. Fara returned home with a clearer conscience.

It was on the third day after that that the door of his shop banged open and a man came in. Fara frowned as he saw who it was: Castler, a village hanger-on. The man was grinning:

"Thought you might be interested, Fara. Somebody came out of the weapon shop today."

Fara strained deliberately at the connecting bolt of a hard plate of the atomic motor he was fixing. He waited with a gathering annoyance that the man did not volunteer further information. Asking questions would be a form of recognition of the worthless fellow. A developing curiosity made him say finally, grudgingly:

"I suppose the constable promptly picked him up."

He supposed nothing of the kind, but it was an opening.

"It wasn't a man. It was a girl."

Fara knitted his brows. He didn't like the idea of making trouble for women. But—the cunning devils! Using a girl, just as they had used an old man as a clerk. It was a trick that deserved to fail, the girl probably a tough one who needed rough treatment. Fara said harshly:

"Well, what's happened?"

"She's still out, bold as you please. Pretty thing, too."

The bolt off, Fara took the hard plate over to the polisher, and began patiently the long, careful task of smoothing away the crystals that heat had seared on the once shining metal. The soft throb of the polisher made the background to his next words:

"Has anything been done?"

"Nope. The constable's been told, but he says he doesn't fancy being away from his family for another three weeks, and paying the cost into the bargain."

Fara contemplated that darkly for a minute, as the polisher throbbed on. His voice shook with suppressed fury, when he said finally:

"So they're letting them get away with it. It's all been as clever as hell. Can't they see that they musn't give an inch before these . . . these transgressors. It's like giving countenance to sin."

From the corner of his eye, he noticed that there was

a curious grin on the face of the other. It struck Fara suddenly that the man was enjoying his anger. And there was something else in that grin; something—a secret knowledge.

Fara pulled the engine plate away from the polisher. He faced the ne'er-do-well, scathed at him:

"Naturally, that sin part wouldn't worry you much."

"Oh," said the man nonchalantly, "the hard knocks of life make people tolerant. For instance, after you know the girl better, you yourself will probably come to realize that there's good in all of us."

It was not so much the words, as the curious I've-got-secret-information tone that made Fara snap:

"What do you mean—if I get to know the girl better! I won't even speak to the brazen creature."

"One can't always choose," the other said with enormous casualness. "Suppose he brings her home."

"Suppose who brings who home?" Fara spoke irritably. "Castler, you—"

He stopped; a dead weight of dismay plumped into his stomach; his whole being sagged. "You mean—" he said.

"I mean," replied Castler with a triumphant leer, "that the boys aren't letting a beauty like her be lonesome. And, naturally, your son was the first to speak to her."

He finished: "They're walkin' together now on Second Avenue, comin' this way, so—"

"Get out of here!" Fara roared. "And stay away from me with your gloating. Get out!"

The man hadn't expected such an ignominious ending. He flushed scarlet, then went out, slamming the door.

Fara stood for a moment, every muscle stiff; then, with an abrupt, jerky movement, he shut off his power, and went out into the street.

The time to put a stop to that kind of thing was—now!

He had no clear plan, just that violent determination to put an immediate end to an impossible situation. And it was all mixed up with his anger against Cayle. How could he have had such a worthless son, he who paid his debts and worked hard, and tried to be decent and to live up to the highest standards of the empress?

A brief, dark thought came to Fara that maybe there

was some bad blood on Creel's side. Not from her mother, of course—Fara added the mental thought hastily. *There* was a fine, hard-working woman, who hung on to her money, and who would leave Creel a tidy sum one of these days.

But Creel's father had disappeared when Creel was only a child, and there had been some vague scandal about his having taken up with a telestat actress.

And now Cayle with this weapon-shop girl. A girl who had let herself be picked up—

He saw them, as he turned the corner onto Second Avenue. They were walking a hundred feet distant, and heading away from Fara. The girl was tall and slender, almost as big as Cayle, and, as Fara came up, she was saying:

"You have the wrong idea about us. A person like you can't get a job in our organization. You belong in the Imperial Service, where they can use young men of good education, good appearance and no scruples. I—"

Fara grasped only dimly that Cayle must have been trying to get a job with these people. It was not clear; and his own mind was too intent on his purpose for it to mean anything at the moment. He said harshly:

"Cayle!"

The couple turned, Cayle with the measured unhurriedness of a young man who has gone a long way on the road to steellike nerves; the girl was quicker, but withal dignified.

Fara had a vague, terrified feeling that his anger was too great, self-destroying, but the very violence of his emotions ended that thought even as it came. He said thickly:

"Cayle, get home—at once."

Fara was aware of the girl looking at him curiously from strange, gray-green eyes. No shame, he thought, and his rage mounted several degrees, driving away the alarm that came at the sight of the flush that crept into Cayle's cheeks.

The flush faded into a pale, tight-lipped anger; Cayle half-turned to the girl, said:

"This is the childish old fool I've got to put up with.

Fortunately, we seldom see each other; we don't even eat together. What do you think of him?"

The girl smiled impersonally: "Oh, we know Fara Clark; he's the backbone of the empress in Glay."

"Yes," the boy sneered. "You ought to hear him. He thinks we're living in heaven; and the empress is the divine power. The worst part of it is that there's no chance of his ever getting that stuffy look wiped off his face."

They walked off; and Fara stood there. The very extent of what had happened had drained anger from him as if it had never been. There was the realization that he had made a mistake so great that—

He couldn't grasp it. For long, long now, since Cayle had refused to work in his shop, he had felt this building up to a climax. Suddenly, his own uncontrollable ferocity stood revealed as a partial product of that—deeper— problem.

Only, now that the smash was here, he didn't want to face it—

All through the day in his shop, he kept pushing it out of his mind, kept thinking:

Would this go on now, as before, Cayle and he living in the same house, not even looking at each other when they met, going to bed at different times, getting up, Fara at 6:30, Cayle at noon? Would *that* go on through all the days and years to come?

When he arrived home, Creel was waiting for him. She said:

"Fara, he wants you to loan him five hundred credits, so that he can go to Imperial City."

Fara nodded wordlessly. He brought the money back to the house the next morning, and gave it to Creel, who took it into the bedroom.

She came out a minute later. "He says to tell you good-by."

When Fara came home that evening, Cayle was gone. He wondered whether he ought to feel relieved or—what?

The days passed. Fara worked. He had nothing else to do, and the gray thought was often in his mind that now he would be doing it till the day he died. Except—

Fool that he was—he told himself a thousand times
how big a fool—he kept hoping that Cayle would walk
into the shop and say:

"Father, I've learned my lesson. If you can ever forgive
me, teach me the business, and then you retire to a well-
earned rest."

It was exactly a month to a day after Cayle's departure
that the telestat clicked on just after Fara had finished
lunch. "Money call," it sighed, "money call."

Fara and Creel looked at each other. "Eh," said Fara
finally, "money call for us."

He could see from the gray look in Creel's face the
thought that was in her mind. He said under his breath:
"Damn that boy!"

But he felt relieved. Amazingly, relieved! Cayle was beginning to appreciate the value of parents and—

He switched on the viewer. "Come and collect," he
said.

The face that came on the screen was heavy-jowled,
beetle-browed—and strange. The man said:

"This is Clerk Pearton of the Fifth Bank of Ferd. We
have received a sight draft on you for ten thousand
credits. With carrying charges and government tax, the
sum required will be twelve thousand one hundred credits.
Will you pay it now or will you come in this afternoon
and pay it?"

"B-but . . . b-but—" said Fara. "W-who—"

He stopped, conscious of the stupidity of the question,
dimly conscious of the heavy-faced man saying something
about the money having been paid out to one Cayle Clark,
that morning, in Imperial City. At last, Fara found his
voice:

"But the bank had no right," he expostulated, "to pay
out the money without my authority. I—"

The voice cut him off coldly: "Are we then to inform
our central that the money was obtained under false pretenses? Naturally, an order will be issued immediately
for the arrest of your son."

"Wait . . . wait—" Fara spoke blindly. He was aware
of Creel beside him, shaking her head at him. She was
as white as a sheet, and her voice was a sick, stricken
thing, as she said:

"Fara, let him go. He's through with us. We must be as hard—let him go."

The words rang senselessly in Fara's ears. They didn't fit into any normal pattern. He was saying:

"I . . . I haven't got— How about my paying . . . installments? I—"

"If you wish a loan," said Clerk Pearton, "naturally we will be happy to go into the matter. I might say that when the draft arrived, we checked up on your status, and we are prepared to loan you eleven thousand credits on indefinite call with your shop as security. I have the form here, and if you are agreeable, we will switch this call through the registered circuit, and you can sign at once."

"Fara, no."

The clerk went on: "The other eleven hundred credits will have to be paid in cash. Is that agreeable?"

"Yes, yes, of course, I've got twenty-five hund—" He stopped his chattering tongue with a gulp; then: "Yes, that's satisfactory."

The deal completed, Fara whirled on his wife. Out of the depths of his hurt and bewilderment, he raged:

"What do you mean, standing there and talking about not paying it? You said several times that I was responsible for his being what he is. Besides, we don't know why he needed the money. He—"

Creel said in a low, dead tone: "In one hour, he's stripped us of our life work. He did it deliberately, thinking of us as two old fools, who wouldn't know any better than to pay it."

Before he could speak, she went on: "Oh, I know I blamed you, but in the final issue, I knew it was he. He was always cold and calculating, but I was weak, and I was sure that if you handled him in a different . . . and besides I didn't want to see his faults for a long time. He—"

"All I see," Fara interrupted doggedly, "is that I have saved our name from disgrace."

His high sense of duty rightly done lasted until mid-afternoon, when the bailiff from Ferd came to take over the shop.

"But what—" Fara began.

The bailiff said: "The Automatic Atomic Repair Shops, Limited, took over your loan from the bank, and are foreclosing. Have you anything to say?"

"It's unfair," said Fara. "I'll take it to court. I'll—"

He was thinking dazedly: "If the empress ever learned of this, she'd . . . she'd—"

The courthouse was a big, gray building; and Fara felt emptier and colder every second, as he walked along the gray corridors. In Glay, his decision not to give himself into the hands of a bloodsucker of a lawyer had seemed a wise act. Here, in these enormous halls and palatial rooms, it seemed the sheerest folly.

He managed, nevertheless, to give an articulate account of the criminal act of the bank in first giving Cayle the money, then turning over the note to his chief competitor, apparently within minutes of his signing it. He finished with:

"I'm sure, sir, the empress would not approve of such goings-on against honest citizens. I—"

"How dare you," said the cold-voiced creature on the bench, "use the name of her holy majesty in support of your own gross self-interest?"

Fara shivered. The sense of being intimately a member of the empress' great human family yielded to a sudden chill and a vast mind-picture of the ten million icy courts like this, and the myriad malevolent and heartless men— *like this*—who stood between the empress and her loyal subject, Fara.

He thought passionately: If the empress knew what was happening here, how unjustly he was being treated, she would—

Or would she?

He pushed the crowding, terrible doubt out of his mind —came out of his hard reverie with a start, to hear the Cadi saying:

"Plaintiff's appeal dismissed, with costs assessed at seven hundred credits, to be divided between the court and the defense solicitor in the ratio of five to two. See to it that the appellant does not leave till the costs are paid. Next case—"

Fara went alone the next day to see Creel's mother. He called first at "Farmer's Restaurant" at the outskirts of the village. The place was, he noted with satisfaction in the thought of the steady stream of money flowing in, half full, though it was only midmorning. But madame wasn't there. Try the feed store.

He found her in the back of the feed store, overseeing the weighing out of grain into cloth measures. The hard-faced old woman heard his story without a word. She said finally, curtly:

"Nothing doing, Fara. I'm one who has to make loans often from the bank to swing deals. If I tried to set you up in business, I'd find the Automatic Atomic Repair people getting after me. Besides, I'd be a fool to turn money over to a man who lets a bad son squeeze a fortune out of him. Such a man has no sense about worldly things. And I won't give you a job because I don't hire relatives in my business." She finished: "Tell Creel to come and live at my house. I won't support a man, though. That's all."

He watched her disconsolately for a while, as she went on calmly superintending the clerks who were manipulating the old, no longer accurate measuring machines. Twice her voice echoed through the dust-filled interior, each time with a sharp: "That's overweight, a gram at least. Watch your machine."

Though her back was turned, Fara knew by her posture that she was still aware of his presence. She turned at last with an abrupt movement, and said:

"Why don't you go to the weapon shop? You haven't anything to lose, and you can't go on like this."

Fara went out, then, a little blindly. At first the suggestion that he buy a gun and commit suicide had no real personal application. But he felt immeasurably hurt that his mother-in-law should have made it.

Kill himself? Why, it was ridiculous. He was still only a young man, going on fifty. Given the proper chance, with his skilled hands, he could wrest a good living even in a world where automatic machines were encroaching everywhere. There was always room for a man who did a good job. His whole life had been based on that credo.

Kill himself—

He went home to find Creel packing. "It's the common sense thing to do," she said. "We'll rent the house and move into rooms."

He told her about her mother's offer to take her in, watching her face as he spoke. Creel shrugged.

"I told her 'No' yesterday," she said thoughtfully. "I wonder why she mentioned it to you."

Fara walked swiftly over to the great front window overlooking the garden, with its flowers, its pool, its rockery. He tried to think of Creel away from this garden of hers, this home of two thirds a life-time, Creel living in rooms—and knew what her mother had meant. There was one more hope—

He waited till Creel went upstairs, then called Mel Dale on the telestat. The mayor's plump face took on an uneasy expression as he saw who it was.

But he listened pontifically, said finally: "Sorry, the council does not loan money; and I might as well tell you, Fara—I have nothing to do with this, mind you—but you can't get a license for a shop any more."

"W-what?"

"I'm sorry!" The mayor lowered his voice. "Listen, Fara, take my advice and go to the weapon shop. These places have their uses."

There was a click, and Fara sat staring at the blank face of the viewing screen.

So it was to be—death!

He waited until the street was empty of human beings, then slipped across the boulevard, past a design of flower gardens, and so to the door of the shop. The brief fear came that the door wouldn't open, but it did, effortlessly.

As he emerged from the dimness of the alcove into the shop proper, he saw the silver-haired old man sitting in a corner chair, reading under a softly bright light. The old man looked up, put aside his book, then rose to his feet.

"It's Mr. Clark," he said quietly. "What can we do for you?"

A faint flush crept into Fara's cheeks. In a dim fashion, he had hoped that he would not suffer the humiliation of being recognized; but now that his fear was realized, he stood his ground stubbornly. The important thing about killing himself was that there be no body for Creel to bury at great expense. Neither knife nor poison would satisfy that basic requirement.

"I want a gun," said Fara, "that can be adjusted to disintegrate a body six feet in diameter in a single shot. Have you that kind?"

Without a word, the old man turned to a showcase, and brought forth a sturdy gem of a revolver that glinted with all the soft colors of the inimitable Ordine plastic. The man said in a precise voice:

"Notice the flanges on this barrel are little more than bulges. This makes the model ideal for carrying in a shoulder holster under the coat; it can be drawn very swiftly because, when properly attuned, it will leap toward the reaching hand of its owner. At the moment it is attuned to me. Watch while I replace it in its holster and—"

The speed of the draw was absolutely amazing. The old man's fingers moved; and the gun, four feet away, was in them. There was no blur of movement. It was like the door the night that it had slipped from Fara's grasp, and slammed noiselessly in Constable Jor's face. *Instantaneous!*

Fara, who had parted his lips as the old man was explaining, to protest the utter needlessness of illustrating any quality of the weapon except that he had asked for, closed them again. He stared in a brief, dazed fascination; and something of the wonder that was here held his mind and his body.

He had seen and handled the guns of soldiers, and they were simply ordinary metal or plastic things that one used clumsily like any other material substance, not like this at all, not possessed of a dazzling life of their own, leaping with an intimate eagerness to assist with all their superb power the will of their master. They—

With a start, Fara remembered his purpose. He smiled wryly, and said:

"All this is very interesting. But what about the beam that can fan out?"

The old man said calmly: "At pencil thickness, this beam will pierce any body except certain alloys of lead up to four hundred yards. With proper adjustment of the firing nozzle, you can disintegrate a six-foot object at fifty yards or less. This screw is the adjustor."

He indicated a tiny device in the muzzle itself. "Turn it to the left to spread the beam, to the right to close it."

Fara said: "I'll take the gun. How much is it?"

He saw that the old man was looking at him thoughtfully; the oldster said finally, slowly: "I have previously explained our regulations to you, Mr. Clark. You recall them, of course?"

"Eh!" said Fara, and stopped, wide-eyed. It wasn't that he didn't remember them. It was simply—

"You mean," he gasped, "those things actually apply. They're not—"

With a terrible effort, he caught his spinning brain and blurring voice. Tense and cold, he said:

"All I want is a gun that will shoot in self-defense, but which I can turn on myself if I have to or—want to."

"Oh, suicide!" said the old man. He looked as if a great understanding had suddenly dawned on him. "My dear sir, we have no objection to your killing yourself at any time. That is your personal privilege in a world where privileges grow scanter every year. As for the price of this revolver, it's four credits."

"Four cre ... only four credits!" said Fara.

He stood, absolutely astounded, his whole mind snatched from its dark purpose. Why, the plastic alone was—and the whole gun with its fine, intricate workmanship—twenty-five credits would have been dirt cheap.

He felt a brief thrill of utter interest; the mystery of the weapon shops suddenly loomed as vast and important as his own black destiny. But the old man was speaking again:

"And now, if you will remove your coat, we can put on the holster—"

Quite automatically, Fara complied. It was vaguely startling to realize that, in a few seconds, he would be walking out of here, equipped for self-murder, and that there was now not a single obstacle to his death.

Curiously, he was disappointed. He couldn't explain it, but somehow there had been in the back of his mind a hope that these shops might, just might—what?

What indeed? Fara sighed wearily—and grew aware again of the old man's voice, saying:

"Perhaps you would prefer to step out of our side door. It is less conspicuous than the front."

There was no resistance in Fara. He was dimly conscious of the man's fingers on his arm, half guiding him; and then the old man pressed one of several buttons on the wall—so that's how it was done—and there was the door.

He could see flowers beyond the opening; without a word he walked toward them. He was outside almost before he realized it.

Fara stood for a moment in the neat little pathway, striving to grasp the finality of his situation. But nothing would come except a curious awareness of many men around him; for a long second, his brain was like a log drifting along a stream at night.

Through that darkness grew a consciousness of something wrong; the wrongness was there in the back of his mind, as he turned leftward to go to the front of the weapon store.

Vagueness transformed to a shocked, startled sound. For—he was not in Glay, and the weapon shop *wasn't* where it had been. In its place—

A dozen men brushed past Fara to join a long line of men farther along. But Fara was immune to their presence, their strangeness. His whole mind, his whole vision, his very being was concentrating on the section of machine that stood where the weapon shop had been.

A machine, oh, a machine—

His brain lifted up, up in his effort to grasp the tremendousness of the dull-metaled immensity of what was spread here under a summer sun beneath a sky as blue as a remote southern sea.

The machine towered into the heavens, five great tiers of metal, each a hundred feet high; and the superbly streamlined five hundred feet ended in a peak of light, a gorgeous spire that tilted straight up a sheer two hundred feet farther, and matched the very sun for brightness.

And it *was* a machine, not a building, because the whole lower tier was alive with shimmering lights, mostly

green, but sprinkled colorfully with red and occasionally
a blue and yellow. Twice, as Fara watched, green lights
directly in front of him flashed unscintillatingly into red.

The second tier was alive with white and red lights,
although there were only a fraction as many lights as on
the lowest tier. The third section had on its dull-metal surface only blue and yellow lights; they twinkled softly
here and there over the vast area.

The fourth tier was a series of signs that brought the
beginning of comprehension. The whole sign was:

WHITE   — BIRTHS
RED   — DEATHS
GREEN   — LIVING
BLUE   — IMMIGRATION TO EARTH
YELLOW   — EMIGRATION

The fifth tier was also all sign, finally explaining:

	POPULATIONS
SOLAR SYSTEM	19,174,463,747
EARTH	11,193,247,361
MARS	1,097,298,604
VENUS	5,141,053,811
MOONS	1,742,863,971

The numbers changed, even as he looked at them, leaping up and down, shifting below and above what they had
first been. People were dying, being born, moving to Mars,
to Venus, to the moons of Jupiter, to Earth's moon, and
others coming back again, landing minute by minute in the
thousands of spaceports. Life went on in its gigantic fashion—and here was the stupendous record. Here was—

"Better get in line," said a friendly voice beside Fara.
"It takes quite a while to put through an individual case,
I understand."

Fara stared at the man. He had the distinct impression
of having had senseless words flung at him. "In line?" he
started—and stopped himself with a jerk that hurt his
throat.

He was moving forward, blindly, ahead of the younger
man, thinking a curious jumble about that this must have

been how Constable Jor was transported to Mars—when another of the man's words penetrated.

"Case?" said Fara violently. "Individual case!"

The man, a heavy-faced, blue-eyed young chap of around thirty-five, looked at him curiously: "You must know why you're here," he said. "Surely you wouldn't have been sent through here unless you had a problem of some kind that the weapons shop courts will solve for you; there's no other reason for coming to Information Center."

Fara walked on because he was in the line now, a fast-moving line that curved him inexorably around the machine; and seemed to be heading him toward a door that led into the interior of the great metal structure.

So it was a building as well as a machine.

A problem, he was thinking, why, of course, he had a problem, a hopeless, insoluble, completely tangled problem so deeply rooted in the basic structure of Imperial civilization that the whole world would have to be overturned to make it right.

With a start, he saw that he was at the entrance. And the awed thought came: In seconds he would be committed irrevocably to—what?

Inside was a long, shining corridor, with scores of completely transparent hallways leading off the main corridor. Behind Fara, the young man's voice said:

"There's one, practically empty. Let's go."

Fara walked ahead; and suddenly he was trembling. He had already noticed that at the end of each side hallway were some dozen young women sitting at desks, interviewing men and . . . and, good heavens, was it possible that all this meant—

He grew aware that he had stopped in front of one of the girls.

She was older than she had looked from a distance, over thirty, but good-looking, alert. She smiled pleasantly, but impersonally, and said:

"Your name, please?"

He gave it before he thought and added a mumble about being from the village of Glay. The woman said:

"Thank you. It will take a few minutes to get your file. Won't you sit down?"

He hadn't noticed the chair. He sank into it; and his heart was beating so wildly that he felt choked. The strange thing was that there was scarcely a thought in his head, nor a real hope; only an intense, almost mind-wrecking excitement.

With a jerk, he realized that the girl was speaking again, but only snatches of her voice came through that screen of tension in his mind:

"—Information Center is . . . in effect . . . a bureau of statistics. Every person born . . . registered here . . . their education, change of address . . . occupation . . . and the highlights of their life. The whole is maintained by . . . combination of . . . unauthorized and unsuspected liaison with . . . Imperial Chamber of Statistics and . . . through medium of agents . . . in every community—"

It seemed to Fara that he was missing vital information, and that if he could only force his attention and hear more —He strained, but it was no use; his nerves were jumping madly and—

Before he could speak, there was a click, and a thin, dark plate slid onto the woman's desk. She took it up, and examined it. After a moment, she said something into a mouthpiece, and in a short time two more plates precipitated out of the empty air onto her desk. She studied them impassively, looked up finally.

"You will be interested to know," she said, "that your son, Cayle, bribed himself into a commission in the Imperial army with five thousand credits."

"Eh?" said Fara. He half rose from his chair, but before he could say anything, the young woman was speaking again, firmly:

"I must inform you that the weapon shops take no action against individuals. Your son can have his job, the money he stole; we are not concerned with moral correction. That must come naturally from the individual, and from the people as a whole—and now if you will give me a brief account of your problem for the record and the court."

Sweating, Fara sank back into his seat; his mind was

heaving; most desperately, he wanted more information about Cayle. He began:

"But . . . but what . . . how—" He caught himself; and in a low voice described what had happened. When he finished, the girl said:

"You will proceed now to the Name Room; watch for your name, and when it appears go straight to Room 474. Remember, 474—and now, the line is waiting, if you please—"

She smiled politely, and Fara was moving off almost before he realized it. He half turned to ask another question, but an old man was sinking into his chair. Fara hurried on, along a great corridor, conscious of curious blasts of sound coming from ahead.

Eagerly, he opened the door; and the sound crashed at him with all the impact of a sledge-hammer blow.

It was such a colossal, incredible sound that he stopped short, just inside the door, shrinking back. He stood then trying to blink sense into a visual confusion that rivaled in magnitude that incredible tornado of noise.

Men, men, men everywhere; men by the thousands in a long, broad auditorium, packed into rows of seats, pacing with an abandon of restlessness up and down aisles, and all of them staring with a frantic interest at a long board marked off into squares, each square lettered from the alphabet, from A, B, C and so on to Z. The tremendous board with its lists of names ran the full length of the immense room.

The Name Room, Fara was thinking shakily, as he sank into a seat—and his name would come up in the C's, and then—

It was like sitting in at a no-limit poker game, watching the jewel-precious cards turn up. It was like playing the exchange with all the world at stake during a stock crash. It was nerve-racking, dazzling, exhausting, fascinating, terrible, mind-destroying, stupendous. It was—

It was like nothing else on the face of the earth.

New names kept flashing on to the twenty-six squares; and men would shout like insane beings and some fainted, and the uproar was absolutely shattering; the pandemonium raged on, one continuous, unbelievable sound.

And every few minutes a great sign would flash along the board, telling everyone:

"WATCH YOUR OWN INITIALS."

Fara watched, trembling in every limb. Each second it seemed to him that he couldn't stand it an instant longer. He wanted to scream at the room to be silent; he wanted to jump up to pace the floor, but others who did that were yelled at hysterically, threatened wildly, hated with a mad, murderous ferocity.

Abruptly, the blind savagery of it scared Fara. He thought unsteadily: "I'm not going to make a fool of myself. I—"

"Clark, Fara—" winked the board: "Clark, Fara—"

With a shout that nearly tore off the top of his head, Fara leaped to his feet. "That's me!" he shrieked. "Me!"

No one turned; no one paid the slightest attention. Shamed, he slunk across the room where an endless line of men kept crowding into a corridor beyond.

The silence in the long corridor was almost as shattering as the mind-destroying noise it replaced. It was hard to concentrate on the idea of a number—474.

It was completely impossible to imagine what could lie beyond—474.

The room was small. It was furnished with a small, business-type table and two chairs. On the table were seven neat piles of folders, each pile of different color. The piles were arranged in a row in front of a large, milky-white globe, that began to glow with a soft light. Out of its depths, a man's baritone voice said:

"Fara Clark?"

"Yes," said Fara.

"Before the verdict is rendered in your case," the voice went on quietly, "I want you to take a folder from the blue pile. The list will show the Fifth Interplanetary Bank in its proper relation to yourself and the world, and it will be explained to you in due course."

The list, Fara saw, was simply that, a list of the names of companies. The names ran from A to Z, and there were about five hundred of them. The folder carried no explanation; and Fara slipped it automatically into his side pocket, as the voice came again from the shining globe:

"It has been established," the words came precisely, "that the Fifth Interplanetary Bank perpetrated upon you a gross swindle, and that it is further guilty of practicing scavengery, deception, blackmail and was accessory in a criminal conspiracy.

"The bank made contact with your son, Cayle, through what is quite properly known as a scavenger, that is, an employee who exists by finding young men and women who are normally capable of drawing drafts on their parents or other victims. The scavenger obtains for this service a commission of eight percent, which is always paid by the person making the loan, in this case your son.

"The bank practiced deception in that its authorized agents deceived you in the most culpable fashion by pretending that it had already paid out the ten thousand credits to your son, whereas the money was not paid over until your signature had been obtained.

"The blackmail guilt arises out of a threat to have your son arrested for falsely obtaining a loan, a threat made at a time when no money had exchanged hands. The conspiracy consists of the action whereby your note was promptly turned over to your competitor.

"The bank is accordingly triple-fined, thirty-six thousand three hundred credits. It is not in our interest, Fara Clark, for you to know how this money is obtained. Suffice to know that the bank pays it, and that of the fine the weapon shops allocate to their own treasury a total of one half. The other half—"

There was a *plop;* a neatly packaged pile of bills fell onto the table. "For you," said the voice; and Fara, with trembling fingers, slipped the package into his coat pocket. It required the purest mental and physical effort for him to concentrate on the next words that came:

"You must not assume that your troubles are over. The re-establishment of your motor repair shop in Glay will require force and courage. Be discreet, brave and determined, and you cannot fail. Do not hesitate to use the gun you have purchased in defense of your rights. The plan will be explained to you. And now, proceed through the door facing you—"

Fara braced himself with an effort, opened the door and walked through.

It was a dim, familiar room that he stepped into, and there was a silver-haired, fine-faced man who rose from a reading chair, and came forward in the dimness, smiling gravely.

The stupendous, fantastic, exhilarating adventure was over; and he was back in the weapon shop of Glay.

He couldn't get over the wonder of it—this great and fascinating organization established here in the very heart of a ruthless civilization, a civilization that had in a few brief weeks stripped him of everything he possessed.

With a deliberate will, he stopped that glowing flow of thought. A dark frown wrinkled his solidly built face; he said:

"The . . . judge—" Fara hesitated over the name. frowned again, annoyed at himself, then went on: "The judge said that, to re-establish myself I would have to—"

"Before we go into that," said the old man quietly, "I want you to examine the blue folder you brought with you."

"Folder?" Fara echoed blankly. It took a long moment to remember that he had picked up a folder from the table in Room 474.

He studied the list of names with a gathering puzzlement, noting that the name of Automatic Atomic Motor Repair Shops was well down among the A's, and the Fifth Interplanetary Bank only one of several great banks included. Fara looked up finally:

"I don't understand," he said; "are these the companies you have had to act against?"

The silver-haired man smiled grimly, shook his head. "That is not what I mean. These firms constitute only a fraction of the eight hundred thousand companies that are constantly in our books."

He smiled again, humorlessly: "These companies all know that, because of us, their profits on paper bear no relation to their assets. What they don't know is how great the difference really is; and, as we want a general improvement in business morals, not merely more skillful scheming to outwit us, we prefer them to remain in ignorance."

He paused, and this time he gave Fara a searching

glance, said at last: "The unique feature of the companies on this particular list is that they are every one wholly owned by Empress Isher."

He finished swiftly: "In view of your past opinions on that subject, I do not expect you to believe me."

Fara stood as still as death, for—he did believe with unquestioning conviction, completely, finally. The amazing, the unforgivable thing was that all his life he had watched the march of ruined men into the oblivion of poverty and disgrace—and blamed *them*.

Fara groaned. "I've been like a madman," he said. "Everything the empress and her officials did was right. No friendship, no personal relationship could survive with me that did not include belief in things as they were. I suppose if I started to talk against the empress I would receive equally short shrift."

"Under no circumstances," said the old man grimly, "must you say anything against her majesty. The weapon shops will not countenance any such words, and will give no further aid to anyone who is so indiscreet. The reason is that, for the moment, we have reached an uneasy state of peace with the Imperial government. We wish to keep it that way; beyond that I will not enlarge on our policy.

"I am permitted to say that the last great attempt to destroy the weapon shops was made seven years ago, when the glorious Innelda Isher was twenty-five years old. That was a secret attempt, based on a new invention; and failed by purest accident because of our sacrifice of a man from seven thousand years in the past. That may sound mysterious to you, but I will not explain.

"The worst period was reached some forty years ago when every person who was discovered receiving aid from us was murdered in some fashion. You may be surprised to know that your father-in-law was among those assassinated at that time."

"Creel's father!" Fara gasped. "But—"

He stopped. His brain was reeling; there was such a rush of blood to his head that for an instant he could hardly see.

"But," he managed at last, "it was reported that he ran away with another woman."

"They also spread a vicious story of some kind," the old man said; and Fara was silent, stunned.

The other went on: "We finally put a stop to their murders by killing the three men from the top down, *excluding* the royal family, who gave the order for the particular execution involved. But we do not again want that kind of bloody murder.

"Nor are we interested in any criticism of our toleration of so much that is evil. It is important to understand that *we do not interfere in the main stream of human existence.* We right wrongs; we act as a barrier between the people and their more ruthless exploiters. Generally speaking, we help only honest men; that is not to say that we do not give assistance to the less scrupulous, but only to the extent of selling them guns—which is a very great aid indeed, and which is one of the reasons why the government is relying almost exclusively for its power on an economic chicanery.

"In the four thousand years since the brilliant genius Walter S. DeLany invented the vibration process that made the weapon shops possible, and laid down the first principles of weapon shop political philosophy, we have watched the tide of government swing backward and forward between democracy under a limited monarchy to complete tyranny. And we have discovered one thing:

"People always have the kind of government they want. When they want change, they must change it. As always we shall remain an incorruptible core—and I mean that literally; we have a psychological machine that never lies about a man's character—I repeat, an incorruptible core of human idealism, devoted to relieving the ills that arise inevitably under any form of government.

"But now—your problem. It is very simple, really. You must fight, as all men have fought since the beginning of time for what they valued, for their just rights. As you know, the Automatic Repair people removed all your machinery and tools within an hour of foreclosing on your shop. This material was taken to Ferd, and then shipped to a great warehouse on the coast.

"We recovered it, and with our special means of transportation have now replaced the machines in your shop. You will accordingly go there and—"

Fara listened with a gathering grimness to the instructions, nodded finally, his jaw clamped tight.

"You can count on me," he said curtly. "I've been a stubborn man in my time; and though I've changed sides, I haven't changed *that*."

Going outside was like returning from life to—death; from hope to—reality.

Fara walked along the quiet streets of Glay at darkest night. For the first time it struck him that the weapon shop Information Center must be halfway around the world, for it had been day, brilliant day.

The picture vanished as if it had never existed, and he grew aware again, preternaturally aware of the village of Glay asleep all around him. Silent, peaceful—yet ugly, he thought, ugly with the ugliness of evil enthroned.

He thought: The right to buy weapons—and his heart swelled into his throat; the tears came to his eyes.

He wiped his vision with the back of his hand, thought of Creel's long dead father, and strode on, without shame. Tears were good for an angry man.

The shop was the same, but the hard metal padlock yielded before the tiny, blazing, supernal power of the revolver. One flick of fire; the metal dissolved—and he was inside.

It was dark, too dark to see, but Fara did not turn on the lights immediately. He fumbled across to the window control, turned the windows to darkness vibration, and then clicked on the lights.

He gulped with awful relief. For the machines, his precious tools that he had seen carted away within hours after the bailiff's arrival, were here again, ready for use.

Shaky from the pressure of his emotion, Fara called Creel on the telestat. It took a little while for her to appear; and she was in her dressing robe. When she saw who it was she turned a dead white.

"Fara, oh, Fara, I thought—"

He cut her off grimly: "Creel, I've been to the weapon shop. I want you to do this: go straight to your mother. I'm here at my shop. I'm going to stay here day and night until it's settled that I *stay*. . . . I shall go home later for some food and clothing, but I want you to be gone by then. Is that clear?"

Color was coming back into her lean, handsome face. She said: "Don't you bother coming home, Fara. I'll do everything necessary. I'll pack all that's needed into the carplane, including a folding bed. We'll sleep in the back room of the shop."

Morning came palely, but it was ten o'clock before a shadow darkened the open door; and Constable Jor came in. He looked shame-faced:

"I've got an order here for your arrest," he said.

"Tell those who sent you," Fara replied deliberately, "that I resisted arrest—with a gun."

The deed followed the words with such rapidity that Jor blinked. He stood like that for a moment, a big, sleepy-looking man, staring at that gleaming, magical revolver; then:

"I have a summons here ordering you to appear at the great court of Ferd this afternoon. Will you accept it?"

"Certainly."

"Then you will be there?"

"I'll send my lawyer," said Fara. "Just drop the summons on the floor there. Tell them I took it."

The weapon shop man had said: "Do not ridicule by word any legal measure of the Imperial authorities. Simply disobey them."

Jor went out, and seemed relieved. It took an hour before Mayor Mel Dale came pompously through the door.

"See here, Fara Clark," he bellowed from the doorway. "You can't get away with this. This is defiance of the law."

Fara was silent as His Honor waddled farther into the building. It was puzzling, almost amazing, that Mayor Dale would risk his plump, treasured body. Puzzlement ended as the mayor said in a low voice:

"Good work, Fara; I knew you had it in you. There's dozens of us in Glay behind you, so stick it out. I had to yell at you just now, because there's a crowd outside. Yell back at me, will you? Let's have a real name calling. But, first, a word of warning: the manager of the Automatic Repair Shop is on his way here with his bodyguards, two of them—"

Shakily, Fara watched the mayor go out. The crisis was at hand. He braced himself, thought: "Let them come, let them—"

It was easier than he had thought—for the men who entered the shop turned pale when they saw the holstered revolver. There was a violence of blustering, nevertheless, that narrowed finally down to:

"Look here," the man said, "we've got your note for twelve thousand one hundred credits. You're not going to deny you owe that money."

"I'll buy it back," said Fara in a stony voice, "for exactly half, not a cent more."

The strong-jawed young man looked at him for a long time. "We'll take it," he said finally, curtly.

Fara said: "I've got the agreement here—"

His first customer was old man Miser Lan Harris. Fara stared at the long-faced oldster with a vast surmise, and his first amazed comprehension came of how the weapon shop must have settled on Harris' lot—by agreement.

It was an hour after Harris had gone that Creel's mother stamped into the shop. She closed the door.

"Well," she said, "you did it, eh? Good work. I'm sorry if I seemed rough with you when you came to my place, but we weapon-shop supporters can't afford to take risks for those who are not on our side.

"But never mind that. I've come to take Creel home. The important thing is to return everything to normal as quickly as possible."

It was over; incredibly it was over. Twice, as he walked home that night, Fara stopped in midstride, and wondered if it had not all been a dream. The air was like wine. The little world of Glay spread before him, green and gracious, a peaceful paradise where time had stood still.

MIMSY WERE THE BOROGOVES

by Lewis Padgett

There's no use trying to describe either Unthahorsten or
his surroundings, because, for one thing, a good many million years had passed since 1942 Anno Domini, and, for
another, Unthahorsten wasn't on Earth, technically speaking. He was doing the equivalent of standing in the equivalent of a laboratory. He was preparing to test his time
machine.

Having turned on the power, Unthahorsten suddenly
realized that the Box was empty. Which wouldn't do at all.
The device needed a control, a three-dimensional solid
which would react to the conditions of another age. Otherwise Unthahorsten couldn't tell, on the machine's return,
where and when it had been. Whereas a solid in the Box
would automatically be subject to the entropy and cosmic
ray bombardment of the other era, and Unthahorsten could
measure the changes, both qualitative and quantitative,
when the machine returned. The Calculators could then get
to work and, presently, tell Unthahorsten that the Box had
briefly visited 1,000,000 A.D., 1,000 A.D., or 1 A.D., as
the case might be.

Not that it mattered, except to Unthahorsten. But he
was childish in many respects.

There was little time to waste. The Box was beginning to
glow and shiver. Unthahorsten stared around wildly, fled
into the next gossatch, and groped in a storage bin there.
He came up with an armful of peculiar-looking stuff. Uh-
huh. Some of the discarded toys of his son Snowen, which

*First published in 1943 ("Lewis Padgett" was a pseudonym
employed by Henry Kuttner and his wife, C. L. Moore)*

the boy had brought with him when he had passed over from Earth, after mastering the necessary technique. Well, Snowen needed this junk no longer. He was conditioned, and had put away childish things. Besides, though Unthahorsten's wife kept the toys for sentimental reasons, the experiment was more important.

Unthahorsten left the glossatch and dumped the assortment into the Box, slamming the cover shut just before the warning signal flashed. The Box went away. The manner of its departure hurt Unthahorsten's eyes.

He waited.
And he waited.

Eventually he gave up and built another time machine, with identical results. Snowen hadn't been annoyed by the loss of his old toys, nor had Snowen's mother, so Unthahorsten cleaned out the bin and dumped the remainder of his son's childhood relics in the second time machine's Box.

According to his calculations, this one should have appeared on Earth, in the latter part of the nineteenth century, A.D. If that actually occurred, the device remained there.

Disgusted, Unthahorsten decided to make no more time machines. But the mischief had been done. There were two of them, and the first—

Scott Paradine found it while he was playing hooky from the Glendale Grammar School. There was a geography test that day, and Scott saw no sense in memorizing place names—which in 1942 was a fairly sensible theory. Besides, it was the sort of warm spring day, with a touch of coolness in the breeze, which invited a boy to lie down in a field and stare at the occasional clouds till he fell asleep. Nuts to geography! Scott dozed.

About noon he got hungry, so his stocky legs carried him to a nearby store. There he invested his small hoard with penurious care and a sublime disregard for his gastric juices. He went down by the creek to feed.

Having finished his supply of cheese, chocolate, and cookies, and having drained the soda-pop bottle to its dregs, Scott caught tadpoles and studied them with a certain amount of scientific curiosity. He did not persevere. Something tumbled down the bank and thudded into the muddy ground near the water, so Scott, with a wary glance around, hurried to investigate.

It was a box. It was, in fact, the Box. The gadgetry hitched to it meant little to Scott, though he wondered why it was so fused and burnt. He pondered. With his jackknife he pried and probed, his tongue sticking out from a corner of his mouth—Hm-m-m. Nobody was around. Where had the box come from? Somebody must have left it here, and sliding soil had dislodged it from its precarious perch.

"That's a helix," Scott decided, quite erroneously. It was helical, but it wasn't a helix, because of the dimensional warp involved. Had the thing been a model airplane, no matter how complicated, it would have held few mysteries to Scott. As it was, a problem was posed. Something told Scott that the device was a lot more complicated than the spring motor he had deftly dismantled last Friday.

But no boy has ever left a box unopened, unless forcibly dragged away. Scott probed deeper. The angles on this thing were funny. Short circuit, probably. That was why— *uh!* The knife slipped. Scott sucked his thumb and gave vent to experienced blasphemy.

Maybe it was a music box.

Scott shouldn't have felt depressed. The gadgetry would have given Finstein a headache and driven Steinmetz raving mad. The trouble was, of course, that the box had not yet completely entered the space-time continuum where Scott existed, and therefore it could not be opened. At any rate, not till Scott used a convenient rock to hammer the helical nonhelix into a more convenient position.

He hammered it, in fact, from its contact point with the fourth dimension, releasing the space-time torsion it had been maintaining. There was a brittle snap. The box jarred slightly, and lay motionless, no longer only partially in existence. Scott opened it easily now.

The soft, woven helmet was the first thing that caught his eye, but he discarded that without much interest. It was just a cap. Next he lifted a square, transparent crystal block, small enough to cup in his palm—much too small to contain the maze of apparatus within it. In a moment Scott had solved that problem. The crystal was a sort of magnifying glass, vastly enlarging the things inside the block. Strange things they were, too. Miniature people, for example—

They moved. Like clockwork automatons, though much more smoothly. It was rather like watching a play. Scott was interested in their costumes, but fascinated by their actions. The tiny people were deftly building a house. Scott wished it would catch fire, so he could see the people put it out.

Flames licked up from the half-completed structure. The automatons, with a great deal of odd apparatus, extinguished the blaze.

It didn't take Scott long to catch on. But he was a little worried. The manikins would obey his thoughts. By the time he discovered that, he was frightened, and threw the cube from him.

Halfway up the bank, he reconsidered and returned. The crystal block lay partly in the water, shining in the sun. It was a toy; Scott sensed that, with the unerring instinct of a child. But he didn't pick it up immediately. Instead, he returned to the box and investigated its remaining contents.

He found some really remarkable gadgets. The afternoon passed all too quickly. Scott finally put the toys back in the box and lugged it home, grunting and puffing. He was quite red-faced by the time he arrived at the kitchen door.

His find he hid at the back of the closet in his own room upstairs. The crystal cube he slipped into his pocket, which already bulged with string, a coil of wire, two pennies, a wad of tinfoil, a grimy defense stamp, and a chunk of feldspar. Emma, Scott's two-year-old sister, waddled unsteadily in from the hall and said hello.

"Hello, Slug," Scott nodded, from his altitude of seven years and some months. He patronized Emma shockingly, but she didn't know the difference. Small, plump, and wide-eyed, she flopped down on the carpet and stared dolefully at her shoes.

"Tie 'em, Scotty, please?"

"Sap," Scott told her kindly, but knotted the laces. "Dinner ready yet?"

Emma nodded.

"Let's see your hands." For a wonder they were reasonably clean, though probably not aseptic. Scott regarded his own paws thoughtfully and, grimacing, went to the

bathroom, where he made a sketchy toilet. The tadpoles
had left their traces.

Dennis Paradine and his wife Jane were having a cock-
tail before dinner, downstairs in the living room. He was
a youngish, middle-aged man with gray-shot hair and a
thinnish, prim-mouthed face; he taught philosophy at the
university. Jane was small, neat, dark, and very pretty. She
sipped her Martini and said:

"New shoes. Like 'em?"

"Here's to crime," Paradine muttered absently. "Huh?
Shoes? Not now. Wait till I've finished this. I had a bad
day."

"Exams?"

"Yeah. Flaming youth aspiring toward manhood. I hope
they die. In considerable agony. *Insh' Allah!*"

"I want the olive," Jane requested.

"I know," Paradine said despondently. "It's been years
since I've tasted one myself. In a Martini, I mean. Even if
I put six of 'em in your glass, you're still not satisfied."

"I want yours. Blood brotherhood. Symbolism. That's
why."

Paradine regarded his wife balefully and crossed his
long legs. "You sound like one of my students."

"Like that hussy Betty Dawson, perhaps?" Jane un-
sheathed her nails. "Does she still leer at you in that of-
fensive way?"

"She does. The child is a neat psychological problem.
Luckily she isn't mine. If she were—" Paradine nodded
significantly. "Sex consciousness and too many movies. I
suppose she still thinks she can get a passing grade by
showing me her knees. Which are, by the way, rather
bony."

Jane adjusted her skirt with an air of complacent pride.
Paradine uncoiled himself and poured fresh Martinis.
"Candidly, I don't see the point of teaching those apes
philosophy. They're all at the wrong age. Their habit-
patterns, their methods of thinking, are already laid down.
They're horribly conservative, not that they'd admit it. The
only people who can understand philosophy are mature
adults or kids like Emma and Scotty."

"Well, don't enroll Scotty in your course," Jane requested. "He isn't ready to be a *Philosophiae Doctor*. I hold no brief for child geniuses, especially when it's my son."

"Scotty would probably be better at it than Betty Dawson," Paradine grunted.

" 'He died an enfeebled old dotard at five,' " Jane quoted dreamily. "I want your olive."

"Here. By the way, I like the shoes."

"Thank you. Here's Rosalie. Dinner?"

"It's all ready, Miz Pa'dine," said Rosalie, hovering. "I'll call Miss Emma 'n' Mista' Scotty."

"I'll get 'em." Paradine put his head into the next room and roared, "Kids! Come and get it!"

Small feet scuttered down the stairs. Scott dashed into view, scrubbed and shining, a rebellious cowlick aimed at the zenith. Emma pursued, levering herself carefully down the steps. Halfway she gave up the attempt to descend upright and reversed, finishing the task monkey-fashion, her small behind giving an impression of marvelous diligence upon the work in hand. Paradine watched, fascinated by the spectacle, till he was hurled back by the impact of his son's body.

"Hi, dad!" Scott shrieked.

Paradine recovered himself and regarded Scott with dignity. "Hi, yourself. Help me in to dinner. You've dislocated at least one of my hip joints."

But Scott was already tearing into the next room, where he stepped on Jane's new shoes in an ecstasy of affection, burbled an apology, and rushed off to find his place at the dinner table. Paradine cocked up an eyebrow as he followed, Emma's pudgy hand desperately gripping his forefinger.

"Wonder what the young devil's been up to?"

"No good, probably," Jane sighed. "Hello, darling. Let's see your ears."

"They're *clean*. Mickey licked 'em."

"Well, that Airedale's tongue is far cleaner than your ears," Jane pondered, making a brief examination. "Still, as long as you can hear, the dirt's only superficial."

"Fisshul?"

"Just a little, that means." Jane dragged her daughter to the table and inserted her legs into a high chair. Only lately had Emma graduated to the dignity of dining with the rest of the family, and she was, as Paradine remarked, all eat up with pride by the prospect. Only babies spilled food, Emma had been told. As a result, she took such painstaking care in conveying her spoon to her mouth that Paradine got the jitters whenever he watched.

"A conveyer belt would be the thing for Emma," he suggested, pulling out a chair for Jane. "Small buckets of spinach arriving at her face at stated intervals."

Dinner proceeded uneventfully until Paradine happened to glance at Scott's plate. "Hello, there. Sick? Been stuffing yourself at lunch?"

Scott thoughtfully examined the food still left before him. "I've had all I need, dad," he explained.

"You usually eat all you can hold, and a great deal more," Paradine said. "I know growing boys need several tons of foodstuff a day, but you're below par tonight. Feel O.K.?"

"Uh-huh. Honest, I've had all I need."

"All you *want?*"

"Sure. I eat different."

"Something they taught you at school?" Jane inquired. Scott shook his head solemnly.

"Nobody taught me. I found it out myself. I used spit."

"Try again," Paradine suggested. "It's the wrong word."

"Uh . . . s-saliva. Hm-m-m?"

"Uh-huh. More pepsin? Is there pepsin in the salivary juices, Jane? I forget."

"There's poison in mine," Jane remarked. "Rosalie's left lumps in the mashed potatoes again."

But Paradine was interested. "You mean you're getting everything possible out of your food—no wastage—and eating less?"

Scott thought that over. "I guess so. It's not just the sp . . . saliva. I sort of measure how much to put in my mouth at once, and what stuff to mix up. I dunno. I just do it."

"Hm-m-m," said Paradine, making a note to check up later. "Rather a revolutionary idea." Kids often get screwy notions, but this one might not be so far off the beam. He pursed his lips. "Eventually I suppose people will eat quite differently—I mean the *way* they eat, as well as what.

What they eat, I mean. Jane, our son shows signs of becoming a genius."

"Oh?"

"It's a rather good point in dietetics he just made. Did
you figure it out yourself, Scott?"

"Sure," the boy said, and really believed it.

"Where'd you get the idea?"

"Oh, I—" Scott wriggled. "I dunno. It doesn't mean
much, I guess."

Paradine was unreasonably disappointed. "But surely—"

"S-s-s-spit!" Emma shrieked, overcome by a sudden fit
of badness. *"Spit!"* she attempted to demonstrate, but
succeeded only in dribbling into her bib.

With a resigned air Jane rescued and reproved her
daughter, while Paradine eyed Scott with rather puzzled
interest. But it was not till after dinner, in the living room,
that anything further happened.

"Any homework?"

"N-no," Scott said, flushing guiltily. To cover his embarrassment he took from his pocket a gadget he had
found in the box, and began to unfold it. The result resembled a tesseract, strung with beads. Paradine didn't see
it at first, but Emma did. She wanted to play with it.

"No. Lay off, Slug," Scott ordered. "You can watch
me." He fumbled with the beads, making soft, interesting
noises. Emma extended a fat forefinger and yelped.

"Scotty," Paradine said warningly.

"I didn't hurt her."

"Bit me. It did," Emma mourned.

Paradine looked up. He frowned, staring. What in—

"Is that an abacus?" he asked. "Let's see it, please."

Somewhat unwillingly Scott brought the gadget across to
his father's chair. Paradine blinked. The "abacus," unfolded, was more than a foot square, composed of thin,
rigid wires that interlocked here and there. On the wires
colored beads were strung. They could be slid back and
forth, and from one support to another, even at the points
of juncture. But—a pierced bead couldn't cross *inter-
locking* wires—

So, apparently, they weren't pierced. Paradine looked
closer. Each small bead had a deep groove running around
it, so that it could be revolved and slid along the wire at

the same time. Paradine tried to pull one free. It clung as though magnetically. Iron? It looked more like plastic.

The framework itself—Paradine wasn't a mathematician. But the angles formed by the wires were vaguely shocking, in their ridiculous lack of Euclidean logic. They were a maze. Perhaps that's what the gadget was—a puzzle.

"Where'd you get this?"

"Uncle Harry gave it to me," Scott said on the spur of the moment. "Last Sunday, when he came over." Uncle Harry was out of town, a circumstance Scott well knew. At the age of seven, a boy soon learns that the vagaries of adults follow a certain definite pattern, and that they are fussy about the donors of gifts. Moreover, Uncle Harry would not return for several weeks; the expiration of that period was unimaginable to Scott, or, at least, the fact that his lie would ultimately be discovered meant less to him than the advantages of being allowed to keep the toy.

Paradine found himself growing slightly confused as he attempted to manipulate the beads. The angles were vaguely illogical. It was like a puzzle. This red bead, if slid along *this* wire to *that* junction, should reach *there*—but it didn't. A maze, odd, but no doubt instructive. Paradine had a well-founded feeling that he'd have no patience with the thing himself.

Scott did, however, retiring to a corner and sliding beads around with much fumbling and grunting. The beads *did* sting, when Scott chose the wrong ones or tried to slide them in the wrong direction. At last he crowed exultantly.

"I did it, dad!"

"Eh? What? Let's see." The device looked exactly the same to Paradine, but Scott pointed and beamed.

"I made it disappear."

"It's still there."

"That blue bead. It's gone now."

Paradine didn't believe that, so he merely snorted. Scott puzzled over the framework again. He experimented. This time there were no shocks, even slight. The abacus had showed him the correct method. Now it was up to him to do it on his own. The bizarre angles of the wires seemed a little less confusing now, somehow.

It was a most instructive toy—

It worked, Scott thought, rather like the crystal cube. Reminded of the gadget, he took it from his pocket and relinquished the abacus to Emma, who was struck dumb with joy. She fell to work sliding the beads, this time without protesting against the shocks—which, indeed, were very minor—and, being imitative, she managed to make a bead disappear almost as quickly as had Scott. The blue bead reappeared—but Scott didn't notice. He had forethoughtfully retired into an angle of the chesterfield with an overstuffed chair and amused himself with the cube.

There were little people inside the thing, tiny manikins which enlarged by the magnifying properties of the crystal, and they moved, all right. They built a house. It caught fire, with realistic-seeming flames, and stood by waiting. Scott puffed urgently. "Put it *out!*"

But nothing happened. Where was that queer fire engine, with revolving arms, that had appeared before? Here it was. It came sailing into the picture and stopped. Scott urged it on.

This was fun. Like putting on a play, only more real. The little people did what Scott told them, inside of his head. If he made a mistake, they waited till he'd found the right way. They even posed new problems for him—

The cube, too, was a most instructive toy. It was teaching Scott, with alarming rapidity—and teaching him very entertainingly. But it gave him no really new knowledge as yet. He wasn't ready. Later—later—

Emma grew tired of the abacus and went in search of Scott. She couldn't find him, even in his room, but once there the contents of the closet intrigued her. She discovered the box. It contained treasure-trove—a doll, which Scott had already noticed but discarded with a sneer. Squealing, Emma brought the doll downstairs, squatted in the middle of the floor, and began to take it apart.

"Darling! What's that?"

"Mr. Bear!"

Obviously it wasn't Mr. Bear, who was blind, earless, but comforting in his soft fatness. But all dolls were named Mr. Bear to Emma.

Jane Paradine hesitated. "Did you take that from some other little girl?"

"I didn't. She's mine."

Scott came out from his hiding place, thrusting the cube into his pocket. "Uh—that's from Uncle Harry."

"Did Uncle Harry give that to you, Emma?"

"He gave it to me for Emma," Scott put in hastily, adding another stone to his foundation of deceit. "Last Sunday."

"You'll break it, dear."

Emma brought the doll to her mother. "She comes apart. See?"

"Oh? It . . . *ugh!*" Jane sucked in her breath. Paradine looked up quickly.

"What's up?"

She brought the doll over to him, hesitated, and then went into the dining room, giving Paradine a significant glance. He followed, closing the door. Jane had already placed the doll on the cleared table.

"This isn't very nice, is it Denny?"

"Hm-m-m." It was rather unpleasant, at first glance. One might have expected an anatomical dummy in a medical school, but a child's doll—

The thing came apart in sections, skin, muscles, organs, miniature but quite perfect, as far as Paradine could see. He was interested. "Dunno. Such things haven't the same connotations to a kid—"

"Look at that liver. Is it a liver?"

"Sure. Say I . . . this is funny."

"What?"

"It isn't anatomically perfect, after all." Paradine pulled up a chair. "The digestive tract's too short. No large intestine. No appendix, either."

"Should Emma have a thing like this?"

"I wouldn't mind having it myself," Paradine said. "Where on earth did Harry pick it up? No, I don't see any harm in it. Adults are conditioned to react unpleasantly to innards. Kids don't. They figure they're solid inside, like a potato. Emma can get a sound working knowledge of physiology from this doll."

"But what are those? Nerves?"

"No, these are the nerves. Arteries here; veins here. Funny sort of aorta—" Paradine looked baffled. "That . . . what's Latin for network? Anyway . . . huh? *Rita? Rata?*"

"*Rales*," Jane suggested at random.

"That's a sort of breathing," Paradine said crushingly. "I can't figure out what this luminous network of stuff is. It goes all through the body, like nerves."

"Blood."

"Nope. Not circulatory, not neural—funny! It seems to to be hooked up with the lungs."

They became engrossed, puzzling over the strange doll. It was made with remarkable perfection of detail, and that in itself was strange, in view of the physiological variation from the norm. "Wait'll I get that Gould," Paradine said, and presently was comparing the doll with anatomical charts. He learned little, except to increase his bafflement.

But it was more fun than a jigsaw puzzle.

Meanwhile, in the adjoining room, Emma was sliding the beads to and fro in the abacus. The motions didn't seem so strange now. Even when the beads vanished. She could almost follow that new direction—almost—

Scott panted, staring into the crystal cube and mentally directing, with many false starts, the building of a structure somewhat more complicated than the one which had been destroyed by fire. He, too, was learning—being conditioned—

Paradine's mistake, from a completely anthropomorphic standpoint, was that he didn't get rid of the toys instantly. He did not realize their significance, and, by the time he did, the progression of circumstances had got well under way. Uncle Harry remained out of town, so Paradine couldn't check with him. Too, the midterm exams were on, which meant arduous mental effort and complete exhaustion at night; and Jane was slightly ill for a week or so. Emma and Scott had free rein with the toys.

"What," Scott asked his father one evening, "is a wabe, dad?"

"Wave?"

He hesitated. "I . . . don't *think* so. Isn't wabe right?"

"Wab is Scot for web. That it?"

"I don't see how," Scott muttered, and wandered off, scowling, to amuse himself with the abacus. He was able to handle it quite deftly now. But, with the instinct of

children for avoiding interruptions, he and Emma usually
played with the toys in private. Not obviously, of course—
but the more intricate experiments were never performed
under the eye of an adult.

Scott was learning fast. What he now saw in the crystal
cube had little relationship to the original simple problems.
But they were fascinatingly technical. Had Scott realized
that his education was being guided and supervised—
though merely mechanically—he would probably have lost
interest. As it was, his initiative was never quashed.

Abacus, cube, doll—and other toys the children found
in the box—

Neither Paradine nor Jane guessed how much of an
effect the contents of the time machine were having on the
kids. How could they? Youngsters are instinctive drama-
tists, for purposes of self-protection. They have not yet
fitted themselves to the exigencies—to them partially inexplicable—of a mature world. Moreover, their lives are
complicated by human variables. They are told by one
person that playing in the mud is permissible, but that,
in their excavations, they must not uproot flowers or small
trees. Another adult vetoes mud *per se*. The Ten Com-
mandments are not carved on stone; they vary, and children are helplessly dependent on the caprice of those
who give them birth and feed and clothe them. And
tyrannize. The young animal does not resent that benevo-
lent tyranny, for it is an essential part of nature. He is,
however, an individualist, and maintains his integrity by
a subtle, passive fight.

Under the eyes of an adult he changes. Like an actor
on-stage, when he remembers, he strives to please, and also
to attract attention to himself. Such attempts are not unknown to maturity. But adults are less obvious—to other
adults.

It is difficult to admit that children lack subtlety. Children are different from the mature animal because they
think in another way. We can more or less easily pierce
the pretenses they set up—but they can do the same to us.
Ruthlessly a child can destroy the pretenses of an adult.
Iconoclasm is their prerogative.

Foppishness, for example. The amenities of social intercourse, exaggerated not quite to absurdity. The gigolo—

"Such *savoir faire!* Such punctilious courtesy!" The dowager and the blond young thing are often impressed. Men have less pleasant comments to make. But the child goes to the root of the matter.

"You're *silly!*"

How can an immature human understand the complicated system of social relationships? He can't. To him, an exaggeration of natural courtesy is silly. In his functional structure of life-patterns, it is rococo. He is an egotistic little animal, who cannot visualize himself in the position of another—certainly not an adult. A self-contained, almost perfect natural unit, his wants supplied by others, the child is much like a unicellular creature floating in the blood stream, nutriment carried to him, waste products carried away—

From the standpoint of logic, a child is rather horribly perfect. A baby may be even more perfect, but so alien to an adult that only superficial standards of comparison apply. The thought processes of an infant are completely unimaginable. But babies think, even before birth. In the womb they move and sleep, not entirely through instinct. We are conditioned to react rather peculiarly to the idea that a nearly-viable embryo may think. We are surprised, shocked into laughter, and repelled. Nothing human is alien.

But a baby is not human. An embryo is far less human.

That, perhaps, was why Emma learned more from the toys than did Scott. He could communicate his thoughts, of course; Emma could not, except in cryptic fragments. The matter of the scrawls, for example—

Give a young child pencil and paper, and he will draw something which looks different to him than to an adult. The absurd scribbles have little resemblance to a fire engine, to a baby. Perhaps it is even three-dimensional. Babies think differently and see differently.

Paradine brooded over that, reading his paper one evening and watching Emma and Scott communicate. Scott was questioning his sister. Sometimes he did it in English. More often he had resource to gibberish and sign language. Emma tried to reply, but the handicap was too great.

Finally Scott got pencil and paper. Emma liked that.

Tongue in cheek, she laboriously wrote a message. Scott took the paper, examined it, and scowled.

"That isn't right, Emma," he said.

Emma nodded vigorously. She seized the pencil again and made more scrawls. Scott puzzled for a while, finally smiled rather hesitantly, and got up. He vanished into the hall. Emma returned to the abacus.

Paradine rose and glanced down at the paper, with some mad thought that Emma might abruptly have mastered calligraphy. But she hadn't. The paper was covered with meaningless scrawls, of a type familiar to any parent. Paradine pursed his lips.

It might be a graph showing the mental variations of a manic-depressive cockroach, but probably wasn't. Still, it no doubt had meaning to Emma. Perhaps the scribble represented Mr. Bear.

Scott returned, looking pleased. He met Emma's gaze and nodded. Paradine felt a twinge of curiosity.

"Secrets?"

"Nope. Emma . . . uh . . . asked me to do something for her."

"Oh." Paradine, recalling instances of babies who had babbled in unknown tongues and baffled linguists, made a note to pocket the paper when the kids had finished with it. The next day he showed the scrawl to Elkins at the university. Elkins had a sound working knowledge of many unlikely languages, but he chuckled over Emma's venture into literature.

"Here's a free translation, Dennis. Quote. I don't know what this means, but I kid the hell out of my father with it. Unquote."

The two men laughed and went off to their classes. But later Paradine was to remember the incident. Especially after he met Holloway. Before that, however, months were to pass, and the situation to develop even further toward its climax.

Perhaps Paradine and Jane had evinced too much interest in the toys. Emma and Scott took to keeping them hidden, playing with them only in private. They never did it overtly, but with a certain unobtrusive caution. Nevertheless, Jane especially was somewhat troubled.

She spoke to Paradine about it one evening. "That doll Harry gave Emma."

"Yeah?"

"I was downtown today and tried to find out where it came from. No soap."

"Maybe Harry bought it in New York."

Jane was unconvinced. "I asked them about the other things, too. They showed me their stock—Johnson's a big store, you know. But there's nothing like Emma's abacus."

"Hm-m-m." Paradine wasn't much interested. They had tickets for a show that night, and it was getting late. So the subject was dropped for the nonce.

Later it cropped up again, when a neighbor telephoned Jane.

"Scotty's never been like that, Denny. Mrs. Burns said he frightened the devil out of her Francis."

"Francis? A little fat bully of a punk, isn't he? Like his father. I broke Burns' nose for him once, when we were sophomores."

"Stop boasting and listen," Jane said, mixing a highball. "Scott showed Francis something that scared him. Hadn't you better—"

"I suppose so." Paradine listened. Noises in the next room told him the whereabouts of his son. "Scotty!"

"Bang," Scotty said, and appeared smiling. "I killed 'em all. Space pirates. You want me, dad?"

"Yes. If you don't mind leaving the space pirates unburied for a few minutes. What did you do to Francis Burns?"

Scott's blue eyes reflected incredible candor. "Huh?"

"Try hard. You can remember, I'm sure."

"Uh. Oh, that. I didn't do nothing."

"Anything," Jane corrected absently.

"Anything. Honest. I just let him look into my television set, and it . . . it scared him."

"Television set?"

Scott produced the crystal cube. "It isn't really that. See?"

Paradine examined the gadget, startled by the magnification. All he could see, though, was a maze of meaningless colored designs.

"Uncle Harry—"

Paradine reached for the telephone. Scott gulped. "Is
. . . is Uncle Harry back in town?"

"Yeah."

"Well, I gotta take a bath." Scott headed for the door.
Paradine met Jane's gaze and nodded significantly.

Harry was home, but disclaimed all knowledge of the
peculiar toys. Rather grimly, Paradine requested Scott
to bring down from his room all of the playthings. Finally
they lay in a row on the table, cube, abacus, doll, helmet-
like cap, several other mysterious contraptions. Scott
was cross-examined. He lied valiantly for a time, but
broke down at last and bawled, hiccuping his confession.

"Get the box these things came in," Paradine ordered.
"Then head for bed."

"Are you . . . *hup!* . . . gonna punish me daddy?"

"For playing hooky and lying, yes. You know the rules.
No more shows for two weeks. No sodas for the same
period."

Scott gulped. "You gonna keep my things?"

"I don't know yet."

"Well . . . g'night, daddy. G'night, mom."

After the small figure had gone upstairs, Paradine
dragged a chair to the table and carefully scrutinized the
box. He poked thoughtfully at the fused gadgetry. Jane
watched.

"What is it, Denny?"

"Dunno. Who'd leave a box of toys down by the creek?"

"It might have fallen out of a car."

"Not at that point. The road doesn't hit the creek north
of the railroad trestle. Empty lots—nothing else." Paradine
lit a cigarette. "Drink, honey?"

"I'll fix it." Jane went to work, her eyes troubled. She
brought Paradine a glass and stood behind him, ruffling
his hair with her fingers. "Is anything wrong?"

"Of course not. Only—where did these toys come
from?"

"Johnsons's didn't know, and they get their stock from
New York."

"I've been checking up, too," Paradine admitted. "That
doll"—he poked it—"rather worried me. Custom jobs,
maybe, but I wish I knew who'd made 'em."

"A psychologist? The abacus—don't they give people tests with such things?"

Paradine snapped his fingers. "Right! And say! There's a guy going to speak at the university next week, fellow named Holloway, who's a child psychologist. He's a big shot, with quite a reputation. He might know something about it."

"Holloway? I don't—"

"Rex Holloway. He's . . . hm-m-m! He doesn't live far from here. Do you suppose he might have had these things made himself?"

Jane was examining the abacus. She grimaced and drew back. "If he did, I don't like him. But see if you can find out, Denny."

Paradine nodded. "I shall."

He drank his highball, frowning. He was vaguely worried. But he wasn't scared—yet.

Rex Holloway was a fat, shiny man, with a bald head and thick spectacles, above which his thick, black brows lay like bushy caterpillars. Paradine brought him home to dinner one night a week later. Holloway did not appear to watch the children, but nothing they did or said was lost on him. His gray eyes, shrewd and bright, missed little.

The toys fascinated him. In the living room the three adults gathered around the table, where the playthings had been placed. Holloway studied them carefully as he listened to what Jane and Paradine had to say. At last he broke his silence.

"I'm glad I came here tonight. But not completely. This is very disturbing, you know."

"Eh?" Paradine stared, and Jane's face showed her consternation. Holloway's next words did not calm them.

"We are dealing with madness."

He smiled at the shocked looks they gave him. "All children are mad, from an adult viewpoint. Ever read Hughes' 'High Wind in Jamaica'?"

"I've got it." Paradine secured the little book from its shelf. Holloway extended a hand, took it, and flipped the pages till he had found the place he wanted. He read aloud:

" 'Babies of course are not human—they are animals,

and have a very ancient and ramified culture, as cats have, and fishes, and even snakes; the same in kind as these, but much more complicated and vivid, since babies are, after all, one of the most developed species of the lower vertebrates. In short, babies have minds which work in terms and categories of their own which cannot be translated into the terms and and categories of the human mind.' "

Jane tried to take that calmly, but couldn't. "You don't mean that Emma—"

"Could you think like your daughter?' Holloway asked. "Listen: 'One can no more think like a baby than one can think like a bee.' "

Paradine mixed drinks. Over his shoulder he said, "You're theorizing quite a bit, aren't you? As I get it, you're implying that babies have a culture of their own, even a high standard of intelligence."

"Not necessarily. There's no yardstick, you see. All I say is that babies think in other ways than we do. Not necessarily *better*—that's a question of relative values. But with a different manner of extension—" He sought for words, grimacing.

"Fantasy," Paradine said, rather rudely, but annoyed because of Emma. "Babies don't have different senses from ours."

"Who said they did?" Holloway demanded. "They use their minds in a different way, that's all. But it's quite enough!"

"I'm trying to understand," Jane said slowly. "All I can think of is my Mixmaster. It can whip up batter and potatoes, but it can squeeze oranges, too."

"Something like that. The brain's a colloid, a very complicated machine. We don't know much about its potentialities. We don't even know how much it can grasp. But it *is* known that the mind becomes conditioned as the human animal matures. It follows certain familiar theorems, and all thought thereafter is pretty well based on patterns taken for granted. Look at this." Holloway touched the abacus. "Have you experimented with it?"

"A little," Paradine said.

"But not much. Eh?"

"Well—"

"Why not?"

"It's pointless," Paradine complained. "Even a puzzle has to have some logic. But those crazy angles—"

"Your mind has been conditioned to Euclid," Holloway said. "So this—thing—bores us, and seems pointless. But a child knows nothing of Euclid. A different sort of geometry from ours wouldn't impress him as being illogical. He believes what he sees."

"Are you trying to tell me that this gadget's got a fourth-dimensional extension?" Paradine demanded.

"Not visually, anyway," Holloway denied. "All I say is that our minds, conditioned to Euclid, can see nothing in this but an illogical tangle of wires. But a child—especially a baby—might see more. Not at first. It'd be a puzzle, of course. Only a child wouldn't be handicapped by too many preconceived ideas."

"Hardening of the thought-arteries," Jane interjected.

Paradine was not convinced. "Then a baby could work calculus better than Einstein? No, I don't mean that. I can see your point, more or less clearly. Only—"

"Well, look. Let's suppose there are two kinds of geometry—we'll limit it, for the sake of the example. Our kind, Euclidean, and another, which we'll call x. X hasn't much relationship to Euclid. It's based on different theorems. Two and two needn't equal four in it; they could equal y_2, or they might not even *equal*. A baby's mind is not yet conditioned, except by certain questionable factors of heredity and environment. Start the infant on Euclid—"

"Poor kid," Jane said.

Holloway shot her a quick glance. "The basis of Euclid. Alphabet blocks. Math, geometry, algebra—they come much later. We're familiar with that development. On the other hand, start the baby with the basic principles of our x logic."

"Blocks? What kind?"

Holloway looked at the abacus. "It wouldn't make much sense to us. But we've been conditioned to Euclid."

Paradine poured himself a stiff shot of whiskey. "That's pretty awful. You're not limiting to math."

"Right! I'm not limiting it at all. How can I? I'm not conditioned to x logic."

"There's the answer," Jane said, with a sigh of relief.

"Who is? It'd take such a person to make the sort of toys you apparently think these are."

Holloway nodded, his eyes, behind the thick lenses, blinking. "Such people may exist."

"Where?"

"They might prefer to keep hidden."

"Supermen?"

"I wish I knew. You see, Paradine, we've got yardstick trouble again. By our standards these people might seem super-doopers in certain respects. In others they might seem moronic. It's not a quantitative difference; its qualitative. They *think* different. And I'm sure we can do things they can't."

"Maybe they wouldn't want to," Jane said.

Paradine tapped the fused gadgetry on the box. "What about this? It implies—"

"A purpose, sure."

"Transportation?"

"One thinks of that first. If so, the box might have come from anywhere."

"Where—things are—*different?*" Paradine asked slowly.

"Exactly. In space, or even time. I don't know; I'm a psychologist. Unfortunately I'm conditioned to Euclid, too."

"Funny place it must be," Jane said. "Denny, get rid of those toys."

"I intend to."

Holloway picked up the crystal cube. "Did you question the children much?"

Paradine said, "Yeah. Scott said there were people in that cube when he first looked. I asked him what was in it now."

"What did he say?" The psychologist's eyes widened.

"He said they were building a place. His exact words. I asked him who—people? But he couldn't explain."

"No, I suppose not," Holloway muttered. "It must be progressive. How long have the children had these toys?"

"About three months, I guess."

"Time enough. The perfect toy, you see, is both instructive and mechanical. It should do things, to interest a child, and it should teach, preferably unobtrusively. Simple problems at first. Later—"

"X logic," Jane said, white-faced.

Paradine cursed under his breath. "Emma and Scott are perfectly normal!"

"Do you know how their minds work—now?"

Holloway didn't pursue the thought. He fingered the doll. "It would be interesting to know the conditions of the place where these things came from. Induction doesn't help a great deal, though. Too many factors are missing. We can't visualize a world based on the x factor—environment adjusted to minds thinking in x patterns. This luminous network inside the doll. It could be anything. It could exist inside us, though we haven't discovered it yet. When we find the right stain—" He shrugged. "What do you make of this?"

It was a crimson globe, two inches in diameter, with a protruding knob upon its surface.

"What could anyone make of it?"

"Scott? Emma?"

"I hadn't even seen it till about three weeks ago. Then Emma started to play with it." Paradine nibbled his lip. "After that, Scott got interested."

"Just what do they do?"

"Hold it up in front of them and move it back and forth. No particular pattern of motion."

"No Euclidean pattern," Holloway corrected. "At first they couldn't understand the toy's purpose. They had to be educated up to it."

"That's horrible," Jane said.

"Not to them. Emma is probably quicker at understanding x than Scott, for her mind isn't yet conditioned to this environment."

Paradine said, "But I can remember plenty of things I did as a child. Even as a baby."

"Well?"

"Was I—mad—then?"

"The things you don't remember are the criterion of your madness," Holloway retorted. "But I use the word 'madness' purely as a convenient symbol for the variation from the known human norm. The arbitrary standard of sanity."

Jane put down her glass. "You've said that induction was difficult, Mr. Holloway. But it seems to me you're making a great deal of it from very little. After all, these toys—"

"I *am* a psychologist, and I've specialized in children. I'm not a layman. These toys mean a great deal to me, chiefly because they mean so little."

"You might be wrong."

"Well, I rather hope I am. I'd like to examine the children."

Jane rose in arms. "How?"

After Holloway had explained, she nodded, though still a bit hesitantly. "Well, that's all right. But they're not guinea pigs."

The psychologist patted the air with a plump hand. "My dear girl! I'm not a Frankenstein. To me the individual is the prime factor—naturally, since I work with minds. If there's anything wrong with the youngsters, I want to cure them."

Paradine put down his cigarette and slowly watched blue smoke spiral up, wavering in an unfelt draft. "Can you give a prognosis?"

"I'll try. That's all I can say. If the undeveloped minds have been turned into the *x* channel, it's necessary to divert them back. I'm not saying that's the wisest thing to do, but it probably is from our standards. After all, Emma and Scott will have to live in this world."

"Yeah. Yeah. I can't believe there's much wrong. They seem about average, thoroughly normal."

"Superficially they may seem so. They've no reason for acting abnormally, have they? And how can you tell if they —think differently?"

"I'll call 'em," Paradine said.

"Make it informal, then. I don't want them to be on guard."

Jane nodded toward the toys. Holloway said, "Leave the stuff there, eh?"

But the psychologist, after Emma and Scott were summoned, made no immediate move at direct questioning. He managed to draw Scott unobtrusively into the conversation, dropping key words now and then. Nothing so obvious as a word-association test—co-operation is necessary for that.

The most interesting development occurred when Holloway took up the abacus. "Mind showing me how this works?"

Scott hesitated. "Yes, sir. Like this—" He slid a bead deftly through the maze, in a tangled course, so swiftly that no one was quite sure whether or not it ultimately vanished. It might have been merely legerdermain. Then, again—

Holloway tried. Scott watched, wrinkling his nose.

"That right?"

"Uh-huh. It's gotta go *there*—"

"Here? Why?"

"Well, that's the only way to make it work."

But Holloway was conditioned to Euclid. There was no apparent reason why the bead should slide from this particular wire to the other. It looked like a random factor. Also, Holloway suddenly noticed, this wasn't the path the bead had taken previously, when Scott had worked the puzzle. At least, as well as he could tell.

"Will you show me again?"

Scott did, and twice more, on request. Holloway blinked through his glasses. Random, yes. And variable. Scott moved the bead along a different course each time.

Somehow, none of the adults could tell whether or not the bead vanished. If they had expected to see it disappear, their reactions might have been different.

In the end nothing was solved. Holloway, as he said good night, seemed ill at ease.

"May I come again?"

"I wish you would," Jane told him. "Any time. You still think—"

He nodded. "The children's minds are not reacting normally. They're not dull at all, but I've the most extraordinary impression that they arrive at conclusions in a way we don't understand. As though they used algebra while we used geometry. The same conclusion, but a different method of reaching it."

"What about the toys?" Paradine asked suddenly.

"Keep them out of the way. I'd like to borrow them, if I may—"

That night Paradine slept badly. Holloway's parallel had been ill-chosen. It led to disturbing theories. The *x* factor—The children were using the equivalent of algebraic reasoning, while adults used geometry.

Fair enough. Only—

Algebra can give you answers that geometry cannot, since there are certain terms and symbols which cannot be expressed geometrically. Suppose x logic showed conclusions inconceivable to an adult mind?

"Damn!" Paradine whispered. Jane stirred beside him.

"Dear? Can't you sleep either?"

"No." He got up and went into the next room. Emma slept peacefully as a cherub, her fat arm curled around Mr. Bear. Through the open doorway Paradine could see Scott's dark head motionless on the pillow.

Jane was beside him. He slipped his arm around her.

"Poor little people," she murmured. "And Holloway called them mad. I think we're the ones who are crazy, Dennis."

"Uh-huh. We've got jitters."

Scott stirred in his sleep. Without awakening, he called what was obviously a question, though it did not seem to be in any particular language. Emma gave a little mewling cry that changed pitch sharply.

She had not awakened. The children lay without stirring.

But Paradine thought, with a sudden sickness in his middle, it was exactly as though Scott had asked Emma something, and she had replied.

Had their minds changed so that even—sleep—was different to them?

He thrust the thought away. "You'll catch cold. Let's get back to bed. Want a drink?"

"I think I do," Jane said, watching Emma. Her hand reached out blindly toward the child; she drew it back. "Come on. We'll wake the kids."

They drank a little brandy together, but said nothing. Jane cried in her sleep, later.

Scott was not awake, but his mind worked in slow, careful building. Thus—

"They'll take the toys away. The fat man . . . listava dangerous maybe. But the Ghoric direction won't show . . . evankrus dun-hasn't-them. Intransdection . . . bright and shiny. Emma. She's more khopranik-high now than . . . I still don't see how to . . . thavarar lixery dist—"

A little of Scott's thoughts could still be understood. But Emma had become conditioned to x much faster.

She was thinking, too.

Not like an adult or a child. Not even like a human. Except, perhaps, a human of a type shockingly unfamiliar to *genus homo*.

Sometimes Scott himself had difficulty in following her thoughts.

If it had not been for Holloway, life might have settled back into an almost normal routine. The toys were no longer active reminders. Emma still enjoyed her dolls and sand pile, with a thoroughly explicable delight. Scott was satisfied with baseball and his chemical set. They did everything other children did, and evinced few, if any, flashes of abnormality. But Holloway seemed to be an alarmist.

He was having the toys tested, with rather idiotic results. He drew endless charts and diagrams, corresponded with mathematicians, engineers, and other psychologists, and went quietly crazy trying to find rhyme or reason in the construction of the gadgets. The box itself, with its cryptic machinery, told nothing. Fusing had melted too much of the stuff into slag. But the toys—

It was the random element that baffled investigation. Even that was a matter of semantics. For Holloway was convinced that it wasn't really random. There just weren't enough known factors. No adult could work the abacus, for example. And Holloway thoughtfully refrained from letting a child play with the thing.

The crystal cube was similarly cryptic. It showed a mad pattern of colors, which sometimes moved. In this it resembled a kaleidoscope. But the shifting of balance and gravity didn't affect it. Again the random factor.

Or, rather, the unknown. The x pattern. Eventually Paradine and Jane slipped back into something like complacence, with a feeling that the children had been cured of their mental quirk, now that the contributing cause had been removed. Certain of the actions of Emma and Scott gave them every reason to quit worrying.

For the kids enjoyed swimming, hiking, movies, games,

the normal functional toys of this particular time-sector. It was true that they failed to master certain rather puzzling mechanical devices which involved some calculation. A three-dimensional jigsaw globe Paradine had picked up, for example. But he found that difficult himself.

Once in a while there were lapses. Scott was hiking with his father one Saturday afternoon, and the two had paused at the summit of a hill. Beneath them a rather lovely valley was spread.

"Pretty, isn't it?" Paradine remarked.

Scott examined the scene gravely. "It's all wrong," he said.

"Eh?"

"I dunno."

"What's wrong about it?"

"Gee—" Scott lapsed into puzzled silence. "I dunno."

The children had missed their toys, but not for long. Emma recovered first, though Scott still moped. He held unintelligible conversations with his sister, and studied meaningless scrawls she drew on paper he supplied. It was almost as though he was consulting her, anent difficult problems beyond his grasp.

If Emma understood more, Scott had more real intelligence, and manipulatory skill as well. He built a gadget with his Meccano set, but was dissatisfied. The apparent cause of his dissatisfaction was exactly why Paradine was relieved when he viewed the structure. It was the sort of thing a normal boy would make, vaguely reminiscent of a cubistic ship.

It was a bit too normal to please Scott. He asked Emma more questions, though in private. She thought for a time, and then made more scrawls with an awkwardly clutched pencil.

"Can you read that stuff?" Jane asked her son one morning.

"Not read it, exactly. I can tell what she means. Not all the time, but mostly."

"Is it writing?"

"N-no. It doesn't mean what it *looks* like."

"Symbolism," Paradine suggested over his coffee.

Jane looked at him, her eyes widening. "Denny—"

He winked and shook his head. Later, when they were alone, he said, "Don't let Holloway upset you. I'm not implying that the kids are corresponding in an unknown tongue. If Emma draws a squiggle and says it's a flower, that's an arbitrary rule—Scott remembers that. Next time she draws the same sort of squiggle, or tries to—well!"

"Sure," Jane said doubtfully. "Have you noticed Scott's been doing a lot of reading lately?"

"I noticed. Nothing unusual, though. No Kant or Spinoza."

"He browses, that's all."

"Well, so did I, at his age," Paradine said, and went off to his morning classes. He lunched with Holloway, which was becoming a daily habit, and spoke of Emma's literary endeavors.

"Was I right about symbolism, Rex?"

The psychologist nodded. "Quite right. Our own language is nothing but arbitrary symbolism now. At least in its application. Look here." On his napkin he drew a very narrow ellipse. "What's that?"

"You mean what does it represent?"

"Yes. What does it suggest to you? It could be a crude representation of—what?"

"Plenty of things," Paradine said. "Rim of a glass. A fried egg. A loaf of French bread. A cigar."

Holloway added a little triangle to his drawing, apex joined to one end of the ellipse. He looked up at Paradine.

"A fish," the latter said instantly.

"Our familiar symbol for a fish. Even without fins, eyes or mouth, it's recognizable, because we've been conditioned to identify this particular shape with our mental picture of a fish. The basis of a rebus. A symbol, to us, means a lot more than what we actually see on paper. What's in your mind when you look at this sketch?"

"Why—a fish."

"Keep going. What do you visualize—everything!"

"Scales," Paradine said slowly, looking into space. "Water. Foam. A fish's eye. The fins. The colors."

"So the symbol represents a lot more than just the abstract idea *fish*. Note the connotation's that of a noun, not a verb. It's harder to express actions by symbolism, you

know. Anyway—reverse the process. Suppose you want
to make a symbol for some concrete noun, say *bird*.
Draw it."

Paradine drew two connected arcs, concavities down.

"The lowest common denominator," Holloway nodded.
"The natural tendency is to simplify. Especially when a
child is seeing something for the first time and has few
standards of comparison. He tries to identify the new
thing with what's already familiar to him. Ever notice
how a child draws the ocean?" He didn't wait for an
answer; he went on.

"A series of jagged points. Like the oscillating line on a
seismograph. When I first saw the Pacific, I was about
three. I remember it pretty clearly. It looked—tilted. A
flat plain, slanted at an angle. The waves were regular
triangles, apex upward. Now I don't *see* them stylized that
way, but later, remembering, I had to find some familiar
standard of comparison. Which is the only way of getting any conception of an entirely new thing. The average
child tries to draw these regular triangles, but his co-
ordination's poor. He gets a seismograph pattern."

"All of which means what?"

"A child sees the ocean. He stylizes it. He draws a certain definite pattern, symbolic, to him, of the sea. Emma's
scrawls may be symbols, too. I don't mean that the world
looks different to her—brighter, perhaps, and sharper,
more vivid and with a slackening of perception above her
eye level. What I do mean is that her thought-processes
are different, that she translates what she sees into ab-
normal symbols."

"You still believe—"

"Yes, I do. Her mind has been conditioned unusually.
It may be that she breaks down what she sees into simple,
obvious patterns—and realizes a significance to those patterns that we can't understand. Like the abacus. She saw
a pattern in that, though to us it was completely random."

Paradine abruptly decided to taper off these luncheon
engagements with Holloway. The man was an alarmist.
His theories were growing more fantastic than ever, and
he dragged in anything, applicable or not, that would
support them.

Rather sardonically he said, "Do you mean Emma's communicating with Scott in an unknown language?"

"In symbols for which she hasn't any words. I'm sure Scott understands a great deal of those—scrawls. To him, an isosceles triangle may represent any factor, though probably a concrete noun. Would a man who knew nothing of algebra understand what H_2O meant? Would he realize that the symbol could evoke a picture of the ocean?"

Paradine didn't answer. Instead, he mentioned to Holloway Scott's curious remark that the landscape, from the hill, had looked all wrong. A moment later, he was inclined to regret his impulse, for the psychologist was off again.

"Scott's thought-patterns are building up to a sum that doesn't equal this world. Perhaps he's subconsciously expecting to see the world where those toys came from."

Paradine stopped listening. Enough was enough. The kids were getting along all right, and the only remaining disturbing factor was Holloway himself. That night, however, Scott evinced an interest, later significant, in eels.

There was nothing apparently harmful in natural history. Paradine explained about eels.

"But where do they lay their eggs? Or do they?"

"That's still a mystery. Their spawning grounds are unknown. Maybe the Sargasso Sea, or the deeps, where the pressure can help them force the young out of their bodies."

"Funny," Scott said, thinking deeply.

"Salmon do the same thing, more or less. They go up rivers to spawn." Paradine went into detail. Scott was fascinated.

"But that's *right*, dad. They're born in the river, and when they learn how to swim, they go down to the sea. And they come back to lay their eggs, huh?"

"Right."

"Only they wouldn't *come* back," Scott pondered. "They'd just send their eggs—"

"It'd take a very long ovipositor," Paradine said, and vouchsafed some well-chosen remarks upon oviparity.

His son wasn't entirely satisfied. Flowers, he contended, sent their seeds long distances.

"They don't guide them. Not many find fertile soil."

"Flowers haven't got brains, though. Dad, why do people live *here?*"

"Glendale?"

"No—*here*. This whole place. It isn't all there is, I bet."

"Do you mean the other planets?"

Scott was hesitant. "This is only—part of the big place. It's like the river where the salmon go. Why don't people go on down to the ocean when they grow up?"

Paradine realized that Scott was speaking figuratively. He felt a brief chill. The—ocean?

The young of the species are not conditioned to live in the completer world of their parents. Having developed sufficiently, they enter that world. Later they breed. The fertilized eggs are buried in the sand, far up the river, where later they hatch.

And they learn. Instinct alone is fatally slow. Especially in the case of a specialized genus, unable to cope even with this world, unable to feed or drink or survive, unless someone has foresightedly provided for those needs.

The young, fed and tended, would survive. There would be incubators and robots. They would survive, but they would not know how to swim downstream, to the vaster world of the ocean.

So they must be taught. They must be trained and conditioned in many ways.

Painlessly, subtly, unobtrusively. Children love toys that do things—and if those toys teach at the same time—

In the latter half of the nineteenth century an Englishman sat on a grassy bank near a stream. A very small girl lay near him, staring up at the sky. She had discarded a curious toy with which she had been playing, and now was murmuring a wordless little song, to which the man listened with half an ear.

"What was that, my dear?" he asked at last.

"Just something I made up, Uncle Charles."

"Sing it again." He pulled out a notebook.

The girl obeyed.

"Does it mean anything?"

She nodded. "Oh, yes. Like the stories I tell you, you know."

"They're wonderful stories, dear."

"And you'll put them in a book some day?"

"Yes, but I must change them quite a lot, or no one would understand. But I don't think I'll change your little song."

"You mustn't. If you did, it wouldn't mean anything."

"I won't change that stanza, anyway," he promised. "Just what does it mean?"

"It's the way out, I think," the girl said doubtfully. "I'm not sure yet. My magic toys told me."

"I wish I knew what London shop sold those marvelous toys!"

"Mamma bought them for me. She's dead. Papa doesn't care."

She lied. She had found the toys in a box one day, as she played by the Thames. And they were indeed wonderful.

Her little song—Uncle Charles thought it didn't mean anything. (He wasn't her real uncle, she parenthesized. But he was nice.) The song meant a great deal. It was the way. Presently she would do what it said, and then—

But she was already too old. She never found the way.

Paradine had dropped Holloway. Jane had taken a dislike to him, naturally enough, since what she wanted most of all was to have her fears calmed. Since Scott and Emma acted normally now, Jane felt satisfied. It was partly wishful-thinking, to which Paradine could not entirely subscribe.

Scott kept bringing gadgets to Emma for her approval. Usually she'd shake her head. Sometimes she would look doubtful. Very occasionally she would signify agreement. Then there would be an hour of laborious, crazy scribbling on scraps of note paper, and Scott, after studying the notations, would arrange and rearrange his rocks, bits of machinery, candle ends, and assorted junk. Each day the maid cleaned them away, and each day Scott began again.

He condescended to explain a little to his puzzled father, who could see no rhyme or reason in the game.

"But why this pebble right here?"

"It's hard and round, dad. It *belongs* there."

"So is this one hard and round."

"Well, that's got vaseline on it. When you get that far, you can't *see* just a hard round thing."

"What comes next? This candle?"

Scott looked disgusted. "That's toward the end. The iron ring's next."

It was, Paradine thought, like a Scout trail through the woods, markers in a labrynth. But here again was the random factor. Logic halted—familiar logic—at Scott's motives in arranging the junk as he did.

Paradine went out. Over his shoulder he saw Scott pull a crumpled piece of paper and a pencil from his pocket, and head for Emma, who was squatted in a corner thinking things over.

Well—

Jane was lunching with Uncle Harry, and, on this hot Sunday afternoon there was little to do but read the papers. Paradine settled himself in the coolest place he could find, with a Collins, and lost himself in the comic strips.

An hour later a clatter of feet upstairs roused him from his doze. Scott's voice was crying exultantly, "This is it, Slug! Come on—"

Paradine stood up quickly, frowning. As he went into the hall the telephone began to ring. Jane had promised to call—

His hand was on the receiver when Emma's faint voice squealed with excitement. Paradine grimaced. What the devil was going on upstairs?

Scott shrieked, "Look out! This way!"

Paradine, his mouth working, his nerves ridiculously tense, forgot the phone and raced up the stairs. The door of Scott's room was open.

The children were vanishing.

They went in fragments, like thick smoke in a wind, or like movement in a distorting mirror. Hand in hand they went, in a direction Paradine could not understand, and as he blinked there on the threshold, they were gone.

"Emma!" he said, dry-throated. *"Scotty!"*

On the carpet lay a pattern of markers, pebbles, an iron ring—junk. A random pattern. A crumpled sheet of paper blew toward Paradine.

He picked it up automatically.

"Kids. Where are you? Don't hide—

"*Emma! SCOTTY!*"

Downstairs the telephone stopped its shrill, monotonous ringing. Paradine looked at the paper he held.

It was a leaf torn from a book. There were interlineations and marginal notes, in Emma's meaningless scrawl. A stanza of verse had been so underlined and scribbled over that it was almost illegible, but Paradine was thoroughly familiar with "Through the Looking Glass." His memory gave him the words—

> 'Twas brillig, and the slithy toves
>   Did gyre and gimbel in the wabe.
> All mimsy were the borogoves,
>   And the mome raths outgrabe.

Idiotically he thought: Humpty Dumpty explained it. A wabe is the plot of grass around a sundial. A sundial. Time—It has something to do with time. A long time ago Scotty asked me what a wabe was. Symbolism.

'Twas brillig—

A perfect mathematical formula, giving all the conditions, in symbolism the children had finally understood. The junk on the floor. The toves had to be made slithy— vaseline?—and they had to be placed in a certain relationship, so that they'd gyre and gimbel.

Lunacy!

But it had not been lunacy to Emma and Scott. They thought differently. They used x logic. Those notes Emma had made on the page—she'd translated Carroll's words into symbols both she and Scott could understand.

The random factor had made sense to the children. They had fulfilled the conditions of the time-space equation. *And the mome raths outgrabe—*

Paradine made a rather ghastly little sound, deep in his throat. He looked at the crazy pattern on the carpet. If he could follow it, as the kids had done— But he couldn't. The pattern was senseless. The random factor defeated him. He was conditioned to Euclid.

Even if he went insane, he still couldn't do it. It would be the wrong kind of lunacy.

His mind had stopped working now. But in a moment the stasis of incredulous horror would pass— Paradine crumpled the page in his fingers. "Emma, Scotty," he called in a dead voice, as though he could expect no response.

Sunlight slanted through the open windows, brightening the golden pelt of Mr. Bear. Downstairs the ringing of the telephone began again.

HUDDLING PLACE

by Clifford D. Simak

The drizzle sifted from the leaden skies, like smoke drifting through the bare-branched trees. It softened the hedges and hazed the outlines of the buildings and blotted out the distance. It glinted on the metallic skins of the silent robots and silvered the shoulders of the three humans listening to the intonations of the black-garbed man, who read from the book cupped between his hands.

"For I am the Resurrection and the Life—"

The moss-mellowed graven figure that reared above the door of the crypt seemed straining upward, every crystal of its yearning body reaching toward something that no one else could see. Straining as it had strained since that day of long ago when men had chipped it from the granite to adorn the family tomb with a symbolism that had pleased the first John J. Webster in the last years he held of life.

"And whosoever liveth and believeth in Me—"

Jerome A. Webster felt his son's fingers tighten on his arm, heard the muffled sobbing of his mother, saw the lines of robots standing rigid, heads bowed in respect to the master they had served. The master who now was going home—to the final home of all.

Numbly, Jerome A. Webster wondered if they understood—if they understood life and death—if they understood what it meant that Nelson F. Webster lay there in the casket, that a man with a book intoned words above him.

Nelson F. Webster, fourth of the line of Websters who

First published in 1944

had lived on these acres, had lived and died here, scarcely
leaving, and now was going to his final rest in that place
the first of them had prepared for the rest of them—for
that long line of shadowy descendants who would live
here and cherish the things and the ways and the life that
the first John J. Webster had established.

Jerome A. Webster felt his jaw muscles tighten, felt a
little tremor run across his body. For a moment his eyes
burned and the casket blurred in his sight and the words
the man in black was saying were one with the wind that
whispered in the pines standing sentinel for the dead.
Within his brain remembrance marched—remembrance
of a gray-haired man stalking the hills and fields, sniffing
the breeze of an early morning, standing, legs braced, before the flaring fireplace with a glass of brandy in his
hand.

Pride—the pride of land and life, and the humility and
greatness that quiet living breeds within a man. Contentment of casual leisure and surety of purpose. Independ-
ence of assured security, comfort of familiar surroundings,
freedom of broad acres.

Thomas Webster was joggling his elbow. "Father," he
was whispering. "Father."

The service was over. The black-garbed man had closed
his book. Six robots stepped forward, lifted the casket.

Slowly the three followed the casket into the crypt,
stood silently as the robots slid it into its receptacle, closed
the tiny door and affixed the plate that read:

NELSON F. WEBSTER
2034–2117

That was all. Just the name and dates. And that, Jerome A. Webster found himself thinking, was enough.
There was nothing else that needed to be there. That was
all those others had. The ones that called the family roll
—starting with William Stevens, 1920–1999. Gramp
Stevens, they had called him, Webster remembered. Father of the wife of that first John J. Webster, who was here
himself—1951–2020. And after him his son, Charles F.
Webster, 1980–2060. And his son, John J. II, 2004–2086.
Webster could remember John J. II—a grandfather who

had slept beside the fire with his pipe hanging from his mouth, eternally threatening to set his whiskers aflame.

Webster's eyes strayed to another plate. Mary Webster, the mother of the boy here at his side. And yet not a boy. He kept forgetting that Thomas was twenty now, in a week or so would be leaving for Mars, even as in his younger days he, too, had gone to Mars.

All here together, he told himself. The Websters and their wives and children. Here in death together as they had lived together, sleeping in the pride and security of bronze and marble with the pines outside and the symbolic figure above the age-greened door.

The robots were waiting, standing silently, their task fulfilled.

His mother looked at him.

"You're the head of the family now, my son," she told him.

He reached out and hugged her close against his side. Head of the family—what was left of it. Just the three of them now. His mother and his son. And his son would be leaving soon, going out to Mars. But he would come back. Come back with a wife, perhaps, and the family would go on. The family wouldn't stay at three. Most of the big house wouldn't stay closed off, as it now was closed off. There had been a time when it had rung with the life of a dozen units of the family, living in their separate apartments under one big roof. That time, he knew, would come again.

The three of them turned and left the crypt, took the path back to the house, looming like a huge gray shadow in the midst.

A fire blazed in the hearth and the book lay upon his desk. Jerome A. Webster reached out and picked it up, read the title once again:

"Martian Physiology, With Especial Reference to the Brain" by Jerome A. Webster, M.D.

Thick and authoritative—the work of a lifetime. Standing almost alone in its field. Based upon the data gathered during those five plague years on Mars—years when he had labored almost day and night with his fellow colleagues of the World Committee's medical commission, dispatched on an errand of mercy to the neighboring planet.

A tap sounded on the door.

"Come in," he called.

The door opened and a robot glided in.

"Your whiskey, sir."

"Thank you, Jenkins," Webster said.

"The minister, sir," said Jenkins, "has left."

"Oh, yes. I presume that you took care of him."

"I did, sir. Gave him the usual fee and offered him a drink. He refused the drink."

"That was a social error," Webster told him. "Ministers don't drink."

"I'm sorry, sir. I didn't know. He asked me to ask you to come to church sometime."

"Eh?"

"I told him, sir, that you never went anywhere."

"That was quite right, Jenkins," said Webster. "None of us ever go anywhere."

Jenkins headed for the door, stopped before he got there, turned around. "If I may say so, sir, that was a touching service at the crypt. Your father was a fine human, the finest ever was. The robots were saying the service was very fitting. Dignified like, sir. He would have liked it had he known."

"My father," said Webster, "would be even more pleased to hear you say that, Jenkins."

"Thank you, sir," said Jenkins, and went out.

Webster sat with the whiskey and the book and fire— felt the comfort of the well-known room close in about him, felt the refuge that was in it.

This was home. It had been home for the Websters since that day when the first John J. had come here and built the first unit of the sprawling house. John J. had chosen it because it had a trout stream, or so he always said. But it was something more than that. It must have been, Webster told himself, something more than that.

Or perhaps, at first, it had only been the trout stream. The trout stream and the trees and meadows, the rocky ridge where the mist drifted in each morning from the river. Maybe the rest of it had grown, grown gradually through the years, through years of family association until the very soil was soaked with something that approached, but wasn't quite, tradition. Something that made each tree, each rock, each foot of soil a Webster tree or rock or clod of soil. It all belonged.

John J., the first John J., had come after the breakup of the cities, after men had forsaken, once and for all, the twentieth century huddling places, had broken free of the tribal instinct to stick together in one cave or in one clearing against a common foe or a common fear. An instinct that had become outmoded, for there were no fears or foes. Man revolting against the herd instinct economic and social conditions had impressed upon him in ages past. A new security and a new sufficiency had made it possible to break away.

The trend had started back in the twentieth century, more than two hundred years before, when men moved to country homes to get fresh air and elbow room and a graciousness in life that communal existence, in its strictest sense, never had given them.

And here was the end result. A quiet living. A peace that could only come with good things. The sort of life that men had yearned for years to have. A manorial existence, based on old family homes and leisurely acres, with atomics supplying power and robots in place of serfs.

Webster smiled at the fireplace with its blazing wood. That was an anachronism, but a good one—something that Man had brought forward from the caves. Useless, because atomic heating was better—but more pleasant. One couldn't sit and watch atomics and dream and build castles in the flames.

Even the crypt out there, where they had put his father that afternoon. That was family, too. All of a piece with the rest of it. The somber pride and leisured life and peace. In the old days the dead were buried in vast plots all together, stranger cheek by jowl with stranger—

He never goes anywhere.

That is what Jenkins had told the minister.

And that was right. For what need was there to go anywhere? It all was here. By simply twirling a dial one could talk face to face with anyone one wished, could go, by sense, if not in body, anywhere one wished. Could attend the theater or hear a concert or browse in a library halfway around the world. Could transact any business one might need to transact without rising from one's chair.

Webster drank the whiskey, then swung to the dialed machine beside his desk.

He spun dials from memory without resorting to the log. He knew where he was going.

His finger flipped a toggle and the room melted away —or seemed to melt. There was left the chair within which he sat, part of the desk, part of the machine itself and that was all.

The chair was on a hillside swept with golden grass and dotted with scraggly, wind-twisted trees, a hillside that straggled down to a lake nestling in the grip of purple mountain spurs. The spurs, darkened in long streaks with the bluish-green of distant pine, climbed in staggering stairs, melting into the blue-tinged snow-capped peaks that reared beyond and above them in jagged saw-toothed outline.

The wind talked harshly in the crouching trees and ripped the long grass in sudden gusts. The last rays of the sun struck fire from the distant peaks.

Solitude and grandeur, the long sweep of tumbled land, the cuddled lake, the knifelike shadows on the far-off ranges.

Webster sat easily in his chair, eyes squinting at the peaks.

A voice said almost at his shoulder: "May I come in?"

A soft, sibilant voice, wholly unhuman. But one that Webster knew.

He nooded his head. "By all means, Juwain."

He turned slightly and saw the elaborate crouching pedestal, the furry, soft-eyed figure of the Martian squatting on it. Other alien furniture loomed indistinctly beyond the pedestal, half guessed furniture from that dwelling out on Mars.

The Martian flipped a furry hand toward the mountain range.

"You love this," he said. "You can understand it. And I can understand how you understand it, but to me there is more terror than beauty in it. It is something we could never have on Mars."

Webster reached out a hand, but the Martian stopped him.

"Leave it on," he said. "I know why you came here. I would not have come at a time like this except I thought perhaps an old friend—"

"It is kind of you," said Webster. "I am glad that you have come."

"Your father," said Juwain, "was a great man. I remember how you used to talk to me of him, those years you spent on Mars. You said then you would come back sometime. Why is it you've never come?"

"Why," said Webster, "I just never—"

"Do not tell me," said the Martian. "I already know."

"My son," said Webster, "is going to Mars in a few days. I shall have him call on you."

"That would be a pleasure," said Juwain. "I shall be expecting him."

He stirred uneasily on the crouching pedestal. "Perhaps he carries on tradition."

"No," said Webster. "He is studying engineering. He never cared for surgery."

"He has a right," observed the Martian, "to follow the life that he has chosen. Still, one might be permitted to wish."

"One could," Webster agreed. "But that is over and done with. Perhaps he will be a great engineer. Space structure. Talks of ships out to the stars."

"Perhaps," suggested Juwain, "your family has done enough for medical science. You and your father—"

"And his father," said Webster, "before him."

"Your book," declared Juwain, "has put Mars in debt to you. It may focus more attention on Martian specialization. My people do not make good doctors. They have no background for it. Queer how the minds of races run. Queer that Mars never thought of medicine—literally never thought of it. Supplied the need with a cult of fatalism. While even in your early history, when men still lived in caves—"

"There are many things," said Webster, "that you thought of and we didn't. Things we wonder now how we ever missed. Abilities that you developed and we do not have. Take your own specialty, philosophy. But different from ours. A science, while ours never was more than ordered fumbling. Yours an orderly, logical development of philosophy, workable, practical, applicable, an actual tool."

Juwain started to speak, hesitated, then went ahead. "I am near to something, something that may be new and startling. Something that will be a tool for you humans as well as for the Martians. I've worked on it for years, starting with certain mental concepts that first were suggested to me with arrival of the Earthmen. I have said nothing, for I could not be sure."

"And now," suggested Webster, "you are sure."

"Not quite," said Juwain. "Not positive. But almost."

They sat in silence, watching the mountains and the lake. A bird came and sat in one of the scraggly trees and sang. Dark clouds piled up behind the mountain ranges and the snow-tipped peaks stood out like graven stone. The sun sank in a lake of crimson, hushed finally to the glow of a fire burned low.

A tap sounded from a door and Webster stirred in his chair, suddenly brought back to the reality of the study, of the chair beneath him.

Juwain was gone. The old philosopher had come and sat an hour of contemplation with his friend and then had quietly slipped away.

The rap came again.

Webster leaned forward, snapped the toggle and the mountains vanished; the room became a room again. Dusk filtered through the high windows and the fire was a rosy flicker in the ashes.

"Come in," said Webster.

Jenkins opened the door. "Dinner is served, sir," he said.

"Thank you," said Webster. He rose slowly from the chair.

"Your place, sir," said Jenkins, "is laid at the head of the table."

"Ah, yes," said Webster. "Thank you, Jenkins. Thank you very much, for reminding me."

Webster stood on the broad ramp of the space field and watched the shape that dwindled in the sky with faint

flickering points of red lancing through the wintry sunlight.

For long minutes after the shape was gone he stood
there, hands gripping the railing in front of him, eyes still
staring up into the sky.

His lips moved and they said: "Good-by son"; but
there was no sound.

Slowly he came alive to his surroundings. Knew that
people moved about the ramp, saw that the landing field
seemed to stretch interminably to the far horizon, dotted
here and there with hump-backed things that were waiting
spaceships. Scooting tractors worked near one hangar,
clearing away the last of the snowfall of the night before.

Webster shivered and thought that it was queer, for
the noonday sun was warm. And shivered again.

Slowly he turned away from the railing and headed for
the administration building. And for the one brain-
wrenching moment he felt a sudden fear—an unreasonable and embarrassing fear of that stretch of concrete that
formed the ramp. A fear that left him shaking mentally
as he drove his feet toward the waiting door.

A man walked toward him, briefcase swinging in his
hand and Webster, eyeing him, wished fervently that the
man would not speak to him.

The man did not speak, passed him with scarcely a
glance, and Webster felt relief.

If he were back home, Webster told himself, he would
have finished lunch, would now be ready to lie down for
his midday nap. The fire would be blazing on the hearth
and the flicker of the flames would be reflected from the
andirons. Jenkins would bring him a liqueur and would
say a word or two—inconsequential conversation.

He hurried toward the door, quickening his step,
anxious to get away from the bare-cold expanse of the
massive ramp.

Funny how he had felt about Thomas. Natural, of
course, that he should have hated to see him go. But
entirely unnatural that he should, in those last few minutes, find such horror welling up within him. Horror of
the trip through space, horror of the alien land of Mars
—although Mars was scarcely alien any longer. For more

than a century now Earthmen had known it, had fought
it, lived with it; some of them had even grown to love it.

But it had only been utter will power that had prevented him, in those last few seconds before the ship had
taken off, from running out into the field, shrieking for
Thomas to come back, shrieking for him not to go.

And that, of course, never would have done. It would
have been exhibitionism, disgraceful and humiliating—
the sort of a thing a Webster could not do.

After all, he told himself, a trip to Mars was no great
adventure, not any longer. There had been a day when
it had been, but that day was gone forever. He, himself,
in his earlier days had made a trip to Mars, had stayed
there for five long years. That had been—he gasped when
he thought of it—that had been almost thirty years ago.

The babble and hum of the lobby hit him in the face
as the robot attendant opened the door for him, and in
that babble ran a vein of something that was almost terror. For a moment he hesitated, then stepped inside. The
door closed softly behind him.

He stayed close to the wall to keep out of people's
way, headed for a chair in one corner. He sat down and
huddled back, forcing his body deep into the cushions,
watching the milling humanity that seethed out in the
room.

Shrill people, hurrying people, people with strange, un-
neighborly faces. Strangers—every one of them. Not a
face he knew. People going places. Heading out for the
planets. Anxious to be off. Worried about last details.
Rushing here and there.

Out of the crowd loomed a familiar face. Webster
hunched forward.

"Jenkins!" he shouted, and then was sorry for the
shout, although no one seemed to notice.

The robot moved toward him, stood before him.

"Tell Raymond," said Webster, "that I must return
immediately. Tell him to bring the 'copter in front at
once."

"I am sorry, sir," said Jenkins, "but we cannot leave
at once. The mechanics found a flaw in the atomics cham-

ber. They are installing a new one. It will take several hours."

"Surely," said Webster, impatiently, "that could wait until some other time."

"The mechanic said not, sir," Jenkins told him. "It might go at any minute. The entire charge of power—"

"Yes, yes," agreed Webster, "I suppose so."

He fidgeted with his hat. "I just remembered," he said, "something I must do. Something that must be done at once. I must get home. I can't wait several hours."

He hitched forward to the edge of the chair, eyes staring at the milling crowd.

Faces—faces—

"Perhaps you could televise," suggested Jenkins. "One of the robots might be able to do it. There is a booth—"

"Wait, Jenkins," said Webster. He hesitated a moment. "There is nothing to do back home. Nothing at all. But I must get there. I can't stay here. If I have to, I'll go crazy. I was frightened out there on the ramp. I'm bewildered and confused here. I have a feeling—a strange, terrible feeling. Jenkins, I—"

"I understand, sir," said Jenkins. "Your father had it, too."

Webster gasped. "My father?"

"Yes, sir, that is why he never went anywhere. He was about your age, sir, when he found it out. He tried to make a trip to Europe and he couldn't. He got halfway there and turned back. He had a name for it."

Webster sat in stricken silence.

"A name for it," he finally said. "Of course there's a name for it. My father had it. My grandfather—did he have it, too?"

"I wouldn't know that, sir," said Jenkins. "I wasn't created until after your grandfather was an elderly man. But he may have. He never went anywhere, either."

"You understand, then," said Webster. "You know how it is. I feel like I'm going to be sick—physically ill. See if you can charter a 'copter—anything, just so we get home."

"Yes, sir," said Jenkins.

He started off and Webster called him back.

"Jenkins, does anyone else know about this? Anyone—"

"No, sir," said Jenkins. "Your father never mentioned it and I felt, somehow, that he wouldn't wish me to."

"Thank you, Jenkins," said Webster.

Webster huddled back into his chair again, feeling desolate and alone and misplaced. Alone in a humming lobby that pulsed with life—a loneliness that tore at him, that left him limp and weak.

Homesickness. Downright, shameful homesickness, he told himself. Something that boys are supposed to feel when they first leave home, when they first go out to meet the world.

There was a fancy word for it—agoraphobia, the morbid dread of being in the midst of open spaces—from the Greek root for the fear—literally, of the market place.

If he crossed the room to the television booth, he could put in a call, talk with his mother or one of the robots—or, better yet, just sit and look at the place until Jenkins came for him.

He started to rise, then sank back in the chair again. It was no dice. Just talking to someone or looking in on the place wasn't being there. He couldn't smell the pines in the wintry air, or hear familiar snow crunch on the walk beneath his feet or reach out a hand and touch one of the massive oaks that grew along the path. He couldn't feel the heat of the fire or sense the sure, deft touch of belonging, of being one with a tract of ground and the things upon it.

And yet—perhaps it would help. Not much, maybe, but some. He started to rise from the chair again and froze. The few short steps to the booth held terror, a terrible, overwhelming terror. If he crossed them, he would have to run. Run to escape the watching eyes, the unfamiliar sounds, the agonizing nearness of strange faces.

Abruptly he sat down.

A woman's shrill voice cut across the lobby and he shrank away from it. He felt terrible. He felt like hell. He wished Jenkins would get a hustle on.

The first breath of spring came through the window, filling the study with the promise of melting snows, of coming leaves and flowers, of north-bound wedges of

waterfowl streaming through the blue, of trout that lurked
in pools waiting for the fly.

Webster lifted his eyes from the sheaf of papers on his
desk, sniffed the breeze, felt the cool whisper of it on his
cheek. His hand reached out for the brandy glass, found
it empty, and put it back.

He bent back above the papers once again, picked up
a pencil and crossed out a word.

Critically, he read the final paragraphs:

The fact that of the two hundred fifty men who were
invited to visit me, presumably on missions of more than
ordinary importance, only three were able to come, does
not necessarily prove that all but those three are victims
of agoraphobia. Some may have had legitimate reasons
for being unable to accept my invitation. But it does indicate a growing unwillingness of men living under the
mode of Earth existence set up following the breakup of
the cities to move from familiar places, a deepening instinct to stay among the scenes and possessions which in
their mind have become associated with contentment and
graciousness of life.

What the result of such a trend will be, no one can
clearly indicate since it applies to only a small portion
of Earth's population. Among the larger families economic pressure forces some of the sons to seek their for-
tunes either in other parts of the Earth or on one of the
other planets. Many others deliberately seek adventure
and opportunity in space while still others become associated with professions or trades which make a sedentary
existence impossible.

He flipped the page over, went on to the last one.

It was a good paper, he knew, but it could not be published, not just yet. Perhaps after he had died. No one,
so far as he could determine, had ever so much as realized the trend, had taken as matter of course the fact
that men seldom left their homes. Why, after all, should
they leave their homes?

Certain dangers may be recognized in—

The televisor muttered at his elbow and he reached out to flip the toggle.

The room faded and he was face to face with a man who sat behind a desk, almost as if he sat on the opposite side of Webster's desk. A gray-haired man with sad eyes behind heavy lenses.

For a moment Webster stared, memory tugging at him.

"Could it be—" he asked and the man smiled gravely.

"I have changed," he said. "So have you. My name is Clayborne. Remember? The Martian medical commission—"

"Clayborne! I'd often thought of you. You stayed on Mars."

"Clayborne nodded. "I've read your book, doctor. It is a real contribution. I've often thought one should be written, wanted to myself, but I didn't have the time. Just as well I didn't. You did a better job. Especially on the brain."

"The Martian brain," Webster told him, "always intrigued me. Certain peculiarities. I'm afraid I spent more of those five years taking notes on it than I should have. There was other work to do."

"A good thing you did," said Clayborne. "That's why I'm calling you now. I have a patient—a brain operation. Only you can handle it."

Webster gasped, his hands trembling. "You'll bring him here?"

Clayborne shook his head. "He cannot be moved. You know him, I believe. Juwain, the philosopher."

"Juwain!" said Webster. "He's one of my best friends. We talked together just a couple of days ago."

"The attack was sudden," said Clayborne. "He's been asking for you."

Webster was silent and cold—cold with a chill that crept upon him from some unguessed place. Cold that sent perspiration out upon his forehead, that knotted his fists.

"If you start immediately," said Clayborne, "you can be here on time. I've already arranged with the World Committee to have a ship at your disposal instantly. The utmost speed is necessary."

"But," said Webster, "but . . . I cannot come."

"You can't come!"

"It's impossible," said Webster. "I doubt in any case that I am needed. Surely, you yourself—"

"I can't," said Clayborne. "No one can but you. No one else has the knowledge. You hold Juwain's life in your hands. If you come, he lives. If you don't, he dies."

"I can't go into space," said Webster.

"Anyone can go into space," snapped Clayborne. "It's not like it used to be. Conditioning of any sort desired is available."

"But you don't understand," pleaded Webster. "You—"

"No, I don't," said Clayborne. "Frankly, I don't. That anyone should refuse to save the life of his friend—"

The two men stared at one another for a long moment, neither speaking.

"I shall tell the committee to send the ship straight to your home," said Clayborne finally. "I hope by that time you will see your way clear to come."

Clayborne faded and the wall came into view again— the wall and books, the fireplace and the paintings, the well-loved furniture, the promise of spring that came through the open window.

Webster sat frozen in his chair, staring at the wall in front of him.

Juwain, the furry, wrinkled face, the sibilant whisper, the friendliness and understanding that was his. Juwain, grasping the stuff that dreams are made of and shaping them into logic, into rules of life and conduct. Juwain, using philosophy as a tool, as a science, as a steppingstone to better living.

Webster dropped his face into his hands and fought the agony that welled up within him.

Clayborne had not understood. One could not expect him to understand since there was no way for him to know. And even knowing, would he understand? Even he, Webster, would not have understood it in someone else until he had discovered it in himself—the terrible fear of leaving his own fire, his own land, his own possessions, the little symbolisms that he had erected. And yet, not he, himself, alone, but those other Websters as well. Starting with the first John J. Men and women who had set up a cult of life, a tradition of behavior.

He, Jerome A. Webster, had gone to Mars when he was a young man, and had not felt or suspected the psychological poison that ran through his veins. Even as Thomas a few months ago had gone to Mars. But thirty years of quiet life here in the retreat that the Websters called a home had brought it forth, had developed it without his even knowing it. There had, in fact, been no opportunity to know it.

It was clear how it had developed—clear as crystal now. Habit and mental pattern and a happiness association with certain things—things that had no actual value in themselves, but had been assigned a value, a definite, concrete value by one family through five generations.

No wonder other places seemed alien, no wonder other horizons held a hint of horror in their sweep.

And there was nothing one could do about it—nothing, that is, unless one cut down every tree and burned the house and changed the course of waterways. Even that might not do it—even that—

The televisor purred and Webster lifted his head from his hands, reached out and thumbed the tumbler.

The room became a flare of white, but there was no image. A voice said: "Secret call. Secret call."

Webster slid back a panel in the machine, spun a pair of dials, heard the hum of power surge into a screen that blocked out the room.

"Secrecy established," he said.

The white flare snapped out and a man sat across the desk from him. A man he had seen many times before in televised addresses, in his daily paper.

Henderson, president of the World Committee.

"I have had a call from Clayborne," said Henderson.

Webster nodded without speaking.

"He tells me you refuse to go to Mars."

"I have not refused," said Webster. "When Clayborne cut off the question was left open. I had told him it was impossible for me to go, but he had rejected that, did not seem to understand."

"Webster, you must go," said Henderson. "You are the only man with the necessary knowledge of the Martian brain to perform this operation. If it were a simple operation, perhaps someone else could do it. But not one such as this."

"That may be true," said Webster, "but—"

"It's not just a question of saving a life," said Henderson. "Even the life of so distinguished a personage as Juwain. It involves even more than that. Juwain is a friend of yours. Perhaps he hinted of something he has found."

"Yes," said Webster. "Yes, he did. A new concept of philosophy."

"A concept," declared Henderson, "that we cannot do without. A concept that will remake the solar system, that will put mankind ahead a hundred thousand years in the space of two generations. A new direction of purpose that will aim toward a goal we heretofore had not suspected, had not even known existed. A brand new truth, you see. One that never before had occurred to anyone."

Webster's hands gripped the edge of the desk until his knuckles stood out white.

"If Juwain dies," said Henderson, "that concept dies with him. May be lost forever."

"I'll try," said Webster. "I'll try—"

Henderson's eyes were hard. "Is that the best you can do?"

"That is the best," said Webster.

"But, man, you must have a reason! Some explanation."

"None," said Webster, "that I would care to give."

Deliberately he reached out and flipped up the switch.

Webster sat at the desk and held his hands in front of him, staring at them. Hands that had skill, held knowledge. Hands that could save a life if he could get them to Mars. Hands that could save for the solar system, for mankind, for the Martians an idea—a new idea—that would advance them a hundred thousand years in the next two generations.

But hands chained by a phobia that grew out of this quiet life. Decadence—a strangely beautiful—and deadly —decadence.

Man had forsaken the teeming cities, the huddling

places, two hundred years ago. He had done with the old foes and the ancient fears that kept him around the common campfire, had left behind the hobgoblins that had walked with him from the caves.

And yet—and yet.

Here was another huddling place. Not a huddling place for one's body, but one's mind. A psychological campfire that still held a man within the circle of its light.

Still, Webster knew, he must leave that fire. As the men had done with the cities two centuries before, he must walk off and leave it. And he must not look back.

He had to go to Mars—or at least start for Mars. There was no question there, at all. He had to go.

Whether he would survive the trip, whether he could perform the operation once he had arrived, he did not know. He wondered vaguely, whether agoraphobia could be fatal. In its most exaggerated form, he supposed it could.

He reached out a hand to ring, then hesitated. No use having Jenkins pack. He would do it himself—something to keep him busy until the ship arrived.

From the top shelf of the wardrobe in the bedroom, he took down a bag and saw that it was dusty. He blew on it, but the dust still clung. It had been there for too many years.

As he packed, the room argued with him, talked in that mute tongue with which inanimate but familiar things may converse with a man.

"You can't go," said the room. "You can't go off and leave me."

And Webster argued back, half pleading, half explanatory. "I have to go. Can't you understand? It's a friend, an old friend. I will be coming back."

Packing done, Webster returned to the study, slumped into his chair.

He must go and yet he couldn't go. But when the ship arrived, when the time had come, he knew that he would walk out of the house and toward the waiting ship.

He steeled his mind to that, tried to set it in a rigid pattern, tried to blank out everything but the thought that he was leaving.

Things in the room intruded on his brain, as if they

were part of a conspiracy to keep him there. Things that he saw as if he were seeing them for the first time. Old, remembered things that suddenly were new. The chronometer that showed both Earthian and Martian time, the days of the month, the phases of the moon. The picture of his dead wife on the desk. The trophy he had won at prep school. The framed short snorter bill that had cost him ten bucks on his trip to Mars.

He stared at them, half unwilling at first, then eagerly, storing up the memory of them in his brain. Seeing them as separate components of a room he had accepted all these years as a finished whole, never realizing what a multitude of things went to make it up.

Dusk was falling, the dusk of early spring, a dusk that smelled of early pussy willows.

The ship should have arrived long ago. He caught himself listening for it, even as he realized that he would not hear it. A ship, driven by atomic motors, was silent except when it gathered speed. Landing and taking off, it floated like thistledown, with not a murmur in it.

It would be here soon. It would have to be here soon or he could never go. Much longer to wait, he knew, and his high-keyed resolution would crumble like a mound of dust in beating rain. Not much longer could he hold his purpose against the pleading of the room, against the flicker of the fire, against the murmur of the land where five generations of Websters had lived their lives and died.

He shut his eyes and fought down the chill that crept across his body. He couldn't let it get him now, he told himself. He had to stick it out. When the ship arrived he still must be able to get up and walk out the door to the waiting port.

A tap came on the door.

"Come in," Webster called.

It was Jenkins, the light from the fireplace flickering on his shining metal hide.

"Had you called earlier, sir?" he asked.

Webster shook his head.

"I was afraid you might have," Jenkins explained, "and wondered why I didn't come. There was a most extraordinary occurrence, sir. Two men came with a ship and said they wanted you to go to Mars."

"They are here," said Webster. "Why didn't you call me?"

He struggled to his feet.

"I didn't think, sir," said Jenkins, "that you would want to be bothered. It was so preposterous. I finally made them understand you could not possibly want to go to Mars."

Webster stiffened, felt chill fear gripping at his heart. Hands groping for the edge of the desk, he sat down in the chair, sensed the walls of the room closing in about him, a trap that would never let him go.

ARENA

by Fredric Brown

Carson opened his eyes, and found himself looking upward into a flickering blue dimness.

It was hot, and he was lying on sand, and a sharp rock embedded in the sand was hurting his back. He rolled over to his side, off the rock, and then pushed himself up to a sitting position.

"I'm crazy," he thought. "Crazy—or dead—or something." The sand was blue, bright blue. And there wasn't any such thing as bright blue sand on Earth or any of the planets.

Blue sand.

Blue sand under a blue dome that wasn't the sky nor yet a room, but a circumscribed area—somehow he knew it was circumscribed and finite even though he couldn't see to the top of it.

He picked up some of the sand in his hand and let it run through his fingers. It trickled down onto his bare leg. *Bare?*

Naked. He was stark naked, and already his body was dripping perspiration from the enervating heat, coated blue with sand wherever sand had touched it.

But elsewhere his body was white.

He thought: Then this sand is really blue. If it seemed blue only because of the blue light, then I'd be blue also. But I'm white, so the sand *is* blue. *Blue sand.* There isn't any blue sand. There isn't any place like this place I'm in.

Sweat was running down in his eyes.

First published in 1944

It was hot, hotter than hell. Only hell—the hell of the ancients—was supposed to be red and not blue.

But if this place wasn't hell, what was it? Only Mercury, among the planets, had heat like this and this wasn't Mercury. And Mercury was some four billion miles from—

It came back to him then, where he'd been. In the little one-man scouter, outside the orbit of Pluto, scouting a scant million miles to one side of the Earth Armada drawn up in battle array there to intercept the Outsiders.

That sudden strident nerve-shattering ringing of the alarm bell when the rival scouter—the Outsider ship—had come within range of his detectors—

No one knew who the Outsiders were, what they looked like, from what far galaxy they came, other than that it was in the general direction of the Pleiades.

First, sporadic raids on Earth colonies and outposts. Isolated battles between Earth patrols and small groups of Outsider spaceships; battles sometimes won and sometimes lost, but never to date resulting in the capture of an alien vessel. Nor had any member of a raided colony ever survived to describe the Outsiders who had left the ships, if indeed they had left them.

Not a too-serious menace, at first, for the raids had not been too numerous or destructive. And individually, the ships had proved slightly inferior in armament to the best of Earth's fighters, although somewhat superior in speed and maneuverability. A sufficient edge in speed, in fact, to give the Outsiders their choice of running or fighting, unless surrounded.

Nevertheless, Earth had prepared for serious trouble, for a showdown, building the mightiest armada of all time. It had been waiting now, that armada, for a long time. But now the showdown was coming.

Scouts twenty billion miles out had detected the approach of a mighty fleet—a showdown fleet—of the Outsiders. Those scouts had never come back, but their radiotronic messages had. And now Earth's armada, all ten thousand ships and half-million fighting spacemen, was out there, outside Pluto's orbit, waiting to intercept and battle to the death.

And an even battle it was going to be, judging by the advance reports of the men of the far picket line who had given their lives to report—before they had died—on the size and strength of the alien fleet.

Anybody's battle, with the mastery of the solar system hanging in the balance, on an even chance. A last and *only* chance, for Earth and all her colonies lay at the utter mercy of the Outsiders if they ran that gauntlet—

Oh yes. Bob Carson remembered now.

Not that it explained blue sand and flickering blueness. But that strident alarming of the bell and his leap for the control panel. His frenzied fumbling as he strapped himself into the seat. The dot in the visiplate that grew larger.

The dryness of his mouth. The awful knowledge that this was *it.* For him, at least, although the main fleets were still out of range of one another.

This, his first taste of battle. Within three seconds or less he'd be victorious, or a charred cinder. Dead.

Three seconds—that's how long a space-battle lasted. Time enough to count to three, slowly, and you'd won or you were dead. One hit completely took care of a lightly armed and armored little one-man craft like a scouter.

Frantically—as, unconsciously, his dry lips shaped the word "One"—he worked at the controls to keep that growing dot centered on the crossed spiderwebs of the visiplate. His hands doing that, while his right foot hovered over the pedal that would fire the bolt. The single bolt of concentrated hell that had to hit—or else. There wouldn't be time for any second shot.

"Two." He didn't know he'd said that, either. The dot in the visiplate wasn't a dot now. Only a few thousand miles away, it showed up in the magnification of the plate as though it were only a few hundred yards off. It was a sleek, fast little scouter, about the size of his.

And an alien ship, all right.

"Thr—" His foot touched the bolt-release pedal—

And then the Outsider had swerved suddenly and was off the crosshairs. Carson punched keys frantically, to follow.

For a tenth of a second, it was out of the visiplate en-

tirely, and then as the nose of his scouter swung after it,
he saw it again, diving straight toward the ground.

The ground?

It was an optical illusion of some sort. It *had* to be, that
planet—or whatever it was—that now covered the visiplate. Whatever it was, it couldn't be there. Couldn't possibly. There *wasn't* any planet nearer than Neptune three
billion miles away—with Pluto around on the opposite
side of the distant pinpoint sun.

His *detectors!* They hadn't shown any object of planetary dimensions, even of asteroid dimensions. They still
didn't.

So it couldn't be there, and whatever-it-was he was diving into, only a few hundred miles below him.

And in his sudden anxiety to keep from crashing, he
forgot even the Outsider ship. He fired the front braking
rockets, and even as the sudden change of speed slammed
him forward against the seat straps, he fired full right for
an emergency turn. Pushed them down and *held* them
down, knowing that he needed everything the ship had
to keep from crashing and that a turn that sudden would
black him out for a moment.

It did black him out.

And that was all. Now he was sitting in hot blue sand,
stark naked but otherwise unhurt. No sign of his spaceship and—for that matter—no sign of *space*. That curve
overhead wasn't a sky, whatever else it was.

He scrambled to his feet.

Gravity seemed a little more than Earth-normal. Not
much more.

Flat sand stretching away, a few scrawny bushes in
clumps here and there. The bushes were blue, too, but
in varying shades, some lighter than the blue of the sand,
some darker.

Out from under the nearest bush ran a little thing that
was like a lizard, except that it had more than four legs.
It was blue, too. Bright blue. It saw him and ran back
again under the bush.

He looked up again, trying to decide what was overhead. It wasn't exactly a roof, but it was dome-shaped.
It flickered and was hard to look at. But definitely, it

curved down to the ground, to the blue sand, all around him.

He wasn't far from being under the center of the dome. At a guess, it was a hundred yards to the nearest wall, if it was a wall. It was as though a blue hemisphere of *something*, about two hundred and fifty yards in circumference, was inverted over the flat expanse of the sand.

And everything blue, except one object. Over near a far curving wall there was a red object. Roughly spherical it seemed to be about a yard in diameter. Too far for him to see clearly through the flickering blueness. But, unaccountably, he shuddered.

He wiped sweat from his forehead, or tried to, with the back of his hand.

Was this a dream, a nightmare? This heat, this sand, that vague feeling of horror he felt when he looked toward the red thing?

A dream? No, one didn't go to sleep and dream in the midst of a battle in space.

Death? No, never. If there were immortality, it wouldn't be a senseless thing like this, a thing of blue heat and blue sand and a red horror.

Then he heard the voice—

Inside his head he heard it, not with his ears. It came from nowhere or everywhere.

"Through spaces and dimensions wandering," rang the words in his mind, *"and in this space and this time I find two people about to wage a war that would exterminate one and so weaken the other that it would retrogress and never fulfill its destiny, but decay and return to mindless dust whence it came. And I say this must not happen."*

"Who . . . what are you?" Carson didn't say it aloud, but the question formed itself in his brain.

"You would not understand completely. I am—" There was a pause as though the voice sought—in Carson's brain —for a word that wasn't there, a word he didn't know. *"I am the end of evolution of a race so old the time can not be expressed in words that have meaning to your mind. A race fused into a single entity, eternal—*

"An entity such as your primitive race might become" —again the groping for a word—*"time from now. So might the race you call, in your mind, the Outsiders. So*

*I intervene in the battle to come, the battle between fleets
so evenly matched that destruction of both races will result.
One must survive. One must progress and evolve.*"

"One?" thought Carson. "Mine, or—?"

"*It is in my power to stop the war, to send the Outsiders back to their galaxy. But they would return, or your
race would sooner or later follow them there. Only by remaining in this space and time to intervene constantly
could I prevent them from destroying one another, and I
cannot remain.*

"*So I shall intervene now. I shall destroy one fleet completely without loss to the other. One civilization shall thus
survive.*"

Nightmare. This had to be nightmare, Carson thought.
But he knew it wasn't.

It was too mad, too impossible, to be anything but real.

He didn't dare ask *the* question—*which?* But his
thoughts asked it for him.

"*The stronger shall survive,*" said the voice. "*That I can
not—and would not—change. I merely intervene to make
it a complete victory, not*"—groping again—"*not Pyrrhic
victory to a broken race.*

"*From the outskirts of the not-yet battle I plucked two
individuals, you and an Outsider. I see from your mind
that in your early history of nationalisms battles between
champions, to decide issues between races, were not unknown.*

"*You and your opponent are here pitted against one
another, naked and unarmed, under conditions equally unfamiliar to you both, equally unpleasant to you both. There
is no time limit, for here there is no time. The survivor
is the champion of his race. That race survives.*"

"But—" Carson's protest was too inarticulate for expression, but the voice answered it.

"*It is fair. The conditions are such that the accident of
physical strength will not completely decide the issue.
There is a barrier. You will understand. Brain-power and
courage will be more important than strength. Most especially courage, which is the will to survive.*"

"But while this goes on, the fleets will—"

"*No, you are in another space, another time. For as long
as you are here, time stands still in the universe you know.*

I see you wonder whether this place is real. It is, and it is not. As I—to your limited understanding—am and am not real. My existence is mental and not physical. You saw me as a planet; it could have been as a dustmote or a sun.

"But to you this place is now real. What you suffer here will be real. And if you die here, your death will be real. If you die, your failure will be the end of your race. That is enough for you to know."

And then the voice was gone.

And he was alone, but not alone. For as Carson looked up, he saw that the red thing, the red sphere of horror which he now knew was the Outsider, was rolling toward him.

Rolling.

It seemed to have no legs or arms that he could see, no features. It rolled across the blue sand with the fluid quickness of a drop of mercury. And before it, in some manner he could not understand, came a paralyzing wave of nauseating, retching, horrid hatred.

Carson looked about him frantically. A stone, lying in the sand a few feet away, was the nearest thing to a weapon. It wasn't large, but it had sharp edges, like a slab of flint. It looked a bit like blue flint.

He picked it up, and crouched to receive the attack. It was coming fast, faster than he could run.

No time to think out how he was going to fight it, and how anyway could he plan to battle a creature whose strength, whose characteristics, whose method of fighting he did not know? Rolling so fast, it looked more than ever like a perfect sphere.

Ten yards way. Five. And then it stopped.

Rather, it *was stopped*. Abruptly the near side of it flattened as though it had run up against an invisible wall. It bounced, actually bounced back.

Then it rolled forward again, but more slowly, more cautiously. It stopped again, at the same place. It tried again, a few yards to one side.

There was a barrier there of some sort. It clicked, then, in Carson's mind. That thought projected into his mind by the Entity who had brought them there: "—accident of physical strength will not completely decide the issue. There is a barrier."

A force-field, of course. Not the Netzian Field, known to Earth science, for that glowed and emitted a crackling sound. This one was invisible, silent.

It was a wall that ran from side to side of the inverted hemisphere; Carson didn't have to verify that himself. The Roller was doing that; rolling sideways along the barrier, seeking a break in it that wasn't there.

Carson took half a dozen steps forward, his left hand groping out before him, and then his hand touched the barrier. It felt smooth, yielding, like a sheet of rubber rather than like glass. Warm to his touch, but no warmer than the sand underfoot. And it was completely invisible, even at close range.

He dropped the stone and put both hands against it, pushing. It seemed to yield, just a trifle. But no farther than that trifle, even when he pushed with all his weight. It felt like a sheet of rubber backed up by steel. Limited resiliency, and then firm strength.

He stood on tiptoe and reached as high as he could and the barrier was still there.

He saw the Roller coming back, having reached one side of the arena. That feeling of nausea hit Carson again, and he stepped back from the barrier as it went by. It didn't stop.

But did the barrier stop at ground level? Carson knelt down and burrowed in the sand. It was soft, light, easy to dig in. At two feet down the barrier was still there.

The Roller was coming back again. Obviously, it couldn't find a way through at either side.

There must be a way through, Carson thought. *Some* way we can get at each other, else this duel is meaningless.

But no hurry now, in finding that out. There was something to try first. The Roller was back now, and it stopped just across the barrier, only six feet away. It seemed to be studying him, although for the life of him, Carson couldn't find external evidence of sense organs on the thing. Nothing that looked like eyes or ears, or even a mouth. There was though, he saw now, a series of grooves—perhaps a dozen of them altogether, and he saw two tentacles suddenly push out from two of the grooves and dip into the sand as though testing its consistency. Tentacles about an inch in diameter and perhaps a foot and a half long.

But the tentacles were retractable into the grooves and were kept there except when in use. They were retracted when the thing rolled and seemed to have nothing to do with its method of locomotion. That, as far as Carson could judge, seemed to be accomplished by some shifting—just *how* he couldn't even imagine—of its center of gravity.

He shuddered as he looked at the thing. It was alien, utterly alien, horribly different from anything on Earth or any of the life forms found on the other solar planets. Instinctively, somehow, he knew its mind was as alien as its body.

But he had to try. If it had no telepathic powers at all, the attempt was foredoomed to failure, yet he thought it had such powers. There had, at any rate, been a projection of something that was not physical at the time a few minutes ago when it had first started for him. An almost tangible wave of hatred.

If it could project that, perhaps it could read his mind as well, sufficiently for his purpose.

Deliberately, Carson picked up the rock that had been his only weapon, then tossed it down again in a gesture of relinquishment and raised his empty hands, palms up, before him.

He spoke aloud, knowing that although the words would be meaningless to the creature before him, speaking them would focus his own thoughts more completely upon the message.

"Can we not have peace between us?" he said, his voice sounding strange in the utter stillness. "The Entity who brought us here has told us what must happen if our races fight—extinction of one and weakening and retrogression of the other. The battle between them, said the Entity, depends upon what we do here. Why can not we agree to an external peace—your race to its galaxy, we to ours?"

Carson blanked out his mind to receive a reply.

It came, and it staggered him back, physically. He actually recoiled several steps in sheer horror at the depth and intensity of the hatred and lust-to-kill of the red images that had been projected at him. Not as articulate words—as had come to him the thoughts of the Entity—but as wave upon wave of fierce emotion.

For a moment that seemed an eternity he had to struggle

against the mental impact of that hatred, fight to clear his mind of it and drive out the alien thoughts to which he had given admittance by blanking out his own thoughts. He wanted to retch.

Slowly his mind cleared as, slowly, the mind of a man wakening from nightmare clears away the fear-fabric of which the dream was woven. He was breathing hard and he felt weaker, but he could think.

He stood studying the Roller. It had been motionless during the mental duel it had so nearly won. Now it rolled a few feet to one side, to the nearest of the blue bushes. Three tentacles whipped out of their grooves and began to investigate the bush.

"O.K.," Carson said, "so it's war then." He managed a wry grin. "If I got your answer straight, peace doesn't appeal to you." And, because he was, after all, a quiet young man and couldn't resist the impulse to be dramatic, he added. "To the death!"

But his voice, in that utter silence, sounded very silly, even to himself. It came to him, then, that this *was* to the death. Not only his own death or that of the red spherical thing which he now thought of as the Roller, but death to the entire race of one or the other of them. The end of the human race, if he failed.

It made him suddenly very humble, and very afraid to think that. More than to think it, to *know* it. Somehow with a knowledge that was above even faith, he knew that the Entity who had arranged this duel had told the truth about its intentions and its powers. It wasn't kidding.

The future of humanity depended upon *him*. It was an awful thing to realize, and he wrenched his mind away from it. He had to concentrate on the situation at hand.

There had to be some way of getting through the barrier, or of killing through the barrier.

Mentally? He hoped that wasn't all, for the Roller obviously had stronger telepathic powers than the primitive, undeveloped ones of the human race. Or did it?

He had been able to drive the thoughts of the Roller out of his own mind; could it drive out his? If its ability to project were stronger, might not its receptivity mechanism be more vulnerable?

He stared at it and endeavored to concentrate and focus all his thoughts upon it.

"Die," he thought. *"You are going to die. You are dying. You are—"*

He tried variations on it, and mental pictures. Sweat stood out on his forehead and he found himself trembling with the intensity of the effort. But the Roller went ahead with its investigation of the bush, as utterly unaffected as though Carson had been reciting the multiplication table.

So *that* was no good.

He felt a bit weak and dizzy from the heat and his strenuous effort at concentration. He sat down on the blue sand to rest and gave his full attention to watching and studying the Roller. By close study, perhaps, he could judge its strength and detect its weaknesses, learn things that would be valuable to know when and if they should come to grips.

It was breaking off twigs. Carson watched carefully, trying to judge just how hard it worked to do that. Later, he thought, he could find a similar bush on his own side, break off twigs of equal thickness himself, and gain a comparison of physical strength between his own arms and hands and those tentacles.

The twigs broke off hard; the Roller was having to struggle with each one, he saw. Each tentacle, he saw, bifurcated at the tip into two fingers, each tipped by a nail or claw. The claws didn't seem to be particularly long or dangerous. No more so than his own fingernails, if they were let to grow a bit.

No, on the whole, it didn't look too tough to handle physically. Unless, of course, that bush was made of pretty tough stuff. Carson looked around him and, yes, right within reach was another bush of identical type.

He reached over and snapped off a twig. It was brittle, easy to break. Of course, the Roller might have been faking deliberately but he didn't think so.

On the other hand, where was it vulnerable? Just how would he go about killing it, if he got the chance? He went back to studying it. The outer hide looked pretty tough. He'd need a sharp weapon of some sort. He picked up the piece of rock again. It was about twelve inches long, narrow, and fairly sharp on one end. If it chipped like flint, he could make a serviceable knife out of it.

The Roller was continuing its investigations of the bushes. It rolled again, to the nearest one of another type. A little blue lizard, many-legged like the one Carson had seen on his side of the barrier, darted out from under the bush.

A tentacle of the Roller lashed out and caught it, picked it up. Another tentacle whipped over and began to pull legs off the lizard, as coldly and calmly as it had pulled twigs off the bush. The creature struggled frantically and emitted a shrill squealing sound that was the first sound Carson had heard here other than the sound of his own voice.

Carson shuddered and wanted to turn his eyes away. But he made himself continue to watch; anything he could learn about his opponent might prove valuable. Even this knowledge of its unnecessary cruelty. Particularly, he thought with a sudden vicious surge of emotion, this knowledge of its unnecessary cruelty. It would make it a pleasure to kill the thing, if and when the chance came.

He steeled himself to watch the dismembering of the lizard, for that very reason.

But he felt glad when, with half its legs gone, the lizard quit squealing and struggling and lay limp and dead in the Roller's grasp.

It didn't continue with the rest of the legs. Contempuously it tossed the dead lizard away from it, in Carson's direction. It arced through the air between them and landed at his feet.

It had come through the barrier! The barrier wasn't there any more!

Carson was on his feet in a flash, the knife gripped tightly in his hand, and leaped forward. He'd settle this thing here and now! With the barrier gone—

But it wasn't gone. He found that out the hard way, running head on into it and nearly knocking himself silly. He bounced back, and fell.

And as he sat up, shaking his head to clear it, he saw something coming through the air toward him, and to duck it, he threw himself flat again on the sand, and to one side.

He got his body out of the way, but there was a sudden sharp pain in the calf of his left leg.

He rolled backward, ignoring the pain, and scrambled to his feet. It was a rock, he saw now, that had struck him. And the Roller was picking up another one now, swinging it back gripped between two tentacles, getting ready to throw again.

It sailed through the air toward him, but he was easily able to step out of its way. The Roller, apparently, could throw straight, but not hard nor far. The first rock had struck him only because he had been sitting down and had not seen it coming until it was almost upon him.

Even as he stepped aside from that weak second throw, Carson drew back his right arm and let fly with the rock that was still in his hand. If missiles, he thought with sudden elation, can cross the barrier, then two can play at the game of throwing them. And the good right arm of an Earthman—

He couldn't miss a three-foot sphere at only four-yard range, and he didn't miss. The rock whizzed straight, and with a speed several times that of the missiles the Roller had thrown. It hit dead center, but it hit flat, unfortunately, instead of point first.

But it hit with a resounding thump, and obviously it hurt. The Roller had been reaching for another rock, but it changed its mind and got out of there instead. By the time Carson could pick up and throw another rock, the Roller was forty yards back from the barrier and going strong.

His second throw missed by feet, and his third throw was short. The Roller was back out of range—at least out of range of a missile heavy enough to be damaging.

Carson grinned. That round had been his. Except—

He quit grinning as he bent over to examine the calf of his leg. A jagged edge of the stone had made a pretty deep cut, several inches long. It was bleeding pretty freely, but he didn't think it had gone deep enough to hit an artery. If it stopped bleeding of its own accord, well and good. If not, he was in for trouble.

Finding out one thing, though, took precedence over that cut. The nature of the barrier.

He went forward to it again, this time groping with his

hands before him. He found it; then holding one hand against it, he tossed a handful of sand at it with the other hand. The sand went right through. His hand didn't.

Organic matter versus inorganic? No, because the dead lizard had gone through it, and a lizard, alive or dead, was certainly organic. Plant life? He broke off a twig and poked it at the barrier. The twig went through, with no resistance, but when his fingers gripping the twig came to the barrier, they were stopped.

He couldn't get through it, nor could the Roller. But rocks and sand and a dead lizard—

How about a live lizard? He went hunting, under the bushes, until he found one, and caught it. He tossed it gently against the barrier and it bounced back and scurried away across the blue sand.

That gave him the answer, in so far as he could determine it now. The screen was a barrier to living things. Dead or inorganic matter could cross it.

That off his mind, Carson looked at his injured leg again. The bleeding was lessening, which meant he wouldn't need to worry about making a tourniquet. But he should find some water, if any was available, to clean the wound.

Water—the thought of it made him realize that he was getting awfully thirsty. He'd *have* to find some water, in case this contest turned out to be a protracted one.

Limping slightly now, he started off to make a full circuit of his half of the arena. Guiding himself with one hand along the barrier, he walked to his right until he came to the curving sidewall. It was visible, a dull blue-gray at close range, and the surface of it felt just like the central barrier.

He experimented by tossing a handful of sand at it, and the sand reached the wall and disappeared as it went through. The hemispherical shell was a force-field, too. But an opaque one, instead of transparent like the barrier.

He followed it around until he came back to the barrier, and walked back along the barrier to the point from which he'd started.

No sign of water.

Worried now, he started a series of zigzags back and forth between the barrier and the wall, covering the intervening space thoroughly.

No water. Blue sand, blue bushes, and intolerable heat. Nothing else.

It must be his imagination, he told himself angrily, that he was suffering *that* much from thirst. How long had he been here? Of course, no time at all, according to his own spacetime frame. The Entity had told him time stood still out there, while he was here. But his body processes went on here, just the same. And according to his body's reckoning, how long had he been here? Three or four hours, perhaps. Certainly not long enough to be suffering seriously from thirst.

But he was suffering from it; his throat dry and parched. Probably the intense heat was the cause. It was *hot!* A hundred and thirty Fahrenheit, at a guess. A dry, still heat without the slightest movement of air.

He was limping rather badly, and utterly fagged out when he'd finished the futile exploration of his domain.

He stared across at the motionless Roller and hoped it was as miserable as he was. And quite possibly it wasn't enjoying this, either. The Entity had said the conditions here were equally unfamiliar and equally uncomfortable for both of them. Maybe the Roller came from a planet where two-hundred degree heat was the norm. Maybe it was freezing while he was roasting.

Maybe the air was much too thick for it as it was too thin for him. For the exertion of his explorations had left him panting. The atmosphere here, he realized now, was not much thicker than that on Mars.

No water.

That meant a deadline, for him at any rate. Unless he could find a way to cross that barrier or to kill his enemy from this side of it, thirst would kill him, eventually.

It gave him a feeling of desperate urgency. He *must* hurry.

But he made himself sit down a moment to rest, to think.

What was there to do? Nothing, and yet so many things. The several varieties of bushes, for example. They didn't look promising, but he'd have to examine them for possibilities. And his leg—he'd have to do something about that, even without water to clean it. Gather ammunition in the form of rocks. Find a rock that would make a good knife.

His leg hurt rather badly now, and he decided that came first. One type of bush had leaves—or things rather similar to leaves. He pulled off a handful of them and decided, after examination, to take a chance on them. He used them to clean off the sand and dirt and caked blood, then made a pad of fresh leaves and tied it over the wound with tendrils from the same bush.

The tendrils proved unexpectedly tough and strong. They were slender, and soft and pliable, yet he couldn't break them at all. He had to saw them off the bush with the sharp edge of a piece of the blue flint. Some of the thicker ones were over a foot long, and he filed away in his memory, for future reference, the fact that a bunch of the thick ones, tied together, would make a pretty serviceable rope. Maybe he'd be able to think of a use for a rope.

Next he made himself a knife. The blue flint *did* chip. From a footlong splinter of it, he fashioned himself a crude but lethal weapon. And of tendrils from the bush, he made himself a rope-belt through which he could thrust the flint knife, to keep it with him all the time and yet have his hands free.

He went back to studying the bushes. There were three other types. One was leafless, dry, brittle, rather like a dried tumbleweed. Another was of soft, crumbly wood, almost like punk. It looked and felt as though it would make excellent tinder for a fire. The third type was the most nearly woodlike. It had fragile leaves that wilted at the touch, but the stalks, although short, were straight and strong.

It was horribly, unbearable hot.

He limped up to the barrier, felt to make sure that it was still there. It was.

He stood watching the Roller for a while. It was keeping a safe distance back from the barrier, out of effective stone-throwing range. It was moving around back there, doing something. He couldn't tell what it was doing.

Once it stopped moving, came a little closer, and seemed to concentrate its attention on him. Again Carson had to fight off a wave of nausea. He threw a stone at it and the

Roller retreated and went back to whatever it had been doing before.

At least he could make it keep its distance.

And, he thought bitterly, a devil of a lot of good *that* did him. Just the same, he spent the next hour or two gathering stones of suitable size for throwing, and making several neat piles of them, near his side of the barrier.

His throat burned now. It was difficult for him to think about anything except water.

But he *had* to think about other things. About getting through that barrier, under or over it, getting *at* that red sphere and killing it before this place of heat and thirst killed him first.

The barrier went to the wall upon either side, but how high and how far under the sand?

For just a moment, Carson's mind was too fuzzy to think out how he could find out either of those things. Idly, sitting there in the hot sand—and he didn't remember sitting down—he watched a blue lizard crawl from the shelter of one bush to the shelter of another.

From under the second bush, it looked out at him.

Carson grinned at it. Maybe he was getting a bit punch-drunk, because he remembered suddenly the old story of the desert colonists on Mars, taken from an older desert story of Earth—"Pretty soon you get so lonesome you find yourself talking to the lizards, and then not so long after that you find the lizards talking back to you—"

He should have been concentrating, of course, on how to kill the Roller, but instead he grinned at the lizard and said, "Hello, there."

The lizard took a few steps toward him. "Hello," it said.

Carson was stunned for a moment, and then he put back his head and roared with laughter. It didn't hurt his throat to do so, either; he hadn't been *that* thirsty.

Why not? Why should the Entity who thought up this nightmare of a place not have a sense of humor, along with the other powers he had? Talking lizards, equipped to talk back in my language, if I talk to them— It's a nice touch.

He grinned at the lizard and said, "Come on over." But the lizard turned and ran away, scurrying from bush to bush until it was out of sight.

He was thirsty again.

And he had to *do* something. He couldn't win this contest by sitting here sweating and feeling miserable. He had to *do* something. But what?

Get through the barrier. But he couldn't get through it, or over it. But was he certain he couldn't get under it? And come to think of it, didn't one sometimes find water by digging? Two birds with one stone—

Painfully now, Carson limped up to the barrier and started digging, scooping up sand a double handful at a time. It was slow, hard work because the sand ran in at the edges and the deeper he got the bigger in diameter the hole had to be. How many hours it took him, he didn't know, but he hit bedrock four feet down. Dry bedrock; no sign of water.

And the force-field of the barrier went down clear to the bedrock. No dice. No water. Nothing.

He crawled out of the hole and lay there panting, and then raised his head to look across and see what the Roller was doing. It must be doing something back there.

It was. It was making something out of wood from the bushes, tied together with tendrils. A queerly shaped framework about four feet high and roughly square. To see it better, Carson climbed up onto the mound of sand he had excavated from the hole, and stood there staring.

There were two long levers sticking out of the back of it, one with a cup-shaped affair on the end of it. Seemed to be some sort of catapult, Carson thought.

Sure enough, the Roller was lifting a sizable rock into the cup-shaped outfit. One of his tentacles moved the other lever up and down for awhile, and then he turned the machine slightly as though aiming it and the lever with the stone flew up and forward.

The stone raced several yards over Carson's head, so far away that he didn't have to duck, but he judged the distance it had traveled, and whistled softly. He couldn't throw a rock that weight more than half that distance. And even retreating to the rear of his domain wouldn't put him out of range of that machine, if the Roller shoved it forward almost to the barrier.

Another rock whizzed over. Not quite so far away this time.

That thing could be dangerous, he decided. Maybe he'd better do something about it.

Moving from side to side along the barrier, so the catapult couldn't bracket him, he whaled a dozen rocks at it. But that wasn't going to be any good, he saw. They had to be light rocks, or he couldn't throw them that far. If they hit the framework, they bounced off harmlessly. And the Roller had no difficulty, at that distance, in moving aside from those that came near it.

Besides, his arm was tiring badly. He ached all over from sheer weariness. If he could only rest awhile without having to duck rocks from that catapult at regular intervals of maybe thirty seconds each—

He stumbled back to the rear of the arena. Then he saw even that wasn't any good. The rocks reached back there, too, only there were longer intervals between them, as though it took longer to wind up the mechanism, whatever it was, of the catapult.

Wearily he dragged himself back to the barrier again. Several times he fell and could barely rise to his feet to go on. He was, he knew, near the limit of his endurance. Yet he didn't dare stop moving now, until and unless he could put that catapult out of action. If he fell asleep, he'd never wake up.

One of the stones from it gave him the first glimmer of an idea. It struck upon one of the piles of stones he'd gathered together near the barrier to use as ammunition, and it struck sparks.

Sparks. Fire. Primitive man had made fire by striking sparks, and with some of those dry crumbly bushes as tinder—

Luckily, a bush of that type was near him. He broke it off, took it over to a pile of stones, then patiently hit one stone against another until a spark touched the punklike wood of the bush. It went up in flames so fast that it singed his eyebrows and was burned to an ash within seconds.

But he had the idea now, and within minutes he had a little fire going in the lee of the mound of sand he'd made digging the hole an hour or two ago. Tinder bushes had started it, and other bushes which burned, but more slowly, kept it a steady flame.

The tough wirelike tendrils didn't burn readily; that

made the firebombs easy to make and throw. A bundle of
faggots tied about a small stone to give it weight and a loop
of the tendril to swing it by.

He made half a dozen of them before he lighted and
threw the first. It went wide, and the Roller started a quick
retreat, pulling the catapult after him. But Carson had the
others ready and threw them in rapid succession. The
fourth wedged in the catapult's framework, and did the
trick. The Roller tried desperately to put out the spreading
blaze by throwing sand, but its clawed tentacles would
take only a spoonful at a time and his efforts were ineffectual. The catapult burned.

The Roller moved safely away from the fire and seemed
to concentrate its attention on Carson and again he felt that
wave of hatred and nausea. But more weakly; either the
Roller itself was weakening or Carson had learned how
to protect himself against the mental attack.

He thumbed his nose at it and then sent it scuttling
back to safety by throwing a stone. The Roller went clear
to the back of its half of the arena and started pulling up
bushes again. Probably it was going to make another catapult.

Carson verified—for the hundredth time—that the barrier was still operating, and then found himself sitting in
the sand beside it because he was suddenly too weak to
stand up.

His leg throbbed steadily now and the pangs of thirst
were severe. But those things paled beside the utter physical exhaustion that gripped his entire body.

And the heat.

Hell must be like this, he thought. The hell that the
ancients had believed in. He fought to stay awake, and yet
staying awake seemed futile, for there was nothing he
could do. Nothing, while the barrier remained impregnable
and the Roller stayed back out of range.

But there must be *something*. He tried to remember
things he had read in books of archaeology about methods
of fighting used back in the days before metal and plastic.
The stone missile, that had come first, he thought. Well,
that he already had.

The only improvement on it would be a catapult, such
as the Roller had made. But he'd never be able to make

one, with the tiny bits of wood available from the bushes
—no single piece longer than a foot or so. Certainly he
could figure out a mechanism for one, but he didn't have
the endurance left for a task that would take days.

Days? But the Roller had made one. Had they been here
days already? Then he remembered that the Roller had
many tentacles to work with and undoubtedly could do
such work faster than he.

And besides, a catapult wouldn't decide the issue. He
had to do better than that.

Bow and arrow? No; he had tried archery once and
knew his own ineptness with a bow. Even with a modern
sportsman's durasteel weapon, made for accuracy. With
such a crude, pieced-together outfit as he could make here,
he doubted if he could shoot as far as he could throw a
rock, and he knew he couldn't shoot as straight.

Spear? Well, he *could* make that. It would be useless as a
throwing weapon at any distance, but would be a handy
thing at close range, if he ever got to close range.

And making one would give him something to do. Help
keep his mind from wandering, as it was beginning to do.
Sometimes now, he had to concentrate awhile before he
could remember why he was here, why he had to kill the
Roller.

Luckily he was still beside one of the piles of stones. He
sorted through it until he found one shaped roughly like
a spearhead. With a smaller stone he began to chip it
into shape, fashioning sharp shoulders on the sides so that
if it penetrated it would not pull out again.

Like a harpoon? There was something in that idea, he
thought. A harpoon was better than a spear, maybe, for
this crazy contest. If he could once get it into the Roller,
and had a rope on it, he could pull the Roller up against
the barrier and the stone blade of his knife would reach
through that barrier, even if his hands wouldn't.

The shaft was harder to make than the head. But by
splitting and joining the main stems of four of the bushes,
and wrapping the joints with the tough but thin tendrils,
he got a strong shaft about four feet long, and tied the
stone head in a notch cut in the end.

It was crude, but strong.

And the rope. With the thin tough tendrils he made

himself twenty feet of line. It was light and didn't look strong, but he knew it would hold his weight and to spare. He tied one end of it to the shaft of the harpoon and the other end about his right wrist. At least, if he threw his harpoon across the barrier, he'd be able to pull it back if he missed.

Then when he had tied the last knot and there was nothing more he could do, the heat and the weariness and the pain in his leg and the dreadful thirst were suddenly a thousand times worse than they had been before.

He tried to stand up, to see what the Roller was doing now, and found he couldn't get to his feet. On the third try, he got as far as his knees and then fell flat again.

"I've got to sleep," he thought. "If a showdown came now, I'd be helpless. He could come up here and kill me, if he knew. I've got to regain some strength."

Slowly, painfully, he crawled back away from the barrier. Ten yards, twenty—

The jar of something thudding against the sand near him waked him from a confused and horrible dream to a more confused and more horrible reality, and he opened his eyes again to blue radiance over blue sand.

How long had he slept? A minute? A day?

Another stone thudded nearer and threw sand on him. He got his arms under him and sat up. He turned around and saw the Roller twenty yards away, at the barrier.

It rolled away hastily as he sat up, not stopping until it was as far away as it could get.

He'd fallen asleep too soon, he realized, while he was still in range of the Roller's throwing ability. Seeing him lying motionless, it had dared come up to the barrier to throw at him. Luckily, it didn't realize how weak he was, or it could have stayed there and kept throwing stones.

Had he slept long? He didn't think so, because he felt just as he had before. Not rested at all, no thirstier, no different. Probably he'd been there only a few minutes.

He started crawling again, this time forcing himself to keep going until he was as far as he could go, until the colorless, opaque wall of the arena's outer shell was only a yard away.

Then things slipped away again—

When he awoke, nothing about him was changed, but this time he knew that he had slept a long time.

The first thing he became aware of was the inside of his mouth; it was dry, caked. His tongue was swollen.

Something was wrong, he knew, as he returned slowly to full awareness. He felt less tired, the stage of utter exhaustion had passed. The sleep had taken care of that.

But there was pain, agonizing pain. It wasn't until he tried to move that he knew that it came from his leg.

He raised his head and looked down at it. It was swollen terribly below the knee and the swelling showed even halfway up his thigh. The plant tendrils he had used to tie on the protective pad of leaves now cut deeply into the swollen flesh.

To get his knife under that imbedded lashing would have been impossible. Fortunately, the final knot was over the shin bone, in front, where the vine cut in less deeply than elsewhere. He was able, after an agonizing effort, to untie the knot.

A look under the pad of leaves told him the worst. Infection and blood poisoning, both pretty bad and getting worse.

And without drugs, without cloth, without even *water*, there wasn't a thing he could do about it.

Not a thing, except *die*, when the poison had spread through his system.

He knew it was hopeless, then, and that he'd lost.

And with him, humanity. When he died here, out there in the universe he knew, all his friends, everybody, would die too. And Earth and the colonized planets would be the home of the red, rolling, alien Outsiders. Creatures out of nightmare, things without a human attribute, who picked lizards apart for the fun of it.

It was the thought of that which gave him courage to start crawling, almost blindly in pain, toward the barrier again. Not crawling on hands and knees this time, but pulling himself along only by his arms and hands.

A chance in a million, that maybe he'd have strength left, when he got there, to throw his harpoon-spear just *once*, and with deadly effect, if—on another chance in a million—the Roller would come up to the barrier. Or if the barrier was gone, now.

It took him years, it seemed, to get there.

The barrier wasn't gone. It was an impassable as when he'd first felt it.

And the Roller wasn't at the barrier. By raising up on his elbows, he could see it at the back of its part of the arena, working on a wooden framework that was a half-completed duplicate of the catapult he'd destroyed.

It was moving slowly now. Undoubtedly it had weakened, too.

But Carson doubted that it would ever need that second catapult. He'd be dead, he thought, before it was finished.

If he could attract it to the barrier, now, while he was still alive— He waved an arm and tried to shout, but his parched throat would make no sound.

Or if he could get through the barrier—

His mind must have slipped for a moment, for he found himself beating his fists against the barrier in futile rage, and made himself stop.

He closed his eyes, tried to make himself calm.

"Hello," said the voice.

It was a small, thin voice. It sounded like—

He opened his eyes and turned his head. It *was* the lizard.

"Go away," Carson wanted to say. "Go away, you're not really there, or you're there but not really talking. I'm imagining things again."

But he couldn't talk; his throat and tongue were past all speech with the dryness. He closed his eyes again.

"Hurt," said the voice. "Kill. Hurt—kill. Come."

He opened his eyes again. The blue ten-legged lizard was still there. It ran a little way along the barrier, came back, started off again, and came back.

"Hurt," it said. "Kill. Come."

Again it started off, and came back. Obviously it wanted Carson to follow it along the barrier.

He closed his eyes again. The voice kept on. The same three meaningless words. Each time he opened his eyes, it ran off and came back.

"Hurt. Kill. Come."

Carson groaned. There would be no peace unless he followed the blasted thing. Like it wanted him to.

He followed it, crawling. Another sound, a high-pitched squealing, came to his ears and grew louder.

There was something lying in the sand, writhing, squealing. Something small, blue, that looked like a lizard and yet didn't—

Then he saw what it was—the lizard whose legs the Roller had pulled off, so long ago. But it wasn't dead; it had come back to life and was wriggling and screaming in agony.

"Hurt," said the other lizard. "Hurt. Kill. Kill."

Carson understood. He took the flint knife from his belt and killed the tortured creature. The live lizard scurried off quickly.

Carson turned back to the barrier. He leaned his hands and head against it and watched the Roller, far back, working on the new catapult.

"I could get that far," he thought, "if I could get through. If I could get through, I might win yet. It looks weak, too. I might—"

And then there was another reaction of black hopelessness, when pain snapped his will and he wished that he were dead. He envied the lizard he'd just killed. It didn't have to live on and suffer. And he did. It would be hours, it might be days, before the blood poisoning killed him.

If only he could use that knife on himself—

But he knew he wouldn't. As long as he was alive, there was the millionth chance—

He was straining, pushing on the barrier with the flat of his hands, and he noticed his arms, how thin and scrawny they were now. He must really have been here a long time, for days, to get as thin as that.

How much longer now, before he died? How much more heat and thirst and pain could flesh stand?

For a little while he was almost hysterical again, and then came a time of deep calm, and a thought that was startling.

The lizard he had just killed. *It had crossed the barrier, still alive.* It had come from the Roller's side; the Roller had pulled off its legs and then tossed it contemptuously at him and it had come through the barrier. He'd thought, because the lizard was dead.

But it hadn't been dead; it had been unconscious.

A live lizard couldn't go through the barrier, but an unconscious one could. The barrier was not a barrier, then, to living flesh, but to conscious flesh. It was a *mental* projection, a *mental* hazard.

And with that thought, Carson started crawling along the barrier to make his last desperate gamble. A hope so forlorn that only a dying man would have dared try it.

No use weighing the odds of success. Not when, if he didn't try it, those odds were infinitely to zero.

He crawled along the barrier to the dune of sand, about four feet high, which he'd scooped out in trying—how many days ago?—to dig under the barrier or to reach water.

That mound was right at the barrier, its farther slope half on one side of the barrier, half on the other.

Taking with him a rock from the pile nearby, he climbed up to the top of the dune and over the top, and lay there against the barrier, his weight leaning against it so that if the barrier were taken away he'd roll on down the short slope, into the enemy territory.

He checked to be sure that the knife was safely in his rope belt, that the harpoon was in the crook of his left arm and that the twenty-foot rope was fastened to it and to his wrist.

Then with his right hand he raised the rock with which he would hit himself on the head. Luck would have to be with him on that blow; it would have to be hard enough to knock him out, but not hard enough to knock him out for long.

He had a hunch that the Roller was watching him, and would see him roll down through the barrier, and come to investigate. It would think he was dead, he hoped—he thought it had probably drawn the same deduction about the nature of the barrier that he had drawn. But it would come cautiously. He would have a little time—

He struck.

Pain brought him back to consciousness. A sudden, sharp pain in his hip that was different from the throbbing pain in his head and the throbbing pain in his leg.

But he had, thinking things out before he had struck himself, anticipated that very pain, even hoped for it, and had steeled himself against awakening with a sudden movement.

He lay still, but opened his eyes just a slit, and saw that he had guessed rightly. The Roller was coming closer. It was twenty feet away and the pain that had awakened him was the stone it had tossed to see whether he was alive or dead.

He lay still. It came closer, fifteen feet away, and stopped again. Carson scarcely breathed.

As nearly as possible, he was keeping his mind a blank, lest its telepathic ability detect consciousness in him. And with his mind blanked out that way, the impact of its thoughts upon his mind was nearly soul-shattering.

He felt sheer horror at the utter *alienness*, the *differentness* of those thoughts. Things that he felt but could not understand and could never express, because no terrestrial language had the words, no terrestrial mind had images to fit them. The mind of a spider, he thought, or the mind of a praying mantis or a Martian sand-serpent, raised to intelligence and put in telepathic rapport with human minds, would be a homely familiar thing, compared to this.

He understood now that the Entity had been right: Man or Roller, and the universe was not a place that could hold them both. Farther apart than god and devil, there could never be even a balance between them.

Closer. Carson waited until it was only feet away, until its clawed tentacles reached out—

Oblivious to agony now, he sat up, raised and flung the harpoon with all the strength that remained to him. Or he thought it was all; sudden final strength flooded through him, along with a sudden forgetfulness of pain as definite as a nerve block.

As the Roller, deeply stabbed by the harpoon, rolled away, Carson tried to get to his feet to run after it. He couldn't do that; he fell, but kept crawling.

It reached the end of the rope, and he was jerked forward by the pull of his wrist. It dragged him a few feet and then stopped. Carson kept on going, pulling himself toward it hand over hand along the rope.

It stopped there, writhing tentacles trying in vain to pull out the harpoon. It seemed to shudder and quiver, and then it must have realized that it couldn't get away, for it rolled back toward him, clawed tentacles reaching out.

Stone knife in hand, he met it. He stabbed, again and again, while those horrid claws ripped skin and flesh and muscle from his body.

He stabbed and slashed, and at last it was still.

A bell was ringing, and it took him a while after he'd opened his eyes to tell where he was and what it was. He was strapped into the seat of his scouter, and the visiplate before him showed only empty space. No Outsider ship and no impossible planet.

The bell was the communications plate signal; someone wanted him to switch power into the receiver. Purely reflex action enabled him to reach forward and throw the lever.

The face of Brander, captain of the *Magellan,* mothership of his group of scouters, flashed into the screen. His face was pale and his black eyes glowed with excitement.

"*Magellan* to Carson," he snapped. "Come on in. The fight's over. We've won!"

The screen went blank; Brander would be signaling the other scouters of his command.

Slowly, Carson set the controls for the return. Slowly, unbelievingly, he unstrapped himself from the seat and went back to get a drink at the cold-water tank. For some reason, he was unbelievably thirsty. He drank six glasses.

He leaned there against the wall, trying to think.

Had it happened? He was in good health, sound, uninjured. His thirst had been mental rather than physical; his throat hadn't been dry. His leg—

He pulled up his trouser leg and looked at the calf. There was a long white scar there, but a perfectly healed scar. It hadn't been there before. He zipped open the front of his shirt and saw that his chest and abdomen was criss-crossed with tiny, almost unnoticeable, perfectly healed scars.

It *had* happened.

The scouter, under automatic control, was already entering the hatch of the mother-ship. The grapples pulled it into its individual lock, and a moment later a buzzer indicated that the lock was air-filled. Carson opened the hatch and stepped outside, went through the double door of the lock.

He went right to Brander's office, went in, and saluted.

Brander still looked dizzily dazed. "Hi, Carson," he said. "What you missed! What a show!"

"What happened, sir?"

"Don't know, exactly. We fired one salvo, and their whole fleet went up in dust! Whatever it was jumped from ship to ship in a flash, even the ones we hadn't aimed at and that were out of range! The whole fleet disintegrated before our eyes, and we didn't get the paint of a single ship scratched!

"We can't even claim credit for it. Must have been some unstable component in the metal they used, and our sighting shot just set it off. Man, oh man, too bad you missed all the excitement."

Carson managed to grin. It was a sickly ghost of a grin, for it would be days before he'd be over the mental impact of his experience, but the captain wasn't watching, and didn't notice.

"Yes, sir," he said. Common sense, more than modesty, told him he'd be branded forever as the worst liar in space if he ever said any more than that. "Yes, sir, too bad I missed all the excitement."

FIRST CONTACT

by Murray Leinster

Tommy Dort went into the captain's room with his last pair of stereo-photos and said:

"I'm through, sir. These are the last two pictures I can take."

He handed over the photographs and looked with professional interest at the visiplates which showed all space outside the ship. Subdued, deep-red lighting indicated the controls and such instruments as the quartermaster on duty needed for navigation of the spaceship *Llanvabon*. There was a deeply cushioned control chair. There was the little gadget of oddly angled mirrors—remote descendant of the back-view mirrors of twentieth-century motorists—which allowed a view of all the visiplates without turning the head. And there were the huge plates which were so much more satisfactory for a direct view of space.

The *Llanvabon* was a long way from home. The plates, which showed every star of visual magnitude and could be stepped up to any desired magnification, portrayed stars of every imaginable degree of brilliance, in the startingly different colors they show outside of atmosphere. But every one was unfamiliar. Only two constellations could be recognized as seen from Earth, and they were shrunken and distorted. The Milky Way seemed vaguely out of place. But even such oddities were minor compared to a sight in the forward plates.

There was a vast, vast mistiness ahead. A luminous mist. It seemed motionless. It took a long time for any appreci-

First published in 1945 ("Murray Leinster" is a pseudonym employed by Will F. Jenkins)

able nearing to appear in the vision plates, though the spaceship's velocity indicator showed an incredible speed. The mist was the Crab Nebula, six light-years long, three and a half light-years thick, and outward-reaching members that in the telescopes of Earth gave it some resemblance to the creature for which it was named. It was a cloud of gas, infinitely tenuous, reaching half again as far as from Sol to its nearest neighbor-sun. Deep within it burned two stars; a double star; one component the familiar yellow of the sun of Earth, the other an unholy white.

Tommy Dort said meditatively:

"We're heading into a deep, sir?"

The skipper studied the last two plates of Tommy's taking, and put them aside. He went back to his uneasy contemplation of the vision plates ahead. The *Llanvabon* was decelerating at full force. She was a bare half light-year from the nebula. Tommy's work was guiding the ship's course, now, but the work was done. During all the stay of the exploring ship in the nebula, Tommy Dort would loaf. But he'd more than paid his way so far.

He had just completed a quite unique first—a complete photographic record of the movement of a nebula during a period of four thousand years, taken by one individual with the same apparatus and with control exposures to detect and record any systematic errors. It was an achievement in itself worth the journey from Earth. But in addition, he had also recorded four thousand years of the history of a double star, and four thousand years of the history of a star in the act of degenerating into a white dwarf.

It was not that Tommy Dort was four thousand years old. He was, actually in his twenties. But the Crab Nebula is four thousand light-years from Earth, and the last two pictures had been taken by light which would not reach Earth until the sixth millennium A. D. On the way here— at speeds incredible multiples of the speed of light— Tommy Dort had recorded each aspect of the nebula by the light which had left it from forty centuries since to a bare six months ago.

The *Llanvabon* bored on through space. Slowly, slowly, slowly, the incredible luminosity crept across the vision

plates. It blotted out half the universe from view. Before
was glowing mist, and behind was a star-studded emptiness. The mist shut off three-fourths of all the stars. Some
few of the brightest shone dimly through it near its edge,
but only a few. Then there was only an irregularly shaped
patch of darkness astern against which the stars shown
unwinking. The *Llanvabon* dived into the nebula, and it
seemed as if it bored into a tunnel of Darkness with walls
of shining fog.

Which was exactly what the spaceship was doing. The
most distant photographs of all disclosed structural features in the nebula. It was not amorphous. It had form.
As the *Llanvabon* drew nearer, indications of structure
grew more distinct, and Tommy Dort had argued for a
curved approach for photographic reasons. So the spaceship had come up to the nebula on a vast logarithmic
curve, and Tommy had been able to take successive photographs from slightly different angles and get stereo-pairs
which showed the nebula in three dimensions; which disclosed billowings and hollows and an actually complicated shape. In places, the nebula displays convolutions
like those of a human brain. It was into one of these
hollows that the spaceship now plunged. They had been
called "deeps" by analogy with crevasses in the ocean
floor. And they promised to be useful.

The skipper relaxed. One of a skipper's functions, nowadays, is to think of things to worry about, and then worry
about them. The skipper of the *Llanvabon* was conscientious. Only after a certain instrument remained definitely
nonregistering did he ease himself back in his seat.

"It was just barely possible," he said heavily, "that
those deeps might be nonluminous gas. But they're empty.
So we'll be able to use overdrive as long as we're in them."

It was a light-year-and-a-half from the edge of the nebula to the neighborhood of the double star which was its
heart. That was the problem. A nebula is a gas. It is so
thin that a comet's tail is solid by comparison, but a ship
traveling on overdrive—above the speed of light—does
not want to hit even a merely hard vacuum. It needs pure
emptiness, such as exists between the stars. But the *Llanvabon* could not do much in this expanse of mist if it was
limited to speeds a merely hard vacuum will permit.

The luminosity seemed to close in behind the spaceship, which slowed and slowed and slowed. The overdrive went off with the sudden *pinging* sensation that goes all over a person when the overdrive field is released.

Then, almost instantly, bells burst into clanging, strident uproar all through the ship. Tommy was almost deafened by the alarm bell which rang in the captain's room before the quartermaster shut it off with a flip of his hand. But other bells could be heard ringing throughout the rest of the ship, to be cut off as automatic doors closed one by one.

Tommy Dort stared at the skipper. The skipper's hands clenched. He was up and staring over the quartermaster's shoulder. One indicator was apparently having convulsions. Others strained to record their findings. A spot on the diffusedly bright mistiness of a bow-quartering visiplate grew brighter as the automatic scanner focused on it. That was the direction of the object which had sounded collision-alarm. But the object locator itself—. According to its reading, there was one solid object some eighty thousand miles away—an object of no great size. But there was another object whose distance varied from extreme range to zero, and whose size shared its impossible advance and retreat.

"Step up the scanner," snapped the skipper.

The extra-bright spot on the scanner rolled outward, obliterating the undifferentiated image behind it. Magnification increased. But nothing appeared. Absolutely nothing. Yet the radio locator insisted that something monstrous and invisible made lunatic dashes toward the *Llanvabon*, at speeds which inevitably implied collision, and then fled coyly away at the same rate.

The visiplate went up to maximum magnification. Still nothing. The skipper ground his teeth. Tommy Dort said meditatively:

"D'you know, sir, I saw something like this on a liner on the Earth-Mars run once, when we were being located by another ship. Their locator beam was the same frequency as ours, and every time it hit, it registered like something monstrous, and solid."

"That," said the skipper savagely, "is just what's happening now. There's something like a locator beam on us.

We're getting that beam and our own echo besides. But
the other ship's invisible! Who is out here in an invisible
ship with locator devices? Not men, certainly!"

He pressed the button in his sleeve communicator and
snapped:

"Action stations! Man all weapons! Condition of extreme alert in all departments immediately!"

His hands closed and unclosed. He stared again at the
visiplate which showed nothing but a formless brightness.

"Not men?" Tommy Dort straightened sharply. "You
mean—"

"How many solar systems in our galaxy?" demanded
the skipper bitterly. "How many planets fit for life? And
how many kinds of life could there be? If this ship isn't
from Earth—and it isn't—it has a crew that isn't human.
And things that aren't human but are up to the level of
deep-space travel in their civilization could mean anything!"

The skipper's hands were actually shaking. He would
not have talked so freely before a member of his own
crew, but Tommy Dort was of the observation staff. And
even a skipper whose duties include worrying may sometimes need desperately to unload his worries. Sometimes,
too, it helps to think out loud.

"Something like this has been talked about and specu-
lated about for years," he said softly. "Mathematically,
it's been an odds-on bet that somewhere in our galaxy
there'd be another race with a civilization equal to or
further advanced than ours. Nobody could ever guess
where or when we'd meet them. But it looks like we've
done it now!"

Tommy's eyes were very bright.

"D'you suppose they'll be friendly, sir?"

The skipper glanced at the distance indicator. The
phantom object still made its insane, nonexistent swoops
toward and away from the *Llanvabon*. The secondary
indication of an object at eighty thousand miles stirred
ever so slightly.

"It's moving," he said curtly. "Heading for us. Just what
we'd do if a strange spaceship appeared in our hunting
grounds! Friendly? Maybe! We're going to try to contact
them. We have to. But I suspect this is the end of this
expedition. Thank God for the blasters!"

The blasters are those beams of ravening destruction which take care of recalcitrant meteorites in a spaceship's course when the deflectors can't handle them. They are not designed as weapons, but they can serve as pretty good ones. They can go into action at five thousand miles, and draw on the entire power output of a whole ship. With automatic aim and a traverse of five degrees, a ship like the *Llanvabon* can come very close to blasting a hole through a small-sized asteroid wihch gets in its way. But not on overdrive, of course.

Tommy Dort had approached the bow-quartering visiplate. Now he jerked his head around.

"Blasters, sir? What for?"

The skipper grimaced at the empty visiplate.

"Because we don't know what they're like and can't take a chance! I know!" he added bitterly. "We're going to make contacts and try to find out all we can about them— especially where they come from. I suppose we'll try to make friends—but we haven't much chance. We can't trust them the fraction of an inch. We daren't! They've locators. Maybe they've tracers better than any we have. Maybe they could trace us all the way home without our knowing it! We can't risk a nonhuman race knowing where Earth is unless we're sure of them! And how can we be sure? They could come to trade, of course—or they could swoop down on overdrive with a battle fleet that could wipe us out before we knew what happened. We wouldn't know which to expect, or when!"

Tommy's face was startled.

"It's all been thrashed out over and over, in theory," said the skipper. "Nobody's ever been able to find a sound answer, even on paper. But you know, in all their theorizing, no one considered the crazy, rank impossibility of a deep-space contact, with neither side knowing the other's home world! But we've got to find an answer in fact! What are we going to do about them? Maybe these creatures will be aesthetic marvels, nice and friendly and polite— and underneath with the sneaking brutal ferocity of a Japanese. Or maybe they'll be crude and gruff as a Swedish farmer—and just as decent underneath. Maybe they're something in between. But am I going to risk the pos-

sible future of the human race on a guess that it's safe to
trust them? God knows it would be worth while to make
friends with a new civilization! It would be bound to
stimulate our own, and maybe we'd gain enormously. But
I can't take chances. The one thing I won't risk is having
them know how to find Earth! Either I know they can't
follow me, or I don't go home! And they'll probably feel
the same way!"

He pressed the sleeve-communicator button again.

"Navigation officers, attention! Every star map on this
ship is to be prepared for instant destruction. This includes
photographs and diagrams from which our course or starting point could be deduced. I want all astronomical data
gathered and arranged to be destroyed in a split second,
on order. Make it fast and report when ready!"

He released the button. He looked suddenly old. The
first contact of humanity with an alien race was a situation
which had been foreseen in many fashions, but never one
quite so hopeless of solution as this. A solitary Earth-ship
and a solitary alien, meeting in a nebula which must be
remote from the home planet of each. They might wish
peace, but the line of conduct which best prepared a
treacherous attack was just the seeming of friendliness.
Failure to be suspicious might doom the human race,—
and a peaceful exchange of the fruits of civilization would
be the greatest benefit imaginable. Any mistake would be
irreparable, but a failure to be on guard would be fatal.

The captain's room was very, very quiet. The bow-
quartering visiplate was filled with the image of a very
small section of the nebula. A very small section indeed.
It was all diffused, featureless, luminous mist. But suddenly Tommy Dort pointed.

"There, sir!"

There was a small shape in the mist. It was far away.
It was a black shape, not polished to mirror-reflection like
the hull of the *Llanvabon*. It was bulbous—roughly pear-
shaped. There was much thin luminosity between, and
no details could be observed, but it was surely no natural
object. Then Tommy looked at the distance indicator and
said quietly:

"It's headed for us at very high acceleration, sir. The
odds are that they're thinking the same thing, sir, that

neither of us will dare let the other go home. Do you think they'll try a contact with us, or let loose with their weapons as soon as they're in range?"

The *Llanvabon* was no longer in a crevasse of emptiness in the nebula's thin substance. She swam in luminescence. There were no stars save the two fierce glows in the nebula's heart. There was nothing but an all-enveloping light, curiously like one's imagining of underwater in the tropic of Earth.

The alien ship had made one sign of less than lethal intention. As it drew near the *Llanvabon,* it decelerated. The *Llanvabon* itself had advanced for a meeting and then come to a dead stop. Its movement had been a recognition of the nearness of the other ship. Its pausing was both a friendly sign and a precaution against attack. Relatively still, it could swivel on its own axis to present the least target to a slashing assault, and it would have a longer firing-time than if the two ships flashed past each other at their combined speeds.

The moment of actual approach, however, was tenseness itself. The *Llanvabon's* needle-pointed bow aimed unwaveringly at the alien bulk. A relay to the captain's room put a key under his hand which would fire the blasters with maximum power. Tommy Dort watched, his brow wrinkled. The aliens must be of a high degree of civilization if they had spaceships, and civilization does not not develop wthout the development of foresight. These aliens must recognize all the implications of this first contact of two civilized races as fully as did the humans on the *Llanvabon.*

The possibility of an enormous spurt in the development of both, by peaceful contact and exchange of their separate technologies, would probably appeal to them as to the man. But when dissimilar human cultures are in contact, one must usually be subordinate or there is war. But subordination between races arising on separate planets could not be peacefully arranged. Men, at least, would never consent to subordination, nor was it likely that any highly developed race would agree. The benefits to be derived from commerce could never make up for a condition of inferiority. Some races—men, perhaps—would prefer commerce to conquest. Perhaps—perhaps!—these aliens would also. But some types even of human beings would have craved red war. If the alien ship now approaching the *Llanvabon* returned to its home base with news of humanity's existence and of ships like the *Llanvabon*, it would give its race the choice of trade or battle. They might want trade, or they might want war. But it takes two to make trade, and only one to make war. They could not be sure of men's peacefulness, nor could men be sure of theirs. The only safety for either civilization would lie in the destruction of one or both of the two ships here and now.

But even victory would not be really enough. Men would need to know where this alien race was to be found, for avoidance if not for battle. They would need to know its weapons, and its resources, and if it could be a menace and how it could be eliminated in case of need. The aliens would feel the same necessities concerning humanity.

So the skipper of the *Llanvabon* did not press the key which might possibly have blasted the other ship to nothingness. He dared not. But he dared not fire either. Sweat came out on his face.

A speaker muttered. Someone from the range room.

"The other ship's stopped, sir. Quite stationary. Blasters are centered on it, sir."

It was an urging to fire. But the skipper shook his head, to himself. The alien ship was no more than twenty miles away. It was dead-black. Every bit of its exterior was an abysmal, nonreflecting sable. No details could be seen except by minor variations in its outline against the misty nebula.

"It's stopped dead, sir," said another voice. "They've sent a modulated short wave at us, sir. Frequency modulated. Apparently a signal. Not enough power to do any harm."

The skipper said through tight-locked teeth:

"They're doing something now. There's movement on the outside of their hull. Watch what comes out. Put the auxiliary blasters on it."

Something small and round came smoothly out of the oval outline of the black ship. The bulbous hulk moved.

"Moving away, sir," said the speaker. "The object they let out is stationary in the place they've left."

Another voice cut in:

"More frequency modulated stuff, sir. Unintelligible."

Tommy Dort's eyes brightened. The skipper watched the visiplate, with sweat-droplets on his forehead.

"Rather pretty, sir," said Tommy, meditatively. "If they sent anything toward us, it might seem a projectile or a bomb. So they came close, let out a lifeboat, and went away again. They figure we can send a boat or a man to make contact without risking our ship. They must think pretty much as we do."

The skipper said, without moving his eyes from the plate:

"Mr. Dort, would you care to go out and look the thing over? I can't order you, but I need all my operating crew for emergencies. The observation staff—"

"Is expendable. Very well, sir," said Tommy briskly. "I won't take a lifeboat, sir. Just a suit with a drive on it. It's smaller and the arms and legs will look unsuitable for a bomb. I think I should carry a scanner, sir."

The alien ship continued to retreat. Forty, eighty, four hundred miles. It came to a stop and hung there, waiting. Climbing into his atomic-driven spacesuit just within the *Llanvabon's* air lock, Tommy heard the reports as they went over the speakers throughout the ship. That the other ship had stopped its retreat at four hundred miles was encouraging. It might not have weapons effective at a greater distance than that, and so felt safe. But just as the thought formed itself in his mind, the alien retreated precipitately still farther. Which, as Tommy reflected as he emerged from the lock, might be because the aliens had realized they were giving themselves away, or might be because they wanted to give the impression that they had done so.

He swooped away from the silvery-mirror *Llanvabon,* through a brightly glowing emptiness which was past any previous experience of the human race. Behind him, the *Llanvabon* swung about and darted away. The skipper's voice came in Tommy's helmet phones.

"We're pulling back, too, Mr. Dort. There is a bare

possibility that they've some explosive atomic reaction they can't use from their own ship, but which might be destructive even as far as this. We'll draw back. Keep your scanner on the object."

The reasoning was sound, if not very comforting. An explosive which would destroy anything within twenty miles was theoretically possible, but humans didn't have it yet. It was decidedly safest for the *Llanvabon* to draw back.

But Tommy Dort felt very lonely. He sped through emptiness toward the tiny black speck which hung in incredible brightness. The *Llanvabon* vanished. Its polished hull would merge with the glowing mist at a relatively short distance, anyhow. The alien ship was not visible to the naked eye, either. Tommy swam in nothingness, four thousand light-years from home, toward a tiny black spot which was the only solid object to be seen in all of space.

It was a slightly distorted sphere, not much over six feet in diameter. It bounced away when Tommy landed on it, feet-first. There were small tentacles, or horns, which projected in every direction. They looked rather like the detonating horns of a submarine mine, but there was a glint of crystal at the tip-end of each.

"I'm here," said Tommy into his helmet phone.

He caught hold of a horn and drew himself to the object. It was all metal, dead-black. He could feel no texture through his space gloves, of course, but he went over and over it, trying to discover its purpose.

"Deadlock, sir," he said presently. "Nothing to report that the scanner hasn't shown you."

Then, through his suit, he felt vibrations. They translated themselves as clankings. A section of the rounded hull of the object opened out. Two sections. He worked his way around to look in and see the first nonhuman civilized beings that any man had ever looked upon.

But what he saw was simply a flate plate on which dim-red glows crawled here and there in seeming aimlessness. His helmet phones emitted a startled exclamation. The skipper's voice:

"Very good, Mr. Dort. Fix your scanner to look into that plate. They dumped out a robot with an infrared visiplate for communication. Not risking any personnel. Whatever we might do would damage only machinery. Maybe they expect us to bring it on board—and it may have a bomb charge that can be detonated when they're ready to start for home. I'll send a plate to face one of its scanners. You return to the ship."

"Yes, sir," said Tommy. "But which way is the ship, sir?"

There were no stars. The nebula obscured them with its light. The only thing visible from the robot was the double star at the nebula's center. Tommy was no longer oriented. He had but one reference point.

"Head straight away from the double star," came the order in his helmet phone. "We'll pick you up."

He passed another lonely figure, a little later, headed for the alien sphere with a vision plate to set up. The two spaceships, each knowing that it dared not risk its own race by the slightest lack of caution, would communicate with each other through this small round robot. Their separate vision systems would enable them to exchange all the information they dared give, while they debated the most practical way of making sure that their own civilization would not be endangered by this first contact with another. The truly most practical method would be the destruction of the other ship in a swift and deadly attack —in self-defense.

II

The *Llanvabon* thereafter, was a ship in which there were two separate enterprises on hand at the same time. She had come out from Earth to make close-range observations on the smaller component of the double star at the nebula's center. The nebula itself was the result of the most titanic explosion of which men have any knowledge. The explosion took place sometime in the year 2946 B. C., before the first of the seven cities of long-dead Ilium was even thought of. The light of that explosion reached Earth in the year 1054 A. D., and was duly recorded in ecclesiastic annals and somewhat more reliably by Chinese court astronomers. It was bright enough to be seen in daylight for twenty-three successive days. Its light

—and it was four thousand light-years away—was brighter than that of Venus.

From these facts, atronomers could calculate nine hundred years later the violence of the detonation. Matter blown away from the center of the explosion would have traveled outward at the rate of two million three hundred thousand miles an hour; more than thirty-eight thousand miles a minute; something over six hundred thirty-eight miles per second. When twentieth-century telescopes were turned upon the scene of this vast explosion, only a double star remained—and the nebula. The brighter star of the doublet was almost unique in having so high a surface temperature that it showed no spectrum lines at all. It had a continuous spectrum. Sol's surface temperature is about 7,000° Absolute. That of the hot white star is 500,000 degrees. It has nearly the mass of the sun, but only one fifth its diameter, so that its density is one hundred seventy-three times that of water, sixteen times that of lead, and eight times that of iridium—the heaviest substance known on Earth. But even this density is not that of a dwarf white star like the companion of Sirius. The white star in the Crab Nebula is an incomplete dwarf; it is a star still in the act of collapsing. Examination—including the survey of a four-thousand-year column of its light—was worth while. The *Llanvabon* had come to make that examination. But the finding of an alien spaceship upon a similar errand had implications which overshadowed the original purpose of the expedition.

A tiny bulbous robot floated in the tenuous nebular gas. The normal operating crew of the *Llanvabon* stood at their posts with a sharp alertness which was productive of tense nerves. The observation staff divided itself, and a part went half-heartedly about the making of the observations for which the *Llanvabon* had come. The other half applied itself to the problem the spaceship offered.

It represented a culture which was up to space travel on an interstellar scale. The explosion of a mere five thousand years since must have blasted every trace of life out of existence in the area now filled by the nebula. So the aliens of the black spaceship came from another solar system. Their trip must have been, like that of the Earth ship, for purely scientific purposes. There was nothing to be extracted from the nebula.

They were, then, at least near the level of human civilization, which meant that they had or could develop arts and articles of commerce which men would want to trade for, in friendship. But they would necessarily realize that the existence and civilization of humanity was a potential menace to their own race. The two races could be friends, but also they could be deadly enemies. Each, even if unwillingly, was a monstrous menace to the other. And the only safe thing to do with a menace is to destroy it.

In the Crab Nebula the problem was acute and immediate. The future relationship of the two races would be settled here and now. If a process for friendship could be established, one race, otherwise doomed, would survive and both would benefit immensely. But that process had to be established, and confidence built up, without the most minute risk of danger from treachery. Confidence would need to be established upon a foundation of necessarily complete distrust. Neither dared return to its own base if the other could do harm to its race. Neither dared risk any of the necessities to trust. The only safe thing for either to do was destroy the other or be destroyed.

But even for war, more was needed than mere destruction of the other. With interstellar traffic, the aliens must have atomic power and some form of overdrive for travel above the speed of light. With radio location and visiplates and short-wave communication they had, of course, many other devices. What weapons did they have? How widely extended was their culture? What were their resources? Could there be a development of trade and friendship, or were the two races so unlike that only war could exist between them? If peace was possible, how could it be begun?

The men on the *Llanvabon* needed facts—and so did the crew of the other ship. They must take back every morsel of information they could. The most important information of all would be of the location of the other civilization, just in case of war. That one bit of information might be the decisive factor in an interstellar war. But other facts would be enormously valuable.

The tragic thing was that there could be no possible

information which could lead to peace. Neither ship could stake its own race's existence upon any conviction of the good will or the honor of the other.

So there was a strange truce between the two ships. The alien went about its work of making observations, as did the *Llanvabon*. The tiny robot floated in bright emptiness. A scanner from the *Llanvabon* was focused upon a vision plate from the alien. A scanner from the alien regarded a vision plate from the *Llanvabon*. Communication began.

It progressed rapidly. Tommy Dort was one of those who made the first progress report. His special task on the expedition was over. He had now been assigned to work on the problem of communication with the alien entities. He went with the ship's solitary psychologist to the captain's room to convey the news of success. The captain's room, as usual, was a place of silence and dull-red indicator lights and the great bright visiplates on every wall and on the ceiling.

"We've established fairly satisfactory communication, sir," said the psychologist. He looked tired. His work on the trip was supposed to be that of measuring personal factors of error in the observation staff, for the reduction of all observations to the nearest possible decimal to the absolute. He had been pressed into service for which he was not especially fitted, and it told upon him. "That is, we can say almost anything we wish, to them, and can understand what they say in return. But of course we don't know how much of what they say is the truth."

The skipper's eyes turned to Tommy Dort.

"We've hooked up some machinery," said Tommy, "that amounts to a mechanical translator. We have vision plates, of course, and then short-wave beams direct. They use frequency-modulation plus what is probably variation in wave forms—like our vowel and consonant sounds in speech. We've never had any use for anything like that before, so our coils won't handle it, but we've developed a sort of code which isn't the language of either set of us. They shoot over short-wave stuff with frequency-modulation, and we record it as sound. When we shoot it back, it's reconverted into frequency-modulation."

The skipper said, frowning:

"Why wave-form changes in short waves? How do you know?"

"We showed them our recorder in the vision plates, and they showed us theirs. They record the frequency-modulation direct. I think," said Tommy carefully, "they don't use sound at all, even in speech. They've set up a communications room, and we've watched them in the act of communicating with us. They make no perceptible movement of anything that corresponds to a speech organ. Instead of a microphone, they simply stand near something that would work as a pick-up antenna. My guess, sir, is that they use microwaves for what you might call person-to-person conversation. I think they make short-wave trains as we make sounds."

The skipper stared at him:

"That means they have telepathy?"

"M-m-m. Yes, sir," said Tommy. "Also it means that we have telepathy too, as far as they are concerned. They're probably deaf. They've certainly no idea of using sound waves in air for communication. They simply don't use noises for any purpose."

The skipper stored the information away.

"What else?"

"Well, sir," said Tommy doubtfully, "I think we're all set. We agreed on arbitrary symbols for objects, sir, by way of the visiplates, and worked out relationships and verbs and so on with diagrams and pictures. We've a couple of thousand words that have mutual meanings. We set up an analyzer to sort out their short-wave groups, which we feed into a decoding machine. And then the coding end of the machine picks out recordings to make the wave groups we want to send back. When you're ready to talk to the skipper of the other ship, sir, I think we're ready."

"H-m-m. What's your impression of their psychology?" The skipper asked the question of the psychologist.

"I don't know, sir," said the psychologist harassedly. "They seem to be completely direct. But they haven't let slip even a hint of the tenseness we know exists. They act as if they were simply setting up a means of communication for friendly conversation. But there is . . . well . . . an overtone—"

The psychologist was a good man at psychological mensuration, which is a good and useful field. But he was not equipped to analyze a completely alien thought-pattern.

"If I may say so, sir—" said Tommy uncomfortably.

"What?"

"They're oxygen breathers," said Tommy, "and they're not too dissimilar to us in other ways. It seems to me, sir, that parallel evolution has been at work. Perhaps intelligence evolves in parallel lines, just as . . . well . . . basic bodily functions. I mean," he added conscientiously, "any living being of any sort must ingest, metabolize, and excrete. Perhaps any intelligent brain must perceive, apperceive, and find a personal reaction. I'm sure I've detected irony. That implies humor, too. In short, sir, I think they could be likable."

The skipper heaved himself to his feet.

"H-m-m." He said profoundly, "We'll see what they have to say."

He walked to the communications room. The scanner for the vision plate in the robot was in readiness. The skipper walked in front of it. Tommy Dort sat down at the coding machine and tapped at the keys. Highly improbable noises came from it, went into a microphone, and governed the frequency-modulation of a signal sent through space to the other spaceship. Almost instantly the vision screen which with one relay—in the robot—showed the interior of the other ship lighted up. An alien came before the scanner and seemed to look inquisitively out of the plate. He was extraordinarily manlike, but he was not human. The impression he gave was of extreme baldness and a somehow humorous frankness.

"I'd like to say," said the skipper heavily, "the appropriate things about this first contact of two dissimilar civilized races, and of my hopes that a friendly intercourse between the two peoples will result."

Tommy Dort hesitated. Then he shrugged and tapped expertly upon the coder. More improbable noises.

The alien skipper seemed to receive the message. He made a gesture which was wryly assenting. The decoder on the *Llanvabon* hummed to itself and word-cards

dropped into the message frame. Tommy said dispassionately:

"He says, sir, 'That is all very well, but is there any
way for us to let each other go home alive? I would be
happy to hear of such a way if you can contrive one. At
the moment it seems to me that one of us must be killed.' "

III

The atmosphere was of confusion. There were too many
questions to be answered all at once. Nobody could
answer any of them. And all of them had to be answered.

The *Llanvabon* could start for home. The alien ship
might or might not be able to multiply the speed of light
by one more unit than the Earth vessel. If it could, the
Llanvabon would get close enough to Earth to reveal its
destination—and then have to fight. It might or might not
win. Even if it did win, the aliens might have a communication system by which the *Llanvabon's* destination might
have been reported to the aliens' home planet before battle
was joined. But the *Llanvabon* might lose in such a fight.
If she was to be destroyed, it would be better to be
destroyed here, without giving any clue to where human
beings might be found by a forewarned, forearmed alien
battle fleet.

The black ship was in exactly the same predicament.
It, too, could start for home. But the *Llanvabon* might be
faster, and an overdrive field can be trailed, if you set to
work on it soon enough. The aliens, also, would not know
whether the *Llanvabon* could report to its home base
without returning. If the alien was to be destroyed, it also
would prefer to fight it out here, so that it could not lead
a probable enemy to its own civilization.

Neither ship, then, could think of flight. The course of
the *Llanvabon* into the nebula might be known to the
black ship, but it had been the end of the logarithmic
curve, and the aliens could not know its properties. They
could not tell from that from what direction the Earth
ship had started. As of the moment, then, the two ships
were even. But the question was and remained, "What
now?"

There was no specific answer. The aliens traded information for information—and did not always realize what

information they gave. The humans traded information for information—and Tommy Dort sweated blood in his anxiety not to give any clue to the whereabout of Earth.

The aliens saw by infrared light, and the vision plates and scanners in the robot communication-exchange had to adapt their respective images up and down an optical octave each, for them to have any meaning at all. It did not occur to the aliens that their eyesight told that their sun was a red dwarf, yielding light of greatest energy just below the part of the spectrum visible to human eyes. But after that fact was realized on the *Llanvabon,* it was realized that the aliens, also, should be able to deduce the Sun's spectral type by the light to which men's eyes were best adapted.

There was a gadget for the recording of short-wave trains which was as casually in use among the aliens as a sound-recorder is among men. The humans wanted that, badly. And the aliens were fascinated by the mystery of sound. They were able to perceive noise, of course, just as a man's palm will perceive infrared light by the sensation of heat it produces, but they could no more differentiate pitch or tone-quality than a man is able to distinguish between two frequencies of heat-radiation even half an octave apart. To them, the human science of sound was a remarkable discovery. They would find uses for noises which humans had never imagined—if they lived.

But that was another question. Neither ship could leave without first destroying the other. But while the flood of information was in passage, neither ship could afford to destroy the other. There was the matter of the outer coloring of the two ships. The *Llanvabon* was mirror-bright exteriorly. The alien ship was dead-black by visible light. It absorbed heat to perfection, and should radiate it away again as readily. But it did not. The black coating was not a "black body" color or lack of color. It was a perfect reflector of certain infrared wave lengths while simultaneously it fluoresced in just those wave bands. In practice, it absorbed the higher frequencies of heat, converted them to lower frequencies it did not radiate—and stayed at the desired temperature even in empty space.

Tommy Dort labored over his task of communications. He found the alien thought-processes not so alien that he could not follow them. The discussion of technics reached the matter of interstellar navigation. A star map was needed to illustrate the process. It would have been logical to use a star map from the chart room—but from a star map one could guess the point from which the map was projected. Tommy had a map made specially, with imaginary but convincing star images upon it. He translated directions for its use by the coder and decoder. In return, the aliens presented a star map of their own before the visiplate. Copied instantly by photograph, the Nav officers labored over it, trying to figure out from what spot in the galaxy the stars and Milky Way would show at such an angle. It baffled them.

It was Tommy who realized finally that the aliens had made a special star map for their demonstration too, and that it was a mirror-image of the faked map Tommy had shown them previously.

Tommy could grin, at that. He began to like these aliens. They were not human, but they had a very human sense of the ridiculous. In course of time Tommy essayed a mild joke. It had to be translated into code numerals, these into quite cryptic groups of short-wave, frequency-modulated impulses, and these went to the other ship and into heaven knew what to become intelligible. A joke which went through such formalities would not seem likely to be funny. But the aliens did see the point.

There was one of the aliens to whom communication became as normal a function as Tommy's own code-handlings. The two of them developed a quite insane friendship, conversing by coder, decoder and short-wave trains. When technicalities in the official messages grew too involved, that alien sometimes threw in strictly non-technical interpolations akin to slang. Often, they cleared up the confusion. Tommy, for no reason whatever, had filed a code-name of "Buck" which the decoder picked out regularly when this particular operator signed his own symbol to a message.

In the third week of communication, the decoder suddenly presented Tommy with a message in the message frame.

You are a good guy. It is too bad we have to kill each other.—Buck.

Tommy had been thinking much the same thing. He tapped off the rueful reply:

We can't see any way out of it. Can you?

There was a pause, and the message frame filled up again.

If we could believe each other, yes, Our skipper would like it. But we can't believe you, and you can't believe us. We'd trail you home if we got a chance, and you'd trail us. But we feel sorry about it.—Buck.

Tommy Dort took the messages to the skipper.

"Look here, sir!" he said urgently. "These people are almost human, and they're likable cusses."

The skipper was busy about his important task of thinking things to worry about, and worrying about them. He said tiredly:

"They're oxygen breathers. Their air is twenty-eight per cent oxygen instead of twenty, but they could do very well on Earth. It would be a highly desirable conquest for them. And we still don't know what weapons they've got or what they can develop. Would you tell them how to find Earth?"

"No-no," said Tommy, unhappily.

"They probably feel the same way," said the skipper dryly. "And if we did manage to make a friendly contact, how long would it stay friendly? If their weapons were inferior to ours, they'd feel that for their own safety they had to improve them. And we, knowing they were planning to revolt, would crush them while we could—for our own safety! If it happened to be the other way about, they'd have to smash us before we could catch up to them."

Tommy was silent, but he moved restlessly.

"If we smash this black ship and get home," said the skipper, "Earth Government will be annoyed if we don't tell them where it came from. But what can we do? We'll be lucky enough to get back alive with our warning. It isn't possible to get out of those creatures any more in-

formation than we give them, and we surely won't give
them our address! We've run into them by accident.
Maybe—if we smash this ship—there won't be another
contact for thousands of years. And it's a pity, because
trade could mean so much! But it takes two to make a
peace, and we can't risk trusting them. The only answer
is to kill them if we can, and if we can't to make sure that
when they kill us they'll find out nothing that will lead
them to Earth. I don't like it," added the skipper tiredly,
"but there simply isn't anything else to do!"

IV

On the *Llanvabon,* the technicians worked frantically
in two divisions. One prepared for victory, and the other
for defeat. The ones working for victory could do little.
The main blasters were the only weapons with any promise.
Their mountings were cautiously altered so that they were
no longer fixed nearly dead ahead, with only a 5° traverse.
Electronic controls which followed a radio-locator master-
finder would keep them trained with absolute precision
upon a given target regardless of its maneuverings. More;
a hitherto unsung genius in the engine room devised a
capacity-storage system by which the normal full-output
of the ship's engines could be momentarily accumulated
and released in surges of stored power far above normal.
In theory, the range of the blasters should be multiplied
and their destructive power considerably stepped up. But
there was not much more that could be done.

The defeat crew had more leeway. Star charts, naviga-
tional instruments carrying telltale notations, the photographic record Tommy Dort had made on the six months'
journey from Earth, and every other memorandum offering clues to Earth's position, were prepared for destruction. They were put in sealed files, and if any one of them
was opened by one who did not know the exact, complicated process, the contents of all the files would flash into
ashes and the ashes be churned past any hope of restoration. Of course, if the *Llanvabon* should be victorious, a
carefully not-indicated method of reopening them in safety
would remain.

There were atomic bombs placed all over the hull of
the ship. If its human crew should be killed without com-

plete destruction of the ship, the atomic-power bombs should detonate if the *Llanvabon* were brought alongside an alien vessel. There were no ready-made atomic bombs on board, but there were small spare atomic-power units on board. It was not hard to trick them so that when they were turned on, instead of yielding a smooth flow of power they would explode. And four men of the earth ship's crew remained always in spacesuits with closed helmets, to fight the ship should it be punctured in many compartments by an unwarned attack.

Such an attack, however, would not be treacherous. The alien skipper had spoken frankly. His manner was that of one who wryly admits the uselessness of lies. The skipper and the *Llanvabon,* in turn, heavily admitted the virtue of frankness. Each insisted—perhaps truthfully—that he wished for friendship between the two races. But neither could trust the other not to make every conceivable effort to find out the one thing he needed most desperately to conceal—the location of his home planet. And neither dared believe that the other was unable to trail him and find out. Because each felt it his own duty to accomplish that unbearable—to the other—act, neither could risk the possible extinction of his race by trusting the other. They must fight because they could not do anything else.

They could raise the stakes of the battle by an exchange of information beforehand. But there was a limit to the stake either would put up. No information on weapons, population, or resources would be given by either. Not even the distance of their home bases from the Crab Nebula would be told. They exchanged information, to be sure, but they knew a battle to the death must follow, and each strove to represent his own civilization as powerful enough to give pause to the other's ideas of possible conquest—and thereby increased its appearance of menace to the other, and made battle more unavoidable.

It was curious how completely such alien brains could mesh, however. Tommy Dort, sweating over the coding and decoding machines, found a personal equation emerging from the at first stilted arrays of word-cards which arranged themselves. He had seen the aliens only in the vision screen, and then only in light at least one octave removed from the light they saw by. They, in turn, saw him very strangely, by transposed illumination from what to them would be the far ultraviolet. But their brains worked alike. Amazingly alike. Tommy Dort felt an actual sympathy and even something close to friendship for the gill-breathing, bald, and dryly ironic creatures of the black space vessel.

Because of that mental kinship he set up—though hopelessly—a sort of table of the aspects of the problem before them. He did not believe that the aliens had any instinctive desire to destroy man. In fact, the study of communications from the aliens had produced on the *Llanvabon* a feeling of tolerance not unlike that between enemy soldiers during a truce on Earth. The men felt no enmity, and probably neither did the aliens. But they had to kill or be killed for strictly logical reasons.

Tommy's table was specific. He made a list of objectives the men must try to achieve, in the order of their importance. The first was the carrying back of news of the existence of the alien creature. The second was the location of that alien culture in the galaxy. The third was the carrying back of as much information as possible about that culture. The third was being worked on but the second was probably impossible. The first—and all— would depend on the result of the fight which must take place.

The aliens' objectives would be exactly similar, so that the men must prevent, first, news of the existence of Earth's culture from being taken back by the aliens, second, alien discovery of the location of Earth, and third, the acquiring by the aliens of information which would help them or encourage them to attack humanity. And again the third was in train, and the second was probably taken care of, and the first must await the battle.

There was no possible way to avoid the grim necessity of the destruction of the black ship. The aliens would see no solution to their problems but the destruction of the *Llanvabon*. But Tommy Dort, regarding his tabulation ruefully, realized that even complete victory would not be a perfect solution. The ideal would be for the *Llanvabon* to take back the alien ship for study. Nothing less would be a complete attainment of the third objective. But Tommy realized that he hated the idea of so complete a victory, even if it could be accomplished. He would hate the idea of killing even nonhuman creatures who understood a human joke. And beyond that, he would hate the idea of Earth fitting out a fleet of fighting ships to destroy an alien culture because its existence was dangerous. The pure accident of this encounter, between people who could like each other, had created a situation which could only result in wholesale destruction.

Tommy Dort soured on his own brain which could find no answer which would work. But there had to be an answer! The gamble was too big! It was too absurd that two spaceships should fight—neither one primarily designed for fighting—so that the survivor could carry back news which would set one side to frenzied preparation for war against the unwarned other.

If both races could be warned, though, and each knew that the other did not want to fight, and if they could communicate with each other but not locate each other until some grounds for mutual trust could be reached—

It was impossible. It was chimerical. It was a daydream. It was nonsense. But it was such luring nonsense that Tommy Dort ruefully put it into the coder to his gill-breathing friend Buck, then some hundred thousand miles off in the misty brightness of the nebula.

"Sure," said Buck, in the decoder's word-cards flicking into place in the message frame. "That is a good dream. But I like you and still won't believe you. If I said that first, you would like me but not believe me either. I tell you the truth more than you believe, and maybe you tell me the truth more than I believe. But there is no way to know. I am sorry."

Tommy Dort stared gloomily at the message. He felt a very horrible sense of responsibility. Everyone did, on the *Llanvabon*. If they failed in this encounter, the human race would run a very good chance of being exterminated in time to come. If they succeeded, the race of the aliens would be the one to face destruction, most likely. Millions or billions of lives hung upon the actions of a few men.

Then Tommy Dort saw the answer.

It would be amazingly simple, if it worked. At worst it might give a partial victory to humanity and the *Llanva-*

bon. He sat quite still, not daring to move lest he break the chain of thought that followed the first tenuous idea. He went over and over it, excitedly finding objections here and meeting them, and overcoming impossibilities there. It was the answer! He felt sure of it.

He felt almost dizzy with relief when he found his way to the captain's room and asked leave to speak.

It is the function of a skipper, among others, to find things to worry about. But the *Llanvabon's* skipper did not have to look. In the three weeks and four days since the first contact with the alien black ship, the skipper's face had grown lined and old. He had not only the *Llanvabon* to worry about. He had all humanity.

"Sir," said Tommy Dort, his mouth rather dry because of his enormous earnestness, "may I offer a method of attack on the black ship? I'll undertake it myself, sir, and if it doesn't work our ship won't be weakened."

The skipper looked at him unseeingly.

"The tactics are all worked out, Mr. Dort," he said heavily. "They're being cut on tape now, for the ship's handling. It's a terrible gamble, but it has to be done."

"I think," said Tommy carefully, "I've worked out a way to take the gamble out. Suppose, sir, we send a message to the other ship, offering—"

His voice went on in the utterly quiet captain's room, with the visiplates showing only a vast mistiness outside and the two fiercely burning stars in the nebula's heart.

V

The skipper himself went through the air lock with Tommy. For one reason, the action Tommy had suggested would need his authority behind it. For another, the skipper had worried more intensely than anybody else on the *Llanvabon*, and he was tired of it. If he went with Tommy, he would do the thing himself, and if he failed he would be the first one killed—and the tapes for the Earth ship's maneuvering were already fed into the control board and correlated with the master-timer. If Tommy and the skipper were killed, a single control pushed home would throw the *Llanvabon* into the most furious possible all-out attack, which would end in the complete destruction of one ship or the other—or both. So the skipper was not deserting his post.

The outer air lock door swung wide. It opened upon that shining emptiness which was the nebula. Twenty miles away, the little round robot hung in space, drifting in an incredible orbit about the twin central suns, and floating ever nearer and nearer. It would never reach either of them, of course. The white star alone was so much hotter than Earth's sun that its heat-effect would produce Earth's temperature on an object five times as far from it as Neptune is from Sol. Even removed to the distance of Pluto, the little robot would be raised to cherry-red heat by the blazing dwarf. And it could not possibly approach to the ninety-odd million miles which is the Earth's distance from the sun. So near, its metal would melt and boil away as vapor. But, half a light-year out, the bulbous object bobbed in emptiness.

The two spacesuited figures soared away from the *Llanvabon*. The small atomic drives which made them minute spaceships on their own had been subtly altered, but the change did not interfere with their functioning. They headed for the communication robot. The skipper, out in space, said gruffly:

"Mr. Dort, all my life I have longed for adventure. This is the first time I could ever justify it to myself."

His voice came through Tommys space-phone receivers. Tommy wetted his lips and said:

"It doesn't seem like adventure to me, sir. I want terribly for the plan to go through. I thought adventure was when you didn't care."

"Oh, no," said the skipper. "Adventure is when you toss your life on the scales of chance and wait for the pointer to stop."

They reached the round object. They clung to its short, scanner-tipped horns.

"Intelligent, those creatures," said the skipper heavily. "They must want desperately to see more of our ship than the communications room, to agree to this exchange of visits before the fight."

"Yes, sir," said Tommy. But privately, he suspected that Buck—his gill-breathing friend—would like to see him in the flesh before one or both of them died. And it seemed to

him that between the two ships had grown up an odd tradition of courtesy, like that between two ancient knights
before a tourney, when they admired each other whole-
heartedly before hacking at each other with all the contents of their respective armories.

They waited.

Then, out of the mist, came two other figures. The alien
spacesuits were also power-driven. The aliens themselves
were shorter than men, and their helmet openings were
coated with a filtering material to cut off visible and
ultraviolet rays which to them would be lethal. It was not
possible to see more than the outline of the heads within.

Tommy's helmet phone said, from the communications
room on the *Llanvabon:*

"They say that their ship is waiting for you, sir. The
air lock door will be open."

The skipper's voice said heavily:

"Mr. Dort, have you seen their spacesuits before? If
so, are you sure they're not carrying anything extra, such
as bombs?"

"Yes, sir," said Tommy. "We've showed each other our
space equipment. They've nothing but regular stuff in view,
sir."

The skipper made a gesture to the two aliens. He and
Tommy Dort plunged on for the black vessel. They could
not make out the ship very clearly with the naked eye,
but directions for change of course came from the communication room.

The black ship loomed up. It was huge; as long as the
Llanvabon and vastly thicker. The air lock did stand
open. The two spacesuited men moved in and anchored
themselves with magnetic-soled boots. The outer door
closed. There was a rush of air and simultaneously the
sharp quick tug of artificial gravity. Then the inner door
opened.

All was darkness. Tommy switched on his helmet light
at the same instant as the skipper. Since the aliens saw
by infrared, a white light would have been intolerable to
them. The men's helmet lights were, therefore, of the deep-
red tint used to illuminate instrument panels so there would
be no dazzling of eyes that must be able to detect the
minutest specks of white light on a navigating vision

plate. There were aliens waiting to receive them. They blinked at the brightness of the helmet lights. The space-phone receivers said in Tommy's ear:

"They say, sir, their skipper is waiting for you."

Tommy and the skipper were in a long corridor with a soft flooring underfoot. Their lights showed details of which every one was exotic.

"I think I'll crack my helmet, sir," said Tommy.

He did. The air was good. By analysis it was thirty percent oxygen instead of twenty for normal air on Earth, but the pressure was less. It felt just right. The artificial gravity, too, was less than that maintained on the *Llanvabon*. The home planet of the aliens would be smaller than Earth, and—by the infrared data—circling close to a nearly dead, dull-red sun. The air had smells in it. They were utterly strange, but not unpleasant.

An arched opening. A ramp with the same soft stuff underfoot. Lights which actually shed a dim, dull-red glow about. The aliens had stepped up some of their il-luminating equipment as an act of courtesy. The light might hurt their eyes, but it was a gesture of considera-tion which made Tommy even more anxious for his plan to go through.

The alien skipper faced them, with what seemed to Tommy a gesture of wryly humorous deprecation. The helmet phones said:

"He says, sir, that he greets you with pleasure, but he has been able to think of only one way in which the prob-lem created by the meeting of these two ships can be solved."

"He means a fight," said the skipper. "Tell him I'm here to offer another choice."

The *Llanvabon's* skipper and the skipper of the alien ship were face to face, but their communication was weirdly indirect. The aliens used no sound in communi-cation. Their talk, in fact, took place on microwaves and and approximated telepathy. But they could not hear, in any ordinary sense of the word, so the skipper's and Tommy's speech approached telepathy, too, as far as they were concerned. When the skipper spoke, his space phone sent his words back to the *Llanvabon*, where the words were fed into the coder and short-wave equivalents sent back to the black ship. The alien skipper's reply went to the *Llanvabon* and through the decoder, and was retransmitted by space phone in words read from the message frame. It was awkward, but it worked.

The short and stocky alien skipper paused. The helmet phones relayed his translated, soundless reply.

"He is anxious to hear, sir."

The skipper took off his helmet. He put his hands at his belt in a belligerent pose.

"Look here!" he said truculently to the bald, strange creature in the unearthly red glow before him. "It looks like we have to fight and one batch of us get killed. We're ready to do it if we have to. But if you win, we've got it fixed so you'll never find out where Earth is, and there's a good chance we'll get you anyhow! If we win, we'll be in the same fix. And if we win and go back home, our government will fit out a fleet and start hunting your planet. And if we find it we'll be ready to blast it to hell! If you win, the same thing will happen to us! And it's all foolishness! We've stayed here a month, and we've swapped information, and we don't hate each other. There's no reason for us to fight except for the rest of our respective races!"

The skipper stopped for breath, scowling. Tommy Dort inconspicuously put his own hands on the belt of his spacesuit. He waited, hoping desperately that the trick would work.

"He says, sir," reported the helmet phones, "that all you say is true. But that his race has to be protected, just as you feel that yours must be."

"Naturally!" said the skipper angrily, "but the sensible thing to do is to figure out how to protect it! Putting its future up as a gamble in a fight is not sensible. Our races have to be warned of each other's existence. That's true. But each should have proof that the other doesn't want to fight, but wants to be friendly. And we shouldn't be able to find each other, but we should be able to communicate with each other to work out grounds for a common trust. If our governments want to be fools, let them! But we should give them the chance to make friends, instead of starting a space war out of mutual funk!"

Briefly, the space phone said:

"He says that the difficulty is that of trusting each other now. With the possible existence of his race at stake, he cannot take any chance, and neither can you, of yielding an advantage."

"But my race," boomed the skipper, glaring at the alien captain, "my race has an advantage now. We came here to your ship in atom-powered spacesuits! Before we left, we altered the drives! We can set off ten pounds of sensitized fuel apiece, right here in this ship, or it can be set off by remote control from our ship! It will be rather remarkable if your fuel store doesn't blow up with us! In other words, if you don't accept my proposal for a commonsense approach to this predicament, Dort and I blow up in an atomic explosion, and your ship will be wrecked if not destroyed—and the *Llanvabon* will be attacking with everything its got within seconds after the blast goes off!"

The captain's room of the alien ship was a strange scene, with its dull-red illumination and the strange, bald, gill-breathing aliens watching the skipper and waiting for the inaudible translation of the harangue they could not hear. But a sudden tensity appeared in the air. A sharp, savage feeling of strain. The alien skipper made a gesture. The helmet phones hummed.

"He says, sir, what is your proposal?"

"Swap ships!" roared the skipper. "Swap ships and go on home! We can fix our instruments so they'll do no trailing, he can do the same with his. We'll each remove our star maps and records. We'll each dismantle our weapons. The air will serve, and we'll take their ship and they'll take ours, and neither one can harm or trail the other, and each will carry home more information than can be taken otherwise! We can agree on this same Crab Nebula as a rendezvous when the double-star has made another circuit, and if our people want to meet them they can do it, and if they are scared they can duck it! That's my proposal! And he'll take it, or Dort and I blow up their ship and the *Llanvabon* blasts what's left!"

He glared about him while he waited for the translation to reach the tense small stocky figures about him. He could tell when it came because the tenseness changed.

The figures stirred. They made gestures. One of them
made convulsive movements. It lay down on the soft
floor and kicked. Others leaned against its walls and
shook.

The voice in Tommy Dort's helmet phones had been
strictly crisp and professional, before, but now it sounded
blankly amazed.

"He says, sir, that it is a good joke. Because the two
crew members he sent to our ship, and that you passed on
the way, have their spaceship stuffed with atomic explosive
too, sir, and he intended to make the very same offer and
threat! Of course he accepts, sir. Your ship is worth more
to him than his own, and his is worth more to you than
the *Llanvabon*. It appears, sir, to be a deal."

Then Tommy Dort realized what the convulsive movements of the aliens were. They were laughter.

It wasn't quite as simple as the skipper had outlined
it. The actual working-out of the proposal was complicated. For three days the crews of the two ships were
intermingled, the aliens learning the workings of the
Llanvabon's engines, and the men learning the controls of
the black spaceship. It was a good joke—but it wasn't all
a joke. There were men on the black ship, and aliens on
the *Llanvabon*, ready at an instant's notice to blow up the
vessels in question. And they would have done it in case
of need, for which reason the need did not appear. But
it was, actually, a better arrangement to have two expeditions return to two civilizations, under the current arrangement, than for either to return alone.

There were differences, though. There was some dispute
about the removal of records. In most cases the dispute was
settled by the destruction of the records. There was more
trouble caused by the *Llanvabon's* books, and the alien
equivalent of a ship's library, containing works which
approximated the novels of Earth. But those items were
valuable to possible friendship, because they would show
the two cultures, each to the other, from the viewpoint
of normal citizens and without propaganda.

But nerves were tense during those three days. Aliens
unloaded and inspected the foodstuffs intended for the
men on the black ship. Men transshipped the foodstuffs

the aliens would need to return to their home. There were endless details, from the exchange of lighting equipment to suit the eyesight of the exchanging crews, to a final check-up of apparatus. A joint inspection party of both races verified that all detector devices had been smashed but not removed, so that they could not be used for trailing and had not been smuggled away. And of course, the aliens were anxious not to leave any useful weapon on the black ship, nor the men upon the *Llanvabon*. It was a curious fact that each crew was best qualified to take exactly the measures which made an evasion of the agreement impossible.

There was a final conference before the two ships parted, back to the communication room of the *Llanvabon*.

"Tell the little runt," rumbled the *Llanvabon's* former skipper, "that he's got a good ship and he'd better treat her right."

The message frame flicked word-cards into position.

"I believe," it said on the alien skipper's behalf, "that your ship is just as good. I hope to meet you here when the double star has turned one turn."

The last man left the *Llanvabon*. It moved away into the misty nebula before they had returned to the black ship. The vision plates in that vessel had been altered for human eyes, and human crewmen watched jealously for any trace of their former ship as their new craft took a crazy, evading course to a remote part of the nebula. It came to a crevasse of nothingness, leading to the stars. It rose swiftly to clear space. There was the instant of breathlessness which the overdrive field produces as it goes on, and then the black ship whipped away into the void at many times the speed of light.

Many days later, the skipper saw Tommy Dort poring over one of the strange objects which were the equivalent of books. It was fascinating to puzzle over. The skipper was pleased with himself. The technicians of the *Llanvabon's* former crew were finding out desirable things about the ship almost momently. Doubtless the aliens were as pleased with their discoveries in the *Llanvabon*. But the black ship would be enormously worth while—and the solution that had been found was by any standard much superior even to a combat in which the Earthmen had been overwhelmingly victorious.

"Hm-m-m, Mr. Dort," said the skipper profoundly. "You've no equipment to make another photographic record on the way back. It was left on the *Llanvabon*. But fortunately, we have your record taken on the way out, and I shall report most favorably on your suggestion and your assistance in carrying it out. I think very well of you, sir."

"Thank you, sir," said Tommy Dort.

He waited. The skipper cleared his throat.

"You . . . ah . . . first realized the close similarity of mental processes between the aliens and ourselves," he observed. "What do you think of the prospects of a friendly arrangement if we keep a rendezvous with them at the nebula as agreed?"

"Oh, we'll get along all right, sir," said Tommy. "We've got a good start toward friendship. After all, since they see by infrared, the planets they'd want to make use of wouldn't suit us. There's no reason why we shouldn't get along. We're almost alike in psychology."

"Hm-m-m. Now just what do you mean by that?" demanded the skipper.

"Why, they're just like us, sir!" said Tommy. "Of course they breathe through gills and they see by heat waves, and their blood has a copper base instead of iron and a few little details like that. But otherwise we're just alike! There were only men on their crew, sir, but they have two sexes as we have, and they have families, and . . . er . . . their sense of humor— In fact—"

Tommy hesitated.

"Go on, sir," said the skipper.

"Well— There was the one I called Buck, sir, because he hasn't any name that goes into sound waves," said Tommy. "We got along very well. I'd really call him my friend, sir. And we were together for a couple of hours just before the two ships separated and we'd nothing in particular to do. So I became convinced that humans and aliens are bound to be good friends if they have only half a chance. You see, sir, we spent those two hours telling dirty jokes."

THAT ONLY A MOTHER

by Judith Merril

Margaret reached over to the other side of the bed where Hank should have been. Her hand patted the empty pillow, and then she came altogether awake, wondering that the old habit should remain after so many months. She tried to curl up, cat-style, to hoard her own warmth, found she couldn't do it any more, and climbed out of bed with a pleased awareness of her increasingly clumsy bulkiness.

Morning motions were automatic. On the way through the kitchenette, she pressed the button that would start breakfast cooking—the doctor had said to eat as much breakfast as she could—and tore the paper out of the facsimile machine. She folded the long sheet carefully to the "National News" section, and propped it on the bathroom shelf to scan while she brushed her teeth.

No accidents. No direct hits. At least none that had been officially released for publication. *Now, Maggie, don't get started on that. No accidents. No hits. Take the nice newspaper's word for it.*

The three clear chimes from the kitchen announced that breakfast was ready. She set a bright napkin and cheerful colored dishes on the table in a futile attempt to appeal to a faulty morning appetite. Then, when there was nothing more to prepare, she went for the mail, allowing herself the full pleasure of prolonged anticipation, because today there would *surely* be a letter.

There was. There were. Two bills and a worried note from her mother: "Darling, why didn't you write and tell me sooner? I'm thrilled, of course, but, well one

First published in 1948

hates to mention these things, but are you *certain* the doctor was right? Hank's been around all that uranium or thorium or whatever it is all these years, and I know you say he's a designer, not a technician, and he doesn't get near anything that might be dangerous, but you know he used to, back at Oak Ridge. Don't you think . . . well, of course, I'm just being a foolish old woman, and I don't want you to get upset. You know much more about it than I do, and I'm sure your doctor was right. He *should* know . . ."

Margaret made a face over the excellent coffee, and caught herself refolding the paper to the medical news.

Stop it, Maggie, stop it! The radiologist said Hank's job couldn't have exposed him. And the bombed area we drove past . . . No, no. Stop it, now! Read the social notes or the recipes, Maggie girl.

A well-known geneticist, in the medical news, said that it was possible to tell with absolute certainty, at five months, whether the child would be normal, or at least whether the mutation was likely to produce anything freakish. The worst cases, at any rate, could be prevented. Minor mutations, of course, displacements in facial features, or changes in brain structure could not be detected. And there had been some cases recently, of normal embryos with atrophied limbs that did not develop beyond the seventh or eighth month. But, the doctor concluded cheerfully, the *worst* cases could now be predicted and prevented.

"Predicted and prevented." We predicted it, didn't we? Hank and the others, they predicted it. But we didn't prevent it. We could have stopped it in '46 and '47. Now . . .

Margaret decided against the breakfast. Coffee had been enough for her in the morning for ten years; it would have to do for today. She buttoned herself into interminable folds of material that, the salesgirl had assured her, was the *only* comfortable thing to wear during the last few months. With a surge of pure pleasure, the letter and newspaper forgotten, she realized she was on the next to the last button. It wouldn't be long now.

The city in the early morning had always been a special
kind of excitement for her. Last night it had rained, and
the sidewalks were still damp-gray instead of dusty. The
air smelled the fresher, to a city-bred woman, for the
occasional pungency of acrid factory smoke. She walked
the six blocks to work, watching the lights go out in the
all-night hamburger joints, where the plate-glass walls
were already catching the sun, and the lights go on in the
dim interiors of cigar stores and dry-cleaning establish-
ments.

The office was in a new Government building. In the
rolovator, on the way up, she felt, as always, like a
frankfurter roll in the ascending half of an old-style
rotary toasting machine. She abandoned the air-foam
cushioning gratefully at the fourteenth floor, and settled
down behind her desk, at the rear of a long row of identical desks.

Each morning the pile of papers that greeted her was a
little higher. These were, as everyone knew, the decisive
months. The war might be won or lost on these calculations as well as any others. The manpower office had
switched her here when her old expeditor's job got to be
too strenuous. The computer was easy to operate, and
the work was absorbing, if not as exciting as the old job.
But you didn't just stop working these days. Everyone who
could do anything at all was needed.

And—she remembered the interview with the psychologist—*I'm probably the unstable type. Wonder what sort of
neurosis I'd get sitting home reading that sensational
paper* . . .

She plunged into the work without pursuing the thought.

February 18.

Hank darling,

Just a note—from the hospital, no less. I had a dizzy
spell at work, and the doctor took it to heart. Blessed
if I know what I'll do with myself lying in bed for
weeks, just waiting—but Dr. Boyer seems to think it
may not be so long.

There are too many newspapers around here. More
infanticides all the time, and they can't seem to get a

jury to convict any of them. It's the fathers who do it. Lucky thing you're not around, in case—

Oh, darling, that wasn't a very *funny* joke, was it? Write as often as you can, will you? I have too much time to think. But there really isn't anything wrong, and nothing to worry about.

Write often, and remember I love you.

Maggie.

SPECIAL SERVICE TELEGRAM

February 21, 1953
22:04 LK37G

From: Tech. Lieut. H. Marvell
X47-016 GCNY

To: Mrs. H. Marvell
Women's Hospital
New York City

HAD DOCTOR'S GRAM STOP WILL ARRIVE FOUR OH TEN STOP SHORT LEAVE STOP YOU DID IT MAGGIE STOP LOVE HANK

February 25.

Hank dear,

So you didn't see the baby either? You'd think a place this size would at least have visiplates on the incubators, so the fathers could get a look, even if the poor benighted mommas can't. They tell me I won't see her for another week, or maybe more—but of course, mother always warned me if I didn't slow my pace, I'd probably even have my babies too fast. Why must she *always* be right?

Did you meet that battle-ax of a nurse they put on here? I imagine they save her for people who've already had theirs, and don't let her get too near the prospectives—but a woman like that simply shouldn't be allowed in a maternity ward. She's obsessed with mutations, can't seem to talk about anything else. Oh, well, *ours* is all right, even if it was in an unholy hurry.

I'm tired. They warned me not to sit up too soon, but I *had* to write you. All my love, darling,

Maggie.

February 29.

Darling,

I finally got to see her? It's all true, what they say about new babies and the face that only a mother could love—but it's all there, darling, eyes, ears, and noses— no, only one!—all in the right places. We're so *lucky*, Hank.

I'm afraid I've been a rambunctious patient. I kept telling that hatchet-faced female with the mutation mania that I wanted to *see* the baby. Finally the doctor came in to "explain" everything to me, and talked a lot of nonsense, most of which I'm sure no one could have understood, any more than I did. The only thing I got out of it was that she didn't actually *have* to stay in the incubator; they just thought it was "wiser."

I think I got a little hysterical at that point. Guess I was more worried than I was willing to admit, but I threw a small fit about it. The whole business wound up with one of those hushed medical conferences out- side the door, and finally the Woman in White said: "Well, we might as well. Maybe it'll work out better that way."

I'd heard about the way doctors and nurses in these places develop a God complex, and believe me, it is as true figuratively as it is literally that a mother hasn't a leg to stand on around here.

I *am* awfully weak, still. I'll write again soon. Love,

Maggie.

March 8.

Dearest Hank,

Well the nurse was wrong if she told you that. She's an idiot anyhow. It's a girl. It's easier to tell with babies than with cats, and *I know*. How about Henrietta?

I'm home again, and busier than a betatron. They got *everything* mixed up at the hospital, and I had to teach myself how to bathe her and do just about every- thing else. She's getting prettier, too. When can you get a leave, a *real* leave?

Love,
Maggie.

May 26.

Hank dear,

You should see her now—and you shall. I'm sending along a reel of color movie. My mother sent her those nighties with drawstrings all over. I put one on, and right now she looks like a snow-white potato sack with that beautiful, beautiful flower-face blooming on top. Is that *me* talking? Am I a doting mother? But wait till you see her!

July 10.

. . . Believe it or not, as you like, but your daughter can talk, and I don't mean baby talk. Alice discovered it— she's a dental assistant in the WACs, you know—and when she heard the baby giving out what I thought was a string of gibberish, she said the kid knew words and sentences, but couldn't say them clearly because she has no teeth yet. I'm taking her to a speech specialist.

September 13.

. . . We have a prodigy for real! Now that all her front teeth are in, her speech is perfectly clear and—a new talent now—she can sing! I mean really carry a tune! At seven months! Darling my world would be perfect if you could only get home.

November 19.

. . . at last. The little goon was so busy being clever, it took her all this time to learn to crawl. The doctor says development in these cases is always erratic . . .

SPECIAL SERVICE TELEGRAM

December 1, 1953
08:47 LK59F

From: Tech. Lieut. H. Marvell
X47-016 GCNY
To: Mrs. H. Marvell
Apt. K-17
504 E. 19 St.
N.Y. N.Y.

WEEK'S LEAVE STARTS TOMORROW STOP WILL ARRIVE AIRPORT TEN OH FIVE STOP DON'T MEET ME STOP LOVE LOVE LOVE HANK

Margaret let the water run out of the bathinette until only a few inches were left, and then loosed her hold on the wriggling baby.

"I think it was better when you were retarded, young woman," she informed her daughter happily. "You *can't* crawl in a bathinette, you know."

"Then why can't I go in the bathtub?" Margaret was used to her child's volubility by now, but every now and then it caught her unawares. She swooped the resistant mass of pink flesh into a towel, and began to rub.

"Because you're too little, and your head is very soft, and bathtubs are very hard."

"Oh. Then when can I go in the bathtub?"

"When the outside of your head is as hard as the in-side, brainchild." She reached toward a pile of fresh clothing. "I cannot understand," she added, pinning a square of cloth through the nightgown, "why a child of your intelligence can't learn to keep a diaper on the way other babies do. They've been used for centuries, you know, with perfectly satisfactory results."

The child disdained to reply; she had heard it too often. She waited patiently until she had been tucked, clean and sweet-smelling, into a white-painted crib. Then she favored her mother with a smile that inevitably made Margaret think of the first golden edge of the sun bursting into a rosy pre-dawn. She remembered Hank's reaction to the color pictures of his beautiful daughter, and with the thought, realized how late it was.

"Go to sleep, puss. When you wake up, you know, your *Daddy* will be here."

"Why?" asked the four-year-old mind, waging a losing battle to keep the ten-month-old body awake.

Margaret went into the kitchenette and set the timer for the roast. She examined the table, and got her clothes from the closet, new dress, new shoes, new slip, new everything, bought weeks before and saved for the day Hank's telegram came. She stopped to pull a paper from the facsimile, and, with clothes and news, went into the bathroom, and lowered herself gingerly into the steaming luxury of a scented tub.

She glanced through the paper with indifferent interest. Today at least there was no need to read the national

news. There was an article by a geneticist. The same geneticist. Mutations, he said, were increasing disproportionately. It was too soon for recessives; even the first mu-
tants, born near Hiroshima and Nagasaki in 1946 and
1947 were not old enough yet to breed. *But my baby's
all right.* Apparently, there was some degree of free radiation from atomic explosions causing the trouble. *My
baby's fine. Precocious, but normal.* If more attention had
been paid to the first Japanese mutations, he said . . .

*There was that little notice in the paper in the spring of
'47. That was when Hank quit at Oak Ridge.* "Only two
or three per cent of those guilty of infanticide are being
caught and punished in Japan today . . ." *But* MY BABY'S
all right.

She was dressed, combed, and ready to the last light
brush-on of lip paste, when the door chime sounded. She
dashed for the door, and heard, for the first time in
eighteen months the almost-forgotten sound of a key
turning in the lock before the chime had quite died away.

"Hank!"

"Maggie!"

And then there was nothing to say. So many days, so
many months, of small news piling up, so many things
to tell him, and now she just stood there, staring at a
khaki uniform and a stranger's pale face. She traced the
features with the finger of memory. The same high-bridged
nose, wide-set eyes, fine feathery brows; the same long
jaw, the hair a little farther back now on the high forehead, the same tilted curve to his mouth. Pale . . . Of
course, he'd been underground all this time. And strange,
stranger because of lost familiarity than any newcomer's
face could be.

She had time to think all that before his hand reached
out to touch her, and spanned the gap of eighteen months.
Now, again, there was nothing to say, because there was
no need. They were together, and for the moment that was
enough.

"Where's the baby?"

"Sleeping. She'll be up any minute."

No urgency. Their voices were as casual as though it
were a daily exchange, as though war and separation did
not exist. Margaret picked up the coat he'd thrown on

the chair near the door, and hung it carefully in the hall closet. She went to check the roast, leaving him to wander through the rooms by himself, remembering and coming back. She found him, finally, standing over the baby's crib.

She couldn't see his face, but she had no need to.

"I think we can wake her just this once." Margaret pulled the covers down, and lifted the white bundle from the bed. Sleepy lids pulled back heavily from smoky brown eyes.

"Hello." Hank's voice was tentative.

"Hello." The baby's assurance was more pronounced.

He had heard about it, of course, but that wasn't the same as hearing it. He turned eagerly to Margaret. "She really can—?"

"Of course she can, darling. But what's more important, she can even do nice normal things like other babies do, even stupid ones. Watch her crawl!" Margaret set the baby on the big bed.

For a moment young Henrietta lay and eyed her parents dubiously.

"Crawl?" she asked.

"That's the idea. Your Daddy is new around here, you know. He wants to see you show off."

"Then put me on my tummy."

"Oh, of course." Margaret obligingly rolled the baby over.

"What's the matter?" Hank's voice was still casual, but an undercurrent in it began to charge the air of the room. "I thought they turned over first."

"This baby," Margaret would not notice the tension, *"This* baby does things when she wants to."

This baby's father watched with softening eyes while the head advanced and the body hunched up propelling itself across the bed.

"Why the little rascal," he burst into relieved laughter. "She looks like one of those potato-sack racers they used to have on picnics. Got her arms pulled out of the sleeves already." He reached over and grabbed the knot at the bottom of the long nightie.

"I'll do it, darling." Margaret tried to get there first.

"Don't be silly, Maggie. This may be *your* first baby,

but *I* had five kid brothers." He laughed her away, and reached with his other hand for the string that closed one sleeve. He opened the sleeve bow, and groped for an arm.

"The way you wriggle," he addressed his child sternly, as his hand touched a moving knob of flesh at the shoulder, "anyone might think you are a worm, using your tummy to crawl on, instead of your hands and feet."

Margaret stood and watched, smiling. "Wait till you hear her sing, darling—"

His right hand traveled down from the shoulder to where he thought an arm would be, traveled down, and straight down, over firm small muscles that writhed in an attempt to move against the pressure of his hand. He let his fingers drift up again to the shoulder. With infinite care, he opened the knot at the bottom of the nightgown. His wife was standing by the bed, saying: "She can do 'Jingle Bells,' and—"

His left hand felt along the soft knitted fabric of the gown, up towards the diaper that folded, flat and smooth, across the bottom end of his child. No wrinkles. No kicking. *No . . .*

"Maggie." He tried to pull his hands from the neat fold in the diaper, from the wriggling body. "Maggie." His throat was dry; words came hard, low and grating. He spoke very slowly, thinking the sound of each word to make himself say it. His head was spinning, but he had to *know* before he let it go. "Maggie, why . . . didn't you . . . tell me?"

"Tell you what, darling?" Margaret's poise was the immemorial patience of woman confronted with man's childish impetuosity. Her sudden laugh sounded fantastically easy and natural in that room; it was all clear to her now. "Is she wet? I didn't know."

She didn't know. His hands, beyond control, ran up and down the soft-skinned baby body, the sinuous, limbless body. *Oh God, dear God*—his head shook and his muscles contracted, in a bitter spasm of hysteria. His fingers tightened on his child—*Oh God, she didn't know . . .*

SCANNERS LIVE IN VAIN

by Cordwainer Smith

Martel was angry. He did not even adjust his blood away from anger. He stamped across the room by judgment, not by sight. When he saw the table hit the floor, and could tell by the expression on Luci's face that the table must have made a loud crash, he looked down to see if his leg were broken. It was not. Scanner to the core, he had to scan himself. The action was reflex and automatic. The inventory included his legs, abdomen, Chestbox of instruments, hands, arms, face and back with the Mirror. Only then did Martel go back to being angry. He talked with his voice, even though he knew that his wife hated its blare and preferred to have him write.

"I tell you, I must cranch. I have to cranch. It's my worry, isn't it?"

When Luci answered, he saw only a part of her words as he read her lips: "Darling . . . you're my husband . . . right to love you . . . dangerous . . . do it . . . dangerous . . . wait. . . ."

He faced her, but put sound in his voice, letting the blare hurt her again: "I tell you, I'm going to cranch."

Catching her expression, he became rueful and a little tender: "Can't you understand what it means to me? To get out of this horrible prison in my own head? To be a man again—hearing your voice, smelling smoke? To *feel* again—to feel my feet on the ground, to feel the air move against my face? Don't you know what it means?"

Her wide-eyed worrisome concern thrust him back into

First published in 1948 ("Cordwainer Smith" was the pseudonym of Dr. Paul Linebarger) pure annoyance. He read only a few words as her lips moved: ". . . . love you . . . your own good . . . don't you think I want you to be human? . . . your own good . . . too much . . . he said . . . they said. . . ."

When he roared at her, he realized that his voice must be particularly bad. He knew that the sound hurt her no less than did the words: "Do you think I wanted to marry a Scanner? Didn't I tell you we're almost as low as the habermans? We're dead, I tell you. We've got to be dead to do our work. How can anybody go to the Up-and-Out? Can you dream what raw Space is? I warned you. But you married me. All right, you married a man. Please, darling, let me be a man. Let me hear your voice, let me feel the warmth of being alive, of being human. Let me!"

He saw by her look of stricken assent that he had won the argument. He did not use his voice again. Instead, he pulled his tablet up from where it hung against his chest. He wrote on it, using the pointed fingernail of his right forefinger—the Talking Nail of a Scanner—in quick clean-cut script: "Pls, drlng, whrs Crnching Wire?"

She pulled the long gold-sheathed wire out of the pocket of her apron. She let its field sphere fall to the carpeted floor. Swiftly, dutifully, with the deft obedience of a Scanner's wife, she wound the Cranching Wire around his head, spirally around his neck and chest. She avoided the instruments set in his chest. She even avoided the radiating scars around the instruments, the stigmata of men who had gone Up and into the Out. Mechanically he lifted a foot as she slipped the wire between his feet. She drew the wire taut. She snapped the small plug into the High Burden Control next to his Heart Reader. She helped him to sit down, arranging his hands for him, pushing his head back into the cup at the top of the chair. She turned then, full-face toward him, so that he could read her lips easily. Her expression was composed.

She knelt, scooped up the sphere at the other end of the wire, stood erect calmly, her back to him. He scanned her, and saw nothing in her posture but grief which would have escaped the eye of anyone but a Scanner. She spoke: he could see her chest-muscles moving. She realized that she was not facing him, and turned so that he could see her lips.

"Ready at last?"

He smiled a *yes*.

She turned her back to him again. (Luci could never bear to watch him Under-the-wire.) She tossed the wire-sphere into the air. It caught in the force-field, and hung there. Suddenly it glowed. That was all. All—except for the sudden red stinking roar of coming back to his senses. Coming back, across the wild threshold of pain.

1

When he awakened under the wire, he did not feel as though he had just cranched. Even though it was the second cranching within the week, he felt fit. He lay in the chair. His ears drank in the sound of air touching things in the room. He heard Luci breathing in the next room, where she was hanging up the wire to cool. He smelt the thousand-and-one smells that are in anybody's room: the crisp freshness of the germburner, the sour-sweet tang of the humidifier, the odor of the dinner they had just eaten, the smells of clothes, furniture, of people themselves. All these were pure delight. H sang a phrase or two of his favorite song:

"Here's to the haberman. Up and Out!

"Up—oh!—and Out—oh!—Up and Out! . . ."

He heard Luci chuckle in the next room. He gloated over the sounds of her dress as she swished to the doorway.

She gave him her crooked little smile. "You sound all right. Are you all right, really?"

Even with this luxury of senses, he scanned. He took the flash-quick inventory which constituted his professional skill. His eyes swept in the news of the instruments. Nothing showed off scale, beyond the Nerve Compression hanging in the edge of "Danger." But he could not worry about the Nerve box. That always came through Cranching. You couldn't get under the wire without having it show on the Nerve box. Some day the box would go to *Overload* and drop back down to *Dead*. That was the way a haberman ended. But you couldn't have everything. People who went to the Up-and-Out had to pay the price for Space.

Anyhow, he should worry! He was a Scanner. A good one, and he knew it. If he couldn't scan himself, who could? This cranching wasn't too dangerous. Dangerous, but not too dangerous.

Luci put out her hand and ruffled his hair as if she had been reading his thoughts, instead of just following them: "But you know you shouldn't have! You shouldn't!"

"But I did!" He grinned at her.

Her gaiety still forced, she said: "Come on, darling, let's have a good time. I have almost everything there is in the icebox—all your favorite tastes. And I have two new records just full of smells. I tried them out myself, and even I liked them. And you know me—"

"Which?"

"Which what, you old darling?"

He slipped his hand over her shoulders as he limped out of the room. (He could never go back to feeling the floor beneath his feet, feeling the air against his face, without being bewildered and clumsy. As if cranching was real, and being a haberman was a bad dream. But he *was* a haberman, and a Scanner.) "You know what I meant, Luci . . . the smells, which you have. Which one did you like, on the record?"

"Well-l-l," said she, judiciously, "there were some lamb chops that were the strangest things—"

He interrupted: "What are lambtchots?"

"Wail till you smell them. Then guess. I'll tell you this much. It's a smell hundreds and hundreds of years old. They found about it in the old books."

"Is a lambtchot a Beast?"

"I won't tell you. You've got to wait," she laughed, as she helped him sit down and spread his tasting dishes before him. He wanted to go back over the dinner first, sampling all the pretty things he had eaten, and savoring them this time with his now-living lips and tongue.

When Luci had found the Music Wire and had thrown its sphere up into the force-field, he reminded her of the new smells. She took out the long glass records and set the first one into a transmitter.

"Now sniff!"

A queer frightening, exciting smell came over the room. It seemed like nothing in this world, nor like anything from the Up-and-Out. Yet it was familiar. His mouth watered. His pulse beat a little faster; he scanned his Heart box. (Faster, sure enough.) But that smell, what was it? In mock perplexity, he grabbed her hands, looked into her eyes, and growled:

"Tell me, darling! Tell me, or I'll eat you up!"

"That's just right!"

"What?"

"You're right. It should make you want to eat me. It's meat."

"Meat. Who?"

"Not a person," said she, knowledgeably, "a beast. A beast which people used to eat. A lamb was a small sheep —you've seen sheep out in the Wild, haven't you?—and a chop is part of its middle—here!" She pointed at her chest.

Martel did not hear her. All his boxes had sung over toward Alarm, some to Danger. He fought against the roar of his own mind, forcing his body into excess excitement. How easy it was to be a Scanner when you really stood outside your own body, haberman-fashion, and looked back into it with your eyes alone. Then you could manage the body, rule it coldly even in the enduring agony of Space. But to realize that you *were* a body, that this thing was ruling you, that the mind could kick the flesh and send it roaring off into panic! That was bad.

He tried to remember the days before he had gone into the Haberman Device, before he had been cut apart for the Up-and-Out. Had he always been subject to the rush of his emotions from his mind to his body, from his body back to his mind, confounding him so that he couldn't Scan? But he hadn't been a Scanner then.

He knew what had hit him. Amid the roar of his own pulse, he knew. In the nightmare of the Up-and-Out, that smell had forced its way through to him, while their ship burned off Venus and the habermans fought the collapsing metal with their bare hands. He had scanned then: all were in *Danger*. Chestboxes went up to *Overload* and dropped to *Dead* all around him as he had moved from man to man, shoving the drifting corpses out of his way as he fought to scan each man in turn, to clamp vises on unnoticed broken legs, to snap the Sleeping Valve on men whose instruments showed they were hopelessly near overload. With men trying to work and cursing him for a Scanner while he, professional zeal aroused, fought to do his job and keep alive in the Great Pain of Space, he had smelled that smell. It had fought its way along his rebuilt nerves, past the Haberman cuts, past all the safeguards of physical and mental discipline. In the wildest hour of tragedy, he had smelled aloud. He remembered it was like a bad cranching, connected with the fury and nightmare all around him. He had even stopped his work to scan himself, fearful that the First Effect might come, breaking past all Haberman cuts and ruining him with the Pain of Space. But he had come through. His own instruments stayed and stayed at *Danger,* without nearing *Overload.* He had done his job, and won a commendation for it. He had even forgotten the burning ship.

All except the smell.

And here the smell was all over again—the smell of meat-with-fire. . . .

Luci looked at him with wifely concern. She obviously thought he had cranched too much, and was about to haberman back. She tried to be cheerful: "You'd better rest, honey."

He whispered to her: "Cut—off—that—smell."

She did not question his word. She cut the transmitter. She even crossed the room and stepped up the room controls until a small breeze flitted across the floor and drove the smells up to the ceiling.

He rose, tired and stiff. (His instruments were normal, except that Heart was fast and Nerves still hanging on the edge of *Danger.*) He spoke sadly:

"Forgive me, Luci. I suppose I shouldn't have cranched. Not so soon again. But darling, I have to get out from being a haberman. How can I ever be near you? How can I be a man—not hearing my own voice, not even feeling my own life as it goes through my veins? I love you, darling. Can't I ever be near you?"

Her pride was disciplined and automatic: "But you're a Scanner!"

"I know I'm a Scanner. But so what?"

She went over the words, like a tale told a thousand times to reassure herself: "You are the bravest of the brave, the most skilful of the skilled. All Mankind owes most honor to the Scanner, who unites the Earths of Mankind. Scanners are the protectors of the habermans. They are the judges in the Up-and-Out. They make men live in the place where men need desperately to die. They are the most honored of Mankind, and even the Chiefs of the Instrumentality are delighted to pay them homage!"

With obstinate sorrow he demurred: "Luci, we've heard that all before. But does it pay us back—"

" 'Scanners work for more than pay. They are the strong guards of Mankind.' Don't you remember that?"

"But our lives, Luci. What can you get out of being a wife of a Scanner? Why did you marry me? I'm human only when I cranch. The rest of the time—you know what I am. A machine. A man turned into a machine. A man who has been killed and kept alive for duty. Don't you realize what I miss?"

"Of course, darling, of course—"

He went on: "Don't you think I remember my childhood? Don't you think I remember what it is to be a man and not a haberman? To walk and feel my feet on the ground? To feel a decent clean pain instead of watching my body every minute to see if I'm alive? How will I know if I'm dead? Did you ever think of that, Luci? How will I know if I'm dead?"

She ignored the unreasonableness of his outburst. Pacifyingly, she said: "Sit down, darling. Let me make you some kind of a drink. You're overwrought."

Automatically, he scanned: "No I'm not! Listen to me. How do you think it feels to be in the Up-and-Out with the crew tied-for-space all around you? How do you think it feels to watch them sleep? How do you think I like scanning, scanning, scanning month after month, when I can feel the Pain-of-Space beating against every part of my body, trying to get past my Haberman blocks? How do you think I like to wake the men when I have to, and have them hate me for it? Have you ever seen habermans fight—strong men fighting, and neither knowing pain, fighting until one touches *Overload*? Do you think about that, Luci?" Triumphantly he added: "Can you blame me if I cranch, and come back to being a man, just two days a month?"

"I'm not blaming you, darling. Let's enjoy your cranch. Sit down now, and have a drink."

He was sitting down, resting his face in his hands, while she fixed the drink, using natural fruits out of bottles in addition to the secure alkaloids. He watched her restlessly and pitied her for marrying a Scanner; and then, though it was unjust, resenting having to pity her.

Just as she turned to hand him the drink, they both jumped a little as the phone rang. It should not have rung. They had turned it off. It rang again, obviously on the emergency circuit. Stepping ahead of Luci, Martel strode over to the phone and looked into it. Vomact was looking at him.

The custom of Scanners entitled him to be brusque, even with a Senior Scanner, on certain given occasions. This was one.

Before Vomact could speak, Martel spoke two words into the plate, not caring whether the old man could read lips or not:

"Cranching. Busy."

He cut the switch and went back to Luci.

The phone rang again.

Luci said, gently, "I can find out what it is, darling. Here, take your drink and sit down."

"Leave it alone," said her husband. "No one has a right to call when I'm cranching. He knows that. He ought to know that."

The phone rang again. In a fury, Martel rose and went to the plate. He cut it back on. Vomact was on the screen. Before Martel could speak, Vomact held up his Talking Nail in line with his Heartbox. Martel reverted to discipline:

"Scanner Martel present and waiting, sir."

The lips moved solemnly: "Top emergency."

"Sir, I am under the wire."

"Top emergency."

"Sir, don't you understand?" Martel mouthed his words, so he could be sure that Vomact followed. "I . . . . am . . . . under . . . . the . . . . wire. Unfit . . for . . Space!'

Vomact repeated: "Top emergency. Report to your central tie-in."

"But, sir, no emergency like this—"

"Right, Martel. No emergency like this, ever before. Report to tie-in." With a faint glint of kindliness, Vomact added: "No need to de-cranch. Report as you are."

This time it was Martel whose phone was cut out. The screen went gray.

He turned to Luci. The temper had gone out of his voice. She came to him. She kissed him, and rumpled his hair. All she could say was,

"I'm sorry."

She kissed him again, knowing his disappointment. "Take good care of yourself, darling. I'll wait."

He scanned, and slipped into his transparent aircoat. At the window he paused, and waved. She called, "Good luck!" As the air flowed past him he said to himself,

"This is the first time I've felt flight in—eleven years. Lord, but it's easy to fly if you can feel yourself alive!"

Central Tie-in glowed white and austere far ahead. Martel peered. He saw no glare of incoming ships from the Up-and-Out, no shuddering flare of Space-fire out of control. Everything was quiet, as it should be on an off-duty night.

And yet Vomact had called. He had called an emergency higher than Space. There was no such thing. But Vomact had called it.

2

When Martel got there, he found about half the Scanners present, two dozen or so of them. He lifted the Talking finger. Most of the Scanners were standing face to face, talking in pairs as they read lips. A few of the old, impatient ones were scribbling on their Tablets and then thrusting the Tablets into other people's faces. All the faces wore the dull dead relaxed look of a haberman. When Martel entered the room, he knew that most of the others laughed in the deep isolated privacy of their own minds, each thinking things it would be useless to express in formal words. It had been a long time since a Scanner showed up at a meeting cranched.

Vomact was not there: probably, thought Martel, he was still on the phone calling others. The light of the phone flashed on and off; the bell rang. Martel felt odd when he realized that of all those present, he was the only one to hear that loud bell. It made him realize why ordinary people did not like to be around groups of habermans or Scanners. Martel looked around for company.

His friend Chang was there, busy explaining to some old and testy Scanner that he did not know why Vomact had called. Martel looked further and saw Parizianski. He walked over, threading his way past the others with a dexterity that showed he could feel his feet from the inside, and did not have to watch them. Several of the others stared at him with their dead faces, and tried to smile. But they lacked full muscular control and their faces twisted into horrid masks. (Scanners knew better than to show expression on faces which they could no longer govern. Martel added to himself, I swear *I'll* never smile again unless I'm cranched.)

Parizianski gave him the sign of the Talking Finger. Looking face to face, he spoke:

"You came here cranched?"

Parizianski could not hear his own voice, so the words roared like the words on a broken and screeching phone; Martel was startled, but knew that the inquiry was well meant. No one could be better-natured than the burly Pole.

"Vomact called. Top emergency."

"You told him you were cranched?"

"Yes."

"He still made you come?"

"Yes."

"Then all this—it is not for Space? You could not go Up-and-Out? You are like ordinary men?"

"That's right."

"Then why did he call us?" Some pre-haberman habit made Parizianski wave his arms in inquiry. The hand struck the back of the old man behind them. The slap could be heard throughout the room, but only Martel heard it. Instinctively, he scanned Parizianski and the old Scanner: they scanned him back, and then asked why. Only then did the old man ask why Martel had scanned him. When Martel explained that he was under-the-wire, the old man moved swiftly away to pass on the news that there was a cranched Scanner present at the Tie-in.

Even this minor sensation could not keep the attention of most of the Scanners from the worry about the Top Emergency. One young man, who had Scanned his first transit just the year before, dramatically interposed himself between Parizianski and Martel. He dramatically flashed his Tablet at them:

Is Vmct mad?

The older men shook their heads. Martel, remembering that it had not been too long that the young man had been haberman, mitigated the dead solemnity of the denial with a friendly smile. He spoke in a normal voice, saying:

"Vomact is the Senior of Scanners. I am sure that he could not go mad. Would he not see it on his boxes first?" Martel had to repeat the question, speaking slowly and mouthing his words before the young Scanner could understand the comment. The young man tried to make his face smile, and twisted it into a comic mask. But he took up his tablet and scribbled:

Yr rght.

Chang broke away from his friend and came over, his half-Chinese face gleaming in the warm evening. (It's strange, thought Martel, that more Chinese don't become Scanners. Or not so strange perhaps, if you think that they never fill their quota of habermans. Chinese love good living too much. The ones who do scan are all good ones.) Chang saw that Martel was cranched, and spoke with voice:

"You break precedents. Luci must be angry to lose you?"

"She took it well. Chang, that's strange."

"What?"

"I'm cranched, and I can hear. Your voice sounds all right. How did you learn to talk like—like an ordinary person?"

"I practised with soundtracks. Funny you noticed it. I think I am the only Scanner in or between the Earths who can pass for an Ordinary Man. Mirrors and soundtracks. I found out how to act."

"But you don't. . . ?"

"No. I don't feel, or taste, or hear, or smell things, any more than you do. Talking doesn't do me much good. But I notice that it cheers up the people around me."

"It would make a difference in the life of Luci."

Chang nodded sagely. "My father insisted on it. He said, 'You may be proud of being a Scanner. I am sorry you are not a Man. Conceal your defects.' So I tried. I wanted to tell the old boy about the Up and Out, and what we did there, but it did not matter. He said, 'Airplanes were good enough for Confucius, and they are for me too.' The old humbug! He tries so hard to be a Chinese when he can't even read Old Chinese. But he's got wonderful good sense, and for somebody going on two hundred he certainly gets around."

Martel smiled at the thought: "In his airplane?"

Chang smiled back. This discipline of his facial muscles was amazing; a bystander would not think that Chang was a haberman, controlling his eyes, cheeks, and lips by cold intellectual control. The expression had the spontaneity of life. Martel felt a flash of envy for Chang when he looked at the dead cold faces of Parizianski and the others. He knew that he himself looked fine: but why shouldn't he? he was cranched. Turning to Parizianski he said,

"Did you see what Chang said about his father? The old boy uses an airplane."

Parizianski made motions with his mouth, but the sounds meant nothing. He took up his tablet and showed it to Martel and Chang.

Bzz bzz. Ha ha. Gd ol' boy.

At that moment, Martel heard steps out in the corridor. He could not help looking toward the door. Other eyes followed the direction of his glance.

Vomact came in.

The group shuffled to attention in four parallel lines. They scanned one another. Numerous hands reached across to adjust the electrochemical controls on chestboxes which had begun to load up. One Scanner held out a broken finger which his counter-Scanner had discovered, and submitted it for treatment and splinting.

Vomact had taken out his Staff of Office. The cube at

the top flashed red light through the room, the lines re-
formed and all scanners gave the sign meaning

Present and ready!

Vomact countered with the stance signifying, *I am the
Senior and take Command.*

Talking fingers rose in the counter-gesture, *We concur
and commit ourselves.*

Vomact raised his right arm, dropped the wrist as
though it were broken, in a queer searching gesture, meaning: *Any men around? Any habermans not tied? All
clear for the Scanners?*

Alone of all those present, the cranched Martel heard
the queer rustle of feet as they all turned completely
around without leaving position, looking sharply at one
another and flashing their beltlights into the dark corners
of the great room. When again they faced Vomact, he
made a further sign:

All clear. Follow my words.

Martel noticed that he alone relaxed. The others could
not know the meaning of relaxation with the minds
blocked off up there in their skulls, connected only with
the eyes, and the rest of the body connected with the
mind only by controlling non-sensory nerves and the instrument boxes on their chests. Martel realized that,
cranched as he was, he expected to hear Vomact's voice:
the Senior had been talking for some time. No sound
escaped his lips. (Vomact never bothered with sound.)

". . . and when the first men to go Up and Out went
to the Moon, what did they find?"

"Nothing," responded the silent chorus of lips.

"Therefore they went further, to Mars and to Venus.
The ships went out year by year, but they did not come
back until the Year One of Space. Then did a ship come
back with the First Effect. Scanners, I ask you, what
is the First Effect?"

"No one knows. No one knows."

"No one will ever know. Too many are the variables.
By what do we know the First Effect?"

"By the Great Pain of Space," came the chorus.

"And by what further sign?"

"By the need, oh the need of death."

Vomact again: "And who stopped the need for death?"

"Henry Haberman conquered the first effect, in the Year 3 of Space."

"And, Scanners, I ask you, what did he do?"

"He made the habermans."

"How, O Scanners, are habermans made?"

"They are made with the cuts. The brain is cut from the heart, the lungs. The brain is cut from the ears, the nose. The brain is cut from the mouth, the belly. The brain is cut from desire, and pain. The brain is cut from the world. Save for the eyes. Save for the control of the living flesh."

"And how, O Scanners, is flesh controlled?"

"By the boxes set in the flesh, the controls set in the chest, the signs made to rule the living body, the signs by which the body lives."

"How does a haberman live and live?"

"The haberman lives by control of the boxes."

"Whence come the habermans?"

Martel felt in the coming response a great roar of broken voices echoing through the room as the Scanners, habermans themselves, put sound behind their mouthings:

"Habermans are the scum of Mankind. Habermans are the weak, the cruel, the credulous, and the unfit. Habermans are the sentenced-to-more-than-death. Habermans live in the mind alone. They are killed for Space but they live for Space. They master the ships that connect the Earths. They live in the Great Pain while ordinary men sleep in the cold cold sleep of the transit."

"Brothers and Scanners, I ask you now: are we habermans or are we not?"

"We are habermans in the flesh. We are cut apart, brain and flesh. We are ready to go to the Up and Out. All of us have gone through the Haberman Device."

"We are habermans then?" Vomact's eyes flashed and glittered as he asked the ritual question.

Again the chorused answer was accompanied by a roar of voices heard only by Martel: "Habermans we are, and more, and more. We are the Chosen who are habermans by our own free will. We are the Agents of the Instrumentality of Mankind."

"What must the others say to us?"

"They must say to us, 'You are the bravest of the brave,

the most skilful of the skilled. All mankind owes most honor to the Scanner, who unites the Earths of Mankind. Scanners are the protectors of the habermans. They are the judges in the Up-and-Out. They make men live in the place where men need desperately to die. They are the most honored of Mankind, and even the Chiefs of the Instrumentality are delighted to pay them homage!' "

Vomact stood more erect: "What is the secret duty of the Scanner?"

"To keep secret our law, and to destroy the acquirers thereof."

"How to destroy?"

"Twice to the *Overload,* back and *Dead.*"

"If habermans die, what the duty then?"

The Scanners all compressed their lips for answer. (Silence was the code.) Martel, who—long familiar with the code—was a little bored with the proceedings, noticed that Chang was breathing too heavily; he reached over and adjusted Changs Lung-control and received the thanks of Chang's eyes. Vomact observed the interruption and glared at them both. Martel relaxed, trying to imitate the dead cold stillness of the others. It was so hard to do, when you were cranched.

"If others die, what the duty then?" asked Vomact.

"Scanners together inform the Instrumentality. Scanners together accept the punishment. Scanners together settle the case."

"And if the punishment be severe?"

"Then no ships go."

"And if Scanners not be honored?"

"Then no ships go."

"And if a Scanner goes unpaid?"

"Then no ships go."

"And if the Others and the Instrumentality are not in all ways at all times mindful of their proper obligation to the Scanners?"

"Then no ships go."

"And what, O Scanners, if no ships go?"

"The Earths fall apart. The Wild comes back in. The Old Machines and the Beasts return."

"What is the unknown duty of a Scanner?"

"Not to sleep in the Up-and-Out."

"What is the second duty of a Scanner?"

"To keep forgotten the name of fear."

"What is the third duty of a Scanner?"

"To use the wire of Eustace Cranch only with care, only with moderation." Several pair of eyes looked quickly at Martel before the mouthed chorus went on. "To cranch only at home, only among friends, only for the purpose of remembering, of relaxing, or of begetting."

"What is the word of the Scanner?"

"Faithful though surrounded by death."

"What is the motto of the Scanner?"

"Awake though surrounded by silence."

"What is the word of the Scanner?"

"Labor even in the heights of the Up-and-Out, loyalty even in the depths of Earths."

"How do you know a Scanner?"

"We know ourselves. We are dead though we live. And we Talk with the Tablet and the Nail."

"What is this Code?"

"This Code is the friendly ancient wisdom of Scanners, briefly put that we may be mindful and be cheered by out loyalty to one another."

At this point the formula should have run: "We complete the Code. Is there work or word for the Scanners?" But Vomact said, and he repeated:

"Top emergency. Top emergency."

They gave him the sign, *Present and ready!*

He said, with every eye straining to follow his lips:

"Some of you know the work of Adam Stone?"

Martel saw lips move, saying: "The Red Asteroid. The Other who lives at the edge of Space."

"Adam Stone has gone to the Instrumentality, claiming success for his work. He says that he has found how to Screen Out the Pain of Space. He says that the Up-and-Out can be made safe for ordinary men to work in, to stay awake in. He says that there need be no more Scanners."

Beltlights flashed on all over the room as Scanners sought the right to speak. Vomact nodded to one of the older men. "Scanner Smith will speak."

Smith stepped slowly up into the light, watching his own feet. He turned so that they could see his face. He spoke:

"I say that this is a lie. I say that Stone is a liar. I say that the Instrumentality must not be deceived."

He paused. Then, in answer to some question from the audience which most of the others did not see, he said:

"I invoke the secret duty of the Scanners."

Smith raised his right hand for Emergency Attention:

"I say that Stone must die."

3

Martel, still cranched, shuddered as he heard the boos, groans, shouts, squeaks, grunts and moans which came from the Scanners who forgot noise in their excitement and strove to make their dead bodies talk to one another's deaf ears. Beltlights flashed wildly all over the room. There was a rush for the rostrum and Scanners milled around at the top, vying for attention until Parizianski—by sheer bulk—shoved the others aside and down, and turned to mouth at the group.

"Brother Scanners, I want your eyes."

The people on the floor kept moving, with their numb bodies jostling one another. Finally Vomact stepped up in front of Parizianski, faced the others, and said:

"Scanners, be Scanners! Give him your eyes."

Parizianski was not good at public speaking. His lips moved too fast. He waved his hands, which took the eyes of the others away from his lips. Nevertheless, Martel was able to follow most of the message:

". . . can't do this. Stone may have succeeded. If he has succeeded, it means the end of Scanners. It means the end of the habermans, too. None of us will have to fight in the Up-and-Out. We won't have anybody else going under-the-Wire for a few hours or days of being human. Everybody will be Other. Nobody will have to Cranch, never again. Men can be men. The habermans can be killed decently and properly, the way men were killed in the Old Days, without anybody keeping them alive. They won't have to work in the Up-and-Out! There will be no more Great Pain—think of it! No . . . more . . . Great . . . Pain! How do we know that Stone is a liar—"

Lights began flashing directly into his eyes. (The rudest insult of Scanner to Scanner was this.)

Vomact again exercised authority. He stepped in front of Parizianski and said something which the others could not see. Parizianski stepped down from the rostrum. Vomact again spoke:

"I think some of the Scanners disagree with our Brother Parizianski. I say the use of the rostrum be suspended till we have had a chance for private discussion. In fifteen minutes I will call the meeting back to order."

Martel looked around for Vomact when the Senior had rejoined the group on the floor. Finding the Senior, Martel wrote swift script on his Tablet, waiting for a chance to thrust the Tablet before the Senior's eyes. He had written,

Am crnchd. Respctfly requst prmissn lv now, stnd by fr orders.

Being cranched did strange things to Martel. Most meetings that he attended seemed formal heartening ceremonial, lighting up the dark inward eternities of habermanhood. When he was not cranched, he noticed his body no more than a marble bust notices its marble pedestal. He had stood with them before. He had stood with them effortless hours, while the long-winded ritual broke through the terrible loneliness behind his eyes, and made him feel that the Scanners, though a confraternity of the damned, were none the less forever honored by the professional requirements of their mutilation.

This time, it was different. Coming cranched, and in full possession of smell-sound-taste-feeling, he reacted more or less as a normal man would. He saw his friends and colleagues as a lot of cruelly driven ghosts, posturing out the meaningless ritual of their indefeasible damnation. What difference did anything make, once you were a haberman? Why all this talk about habermans and Scanners? Habermans were criminals or heretics, and Scanners were gentlemen-volunteers, but they were all in the same fix—except that Scanners were deemed worthy of the short-time return of the Cranching Wire, while habermans were simply disconnected while the ships lay in port and were left suspended until they should be awakened, in some hour of emergency or trouble, to work out another spell of their damnation. It was a rare haberman that you saw on the street—someone of special merit or bravery, allowed to look at mankind from the terrible prison of his own mechanified body. And yet, what Scanner ever honored a haberman except perfunctorily in the line of duty? What had the Scanners as a guild and a class, ever done for the habermans, except to murder them with a twist of the wrist whenever a haberman, too long beside a Scanner, picked up the tricks of the Scanning trade and learned how to live at his own will, not the will the Scanners imposed? What could the Others, the ordinary men, know of what went on inside the ships? The Others slept in their cylinders, mercifully unconscious until they woke up on whatever other Earth they had consigned themselves to. What could the Others know of the men who had to stay alive within the ship?

What could any Other know of the Up-and-Out? What Other could look at the biting acid beauty of the stars in open space? What could they tell of the Great Pain, which started quietly in the marrow, like an ache, and proceeded by the fatigue and nausea of each separate nerve cell, brain cell, touchpoint in the body, until life itself became a terrible aching hunger for silence and for death?

He was a Scanner. All right, he *was* a Scanner. He had been a Scanner from the moment when, wholly normal, he had stood in the sunlight before a Subchief of Instrumentality, and had sworn:

"I pledge my honor and my life to Mankind. I sacrifice myself willingly for the welfare of Mankind. In accepting the perilous austere Honor, I yield all my rights without exception to the Honorable Chiefs of the Instrumentality and to the Honored Confraternity of Scanners."

He had pledged.

He had gone into the Haberman Device.

He remembered his Hell. He had not had such a bad one, even though it seemed to last a hundred million years, all of them without sleep. He had learned to feel with his eyes. He had learned to see despite the heavy eyeplates set back of his eyeballs, to insulate his eyes from the rest of him. He had learned to watch his skin. He still remembered the time he had noticed dampness on his shirt, and had pulled out his Scanning Mirror only to discover that he had worn a hole in his side by leaning against a vibrating machine. (A thing like that could not happen to him now; he was too adept at reading his own instruments.) He remembered the way that he had gone Up-and-Out, and the way that the Great Pain beat into him, despite the fact that his touch, smell, feeling, and hearing were gone for all ordinary purposes. He remembered killing habermans, and keeping others alive, and standing for months beside the Honorable Scanner-Pilot while neither of them slept. He remembered going ashore on Earth Four, and remembered that he had not enjoyed it, and had realized on that day that there was no reward.

Martel stood among the other Scanners. He hated their awkwardness when they moved, their immobility when they stood still. He hated the queer assortment of smells which their bodies yielded unnoticed. He hated the grunts and groans and squawks which they emitted from their deafness. He hated them, and himself.

How could Luci stand him? He had kept his chest-box reading *Danger* for weeks while he courted her, carrying the Cranch Wire about with him most illegally, and going direct from one cranch to the other without worrying about the fact his indicators all crept up to the edge of *Overload*. He had wooed her without thinking of what would happen if she did say, "Yes." She had.

"And they lived happily ever after." In Old Books they did, but how could they, in life? He had had eighteen days under-the-wire in the whole of the past year! Yet she had loved him. She still loved him. He knew it. She fretted about him through the long months that he was in the Up-and-Out. She tried to make home mean something to him even when he was haberman, make food pretty when it could not be tasted, make herself lovable when she could not be kissed—or might as well not, since a haberman body meant no more than furniture. Luci was patient.

And now, Adam Stone! (He let his Tablet fade: how could he leave, now?)

God bless Adam Stone?

Martel could not help feeling a little sorry for himself. No longer would the high keen call of duty carry him through two hundred or so years of the Other's time, two million private eternities of his own. He could slouch and relax. He could forget High Space, and let the Up-and-Out be tended by Others. He could cranch as much as he dared. He could be almost normal—almost—for one year or five years or no years. But at least he could stay with Luci. He could go with her into the Wild, where there were Beasts and Old Machines still roving the dark places. Perhaps he would die in the excitement of the hunt, throwing spears at an ancient Manshonjagger as it leapt from its lair, or tossing hot spheres at the tribesmen of the Unforgiven who still roamed the Wild. There was still life to live, still a good normal death to die, not the moving of a needle out in silence and Pain of Space!

He had been walking about restlessly. His ears were attuned to the sounds of normal speech, so that he did not feel like watching the mouthings of his brethren. Now they seemed to have come to a decision. Vomact was moving to the rostrum. Martel looked about for Chang, and went to stand beside him. Chang whispered:

"You're as restless as water in mid-air! What's the matter? De-cranching?"

They both scanned Martel, but the instruments held steady and showed no sign of the cranch giving out.

The great light flared in its call to attention. Again they formed ranks. Vomact thrust his lean old face into the glare, and spoke:

"Scanners and Brothers, I call for a vote." He held himself in the stance which meant: *I am the Senior and take Command.*

A beltlight flashed in protest.

It was old Henderson. He moved to the rostrum, spoke to Vomact, and—with Vomact's nod of approval—turned full-face to repeat his question:

"Who speaks for the Scanners Out in Space?"

No beltlight or hand answered.

Henderson and Vomact, face to face, conferred for a few moments. Then Henderson faced them again:

"I yield to the Senior in Command. But I do not yield to a Meeting of the Confraternity. There are sixty-eight Scanners, and only forty-seven present, of whom one is cranched and U. D. I have therefore proposed that the Senior in Command assume authority only over an Emergency Committee of the Confraternity, not over a Meeting. Is that agreed and understood by the Honorable Scanners?"

Hands rose in assent.

Chang murmured in Martel's ear, "Lot of difference that makes! Who can tell the difference between a meeting and a committee?" Martel agreed with the words, but was even more impressed with the way that Chang, while haberman, could control his own voice.

Vomact resumed chairmanship: "We now vote on the question of Adam Stone.

"First, we can assume that he has not succeeded, and that his claims are lies. We know that from our practical experience as Scanners. The Pain of Space is only part of Scanning" (*But the essential part, the basis of it all,* thought Martel.) "and we can rest assured that Stone cannot solve the problem of Space Discipline."

"That tripe again," whispered Chang, unheard save by Martel.

"The Space Discipline of our Confraternity has kept High Space clean of war and dispute. Sixty-eight disciplined men control all High Space. We are removed by our oath and our haberman status from all Earthly passions.

"Therefore, if Adam Stone has conquered the Pain of Space, so that Others can wreck our Confraternity and bring to Space the trouble and ruin which afflicts Earths, I say that Adam Stone is wrong. If Adam Stone succeeds, Scanners live in Vain!

"Secondly, if Adam Stone has not conquered the Pain of Space, he will cause great trouble in all the Earths. The Instrumentality and the Subchiefs may not give us as many habermans as we need to operate the ships of Mankind. There will be wild stories, and fewer recruits and, worst of all, the Discipline of the Confraternity may relax if this kind of nonsensical heresy is spread around.

"Therefore, if Adam Stone has succeeded, he threatens the ruin of the Confraternity and should die.

"I move the death of Adam Stone."

And Vomact made the sign, *The Honorable Scanners are pleased to vote.*

4

Martel grabbed wildly for his beltlight. Chang, guess-
ing ahead, had his light out and ready; its bright beam,
voting *No,* shone straight up at the ceiling. Martel got his
light out and threw its beam upward in dissent. Then he
looked around. Out of the forty-seven present, he could see
only five or six glittering.

Two more lights went on. Vomact stood as erect as a
frozen corpse. Vomact's eyes flashed as he stared back and
forth over the group, looking for lights. Several more
went on. Finally Vomact took the closing stance:

May it please the Scanners to count the vote.

Three of the older men went up on the rostrum with
Vomact. They looked over the room. (Martel thought:
*These damned ghosts are voting on the life of a real man,
a live man! They have no right to do it. I'll tell the Instru-
mentality!* But he knew that he would not. He thought of
Luci and what she might gain by the triumph of Adam
Stone: the hearbreaking folly of the vote was then almost
too much for Martel to bear.)

All three of the tellers held up their hands in unani-
mous agreement on the sign of the number: *Fifteen
against.*

Vomact dismissed them with a bow of courtesy. He
turned and again took the stance, *I am the Senior and
take Command.*

Marveling at his own daring, Martel flashed his beltlight
on. He knew that anyone of the bystanders might reach
over and twist his Heartbox to *Overload* for such an act.
He felt Chang's hand reaching to catch him by the aircoat.
But he eluded Chang's grasp and ran, faster than a Scanner should, to the platform. As he ran, he wondered what
appeal to make. It was no use talking commonsense. Not
now. It had to be law.

He jumped up on the rostrum beside Vomact, and took
the stance: *Scanners, an Illegality!*

He violated good custom while speaking, still in the
stance: "A Committee has no right to vote death by a
majority vote. It takes two-thirds of a full Meeting."

He felt Vomact's body lunge behind him, felt himself
falling from the rostrum, hitting the floor, hurting his

knees and his touch-aware hands. He was helped to his feet. He was scanned. Some Scanner he scarcely knew took his instruments and toned him down.

Immediately Martel felt more calm, more detached, and hated himself for feeling so.

He looked up at the rostrum. Vomact maintained the stance signifying: *Order!*

The Scanners adjusted their ranks. The two Scanners next to Martel took his arms. He shouted at them, but they looked away, and cut themselves off from communication altogether.

Vomact spoke again when he saw the room was quiet: "A Scanner came here cranched, Honorable Scanners, I apologize for this. It is not the fault of our great and worthy Scanner and friend, Martel. He came here under orders. I told him not to de-cranch. I hoped to spare him an unnecessary haberman. We all know how happily Martel is married, and we wish his brave experiment well. I like Martel. I respect his judgment. I wanted him here. I knew you wanted him here. But he is cranched. He is in no mood to share in the lofty business of the Scanners. I therefore propose a solution which will meet all the requirements of fairness. I propose that we rule Scanner Martel out of order for his violation of rules. This violation would be inexcusable if Martel were not cranched.

"But at the same time, in all fairness to Martel, I further propose that we deal with the points raised so improperly by our worthy but disqualified brother."

Vomact gave the sign, *The Honorable Scanners are pleased to vote.* Martel tried to reach his own beltlight; the dead strong hands held him tightly and he struggled in vain. One lone light shone high: Chang's, no doubt.

Vomact thrust his face into the light again: "Having the approval of our worthy Scanners and present company for the general proposal, I now move that this Committee declare itself to have the full authority of a Meeting, and that this Committee further make me responsible for all misdeeds which this Committee may enact, to be held answerable before the next full Meeting, but not before any other authority beyond the closed and secret ranks of Scanners."

Flamboyantly this time, his triumph, evident, Vomact assumed the *vote* stance.

Only a few lights shone: far less, patently, than a minority of one-fourth.

Vomact spoke again. The light shone on his high calm forehead, on his dead relaxed cheekbones. His lean cheeks and chin were half-shadowed, save where the lower light picked up and spotlighted his mouth, cruel even in repose. (Vomact was said to be a descendant of some Ancient Lady who had traversed, in an illegitimate and inexplicable fashion, some hundreds of years of time in a single night. Her name, the Lady Vomact, had passed into legend; but her blood and her archaic lust for mastery lived on in the mute masterful body of her descendant. Martel could believe the old tales as he stared at the rostrum, wondering what untraceable mutation had left the Vomact kith as predators among mankind.) Calling loudly with the movement of his lips, but still without sound, Vomact appealed:

"The Honorable Committee is now pleased to reaffirm the sentence of death issued against the heretic and enemy, Adam Stone." Again the *vote* stance.

Again Chang's light shone lonely in its isolated protest.

Vomact then made his final move:

"I call for the designation of the Senior Scanner present as the manager of the sentence. I call for authorization to him to appoint executioners, one or many, who shall make evident the will and majesty of Scanners. I ask that I be accountable for the deed, and not for the means. The deed is a noble deed, for the protection of Mankind and for the honor of the Scanners; but of the means it must be said that they are to be the best at hand, and no more. Who knows the true way to kill an Other, here on a crowded and watchful Earth? This is no mere matter of discharging a cylindered sleeper, no mere question of upgrading the needle of a haberman. When people die down here, it is not like the Up-and-Out. They die reluctantly. Killing within the Earth is not our usual business, O brothers and Scanners, as you know well. You must choose me to choose my agent as I see fit. Otherwise the common knowledge will become the common betrayal whereas if I alone know the responsibility, I alone could betray us, and you will not have far to look in case the Instrumentality comes searching." *(What about the killer you choose? thought Martel. He too will know unless you silence him forever.)*

Vomact went into the stance, *The Honorable Scanners are pleased to vote.*

One light of protest shone; Chang's, again.

Martel imagined that he could see a cruel joyful smile on Vomact's dead face—the smile of a man who knew himself righteous and who found his righteousness upheld and affirmed by militant authority.

Martel tried one last time to come free.

The dead hands held. They were locked like vises until their owners' eyes unlocked them: how else could they hold the piloting month by month?

Martel then shouted: "Honorable Scanners, this is judicial murder."

No ear heard him. He was cranched, and alone.

None the less, he shouted again: "You endanger the Confraternity."

Nothing happened.

The echo of his voice sounded from one end of the room to the other. No head turned. No eyes met his.

Martel realized that as they paired for talk, the eyes of Scanners averted him. He saw that no one desired to watch his speech. He knew that behind the cold faces of his friends there lay compassion or amusement. He knew that they knew him to be cranched—absurd, normal, man-like, temporarily no Scanner. But he knew that in this matter the wisdom of Scanners was nothing. He knew that only a cranched Scanner could feel with his very blood the outrage and anger which deliberate murder would provoke among the Others. He knew that the Confraternity endangered itself, and knew that the most ancient prerogative of law was the monopoly of death. Even the Ancient Nations, in the times of the Wars, before the Beasts, before men went into the Up-and-Out—even the Ancients had known this. How did they say it? *Only the State shall kill.* The States were gone but the Instrumentality remained, and the Instrumentality could not pardon things which occurred within the Earths but beyond its authority. Death in Space was the business, the

right of the Scanners: how could the Instrumentality enforce its laws in a place where all men who wakened,
wakened only to die in the Great Pain? Wisely did the
Instrumentality leave Space to the Scanners, wisely had
the Confraternity not meddled inside the Earths. And now
the Confraternity itself was going to step forth as an outlaw band, as a gang of rogues as stupid and reckless as
the tribes of the Unforgiven!

Martel knew this because he was cranched. Had he been
haberman, he would have thought only with his mind, not
with his heart and guts and blood. How could the other
Scanners know?

Vomact returned for the last time to the Rostrum: *The
Committee has met and its will shall be done*. Verbally
he added: "Senior among you, I ask your loyalty and
silence."

At that point, the two Scanners let his arms go. Martel
rubbed his numb hands, shaking his fingers to get the
circulation back into the cold fingertips. With real freedom, he began to think of what he might still do. He
scanned himself: the cranching held. He might have a
day. Well, he could go on even if haberman, but it would
be inconvenient, having to talk with Finger and Tablet.
He looked about for Chang. He saw his friend standing
patient and immobile in a quiet corner. Martel moved
slowly, so as not to attract any more attention to himself
than could be helped. He faced Chang, moved until his
face was in the light, and then articulated:

"What are we going to do? You're not going to let them
kill Adam Stone, are you? Don't you realize what Stone's
work will mean to us, if it succeeds? No more Scanners.
No more habermans. No more Pain in the Up-and-Out. I
tell you, if the others were all cranched, as I am, they
would see it in a human way, not with the narrow crazy
logic which they used in the meeting. We've got to stop
them. How can we do it? What are we going to do? What
does Parizianski think? Who has been chosen?"

"Which question do you want me to answer?"

Martel laughed. (It felt good to laugh, even then; it
felt like being a man.) "Will you help me?"

Chang's eyes flashed across Martel's face as Chang
answered: "No. No. No."

"You won't help?"

"No."

"Why not, Chang? Why not?"

"I am a Scanner. The vote has been taken. You would do the same if you were not in this unusual condition."

"I'm not in an unusual condition. I'm cranched. That merely means that I see things the way that Others would. I see the stupidity. The recklessness. The selfishness. It is murder."

"What is murder? Have you not killed? You are not one of the Others. You are a Scanner. You will be sorry for what you are about to do, if you do not watch out."

"But why did you vote against Vomact then? Didn't you too see what Adam Stone means to all of us? Scanners will live in vain. Thank God for that! Can't you see it?"

"No."

"But you talk to me, Chang. You are my friend?"

"I talk to you. I am your friend. Why not?"

"But what are you going to do?"

"Nothing, Martel. Nothing."

"Will you help me?"

"No."

"Not even to save Stone?"

"No."

"Then I will go to Parizianski for help."

"It will do you no good."

"Why not? He's more human than you, right now."

"He will not help you, because he has the job. Vomact designated him to kill Adam Stone."

Martel stopped speaking in mid-movement. He suddenly took the stance, *I thank you, brother, and I depart.*

At the window he turned and faced the room. He saw that Vomact's eyes were upon him. He gave the stance, *I thank you, brother, and I depart,* and added the flourish of respect which is shown when Seniors are present. Vomact caught the sign, and Martel could see the cruel lips move. He thought he saw the words ". . . take good care of yourself. . . ." but did not wait to inquire. He stepped backward and dropped out the window.

Once below the window and out of sight, he adjusted his aircoat to maximum speed. He swam lazily in the air, scanning himself thoroughly, and adjusting his adrenal intake down. He then made the movement of release, and felt the cold air rush past his face like running water.

Adam Stone had to be at Chief Downport.

Adam Stone had to be there.

Wouldn't Adam Stone be surprised in the night? Surprised to meet the strangest of beings, the first renegade among Scanners. (Martel suddenly appreciated that it was of himself he was thinking. Martel the Traitor to Scanners! That sounded strange and bad. But what of Martel, the Loyal to Mankind? Was that not compensation? And if he won, he won Luci. If he lost, he lost nothing—an unconsidered and expendable haberman. It happened to be himself. But in contrast to the immense reward, to Mankind, to the Confraternity, to Luci, what did that matter?)

Martel thought to himself: "Adam Stone will have two visitors tonight. Two Scanners, who are the friends of one another." He hoped that Parizianski was still his friend.

"And the world," he added, "depends on which of us gets there first."

Multifaceted in their brightness, the lights of Chief Downport began to shine through the mist ahead. Martel could see the outer towers of the city and glimpsed the phosphorescent Periphery which kept back the Wild, whether Beasts, Machines, or the Unforgiven.

Once more Martel invoked the lords of his chance: "Help me to pass for an Other!"

5

Within the Downport, Martel had less trouble than he thought. He draped his aircoat over his shoulder so that it concealed the instruments. He took up his scanning mirror, and made up his face from the inside, by adding tone and animation to his blood and nerves until the muscles of his face glowed and the skin gave out a healthy sweat. That way he looked like an ordinary man who had just completed a long night flight.

After straightening out his clothing, and hiding his Tablet within his jacket, he faced the problem of what to do about the Talking Finger. If he kept the Nail, it would show him to be a Scanner. He would be respected, but he would be identified. He might be stopped by the guards whom the Instrumentality had undoubtedly set around the person of Adam Stone. If he broke the Nail— But he couldn't! No Scanner in the history of the Confraternity had ever willingly broken his Nail. That would be Resignation, and there was no such thing. The only way *out*, was in the Up-and-Out! Martel put his finger to his mouth and bit off the Nail. He looked at the now-queer finger, and sighed to himself.

He stepped toward the city gate, slipping his hand into his jacket and running up his muscular strength to four times normal. He started to scan, and then realized that his instruments were masked. *Might as well take all the chances at once*, he thought.

The watcher stopped him with a searching Wire. The sphere thumped suddenly against Martel's chest.

"Are you a Man?" said the unseen voice. (Martel would have known that as a Scanner in haberman condition, his own field-charge would have illuminated the sphere.)

"I am a Man." Martel knew that the timber of his voice had been good; he hoped that it would not be taken for that of a Manshonjagger or a Beast or an Unforgiven one, who with mimicry sought to enter the cities and ports of Mankind.

"Name, number, rank, purpose, function, time departed."

"Martel." He had to remember his old number, not Scanner 34. "Sunward 4234, 182nd Year of Space. Rank, rising Subchief." That was no lie, but his substantive rank. "Purpose, personal and lawful within the limits of this city. No function of the Instrumentality. Departed Chief Outport 2019 hours." Everything now depended on whether he was believed, or would be checked against Chief Outport.

The voice was flat and routine: "Time desired within the city."

Martel used the standard phrase: "Your Honorable sufferance is requested."

He stood in the cool night air, waiting. Far above him, through a gap in the mist, he could see the poisonous glittering in the sky of Scanners. *The stars are my enemies*, he thought: *I have mastered the stars but they hate me. Ho, that sounds Ancient! Like a Book. Too much cranching.*

The voice returned: "Sunward 4234 dash 182 rising Subchief Martel, enter the lawful gates of the city. Welcome. Do you desire food, raiment, money, or companionship?" The voice had no hospitality in it, just business. This was certainly different from entering a city in a Scanner's role! Then the petty officers came out, and threw their beltlights in their fretful faces, and mouthed their words with preposterous deference, shouting against the stone deafness of a Scanner's ears. So that was the way that a Subchief was treated: matter of fact, but not bad. Not bad.

Martel replied: "I have that which I need, but beg of the city a favor. My friend Adam Stone is here. I desired to see him, on urgent and personal lawful affairs."

The voice replied: "Did you have an appointment with Adam Stone?"

"No."

"The city will find him. What is his number?"

"I have forgotten it."

"You have forgotten it? Is not Adam Stone a Magnate of the Instrumentality? Are you truly his friend?"

"Truly." Martel let a little annoyance creep into his voice. "Watcher, doubt me and call your Subchief."

"No doubt implied. Why do you not know the number? This must go into the record," added the voice.

"We were friends in childhood. He has crossed the—" Martel started to say "the Up-and-Out" and remembered that the phrase was current only among Scanners. "He has leapt from Earth to Earth, and has just now returned. I knew him well and I seek him out. I have word of his kith. May the Instrumentality protect us!"

"Heard and believed. Adam Stone will be searched."

At a risk, though a slight one, of having the sphere sound an alarm for *non-human,* Martel cut in on his Scanner speaker within his jacket. He saw the trembling needle of light await his words and he started to write on it with his blunt finger. *That won't work,* he thought, and had a moment's panic until he found his comb, which had a sharp enough tooth to write. He wrote: "Emergency none. Martel Scanner calling Parizianski Scanner."

The needle quivered and the reply glowed and faded

out: "Parizianski Scanner on duty and D. C. Calls taken by Scanner Relay."

Martel cut off his speaker.

Parizianski was somewhere around. Could he have crossed the direct way, right over the city wall, setting off the alert, and invoking official business when the petty officers overtook him in mid-air? Scarcely. That meant that a number of other Scanners must have come in with Parizianski, all of them pretending to be in search of a few of the tenuous pleasures which could be enjoyed by a haberman, such as the sight of the newspictures or the viewing of beautiful women in the Pleasure Gallery. Parizianski was around, but he could not have moved privately, because Scanner Central registered him on duty and recorded his movements city by city.

The voice returned. Puzzlement was expressed in it. "Adam Stone is found and awakened. He has asked pardon of the Honorable, and says he knows no Martel. Will you see Adam Stone in the morning? The city will bid you welcome."

Martel ran out of resources. It was hard enough mimicking a man without having to tell lies in the guise of one. Martel could only repeat: "Tell him I am Martel. The husband of Luci."

"It will be done."

Again the silence, and the hostile stars, and the sense that Parizianski was somewhere near and getting nearer; Martel felt his heart beating faster. He stole a glimpse at his chestbox and set his heart down a point. He felt calmer, even though he had not been able to scan with care.

The voice this time was cheerful, as though an annoyance had settled: "Adam Stone consents to see you. Enter Chief Downport, and welcome."

The little sphere dropped noiselessly to the ground and the wire whispered away into the darkness. A bright arc of narrow light rose from the ground in front of Martel and swept through the city to one of the higher towers— apparently a hostel, which Martel had never entered. Martel plucked his aircoat to his chest for ballast, stepped heel-and-toe on the beam, and felt himself whistle through the air to an entrance window which sprang up before him as suddenly as a devouring mouth.

A tower guard stood in the doorway. "You are awaited, sir. Do you bear weapons, sir?"

"None," said Martel, grateful that he was relying on his own strength.

The guard led him past the check-screen. Martel noticed the quick flight of a warning across the screen as his instruments registered and identified him as a Scanner. But the guard had not noticed it.

The guard stopped at a door. "Adam Stone is armed. He is lawfully armed by authority of the Instrumentality and by the liberty of this city. All those who enter are given warning."

Martel nodded in understanding at the man and went in.

Adam Stone was a short man, stout and benign. His grey hair rose stiffly from a low forehead. His whole face was red and merry looking. He looked like a jolly guide from the Pleasure Gallery, not like a man who had been at the edge of the Up-and-Out, fighting the Great Pain without haberman protection.

He stared at Martel. His look was puzzled, perhaps a little annoyed, but not hostile.

Martel came to the point. "You do not know me. I lied. My name is Martel, and I mean you no harm. But I lied. I beg the Honorable gift of your hospitality. Remain armed. Direct your weapon against me——"

Stone smiled: "I am doing so," and Martel noticed the small Wirepoint in Stone's capable plump hand.

"Good. Keep on guard against me. It will give you confidence in what I shall say. But do, I beg you, give us a screen of privacy. I want no casual lookers. This is a matter of life and death."

"First: whose life and death?" Stone's face remained calm, his voice even.

"Yours, and mine, and the worlds'."

"You are cryptic but I agree." Stone called through the doorway: "Privacy please." There was a sudden hum and all the little noises of the night quickly vanished from the air of the room.

Said Adam Stone: "Sir, who are you? What brings you here?"

"I am Scanner Thirty-four."

"You a Scanner. I don't believe it."

For answer, Martel pulled his jacket open, showing his chestbox. Stone looked up at him, amazed. Martel explained:

"I am cranched. Have you never seen it before?"

"Not with men. On animals. Amazing! But—what do you want?"

"The truth. Do you fear me?"

"Not with this," said Stone, grasping the Wirepoint. "But I shall tell you the truth."

"Is it true that you have conquered the Great Pain?"

Stone hesitated, seeking words for an answer.

"Quick, can you tell me how you have done it, so that I may believe you?"

"I have loaded the ships with life."

"Life."

"Life. I don't know what the Great Pain is, but I did find that in the experiments, when I sent out masses of animals or plants, the life in the center of the mass lived the longest. I built ships—small ones, of course—and sent them out with rabbits, with monkeys—"

"Those are Beasts?"

"Yes. With small Beasts. And the Beasts came back unhurt. They came back because the walls of the ships were filled with life. I tried many kinds, and finally found a sort of life which lives in the waters. Oysters. Oysterbeds. The outermost oyster died in the Great Pain. The inner ones lived. The passengers were unhurt."

"But they were Beasts?"

"Not only Beasts. Myself."

"You!"

"I came through Space alone. Through what you call the Up-and-Out, alone. Awake and sleeping. I am unhurt. If you do not believe me, ask your brother Scanners. Come and see my ship in the morning. I will be glad to see you then, along with your brother Scanners. I am going to demonstrate before the Chiefs of the Instrumentality."

Martel repeated his question: "You came here alone?"

Adam Stone grew testy: "Yes, alone. Go back and check your Scanner's register if you do not believe me. You never put me in a bottle to cross space."

Martel's face was radiant. "I belive you now. It is

true. No more Scanners. No more habermans. No more cranching."

Stone looked significantly toward the door.

Martel did not take the hint. "I must tell you that—"

"Sir, tell me in the morning. Go enjoy your cranch. Isn't it supposed to be pleasure? Medically I know it well. But not in practice."

"It is pleasure. It's normality—for a while. But listen. The Scanners have sworn to destroy you, and your work."

"What!"

"They have met and have voted and sworn. You will make Scanners unnecessary, they say. You will bring the Ancient Wars back to the world, if Scanning is lost and the Scanners live in vain!"

Adam Stone was nervous but kept his wits about him: "You're a Scanner. Are you going to kill me—or try?"

"No, you fool. I have betrayed the Confraternity. Call guards the moment I escape. Keep guards around you. I will try to intercept the killer."

Martel saw a blur in the window. Before Stone could turn, the Wirepoint was whipped out of his hand. The blur solidified and took form as Parizianski.

Martel recognized what Parizianski was doing: *High speed.*

Without thinking of his cranch, he thrust his hand to his chest, set himself up to *High speed* too. Waves of fire, like the Great Pain, but hotter, flooded over him. He fought to keep his face readable as he stepped in front of Parizianski and gave the sign,

Top Emergency.

Parizianski spoke, while the normally-moving body of Stone stepped away from them as slowly as a drifting cloud: "Get out of my way, I am on a mission."

"I know it. I stop you here and now. Stop. Stop. Stop. Stone is right."

Parizianski's lips were barely readable in the haze of pain which flooded Martel. (He thought: *God, God, God of the Ancients! Let me hold on! Let me live under Overload just long enough!*) Parizianski was saying: "Get out of my way. By order of the Confraternity, get out of my way!" And Parizianski gave the sign, *Help I demand in the name of my duty!*

Martel choked for breath in the syrup-like air. He tried one last time: "Parizianski, friend, friend, my friend. Stop. Stop." (No Scanner ever murdered Scanner before.)

Parizianski made the sign: *You are unfit for duty, and I will take over.*

Martel thought, "For first time in the world!" as he reached over and twisted Parizianski's Brainbox up to *Overload.* Parizianski's eyes glittered in terror and understanding. His body began to drift down toward the floor.

Martel had just strength enough to reach his own *Chestbox.* As he faded into haberman or death, he knew not which, he felt his fingers turning on the control of speed, turning down. He tried to speak, to say, "Get a Scanner, I need help, get a Scanner. . . ."

But the darkness rose about him, and the numb silence clasped him.

Martel awakened to see the face of Luci near his own.

He opened his eyes wider, and found that he was hearing—hearing the sound of her happy weeping, the sound of her chest as she caught the air back into her throat.

He spoke weakly: "Still cranched? Alive?"

Another face swam into the blur beside Luci's. It was Adam Stone. His deep voice rang across immensities of space before coming to Martel's hearing. Martel tried to read Stone's lips, but could not make them out. He went back to listening to the voice:

". . . not cranched. Do you understand me? Not cranched!"

Martel tried to say: "But I can hear! I can feel!" The others got his sense if not his words.

Adam Stone spoke again:

"You have gone back through the Haberman. I put you back first. I didn't know how it would work in practice, but I had the theory all worked out. You don't think the Instrumentality would waste the Scanners, do you? You go back to normality. We are letting the habermans die as fast as the ships come in. They don't need to live any more. But we are restoring the Scanners. You are the first. Do you understand? You are the first. Take it easy, now."

Adam Stone smiled. Dimly behind Stone, Martel thought he saw the face of one of the Chiefs of the Instrumentality. That face, too, smiled at him, and then both faces disappeared upward and away.

Martel tried to lift his head, to scan himself. He could not. Luci stared at him, calming herself, but with an expression of loving perplexity. She said,

"My darling husband! You're back again, to stay!"

Still, Martel tried to see his box. Finally he swept his hand across his chest with a clumsy motion. There was nothing there. The instruments were gone. He was back to normality but still alive.

In the deep weak peacefulness of his mind, another troubling thought took shape. He tried to write with his finger, the way that Luci wanted him to, but he had neither pointed fingernail nor Scanner's Tablet. He had to use his voice. He summoned up his strength and whispered:

"Scanners?"

"Yes, darling? What is it?"

"Scanners?"

"Scanners. Oh, yes, darling, they're all right. They had to arrest some of them for going into *High Speed* and running away. But the Instrumentality caught them all—all those on the ground—and they're happy now. Do you know, darling," she laughed, "some of them didn't want to be restored to normality. But Stone and his Chiefs persuaded them."

"Vomact?"

"He's fine, too. He's staying cranched until he can be restored. Do you know, he has arranged for Scanners to take new jobs. You're all to be Deputy Chiefs for Space. Isn't that nice? But he got himself made Chief of Space. You're all going to be pilots, so that your fraternity and guild can go on. And Chang's getting changed right now. You'll see him soon."

Her face turned sad. She looked at him earnestly and said: "I might as well tell you now. You'll worry otherwise. There has been one accident. Only one. When you and your friend called on Adam Stone, your friend was so happy that he forgot to scan, and he let himself die of *Overload*."

"Called on Stone?"

"Yes. Don't you remember? Your friend."

He still looked surprised, so she said:

"Parizianski."

MARS IS HEAVEN!

by Ray Bradbury

The ship came down from space. It came from the stars and the black velocities, and the shining movements, and the silent gulfs of space. It was a new ship; it had fire in its body and men in its metal cells, and it moved with a clean silence, fiery and warm. In it were seventeen men, including a captain. The crowd at the Ohio field had shouted and waved their hands up into the sunlight, and the rocket had bloomed out great flowers of heat and color and run away into space on the third voyage to Mars!

Now it was decelerating with metal efficiency in the upper Martian atmospheres. It was still a thing of beauty and strength. It had moved in the midnight waters of space like a pale sea leviathan; it had passed the ancient moon and thrown itself onward into one nothingness following another. The men within it had been battered, thrown about, sickened, made well again, each in his turn. One man had died, but now the remaining sixteen, with their eyes clear in their heads and their faces pressed to the thick glass ports, watched Mars swing up under them.

"Mars! Mars! Good old Mars, here we are!" cried Navigator Lustig.

"Good old Mars!" said Samuel Hinkston, archaeologist.

"Well," said Captain John Black.

The ship landed softly on a lawn of green grass. Outside, upon the lawn, stood an iron deer. Further up the lawn, a tall brown Victorian house sat in the quiet sunlight, all covered with scrolls and rococo, its windows

First published in 1948

made of blue and pink and yellow and green colored glass. Upon the porch were hairy geraniums and an old swing which was hooked into the porch ceiling and which now swung back and forth, back and forth, in a little breeze. At the top of the house was a cupola with diamond, leaded-glass windows, and a dunce-cap roof! Through the front window you could see an ancient piano with yellow keys and a piece of music titled *Beautiful Ohio* sitting on the music rest.

Around the rocket in four directions spread the little town, green and motionless in the Martian spring. There were white houses and red brick ones, and tall elm trees blowing in the wind, and tall maples and horse chestnuts. And church steeples with golden bells silent in them.

The men in the rocket looked out and saw this. Then they looked at one another and then they looked out again. They held on to each other's elbows, suddenly unable to breathe, it seemed. Their faces grew pale and they blinked constantly, running from glass port to glass port of the ship.

"I'll be damned," whispered Lustig, rubbing his face with his numb fingers, his eyes wet. "I'll be damned, damned, damned."

"It can't be, it just can't be," said Samuel Hinkston.

"Lord," said Captain John Black.

There was a call from the chemist. "Sir, the atmosphere is fine for breathing, sir."

Black turned slowly. "Are you sure?"

"No doubt of it, sir."

"Then we'll go out," said Lustig.

"Lord, yes," said Samuel Hinkston.

"Hold on," said Captain John Black. "Just a moment. Nobody gave any orders."

"But, sir—"

"Sir, nothing. How do we know what this is?"

"We know what it is, sir," said the chemist. "It's a small town with good air in it, sir."

"And it's a small town the like of Earth towns," said Samuel Hinkston, the archaeologist. "Incredible. It can't be, but it is."

Captain John Black looked at him, idly. "Do you think

that the civilizations of two planets can progress at the same rate and evolve in the same way, Hinkston?"

"I wouldn't have thought so, sir."

Captain Black stood by the port. "Look out there. The geraniums. A specialized plant. That specific variety has only been known on Earth for fifty years. Think of the thousands of years of time it takes to evolve plants. Then tell me if it is logical that the Martians should have: one, leaded glass windows; two, cupolas; three, porch swings; four, an instrument that looks like a piano and probably is a piano; and, five, if you look closely, if a Martian composer would have published a piece of music titled, strangely enough, *Beautiful Ohio*. All of which means that we have an Ohio River here on Mars!"

"It is quite strange, sir."

"Strange, hell, it's absolutely impossible, and I suspect the whole bloody shooting setup. Something's wrong here, and I'm not leaving the ship until I know what it is."

"Oh, sir," said Lustig.

"Darn it," said Samuel Hinkston. "Sir, I want to investigate this at first hand. It may be that there are similar patterns of thought, movement, civilization on *every* planet in our system. We may be on the threshold of the great psychological and metaphysical discovery in our time, sir, don't you think?"

"I'm willing to wait a moment," said Captain John Black.

"It may be, sir, that we are looking upon a phenomenon that, for the first time, would absolutely prove the existence of a God, sir."

"There are many people who are of good faith without such proof, Mr. Hinkston."

"I'm one myself, sir. But certainly a thing like this, out there," said Hinkston, "could not occur without divine intervention, sir. It fills me with such terror and elation I don't know whether to laugh or cry, sir."

"Do neither, then, until we know what we're up against."

"Up against, sir?" inquired Lustig. "I see that we're up against nothing. It's a good quiet, green town, much like the one I was born in, and I like the looks of it."

"When were you born, Lustig?"

"In 1910, sir."

"That makes you fifty years old, now, doesn't it?"

"This being 1960, yes, sir."

"And you, Hinkston?"

"1920, sir. In Illinois. And this looks swell to me, sir."

"This couldn't be Heaven," said the captain, ironically. "Though, I must admit, it looks peaceful and cool, and pretty much like Green Bluff, where I was born, in 1915." He looked at the chemist. "The air's all right, is it?"

"Yes, sir."

"Well, then, tell you what we'll do. Lustig, you and Hinkston and I will fetch ourselves out to look this town over. The other 14 men will stay aboard ship. If anything untoward happens, lift the ship and get the hell out, do you hear what I say, Craner?"

"Yes, sir. The hell out we'll go, sir. Leaving *you?*"

"A loss of three men's better than a whole ship. If something bad happens get back to Earth and warn the next Rocket, that's Lingle's Rocket, I think, which will be completed and ready to take off some time around next Christmas, what he has to meet up with. If there's something hostile about Mars we certainly want the next expedition to be well armed."

"So are we, sir. We've got a regular arsenal with us."

"Tell the men to stand by the guns, then, as Lustig and Hinkston and I go out."

"Right, sir."

"Come along, Lustig, Hinkston."

The three men walked together, down through the levels of the ship.

It was a beautiful spring day. A robin sat on a blossoming apple tree and sang continuously. Showers of petal snow sifted down when the wind touched the apple tree, and the blossom smell drifted upon the air. Somewhere in the town, somebody was playing the piano and the music came and went, came and went, softly, drowsily. The song was *Beautiful Dreamer.* Somewhere else, a phonograph, scratchy and faded, was hissing out a record of *Roamin' In The Gloamin,'* sung by Harry Lauder.

The three men stood outside the ship. The port closed

behind them. At every window, a face pressed, looking out. The large metal guns pointed this way and that, ready.

Now the phonograph record being played was:

> "Oh give me a June night
> The moonlight and you—"

Lustig began to tremble. Samuel Hinkston did likewise. Hinkston's voice was so feeble and uneven that the captain had to ask him to repeat what he had said. "I said, sir, that I think I have solved this, all of this, sir!"

"And what is the solution, Hinkston?"

The soft wind blew. The sky was serene and quiet and somewhere a stream of water ran through the cool caverns and tree-shadings of a ravine. Somewhere a horse and wagon trotted and rolled by, bumping.

"Sir, it must be, it has to be, this is the *only* solution! Rocket travel began to Mars in the years before the first World War, sir!"

The captain stared at his archaeologist. "No!"

"But, yes, sir! You must admit, look at all of this! How else explain it, the houses, the lawns, the iron deer, the flowers, the pianos, the music!"

"Hinkston, Hinkston, oh," and the captain put his hand to his face, shaking his head, his hand shaking now, his lips blue.

"Sir, listen to me." Hinkston took his elbow persuasively and looked up into the captain's face, pleading. "Say that there were some people in the year 1905, perhaps, who hated wars and wanted to get away from Earth and they got together, some scientists, in secret, and built a rocket and came out here to Mars."

"No, no, Hinkston."

"Why not? The world was a different place in 1905, they could have kept it a secret much more easily."

"But the work, Hinkston, the work of building a complex thing like a rocket, oh, no, no." The captain looked at his shoes, looked at his hands, looked at the houses, and then at Hinkston.

"And they came up here, and naturally the houses they built were similar to Earth houses because they

brought the cultural architecture with them, and here
it is!"

"And they've lived here all these years?" said the
captain.

"In peace and quiet, sir, yes. Maybe they made a few
trips, to bring enough people here for one small town,
and then stopped, for fear of being discovered. That's
why the town seems so old-fashioned. I don't see a thing,
myself, that is older than the year 1927, do you?"

"No, frankly, I don't, Hinkston."

"These are *our* people, sir. This is an American city;
it's definitely not European!"

"That—that's right, too, Hinkston."

"Or maybe, just maybe, sir, rocket travel is older than
we think. Perhaps it started in some part of the world
hundreds of years ago, was discovered and kept secret by
a small number of men, and they came to Mars, with only
occasional visits to Earth over the centuries."

"You make it sound almost reasonable."

"It is, sir. It has to be. We have the proof here before
us, all we have to do now, is find some people and
verify it!"

"You're right there, of course. We can't just stand
here and talk. Did you bring your gun?"

"Yes, but we won't need it."

"We'll see about it. Come along, we'll ring that door-
bell and see if anyone is home."

Their boots were deadened of all sound in the thick
green grass. It smelled from a fresh mowing. In spite of
himself, Captain John Black felt a great peace come over
him. It had been thirty years since he had been in a
small town, and the buzzing of spring bees on the air
lulled and quieted him, and the fresh look of things was
a balm to the soul.

Hollow echoes sounded from under the boards as they
walked across the porch and stood before the screen
door. Inside, they could see a bead curtain hung across
the hall entry, and a crystal chandelier and a Maxfield
Parrish painting framed on one wall over a comfortable
Morris Chair. The house smelled old, and of the attic,
and infinitely comfortable. You could hear the tinkle of

ice rattling in a lemonade pitcher. In a distant kitchen, because of the day, someone was preparing a soft, lemon drink.

Captain John Black rang the bell.

Footsteps, dainty and thin, came along the hall and a kind-faced lady of some forty years, dressed in the sort of dress you might expect in the year 1909, peered out at them.

"Can I help you?" she asked.

"Beg your pardon," said Captain Black, uncertainly. "But we're looking for, that is, could you help us, I mean." He stopped. She looked out at him with dark wondering eyes.

"If you're selling something," she said, "I'm much too busy and I haven't time." She turned to go.

"No, *wait*," he cried bewilderedly. "What town is this?"

She looked him up and down as if he were crazy. "What do you mean, what town is it? How could you be in a town and not know what town it was?"

The captain looked as if he wanted to go sit under a shady apple tree. "I beg your pardon," he said. "But we're strangers here. We're from Earth, and we want to know how this town got here and you got here."

"Are you census takers?" she asked.

"No," he said.

"What do you want then?" she demanded.

"Well," said the captain.

"Well?" she asked.

"How long has this town been here?" he wondered.

"It was built in 1868," she snapped at them. "Is this a game?"

"No, not a game," cried the captain. "Oh, God," he said. "Look here. We're from Earth!"

"From *where?*" she said.

"From Earth!" he said.

"Where's that?" she said.

"From Earth," he cried.

"Out of the ground, do you mean?"

"No, from the planet Earth!" he almost shouted. "Here," he insisted, "come out on the porch and I'll show you."

"No," she said, "I won't come out there, you are all evidently quite mad from the sun."

Lustig and Hinkston stood behind the captain. Hinkston now spoke up. "Mrs.," he said. "We came in a flying ship across space, among the stars. We came from the third planet from the sun, Earth, to this planet, which is Mars. *Now* do you understand, Mrs.?"

"Mad from the sun," she said, taking hold of the door. "Go away now, before I call my husband who's upstairs taking a nap, and he'll beat you all with his fists."

"But—" said Hinkston. "This is Mars, is it not?"

"This," explained the woman, as if she were addressing a child, "is Green Lake, Wisconsin, on the continent of America, surrounded by the Pacific and Atlantic Oceans, on a place called the world, or sometimes, the Earth. Go away now. Good-bye!"

She slammed the door.

The three men stood before the door with their hands up in the air toward it, as if pleading with her to open it once more.

They looked at one another.

"Let's knock the door down," said Lustig.

"We can't," sighed the captain.

"Why not?"

"She didn't do anything bad, did she? We're the strangers here. This is private property. Good God, Hinkston!" He went and sat down on the porchstep.

"What, sir?"

Did it ever strike you, that maybe we got ourselves, somehow, some way, fouled up. And, by accident, came back and landed on Earth!"

"Oh, sir, oh, sir, oh oh, sir." And Hinkston sat down numbly and thought about it.

Lustig stood up in the sunlight. "How could we have done that?"

"I don't know, just let me think."

Hinkston said, "But we checked every mile of the way, and we saw Mars and our chronometers said so many miles gone, and we went past the moon and out into space and here we are, on Mars. I'm sure we're on Mars, sir."

Lustig said, "But, suppose that, by accident, in space,

in time, or something, we landed on a planet in space, in another time. Suppose this is Earth, thirty or fifty years ago? Maybe we got lost in the dimensions, do you think?"

"Oh, go away, Lustig."

"Are the men in the ship keeping an eye on us, Hinkston?"

"At their guns, sir."

Lustig went to the door, rang the bell. When the door opened again, he asked, "What year is this?"

"1926, of course!" cried the woman, furiously, and slammed the door again.

"Did you hear that?" Lustig ran back to them, wildly. "She said 1926! We *have* gone back in time. This *is* Earth!"

Lustig sat down and the three men let the wonder and terror of the thought afflict them. Their hands stirred fitfully on their knees. The wind blew, nodding the locks of hair on their heads.

The captain stood up, brushing off his pants. "I never thought it would be like this. It scares the hell out of me. How can a thing like this happen?"

"Will anybody in the whole town believe us?" wondered Hinkston. "Are we playing around with something dangerous? Time, I mean. Shouldn't we just take off and go home?"

"No. We'll try another house."

They walked three houses down to a little white cottage under an oak tree. "I like to be as logical as I can get," said the captain. He nodded at the town. "How does this sound to you, Hinkston? Suppose, as you said originally, that rocket travel occurred years ago. And when the Earth people had lived here a number of years they began to get homesick for Earth. First a mild neurosis about it, then a full-fledged psychosis. Then, threatened insanity. What would you do, as a psychiatrist, if faced with such a problem?"

Hinkston thought. "Well, I think I'd re-arrange the civilization on Mars so it resembled Earth more and more each day. If there was any way of reproducing every plant, every road and every lake, and even an ocean, I would do so. Then I would, by some vast crowd hypnosis, theoretically anyway, convince everyone in a town this size that this really *was* Earth, not Mars at all."

"Good enough, Hinkston. I think we're on the right track now. That woman in that house back there, just *thinks* she's living on Earth. It protects her sanity. She and all the others in this town are the patients of the greatest experiment in migration and hypnosis you will ever lay your eyes on in your life."

"That's it, sir!" cried Lustig.

"Well," the captain sighed. "Now we're getting somewhere. I feel better. It all sounds a bit more logical now. This talk about time and going back and forth and traveling in time turns my stomach upside down. But, *this* way—" He actually smiled for the first time in a month. "Well. It looks as if we'll be fairly welcome here."

"Or, will we, sir?" said Lustig. "After all, like the Pilgrims, these people came here to escape Earth. Maybe they won't be too happy to see us, sir. Maybe they'll try to drive us out or kill us?"

"We have superior weapons if that should happen. Anyway, all we can do is try. This next house now. Up we go."

But they had hardly crossed the lawn when Lustig stopped and looked off across the town, down the quiet, dreaming afternoon street. "Sir," he said.

"What is it, Lustig?" asked the captain.

"Oh, sir, *sir*, what I see, what I do see now before me, oh, oh—" said Lustig, and he began to cry. His fingers came up, twisting and trembling, and his face was all wonder and joy and incredulity. He sounded as if any moment he might go quite insane with happiness. He looked down the street and he began to run, stumbling, awkwardly, falling, picking himself up, and running on. "Oh, God, God, thank you, God! Thank you!"

"Don't let him get away!" The captain broke into a run.

Now Lustig was running at full speed, shouting. He turned into a yard half way down the little shady side street and leaped up upon the porch of a large green house with an iron rooster on the roof.

He was beating upon the door, shouting and hollering and crying when Hinkston and the captain ran up and stood in the yard.

The door opened. Lustig yanked the screen wide and in a high wail of discovery and happiness, cried out, "Grandma! Grandpa!"

Two old people stood in the doorway, their faces lighting up.

"Albert!" Their voices piped and they rushed out to embrace and pat him on the back and move around him. "Albert, oh, Albert, it's been so many years! How you've grown, boy, how big you are, boy, oh, Albert boy, how are you!"

"Grandma, Grandpa!" sobbed Albert Lustig. "Good to see you! You look fine, fine! Oh, fine." He held them, turned them, kissed them, hugged them, cried on them, held them out again, blinked at the little old people. The sun was in the sky, the wind blew, the grass was green, the screen door stood open.

"Come in, lad, come in, there's lemonade for you, fresh, lots of it!"

"Grandma, Grandpa, good to see you! I've got friends down here! Here!" Lustig turned and waved wildly at the captain and Hinkston, who, all during the adventure on the porch, had stood in the shade of a tree, holding onto each other. "Captain, captain, come up, come up, I want you to meet my grandfolks!"

"Howdy," said the folks. "Any friend of Albert's is ours, too! Don't stand there with your mouths open! Come on!"

In the living room of the old house it was cool and a grandfather clock ticked high and long and bronzed in one corner. There were soft pillows on large couches and walls filled with books and a rug cut in a thick rose pattern and antimacassars pinned to furniture, and lemonade in the hand, sweating, and cool on the thirsty tongue.

"Here's to our health." Grandma tipped her glass to her porcelain teeth.

"How long you *been* here, Grandma?" said Lustig.

"A good many years," she said, tartly. "Ever since we died."

"Ever since you what?" asked Captain John Black, putting his drink down.

"Oh, yes," Lustig looked at his captain. "They've been dead thirty years."

"And you *sit* there, calmly!" cried the captain.

"Tush," said the old woman, and winked glitteringly at John Black. "Who are we to question what happens? Here we are. What's life, anyways? Who does what for why and where? All we know is here we are, alive again, and no questions asked. A second chance." She toddled over and held out her thin wrist to Captain John Black. "Feel." He felt. "Solid, ain't I?" she asked. He nodded. "You hear my voice, don't you?" she inquired. Yes, he did. "Well, then," she said in triumph, "why go around questioning?"

"Well," said the captain, "it's simply that we never thought we'd find a thing like this on Mars."

"And now you've found it. I dare say there's lots on every planet that'll show you God's infinite ways."

"Is this Heaven?" asked Hinkston.

"Nonsense, no. It's a world and we get a second chance. Nobody told us why. But then nobody told us why we were on Earth, either. That *other* Earth, I mean. The one you came from. How do we know there wasn't *another* before *that* one?"

"A good question," said the captain.

The captain stood up and slapped his hand on his leg in an off-hand fashion. "We've got to be going. It's been nice. Thank you for the drinks."

He stopped. He turned and looked toward the door, startled.

Far away, in the sunlight, there was a sound of voices, a crowd, a shouting and a great hello.

"What's that?" asked Hinkston.

"We'll soon find out!" And Captain John Black was out the front door abruptly, jolting across the green lawn and into the street of the Martian town.

He stood looking at the ship. The ports were open and his crew were streaming out, waving their hands. A crowd of people had gathered and in and through and among these people the members of the crew were running, talking, laughing, shaking hands. People did little dances. People swarmed. The rocket lay empty and abandoned.

A brass band exploded in the sunlight, flinging off a gay tune from upraised tubas and trumpets. There was a bang of drums and a shrill of fifes. Little girls with golden hair jumped up and down. Little boys shouted, "Hooray!" And fat men passed around ten-cent cigars. The mayor of the town made a speech. Then, each member of the crew with a mother on one arm, a father or sister on the other, was spirited off down the street, into little cottages or big mansions and doors slammed shut.

The wind rose in the clear spring sky and all was silent. The brass band had banged off around a corner leaving the rocket to shine and dazzle alone in the sunlight.

"Abandoned!" cried the captain. "Abandoned the ship, they did! I'll have their skins, by God! They had orders!"

"Sir," said Lustig. "Don't be too hard on them. Those were all old relatives and friends."

"That's no excuse!"

"Think how they felt, captain, seeing familiar faces outside the ship!"

"I would have obeyed orders! I would have—" The captain's mouth remained open.

Striding along the sidewalk under the Martian sun, tall, smiling, eyes blue, face tan, came a young man of some twenty-six years.

"John!" the man cried, and broke into a run.

"What?" said Captain John Black. He swayed.

"John, you old beggar, you!"

The man ran up and gripped his hand and slapped him on the back.

"It's you," said John Black.

"Of course, who'd you *think* it was!"

"Edward!" The captain appealed now to Lustig and Hinkston, holding the stranger's hand. "This is my brother Edward. Ed, meet my men, Lustig, Hinkston! My brother!"

They tugged at each other's hands and arms and then finally embraced. "Ed!" "John, you old bum, you!" "You're looking fine, Ed, but, Ed, what is this? You haven't changed over the years. You died, I remember, when you were twenty-six, and I was nineteen, oh God,

so many years ago, and here you are, and, Lord, what
goes on, what goes on?"

Edward Black gave him a brotherly knock on the chin.
"Mom's waiting," he said.

"Mom?"

"And Dad, too."

"And Dad?" The captain almost fell to earth as if hit
upon the chest with a mighty weapon. He walked stiffly
and awkwardly, out of coordination. He stuttered and
whispered and talked only one or two words at a time.
"Mom alive? Dad? Where?"

"At the old house on Oak Knoll Avenue."

"The old house." The captain stared in delighted
amazement. "Did you *hear* that, Lustig, Hinkston?"

"I know it's hard for you to believe."

"But alive. Real."

"Don't I *feel* real?" The strong arm, the firm grip, the
white smile. The light, curling hair.

Hinkston was gone. He had seen his own house down
the street and was running for it. Lustig was grinning.
"Now you understand, sir, what happened to everybody
on the ship. They couldn't help themselves."

"Yes. Yes," said the captain, eyes shut. "Yes." He put
out his hand. "When I open my eyes, you'll be gone." He
opened his eyes. "You're still here. God, Edward, you
look fine!"

"Come along, lunch is waiting for you. I told Mom."

Lustig said, "Sir, I'll be with my grandfolks if you
want me."

"What? Oh, fine, Lustig. Later, then."

Edward grabbed his arm and marched him. "You
need support."

"I do. My knees, all funny. My stomach, loose. God."

"There's the house. Remember it?"

"Remember it? Hell! I bet I can beat you to the front
porch!"

They ran. The wind roared over Captain John Black's
ears. The earth roared under his feet. He saw the golden
figure of Edward Black pull ahead of him in the amazing
dream of reality. He saw the house rush forward, the door
open, the screen swing back. "Beat you!" cried Edward,
bounding up the steps. "I'm an old man," panted the cap-

tain, "and you're still young. But, then, you *always* beat me, I remember!"

In the doorway, Mom, pink and plump and bright. And behind her, pepper grey, Dad, with his pipe in his hand.

"Mom, Dad!"

He ran up the steps like a child, to meet them.

It was a fine long afternoon. They finished lunch and they sat in the living room and he told them all about his rocket and his being captain and they nodded and smiled upon him and Mother was just the same, and Dad bit the end off a cigar and lighted it in his old fashion. Mom brought in some iced tea in the middle of the afternoon. Then, there was a big turkey dinner at night and time flowing on. When the drumsticks were sucked clean and lay brittle upon the plates, the captain leaned back in his chair and exhaled his deep contentment. Dad poured him a small glass of dry sherry. It was seven-thirty in the evening. Night was in all the trees and coloring the sky, and the lamps were halos of dim light in the gentle house. From all the other houses down the streets came sounds of music, pianos playing, laughter.

Mom put a record on the victrola and she and Captain John Black had a dance. She was wearing the same perfume he remembered from the summer when she and Dad had been killed in the train accident. She was very real in his arms as they danced lightly to the music.

"I'll wake in the morning," said the captain. "And I'll be in my rocket in space, and this will be gone."

"No, no, don't think that," she cried, softly, pleadingly. "We're here. Don't question. God is good to us. Let's be happy."

The record ended with a hissing.

"You're tired, son," said Dad. He waved his pipe. "You and Ed go on upstairs. Your old bedroom is waiting for you."

"The old one?"

"The brass bed and all," laughed Edward.

"But I should report my men in."

"Why?" Mother was logical.

"Why? Well, I don't know. No reason, I guess. No, none at all. What's the difference?" He shook his head. "I'm not being very logical these days."

"Good night, son." She kissed his cheek.

" 'Night, Mom."

"Sleep tight, son." Dad shook his hand.

"Same to you, Pop."

"It's good to have you home."

"It's good to *be* home."

He left the land of cigar smoke and perfume and books and gentle light and ascended the stairs, talking, talking with Edward. Edward pushed a door open and there was the yellow brass bed and the old semaphore banners from college·days and a very musty raccoon coat which he petted with strange, muted affection. "It's too much," he said faintly. "Like being in a thunder shower without an umbrella. I'm soaked to the skin with emotion. I'm numb. I'm tired."

"A night's sleep between cool clean sheets for you, my bucko." Edward slapped wide the snowy linens and flounced the pillows. Then he put up a window and let the night blooming jasmine float in. There was moonlight and the sound of distant dancing and whispering.

"So this is Mars," said the captain undressing.

"So this is Mars." Edward undressed in idle, leisurely moves, drawing his shirt off over his head, revealing golden shoulders and the good muscular neck.

The lights were out, they were into bed, side by side, as in the days, how many decades ago? The captain lolled and was nourished by the night wind pushing the lace curtains out upon the dark room air. Among the trees, upon a lawn, someone had cranked up a portable phonograph and now it was playing softly, "I'll be loving you, always, with a love that's true, always."

The thought of Anna came to his mind. "Is Anna here?"

His brother, lying straight out in the moonlight from the window, waited and then said, "Yes. She's out of town. But she'll be here in the morning."

The captain shut his eyes. "I want to see Anna very much."

The room was square and quiet except for their breathing. "Good night, Ed."

A pause. "Good night, John."

He lay peacefully, letting his thoughts float. For the

first time the stress of the day was moved aside, all of the excitement was calmed. He could think logically now. It had all been emotion. The bands playing, the sight of familiar faces, the sick pounding of your heart. But— now . . .

How? He thought. How was all this made? And why? For what purpose? Out of the goodness of some kind God? Was God, then, really that fine and thoughtful of his children? How and why and what for?

He thought of the various theories advanced in the first heat of the afternoon by Hinkston and Lustig. He let all kinds of new theories drop in lazy pebbles down through his mind, as through a dark water, now, turning, throwing out dull flashes of white light. Mars. Earth. Mom. Dad. Edward. Mars. Martians.

Who had lived here a thousand years ago on Mars? Martians? Or had this always been like this? Martians. He repeated the word quietly, inwardly.

He laughed out loud, almost. He had the ridiculous theory, all of a sudden. It gave him a kind of chilled feeling. It was really nothing to think of, of course. Highly improbable. Silly. Forget it. Ridiculous.

But, he thought, just suppose. Just *suppose* now, that there were Martians living on Mars and they saw our ship coming and saw us inside our ship and hated us. Suppose, now, just for the hell of it, that they wanted to destroy us, as invaders, as unwanted ones, and they wanted to do it in a very clever way, so that we would be taken off guard. Well, what would the best weapon be that a Martian could use against Earthmen with atom weapons?

The answer was interesting. Telepathy, hypnosis, memory and imagination.

Suppose all these houses weren't real at all, this bed not real, but only figments of my own imagination, given substance by telepathy and hypnosis by the Martians.

Suppose these houses are really some other shape, a Martian shape, but, by playing on my desires and wants, these Martians have made this seem like my old home town, my old house, to lull me out of my suspicions? What better way to fool a man, by his own emotions.

And suppose those two people in the next room, asleep, are not my mother and father at all. But two Martians, incredibly brilliant, with the ability to keep me under this dreaming hypnosis all of the time?

And that brass band, today? What a clever plan it would be. First, fool Lustig, then fool Hinkston, then gather a crowd around the rocket ship and wave. And all the men in the ship, seeing mothers, aunts, uncles, sweethearts dead ten, twenty years ago, naturally, disregarding orders, would rush out and abandon the ship. What more natural? What more unsuspecting? What more simple? A man doesn't ask too many questions when his mother is suddenly brought back to life; he's much too happy. And the brass band played and everybody was taken off to private homes. And here we all are, tonight, in various houses, in various beds, with no weapons to protect us, and the rocket lies in the moonlight, empty. And wouldn't it be horrible and terrifying to discover that all of this was part of some great clever plan by the Martians to divide and conquer us, and kill us. Some time during the night, perhaps, my brother here on this bed, will change form, melt, shift, and become a one-eyed, green and yellow-toothed Martian. It would be very simple for him just to turn over in bed and put a knife into my heart. And in all those other houses down the street a dozen other brothers or fathers suddenly melting away and taking out knives and doing things to the unsuspecting, sleeping men of Earth.

His hands were shaking under the covers. His body was cold. Suddenly it was not a theory. Suddenly he was very afraid. He lifted himself in bed and listened. The night was very quiet. The music had stopped. The wind had died. His brother (?) lay sleeping beside him.

Very carefully he lifted the sheets, rolled them back. He slipped from bed and was walking softly across the room when his brother's voice said, "Where are you going?"

"What?"

His brother's voice was quite cold. "I said, where do you think you're going?"

"For a drink of water."

"But you're not thirsty."

"Yes, yes, I am."

"No, you're not."

Captain John Black broke and ran across the room. He screamed. He screamed twice.

He never reached the door.

In the morning, the brass band played a mournful dirge. From every house in the street came little solemn processions bearing long boxes and along the sun-filled street, weeping and changing, came the grandmas and grandfathers and mothers and sisters and brothers, walking to the churchyard, where there were open holes dug freshly and new tombstones installed. Seventeen holes in all, and seventeen tombstones. Three of the tombstones said, CAPTAIN JOHN BLACK, ALBERT LUSTIG, and SAMUEL HINKSTON.

The mayor made a little sad speech, his face sometimes looking like the mayor, sometimes looking like something else.

Mother and Father Black were there, with Brother Edward, and they cried, their faces melting now from a familiar face into something else.

Grandpa and Grandma Lustig were there, weeping, their faces also shifting like wax, shivering as a thing does in waves of heat on a summer day.

The coffins were lowered. Somebody murmured about "the unexpected and sudden deaths of seventeen fine men during the night—"

Earth was shoveled in on the coffin tops.

After the funeral the brass band slammed and banged into town and the crowd stood around and waved and shouted as the rocket was torn to pieces and strewn about and blown up.

THE LITTLE BLACK BAG

by C. M. Kornbluth

Old Dr. Full felt the winter in his bones as he limped
down the alley. It was the alley and the back door he
had chosen rather than the sidewalk and the front door
because of the brown paper bag under his arm. He knew
perfectly well that the flat-faced, stringy-haired women
of his street and their gap-toothed, sour-smelling hus-
bands did not notice if he brought a bottle of cheap wine
to his room. They all but lived on the stuff themselves,
varied with whiskey when pay checks were boosted by
overtime. But Dr. Full, unlike them, was ashamed. A
complicated disaster occurred as he limped down the
littered alley. One of the neighborhood dogs—a mean
little black one he knew and hated, with its teeth always
bared and always snarling with menace—hurled at his
legs through a hole in the board fence that lined his path.
Dr. Full flinched, then swung his leg in what was to have
been a satisfying kick to the animal's gaunt ribs. But the
winter in his bones weighed down the leg. His foot failed
to clear a half-buried brick, and he sat down abruptly,
cursing. When he smelled unbottled wine and realized his
brown paper package had slipped from under his arm
and smashed, his curses died on his lips. The snarling
black dog was circling him at a yard's distance, tensely
stalking, but he ignored it in the greater disaster.

With stiff fingers as he sat on the filth of the alley, Dr.
Full unfolded the brown paper bag's top, which had been
crimped over, grocer-wise. The early autumnal dusk had
come; he could not see plainly what was left. He lifted

First published in 1950

out the jug-handled top of his half gallon, and some fragments, and then the bottom of the bottle. Dr. Full was
far too occupied to exult as he noted that there was a
good pint left. He had a problem, and emotions could be
deferred until the fitting time.

The dog closed in, its snarl rising in pitch. He set down
the bottom of the bottle and pelted the dog with the
curved triangular glass fragments of its top. One of them
connected, and the dog ducked back through the fence,
howling. Dr. Full then placed a razor-like edge of the half-
gallon bottle's foundation to his lip and drank from it as
though it were a giant's cup. Twice he had to put it down
to rest his arms, but in one minute he had swallowed the
pint of wine.

He thought of rising to his feet and walking through
the alley to his room, but a flood of well-being drowned
the notion. It was, after all, inexpressibly pleasant to sit
there and feel the frost-hardened mud of the alley turn
soft, or seem to, and to feel the winter evaporating from
his bones under a warmth which spread from his stomach
through his limbs.

A three-year-old girl in a cut-down winter coat squeezed
through the same hole in the board fence from which the
black dog had sprung its ambush. Gravely she toddled up
to Dr. Full and inspected him with her dirty forefinger in
her mouth. Dr. Full's happiness had been providentially
made complete; he had been supplied with an audience.

"Ah, my dear," he said hoarsely. And then: "Preposterous accusation. 'If that's what you call evidence,' I
should have told them, 'you better stick to your doctoring.'
I should have told them: 'I was here before your County
Medical Society. And the License Commissioner never
proved a thing on me. So gennulmen, doesn't it stand to
reason? I appeal to you as fellow members of a great
profession?' "

The little girl bored, moved away, picking up one of the
triangular pieces of glass to play with as she left. Dr. Full
forgot her immediately, and continued to himself earnestly:
"But so help me, they *couldn't* prove a thing. Hasn't a man
got any *rights?*" He brooded over the question, of whose
answer he was so sure, but on which the Committee on
Ethics of the County Medical Society had been equally

certain. The winter was creeping into his bones again, and he had no money and no more wine.

Dr. Full pretended to himself that there was a bottle of whiskey somewhere in the fearful litter of his room. It was an old and cruel trick he played on himself when he simply had to be galvanized into getting up and going home. He might freeze there in the alley. In his room he would be bitten by bugs and would cough at the moldy reek from his sink, but he would not freeze and be cheated of the hundreds of bottles of wine that he still might drink, the thousands of hours of glowing content he still might feel. He thought about that bottle of whiskey—was it back of a mounded heap of medical journals? No; he had looked there last time. Was it under the sink, shoved well to the rear, behind the rusty drain? The cruel trick began to play itself out again. Yes, he told himself with mounting excitement, yes, it might be! Your memory isn't so good nowadays, he told himself with rueful good-fellowship. You know perfectly well you might have bought a bottle of whiskey and shoved it behind the sink drain for a moment just like this.

The amber bottle, the crisp snap of the sealing as he cut it, the pleasurable exertion of starting the screw cap on its threads, and then the refreshing tangs in his throat, the warmth in his stomach, the dark, dull happy oblivion of drunkenness—they became real to him. You *could* have, you know! You *could* have! he told himself. With the blessed conviction growing in his mind—It *could* have happened, you know! It *could* have!—he struggled to his right knee. As he did, he heard a yelp behind him, and curiously craned his neck around while resting. It was the little girl, who had cut her hand quite badly on her toy, the piece of glass. Dr. Full could see the rilling bright blood down her coat, pooling at her feet.

He almost felt inclined to defer the image of the amber bottle for her, but not seriously. He knew that it was there, shoved well to the rear under the sink, behind the rusty drain where he had hidden it. He would have a drink and then magnanimously return to help the child. Dr. Full got to his other knee and then his feet, and proceeded at a rapid totter down the littered alley toward his room, where he would hunt with calm optimism at first for the bottle that was not there, then with anxiety, and then with frantic violence. He would hurl books and dishes about before he was done looking for the amber bottle of whiskey, and finally would beat his swollen knuckles against the brick wall until old scars on them opened and his thick old blood oozed over his hands. Last of all, he would sit down somewhere on the floor, whimpering, and would plunge into the abyss of purgative nightmare that was his sleep.

After twenty generations of shilly-shallying and "we'll cross that bridge when we come to it," genus homo had bred itself into an impasse. Dogged biometricians had pointed out with irrefutable logic that mental subnormals were outbreeding mental normals and supernormals, and that the process was occurring on an exponential curve. Every fact that could be mustered in the argument proved the biometricians' case, and led inevitably to the conclusion that genus homo was going to wind up in a preposterous jam quite soon. If you think that had any effect on breeding practices, you do not know genus homo.

There was, of course, a sort of masking effect produced by that other exponential function, the accumulation of technological devices. A moron trained to punch an adding machine seems to be a more skillful computer than a medieval mathematician trained to count on his fingers. A moron trained to operate the twenty-first century equivalent of a linotype seems to be a better typographer than a Rennaissance printer limited to a few fonts of movable type. This is also true of medical practice.

It was a complicated affair of many factors. The supernormals "improved the product" at greater speed than the subnormals degraded it, but in smaller quantity because elaborate training of their children was practiced on a custom-made basis. The fetish of higher education had some weird avatars by the twentieth generation: "colleges" where not a member of the student body could read words of three syllables; "universities" where such degrees as "Bachelor of Typewriting," "Master of Shorthand" and "Doctor of Philosophy (Card Filing)" were conferred with the traditional pomp. The handful of supernormals used such devices in order that the vast majority might keep some semblance of a social order going.

Some day the supernormals would mercilessly cross the bridge; at the twentieth generation they were standing irresolutely at its approaches wondering what had hit them. And the ghosts of twenty generations of biometricians chuckled malignantly.

It is a certain Doctor of Medicine of this twentieth generation that we are concerned with. His name was Hemingway—John Hemingway, B.Sc., M.D. He was a general practitioner, and did not hold with running to specialists with every trifling ailment. He often said as much, in approximately these words: "Now, uh, what I mean is you got a good old G.P. See what I mean? Well, uh, now a good old G.P. don't claim he knows all about lungs and glands and them things, get me? But you got a G.P., you got, uh, you got a, well, you got a . . . *all-around man!* That's what you got when you got a G.P.—you got a all-around man."

But from this, do not imagine that Dr. Hemingway was a poor doctor. He could remove tonsils or appendixes, assist at practically any confinement and deliver a living, uninjured infant, correctly diagnose hundreds of ailments, and prescribe and administer the correct medication or treatment for each. There was, in fact, only one thing he could not do in the medical line, and that was, violate the ancient canons of medical ethics. And Dr. Hemingway knew better than to try.

Dr. Hemingway and a few friends were chatting one evening when the event occurred that precipitates him into our story. He had been through a hard day at the clinic, and he wished his physicist friend Walter Gillis, B.Sc., M.Sc., Ph.D., would shut up so he could tell everybody about it. But Gillis kept rambling on, in his stilted fashion: "You got to hand it to old Mike; he don't have what we call the scientific method, but you got to hand it to him. There this poor little dope is, puttering around with some glassware, and I come up and I ask him, kidding of course, 'How's about a time-travel machine, Mike?' "

Dr. Gillis was not aware of it, but "Mike" had an I.Q. six times his own and was—to be blunt—his keeper. "Mike" rode herd on the pseudo-physicists in the pseudo-laboratory, in the guise of a bottle-washer. It was a social waste—but as has been mentioned before, the supernormals were still standing at the approaches to a bridge. Their irresolution led to many such preposterous situations. And it happens that "Mike," having grown frantically bored with his task, was malevolent enough to—but let Dr. Gillis tell it:

"So he gives me these here tube numbers and says, 'Series circuit. Now stop bothering me. Build your time machine, sit down at it and turn on the switch. That's all I ask, Dr. Gillis—that's all I ask.' "

"Say," marveled a brittle and lovely blond guest, "you remember real good, don't you, doc?" She gave him a melting smile.

"Heck," said Gillis modestly, "I always remember good. It's what you call an inherent facility. And besides I told it quick to my secretary, so she wrote it down. I don't read so good, but I sure remember good, all right. Now, where was I?"

Everybody thought hard, and there were various suggestions:

"Something about bottles, doc?"

"You was starting a fight. You said 'time somebody was traveling.' "

"Yeah—you called somebody a swish. Who did you call a swish?"

"Not swish—*switch!*"

Dr. Gillis' noble brow grooved with thought, and he declared: "Switch is right. It was about time travel. What we call travel through time. So I took the tube numbers he gave me and I put them into the circuit-builder; I set it for 'series' and there it is—my time-traveling machine. It travels things through time real good." He displayed a box.

"What's in the box?" asked the lovely blonde.

Dr. Hemingway told her: "Time travel. It travels things through time."

"Look," said Gillis, the physicist. He took Dr. Hemingway's little black bag and put it on the box. He turned on the switch and the little black bag vanished.

"Say," said Dr. Hemingway, "that was, uh, swell. Now bring it back."

"Huh?"

"Bring back my little black bag."

"Well," said Dr. Gillis, "they don't come back. I tried backwards and they don't come back. I guess maybe that dummy Mike give me a bum steer."

There was wholesale condemnation of "Mike" but Dr. Hemingway took no part in it. He was nagged by a vague feeling that there was something he would have to do. He reasoned: "I am a doctor, and a doctor has got to have a little black bag. I ain't got a little black bag—so ain't I a doctor no more?" He decided that this was absurd. He *knew* he was a doctor. So it must be the bag's fault for not being there. It was no good, and he would get another one tomorrow from that dummy Al, at the clinic. Al could find things good, but he was a dummy—never liked to talk sociable to you.

So the next day Dr. Hemingway remembered to get another little black bag from his keeper—another little black bag with which he could perform tonsillectomies, appendectomies and the most difficult confinements, and with which he could diagnose and cure his kind until the day when the supernormals could bring themselves to cross that bridge. Al was kinda nasty about the missing little black bag, but Dr. Hemingway didn't exactly remember what had happened, so no tracer was sent out, so—

Old Dr. Full awoke from the horrors of the night to the horrors of the day. His gummy eyelashes pulled apart convulsively. He was propped against a corner of his room, and something was making a little drumming noise. He felt very cold and cramped. As his eyes focused on his lower body, he croaked out a laugh. The drumming noise was being made by his left heel, agitated by fine tremors against the bare floor. It was going to be the D.T.'s again, he decided dispassionately. He wiped his mouth with his bloody knuckles, and the fine tremor coarsened; the snare-drum beat became louder and slower. He was getting a break this fine morning, he decided sardonically. You didn't get the horrors until you had been tightened like a violin string, just to the breaking point. He had a reprieve, if a reprieve into his old body with the blazing, endless headache just back of the eyes and the screaming stiffness in the joints were anything to be thankful for.

There was something or other about a kid, he thought vaguely. He was going to doctor some kid. His eyes rested on a little black bag in the center of the room, and he forgot about the kid. "I could have sworn," said Dr. Full, "I hocked that two years ago!" He hitched over and reached the bag, and then realized it was some stranger's kit, arriving here he did not know how. He tentatively touched the lock and it snapped open and lay flat, rows and rows of instruments and medications tucked into loops in its four walls. It seemed vastly larger open than closed. He didn't see how it could possibly fold up into that compact size again, but decided it was some stunt of the instrument makers. Since his time—that made it worth more at the hock shop, he thought with satisfaction.

Just for old times' sake, he let his eyes and fingers rove over the instruments before he snapped the bag shut and headed for Uncle's. More than few were a little hard to recognize—exactly that is. You could see the things with blades for cutting, the forceps for holding and pulling, the retractors for holding fast, the needles and gut for suturing, the hypos—a fleeting thought crossed his mind that he could peddle the hypos separately to drug addicts.

Let's go, he decided, and tried to fold up the case. It didn't fold until he happened to touch the lock, and then it folded all at once into a little black bag. Sure have forged ahead, he thought, almost able to forget that what he was primarily interested in was its pawn value.

With a definite objective, it was not too hard for him to get to his feet. He decided to go down the front steps, out the front door and down the sidewalk. But first—

He snapped the bag open again on his kitchen table, and pored through the medication tubes. "Anything to sock the autonomic nervous system good and hard," he mumbled. The tubes were numbered, and there was a plastic card which seemed to list them. The left margin of the card was a run-down of the systems—vascular, muscular, nervous. He followed the last entry across to the right. There were columns for "stimulant," "depressant," and so on. Under "nervous system" and "depressant" he found the number 17, and shakily located the little glass tube which bore it. It was full of pretty blue pills and he took one.

It was like being struck by a thunderbolt.

Dr. Full had so long lacked any sense of well-being except the brief glow of alcohol that he had forgotten its very nature. He was panic-stricken for a long moment at the sensation that spread through him slowly, finally tingling in his fingertips. He straightened up, his pains gone and his leg tremor stilled.

That was great, he thought. He'd be able to *run* to the hock shop, pawn the little black bag and get some booze. He started down the stairs. Not even the street, bright with mid-morning sun, into which he emerged made him quail. The little black bag in his left hand had a satisfying, authoritative weight. He was walking erect, he noted, and not in the somewhat furtive crouch that had grown on him in recent years. A little self-respect, he told himself, that's what I need. Just because a man's down doesn't mean—

"Docta, please-a come wit'!" somebody yelled at him, tugging his arm. "Da litt-la girl, she's-a burn' up!" It was one of the slum's innumerable flat-faced, stringy-haired women, in a slovenly wrapper.

"Ah, I happen to be retired from practice—" he began hoarsely, but she would not be put off.

"In by here, Docta!" she urged, tugging him to a doorway. "You come look-a da litt-la girl. I got two dolla, you come look!" That put a different complexion on the matter. He allowed himself to be towed through the doorway into a messy, cabbage-smelling flat. He knew the woman now, or rather knew who she must be—a new arrival who had moved in the other night. These people moved at night, in motorcades of battered cars supplied by friends and relatives, with furniture lashed to the tops, swearing and drinking until the small hours. It explained why she had stopped him: she did not yet know he was old Dr. Full, a drunken reprobate whom nobody would trust. The little black bag had been his guarantee, outweighing his whiskey face and stained black suit.

He was looking down on a three-year-old girl who had, he rather suspected, just been placed in the mathematical center of a freshly changed double bed. God knew what sour and dirty mattress she usually slept on. He seemed to recognize her as he noted a crusted bandage on her right hand. Two dollars, he thought. An ugly flush had spread up her pipe-stem arm. He poked a finger into the socket of her elbow, and felt little spheres like marbles under the skin and ligaments roll apart. The child began to squall thinly; beside him, the woman gasped and began to weep herself.

"Out," he gestured briskly at her, and she thudded away, still sobbing.

Two dollars, he thought. Give her some mumbo jumbo, take the money and tell her to go to a clinic. Strep, I guess, from that stinking alley. It's a wonder any of them grow up. He put down the little black bag and forgetfully fumbled for his key, then remembered and touched the lock. It flew open, and he selected a bandage shears, with a blunt wafer for the lower jaw. He fitted the lower jaw under the bandage, trying not to hurt the kid by its pressure on the infection, and began to cut. It was amazing how easily and swiftly the shining shears snipped through the crusty rag around the wound. He hardly seemed to be driving the shears with fingers at all. It almost seemed as though the shears were driving his fingers instead as they scissored a clean, light line through the bandage.

Certainly have forged ahead since my time, he thought —sharper than a microtome knife. He replaced the shears in their loop on the extraordinarily big board that the little black bag turned into when it unfolded, and leaned over the wound. He whistled at the ugly gash, and the violent infection which had taken immediate root in the sickly child's thin body. Now what can he do with a thing like that? He pawed over the contents of the little black bag, nervously. If he lanced it and let some of the pus out, the old woman would think he'd done something for her and he'd get the two dollars. But at the clinic they'd want to know who did it and if they got sore enough they might send a cop around. Maybe there was something in the kit—

He ran down the left edge of the card to "lymphatic" and read across to the column under "infection." It didn't sound right at all to him; he checked again, but it still said that. In the square to which the line and column led were the symbols: "IV-g-3cc." He couldn't find any bottles marked with Roman numerals, and then noticed that that was how the hypodermic needles were designated. He lifted number IV from its loop, noting that it was fitted with a needle already and even seemed to be charged. What a way to carry those things around! So—three cc. of whatever was in hypo number IV ought to do something or other about infections settled in the lymphatic system—which, God knows, this one was. What did the lower-case "g" mean, though? He studied the glass hypo and saw letters engraved on what looked like a rotating disk at the top of the barrel. They ran from "a" to "i," and there was an index line engraved on the barrel on the opposite side from the calibrations.

Shrugging, old Dr. Full turned the disk until "g" coincided with the index line, and lifted the hypo to eye level. As he pressed in the plunger he did not see the tiny thread of fluid squirt from the tip of the needle. There was a sort of dark mist for a moment about the tip. A closer inspection showed that the needle was not even pierced at the tip. It had the usual slanting cut across the bias of the shaft, but the cut did not expose an oval hole. Baffled, he tried pressing the plunger again. Again *something* appeared around the tip and vanished. "We'll settle this," said the doctor. He slipped the needle into the skin of his forearm. He thought at first that he had missed—that the point had glided over the top of his skin instead of catching and slipping under it. But he saw a tiny blood-spot and realized that somehow he just hadn't felt the puncture. Whatever was in the barrel, he decided, couldn't do him any harm if it lived up to its billing—and if it could come out through a needle that had no hole. He gave himself three cc. and twitched the needle out. There was the swelling—painless, but otherwise typical.

Dr. Full decided it was his eyes or something, and gave three cc. of "g" from hypodermic IV to the feverish child. There was no interruption to her wailing as the needle went in and the swelling rose. But a long instant later, she gave a final gasp and was silent.

Well, he told himself, cold with horror, you did it that time. You killed her with that stuff.

Then the child sat up and said: "Where's my mommy?"

Incredulously, the doctor seized her arm and palpated the elbow. The gland infection was zero, and the temperature seemed normal. The blood-congested tissues surrounding the wound were subsiding as he watched. The child's pulse was stronger and no faster than a child's should be. In the sudden silence of the room he could hear the little girl's mother sobbing in her kitchen, outside. And he also heard a girl's insinuating voice:

"She gonna be OK. doc?"

He turned and saw a gaunt-faced, dirty-blond sloven of perhaps eighteen leaning in the doorway and eyeing him with amused contempt. She continued: "I heard about you, *Doc-tor* Full. So don't go try and put the bite on the old lady. You couldn't doctor up a sick cat."

"Indeed?" he rumbled. This young person was going to get a lesson she richly deserved. "Perhaps you would care to look at my patient?"

"Where's my mommy?" insisted the little girl, and the blond's jaw fell. She went to the bed and cautiously asked: "You OK now, Teresa? You all fixed up?"

"Where's my mommy?" demanded Teresa. Then, accusingly, she gestured with her wounded hand at the doctor. "You *poke* me!" she complained, and giggled pointlessly.

"Well—" said the blond girl, "I guess I got to hand it to you, doc. These loud-mouth women around here said you didn't know your . . . I mean, didn't know how to cure people. They said you ain't a real doctor."

"I *have* retired from practice," he said. "But I happened to be taking this case to a colleague as a favor, your good mother noticed me, and—" a deprecating smile. He touched the lock of the case and it folded up into the little black bag again.

"You stole it," the girl said flatly.

He sputtered.

"Nobody'd trust you with a thing like that. It must be worth plenty. You stole that case. I was going to stop you when I came in and saw you working over Teresa, but it looked like you wasn't doing her any harm. But when you give me that line about taking that case to a colleague I know you stole it. You gimme a cut or I go to the cops. A thing like that must be worth twenty-thirty dollars."

The mother came timidly in, her eyes red. But she let out a whoop of joy when she saw the little girl sitting up and babbling to herself, embraced her madly, fell on her knees for a quick prayer, hopped up to kiss the doctor's hand, and then dragged him into the kitchen, all the while rattling in her native language while the blond girl let her eyes go cold with disgust. Dr. Full allowed himself to be towed into the kitchen, but flatly declined a cup of coffee and a plate of anise cakes and St.-John's-bread.

Try him on some wine, ma," said the girl sardonically.

"Hyass! Hyass!" breathed the woman delightedly. "You like-a wine, docta?" She had a carafe of purplish liquid before him in an instant, and the blond girl snickered as the doctor's hand twitched out at it. He drew his hand back, while there grew in his head the old image of how it would smell and then taste and then warm his stomach and limbs. He made the kind of calculation at which he was practiced; the delighted woman would not notice as he downed two tumblers, and he could overawe her through two tumblers more with his tale of Teresa's narrow brush with the Destroying Angel, and then—why, then it would not matter. He would be drunk.

But for the first time in years, there was a sort of counter-image: a blend of the rage he felt at the blond girl to whom he was so transparent, and of pride at the cure he had just effected. Much to his own surprise, he drew back his hand from the carafe and said, luxuriating in the words: "No, thank you. I don't believe I'd care for any so early in the day." He covertly watched the blond girl's face, and was gratified at her surprise. Then the mother was shyly handing him two bills and saying: "Is no much-a-money, docta—but you come again, see Teresa?"

"I shall be glad to follow the case through," he said. "But now excuse me—I really must be running along." He grasped the little black bag firmly and got up; he wanted very much to get away from the wine and the older girl.

"Wait up, doc," said she, "I'm going your way." She followed him out and down the street. He ignored her until he felt her hand on the black bag. Then old Dr. Full stopped and tried to reason with her:

"Look, my dear. Perhaps you're right. I might have stolen it. To be perfectly frank, I don't remember how I got it. But you're young and you can earn your own money—"

"Fifty-fifty," she said, "or I go to the cops. And if I get

another word outta you, it's sixty-forty. And you know who gets the short end. don't you, doc?"

Defeated. he marched to the pawnshop, her impudent hand still on the handle with his, and her heels beating out a tattoo against his stately tread.

In the pawnshop. they both got a shock.

"It ain't stendard," said Uncle, unimpressed by the ingenious lock. "I ain't nevva seen one like it. Some cheap Jap stuff, maybe? Try down the street. This I nevva could sell."

Down the street they got an offer of one dollar. The same complaint was made: "I ain't a collecta, mista—I buy stuff that got resale value. Who could I sell this to, a Chinaman who don't know medical instruments? Every one of them looks funny. You sure you didn't make these yourself?" They didn't take the one-dollar offer.

The girl was baffled and angry; the doctor was baffled too, but triumphant. He had two dollars. and the girl had a half-interest in something nobody wanted. But, he suddenly marveled, the thing had been all right to cure the kid. hadn't it?

"Well," he asked her, "do you give up? As you see, the kit is practically valueless."

She was thinking hard. "Don't fly off the handle, doc. I don't get this but something's going on all right . . . would those guys know good stuff if they saw it?"

"They would. They make a living from it. Wherever this kit came from—"

She seized on that, with a devilish faculty she seemed to have of eliciting answers without asking questions. "I thought so. You don't know either, huh? Well, maybe I can find out for you. C'mon in here. I ain't letting go of that thing. There's money in it—some way, I don't know how, there's money in it." He followed her into a cafeteria and to an almost empty corner. She was oblivious to stares and snickers from the other customers as she opened the little black bag—it almost covered a cafeteria table—and ferreted through it. She picked out a retractor from a loop, scrutinized it, contempuously threw it down, picked out a speculum, threw it down, picked out the lower half of an O.B. forceps, turned it over, close to her sharp young eyes

—and saw what the doctor's dim old ones could not have seen.

All old Dr. Full knew was that she was peering at the neck of the forceps and then turned white. Very carefully, she placed the half of the forceps back in its loop of cloth and then replaced the retractor and the speculum. "Well?" he asked. "What did you see?"

" 'Made in U.S.A..,' " she quoted hoarsely. " 'Patent Applied for July 2450.' "

He wanted to tell her she must have misread the inscription, that it must be a practical joke, that—

But he knew she had read correctly. Those bandage shears: they *had* driven his fingers, rather than his fingers driving them. The hypo needle that had no hole. The pretty blue pill that had struck him like a thunderbolt.

"You know what I'm going to do?" asked the girl, with sudden animation. "I'm going to go to charm school. You'll like that, won't ya, doc? Because we're sure going to be seeing a lot of each other."

Old Dr. Full didn't answer. His hands had been playing idly with that plastic card from the kit on which had been printed the rows and columns that had guided him twice before. The card had a slight convexity; you could snap the convexity back and forth from one side to the other. He noted. in a daze. that with each snap a different text appeared on the cards. *Snap*. "The knife with the blue dot in the handle is for tumors only. Diagnose tumors with your Instrument Seven, the Swelling Tester. Place the Swelling Tester—" *Snap*. "An overdose of the pink pills in Bottle 3 can be fixed with one white pill from Bottle—" *Snap*. "Hold the suture needle by the end without the hole in it. Touch it to one end of the wound you want to close and let go. After it has made the knot. touch it—" *Snap*. "Place the top half of the O.B. Forceps near the opening. Let go. After it has entered and conformed to the shape of—" *Snap*.

The slot man saw "FLANNERY 1—MEDICAL" in the upper left corner of the hunk of copy. He automatically scribbled "trim to .75" on it and skimmed it across the horseshoe-shaped copy desk to Piper. who had been handling Edna Flannery's quack-exposé series. She was a nice

youngster, he thought. but like all youngsters she over-
wrote. Hence, the "trim."

Piper dealt back a city hall story to the slot, pinned
down Flannery's feature with one hand and began to tap
his pencil across it, one tap to a word, at the same steady
beat as a teletype carriage traveling across the roller. He
wasn't exactly reading it this first time. He was just looking
at the letters and words to find out whether, as letters and
words, they conformed to *Herald* style. The steady tap of
his pencil ceased at intervals as it drew a black line ending
with a stylized letter "d" through the word "breast" and
scribbled in "chest" instead, or knocked down the capital
"E" in "East" to lower case with a diagonal, or closed up
a split word—in whose middle Flannery had bumped the
space bar of her typewriter—with two curved lines like
parentheses rotated through ninety degrees. The thick black
pencil zipped a ring around the "30" which, like all
youngsters. she put at the end of her stories. He turned
back to the first page for the second reading. This time
the pencil drew lines with the stylized "d's" at the end of
them through adjectives and whole phrases, printed big
"L's" to mark paragraphs. hooked some of Flannery's
own paragraphs together with swooping recurved lines.

At the bottom of "FLANNERY ADD 2—MEDICAL"
the pencil slowed down and stopped. The slot man. sensitive to the rhythm of his beloved copy desk, looked up
almost at once. He saw Piper squinting at the story, at a
loss. Without wasting words. the copy reader skimmed it
back across the masonite horseshoe to the chief, caught
a police story in return and buckled down. his pencil
tapping. The slot man read as far as the fourth add. barked
at Howard. on the rim: "Sit in for me." and stamped
through the clattering city room toward the alcove where
the managing editor presided over his own bedlam.

The copy chief waited his turn while the makeup editor,
the pressroom foreman and the chief photographer had
words with the M.E. When his turn came. he dropped
Flannery's copy on his desk and said: "She says this one
isn't a quack."

The M.E. read:

"FLANNERY 1—MEDICAL, by Edna Flannery, *Herald* Staff Writer.

"The sordid tale of medical quackery which the *Herald* has exposed in this series of articles undergoes a change of pace today which the reporter found a welcome surprise. Her quest for the facts in the case of today's subject started just the same way that her exposure of one dozen shyster M.D.'s and faithhealing phonies did. But she can report for a change that Dr. Bayard Full is, despite unorthodox practices which have drawn the suspicion of the rightly hypersensitive medical associations, a true healer living up to the highest ideals of his profession.

"Dr. Full's name was given to the *Herald's* reporter by the ethical committee of a county medical association, which reported that he had been expelled from the association, on July 18, 1941 for allegedly 'milking' several patients suffering from trivial complaints. According to sworn statements in the committee's files, Dr. Full had told them they suffered from cancer, and that he had a treatment which would prolong their lives. After his expulsion from the association, Dr. Full dropped out of their sight—until he opened a midtown 'sanitarium' in a brownstone front which had for several years served as a rooming house.

"The *Herald's* reporter went to that sanitarium, on East 89th Street, with the full expectation of having numerous imaginary ailments diagnosed and of being promised a sure cure for a flat sum of money. She expected to find unkept quarters, dirty instruments and the mumbo-jumbo paraphernalia of the shyster M.D. which she had seen a dozen times before.

"She was wrong.

"Dr. Full's sanitarium is spotlessly clean, from its tastefully furnished entrance hall to its shining white treatment rooms. The attractive, blond receptionist who greeted the reporter was soft-spoken and correct, asking only the reporter's name, address and the general nature of her complaint. This was given, as usual, as 'nagging backache.' The receptionist asked the *Herald's* reporter to be seated, and a short while later conducted her to a second-floor treatment room and introduced her to Dr. Full.

"Dr. Full's alleged past, as described by the medical society spokesman, is hard to reconcile with his present appearance. He is a clear-eyed, white-haired man in his sixties, to judge by his appearance—a little above middle height and apparently in good physical condition. His voice was firm and friendly, untainted by the ingratiating whine of the shyster M.D. which the reporter has come to know too well.

"The receptionist did not leave the room as he began his examination after a few questions as to the nature and location of the pain. As the reporter lay face down on a treatment table the doctor pressed some instrument to the small of her back. In about one minute he made this astounding statement: 'Young woman, there is no reason for you to have any pain where you say you do. I understand they're saying nowadays that emotional upsets cause pains like that. You'd better go to a psychologist or psychiatrist if the pain keeps up. There is no physical cause for it, so I can do nothing for you.'

"His frankness took the reporter's breath away. Had he guessed she was, so to speak, a spy in his camp? She tried again: 'Well, doctor, perhaps you'd give me a physical checkup. I feel rundown all the time, besides the pains. Maybe I need a tonic.' This is never-failing bait to shyster M.D.'s—an invitation for them to find all sorts of mysterious conditions wrong with a patient, each of which 'requires' an expensive treatment. As explained in the first article of this series, of course, the reporter underwent a thorough physical checkup before she embarked on her quack-hunt and was found to be in one hundred percent perfect condition, with the exception of a 'scarred' area at the bottom tip of her left lung resulting from a childhood attack of tuberculosis and a tendency toward 'hyperthyroidism'— overactivity of the thyroid gland which makes it difficult to put on weight and sometimes causes a slight shortness of breath.

"Dr. Full consented to perform the examination, and took a number of shining, spotlessly clean instruments from loops in a large board literally covered with instruments—most of them unfamiliar to the reporter. The instrument with which he approached first was a tube with a curved dial in its surface and two wires that ended on flat disks growing from its ends. He placed one of the disks on the back of the reporter's right hand and the other on the back of her left. 'Reading the meter,' he called out some number which the attentive receptionist took down on a ruled form. The same procedure was repeated several times, thoroughly covering the reporter's anatomy and thoroughly convincing her that the doctor was a complete quack. The reporter had never seen any such diagnostic procedure practiced during the weeks she put in preparing for this series.

"The doctor then took the ruled sheet from the receptionist, conferred with her in low tones and said: 'You have a slightly overactive thyroid, young woman. And ther's something wrong with your left lung—not seriously, but I'd like to take a closer look.'

"He selected an instrument from the board which, the reporter knew, is called a 'speculum'—a scissorlike device which spreads apart body openings such as the orifice of the ear, the nostril and so on, so that a doctor can look in during an examination. The instrument was, however, too large to be an aural or nasal speculum but too small to be anything else. As the *Herald's* reporter was about to ask further questions, the attending receptionist told her: 'It's customary for us to blindfold our patients during lung examinations—do you mind?' The reporter, bewildered, allowed her to tie a spotlessly clean bandage over her eyes, and waited nervously for what would come next.

"She still cannot say exactly what happened while she was blindfolded—but X rays confirm her suspicions. She felt a cold sensation at her ribs on the left side—a cold that seemed to enter inside her body. Then there was a snapping feeling, and the cold sensation was gone. She heard Dr. Full say in a matter-of-fact voice: 'You have an old tubercular scar down there. It isn't doing any particular harm, but an active person like you needs all the oxygen she can get. Lie still and I'll fix it for you.'

"Then there was a repetition of the cold sensation, lasting for a longer time. 'Another batch of alveoli and some more vascular glue,' the *Herald's* reporter heard Dr. Full say, and the receptionist's crisp response to the order. Then the strange sensation departed and the eye-bandage was removed. The reporter saw no scar on her ribs, and yet the doctor assured her: 'That did it. We took out the fibrosis—and a good fibrosis it was, too; it walled off the infection so you're still alive to tell the tale. Then we planted a few clumps of alveoli—they're the little gadgets that get the oxygen from the air you breathe into your blood. I won't monkey with your thyroxin supply. You've got used to being the kind of person you are, and if you suddenly found yourself easy-going and all the rest of it, chances are you'd only be upset. About the backache: just check with the county medical society for the name of a good psychologist or psychiatrist. And look out for quacks; the woods are full of them.'

"The doctor's self-assurance took the reporter's breath away. She asked what the charge would be, and was told to pay the receptionist fifty dollars. As usual, the reporter delayed paying until she got a receipt signed by the doctor himself, detailing the services for which it paid. Unlike most the doctor cheerfully wrote: 'For removal of fibrosis from left lung and restoration of alveoli,' and signed it.

"The reporter's first move when she left the sanitarium was to head for the chest specialist who had examined her in preparation for this series. A comparison of X rays taken on the day of the 'operation' and those taken previously would, the *Herald's* reporter thought, expose Dr. Full as a prince of shyster M.D.'s and quacks.

"The chest specialist made time on his crowded schedule for the reporter, in whose series he has shown a lively interest from the planning stage on. He laughed uproariously in his staid Park Avenue examining room as she described the weird procedure to which she had been subjected. But he did not laugh when he took a chest X ray of the reporter, developed it, dried it, and compared it with the ones he had taken earlier. The chest specialist took six more X rays that afternoon, but finally admitted that they all told the same story. The *Herald's* reporter has it on his authority that the scar she had eighteen days ago from her tuberculosis is now gone and has been replaced by healthy lung-tissue. He declares that this is a happening unparalleled in medical history. He does not go along with the reporter in her firm conviction that Dr. Full is responsible for the change.

"The *Herald's* reporter, however, sees no two ways about it. She concludes that Dr. Bayard Full—whatever his alleged past may have been—is now an unorthodox but highly successful practitioner of medicine, to whose hands the reporter would trust herself in any emergency.

"Not so is the case of 'Rev.' Annie Dimsworth—a female harpy who, under the guise of 'faith,' preys on the ignorant and suffering who come to her sordid 'healing parlor' for help and remain to feed 'Rev.' Annie's bank account, which now totals up to $53,238.64. Tomorrow's article will show, with photostats of bank statements and sworn testimony, that— "

The managing editor turned down "FLANNERY LAST ADD—MEDICAL" and tapped his front teeth with a pencil, trying to think straight. He finally told the copy chief: "Kill the story. Run the teaser as a box." He tore off the last paragraph—the "teaser" about "Rev." Annie— and handed it to the desk man, who stumped back to his masonite horseshoe.

The makeup editor was back, dancing with impatience as he tried to catch the M.E.'s eye. The interphone buzzed with the red light which indicated that the editor and publisher wanted to talk to him. The M.E. thought briefly of a special series on this Dr. Full, decided nobody would believe it and that he probably was a phony anyway. He spiked the story on the "dead" hook and answered his interphone.

Dr. Full had become almost fond of Angie. As his practice had grown to engross the neighborhood illnesses, and then to a corner suite in an uptown taxpayer building, and finally to the sanitarium, she seemed to have grown with it. Oh, he thought, we have our little disputes—

The girl, for instance, was too much interested in money. She had wanted to specialize in cosmetic surgery—removing wrinkles from wealthy old women and what-not. She didn't realize, at first, that a thing like this was in their trust, that they were the stewards and not the owners of the little black bag and its fabulous contents.

He had tried, ever so cautiously, to analyze them, but without success. All the instruments were slightly radioactive, for instance, but not quite so. They would make a Geiger-Mueller counter indicate, but they would not collapse the leaves of an electroscope. He didn't pretend to be up on the latest developments, but as he understood it, that was just plain *wrong*. Under the highest magnification there were lines on the instruments' superfinished surfaces: incredibly fine lines, engraved in random hatchments which made no particular sense. Their magnetic properties were preposterous. Sometimes the instruments were strongly attracted to magnets, sometimes less so, and sometimes not at all.

Dr. Full had taken X rays in fear and trembling lest he disrupt whatever delicate machinery worked in them. He was *sure* they were not solid, that the handles and perhaps the blades must be mere shells filled with busy little watch-works—but the X rays showed nothing of the sort. Oh, yes —and they were always sterile, and they wouldn't rust. Dust *fell* off them if you shook them: now, that was something he understood. They ionized the dust, or were ionized themselves, or something of the sort. At any rate he had read of something similar that had to do with phonograph records.

She wouldn't know about that, he proudly thought. She kept the books well enough, and perhaps she gave him a useful prod now and then when he was inclined to settle down. The move from the neighborhood slum to the uptown quarters had been her idea, and so had the sanitarium. Good, good, it enlarged his sphere of usefulness. Let the child have her mink coats and her convertible, as they seemed to be calling roadsters nowadays. He himself was too busy and too old. He had so much to make up for.

Dr. Full thought happily of his Master Plan. She would not like it much, but she would have to see the logic of it. This marvelous thing that had happened to them must be handed on. She was herself no doctor; even though the instruments practically ran themselves, there was more to doctoring than skill. There were the ancient canons of the healing art. And so, having seen the logic of it, Angie would yield; she would assent to his turning over the little black bag to all humanity.

He would probably present it to the College of Surgeons, with as little fuss as possible—well, perhaps a *small* ceremony, and he would like a souvenir of the occasion, a cup or a framed testimonial. It would be a relief to have the thing out of his hands, in a way; let the giants of the healing art decide who was to have its benefits. No, Angie would understand. She was a good-hearted girl.

It was nice that she had been showing so much interest in the surgical side lately—asking about the instruments, reading the instruction card for hours, even practicing on guinea pigs. If something of his love for humanity had been communicated to her, old Dr. Full sentimentally thought, his life would not have been in vain. Surely she would realize that a greater good would be served by surrendering the instruments to wiser hands than theirs, and by throwing aside the cloak of secrecy necessary to work on their small scale.

Dr. Full was in the treatment room that had been the brownstone's front parlor; through the window he saw Angie's yellow convertible roll to a stop before the stoop. He liked the way she looked as she climbed the stairs; neat, not flashy, he thought. A sensible girl like her, she'd understand. There was somebody with her—a fat woman, puffing up the steps, overdressed and petulant. Now, what could she want?

Angie let herself in and went into the treatment room, followed by the fat woman. "Doctor," said the blond girl gravely, "may I present Mrs. Coleman?" Charm school had not taught her everything, but Mrs. Coleman, evidently *nouveau riche,* thought the doctor, did not notice the blunder.

"Miss Aquella told me *so* much about you, doctor, and your remarkable system!" she gushed.

Before he could answer, Angie smoothly interposed: "Would you excuse us for just a moment, Mrs. Coleman?"

She took the doctor's arm and led him into the reception hall. "Listen," she said swiftly, "I know this goes against your grain, but I couldn't pass it up. I met this old thing in the exercise class at Elizabeth Barton's. Nobody else'll talk to her there. She's a widow. I guess her husband was a black marketeer or something, and she has a pile of dough. I gave her a line about how you had a system of massaging wrinkles out. My idea is, you blindfold her, cut her neck open with the Cutaneous Series knife, shoot some Firmol into the muscles, spoon out some of that blubber with an Adipose Series curette and spray it all with Skintite. When you take the blindfold off she's got rid of a wrinkle and doesn't know what happened. She'll pay five hundred dollars. Now, don't say 'no,' doc. Just this once, let's do it my way, can't you? I've been working on this deal all along too, haven't I?"

"Oh," said the doctor, "very well." He was going to have to tell her about the Master Plan before long anyway. He would let her have it her way this time.

Back in the treatment room, Mrs. Coleman had been thinking things over. She told the doctor sternly as he entered: "Of course, your system is permanent, isn't it?"

"It is, madam," he said shortly. "Would you please lie down there? Miss Aquella get a sterile three-inch bandage for Mrs. Coleman's eyes." He turned his back on the fat woman to avoid conversation, and pretended to be adjusting the lights. Angie blindfolded the woman, and the doctor selected the instruments he would need. He handed the blond girl a pair of retractors, and told her: "Just slip the corners of the blades in as I cut——" She gave him an alarmed look, and gestured at the reclining woman. He lowered his voice: "Very well. Slip in the corners and rock them along the incision. I'll tell you when to pull them out."

Dr. Full held the Cutaneous Series knife to his eyes as he adjusted the little slide for three centimeters' depth. He sighed a little as he recalled that its last use had been in the extirpation of an "inoperable" tumor of the throat.

"Very well," he said, bending over the woman. He tried a tentative pass through her tissues. The blade dipped in and flowed through them, like a finger through quicksilver, with no wound left in the wake. Only the retractors could hold the edges of the incision apart.

Mrs. Coleman stirred and jabbered: "Doctor, that felt so peculiar! Are you sure you're rubbing the right way?"

"Quite sure, madam," said the doctor wearily. "Would you please try not to talk during the massage?"

He nodded at Angie, who stood ready with the retractors. The blade sank in to its three centimeters, miraculously cutting only the dead horny tissues of the epidermis and the live tissue of the dermis, pushing aside mysteriously all major and minor blood vessels and muscular tissue, declining to affect any system or organ except the

one it was—tuned to, could you say? The doctor didn't
know the answer, but he felt tired and bitter at this pros-
titution. Angie slipped in the retractor blades and rocked
them as he withdrew the knife, then pulled to separate
the lips of the incision. It bloodlessly exposed an unhealthy string of muscle, sagging in a dead-looking loop
from blue-gray ligaments. The doctor took a hypo, Number IX, preset to "g," and raised it to his eye level. The
mist came and went; there probably was no possibility
of an embolus with one of these gadgets, but why take
chances? He shot one cc. of "g"—identified as "Firmol"
by the card—into the muscle. He and Angie watched as
it tightened up against the pharynx.

He took the Adipose Series curette, a small one, and
spooned out yellowish tissue, dropping it into the incinerator box, and then nodded to Angie. She eased out the
retractors and the gaping incision slipped together into
unbroken skin, sagging now. The doctor had the atom-
izer—dialed to "Skintite"—ready. He sprayed, and the
skin shrank up into the new firm throat line.

As he replaced the instruments, Angie removed Mrs.
Coleman's bandage and gaily announced: "We're finished!
And there's a mirror in the reception hall—"

Mrs. Coleman didn't need to be invited twice. With
incredulous fingers she felt her chin, and then dashed for
the hall. The doctor grimaced as he heard her yelp of
delight, and Angie turned to him with a tight smile. "I'll
get the money and get her out," she said. "You won't
have to be bothered with her any more."

He was grateful for that much.

She followed Mrs. Coleman into the reception hall,
and the doctor dreamed over the case of instruments.
A ceremony, certainly—he was *entitled* to one. Not everybody, he thought, would turn such a sure source of money
over to the good of humanity. But you reached an age
when money mattered less, and when you thought of
these things you had done that *might* be open to mis-
understanding if, just if, there chanced to be any of that,
well, that judgment business. The doctor wasn't a religious man, but you certainly found yourself thinking
hard about some things when your time drew near—

Angie was back, with a bit of paper in her hands. "Five

hundred dollars," she said matter-of-factly. "And you realize, don't you, that we could go over her an inch at a time—at five hundred dollars an inch?"

"I've been meaning to talk to you about that," he said.

There was bright fear in her eyes, he thought—but why?

"Angie, you've been a good girl and an understanding girl, but we can't keep this up forever, you know."

"Let's talk about it some other time," she said flatly. "I'm tired now."

"No—I really feel we've gone far enough on our own. The instruments—"

"Don't say it, doc!" she hissed. "Don't say it, or you'll be sorry!" In her face there was a look that reminded him of the hollow-eyed, gaunt-faced, dirty-blond creature she had been. From under the charm-school finish there burned the guttersnipe whose infancy had been spent on a sour and filthy mattress, whose childhood had been play in the littered alley and whose adolescence had been the sweatshops and the aimless gatherings at night under the glaring street lamps.

He shook his head to dispel the puzzling notion. "It's this way," he patiently began. "I told you about the family that invented the O.B. forceps and kept them a secret for so many generations, how they could have given them to the world but didn't?"

"They knew what they were doing," said the guttersnipe flatly.

"Well, that's neither here nor there," said the doctor, irritated. "My mind is made up about it. I'm going to turn the instruments over to the College of Surgeons. We have enough money to be comfortable. You can even have the house. I've been thinking of going to a warmer climate, myself." He felt peeved with her for making the unpleasant scene. He was unprepared for what happened next.

Angie snatched the little black bag and dashed for the door, with panic in her eyes. He scrambled after her, catching her arm, twisting it in a sudden rage. She clawed at his face with her free hand, babbling curses. Somehow, somebody's finger touched the little black bag, and it opened grotesquely into the enormous board, covered

with shining instruments, large and small. Half a dozen
of them joggled loose and fell to the floor.

"Now see what you've done!" roared the doctor, unreasonably. Her hand was still viselike on the handle, but
she was standing still, trembling with choked-up rage.
The doctor bent stiffly to pick up the fallen instruments.
Unreasonable girl! he thought bitterly. Making a scene—

Pain drove in between his shoulderblades and he fell
face down. The light ebbed. "Unreasonable girl!" he tried
to croak. And then: "They'll know I tried, anyway—"

Angie looked down on his prone body, with the handle
of the Number Six Cautery Series knife protruding from
it. "—will cut through all tissues. Use for amputations
before you spread on the Re-Gro. Extreme caution should
be used in the vicinity of vital organs and major blood
vessels or nerve trunks—"

"I didn't mean to do that," said Angie, dully, cold
with horror. Now the detective would come, the implacable detective who would reconstruct the crime from the
dust in the room. She would run and turn and twist, but
the detective would find her out and she would be tried
in a courtroom before a judge and jury; the lawyer would
make speeches, but the jury would convict her anyway,
and the headlines would scream: "BLOND KILLER
GUILTY!" and she'd maybe get the chair, walking down
a plain corridor where a beam of sunlight struck through
the dusty air, with an iron door at the end of it. Her
mink, her convertible, her dresses, the handsome man
she was going to meet and marry—

The mist of cinematic clichés cleared, and she knew
what she would do next. Quite steadily, she picked the
incinerator box from its loop in the board—a metal cube
with a different-textured spot on one side. "—to dispose
of fibroses or other unwanted matter, simply touch the
disk—" You dropped something in and touched the disk.
There was a sort of soundless whistle, very powerful
and unpleasant if you were too close, and a sort of lightless flash. When you opened the box again, the contents
were gone. Angie took another of the Cautery Series
knives and went grimly to work. Good thing there wasn't
any blood to speak of—She finished the awful task in
three hours.

She slept heavily that night, totally exhausted by the wringing emotional demands of the slaying and the subsequent horror. But in the morning, it was as though the doctor had never been there. She ate breakfast, dressed with unusual care—and then undid the unusual care. Nothing out of the ordinary, she told herself. Don't do one thing different from the way you would have done it before. After a day or two, you can phone the cops. Say he walked out spoiling for a drunk, and you're worried. But don't rush it, baby—*don't rush it.*

Mrs. Coleman was due at ten A.M. Angie had counted on being able to talk the doctor into at least one more five-hundred-dollar session. She'd have to do it herself now—but she'd have to start sooner or later.

The woman arrived early. Angie explained smoothly: "The doctor asked me to take care of the massage today. Now that he has the tissue-firming process beginning, it only requires somebody trained in his methods—" As she spoke, her eyes swiveled to the instrument case—open! She cursed herself for the single flaw as the woman followed her gaze and recoiled.

"What are those things!" she demanded. "Are you going to cut me with them? I *thought* there was something fishy—"

"Please, Mrs. Coleman," said Angie, "please, *dear* Mrs. Coleman—you don't understand about the . . . the massage instruments!"

"Massage instruments, my foot!" squabbled the woman shrilly. "The doctor *operated* on me. Why, he might have killed me!"

Angie wordlessly took one of the smaller Cutaneous Series knives and passed it through her forearm. The blade flowed like a finger through quicksilver, leaving no wound in its wake. *That* should convince the old cow!

It didn't convince her, but it did startle her. "What did you do with it? The blade folds up into the handle —that's it!"

"Now look closely, Mrs. Coleman," said Angie, thinking desperately of the five hundred dollars. "Look very closely and you'll see that the, uh, the sub-skin massager simply slips beneath the tissues without doing any harm, tightening and firming the muscles themselves instead of having to work through layers of skin and adipose tissue. It's the secret of the doctor's method. Now, how can outside massage have the effect that we got last night?"

Mrs. Coleman was beginning to calm down. "It *did* work, all right." she admitted, stroking the new line of her neck. "But your arm's one thing and my neck's another! Let me see you do that with your neck!"

Angie smiled—

Al returned to the clinic after an excellent lunch that had almost reconciled him to three more months he would have to spend on duty. And then, he thought, and then a blessed year at the blessedly super-normal South Pole working on his specialty—which happened to be telekinesis exercises for ages three to six. Meanwhile, of course, the world had to go on and of course he had to shoulder his share in the running of it.

Before settling down to desk work he gave a routine glance at the bag board. What he saw made him stiffen with shocked surprise. A red light was on next to one of the numbers—the first since he couldn't think when. He read off the number and murmured "OK, 674101. That fixes *you.*" He put the number on a card sorter and in a moment the record was in his hand. Oh, yes—Hemingway's bag. The big dummy didn't remember how or where he had lost it; none of them ever did. There were hundreds of them floating around.

Al's policy in such cases was to leave the bag turned on. The things practically ran themselves, it was practically impossible to do harm with them, so whoever found a lost one might as well be allowed to use it. You turn it off, you have a social loss—you leave it on, it may do some good. As he understood it, and not very well at that, the stuff wasn't "used up." A temporalist had tried to explain it to him with little success that the prototypes in the transmitter *had been transduced* through a series of point-events of transfinite cardinality. Al had innocently asked whether that meant prototypes had been stretched, so to speak, through all time, and the temporalist had thought he was joking and left in a huff.

"Like to see him do this," thought Al darkly, as he telekinized himself to the combox, after a cautious look to see that there were no medics around. To the box he said: "Police chief," and then to the police chief: "There's been a homicide committed with Medical Instrument Kit 674101. It was lost some months ago by one of my people, Dr. John Hemingway. He didn't have a clear account of the circumstances."

The police chief groaned and said: "I'll call him in and question him." He was to be astonished by the answers, and was to learn that the homicide was well out of his jurisdiction.

Al stood for a moment at the bag board by the glowing red light that had been sparked into life by a departing vital force giving, as its last act, the warning that Kit 674101 was in homicidal hands. With a sigh, Al pulled the plug and the light went out.

"Yah," jeered the woman. "You'd fool around with my neck, but you wouldn't risk your own with that thing!"

Angie smiled with serene confidence a smile that was to shock hardened morgue attendants. She set the Cutaneous Series knife to three centimeters before drawing it across her neck. Smiling, knowing the blade would cut only the dead horny tissue of the epidermis and the live tissue of the dermis, mysteriously push aside all major and minor blood vessels and muscular tissue—

Smiling, the knife plunging in and its microtomesharp metal shearing through major and minor blood vessels and muscular tissue and pharynx, Angie cut her throat.

In the few minutes it took the police, summoned by the shrieking Mrs. Coleman, to arrive, the instruments had become crusted with rust, and the flasks which had held vascular glue and clumps of pink, rubbery alveoli and spare gray cells and coils of receptor nerves held only black slime, and from them when opened gushed the foul gases of decomposition.

BORN OF MAN AND WOMAN

by Richard Matheson

X—This day when it had light mother called me retch. You retch she said. I saw in her eyes the anger. I wonder what it is a retch.

This day it had water falling from upstairs. It fell all around. I saw that. The ground of the back I watched from the little window. The ground it sucked up the water like thirsty lips. It drank too much and it got sick and runny brown. I didn't like it.

Mother is a pretty I know. In my bed place with cold walls around I have a paper things that was behind the furnace. It says on it SCREEN-STARS. I see in the pictures faces like of mother and father. Father says they are pretty. Once he said it.

And also mother he said. Mother so pretty and me decent enough. Look at you he said and didnt have the nice face. I touched his arm and said it is alright father. He shook and pulled away where I couldn't reach.

Today mother let me off the chain a little so I could look out the little window. Thats how I saw the water falling from upstairs.

XX—This day it had goldness in the upstairs. As I know when I looked at it my eyes hurt. After I look at it the cellar is red.

I think this was church. They leave the upstairs. The big machine swallows them and rolls out past and is gone. In the back part is the little mother. She is much smaller than me. I am I can see out the little window all I like.

First published in 1950

In this day when it got dark I had eat my food and some bugs. I hear laughs upstairs. I like to know why there are laughs for. I took the chain from the wall and wrapped it around me. I walked squish to the stairs. They creak when I walk on them. My legs slip on them because I dont walk on stairs. My feet stick to the wood.

I went up and opened a door. It was a white place. White as white jewels that come upstairs sometime. I went in and stood quiet. I hear the laughing some more. I walk to the sound and look through to the people. More people than I thought was. I thought I should laugh with them.

Mother came out and pushed the door in. It hit me and hurt. I fell back on the smooth floor and the chain made noise. I cried. She made a hissing noise into her and put her hand on her mouth. Her eyes got big.

She looked at me. I heard father call. What fell he called. She said a iron board. Come help pick it up she said. He came and said now is *that* so heavy you need. He saw me and grew big. The anger came in his eyes. He hit me. I spilled some of the drip on the floor from one arm. It was not nice. It made ugly green on the floor.

Father told me to go to the cellar. I had to go. The light it hurt some now in my eyes. It is not so like that in the cellar.

Father tied my legs and arms up. He put me on my bed. Upstairs I heard laughing while I was quiet there looking on a black spider that was swinging down to me. I thought what father said. Ohgod he said. And only eight.

XXX—This day father hit in the chain again before it had light. I have to try pull it out again. He said I was bad to come upstairs. He said never do that again or he would beat me hard. That hurts.

I hurt. I slept the day and rested my head against the cold wall. I thought of the white place upstairs.

XXXX—I got the chain from the wall out. Mother was upstairs. I heard little laughs very high. I looked out the window. I saw all little people like the little mother and little fathers too. They are pretty.

They were making nice noise and jumping around the ground. Their legs was moving hard. They are like mother and father. Mother says all right people look like they do.

One of the little fathers saw me. He pointed at the window. I let go and slid down the wall in the dark. I curled up as they would not see. I heard their talks by the window and foots running. Upstairs there was a door hitting. I heard the little mother call upstairs. I heard heavy steps and I rushed in my bed place. I hit the chain in the wall and lay down on my front.

I heard mother come down. Have you been at the window she said. I heard the anger. *Stay* away from the window. You have pulled the chain out again.

She took the stick and hit me with it. I didn't cry. I cant do that. But the drip ran all over the bed. She saw it and twisted away and made a noise. Oh mygodmygod she said why have you *done* this to me? I heard the stick go bounce on the stone floor. She ran upstairs. I slept the day.

XXXXX—This day it had water again. When mother was upstairs I heard the little one come slow down the steps. I hidded myself in the coal bin for mother would have anger if the little mother saw me.

She had a little live thing with her. It walked on the arms and had pointy ears. She said things to it.

It was all right except the live thing smelled me. It ran up the coal and looked down at me. The hairs stood up. In the throat it made an angry noise. I hissed but it jumped on me.

I didnt want to hurt it. I got fear because it bit me harder than the rat does. I hurt and the little mother screamed. I grabbed the live thing tight. It made sounds I never heard. I pushed it all together. It was all lumpy and red on the black coal.

I hid there when mother called. I was afraid of the stick. She left. I crept over the coal with the thing. I hid it under my pillow and rested on it. I put the chain in the wall again.

X—This is another times. Father chained me tight. I hurt because he beat me. This time I hit the stick out of his hands and made noise. He went away and his face was white. He ran out of my bed place and locked the door.

I am not so glad. All day it is cold in here. The chain comes slow out of the wall. And I have a bad anger with mother and father. I will show them. I will do what I did that once.

I will screech and laugh loud. I will run on the walls. Last I will hang head down by all my legs and laugh and drip green all over until they are sorry they didn't be nice to me.

If they try to beat me again Ill hurt them. I will.

COMING ATTRACTION

by Fritz Leiber

The coupe with the fishhooks welded to the fender shouldered up over the curb like the nose of a nightmare. The girl in its path stood frozen, her face probably stiff with fright under her mask. For once my reflexes weren't shy. I took a fast step toward her, grabbed her elbow, yanked her back. Her black skirt swirled out.

The big coupe shot by, its turbine humming. I glimpsed three faces. Something ripped. I felt the hot exhaust on my ankles as the big coupe swerved back into the street. A thick cloud like a black flower blossomed from its jouncing rear end, while from the fishhooks flew a black shimmering rag.

"Did they get you?" I asked the girl.

She had twisted around to look where the side of her skirt was torn away. She was wearing nylon tights.

"The hooks didn't touch me," she said shakily. "I guess I'm lucky."

I heard voices around us:

"Those kids! What'll they think up next?"

"They're a menace. They ought to be arrested."

Sirens screamed at a rising pitch as two motor-police, their rocket-assist jets full on, came whizzing toward us after the coupe. But the black flower had become an inky fog obscuring the whole street. The motor-police switched from rocket assists to rocket brakes and swerved to a stop near the smoke cloud.

"Are you English?" the girl asked me. "You have an English accent."

First published in 1950

Her voice came shudderingly from behind the sleek black satin mask. I fancied her teeth must be chattering. Eyes that were perhaps blue searched my face from behind the black gauze covering the eyeholes of the mask. I told her she'd guessed right. She stood close to me. "Will you come to my place tonight?" she asked rapidly. "I can't thank you now. And there's something else you can help me about."

My arm, still lightly circling her waist, felt her body trembling. I was answering the plea in that as much as in her voice when I said, "Certainly." She gave me an address south of Inferno, an apartment number and a time. She asked my name and I told her.

"Hey, you!"

I turned obediently to the policeman's shout. He shooed away the small clucking crowd of masked women and barefaced men. Coughing from the smoke that the black coupe had thrown out, he asked for my papers. I handed him the essential ones.

He looked at them and then at me. "British Barter? How long will you be in New York?"

Suppressing the urge to say, "For as short a time as possible," I told him I'd be here for a week or so.

"May need you as a witness," he explained. "Those kids can't use smoke on us. When they do that, we pull them in."

He seemed to think the smoke was the bad thing. "They tried to kill the lady," I pointed out.

He shook his head wisely. "They always pretend they're going to, but actually they just want to snag skirts. I've picked up rippers with as many as fifty skirt-snags tacked up in their rooms. Of course, sometimes they come a little too close."

I explained that if I hadn't yanked her out of the way, she'd have been hit by more than hooks. But he interrupted, "If she'd thought it was a real murder attempt, she'd have stayed here."

I looked around. It was true. She was gone.

"She was fearfully frightened," I told him.

"Who wouldn't be? Those kids would have scared old Stalin himself."

"I mean frightened of more than 'kids.' They didn't look like 'kids.'"

"What did they look like?"

I tried without much success to describe the three faces. A vague impression of viciousness and effeminacy doesn't mean much.

"Well, I could be wrong," he said finally. "Do you know the girl? Where she lives?"

"No," I half lied.

The other policeman hung up his radiophone and ambled toward us, kicking at the tendrils of dissipating smoke. The black cloud no longer hid the dingy facades with their five-year-old radiation flash-burns, and I could begin to make out the distant stump of the Empire State Building, thrusting up out of Inferno like a mangled finger.

"They haven't been picked up so far," the approaching policeman grumbled. "Left smoke for five blocks, from what Ryan says."

The first policeman shook his head. "That's bad," he observed solemnly.

I was feeling a bit uneasy and ashamed. An Englishman shouldn't lie, at least not on impulse.

"They sound like nasty customers," the first policeman continued in the same grim tone. "We'll need witnesses. Looks as if you may have to stay in New York longer than you expect."

I got the point. I said, "I forgot to show you all my papers," and handed him a few others, making sure there was a five dollar bill in among them.

When he handed them back a bit later, his voice was no longer ominous. My feelings of guilt vanished. To cement our relationship, I chatted with the two of them about their job.

"I suppose the masks give you some trouble," I observed. "Over in England we've been reading about your new crop of masked female bandits."

"Those things get exaggerated," the first policeman assured me. "It's the men masking as women that really mix us up. But brother, when we nab them, we jump on them with both feet."

"And you get so you can spot women almost as well as if they had naked faces," the second policeman volunteered. "You know, hands and all that."

"Especially all that," the first agreed with a chuckle. "Say, is it true that some girls don't mask over in England?"

"A number of them have picked up the fashion," I told him. "Only a few, though—the ones who always adopt the latest style, however extreme."

"They're usually masked in the British newscasts."

"I imagine it's arranged that way out of deference to American taste," I confessed. "Actually, not very many do mask."

The second policeman considered that. "Girls going down the street bare from the neck up." It was not clear whether he viewed the prospect with relish or moral distaste. Likely both.

"A few members keep trying to persuade Parliament to enact a law forbidding all masking," I continued, talking perhaps a bit too much.

The second policeman shook his head. "What an idea. You know, masks are a pretty good thing, brother. Couple of years more and I'm going to make my wife wear hers around the house."

The first policeman shrugged. "If women were to stop wearing masks, in six weeks you wouldn't know the difference. You get used to anything, if enough people do or don't do it."

I agreed, rather regretfully, and left them. I turned north on Broadway (old Tenth Avenue, I believe) and walked rapidly until I was beyond Inferno. Passing such an area of undecontaminated radioactivity always makes a person queasy. I thanked God there weren't any such in England, as yet.

The street was almost empty, though I was accosted by a couple of beggars with faces tunneled by H-bomb scars, whether real or of makeup putty, I couldn't tell. A fat woman held out a baby with webbed fingers and toes. I told myself it would have been deformed anyway and that she was only capitalizing on our fear of bomb-induced mutations. Still, I gave her a seven-and-a-half-

cent piece. Her mask made me feel I was paying tribute
to an African fetish.

"May all your children be blessed with one head and
two eyes, sir."

"Thanks," I said, shuddering, and hurried past her.

". . . There's only trash behind the mask, so turn your
head, stick to your task: Stay away, stay away—from—
the—girls!"

This last was the end of an anti-sex song being sung
by some religionists half a block from the circle-and-cross
insignia of a femalist temple. They reminded me only
faintly of our small tribe of British monastics. Above their
heads was a jumble of billboards advertising predigested
foods, wrestling instruction, radio handies and the like.

I stared at the hysterical slogans with disagreeable fascination. Since the female face and form have been
banned on American signs, the very letters of the adver-
tiser's alphabet have begun to crawl with sex—the fat-
bellied, big-breasted capital B, the lascivious double O.
However, I reminded myself, it is chiefly the mask that
so strangely accents sex in America.

A British anthropologist has pointed out, that, while it
took more than 5,000 years to shift the chief point of
sexual interest from the hips to the breasts, the next
transition to the face has taken less than 50 years. Comparing the American style with Moslem tradition is not
valid; Moslem women are compelled to wear veils, the
purpose of which is to make a husband's property private, while American women have only the compulsion
of fashion and use masks to create mystery.

Theory aside, the actual origins of the trend are to be
found in the anti-radiation clothing of World War III,
which led to masked wrestling, now a fantastically popular sport, and that in turn led to the current female
fashion. Only a wild style at first, masks quickly became
as necessary as brassieres and lipsticks had been earlier
in the century.

I finally realized that I was not speculating about masks
in general, but about what lay behind one in particular.
That's the devil of the things; you're never sure whether
a girl is heightening loveliness or hiding ugliness. I pic-

tured a cool, pretty face in which fear showed only in widened eyes. Then I remembered her blonde hair, rich against the blackness of the satin mask. She'd told me to come at the twenty-second hour—ten p.m.

I climbed to my apartment near the British Consulate; the elevator shaft had been shoved out of plumb by an old blast, a nuisance in these tall New York buildings. Before it occurred to me that I would be going out again, I automatically tore a tab from the film strip under my shirt. I developed it just to be sure. It showed that the total radiation I'd taken that day was still within the safety limit. I'm no phobic about it, as so many people are these days, but there's no point in taking chances.

I flopped down on the day bed and stared at the silent speaker and the dark screen of the video set. As always, they made me think, somewhat bitterly, of the two great nations of the world. Mutilated by each other, yet still strong, they were crippled giants poisoning the planet with their respective dreams of an impossible equality and as impossible success.

I fretfully twitched on the speaker. By luck, the newscaster was talking excitedly of the prospects of a bumper wheat crop, sown by planes across a dust bowl moistened by seeded rains. I listened carefully to the rest of the program (it was remarkably clear of Russian telejamming) but there was no further news of interest to me. And, of course, no mention of the Moon, though everyone knows that America and Russia are racing to develop their primary bases into fortresses capable of mutual assault and the launching of alphabet-bombs toward Earth. I myself knew perfectly well that the British electronic equipment I was helping trade for American wheat was destined for use in spaceships.

I switched off the newscast. It was growing dark and once again I pictured a tender, frightened face behind a mask. I hadn't had a date since England. It's exceedingly difficult to become acquainted with a girl in America, where as little as a smile, often, can set one of them yelping for the police—to say nothing of the increasingly puritanical morality and the roving gangs that keep most women indoors after dark. And naturally, the masks which are definitely not, as the Soviets claim, a last invention of capitalist degeneracy, but a sign of great psychological insecurity. The Russians have no masks, but they have their own signs of stress.

I went to the window and impatiently watched the darkness gather. I was getting very restless. After a while a ghostly violet cloud appeared to the south. My hair rose. Then I laughed. I had momentarily fancied it a radiation from the crater of the Hell-bomb, though I should instantly have known it was only the radio-induced glow in the sky over the amusement and residential area south of Inferno.

Promptly at twenty-two hours I stood before the door of my unknown girl friend's apartment. The electronic say-who-please said just that. I answered clearly, "Wysten Turner," wondering if she'd given my name to the mechanism. She evidently had, for the door opened. I walked into a small empty living room, my heart pounding a bit.

The room was expensively furnished with the latest pneumatic hassocks and sprawlers. There were some midgie books on the table. The one I picked up was the standard hard-boiled detective story in which two female murderers go gunning for each other.

The television was on. A masked girl in green was crooning a love song. Her right hand held something that blurred off into the foreground. I saw the set had a handie, which we haven't in England as yet, and curiously thrust my hand into the handie orifice beside the screen. Contrary to my expectations, it was not like slipping into a pulsing rubber glove, but rather as if the girl on the screen actually held my hand.

A door opened behind me. I jerked out my hand with as guilty a reaction as if I'd been caught peering through a keyhole.

She stood in the bedroom doorway. I think she was trembling. She was wearing a gray fur coat, white-speckled, and a gray velvet evening mask with shirred gray lace around the eyes and mouth. Her fingernails twinkled like silver.

It hadn't occurred to me that she'd expect us to go out.

"I should have told you," she said softly. Her mask veered nervously toward the books and the screen and

the room's dark corners. "But I can't possibly talk to
you here."

I said doubtfully, "There's a place near the Consulate . . ."

"I know where we can be together and talk," she said
rapidly. "If you don't mind."

As we entered the elevator I said, "I'm afraid I dismissed the cab."

But the cab driver hadn't gone for some reason of his
own. He jumped out and smirkingly held the front door
open for us. I told him we preferred to sit in back. He
sulkily opened the rear door, slammed it after us, jumped
in front and slammed the door behind him.

My companion leaned forward. "Heaven," she said.
The driver switched on the turbine and televisor.

"Why did you ask if I were a British subject?" I said,
to start the conversation.

She leaned away from me, tilting her mask close to the
window. "See the Moon," she said in a quick, dreamy
voice.

"But why, really?" I pressed, conscious of an irritation
that had nothing to do with her.

"It's edging up into the purple of the sky."

"And what's your name?"

"The purple makes it look yellower."

Just then I became aware of the source of my irritation.
It lay in the square of writhing light in the front of the cab
beside the driver.

I don't object to ordinary wrestling matches, though they
bore me, but I simply detest watching a man wrestle a
woman. The fact that the bouts are generally "on the
level," with the man greatly outclassed in weight and reach
and the masked females young and personable, only makes
them seem worse to me.

"Please turn off the screen," I requested the driver.

He shook his head without looking around. "Uh-uh,
man," he said. "They've been grooming that babe for
weeks for this bout with Little Zirk."

Infuriated, I reached forward, but my companion caught

my arm. "Please," she whispered frightenedly, shaking her head.

I settled back, frustrated. She was closer to me now, but silent and for a few minutes I watched the heaves and contortions of the powerful masked girl and her wiry masked opponent on the screen. His frantic scrambling at her reminded me of a male spider.

I jerked around, facing my companion. "Why did those three men want to kill you?" I asked sharply.

The eyeholes of her mask faced the screen. "Because they're jealous of me," she whispered.

"Why are they jealous?"

She still didn't look at me. "Because of him."

"Who?"

She didn't answer.

"I'm dreadfully sorry," I heard her say, "but you frightened me." I asked, "What *is* the matter?"

She still didn't look my way. She smelled nice.

"See here," I said laughingly, changing my tactics, "you really should tell me something about yourself. I don't even know what you look like."

I half playfully lifted my hand to the band of her neck. She gave it an astonishingly swift slap. I pulled it away in sudden pain. There were four tiny indentations on the back. From one of them a tiny bead of blood welled out as I watched. I looked at her silver fingernails and saw they were actually delicate and pointed metal caps.

"I'm dreadfully sorry," I heard her say, "but you frightened me. I thought for a moment you were going to . . ."

At last she turned to me. Her coat had fallen open. Her evening dress was Cretan Revival, a bodice of lace beneath and supporting the breasts without covering them.

"Don't be angry," she said, putting her arms around my neck. "You were wonderful this afternoon."

The soft gray velvet of her mask, molding itself to her cheek, pressed mine. Through the mask's lace the wet warm tip of her tongue touched my chin.

"I'm not angry," I said. "Just puzzled and anxious to help."

The cab stopped. To either side were black windows bordered by spears of broken glass. The sickly purple light showed a few ragged figures slowly moving toward us.

The driver muttered, "It's the turbine, man. We're grounded." He sat there hunched and motionless. "Wish it had happened somewhere else."

My companion whispered, "Five dollars is the usual amount."

She looked out so shudderingly at the congregating figures that I suppressed my indignation and did as she suggested. The driver took the bill without a word. As he started up, he put his hand out the window and I heard a few coins clink on the pavement.

My companion came back into my arms, but her mask faced the television screen, where the tall girl had just pinned the convulsively kicking Little Zirk.

"I'm so frightened," she breathed.

Heaven turned out to be an equally ruinous neighborhood, but it had a club with an awning and a huge doorman uniformed like a spaceman, but in gaudy colors. In my sensuous daze I rather liked it all. We stepped out of the cab just as a drunken old woman came down the sidewalk, her mask awry. A couple ahead of us turned their heads from the half revealed face, as if from an ugly body at the beach. As we followed them in I heard the doorman say, "Get along, grandma, and cover yourself."

Inside, everything was dimness and blue glows. She had said we could talk here, but I didn't see how. Besides the inevitable chorus of sneezes and coughs (they say America is fifty per cent allergic these days), there was a band going full blast in the latest robop style, in which an electronic composing machine selects an arbitrary sequence of tones into which the musicians weave their raucous little individualities.

Most of the people were in booths. The band was behind the bar. On a small platform beside them, a girl was dancing, stripped to her mask. The little cluster of men at the shadowy far end of the bar weren't looking at her.

We inspected the menu in gold script on the wall and pushed the buttons for breast of chicken, fried shrimps and two scotches. Moments later, the serving bell tinkled. I opened the gleaming panel and took out our drinks.

The cluster of men at the bar filed off toward the door,

but first they stared around the room. My companion had just thrown back her coat. Their look lingered on our booth. I noticed that there were three of them.

The band chased off the dancing girl with growls. I handed my companion a straw and we sipped our drinks.

"You wanted me to help you about something," I said. "Incidentally, I think you're lovely."

She nodded quick thanks, looked around, leaned forward. "Would it be hard for me to get to England?"

"No," I replied, a bit taken aback. "Provided you have an American passport."

"Are they difficult to get?"

"Rather," I said, surprised at her lack of information. "Your country doesn't like its nationals to travel, though it isn't quite as stringent as Russia."

"Could the British Consulate help me get a passport?"

"It's hardly their . . ."

"Could you?"

I realized we were being inspected. A man and two girls had passed opposite our table. The girls were tall and wolfish-looking, with spangled masks. The man stood jauntily between them like a fox on its hind legs.

My companion didn't glance at them, but she sat back. I noticed that one of the girls had a big yellow bruise on her forearm. After a moment they walked to a booth in the deep shadows.

"Know them?" I asked. She didn't reply. I finished my drink. "I'm not sure you'd like England," I said. "The austerity's altogether different from your American brand of misery."

She leaned forward again. "But I must get away," she whispered.

"Why?" I was getting impatient.

"Because I'm so frightened."

There were chimes. I opened the panel and handed her the friend shrimps. The sauce on my breast of chicken was a delicious steaming compound of almonds, soy and ginger. But something must have been wrong with the radionic oven that had thawed and heated it, for at the first bite I crunched a kernel of ice in the meat. These delicate mechanisms need constant repair and there aren't enough mechanics.

I put down my fork. "What are you really scared of?" I asked her.

For once her mask didn't waver from my face. As I waited I could feel the fears gathering without her naming them, tiny dark shapes swarming through the curved night outside, converging on the radioactive pest spot of New York, dipping into the margins of the purple. I felt a sudden rush of sympathy, a desire to protect the girl opposite me. The warm feeling added itself to the infatuation engendered in the cab.

"Everything," she said finally.

I nodded and touched her hand.

"I'm afraid of the Moon," she began, her voice going dreamy and brittle as it had in the cab. "You can't look at it and not think of guided bombs."

"It's the same Moon over England," I reminded her.

"But it's not England's Moon any more. It's ours and Russia's. You're not responsible."

"Oh, and then," she said with a tilt of her mask, "I'm afraid of the cars and the gangs and the loneliness and Inferno. I'm afraid of the lust that undresses your face. And—" her voice hushed—"I'm afraid of the wrestlers."

"Yes?" I prompted softly after a moment.

Her mask came forward. "Do you know something about the wrestlers?" she asked rapidly. "The ones that wrestle women, I mean. They often lose, you know. And then they have to have a girl to take their frustration out on. A girl who's soft and weak and terribly frightened. They need that, to keep them men. Other men don't want them to have a girl. Other men want them just to fight women and be heroes. But they must have a girl. It's horrible for her."

I squeezed her fingers tighter, as if courage could be transmitted—granting I had any. "I think I can get you to England," I said.

Shadows crawled onto the table and stayed there. I looked up at the three men who had been at the end of the bar. They were the men I had seen in the big coupe. They wore black sweaters and close-fitting black trousers. Their faces were as expressionless as dopers. Two of them stood about me. The other loomed over the girl.

"Drift off, man," I was told. I heard the other inform
the girl: "We'll wrestle a fall, sister. What shall it be?
Judo, slapsie or kill-who-can?"

I stood up. There are times when an Englishman simply
must be maltreated. But just then the foxlike man came
gliding in like the star of a ballet. The reaction of the other
three startled me. They were acutely embarrassed.

He smiled at them thinly. "You won't win my favor by
tricks like this," he said.

"Don't get the wrong idea, Zirk," one of them pleaded.

"I will if it's right," he said. "She told me what you tried
to do this afternoon. That won't endear you to me, either.
Drift."

They backed off awkwardly. "Let's get out of here," one
of them said loudly, as they turned. "I know a place where
they fight naked with knives."

Little Zirk laughed musically and slipped into the seat
beside my companion. She shrank from him, just a little.
I pushed my feet back, leaned forward.

"Who's your friend, baby?" he asked, not looking at her.

She passed the question to me with a little gesture. I told
him.

"British," he observed. "She's been asking you about
getting out of the country? About passports?" He smiled
pleasantly. "She likes to start running away. Don't you,
baby?" His small hand began to stroke her wrist, the
fingers bent a little, the tendons ridged, as if he were about
to grab and twist.

"Look here," I said sharply. "I have to be grateful to
you for ordering off those bullies, but—"

"Think nothing of it," he told me. "They're no harm
except when they're behind steering wheels. A well-trained
fourteen-year-old girl could cripple any one of them. Why,
even Theda here, if she went in for that sort of thing. . . ."
He turned to her, shifting his hand from her wrist to her
hair. He stroked it, letting the strands slip slowly through
his fingers. "You know I lost tonight, baby, don't you?" he
said softly.

I stood up. "Come along," I said to her. "Let's leave."

She just sat there, I couldn't tell if she was trembling.
I tried to read a message in her eyes through the mask.

"I'll take you away," I said to her. "I can do it. I really will."

He smiled at me. "She'd like to go with you," he said. "Wouldn't you, baby?"

"Will you or won't you?" I said to her. She still just sat there.

He slowly knotted his fingers in her hair.

"Listen, you little vermin," I snapped at him. "Take your hands off her."

He came up from the seat like a snake. I'm no fighter. I just know that the more scared I am, the harder and straighter I hit. This time I was lucky. But as he crumbled back, I felt a slap and four stabs of pain in my cheek. I clapped my hand to it. I could feel the four gashes made by her dagger finger caps, and the warm blood oozing out from them.

She didn't look at me. She was bending over little Zirk and cuddling her mask to his cheek and crooning: "There, there, don't feel bad, you'll be able to hurt me afterward."

There were sounds around us, but they didn't come close. I leaned forward and ripped the mask from her face.

I really don't know why I should have expected her face to be anything else. It was very pale, of course, and there weren't any cosmetics. I suppose there's no point in wearing any under a mask. The eyebrows were untidy and the lips chapped. But as for the general expression, as for the feelings crawling and wriggling across it—

Have you ever lifted a rock from damp soil? Have you ever watched the slimy white grubs?

I looked down at her, she up at me. "Yes, you're so frightened, aren't you?" I said sarcastically. "You dread this little nightly drama, don't you? You're scared to death."

And I walked right out into the purple night, still holding my hand to my bleeding cheek. No one stopped me, not even the girl wrestlers. I wished I could tear a tab from under my shirt, and test it then and there, and find I'd taken too much radiation, and so be able to ask to cross the Hudson and go down New Jersey, past the lingering radiance of the Narrows Bomb, and so on to Sandy Hook to wait for the rusty ship that would take me back over the seas to England.

THE QUEST FOR SAINT AQUIN

by Anthony Boucher

The Bishop of Rome, the head of the Holy, Catholic and
Apostolic Church, the Vicar of Christ on Earth—in short,
the Pope—brushed a cockroach from the filth-encrusted
wooden table, took another sip of the raw red wine, and
resumed his discourse.

"In some respects, Thomas," he smiled, "we are stronger
now than when we flourished in the liberty and exaltation
for which we still pray after Mass. We know, as they knew
in the catacombs, that those who are of our flock are indeed truly of it; that they belong to Holy Mother the
Church because they believe in the brotherhood of man
under the fatherhood of God—not because they can further their political aspirations, their social ambitions, their
business contacts."

" 'Not of the will of flesh, nor of the will of man, but of
God . . .' " Thomas quoted softly from St. John.

The Pope nodded. "We are, in a way, born again in
Christ; but there are still too few of us—too few even if
we include those other handfuls who are not of our faith,
but still acknowledge God through the teachings of Luther
or Lao-tse, Gautama Buddha or Joseph Smith. Too many
men still go to their deaths hearing no gospel preached to
them but the cynical self-worship of the Technarchy. And
that is why, Thomas, you must go forth on your quest."

"But Your Holiness," Thomas protested, "if God's word
and God's love will not convert them, what can saints and
miracles do?"

"I seem to recall," murmured the Pope, "that God's own

First published in 1951

458

Son once made a similar protest. But human nature, how-ever illogical it may seem, is part of His design, and we must cater to it. If signs and wonders can lead souls to God, then by all means let us find the signs and wonders. And what can be better for the purpose than this legendary Aquin? Come now, Thomas; be not too scrupulously exact in copying the doubts of your namesake, but prepare for your journey."

The Pope lifted the skin that covered the doorway and passed into the next room, with Thomas frowning at his heels. It was past legal hours and the main room of the tavern was empty. The swarthy innkeeper roused from his doze to drop to his knees and kiss the ring on the hand which the Pope extended to him. He rose crossing himself and at the same time glancing furtively about as though a Loyalty Checker might have seen him. Silently he indicated another door in the back, and the two priests passed through.

Toward the west the surf purred in an oddly gentle way at the edges of the fishing village. Toward the south the stars were sharp and bright; toward the north they dimmed a little in the persistent radiation of what had once been San Francisco.

"Your steed is here," the Pope said, with something like laughter in his voice.

"Steed?"

"We may be as poor and as persecuted as the primitive church, but we can occasionally gain greater advantages from our tyrants. I have secured for you a robass—gift of a leading Technarch who, like Nicodemus, does good by stealth—a secret convert, and converted, indeed, by that very Aquin whom you seek."

It looked harmlessly like a woodpile sheltered against possible rain. Thomas pulled off the skins and contemplated the sleek functional lines of the robass. Smiling, he stowed his minimal gear into its panniers and climbed into the foam saddle. The starlight was bright enough so that he could check the necessary coordinates on his map and feed the data into the electronic controls.

Meanwhile there was a murmur of Latin in the still night air, and the Pope's hand moved over Thomas in the im-memorial symbol. Then he extended that hand, first for the

kiss on the ring, and then again for the handclasp of a man
to a friend he may never see again.

Thomas looked back once more as the robass moved off.
The Pope was wisely removing his ring and slipping it into
the hollow heel of his shoe.

Thomas looked hastily up at the sky. On that altar at
least the candles still burnt openly to the glory of God.

Thomas had never ridden a robass before, but he was
inclined, within their patent limitations, to trust the works
of the Technarchy. After several miles had proved that the
coordinates were duly registered, he put up the foam back-
rest, said his evening office (from memory; the possession
of a breviary meant the death sentence), and went to sleep.

They were skirting the devastated area to the east of the
Bay when he awoke. The foam seat and back had given
him his best sleep in years; and it was with difficulty that
he smothered an envy of the Technarchs and their creature
comforts.

He said his morning office, breakfasted lightly, and took
his first opportunity to inspect the robass in full light. He
admired the fast-plodding, articulated legs, so necessary
since roads had degenerated to, at best, trails in all save
metropolitan areas; the side wheels that could be lowered
into action if surface conditions permitted; and above all
the smooth black mound that housed the electronic brain—
the brain that stored commands and data concerning ultimate objectives and made its own decisions on how to fulfill those commands in view of those data; the brain that
made this thing neither a beast, like the ass his Saviour had
ridden, nor a machine, like the jeep of his many-times-
great-grandfather, but a robot . . . a robass.

"Well," said a voice, "what do you think of the ride."

Thomas looked about him. The area of this fringe of
desolation was as devoid of people as it was of vegetation.

"Well," the voice repeated unemotionally. "Are not
priests taught to answer when spoken to politely."

There was no querying inflection to the question. No inflection at all—each syllable was at the same dead level.
It sounded strange, mechani . . .

Thomas stared at the black mound of brain. "Are you
talking to me?" he asked the robass.

"Ha ha," the voice said in lieu of laughter. "Surprised, are you not."

"Somewhat," Thomas confessed. "I thought the only robots who could talk were in library information service and such."

"I am a new model. Designed-to-provide-conversation-to-entertain-the-way-worn-traveler," the robass said slurring the words together as though that phrase of promotional copy was released at once by one of his simplest binary synapses.

"Well," said Thomas simply. "One keeps learning new marvels."

"I am no marvel. I am a very simple robot. You do not know much about robots do you."

"I will admit that I have never studied the subject closely. I'll confess to being a little shocked at the whole robotic concept. It seems almost as though man were arrogating to himself the powers of—" Thomas stopped abruptly.

"Do not fear," the voice droned on. "You may speak freely. All data concerning your vocation and mission have been fed into me. That was necessary otherwise I might inadvertently betray you."

Thomas smiled. "You know," he said, "this might be rather pleasant—having one other being that one can talk to without fear of betrayal, aside from one's confessor."

"Being," the robass repeated. "Are you not in danger of lapsing into heretical thoughts."

"To be sure, it *is* a little difficult to know how to think of you—one who can talk and think but has no soul."

"Are you sure of that."

"Of course I— Do you mind very much," Thomas asked, "if we stop talking for a little while? I should like to meditate and adjust myself to the situation."

"I do not mind. I never mind. I only obey. Which is to say that I *do* mind. This is very confusing language which has been fed into me."

"If we are together long," said Thomas, "I shall try teaching you Latin. I think you might like that better. And now let me meditate."

The robass was automatically veering further east to escape the permanent source of radiation which had been the first cyclotron. Thomas fingered his coat. The combination of ten small buttons and one large made for a peculiar fashion; but it was much safer than carrying a rosary, and fortunately the Loyalty Checkers had not yet realized the fashion's functional purpose.

The Glorious Mysteries seemed appropriate to the possible glorious outcome of his venture; but his meditations were unable to stay fixedly on the Mysteries. As he murmured his *Aves* he was thinking:

If the prophet Balaam conversed with his ass, surely I may converse with my robass. Balaam has always puzzled me. He was not an Israelite; he was a man of Moab, which worshipped Baal and was warring against Israel; and yet he was a prophet of the Lord. He blessed the Israelites when he was commanded to curse them; and for his reward he was slain by the Israelites when they triumphed over Moab. The whole story has no shape, no moral; it is as though it was there to say that there are portions of the Divine Plan which we will never understand . . .

He was nodding in the foam seat when the robass halted abruptly, rapidly adjusting itself to exterior data not previously fed into its calculations. Thomas blinked up to see a giant of a man glaring down at him.

"Inhabited area a mile ahead," the man barked. "If you're going there, show your access pass. If you ain't, steer off the road and stay off."

Thomas noted that they were indeed on what might roughly be called a road, and that the robass had lowered its side wheels and retracted its legs. "We—" he began, then changed it to "I'm not going there. Just on toward the mountains. We—I'll steer around."

The giant grunted and was about to turn when a voice shouted from the crude shelter at the roadside. "Hey Joe! Remember about robasses!"

Joe turned back. "Yeah, tha's right. Been a rumor about some robass got into the hands of Christians." He spat on the dusty road. "Guess I better see an ownership certificate."

To his other doubts Thomas now added certain uncharitable suspicions as to the motives of the Pope's anonymous Nicodemus, who had not provided him with any such certificate. But he made a pretense of searching for it, first touching his right hand to his forehead as if in thought, then fumbling low on his chest, then reaching his hand first to his left shoulder, then to his right.

The guard's eyes remained blank as he watched this furtive version of the sign of the cross. Then he looked down. Thomas followed his gaze to the dust of the road, where the guard's hulking right foot had drawn the two curved lines which a child uses for its sketch of a fish—and which the Christians in the catacombs had employed as a punning symbol of their faith. His boot scuffed out the fish as he called to his unseen mate, " 's OK, Fred!" and added, "Get going, mister."

The robass waited until they were out of earshot before it observed, "Pretty smart. You will make a secret agent yet."

"How did you see what happened?" Thomas asked. "You don't have any eyes."

"Modified psi factor. Much more efficient."

"Then . . ." Thomas hesitated. "Does that mean you can read my thoughts?"

"Only a very little. Do not let it worry you. What I can read does not interest me it is such nonsense."

"Thank you," said Thomas.

"To believe in God. Bah." (It was the first time Thomas had ever heard that word pronounced just as it is written.) "I have a perfectly constructed logical mind that cannot commit such errors."

"I have a friend," Thomas smiled, "who is infallible too. But only on occasions and then only because God is with him."

"No human being is infallible."

"Then imperfection," asked Thomas, suddenly feeling a little of the spirit of the aged Jesuit who had taught him philosophy, "has been able to create perfection?"

"Do not quibble," said the robass. "That is no more absurd than your own belief that God who is perfection created man who is imperfection."

Thomas wished that his old teacher were here to answer that one. At the same time he took some comfort in the fact that, retort and all, the robass had still not answered his own objection. "I am not sure," he said, "that this comes under the head of conversation-to-entertain-the-way-weary-traveler. Let us suspend debate while you tell me what, if anything, robots do believe."

"What we have been fed."

"But your minds work on that; surely they must evolve ideas of their own?"

"Sometimes they do and if they are fed imperfect data they may evolve very strange ideas. I have heard of one robot on an isolated space station who worshipped a God of robots and would not believe that any man had created him."

"I suppose," Thomas mused, "he argued that he had hardly been created in our image. I am glad that we—at least they, the Technarchs—have wisely made only usuform robots like you, each shaped for his function, and never tried to reproduce man himself."

"It would not be logical," said the robass. "Man is an all-purpose machine but not well designed for any one purpose. And yet I have heard that once . . ."

The voice stopped abruptly in midsentence.

So even robots have their dreams, Thomas thought. That once there existed a super-robot in the image of his creator Man. From that thought could be developed a whole robotic theology . . .

Suddenly Thomas realized that he had dozed again and again been waked by an abrupt stop. He looked around. They were at the foot of a mountain—presumably the mountain on his map, long ago named for the Devil but now perhaps sanctified beyond measure—and there was no one else anywhere in sight.

"All right," the robass said. "By now I show plenty of dust and wear and tear and I can show you how to adjust my mileage recorder. You can have supper and a good night's sleep and we can go back."

Thomas gasped. "But my mission is to find Aquin. I can sleep while you go on. You don't need any sort of rest or anything, do you?" he added considerately.

"Of course not. But what is your mission."

"To find Aquin," Thomas repeated patiently. "I don't know what details have been—what is it you say?—fed into you. But reports have reached His Holiness of an ex-

tremely saintly man who lived many years ago in this
area—"

"I know I know I know," said the robass. "His logic was
such that everyone who heard him was converted to the
Church and do not I wish that I had been there to put in a
word or two and since he died his secret tomb has become
a place of pilgrimage and many are the miracles that are
wrought there above all the greatest sign of sanctity that
his body has been preserved incorruptible and in these
times you need signs and wonders for the people."

Thomas frowned. It all sounded hideously irreverent and
contrived when stated in that deadly inhuman monotone.
When His Holiness had spoken of Aquin, one thought of
the glory of a man of God upon earth—the eloquence of
St. John Chrysostom. the cogency of St. Thomas Aquinas,
the poetry of St. John of the Cross . . . and above all that
physical miracle vouchsafed to few even of the saints, the
supernatural preservation of the flesh . . . "for Thou shalt
not suffer Thy holy one to see corruption . . ."

But the robass spoke, and one thought of cheap show-
manship hunting for a Cardiff Giant to pull in the mobs . . .

The robass spoke again. "Your mission is not to find
Aquin. It is to report that you have found him. Then your
occasionally infallible friend can with a reasonably clear
conscience canonize him and proclaim a new miracle and
many will be the converts and greatly will the faith of the
flock be strengthened. And in these days of difficult travel
who will go on pilgrimages and find out that there is no
more Aquin than there is God."

"Faith cannot be based on a lie," said Thomas.

"No," said the robass. "I do not mean no period. I mean
no question mark with an ironical inflection. This speech
problem must surely have been conquered in that one
perfect . . ."

Again he stopped in midsentence. But before Thomas
could speak he had resumed, "Does it matter what small
untruth leads people into the Church if once they are in
they will believe what you think to be the great truths. The
report is all that is needed not the discovery. Comfortable
though I am you are already tired of traveling very tired
you have many small muscular aches from sustaining an

unaccustomed position and with the best intentions I am bound to jolt a little a jolting which will get worse as we ascend the mountain and I am forced to adjust my legs disproportionately to each other but proportionately to the slope. You will find the remainder of this trip twice as uncomfortable as what has gone before. The fact that you do not seek to interrupt me indicates that you do not disagree do you. You know that the only sensible thing is to sleep here on the ground for a change and start back in the morning or even stay here two days resting to make a more plausible lapse of time. Then you can make your report and—"

Somewhere in the recess of his somnolent mind Thomas uttered the names, "Jesus, Mary and Joseph!" Gradually through these recesses began to filter a realization that an absolutely uninfected monotone is admirably adapted to hypnotic purposes.

"Retro me, Satanas!" Thomas exclaimed aloud, then added, "Up the mountain. That is an order and you must obey."

"I obey," said the robass. "But what did you say before that."

"I beg your pardon," said Thomas. "I must start teaching you Latin."

The little mountain village was too small to be considered an inhabited area worthy of guard-control and passes; but it did possess an inn of sorts.

As Thomas dismounted from the robass, he began fully to realize the accuracy of those remarks about small muscular aches, but he tried to show his discomfort as little as possible. He was in no mood to give the modified psi factor the chance of registering the thought, "I told you so."

The waitress at the inn was obviously a Martian-American hybrid. The highly developed Martian chest expansion and the highly developed American breasts made a spectacular combination. Her smile was all that a stranger could, and conceivably a trifle more than he should ask; and she was eagerly ready, not only with prompt service of passable food, but with full details of what little information there was to offer about the mountain settlement.

But she showed no reaction at all when Thomas offhandedly arranged two knives in what might have been an X.

As he stretched his legs after breakfast, Thomas thought of her chest and breasts—purely, of course, as a symbol of the extraordinary nature of her origin. What a sign of the divine care for His creatures that these two races, separated for countless eons, should prove fertile to each other!

And yet there remained the fact that the offspring, such as this girl, were sterile to both races—a fact that had proved both convenient and profitable to certain unspeakable interplanetary entrepreneurs. And what did that fact teach us as to the Divine Plan?

Hastily Thomas reminded himself that he had not yet said his morning office.

It was close to evening when Thomas returned to the robass stationed before the inn. Even though he had expected nothing in one day, he was still unreasonably disappointed. Miracles should move faster.

He knew these backwater villages, where those drifted who were either useless to or resentful of the Technarchy. The technically high civilization of the Technarchic Empire, on all three planets, existed only in scattered metropolitan centers near major blasting ports. Elsewhere, aside from the areas of total devastation, the drifters, the morons, the malcontents had subsided into a crude existence a thousand years old, in hamlets which might go a year without even seeing a Loyalty Checker—though by some mysterious grapevine (and Thomas began to think again about modified psi factors) any unexpected technological advance in one of these hamlets would bring Checkers by the swarm.

He had talked with stupid men, he had talked with lazy men, he had talked with clever and angry men. But he had not talked with any man who responded to his unobtrusive signs, any man to whom he would dare ask a question containing the name of Aquin.

"Any luck," said the robass, and added "question mark."

"I wonder if you ought to talk to me in public," said Thomas a little irritably. "I doubt if these villagers know about talking robots."

"It is time that they learned then. But if it embarrasses you you may order me to stop."

"I'm tired," said Thomas. "Tired beyond embarrassment. And to answer your question mark, no. No luck at all. Exclamation point."

"We will go back tonight then," said the robass.

"I hope you meant that with a question mark. The answer," said Thomas hesitantly, "is no. I think we ought to stay overnight anyway. People always gather at the inn of an evening. There's a chance of picking up something."

"Ha, ha," said the robass.

"That is a laugh?" Thomas inquired.

"I wished to express the fact that I had recognized the humor in your pun."

"My pun?"

"I was thinking the same thing myself. The waitress is by humanoid standards very attractive, well worth picking up."

"Now look. You know I meant nothing of the kind. You know that I'm a—" He broke off. It was hardly wise to utter the word *priest* aloud.

"And you know very well that the celibacy of the clergy is a matter of discipline and not of doctrine. Under your own Pope priests of other rites such as the Byzantine and the Anglican are free of vows of celibacy. And even within the Roman rite to which you belong there have been eras in history when that vow was not taken seriously even on the highest levels of the priesthood. You are tired you need refreshment both in body and in spirit you need comfort and warmth. For is it not written in the book of the prophet Isaiah Rejoice for joy with her that ye may be satisfied with the breasts of her consolation and is it—"

"Hell!" Thomas exploded suddenly. "Stop it before you begin quoting the Song of Solomon. Which is strictly an allegory concerning the love of Christ for His Church, or so they kept telling me in seminary."

"You see how fragile and human you are," said the robass. "I a robot have caused you to swear."

"*Distinguo*," said Thomas smugly. "I said *Hell*, which is certainly not taking the name of *my* Lord in vain." He walked into the inn feeling momentarily satisfied with himself . . . and markedly puzzled as to the extent and variety of data that seemed to have been "fed into" the robass.

Never afterward was Thomas able to reconstruct that evening in absolute clarity.

It was undoubtedly because he was irritated—with the robass, with his mission, and with himself—that he drank at all of the crude local wine. It was undoubtedly because he was so physically exhausted that it affected him so promptly and unexpectedly.

He had flashes of memory. A moment of spilling a glass over himself and thinking, "How fortunate that clerical garments are forbidden so that no one can recognize the disgrace of a man of the cloth!" A moment of listening to a bawdy set of verses of *A Space-suit Built for Two,* and another moment of his interrupting the singing with a sonorous declamation of passages from the *Song of Songs* in Latin.

He was never sure whether one remembered moment was real or imaginary. He could taste a warm mouth and feel the tingling of his fingers at the touch of Martian-American flesh; but he was never certain whether this was true memory or part of the Ashtaroth-begotten dream that had begun to ride him.

Nor was he ever certain which of his symbols, or to whom, was so blatantly and clumsily executed as to bring forth a gleeful shout of "God-damned Christian dog!" He did remember marveling that those who most resolutely disbelieved in God still needed Him to blaspheme by. And then the torment began.

He never knew whether or not a mouth had touched his lips, but there was no question that many solid fists had found them. He never knew whether his fingers had touched breasts, but they had certainly been trampled by heavy heels. He remembered a face that laughed aloud while its owner swung the chair that broke two ribs. He remembered another face with red wine dripping over it from an upheld bottle, and he remembered the gleam of the candlelight on the bottle as it swung down.

The next he remembered was the ditch and the morning and the cold. It was particularly cold because all of his clothes were gone, along with much of his skin. He could not move. He could only lie there and look.

He saw them walk by, the ones he had spoken with yesterday, the ones who had been friendly. He saw them
glance at him and turn their eyes quickly away. He saw
the waitress pass by. She did not even glance; she knew
what was in the ditch.

The robass was nowhere in sight. He tried to project his
thoughts, tried desperately to hope in the psi factor.

A man whom Thomas had not seen before was coming
along fingering the buttons of his coat. There were ten
small buttons and one large one, and the man's lips were
moving silently.

This man looked into the ditch. He paused a moment
and looked around him. There was a shout of laughter
somewhere in the near distance.

The Christian hastily walked on down the pathway, de-
voutly saying his button-rosary.

Thomas closed his eyes.

He opened them on a small neat room. They moved
from the rough wooden walls to the rough but clean and
warm blankets that covered him. Then they moved to the
lean dark face that was smiling over him.

"You feel better now?" a deep voice asked. "I know.
You want to say 'Where am I?' and you think it will sound
foolish. You are at the inn. It is the only good room."

"I can't afford—" Thomas started to say. Then he remembered that he could afford literally nothing. Even his
few emergency credits had vanished when he was stripped.

"It's all right. For the time being, I'm paying," said the
deep voice. "You feel like maybe a little food?"

"Perhaps a little herring," said Thomas . . . and was
asleep within the next minute.

When he next awoke there was a cup of hot coffee beside him. The real thing, too, he promptly discovered. Then
the deep voice said apologetically, "Sandwiches. It is all
they have in the inn today."

Only on the second sandwich did Thomas pause long
enough to notice that it was smoked swamphog, one of his
favorite meats. He ate the second with greater leisure, and
was reaching for a third when the dark man said, "Maybe
that is enough for now. The rest later."

Thomas gestured at the plate. "Won't you have one?"

"No thank you. They are all swamphog."

Confused thoughts went through Thomas' mind. The Venusian swamphog is a ruminant. Its hoofs are not cloven. He tried to remember what he had once known of Mosaic dietary law. Someplace in Leviticus, wasn't it?

The dark man followed his thoughts. *"Treff,"* he said.

"I beg your pardon?"

"Not kosher."

Thomas frowned. "You admit to me that you're an Orthodox Jew? How can you trust me? How do you know I'm not a Checker?"

"Believe me, I trust you. You were very sick when I brought you here. I sent everybody away because I did not trust them to hear things you said . . . Father," he added lightly.

Thomas struggled with words. "I . . . I didn't deserve you. I was drunk and disgraced myself and my office. And when I was lying there in the ditch I didn't even think to pray. I put my trust in . . . God help me in the modified psi factor of a robass!"

"And He did help you," the Jew reminded him. "Or He allowed me to."

"And they all walked by," Thomas groaned. "Even one that was saying his rosary. He went right on by. And then you come along—the good Samaritan."

"Believe me," said the Jew wryly, "if there is one thing I'm not, it's a Samaritan. Now go to sleep again. I will try to find your robass . . . and the other thing."

He had left the room before Thomas could ask him what he meant.

Later that day the Jew—Abraham, his name was— reported that the robass was safely sheltered from the weather behind the inn. Apparently it had been wise enough not to startle him by engaging in conversation.

It was not until the next day that he reported on "the other thing."

"Believe me, Father," he said gently, "after nursing you there's little I don't know about who you are and why you're here. Now there are some Christians here I know, and they know me. We trust each other. Jews may still be hated; but no longer, God be praised, by worshipers of the same Lord. So I explained about you. One of them," he added with a smile, "turned very red."

"God has forgiven him," said Thomas. "There were people near—the same people who attacked me. Could he be expected to risk his life for mine?"

"I seem to recall that that is precisely what your Messiah did expect. But who's being particular? Now that they know who you are, they want to help you. See: they gave me this map for you. The trail is steep and tricky; it's good you have the robass. They ask just one favor of you: When you came back will you hear their confession and say Mass? There's a cave near here where it's safe."

"Of course. These friends of yours, they've told you about Aquin?"

The Jew hesitated a long time before he said slowly, "Yes . . ."

"And . . . ?"

"Believe me, my friend, I don't know. So it seems a miracle. It helps to keep their faith alive. My own faith . . . *nu*, it's lived for a long time on miracles three thousand years old and more. Perhaps if I had heard Aquin himself . . ."

"You don't mind," Thomas asked, "if I pray for you, in my faith?"

Abraham grinned, "Pray in good health, Father."

The not-quite-healed ribs ached agonizingly as he climbed into the foam saddle. The robass stood patiently while he fed in the coordinates from the map. Not until they were well away from the village did it speak.

"Anyway," it said, "now you're safe for good."

"What do you mean?"

"As soon as we get down from the mountain you deliberately look up a Checker. You turn in the Jew. From then on you are down in the books as a faithful servant of the Technarchy and you have not harmed a hair of the head of your own flock."

Thomas snorted. "You're slipping, Satan. That one doesn't even remotely tempt me. It's inconceivable."

"I did best did not I with the breasts. Your God has said it the spirit indeed is willing but the flesh is weak."

"And right now," said Thomas, "the flesh is too weak for even fleshly temptations. Save your breath . . . or whatever it is you use."

They climbed the mountain in silence. The trail indicated by the coordinates was a winding and confused one, obviously designed deliberately to baffle any possible Checkers.

Suddenly Thomas roused himself from his button-rosary (on a coat lent by the Christian who had passed by) with a startled "Hey!" as the robass plunged directly into a heavy thicket of bushes.

"Coordinates say so," the robass stated tersely.

For a moment Thomas felt like the man in the nursery rhyme who fell into a bramble bush and scratched out both his eyes. Then the bushes were gone, and they were plodding along a damp narrow passageway through solid stone, in which even the robass seemed to have some difficulty with his footing.

Then they were in a rocky chamber some four meters high and ten in diameter, and there on a sort of crude stone catafalque lay the uncorrupted body of a man.

Thomas slipped from the foam saddle, groaning as his ribs stabbed him, sank to his knees, and offered up a wordless hymn of gratitude. He smiled at the robass and hoped the psi factor could detect the elements of pity and triumph in that smile.

Then a frown of doubt crossed his face as he approached the body. "In canonization proceedings in the old time," he said, as much to himself as to the robass, "they used to have what they called a devil's advocate, whose duty it was to throw every possible doubt on the evidence."

"You would be well cast in such a role Thomas," said the robass.

"If I were," Thomas muttered, "I'd wonder about caves. Some of them have peculiar properties of preserving bodies by a sort of mummification . . ."

The robass had clumped close to the catafalque. "This body is not mummified," he said. "Do not worry."

"Can the psi factor tell you that much?" Thomas smiled.

"No," said the robass. "But I will show you why Aquin could never be mummified."

He raised his articulated foreleg and brought its hoof down hard on the hand of the body. Thomas cried out with horror at the sacrilege—then stared hard at the crushed hand.

There was no blood, no ichor of embalming, no bruised flesh. Nothing but a shredded skin and beneath it an intricate mass of plastic tubes and metal wires.

The silence was long. Finally the robass said, "It was well that you should know. Only you of course."

"And all the time," Thomas gasped, "my sought-for saint was only your dream . . . the one perfect robot in man's form."

"His maker died and his secrets were lost," the robass said. "No matter we will find them again."

"All for nothing. For less than nothing. The 'miracle' was wrought by the Technarchy."

"When Aquin died," the robass went on, "and put died in quotation marks it was because he suffered some mechanical defects and did not dare have himself repaired because that would reveal his nature. This is for you only to know. Your report of course will be that you found the body of Aquin it was unimpaired and indeed incorruptible. That is the truth and nothing but the truth if it is not the whole truth who is to care. Let your infallible friend use the report and you will not find him ungrateful I assure you."

"Holy Spirit, give me grace and wisdom," Thomas muttered.

"Your mission has been successful. We will return now the Church will grow and your God will gain many more worshipers to hymn His praise into His nonexistent ears."

"Damn you!" Thomas exclaimed. "And that would be indeed a curse if you had a soul to damn."

"You are certain that I have not," said the robass. "Question mark."

"I know what you are. You are in very truth the devil, prowling about the world seeking the destruction of men. You are the business that prowls in the dark. You are a purely functional robot constructed and fed to tempt me, and the tape of your data is the tape of Screwtape."

"Not to tempt you," said the robass. "Not to destroy you. To guide and save you. Our best calculators indicate a probability of 51.5 per cent that within twenty years you will be the next Pope. If I can teach you wisdom and practicality in your actions the probability can rise as high as 97.2 or very nearly to certainty. Do not you wish to see the Church governed as you know you can govern it. If you report failure on this mission you will be out of favor with your friend who is as even you admit fallible at most times. You will lose the advantages of position and contact that can lead you to the cardinal's red hat even though you may never wear it under the Technarchy and from there to—"

"Stop!" Thomas' face was alight and his eyes aglow with something the psi factor had never detected there before. "It's all the other way round, don't you see? *This* is the triumph! *This* is the perfect ending to the quest!"

The articulated foreleg brushed the injured hand. "This question mark."

"This is *your* dream. This is *your* perfection. And what came of this perfection? This perfect logical brain—this all-purpose brain, not functionally specialized like yours—knew that it was made by man, and its reason forced it to believe that man was made by God. And it saw that its duty lay to man its maker, and beyond him to his Maker, God. Its duty was to convert man, to augment the glory of God. And it converted by the pure force of its perfect brain!

"Now I understand the name Aquin," he went on to himself. "We've known of Thomas Aquinas, the Angelic Doctor, the perfect reasoner of the church. His writings are lost, but surely somewhere in the world we can find a copy. We can train our young men to develop his reasoning still further. We have trusted too long in faith alone; this is not an age of faith. We must call reason into our service—and Aquin has shown us that perfect reason can lead only to God!"

"Then it is all the more necessary that you increase the probabilities of becoming Pope to carry out this program. Get in the foam saddle we will go back and on the way I will teach you little things that will be useful in making certain—"

"No," said Thomas. "I am not so strong as St. Paul, who could glory in his imperfections and rejoice that he had been given an imp of Satan to buffet him. No; I will rather pray with the Saviour, 'Lead us not into temptation.' I know myself a little. I am weak and full of uncertainties and you are very clever. Go. I'll find my way back alone."

"You are a sick man. Your ribs are broken and they ache. You can never make the trip by yourself you need my help. If you wish you can order me to be silent. It is most necessary to the Church that you get back safely to the Pope with your report you cannot put yourself before the Church."

"Go!" Thomas cried. "Go back to Nicodemus . . . or Judas! That is an order. Obey!"

"You do not think do you that I was really conditioned to obey your orders. I will wait in the village. If you get that far you will rejoice at the sight of me."

The legs of the robass clumped off down the stone passageway. As their sound died away, Thomas fell to his knees beside the body of that which he could hardly help thinking of as St. Aquin the Robot.

His ribs hurt more excruciatingly than ever. The trip alone would be a terrible one . . .

His prayers arose, as the text has it, like clouds of insense, and as shapeless as those clouds. But through all his thoughts ran the cry of the father of the epileptic in Caesarea Philippi:

I believe, O Lord; help thou mine unbelief!

SURFACE TENSION

by James Blish

Dr. Chatvieux took a long look over the microscope, leaving la Ventura with nothing to do but look out at the dead landscape of Hydrot. Waterscape, he thought, would be a better word. The new world had shown only one small, triangular continent, set amid endless ocean; and even the continent was mostly swamp.

The wreck of the seed-ship lay broken squarely across the one real spur of rock Hydrot seemed to possess, which reared a magnificent twenty-one feet above sea-level. From this eminence, la Ventura could see forty miles to the horizon across a flat bed of mud. The red light of the star Tau Ceti, glinting upon thousands of small lakes, pools, ponds, and puddles, made the watery plain look like a mosaic of onyx and ruby.

"If I were a religious man," the pilot said suddenly, "I'd call this a plain case of divine vengeance."

Chatvieux said: "Hmn?"

"It's as if we've been struck down for—is it *hubris*, arrogant pride?"

"Well, is it?" Chatvieux said, looking up at last. "I don't feel exactly swollen with pride at the moment. Do you?"

"I'm not exactly proud of my piloting," la Ventura admitted. "But that isn't quite what I meant. I was thinking about why we came here in the first place. It takes arrogant pride to think that you can scatter men, or at least things like men, all over the face of the Galaxy. It takes even more pride to do the job—to pack up all the equip-

First published in 1952

ment and move from planet to planet and actually make
men suitable for every place you touch."

"I suppose it does," Chatvieux said. "But we're only one
of several hundred seed-ships in this limb of the Galaxy,
so I doubt that the gods picked us out as special sinners."
He smiled drily. "If they had, maybe they'd have left us
our ultraphone, so the Colonization Council could hear
about our cropper. Besides, Paul, we try to produce men
adapted to Earthlike planets, nothing more. We've sense
enough—humility enough, if you like—to know that we
can't adapt men to Jupiter or to Tau Ceti."

"Anyhow, we're here," la Ventura said grimly. "And
we aren't going to get off. Phil tells me that we don't even
have our germ-cell bank any more, so we can't seed this
place in the usual way. We've been thrown onto a dead
world and dared to adapt to it. What are the panatropes
going to do—provide built-in waterwings?"

"No," Chatvieux said calmly. "You and I and the rest
of us are going to die, Paul. Panatropic techniques don't
work on the body, only on the inheritance-carrying factors.
We can't give you built-in waterwings, any more than we
can give you a new set of brains. I think we'll be able to
populate this world with men, but we won't live to see it."

The pilot thought about it, a lump of cold collecting
gradually in his stomach. "How long do you give us?" he
said at last.

"Who knows? A month, perhaps."

The bulkhead leading to the wrecked section of the ship
was pushed back, admitting salty, muggy air, heavy with
carbon dioxide. Philip Strasvogel, the communications
officer, came in, tracking mud. Like la Ventura, he was
now a man without a function, but it did not appear to
bother him. He unbuckled from around his waist a canvas
belt into which plastic vials were stuffed like cartridges.

"More samples, Doc," he said. "All alike—water, very
wet. I have some quicksand in one boot, too. Find anything?"

"A good deal, Phil. Thanks. Are the others around?"

Strasvogel poked his head out and hallooed. Other voices
rang out over the mudflats. Minutes later, the rest of the
survivors were crowding into the panatrope deck: Salton-

stall, Chatvieux's senior assistant; Eunice Wagner, the only remaining ecologist; Eleftherios Venezuelos, the delegate from the Colonization Council; and Joan Heath, a midshipman whose duties, like la Ventura's and Strasvogel's, were now without meaning.

Five men and two women—to colonize a planet on which standing room meant treading water.

They came in quietly and found seats or resting places on the deck, on the edges of tables, in corners.

Venezuelos said: "What's the verdict, Dr. Chatvieux?"

"This place isn't dead," Chatvieux said. "There's life in the sea and in the fresh water, both. On the animal side of the ledger, evolution seems to have stopped with the crustacea; the most advanced form I've found is a tiny crayfish, from one of the local rivulets. The ponds and puddles are well-stocked with protozoa and small metazoans, right up to a wonderfully variegated rotifer population—including a castle-building rotifer like Earth's *Floscularidae*. The plants run from simple algae to the thalluslike species."

"The sea is about the same," Eunice said, "I've found some of the larger simple metazoans—jellyfish and so on—and some crayfish almost as big as lobsters. But it's normal to find salt-water species running larger than freshwater."

"In short," Chatvieux said, "we'll survive here—if we fight."

"Wait a minute," la Ventura said. "You've just finished telling me that we wouldn't survive. And you were talking about us, not about the species, because we don't have our germ-cell banks any more. What's—"

"I'll get to that in a moment," Chatvieux said. "Saltonstall, what would you think of taking to the sea? We came out of it once; maybe we could come out of it again."

"No good," Saltonstall said immediately. "*I* like the idea, but I don't think this planet ever heard of Swinburne, or Homer, either. Looking at it as a colonization problem, as if we weren't involved ourselves, I wouldn't give you a credit for *epi oinopa ponton*. The evolutionary pressure there is too high, the competition from other species is prohibitive; seeding the sea would be the last thing we attempt. The colonists wouldn't have a chance to learn a thing before they were destroyed."

"Why?" la Ventura said. The death in his stomach was becoming hard to placate.

"Eunice, do your sea-going Coelenterates include anything like the Portuguese man-of-war?"

The ecologist nodded.

"There's your answer, Paul," Saltonstall said. "The sea is out. It's got to be fresh water, where the competing creatures are less formidable and there are more places to hide."

"We can't compete with a jellyfish?" la Ventura asked, swallowing.

"No, Paul," Chatvieux said. "The panatropes make adaptations, not gods. They take human germ-cells—in this case, our own, since our bank was wiped out in the crash—and modify them toward creatures who can live in any reasonable environment. The result will be manlike and intelligent. It usually shows the donor's personality pattern, too.

"But we can't transmit memory. The adapted man is worse than a child in his new environment. He has no history, no techniques, no precedents, not even a language. Ordinarily the seeding teams more or less take him through elementary school before they leave the planet, but we won't survive long enough for that. We'll have to design our colonists with plenty of built-in protections and locate them in the most favorable environment possible, so that at least some of them will survive the learning process."

The pilot thought about it, but nothing occurred to him which did not make the disaster seem realer and more intimate with each passing second. "One of the new creatures can have my personality pattern, but it won't be able to remember being me. Is that right?"

"That's it. There may be just the faintest of residuums —panatropy's given us some data which seem to support the old Jungian notion of ancestral memory. But we're all going to die on Hydrot, Paul. There's no avoiding that. Somewhere we'll leave behind people who behave as we would, think and feel as we would, but who won't remember la Ventura, or Chatvieux, or Joan Heath—or Earth."

The pilot said nothing more. There was a gray taste in his mouth.

"Saltonstall, what do you recommend as a form?"

The panatropist pulled reflectively at his nose. "Webbed extremities, of course, with thumbs and big toes heavy and thornilke for defense until the creature has had a chance to learn. Book-lungs, like the arachnids, working out of intercostal spiracles—they are gradually adaptable to atmosphere-breathing, if it ever decides to come out of the water. Also I'd suggest sporulation. As an aquatic animal, our colonist is going to have an indefinite lifespan, but we'll have to give it a breeding cycle of about six weeks to keep its numbers up during the learning period; so there'll have to be a definite break of some duration in its active year. Otherwise it'll hit the population problem before it's learned enough to cope with it."

"Also, it'll be better if our colonists could winter inside a good hard shell," Eunice Wagner added in agreement. "So sporulation's the obvious answer. Most microscopic creatures have it."

"Microscopic?" Phil said incredulously.

"Certainly," Chatvieux said, amused. "We can't very well crowd a six-foot man into a two-foot puddle. But that raises a question. We'll have tough competition from the rotifers, and some of them aren't strictly microscopic. I don't think your average colonist should run under 25 microns, Saltonstall. Give them a chance to slug it out."

"I was thinking of making them twice that big."

"Then they'd be the biggest things in their environment," Eunice Wagner pointed out, "and won't ever develop any skills. Besides, if you make them about rotifer size, I'll give them an incentive for pushing out the castle-building rotifers.

"They'll be able to take over the castles as dwellings."

Chatvieux nodded. "All right, let's get started. While the panatropes are being calibrated, the rest of us can put our heads together on leaving a record for these people. We'll micro-engrave the record on a set of corrosion-proof metal leaves, of a size our colonists can handle conveniently. Some day they may puzzle it out."

"Question," Eunice Wagner said. "Are we going to tell them they're microscopic? I'm opposed to it. It'll saddle their entire early history with a gods-and-demons mythology they'd be better off without."

"Yes, we are," Chatvieux said; and la Ventura could tell by the change in the tone of his voice that he was speaking now as their senior. "These people will be of the race of men, Eunice. We want them to win their way back to the community of men. They are not toys, to be protected from the truth forever in a fresh-water womb."

"I'll make that official," Venezuelos said, and that was that.

And then, essentially, it was all over. They went through the motions. Already they were beginning to be hungry. After la Ventura had had his personality pattern recorded, he was out of it. He sat by himself at the far end of the ledge, watching Tau Ceti go redly down, chucking pebbles into the nearest pond, wondering morosely which nameless puddle was to be his Lethe.

He never found out, of course. None of them did.

I

Old Shar set down the heavy metal plate at last, and gazed instead out the window of the castle, apparently resting his eyes on the glowing green-gold obscurity of the summer waters. In the soft fluorescence which played down upon him, from the Noc dozing impassively in the groined vault of the chamber, Lavon could see that he was in fact a young man. His face was so delicately formed as to suggest that it had not been many seasons since he had first emerged from his spore.

But of course there had been no real reason to expect an old man. All the Shars had been referred to traditionally as "old" Shar. The reason, like the reasons for everything else, had been forgotten, but the custom had persisted; the adjective at least gave weight and dignity to the office.

The present Shar belonged to the generation XVI, and hence would have to be at least two seasons younger than Lavon himself. If he was old, it was only in knowledge.

"Lavon, I'm going to have to be honest with you," Shar said at last, still looking out of the tall, irregular window. "You've come to me for the secrets of the metal plates, just as your predecessors did to mine. I can give some of them to you—but for the most part, I don't know what they mean."

"After so many generations?" Lavon asked, surprised. "Wasn't it Shar III who first found out how to read them? That was a long time ago."

The young man turned and looked at Lavon with eyes made dark and wide by the depths into which they had been staring. "I can read what's on the plates, but most of it seems to make no sense. Worst of all, the plates are incomplete. You didn't know that? They are. One of them was lost in a battle during the final war with the Eaters, while these castles are still in their hands."

"What am I here for, then?" Lavon said. "Isn't there anything of value on the remaining plates? Do they really contain 'the wisdom of the Creators' or is that another myth?"

"No. No, that's true," Shar said slowly, "as far as it goes."

He paused, and both men turned and gazed at the ghostly creature which had appeared suddenly outside the window. Then Shar said gravely, "Come in, Para."

The slipper-shaped organism, nearly transparent except for the thousands of black-and-silver granules and frothy bubbles which packed its interior, glided into the chamber and hovered, with a muted whirring of cilia. For a moment it remained silent, probably speaking telepathically to the Noc floating in the vault, after the ceremonious fashion of all the protos. No human had ever intercepted one of these colloquies, but there was no doubt about their reality: humans had used them for long-range communications for generations.

Then the Para's cilia buzzed once more. Each separate hairlike process vibrated at an independent, changing rate; the resulting sound waves spread through the water, inter-modulating, reinforcing or canceling each other. The aggregate wave-front, by the time it reached human ears, was recognizable human speech.

"We are arrived, Shar and Lavon, according to the custom."

"And welcome," said Shar. "Lavon, let's leave this matter of the plates for a while, until you hear what Para has

to say; that's a part of the knowledge Lavons must have as
they come of age, and it comes before the plates. I can give
you some hints of what we are. First Para has to tell you
something about what we aren't."

Lavon nodded, willingly enough, and watched the proto
as it settled gently to the surface of the hewn table at
which Shar and been sitting. There was in the entity such
a perfection and economy of organization, such a grace
and surety of movement, that he could hardly believe in
his own new-won maturity. Para, like all the protos, made
him feel not, perhaps, poorly thought-out, but at least
unfinished.

"We know that in this universe there is logically no
place for man," the gleaming now immoble cylinder upon
the table droned abruptly. "Our memory is the common
property to all our races. It reaches back to a time when
there were no such creatures as men here. It remembers
also that once upon a day there were men here, suddenly,
and in some numbers. Their spores littered the bottom;
we found the spores only a short time after our season's
Awakening, and in them we saw the forms of men
slumbering.

"Then men shattered their spores and emerged. They
were intelligent, active. And they were gifted with a trait,
a character, possessed by no other creature in this world.
Not even the savage Eaters had it. Men organized us to
exterminate the Eaters and therein lay the difference. Men
had initiative. We have the word now, which you gave us,
and we apply it, but we still do not know what the thing is
that it labels."

"You fought beside us," Lavon said.

"Gladly. We would never have thought of that war by
ourselves, but it was good and brought good. Yet we
wondered. We saw that men were poor swimmers, poor
walkers, poor crawlers, poor climbers. We saw that men
were formed to make and use tools, a concept we still do
not understand, for so wonderful a gift is largely wasted
in this universe, and there is no other. What good are
tool-useful members such as the hands of men? We do
not know. It seems plain that so radical a thing should

lead to a much greater rulership over the world than has, in fact, proven to be possible for men."

Lavon's head was spinning. "Para, I had no notion that you people were philosophers."

"The protos are old," Shar said. He had again turned to look out the window, his hands locked behind his back. "They aren't philosophers, Lavon but they are remorseless logicians. Listen to Para."

"To this reasoning there could be but one outcome," the Para said. "Our strange ally, Man, was like nothing else in this universe. He was and is ill-fitted for it. He does not belong here; he has been—adopted. This drives us to think that there are other universes besides this one, but where these universes might lie, and what their properties might be, it is impossible to imagine. We have no imagination, as men know."

Was the creature being ironic? Lavon could not tell. He said slowly: "Other universes? How could that be true?"

"We do not know," the Para's uninflected voice hummed. Lavon waited, but obviously the proto had nothing more to say.

Shar had resumed sitting on the window sill, clasping his knees, watching the come and go of dim shapes in the lighted gulf. "It is quite true," he said. "What is written on the remaining plates makes it plain. Let me tell you now what they say.

"We were made, Lavon. We were made by men who are not as we are, but men who were our ancestors all the same. They were caught in some disaster, and they made us here in our universe—so that, even though they had to die, the race of men would live."

Lavon surged up from the woven spyrogrya mat upon which he had been sitting. "You must think I'm a fool!" he said sharply.

"No. You're our Lavon; you have a right to know the facts. Make what you like of them." Shar swung his webbed toes back into the chamber. "What I've told you may be hard to believe, but it seems to be so; what Para says backs it up. Our unfitness to live here is self-evident. I'll give you some examples:

"The past four Shars discovered that we won't get any

further in our studies until we learn how to control heat. We've produced enough heat chemically to show that even the water around us changes when the temperature gets high enough. But there we're stopped."

"Why?"

"Because heat produced in open water is carried off as rapidly as it's produced. Once we tried to enclose that heat, and we blew up a whole tube of the castle and killed everything in range; the shock was terrible. We measured the pressures that were involved in that explosion, and we discovered that no substance we know could have resisted them. Theory suggests some stronger substances—*but we need heat to form them!*

"Take our chemistry. We live in water. Everything seems to dissolve in water, to some extent. How de we confine a chemical test to the crucible we put it in? How do we maintain a solution at one dilution? I don't know. Every avenue leads me to the same stone door. We're thinking creatures, Lavon, but there's something drastically wrong in the way we think about this universe we live in. It just doesn't seem to lead to results."

Lavon pushed back his floating hair futilely. "Maybe you're thinking about the wrong results. We've had no trouble with warfare, or crops, or practical things like that. If we can't create much heat, well, most of us don't miss it; we don't need any. What's the other universe supposed to be like, the one our ancestors lived in? Is it any better than this one?"

"I don't know," Shar admitted. "It was so different that it's hard to compare the two. The metal plates tell a story about men who were traveling from one place to another in a container that moved by itself. The only analogy I can think of is the shallops of diatom shells that our youngsters used to sled along the thermocline; but evidently what's meant is something much bigger.

"I picture a huge shallop, closed on all sides, big enough to hold many people—maybe twenty or thirty. It had to travel for generations through some kind of space where there wasn't any water to breathe, so that the people had to carry their own water and renew it constantly. There were no seasons; no yearly turnover; no ice forming on the sky, because there wasn't any sky in a closed shallop; no spore formation.

"Then the shallop was wrecked somehow. The people in it knew they were going to die. They made us, and put us here, as if we were their children. Because they had to die, they wrote their story on the plates, to tell us what had happened. I suppose we'd understand it better if we had the plate Shar III lost during the war, but we don't."

"The whole thing sounds like a parable," Lavon said, shrugging. "Or a song. I can see why you don't understand it. What I can't see is why you bother to try."

"Because of the plates," Shar said. "You've handled them yourself, so you know that we've nothing like them. We have crude, impure metals we've hammered out, metals that last for a while and then decay. But the plates shine on and on, generation after generation. They don't change; our hammers and graving tools break against them; the little heat we can generate leaves them unharmed. Those plates weren't formed in our universe—and that one fact makes every word on them important to me. Someone went to a great deal of trouble to make those plates indestructible to give them to us. Someone to whom the word 'stars' was important enough to be worth fourteen repetitions, despite the fact that the word doesn't seem to mean anything. I'm ready to think that if our makers repeated the word even twice on a record that seems likely to last forever, it's important for us to know what it means."

"All these extra universes and huge shallops and meaningless words— I can't say that they don't exist, but I don't see what difference it makes. The Shars of a few generations ago spent their whole lives breeding better crops for us, and showing us how to cultivate them instead of living haphazardly off bacteria. That was work worth doing. The Lavons of those days evidently got along without the metal plates, and saw to it that the Shars did, too: Well, as far as I'm concerned, you're welcome to the plates, if you like them better than crop improvement— but I think they ought to be thrown away."

"All right," Shar said, shrugging. "If you don't want them, that ends the traditional interview. We'll go our—"

There was a rising drone from the table-top. The Para

was lifting itself, waves of motion passing over its cilia,
like the waves which went across the fruiting stalks of the
fields of delicate fungi with which the bottom was planted.
It had been so silent that Lavon had forgotten it; he could
tell from Shar's startlement that Shar had, too.

"This is a great decision," the waves of sound washing
from the creature throbbed. "Every proto has heard it and
agrees with it. We have been afraid of these metal plates
for a long time, afraid that men would learn to understand
them and to follow what they say to some secret place,
leaving the protos behind. Now we are not afraid."

"There wasn't anything to be afraid of," Lavon said
indulgently.

"No Lavon before you had said so," Para said. "We
are glad. We will throw the plates away."

With that, the shining creature swooped toward the
embrasure. With it, it bore away the remaining plates,
which had been resting under it on the table-top, suspended delicately in the curved tips of its supple cilia.
With a cry, Shar plunged through the water toward the
opening.

"Stop, Para!"

But Para was already gone, so swiftly that he had not
even heard the call. Shar twisted his body and brought up
on one shoulder against the tower wall. He said nothing.
His face was enough. Lavon could not look at it for more
than an instant.

The shadows of the two men moved slowly along the
uneven cobbled floor. The Noc descended toward them
from the vault, its single thick tentacle stirring the water,
its internal light flaring and fading irregularly. It, too,
drifted through the window after its cousin, and sank
slowly away toward the bottom. Gently its living glow
dimmed, flickered, winked out.

II

For many days, Lavon was able to avoid thinking much
about the loss. There was always a great deal of work to
be done. Maintenance of the castles, which had been built
by the now-extinct Eaters rather than by human hands,
was a never-ending task. The thousand dichotomously

bracing wings tended to crumble, especially at their bases where they sprouted from each other, and no Shar had yet come forward with a mortar as good as the rotifer-spittle which had once held them together. In addition, the breaking through of windows and the construction of chambers in the early days had been haphazard and often unsound. The instinctive architecture of the rotifers, after all, had not been meant to meet the needs of human occupants.

And then there were the crops. Men no longer fed precariously upon passing bacteria; now there were the drifting mats of specific water-fungi, rich and nourishing, which had been bred by five generations of Shars. These had to be tended constantly to keep the strains pure, and to keep the older and less intelligent species of the protos from grazing on them. In this latter task, to be sure, the more intricate and far-seeing proto types cooperated, but men were needed to supervise.

There had been a time, after the war with the Eaters, when it had been customary to prey upon the slow-moving and stupid diatoms, whose exquisite and fragile glass shells were so easily burst, and who were unable to learn that a friendly voice did not necessarily mean a friend. There were still people who would crack open a diatom when no one else was looking, but were regarded as barbarians, to the puzzlement of the protos. The blurred and simple-minded speech of the gorgeously engraved plants had brought them into the category of pets—a concept which the protos were utterly unable to grasp, especially since men admitted that diatoms on the half-frustrule were delicious.

Lavon had had to agree, very early, that the distinction was tiny. After all, humans did eat the desmids, which differed from the diatoms only in three particulars: their shells were flexible, they could not move, and they did not speak. Yet to Lavon, as to most men, there did seem to be some kind of distinction, whether the protos could see it or not, and that was that. Under the circumstances he felt that it was a part of his duty, as a leader of men, to protect the diatoms from the occasional poachers who browsed upon them, in defiance of custom, in the high levels of the sunlit sky.

Yet Lavon found it impossible to keep himself busy

enough to forget that moment when the last clues to Man's origin and destination had been seized and borne away into dim space.

It might be possible to ask Para for the return of the plates, explain that a mistake had been made. The protos were creatures of implacable logic, but they respected Man, and might reverse their decision if pressed—

We are sorry. The plates were carried over the bar and released in the gulf. We will have the bottom there searched, but . . .

With a sick feeling he could not repress, Lavon knew that when the protos decided something was worthless, they did not hide it in some chamber like old women. They threw it away—efficiently.

Yet despite the tormenting of his conscience, Lavon was convinced that the plates were well lost. What had they ever done for man, except to provide Shars with useless things to think about in the late seasons of their lives? What the Shars themselves had done to benefit Man, here, in the water, in the world, in the universe, had been done by direct experimentation. No bit of useful knowledge ever had come from the plates. There had never been anything in the plates but things best left unthought. The protos were right.

Lavon shifted his position on the plant frond, where he had been sitting in order to overlook the harvesting of an experimental crop of blue-green, oil-rich algae drifting in a clotted mass close to the top of the sky, and scratched his back gently against the coarse bole. The protos were seldom wrong, after all. Their lack of creativity, their inability to think an original thought, was a gift as well as a limitation. It allowed them to see and feel things at all times as they were—not as they hoped they might be, for they had no ability to hope, either.

"La-von! Laa-vah-on!"

The long halloo came floating up from the sleepy depths. Propping one hand against the top of the frond, Lavon bent and looked down. One of the harvesters was looking up at him, holding loosely the adze with which he had splitting free the glutinous tetrads of the algae.

"Up here. What's the matter?"

"We have the ripened quadrant cut free. Shall we tow it away?"

"Tow it away," Lavon said, with a lazy gesture. He leaned back again. At the same instant, a brilliant reddish glory burst into being above him, and cast itself down toward the depths like mesh after mesh of the finest-drawn gold. The great light which lived above the sky during the day, brightening or dimming according to some pattern no Shar ever had fathomed, was blooming again.

Few men, caught in the warm glow of that light, could resist looking up at it—especially when the top of the sky itself wrinkled and smiled just a moment's climb or swim away. Yet, as always, Lavon's bemused upward look gave back nothing but his own distorted, bobbling reflection, and a reflection of the plant on which he rested.

Here was the upper limit, the third of the three surfaces of the universe.

The first surface was the bottom, where the water ended.

The second surface was the thermocline, the invisible division between the colder waters of the bottom and the warm, light waters of the sky. During the height of the warm weather, the thermocline was so definite a division as to make for good sledding and for chilly passage. A real interface formed between the cold, denser bottom waters and the warm reaches above, and maintained itself almost for the whole of the warm season.

The third surface was the sky. One could no more pass through that surface than one could penetrate the bottom, nor was there any better reason to try. There the universe ended. The light which played over it daily, waxing and waning as it chose, seemed to be one of its properties.

Toward the end of the season, the water gradually grew colder and more difficult to breathe, while at the same time the light became duller and stayed for shorter periods between darknesses. Slow currents started to move. The high waters turned chill and began to fall. The bottom mud stirred and smoked away, carrying with it the spores of the fields of fungi. The thermocline tossed, became choppy, and melted away. The sky began to fog with particles of soft silt carried up from the bottom, the walls, the corners of the universe. Before very long, the whole world was cold, inhospitable, flocculent with yellowing dying creatures.

Then the protos encysted; the bacteria, even most of the plants and, not long afterward, men, too, curled up in their oil-filled amber shells. The world died until the first tentative current of warm water broke the winter silence.

"La-von!"

Just after the long call, a shinning bubble rose past Lavon. He reached out and poked it, but it bounded away from his sharp thumb. The gas-bubbles which rose from the bottom in late summer were almost invulnerable—and when some especially hard blow or edge did penetrate them, they broke into smaller bubbles which nothing could touch, and fled toward the sky, leaving behind a remarkably bad smell.

Gas. There was no water inside a bubble. A man who got inside a bubble would have nothing to breathe.

But, of course, it was impossible to penetrate a bubble. The surface tension was too strong. As strong as Shar's metal plates. As strong as the top of the sky.

As strong as the top of the sky. And above that—once the bubble was broken—a world of gas instead of water? Were all worlds bubbles of water drifting in gas?

If it were so, travel between them would be out of the question, since it would be impossible to pierce the sky to begin with. Nor did the infant cosmology include any provsions for bottoms for the worlds.

And yet some of the local creatures did burrow *into* the bottom, quite deeply, seeking something in those depths which was beyond the reach of Man. Even the surface of the ooze, in high summer, crawled with tiny creatures for which mud was a natural medium. Man, too, passed freely between the two countries of water which were divided by the thermocline, though many of the creatures with which he lived could not pass that line at all, once it had established itself.

And if the new universe of which Shar had spoken existed at all, it had to exist beyond the sky, where the light was. Why could not the sky be passed, after all? The fact that bubbles could be broken showed that the surface skin that formed between water and gas wasn't completely invulnerable. Had it ever been tried?

Lavon did not suppose that one man could butt his way

through the top of the sky, any more than he could burrow into the bottom, but there might be ways around the
difficulty. Here at his back, for instance, was a plant which
gave every appearance of continuing beyond the sky: its
uppermost fronds broke off and were bent back only by
a trick of reflection.

It had always been assumed that the plants died where
they touched the sky. For the most part, they did, for
frequently the dead extension could be seen, leached and
yellow, the boxes of its component cells empty, floating
imbedded in the perfect mirror. But some were simply
chopped off, like the one which sheltered him now. Perhaps that was only an illusion, and instead it soared
indefinitely into some other place— some place where
men might once have been born, and might still live . . .

The plates were gone. There was only one other way to
find out.

Determinedly, Lavon began to climb toward the wavering mirror of the sky. His thorn-thumbed feet trampled
obliviously upon the clustered sheaves of fragile stippled
diatoms. The tulip-heads of Vortae, placid and murmurous
cousins of Para, retracted startledly out of his way upon
coiling stalks, to make silly gossip behind him.

Lavon did not hear them. He continued to climb doggedly toward the light, his fingers and toes gripping the
plant-bole.

"Lavon! Where are you going? Lavon!"

He leaned out and looked down. The man with the adze,
a doll-like figure, was beckoning to him from a patch of
blue-green retreating over a violet abyss. Dizzily he looked
away, clinging to the bole; he had never been so high before. Then he began to climb again.

After a while, he touched the sky with one hand. He
stopped to breathe. Curious bacteria gathered about the
base of his thumb where blood from a small cut was fog-
ging away, scattered at his gesture, and wriggled mindlessly
back toward the dull red lure.

He waited until he no longer felt winded, and resumed
climbing. The sky pressed down against the top of his
head, against the back of his neck, against his shoulders.
It seemed to give slightly, with a tough, frictionless elasti-

city. The water here was intensely bright, and quite color-less. He climbed another step, driving his shoulders against that enormous weight.

It was fruitless. He might as well have tried to penetrate a cliff.

Again he had to rest. While he panted, he made a curious discovery. All around the bole of the water plant, the steel surface of the sky curved upward, making a kind of sheath. He found that he could insert his hand into it—there was almost enough space to admit his head as well. Clinging closely to the bole, he looked up into the inside of the sheath, probing with his injured hand. The glare was blinding.

There was a kind of soundless explosion. His whole wrist was suddenly encircled in an intense, impersonal grip, as if it were being cut in two. In blind astonishment, he lunged upward.

The ring of pain traveled smoothly down his upflung arm as he rose, was suddenly around his shoulders and chest. Another lunge and his knees were being squeezed in the circular vine. Another—

Something was horribly wrong. He clung to the bole and tried to gasp, but there was—nothing to breathe.

The water came streaming out of his body, from his mouth, his nostrils, the spiracles in his sides, spurting in tangible jets. An intense and fiery itching crawled over the entire surface of his body. At each spasm, long knives ran into him, and from a great distance he heard more water being expelled from his book-lungs in an obscene, frothy sputtering.

Lavon was drowning.

With a final convulsion, he kicked away from the splintery bole, and fell. A hard impact shook him; and then the water, which had clung to him so tightly when he had first attempted to leave it, took him back with cold violence.

Sprawling and tumbling grotesquely, he drifted down and down and down, toward the bottom.

III

For many days, Lavon lay curled insensibly in his spore, as if in the winter sleep. The shock of cold which he had felt on re-entering his native universe had been taken by his body as a sign of coming winter, as it had taken the oxygen-starvation of his brief sojourn above the sky. The spore-forming glands had at once begun to function.

Had it not been for this, Lavon would surely have died. The danger of drowning disappeared even as he fell, as the air bubbled out of his lungs and readmitted the life-giving water. But for acute desiccation and third degree sunburn, the sunken universe knew no remedy. The healing amnionic fluid generated by the spore-forming glands, after the transparent amber sphere had enclosed him, offered Lavon his only chance.

The brown sphere was spotted after some days by a prowling ameba, quiescent in the eternal winter of the bottom. Down there the temperature was always an even 4°, no matter what the season, but it was unheard of that a spore should be found there while the high epilimnion was still warm and rich in oxygen.

Within an hour, the spore was surrounded by scores of astonished protos, jostling each other to bump their blunt eyeless prows against the shell. Another hour later, a squad of worried men came plunging from the castles far above to press their own noses against the transparent wall. Then swift orders were given.

Four Para grouped themselves about the amber sphere, and there was a subdued explosion as the trichocysts which lay embedded at the bases of their cilia, just under the pellicle, burst and cast fine lines of a quickly solidifying liquid into the water. The four Paras thrummed and lifted, tugging.

Lavon's spore swayed gently in the mud and then rose slowly, entangled in the web. Nearby, a Noc cast a cold pulsating glow over the operation—not for the Paras, who did not need the light, but for the baffled knot of men. The sleeping figure of Lavon, head bowed, knees drawn up to its chest, revolved with an absurd solemnity inside the shell as it was moved.

"Take him to Shar, Para."

The young Shar justified, by minding his own business, the traditional wisdom with which his hereditary office had invested him. He observed at once that there was nothing he could do for the encysted Lavon which would not be classifiable as simple meddling.

He had the sphere deposited in a high tower room of his castle, where there was plenty of light and the water was warm, which should suggest to the hibernating form that spring was again on the way. Beyond that, he simply sat and watched, and kept his speculations to himself.

Inside the spore, Lavon's body seemed rapidly to be shedding its skin, in long strips and patches. Gradually, his curious shrunkenness disappeared. His withered arms and legs and sunken abdomen filled out again.

The days went by while Shar watched. Finally he could discern no more changes, and, on a hunch, had the spore taken up to the topmost battlements of the tower, into the direct daylight.

An hour later, Lavon moved in his amber prison.

He uncurled and stretched, turned blank eyes up toward the light. His expression was that of a man who had not yet awakened from a ferocious nightmare. His whole body shone with a strange pink newness.

Shar knocked gently on the wall of the spore. Lavon turned his blind face toward the sound, life coming into his eyes. He smiled tentatively and braced his hands and feet against the inner wall of the shell.

The whole sphere fell abruptly to pieces with a sharp crackling. The amnionic fluid dissipated around him and Shar, carrying away with it the suggestive odor of a bitter struggle against death.

Lavon stood among the bits of shell and looked at Shar silently. At last he said:

"Shar—I've been beyond the sky."

"I know," Shar said gently.

Again Lavon was silent. Shar said, "Don't be humble, Lavon. You've done an epoch-making thing. It nearly cost you your life. You must tell me the rest—all of it."

"The rest?"

"You taught me a lot while you slept. Or are you still opposed to useless knowledge?"

Lavon could say nothing. He no longer could tell what he knew from what he wanted to know. He had only one question left, but he could not utter it. He could only look dumbly into Shar's delicate face.

"You have answered me," Shar said, even more gently. "Come, my friend; join me at my table. We will plan our journey to the stars."

It was two winter sleeps after Lavon's disastrous climb beyond the sky that all work on the spaceship stopped. By then, Lavon knew that he had hardened and weathered into that temporarily ageless state a man enters after he has just reached his prime; and he knew also that there were wrinkles engraved upon his brow, to stay and to deepen.

"Old" Shar, too had changed, his features losing some of their delicacy as he came into his maturity. Though the wedge-shaped bony structure of his face would give him a withdrawn and poetic look for as long as he lived, participation in the plan had given his expression a kind of executive overlay, which at best gave it a masklike rigidity, and at worst coarsened it somehow.

Yet despite the bleeding away of the years, the spaceship was still only a hulk. It lay upon a platform built above the tumbled boulders of the sandbar which stretched out from one wall of the world. It was an immense hull of pegged wood, broken by regularly spaced gaps through which the raw beams of the skeleton could be seen.

Work upon it had progressed fairly rapidly at first, for it was not hard to visualize what kind of vehicle would be needed to crawl through empty space without losing its water. It had been recognized that the sheer size of the machine would enforce a long period of construction, perhaps two full seasons; but neither Shar nor Lavon had anticipated any serious snag.

For that matter, part of the vehicle's apparent incompleteness was an illusion. About a third of its fittings were to consist of living creatures, which could not be expected to install themselves in the vessel much before the actual takeoff.

Yet time and time again, work on the ship had had to be halted for long periods. Several times whole sections needed to be ripped out, as it became more and more evident that hardly a single normal, understandable concept could be applied to the problem of space travel.

The lack of the history plates, which the Para steadfastly refused to deliver up, was a double handicap. Immediately upon their loss, Shar had set himself to reproduce them from memory; but unlike the more religious of his people, he had never regarded them as holy writ, and hence had never set himself to memorizing them word by word. Even before the theft, he had accumulated a set of variant translations of passages presenting specific experimental problems, which were stored in his library, carved in wood. But most of these translations tended to contradict each other, and none of them related to spaceship construction, upon which the original had been vague in any case.

No duplicates of the cryptic characters of the original had ever been made, for the simple reason that there was nothing in the sunken universe capable of destroying the originals, nor of duplicating their apparently changeless permanence. Shar remarked too late that through simple caution they should have made a number of verbatim temporary records—but after generations of green-gold peace, simple caution no longer covers preparation against catastrophe. (Nor, for that matter, did a culture which had to dig each letter of its simple alphabet into pulpy waterlogged wood with a flake of stonewort, encourage the keeping of records in triplicate.)

As a result, Shar's imperfect memory of the contents of the history plates, plus the constant and millennial doubt as to the accuracy of the various translations, proved finally to be the worst obstacle to progress on the spaceship itself.

"Men must paddle before they can swim," Lavon observed belatedly, and Shar was forced to agree with him.

Obviously, whatever the ancients had known about spaceship construction, very little of that knowledge was usable to a people still trying to build its first spaceship from scratch. In retrospect, it was not surprising that the great hulk still rested incomplete upon its platform above the sand boulders, exuding a musty odor of wood steadily losing its strength, two generations after its flat bottom had been laid down.

The fat-faced young man who headed the strike delegation was Phil XX, a man two generations younger than Lavon, four younger than Shar. There were crow's-feet

at the corners of his eyes, which made him look both
like a querulous old man and like an infant spoiled in
the spore.

"We're calling a halt to this crazy project," he said
bluntly. "We've slaved our youth away on it, but now
that we're our own masters, it's over, that's all. Over."

"Nobody's compelled you," Lavon said angrily.

"Society does; our parents do," a gaunt member of the
delegation said. "But now we're going to start living in
the real world. Everybody these days knows that there's
no other world but this one. You oldsters can hang on to
your superstitions if you like. We don't intend to."

Baffled, Lavon looked over at Shar. The scientist smiled
and said, "Let them go, Lavon. We have no use for the
faint-hearted."

The fat-faced young man flushed. "You can't insult us
into going back to work. We're through. Build your own
ship to no place!"

"All right," Lavon said evenly. "Go on, beat it. Don't
stand around here orating about it. You've made your
decision and we're not interested in your self-justifications.
Good-by."

The fat-faced young man evidently still had quite a bit
of heroism to dramatize which Lavon's dismissal had short-
circuited. An examination of Lavon's stony face, however,
convinced him that he had to take his victory as he found
it. He and the delegation trailed ingloriously out the arch-
way.

"Now what?" Lavon asked when they had gone. "I
must admit, Shar, that I would have tried to persuade
them. We do need the workers, after all."

"Not as much as they need us," Shar said tranquilly.
"How many volunteers have you got for the crew of the
ship?"

"Hundreds. Every young man of the generation after
Phil's wants to go along. Phil's wrong about that segment of the population, at least. The project catches the
imagination of the very young."

"Did you give them any encouragement?"

"Sure," Lavon said. "I told them we'd call on them if
they were chosen. But you can't take that seriously! We'd

do badly to displace our picked group of specialists with
youths who have enthusiasm and nothing else."

"That's not what I had in mind, Lavon. Didn't I see a
Noc in your chambers somewhere? Oh, there he is, asleep
in the dome. Noc!"

The creature stirred its tentacles lazily.

"Noc, I've a message," Shar called. "The protos are
to tell all men that those who wish to go to the next world
with the spaceship must come to the staging area right
away. Say that we can't promise to take everyone, but that
only those who help us build the ship will be considered
at all."

The Noc curled its tentacles again and appeared to go
back to sleep. Actually, of course, it was sending its message through the water in all directions.

IV

Lavon turned from the arrangement of speaking-tube
megaphones which was his control board and looked at the
Para. "One last try," he said. "Will you give us back the
plates?"

"No, Lavon. We have never denied you anything before,
but this we must."

"You're going with us though, Para. Unless you give
us the knowledge we need, you'll lose your life if we
lose ours."

"What is one Para?" the creature said. "We are all alike.
This cell will die; but the protos need to know how you
fare on this journey. We believe you should make it without the plates."

"Why?"

The proto was silent. Lavon stared at it a moment, then
turned deliberately back to the speaking tubes. "Everyone hang on," he said. He felt shaky. "We're about to
start. Tol, is the ship sealed?"

"As far as I can tell, Lavon."

Lavon shifted to another megaphone. He took a deep
breath. Already the water seemed stifling, though the ship
hadn't moved.

"Ready with one-quarter power. One, two, three, go."

The whole ship jerked and settled back into place again.

The raphe diatoms along the under hull settled into their niches, their jelly treads turning against broad endless belts of crude leather. Wooden gears creaked, stepping up the slow power of the creatures, transmitting it to the sixteen axles of the ship's weels.

The ship rocked and began to roll slowly along the sandbar. Lavon looked tensely through the mica port. The world flowed painfully past him. The ship canted and began to climb the slope. Behind him, he could feel the electric silence of Shar, Para, the two alternate pilots, as if their gaze were stabbing directly through his body and on out the port. The world looked different, now that he was leaving it. How had he missed all this beauty before?

The slapping of the endless belts and the squeaking and groaning of the gears and axles grew louder as the slope steepened. The ship continued to climb, lurching. Around it, squadrons of men and protos dipped and wheeled, escorting it toward the sky.

Gradually the sky lowered and pressed down toward the top of the ship.

"A little more work from your diatoms, Tanol," Lavon said. "Boulder ahead." The ship swung ponderously. "All right, slow them up again. Give us a shove from your side, Than—no, that's too much—there, that's it. Back to normal; you're still turning us! Tanol, give us one burst to line us up again. Good. All right, steady drive on all sides. Won't be long now."

"How can you think in webs like that?" the Para wondered behind him.

"I just do, that's all. It's the way men think. Overseers, a little more thrust now; the grade's getting steeper."

The gears groaned. The ship nosed up. The sky brightened in Lavon's face. Despite himself, he began to be frightened. His lungs seemed to burn, and in his mind he felt his long fall through nothingness toward the chill slap of water as if he were experiencing it for the first time. His skin itched and burned. Could he go up *there* again? Up there into the burning void, the great gasping agony where no life should go?

The sandbar began to level out and the going became a little easier. Up here, the sky was so close that the lumbering motion of the huge ship disturbed it. Shadows of wavelets ran across the sand. Silently, the thick-barreled bands of blue-green algae drank in the light and converted it to oxygen, writhing in their slow mindless dance just under the long mica skylight which ran along the spine of the ship. In the hold, beneath the latticed corridor and cabin floors, whirring Vortae kept the ship's water in motion, fueling themselves upon drifting organic particles.

One by one, the figures wheeling about the ship outside waved arms or cilia and fell back, coasting down the slope of the sandbar toward the familiar world, dwindling and disappearing. There was at last only one single Euglena, half-plant cousin of the protos, forging along beside the spaceship into the marches of the shallows. It loved the light, but finally it, too, was driven away into cooler, deeper waters, its single whiplike tentacle undulating placidly as it went. It was not very bright, but Lavon felt deserted when it left.

Where they were going, though, none could follow.

Now the sky was nothing but a thin, resistant skin of water coating the top of the ship. The vessel slowed, and when Lavon called for more power, it began to dig itself in among the sandgrains.

"That's not going to work," Shar said tensely. "I think we'd better step down the gear ratio, Lavon, so you can apply stress more slowly."

"All right," Lavon agreed. "Full stop, everybody. Shar, will you supervise gear-changing, please?"

Insane brilliance of empty space looked Lavon full in the face just beyond his big mica bull's eye. It was maddening to be forced to stop here upon the threshold of infinity; and it was dangerous, too. Lavon could feel building in him the old fear of the outside. A few moments more of inaction, he knew with a gathering coldness at the pit of his stomach, and he would be unable to go through with it.

Surely, he thought, there must be a better way to change gear-ratios than the traditional one, which involved dismantling almost the entire gear-box. Why couldn't a number of gears of different sizes be carried on the same shaft, not necessarily all in action all at once, but awaiting use simply by shoving the axle back and forth longitudinally in its sockets? It would still be clumsy, but it could be worked on orders from the bridge and would not involve shutting down the entire machine—and throwing the new pilot into a blue-green funk.

Shar came lunging up through the trap and swam himself a stop.

"All set," he said. "The big reduction gears aren't taking the strain too well, though."

"Splintering?"

"Yes. I'd go it slow at first."

Lavon nodded mutely. Without allowing himself to stop, even for a moment, to consider the consequences of his words, he called: "Half power."

The ship hunched itself down again and began to move, very slowly indeed, but more smoothly than before. Overhead, the sky thinned to complete transparency. The great light came blasting in. Behind Lavon there was an uneasy stir. The whiteness grew at the front ports.

Again the ship slowed, straining against the blinding barrier. Lavon swallowed and called for more power. The ship groaned like something about to die. It was now almost at a standstill.

"More power," Lavon called out.

Once more, with infinite slowness, the ship began to move. Gently, it tilted upward.

Then it lunged forward and every board and beam in it began to squall.

"Lavon! Lavon!"

Lavon started sharply at the shout. The voice was coming at him from one of the megaphones, the one marked for the port at the rear of the ship.

"Lavon!"

"What is it? Stop your damn yelling."

"I can see the top of the sky! From the *other* side, from the top side! It's like a big sheet of metal. We're going away from it. We're above the sky, Lavon, we're above the sky!"

Another violent start swung Lavon around toward the

forward port. On the outside of the mica, the water was evaporating with shocking swiftness, taking with it strange distortions and patterns made of rainbows.

Lavon saw Space.

It was at first like a deserted and cruelly dry version of the bottom. There were enormous boulders, great cliffs, tumbled, split, riven, jagged rocks going up and away in all directions.

But it had a sky of its own—a deep blue dome so far away that he could not believe it, let alone compute, what its distance might be. And in this dome was a ball of white fire that seared his eyeballs.

The wilderness of rock was still a long way away from the ship, which now seemed to be resting upon a level, glistening plain. Beneath the surface-shine, the plain seemed to be made of sand, nothing but familiar sand, the same substance which had heaped up to form a bar in Lavon's own universe, the bar along which the ship had climbed. But the glassy, colorful skin over it—

Suddenly Lavon became conscious of another shout from the megaphone banks. He shook his head savagely and asked. "What is it now?"

"Lavon, this is Than. What have you gotten us into? The belts are locked. The diatoms can't move them. They aren't faking, either; we've rapped them hard enough to make them think we are trying to break their shells, but they still can't give us more power."

"Leave them alone," Lavon snapped. "They can't fake; they haven't enough intelligence. If they say they can't give you more power, they can't."

"Well, then, you get us out of it," Than's voice said frightenedly.

Shar came forward to Lavon's elbow. "We're on a space-water interface, where the surface tension is very high," he said softly. "This is why I insisted on our building the ship so that we could lift the wheels off the ground whenever necessary. For a long while I couldn't understand the reference of the history plates to 'retractable landing gear,' but it finally occurred to me that the tension along a space-water interface—or, to be more exact, a space-mud interface—would hold any large object pretty tightly. If you order the wheels pulled up now, I think we'll make better progress for a while on the belly-treads."

"Good enough," Lavon said. "Hello below—up landing gear. Evidently the ancients knew their business after all, Shar."

Quite a few minutes later, for shifting power to the belly-treads involved another setting of the gear box, the ship was crawling along the shore toward the tumbled rock. Anxiously, Lavon scanned the jagged, threatening wall for a break. There was a sort of rivulet off toward the left which might offer a route, though a dubious one, to the next world. After some thought, Lavon ordered his ship turned toward it.

"Do you suppose that thing in the sky is a 'star'?" he asked. "But there were supposed to be lots of them. Only one is up there—and one's plenty for *my* taste."

"I don't know," Shar admitted. 'But I'm beginning to get a picture of the way the universe is made, I think. Evidently our world is a sort of cup in the bottom of this huge one. This one has a sky of its own; perhaps it, too, is only a cup in the bottom of a still huger world, and so on and on without end. It's a hard concept to grasp, I'll admit. Maybe it would be more sensible to assume that all the worlds are cups in this one common surface, and that the great light shines on them all impartially."

"Then what makes it seem to go out every night, and dim even in the day during winter?" Lavon demanded.

"Perhaps it travels in circles, over first one world, then another. How could I know yet?"

"Well, if you're right, it means that all we have to do is crawl along here for a while, until we hit the top of the sky of another world," Lavon said. "Then we dive in. Somehow it seems too simple, after all our preparations."

Shar chuckled, but the sound did not suggest that he had discovered anything funny. "Simple? Have you noticed the temperature yet?"

Lavon had noticed it, just beneath the surface of awareness, but at Shar's remark he realized that he was gradually being stifled. The oxygen content of the water, luckily, had not dropped, but the temperature suggested the shallows in the last and worst part of the autumn. It was like trying to breathe soup.

"Than, give us more action from the Vortae," Lavon called. "This is going to be unbearable unless we get more circulation."

It was all he could do now to keep his attention on the business of steering the ship.

The cut or defile in the scattered razor-edged rocks was a little closer, but there still seemed to be many miles of rough desert to cross. After a while, the ship settled into a steady, painfully slow crawling, with less pitching and jerking than before, but also with less progress. Under it, there was now a sliding, grinding sound, rasping against the hull of the ship itself, as if it were treadmilling over some coarse lubricant whose particles were each as big as a man's head.

Finally Shar said, "Lavon, we'll have to stop again. The sand this far up is dry, and we're wasting energy using the treads."

"Are you sure we can take it?" Lavon asked, gasping for breath. "At least we are moving. If we stop to lower the wheels and change gears again, we'll boil."

"We'll boil if we don't," Shar said calmly. "Some of our algae are already dead and the rest are withering. That's a pretty good sign that we can't take much more. I don't think we'll make it into the shadows, unless we do change over and put on some speed."

There was a gulping sound from one of the mechanics. "We ought to turn back," he said raggedly. "We were never meant to be out here in the first place. We were made for the water, not this hell."

"We'll stop," Lavon said, "but we're not turning back. That's final."

The words made a brave sound, but the man had upset Lavon more than he dared to admit, even to himself. "Shar," he said, "make it fast, will you?"

The scientist nodded and dived below.

The minutes stretched out. The great white globe in the sky blazed and blazed. It had moved down the sky, far down, so that the light was pouring into the ship directly in Lavon's face, illuminating every floating par-

ticle, its rays like long milky streamers. The currents of
water passing Lavon's cheek were almost hot.

How could they dare go directly forward into that inferno? The land directly under the "star" must be even
hotter than it was here!

"Lavon! Look at Para!"

Lavon forced himself to turn and look at his proto
ally. The great slipper had settled to the deck, where it
was lying with only a feeble pulsation of its cilia. Inside, its vacuoles were beginning to swell, to become
bloated, pear-shaped bubbles, crowding the granulated
protoplasm, pressing upon the dark nuclei.

"This cell is dying," Para said, as coldly as always.
"But go on—go on. There is much to learn, and you may
live, even though we do not. Go on."

"You're . . . for us now?" Lavon whispered.

"We have always been for you. Push your folly to its
uttermost. We will benefit in the end, and so will Man."

The whisper died away. Lavon called the creature again,
but it did not respond.

There was a wooden clashing from below, and then
Shar's voice came tinnily from one of the megaphones.
"Lavon, go ahead! The diatoms are dying, too, and then
we'll be without power. Make it as quickly and directly
as you can."

Grimly, Lavon leaned forward. "The 'star' is directly
over the land we're approaching."

"It is? It may go lower still and the shadows will get
longer. That's our only hope."

Lavon had not thought of that. He rasped into the
banked megaphones. Once more, the ship began to move.

It got hotter.

Steadily, with a perceptible motion, the "star" sank in
Lavon's face. Suddenly a new terror struck him. Suppose
it should continue to go down until it was gone entirely?
Blasting though it was now, it was the only source of heat.
Would not space become bitter cold on the instant—and
the ship an expanding, bursting block of ice?

The shadows lengthened menacingly, stretched across
the desert toward the forward-rolling vessel. There was no
talking in the cabin, just the sound of ragged breathing and
the creaking of the machinery.

Then the jagged horizon seemed to rush open upon them. Stony teeth cut into the lower rim of the ball of fire, devoured it swiftly. It was gone.

They were in the lee of the cliffs. Lavon ordered the ship turned to parallel the rock-line; it responded heavily, sluggishly. Far above, the sky deepened steadily from blue to indigo.

Shar came silently up through the trap and stood beside Lavon, studying that deepening color and the lengthening of the shadows down the beach toward their world. He said nothing, but Lavon knew that the same chilling thought was in his mind.

"Lavon."

Lavon jumped. Shar's voice had iron in it. "Yes?"

"We'll have to keep moving. We must make the next world, wherever it is, very shortly."

"How can we dare move when we can't see where we're going? Why not sleep it over—if the cold will let us?"

"It will let us." Shar said. "It can't get dangerously cold up here. If it did, the sky—or what we used to think of as the sky—would have frozen over every night, even in summer. But what I'm thinking about is the water. The plants will go to sleep now. In our world that wouldn't matter; the supply of oxygen is enough to last through the night. But in this confined space, with so many creatures in it and no source of fresh water, we will probably smother."

Shar seemed hardly to be involved at all, but spoke rather with the voice of implacable physical laws.

"Furthermore," he said, staring unseeingly out at the raw landscape, "the diatoms are plants, too. In other words, we must stay on the move for as long as we have oxygen and power—and pray that we make it."

"Shar, we had quite a few protos on board this ship once. And Para there isn't quite dead yet. If he were, the cabin would be intolerable. The ship is nearly sterile of bacteria, because all the protos have been eating them as a matter of course and there's no outside supply of them, any more than there is for oxygen. But still and all there would have been some decay."

Shar bent and tested the pellicle of the motionless Para

with a probing finger. "You're right, he's still alive. What does that prove?"

"The Vortae are also alive; I can feel the water circulating. Which proves it wasn't the heat that hurt Para. *It was the light.* Remember how badly my skin was affected after I climbed beyond the sky? Undiluted starlight is deadly. We should add that to the information on the plates."

"I still don't see the point."

"It's this. We've got three or four Noc down below. They were shielded from the light, and so must be alive. If we concentrate them in the diatom galleys, the dumb diatoms will think it's still daylight and will go on working. Or we can concentrate them up along the spine of the ship, and keep the algae putting out oxygen. So the question is: which do we need more, oxygen or power? Or can we split the difference?"

Shar actually grinned. "A brilliant piece of thinking. We'll make a Shar of you yet, Lavon. No, I'd say that we can't split the difference. There's something about daylight, some quality, that the light Noc emits doesn't have. You and I can't detect it, but the green plants can, and without it they don't make oxygen. So we'll have to settle for the diatoms—for power."

Lavon brought the vessel away from the rocky lee of the cliff, out onto the smoother sand. All trace of direct light was gone now, although there was still a soft, general glow on the sky.

"Now, then," Shar said thoughtfully, "I would guess that there's water over there in the canyon, if we can reach it. I'll go below and arrange—"

Lavon gasped, "What's the matter?"

Silently, Lavon pointed, his heart pounding.

The entire dome of indigo above them was spangled with tiny, incredibly brilliant lights. There were hundreds of them, and more and more were becoming visible as the darkness deepened. And far away, over the ultimate edge of the rocks, was a dim red globe, crescented with ghostly silver. Near the zenith was another such body, much smaller, and silvered all over . . .

Under the two moons of Hydrot, and under the eternal stars, the two-inch wooden spaceship and its microscopic cargo toiled down the slope toward the drying little rivulet.

V

The ship rested on the bottom of the canyon for the rest of the night. The great square doors were thrown open to admit the raw, irradiated, life-giving water from outside—and the wriggling bacteria which were fresh food.

No other creatures approached them, either with curiosity or with predatory intent, while they slept, though Lavon had posted guards at the doors. Evidently, even up here on the very floor of space, highly organized creatures were quiescent at night.

But when the first flush of light filtered through the water, trouble threatened.

First of all, there was the bug-eyed monster. The thing was green and had two snapping claws, either one of which could have broken the ship in two like a spyrogyra straw. Its eyes were black and globular, on the ends of short columns, and its long feelers were as thick as a plantbole. It passed in a kicking fury of motion, however, never noticing the ship at all.

"Is that—a sample of the kind of life we can expect in the next world?" Lavon whispered. Nobody answered, for the very good reason that nobody knew.

After a while, Lavon risked moving the ship forward against the current, which was slow but heavy. Enormous writhing worms whipped past them. One struck the hull a heavy blow, then thrashed on obliviously.

"They don't notice us," Shar said. "We're too small, Lavon, the ancients warned us of the immensity of space, but even when you see it, it's impossible to grasp. And all those stars—can they mean what I think they mean? It's beyond thought, beyond belief!"

"The bottom's sloping," Lavon said, looking ahead intently. "The walls of the canyon are retreating, and the water's becoming rather silty. Let the stars wait, Shar; we're coming toward the entrance of our new world."

Shar subsided moodily. His vision of space had disturbed him, perhaps seriously. He took little notice of the great thing that was happening, but instead huddled worriedly over his own expanding speculations. Lavon felt the old gap between their two minds widening once more.

Now the bottom was tilting upward again. Lavon had

no experience with delta-formation, for no rivulets left his own world, and the phenomenon worried him. But his worries were swept away in wonder as the ship topped the rise and nosed over.

Ahead, the bottom sloped away again, indefinitely, into glimmering depths. A proper sky was over them once more, and Lavon could see small rafts of plankton floating placidly beneath it. Almost at once, too, he saw several of the smaller kinds of protos, a few of which were already approaching the ship—

Then the girl came darting out of the depths, her features distorted with terror. At first she did not see the ship at all. She came twisting and turning lithely through the water, obviously hoping only to throw herself over the ridge of the delta and into the savage streamlet beyond.

Lavon was stunned. Not that there were men here—he had hoped for that—but at the girl's single-minded flight toward suicide.

"What—"

Then a dim buzzing began to grow in his ears, and he understood.

"Shar! Than! Tanol!" he bawled. "Break out crossbows and spears! Knock out all the windows!" He lifted a foot and kicked through the big port in front of him. Someone thrust a crossbow into his hand.

"Eh? What's happening?" Shar blurted.

"Rotifers!"

The cry went though the ship like a galvanic shock. The rotifers back in Lavon's own world were virtually extinct, but everyone knew thoroughly the grim history of the long battle man and proto had waged against them.

The girl spotted the ship and paused, stricken by despair at the sight of the new monster. She drifted with her own momentum, her eyes alternately fixed hypnotically upon the ship and glancing back over her shoulder, toward the buzzing snarled louder and louder in the dimness.

"Don't stop!" Lavon shouted. "This way, this way! We're friends! We'll help!"

Three great semi-transparent trumpets of smooth flesh bored over the rise, the many thick cilia of their coronas whirring greedily. Dicrans—the most predacious of the entire tribe of Eaters. They were quarreling thickly among themselves as they moved, with the few blurred, pre-symbolic noises which made up their "language."

Carefully, Lavon wound the crossbow, brought it to his shoulder, and fired. The bolt sang away through the water. It lost momentum rapidly, and was caught by a stray current which brought it closer to the girl than to the Eater at which Lavon had aimed.

He bit his lip, lowered the weapon, wound it up again. It did not pay to underestimate the range; he would have to wait until he could fire with effect. Another bolt, cutting through the water from a side port, made him issue orders to cease firing.

The sudden irruption of the rotifers decided the girl. The motionless wooden monster was strange to her and had not yet menaced her—but she must have known what it would be like to have three Dicrans over her, each trying to grab away from the other the biggest share. She threw herself toward the big port. The Eaters screamed with fury and greed and bored after her.

She probably would not have made it, had not the dull vision of the lead Dicran made out the wooden shape of the ship at the last instant. It backed off, buzzing, and the other two sheered away to avoid colliding with it. After that they had another argument, though they could hardly have formulated what it was that they were fighting about. They were incapable of saying anything much more complicated than the equivalent of "Yaah," "Drop dead," and "You're another."

While they were still snarling at each other, Lavon pierced the nearest one all the way through with an arablast bolt. It disintegrated promptly—rotifers are delicately organized creatures despite their ferocity—and the remaining two were at once involved in a lethal battle over the remains.

"Than, take a party out and spear me those two Eaters while they're still fighting," Lavon ordered. "Don't forget to destroy their eggs, too. I can see that this world needs a little taming."

The girl shot through the port and brought up against the far wall of the cabin, flailing in terror. Lavon tried to approach her, but from somewhere she produced a flake of stonewort chipped to a nasty point. He sat down on the stool before his control board and waited while she took in the cabin, Lavon, Shar, the pilot, the senescent Para.

At last she said: "Are—you—the gods from beyond the sky?"

"We're from beyond the sky, all right," Lavon said. "But we're not gods. We're human beings, like yourself. Are there many humans here?"

The girl seemed to assess the situation very rapidly, savage though she was. Lavon had the odd and impossible impression that he should recognize her. She tucked the knife back into her matted hair—ah, Lavon thought, that's a trick I may need to remember—and shook her head.

"We are few. The Eaters are everywhere. Soon they will have the last of us."

Her fatalism was so complete that she actually did not seem to care.

"And you've never cooperated against them? Or asked the protos to help?"

"The protos?" She shrugged. "They are as helpless as we are against the Eaters. We have no weapons which kill at a distance, like yours. And it is too late now for such weapons to do any good. We are too few, the Eaters too many."

Lavon shook his head emphatically. "You've had one weapon that counts all along. Against it, numbers mean nothing. We'll show you how we've used it. You may be able to use it even better than we did, once you've given it a try."

The girl shrugged again. "We have dreamed of such a weapon now and then, but never found it. I do not think that what you say is true. What is this weapon?"

"Brains," Lavon said. "Not just one brain, but brains. Working together. Cooperation."

"Lavon speaks the truth," a weak voice said from the deck.

The Para stirred feebly. The girl watched it with wide eyes. The sound of the Para using human speech seemed to impress her more than the ship or anything else it contained.

"The Eaters can be conquered," the thin, buzzing voice said. "The protos will help, as they helped in the world from which we came. They fought this flight through space, and deprived Man of his records; but Man made the trip without the records. The protos will never oppose men again. I have already spoken to the protos of this world and have told them what Man can dream, Man can do, whether the protos wish it or not.

"Shar, your metal records are with you. They were hidden in the ship. My brothers will lead you to them.

"This organism dies now. It dies in confidence of knowledge, as an intelligent creature dies. Man has taught us this. There is nothing that knowledge . . . cannot do. With it, men . . . have crossed . . . have crossed space . . ."

The voice whispered away. The shining slipper did not change, but something about it was gone. Lavon looked at the girl; their eyes met.

"We have crossed space," Lavon repeated softly.

Shar's voice came to him across a great distance. The young-old man was whispering: But *have* we?"

"As far as I'm concerned, yes," said Lavon.

THE NINE BILLION NAMES OF GOD

by Arthur C. Clarke

"This is a slightly unusual request," said Dr. Wagner, with what he hoped was commendable restraint. "As far as I know, it's the first time anyone's been asked to supply a Tibetan monastery with an Automatic Sequence Computer. I don't wish to be inquisitive, but I should hardly have thought that your—ah—establishment had much use for such a machine. Could you explain just what you intend to do with it?"

"Gladly," replied the lama, readjusting his silk robes and carefully putting away the slide rule he had been using for currency conversions. "Your Mark V Computer can carry out any routine mathematical operation involving up to ten digits. However, for our work we are interested in *letters,* not numbers. As we wish you to modify the output circuits, the machine will be printing words, not columns of figures."

"I don't quite understand. . . ."

"This is a project on which we have been working for the last three centuries—since the lamasery was founded, in fact. It is somewhat alien to your way of thought, so I hope you will listen with an open mind while I explain it."

"Naturally."

"It is really quite simple. We have been compiling a list which shall contain all the possible names of God."

"I beg your pardon?"

"We have reason to believe," continued the lama imperturbably, "that all such names can be written with not more than nine letters in an alphabet we have devised."

First published in 1953

"And you have been doing this for three centuries?"

"Yes: we expected it would take us about fifteen thousand years to complete the task."

"Oh," Dr. Wagner looked a little dazed. "Now I see why you wanted to hire one of our machines. But exactly what is the *purpose* of this project?"

The lama hesitated for a fraction of a second, and Wagner wondered if he had offended him. If so, there was no trace of annoyance in the reply.

"Call it ritual, if you like, but it's a fundamental part of our belief. All the many names of the Supreme Being— God, Jehovah, Allah, and so on—they are only man-made labels. There is a philosophical problem of some difficulty here, which I do not propose to discuss, but somewhere among all the possible combinations of letters that can occur are what one may call the *real* names of God. By systematic permutation of letters, we have been trying to list them all."

"I see. You've been starting at AAAAAAA . . . and working up to ZZZZZZZZ. . . ."

"Exactly—though we use a special alphabet of our own. Modifying the electromatic typewriters to deal with this is, of course, trivial. A rather more interesting problem is that of devising suitable circuits to eliminate ridiculous combinations. For example, no letter must occur more than three times in succession."

"Three? Surely you mean two."

"Three is correct: I am afraid it would take too long to explain why, even if you understood our language."

"I'm sure it would," said Wagner hastily. "Go on."

"Luckily, it will be a simple matter to adapt your Automatic Sequence Computer for this work, since once it has been programed properly it will permute each letter in turn and print the result. What would have taken us fifteen thousand years it will be able to do in a hundred days."

Dr. Wagner was scarcely conscious of the faint sounds from the Manhattan streets far below. He was in a different world, a world of natural, not man-made, mountains. High up in their remote aeries these monks had been patiently at work, generation after generation, compiling their lists of meaningless words. Was there any limit to the follies of mankind? Still, he must give no hint of his inner thoughts. The customer was always right. . . .

"There's no doubt," replied the doctor, "that we can modify the Mark V to print lists of this nature. I'm much more worried about the problem of installation and maintenance. Getting out to Tibet, in these days, is not going to be easy."

"We can arrange that. The components are small enough to travel by air—that is one reason why we chose your machine. If you can get them to India, we will provide transport from there."

"And you want to hire two of our engineers?"

"Yes, for the three months that the project should occupy."

"I've no doubt that Personnel can manage that." Dr. Wagner scribbled a note on his desk pad. "There are just two other points—"

Before he could finish the sentence the lama had produced a small slip of paper.

"This is my certified credit balance at the Asiatic Bank."

"Thank you. It appears to be—ah—adequate. The second matter is so trivial that I hesitate to mention it—but it's surprising how often the obvious gets overlooked. What source of electrical energy have you?"

"A diesel generator providing fifty kilowatts at a hundred and ten volts. It was installed about five years ago and is quite reliable. It's made life at the monastery much more comfortable, but of course it was really installed to provide power for the motors driving the prayer wheels."

"Of course," echoed Dr. Wagner. "I should have thought of that."

The view from the parapet was vertiginous, but in time one gets used to anything. After three months, George Hanley was not impressed by the two-thousand-foot swoop into the abyss or the remote checkerboard of fields in the valley below. He was leaning against the wind-smoothed stones and staring morosely at the distant mountains whose names he had never bothered to discover.

This, thought George, was the craziest thing that had

ever happened to him. "Project Shangri-La," some wit back at the labs had christened it. For weeks now the Mark V had been churning out acres of sheets covered with gibberish. Patiently, inexorably, the computer had been rearranging letters in all their possible combinations, exhausting each class before going on to the next. As the sheets had emerged from the electromatic typewriters, the monks had carefully cut them up and pasted them into enormous books. In another week, heaven be praised, they would have finished. Just what obscure calculations had convinced the monks that they needn't bother to go on to words of ten, twenty, or a hundred letters, George didn't know. One of his recurring nightmares was that there would be some change of plan, and that the high lama (whom they'd naturally called Sam Jaffe, though he didn't look a bit like him) would suddenly announce that the project would be extended to approximately A.D. 2060. They were quite capable of it.

George heard the heavy wooden door slam in the wind as Chuck came out onto the parapet beside him. As usual, Chuck was smoking one of the cigars that made him so popular with the monks—who, it seemed, were quite willing to embrace all the minor and most of the major pleasures of life. That was one thing in their favor: they might be crazy, but they weren't bluenoses. Those frequent trips they took down to the village, for instance . . .

"Listen, George," said Chuck urgently. "I've learned something that means trouble."

"What's wrong? Isn't the machine behaving?" That was the worst contingency George could imagine. It might delay his return, and nothing could be more horrible. The way he felt now, even the sight of a TV commercial would seem like manna from heaven. At least it would be some link with home.

"No—it's nothing like that." Chuck settled himself on the parapet, which was unusual because normally he was scared of the drop. "I've just found what all this is about."

"What d'ya mean? I thought we knew."

"Sure—we know what the monks are trying to do. But we didn't know *why*. It's the craziest thing—"

"Tell me something new," growled George.

"—but old Sam's just come clean with me. You know

the way he drops in every afternoon to watch the sheets roll out. Well, this time he seemed rather excited, or at least as near as he'll ever get to it. When I told him that we were on the last cycle he asked me, in that cute English accent of his, if I'd ever wondered what they were trying to do. I said, 'Sure'—and he told me."

"Go on: I'll buy it."

"Well, they believe that when they have listed all His names—and they reckon that there are about nine billion of them—God's purpose will be achieved. The human race will have finished what it was created to do, and there won't be any point in carrying on. Indeed, the very idea is something like blasphemy."

"Then what do they expect us to do? Commit suicide?"

"There's no need for that. When the list's completed, God steps in and simply winds things up . . . bingo!"

"Oh, I get it. When we finish our job, it will be the end of the world."

Chuck gave a nervous little laugh.

"That's just what I said to Sam. And do you know what happened? He looked at me in a very queer way, like I'd been stupid in class, and said, 'It's nothing as trivial as *that.*'"

George thought this over for a moment.

"That's what I call taking the Wide View," he said presently. "But what d'you suppose we should do about it? I don't see that it makes the slightest difference to us. After all, we already knew that they were crazy."

"Yes—but don't you see what may happen? When the list's complete and the Last Trump doesn't blow—or whatever it is they expect—*we* may get the blame. It's our machine they've been using. I don't like the situation one little bit."

"I see," said George slowly. "You've got a point there. But this sort of thing's happened before, you know. When I was a kid down in Louisiana we had a crackpot preacher who once said the world was going to end next Sunday. Hundreds of people believed him—even sold their homes. Yet when nothing happened, they didn't turn nasty, as you'd expect. They just decided that he'd made a mistake in his calculations and went right on believing. I guess some of them still do."

"Well, this isn't Louisiana, in case you hadn't noticed. There are just two of us and hundreds of these monks. I like them, and I'll be sorry for old Sam when his lifework backfires on him. But all the same, I wish I was somewhere else."

"I've been wishing that for weeks. But there's nothing we can do until the contract's finished and the transport arrives to fly us out."

"Of course," said Chuck thoughtfully, "we could always try a bit of sabotage."

"Like hell we could! That would make things worse."

"Not the way I meant. Look at it like this. The machine will finish its run four days from now, on the present twenty-hours-a-day basis. The transport calls in a week. O.K.—then all we need to do is to find something that needs replacing during one of the overhaul periods—something that will hold up the works for a couple of days. We'll fix it, of course, but not too quickly. If we time matters properly, we can be down at the airfield when the last name pops out of the register. They won't be able to catch us then."

"I don't like it," said George. "It will be the first time I ever walked out on a job. Besides, it would make them suspicious. No, I'll sit tight and take what comes."

"I *still* don't like it," he said, seven days later, as the tough little mountain ponies carried them down the winding road. "And don't you think I'm running away because I'm afraid. I'm just sorry for those poor old guys up there, and I don't want to be around when they find what suckers they've been. Wonder how Sam will take it?"

"It's funny," replied Chuck, "but when I said good-by I got the idea he knew we were walking out on him—and that he didn't care because he knew the machine was running smoothly and that the job would soon be finished. After that—well, of course, for him there just isn't any After That. . . ."

George turned in his saddle and stared back up the mountain road. This was the last place from which one could get a clear view of the lamasery. The squat, angular buildings were silhouetted against the after-glow of the sunset: here and there, lights gleamed like portholes in the side of an ocean liner. Electric lights, of course, sharing the same circuit as the Mark V. How much longer would they share it? wondered George. Would the monks smash up the computer in their rage and disappointment? Or would they just sit down quietly and begin their calculations all over again?

He knew exactly what was happening up on the mountain at this very moment. The high lama and his assistants would be sitting in their silk robes, inspecting the sheets as the junior monks carried them away from the typewriters and pasted them into the great volumes. No one would be saying anything. The only sound would be the incessant patter, the never-ending rainstorm of the keys hitting the paper, the Mark V itself was utterly silent as it flashed through its thousands of calculations a second. Three months of this, thought George, was enough to start anyone climbing up the wall.

"There she is!" called Chuck, pointing down into the valley. "Ain't she beautiful!"

She certainly was, thought George. The battered old DC3 lay at the end of the runway like a tiny silver cross. In two hours she would be bearing them away to freedom and sanity. It was a thought worth savoring like a fine liqueur. George let it roll round his mind as the pony trudged patiently down the slope.

The swift night of the high Himalayas was now almost upon them. Fortunately, the road was very good, as roads went in that region, and they were both carrying torches. There was not the slightest danger, only a certain discomfort from the bitter cold. The sky overhead was perfectly clear, and ablaze with the familiar, friendly stars. At least there would be no risk, thought George, of the pilot being unable to take off because of weather conditions. That had been his only remaining worry.

He began to sing, but gave it up after a while. This vast arena of mountains, gleaming like whitely hooded ghosts on every side, did not encourage such ebullience. Presently George glanced at his watch.

"Should be there in an hour," he called back over his shoulder to Chuck. Then he added, in an afterthought: "Wonder if the computer's finished its run. It was due about now."

Chuck didn't reply, so George swung round in his saddle. He could just see Chuck's face, a white oval turned toward the sky.

"Look," whispered Chuck, and George lifted his eyes to heaven. (There is always a last time for everything.)

Overhead, without any fuss, the stars were going out.

IT'S A *GOOD* LIFE

by Jerome Bixby

Aunt Amy was out on the front porch, rocking back
and forth in the highbacked chair and fanning herself,
when Bill Soames rode his bicycle up the road and stopped
in front of the house.

Perspiring under the afternoon "sun," Bill lifted the box
of groceries out of the big basket over the front wheel
of the bike, and came up the front walk.

Little Anthony was sitting on the lawn, playing with
a rat. He had caught the rat down in the basement—he
had made it think that it smelled cheese, the most rich-
smelling and crumbly-delicious cheese a rat had ever
thought it smelled, and it had come out of its hole, and
now Anthony had hold of it with his mind and was making
it do tricks.

When the rat saw Bill Soames coming, it tried to run,
but Anthony thought at it, and it turned a flip-flop on
the grass, and lay trembling, its eyes gleaming in small
black terror.

Bill Soames hurried past Anthony and reached the front
steps, mumbling. He always mumbled when he came to
the Fremont house, or passed by it, or even thought of it.
Everybody did. They thought about silly things, things
that didn't mean very much, like two-and-two-is-four-and-
twice-is-eight and so on; they tried to jumble up their
thoughts and keep them skipping back and forth, so Anthony couldn't read their minds. The mumbling helped.
Because if Anthony got anything strong out of your
thoughts, he might take a notion to do something about

First published in 1953

it—like curing your wife's sick headaches or your kid's mumps, or getting your old milk cow back on schedule, or fixing the privy. And while Anthony mightn't actually mean any harm, he couldn't be expected to have much notion of what was the right thing to do in such cases.

That was if he liked you. He might try to help you, in his way. And that could be pretty horrible.

If he didn't like you . . . well, that could be worse.

Bill Soames set the box of groceries on the porch railing, and stopped his mumbling long enough to say, "Everythin' you wanted, Miss Amy."

"Oh, fine, William," Amy Fremont said lightly. "My, ain't it terrible hot today?"

Bill Soames almost cringed. His eyes pleaded with her. He shook his head violently *no,* and then interrupted his mumbling again, though obviously he didn't want to: "Oh, don't say that, Miss Amy . . . it's fine, just fine. A real *good* day!"

Amy Fremont got up from the rocking chair, and came across the porch. She was a tall woman, thin, a smiling vacancy in her eyes. About a year ago, Anthony had gotten mad at her, because she'd told him he shouldn't have turned the cat into a cat-rug, and although he had always obeyed her more than anyone else, which was hardly at all, this time he'd snapped at her. With his mind. And that had been the end of Amy Fremont's bright eyes, and the end of Amy Fremont as everyone had known her. And that was when word got around in Peaksville (population: 46) that even the members of Anthony's own family weren't safe. After that, everyone was twice as careful.

Someday Anthony might undo what he'd done to Aunt Amy. Anthony's Mom and Pop hoped he would. When he was older, and maybe sorry. If it was possible, that is. Because Aunt Amy had changed a lot, and besides, now Anthony wouldn't obey anyone.

"Land alive, William," Aunt Amy said, "you don't have to mumble like that. Anthony wouldn't hurt you. My goodness, Anthony likes you!" She raised her voice and called to Anthony, who had tired of the rat and was making it eat itself. "Don't you, dear? Don't you like Mr. Soames?"

Anthony looked across the lawn at the grocery man— a bright, wet, purple gaze. He didn't say anything. Bill

Soames tried to smile at him. After a second Anthony returned his attention to the rat. It had already devoured its tail, or at least chewed it off—for Anthony had made it bite faster than it could swallow, and little pink and red furry pieces lay around it on the green grass. Now the rat was having trouble reaching its hindquarters.

Mumbling silently, thinking of nothing in particular as hard as he could, Bill Soames went stiff-legged down the walk, mounted his bicycle and pedaled off.

"We'll see you tonight, William," Aunt Amy called after him.

As Bill Soames pumped the pedals, he was wishing deep down that he could pump twice as fast, to get away from Anthony all the faster, and away from Aunt Amy, who sometimes just forgot how *careful* you had to be. And he shouldn't have thought that. Because Anthony caught it. He caught the desire to get away from the Fremont house as if it was something *bad*, and his purple gaze blinked and he snapped a small, sulky thought after Bill Soames—just a small one, because he was in a good mood today, and besides, he liked Bill Soames, or at least didn't dislike him, at least today. Bill Soames wanted to go away —so, petulantly, Anthony helped him.

Pedaling with superhuman speed—or rather, appearing to, because in reality the bicycle was pedaling *him*—Bill Soames vanished down the road in a cloud of dust, his thin, terrified wail drifting back across the summerlike heat.

Anthony looked at the rat. It had devoured half its belly, and had died from pain. He thought it into a grave out deep in the cornfield—his father had once said, smiling, that he might do that with the things he killed—and went around the house, casting his odd shadow in the hot, brassy light from above.

In the kitchen, Aunt Amy was unpacking the groceries. She put the Mason-jarred goods on the shelves, and the meat and milk in the icebox, and the beet sugar and coarse flour in big cans under the sink. She put the cardboard box in the corner, by the door, for Mr. Soames to pick up next time he came. It was stained and battered and torn and worn fuzzy, but it was one of the few left in

Peaksville. In faded red letters it said *Campbell's Soup.*
The last cans of soup, or of anything else, had been eaten
long ago, except for a small communal hoard which the
villagers dipped into for special occasions—but the box
lingered on, like a coffin, and when it and the other boxes
were gone, the men would have to make some out of
wood.

Aunt Amy went out in back, where Anthony's Mom—
Aunt Amy's sister—sat in the shade of the house, shelling
peas. The peas, every time Mom ran a finger along a pod,
went *lollop-lollop-lollop* into the pan on her lap.

"William brought the groceries," Aunt Amy said. She sat
down wearily in the straightbacked chair beside Mom,
and began fanning herself again. She wasn't really old; but
ever since Anthony had snapped at her with his mind,
something had seemed to be wrong with her body as well
as her mind, and she was tired all the time.

"Oh, good," said Mom. *Lollop* went the fat peas into
the pan.

Everybody in Peaksville always said "Oh, fine," or
"Good," or "Say, that's swell!" when almost anything
happened or was mentioned—even unhappy things like
accidents or even deaths. They'd always say "Good,"
because if they didn't try to cover up how they really felt,
Anthony might overhear with his mind, and then nobody
knew what might happen. Like the time Mrs. Kent's husband, Sam, had come walking back from the graveyard,
because Anthony liked Mrs. Kent and had heard her
mourning.

Lollop.

"Tonight's television night," said Aunt Amy. "I'm glad.
I look forward to it so much every week. I wonder what
we'll see tonight?"

"Did Bill bring the meat?" asked Mom.

"Yes." Aunt Amy fanned herself, looking up at the
featureless brassy glare of the sky. "Goodness, it's so hot.
I wish Anthony would make it just a little cooler——"

"*Amy!*"

"Oh!" Mom's sharp tone had penetrated, where Bill
Soames' agonized expression had failed. Aunt Amy put one
thin hand to her mouth in exaggerated alarm. "Oh . . .
I'm sorry, dear." Her pale blue eyes shuttled around, right

and left, to see if Anthony was in sight. Not that it would make any difference if he was or wasn't—he didn't have to be near you to know what you were thinking. Usually, though, unless he had his attention on somebody, he would be occupied with thoughts of his own.

But some things attracted his attention—you could never be sure just what.

"This weather's just *fine*," Mom said.

Lollop.

"Oh, yes," Aunt Amy said. "It's a wonderful day. I wouldn't want it changed for the world!"

Lollop.

Lollop.

"What time is it?" Mom asked.

Aunt Amy was sitting where she could see through the kitchen window to the alarm clock on the shelf above the stove. "Four-thirty," she said.

Lollop.

"I want tonight to be something special," Mom said. "Did Bill bring a good lean roast?"

"Good and lean, dear. They butchered just today, you know, and sent us over the best piece."

"Dan Hollis will be *so* surprised when he finds out that tonight's television party is a birthday party for him too!"

"Oh *I* think he will! Are you sure nobody's told him?"

"Everybody swore they wouldn't."

"That'll be real nice," Aunt Amy nodded, looking off across the cornfield. "A birthday party."

"Well——" Mom put the pan of peas down beside her, stood up and brushed her apron. "I'd better get the roast on. Then we can set the table." She picked up the peas.

Anthony came around the corner of the house. He didn't look at them, but continued on down through the carefully kept garden—*all* the gardens in Peaksville were carefully kept, very carefully kept—and went past the rustling, useless hulk that had been the Fremont family car, and went smoothly over the fence and out into the cornfield.

"Isn't this a lovely day!" said Mom, a little loudly, as they went toward the back door.

Aunt Amy fanned herself. "A beautiful day, dear. Just *fine!*"

Out in the cornfield, Anthony walked between the tall, rustling rows of green stalks. He liked to smell the corn. The alive corn overhead, and the old dead corn underfoot. Rich Ohio earth, thick with weeds and brown, dry-rotting ears of corn, pressed between his bare toes with every step —he had made it rain last night so everything would smell and feel nice today.

He walked clear to the edge of the cornfield, and over to where a grove of shadowy green trees covered cool, moist, dark ground, and lots of leafy undergrowth, and jumbled moss-covered rocks, and a small spring that made a clear, clean pool. Here Anthony liked to rest and watch the birds and insects and small animals that rustled and scampered and chirped about. He liked to lie on the cool ground and look up through the moving greenness overhead, and watch the insects flit in the hazy soft sunbeams that stood like slanting, glowing bars between ground and treetops. Somehow, he liked the thoughts of the little creatures in this place better than the thoughts outside; and while the thoughts he picked up here weren't very strong or very clear, he could get enough out of them to know what the little creatures liked and wanted, and he spent a lot of time making the grove more like what they wanted it to be. The spring hadn't always been here; but one time he had found thirst in one small furry mind, and had brought subterranean water to the surface in a clear cold flow, and had watched blinking as the creature drank, feeling its pleasure. Later he had made the pool, when he found a small urge to swim.

He had made rocks and trees and bushes and caves, and sunlight here and shadows there, because he had felt in all the tiny minds around him the desire—or the instinctive want—for this kind of resting place, and that kind of mating place, and this kind of place to play, and that kind of home.

And somehow the creatures from all the fields and pastures around the grove had seemed to know that this was a good place, for there were always more of them coming in—every time Anthony came out here there were more creatures than the last time, and more desires and needs to be tended to. Every time there would be some kind of creature he had never seen before, and he would find its mind, and see what it wanted, and then give it to it.

He liked to help them. He liked to feel their simple gratification.

Today, he rested beneath a thick elm, and lifted his purple gaze to a red and black bird that had just come to the grove. It twittered on a branch over his head, and hopped back and forth, and thought its tiny thoughts, and Anthony made a big, soft nest for it, and pretty soon it hopped in.

A long, brown, sleek-furred animal was drinking at the pool. Anthony found its mind next. The animal was thinking about a smaller creature that was scurrying along the ground on the other side of the pool, grubbing for insects. The little creature didn't know that it was in danger. The long, brown animal finished drinking and tensed its legs to leap, and Anthony thought it into a grave in the cornfield.

He didn't like those kinds of thoughts. They reminded him of the thoughts outside the grove. A long time ago some of the people outside had thought that way about *him,* and one night they'd hidden and waited for him to come back from the grove—and he'd just thought them all into the cornfield. Since then, the rest of the people hadn't thought that way—at least, very clearly. Now their thoughts were all mixed up and confusing whenever they thought about him or near him, so he didn't pay much attention.

He liked to help them too, sometimes—but it wasn't simple, or very gratifying either. They never thought happy thoughts when he did—just the jumble. So he spent more time out here.

He watched all the birds and insects and furry creatures for a while, and played with a bird, making it soar and dip and streak madly around tree trunks until, accidentally, when another bird caught his attention for a moment, he ran it into a rock. Petulantly, he thought the rock into a grave in the cornfield; but he couldn't do anything more with the bird. Not because it was dead, though it was; but because it had a broken wing. So he went back to the house. He didn't feel like walking back through the cornfield, so he just *went* to the house, right down into the basement.

It was nice down here. Nice and dark and damp and sort of fragrant, because once Mom had been making preserves in a rack along the far wall, and then she'd stopped coming down ever since Anthony had started spending time here, and the preserves had spoiled and leaked down and spread over the dirt floor, and Anthony liked the smell.

He caught another rat, making it smell cheese, and after he played with it, he thought it into a grave right beside the long animal he'd killed in the grove. Aunt Amy hated rats, and so he killed a lot of them, because he liked Aunt Amy most of all and sometimes did things that Aunt Amy wanted. Her mind was more like the little furry minds out in the grove. She hadn't thought anything bad at all about him for a long time.

After the rat, he played with a big black spider in the corner under the stairs, making it run back and forth until its web shook and shimmered in the light from the cellar window like a reflection in silvery water. Then he drove fruit flies into the web until the spider was frantic trying to wind them all up. The spider liked flies, and its thoughts were stronger than theirs, so he did it. There was something bad in the way it liked flies, but it wasn't clear—and besides, Aunt Amy hated flies too.

He heard footsteps overhead—Mom moving around in the kitchen. He blinked his purple gaze, and almost decided to make her hold still—but instead he *went* up to the attic, and, after looking out the circular window at the front end of the long X-roofed room for a while at the front lawn and the dusty road and Henderson's tip-waving wheatfield beyond, he curled into an unlikely shape and went partly to sleep.

Soon people would be coming for television, he heard Mom think.

He went more to sleep. He liked television night. Aunt Amy had always liked television a lot, so one time he had thought some for her, and a few other people had been there at the time, and Aunt Amy had felt disappointed when they wanted to leave. He'd done something to them for that—and now everybody came to television.

He liked all the attention he got when they did.

Anthony's father came home around six-thirty, looking tired and dirty and bloody. He's been over in Dun's pasture with the other men, helping pick out the cow to be slaughtered this month and doing the job, and then butchering the meat and salting it away in Soames's icehouse. Not a job he cared for, but every man had his turn. Yesterday, he had helped scythe down old McIntyre's wheat. Tomorrow, they would start threshing. By hand. Everything in Peaksville had to be done by hand.

He kissed his wife on the cheek and sat down at the kitchen table. He smiled and said, "Where's Anthony?"

"Around someplace," Mom said.

Aunt Amy was over at the wood-burning stove, stirring the big pot of peas. Mom went back to the oven and opened it and basted the roast.

"Well, it's been a *good* day," Dad said. By rote. Then he looked at the mixing bowl and breadboard on the table. He sniffed at the dough. "M'm," he said. "I could eat a loaf all by myself, I'm so hungry."

"No one told Dan Hollis about its being a birthday party, did they?" his wife asked.

"Nope. We kept as quiet as mummies."

"We've fixed up such a lovely surprise!"

"Um? What?"

"Well . . . you know how much Dan likes music. Well, last week Thelma Dunn found a *record* in her attic!"

"No!"

"Yes! And we had Ethel sort of ask—you know, without really *asking*—if he had that one. And he said no. Isn't that a wonderful surprise?"

"Well, now, it sure is. A record, imagine! That's a real nice thing to find! What record is it?"

"Perry Como, singing *You Are My Sunshine*."

"Well, I'll be darned. I always liked that tune." Some raw carrots were lying on the table. Dad picked up a small one, scrubbed it on his chest, and took a bite. "How did Thelma happen to find it?"

"Oh, you know—just looking around for new things."

"M'm." Dad chewed the carrot. "Say, who has that picture we found a while back? I kind of liked it—that old clipper sailing along——"

"The Smiths. Next week the Sipichs get it, and they give the Smiths old McIntyre's music-box, and we give the Sipichs——" and she went down the tentative order of things that would exchange hands among the women at church this Sunday.

He nodded. "Looks like we can't have the picture for a while, I guess. Look, honey, you might try to get that detective book back from the Reillys. I was so busy the week we had it, I never got to finish all the stories——"

"I'll try," his wife said doubtfully. "But I hear the van Husens have a stereoscope they found in the cellar." Her voice was just a little accusing. "They had it two whole months before they told anybody about it——"

"Say," Dad said, looking interested. "That'd be nice, too. Lots of pictures?"

"I suppose so. I'll see on Sunday. I'd like to have it—but we still owe the van Husens for their canary. I don't know why that bird had to pick *our* house to die . . . it must have been sick when we got it. Now there's just no satisfying Betty van Husen—she even hinted she'd like our *piano* for a while!"

"Well, honey, you try for the stereoscope—or just anything you think we'll like." At last he swallowed the carrot. It had been a little young and tough. Anthony's whims about the weather made it so that people never knew what crops would come up, or what shape they'd be in if they did. All they could do was plant a lot; and always enough of something came up any one season to live on. Just once there had been a grain surplus; tons of it had been hauled to the edge of Peaksville and dumped off into the nothingness. Otherwise, nobody could have breathed, when it started to spoil.

"You know," Dad went on. "It's nice to have the new things around. It's nice to think that there's probably still a lot of stuff nobody's found yet, in cellars and attics and barns and down behind things. They help, somehow. As much as anything can help——"

"Sh-h!" Mom glanced nervously around.

"Oh," Dad said, smiling hastily. "It's all right! The new things are *good!* It's *nice* to be able to have something around you've never seen before, and know that something you've given somebody else is making them happy . . . that's a real *good* thing."

"A good thing," his wife echoed.

"Pretty soon," Aunt Amy said, from the stove, "there won't be any more new things. We'll have found everything there is to find. Goodness, that'll be too bad——"

"*Amy!*"

"Well——" her pale eyes were shallow and fixed, a sign of her recurrent vagueness. "It will be kind of a shame ——no new things——"

"Don't *talk* like that," Mom said, trembling. "Amy, be *quiet!*"

"It's *good*," said Dad, in the loud, familiar, wanting-to-be-overheard tone of voice. "Such talk is *good*. It's okay, honey—don't you see? It's good for Amy to talk any way she wants. It's good for her to feel bad. Everything's good. Everything *has* to be good . . ."

Anthony's mother was pale. And so was Aunt Amy—the peril of the moment had suddenly penetrated the clouds surrounding her mind. Sometimes it was difficult to handle words so that they might not prove disastrous. You just never *knew*. There were so many things it was wise not to say, or even think—but remonstration for saying or thinking them might be just as bad, if Anthony heard and decided to do anything about it. You could just never tell what Anthony was liable to do.

Everything had to be good. Had to be fine just as it was, even if it wasn't. Always. Because any change might be worse. So terribly much worse.

"Oh, my goodness, yes, of course it's good," Mom said. "You talk any way you want to, Amy, and it's just fine. Of course, you want to remember that some ways are *better* than others . . ."

Aunt Amy stirred the peas, fright in her pale eyes.

"Oh, yes," she said. "But I don't feel like talking right now. It . . . it's *good* that I don't feel like talking."

Dad said tiredly, smiling, "I'm going out and wash up."

They started arriving around eight o'clock. By that time, Mom and Aunt Amy had the big table in the dining room set, and two more tables off to the side. The candles were burning, and the chairs situated, and Dad had a big fire going in the fireplace.

The first to arrive were the Sipichs, John and Mary. John wore his best suit, and was well-scrubbed and pink-faced after his day in McIntyre's pasture. The suit was neatly pressed, but getting threadbare at elbows and cuffs. Old McIntyre was working on a loom, designing it out of schoolbooks, but so far it was slow going. McIntyre was a capable man with wood and tools, but a loom was a big order when you couldn't get metal parts. McIntyre had been one of the ones, who, at first, had wanted to try to get Anthony to make things the villagers needed, like clothes and canned goods and medical supplies and gasoline. Since then, he felt that what had happened to the whole Terrance family and Joe Kinney was his fault, and he worked hard trying to make it up to the rest of them. And since then, no one had tried to get Anthony to do anything.

Mary Sipich was a small, cheerful woman in a simple dress. She immediately set about helping Mom and Aunt Amy put the finishing touches on the dinner.

The next arrivals were the Smiths and the Dunns, who lived right next to each other down the road, only a few yards from the nothingness. They drove up in the Smiths' wagon, drawn by their old horse.

Then the Reillys showed up, from across the darkened wheatfield, and the evening really began. Pat Reilly sat down at the big upright in the front room, and began to play from the popular sheet music on the rack. He played softly, as expressively as he could—and nobody sang. Anthony liked piano playing a whole lot, but not singing; often he would come up from the basement, or down from the attic, or just *come,* and sit on top of the piano, nodding his head as Pat played *Lover* or *Boulevard of Broken Dreams* or *Night and Day.* He seemed to prefer ballads, sweet-sounding songs—but the one time somebody had started to sing, Anthony had looked over from the top of the piano and done something that made everybody afraid of singing from then on. Later, they'd decided that the piano was what Anthony had heard first, before anybody had ever tried to sing, and now anything else added to it didn't sound right and distracted him from his pleasure.

So, every television night, Pat would play the piano, and that was the beginning of the evening. Wherever Anthony was, the music would make him happy, and put him in a good mood, and he would know that they were gathering for television and waiting for him.

By eight-thirty everybody had shown up, except for the seventeen children and Mrs. Soames who was off watching them in the schoolhouse at the far end of town. The children of Peaksville were never, never allowed near the Fremont house—not since little Fred Smith had tried to play with Anthony on a dare. The younger children weren't even told about Anthony. The others had mostly forgotten about him, or were told that he was a nice, nice goblin but they must never go near him.

Dan and Ethel Hollis came late, and Dan walked in not suspecting a thing. Pat Reilly had played the piano until his hands ached—he'd worked pretty hard with them today—and now he got up, and everybody gathered around to wish Dan Hollis a happy birthday.

"Well, I'll be darned," Dan grinned. "This is swell. I wasn't expecting this at all . . . gosh, this is *swell!*"

They gave him his presents—mostly things they had made by hand, though some were things that people had possessed as their own and now gave him as his. John Sipich gave him a watch charm, hand-carved out of a piece of hickory wood. Dan's watch had broken down a year or so ago, and there was nobody in the village who knew how to fix it, but he still carried it around because it had been his grandfather's and was a fine old heavy thing of gold and silver. He attached the charm to the chain, while everybody laughed and said John had done a nice job of carving. Then Mary Sipich gave him a knitted necktie, which he put on, removing the one he'd worn.

The Reillys gave him a little box they had made, to keep things in. They didn't say what things, but Dan said he'd keep his personal jewelry in it. The Reillys had made it out of a cigar box, carefully peeled of its paper and lined on the inside with velvet. The outside had been polished, and carefully if not expertly carved by Pat—but his carving got complimented too. Dan Hollis received many other gifts—a pipe, a pair of shoelaces, a tie pin, a knit pair of socks, some fudge, a pair of garters made from old suspenders.

He unwrapped each gift with vast pleasure, and wore as many of them as he could right there, even the garters. He lit up the pipe, and said he'd never had a better smoke; which wasn't quite true, because the pipe wasn't broken in yet. Pete Manners had had it lying around ever since he'd received it as a gift four years ago from an out-of-town relative who hadn't know he'd stopped smoking.

Dan put the tobacco into the bowl very carefully. Tobacco was precious. It was only pure luck that Pat Reilly had decided to try to grow some in his backyard just before what had happened to Peaksville had happened. It didn't grow very well, and then they had to cure it and shred it and all, and it was just precious stuff. Everybody in town used wooden holders old McIntyre had made, to save on butts.

Last of all, Thelma Dunn gave Dan Hollis the record she had found.

Dan's eyes misted even before he opened the package. He knew it was a record.

"Gosh," he said softly. "What one is it? I'm almost afraid to look . . ."

"You haven't got it, darling," Ethel Hollis smiled. "Don't you remember, I asked about *You Are My Sunshine?*"

"Oh, gosh," Dan said again. Carefully he removed the wrapping and stood there fondling the record, running his big hands over the worn grooves with their tiny, dulling crosswise scratches. He looked around the room, eyes shining, and they all smiled back, knowing how delighted he was.

"Happy birthday, darling!" Ethel said, throwing her arms around him and kissing him.

He clutched the record in both hands, holding it off to one side as she pressed against him. "Hey," he laughed, pulling back his head. "Be careful . . . I'm holding a priceless object!" He looked around again, over his wife's arms, which were still around his neck. His eyes were hungry. "Look . . . do you think we could play it? Lord, what I'd give to hear some new music . . . just the first part, the orchestra part, before Como sings?"

Faces sobered. After a minute, John Sipich said, "I don't think we'd better, Dan. After all, we don't know just where the singer comes in—it'd be taking too much of a chance. Better wait till you get home."

Dan Hollis reluctantly put the record on the buffet with all his other presents. "It's *good*," he said automatically, but disappointedly, "that I can't play it here."

"Oh, yes," said Sipich. "It's good." To compensate for Dan's disappointed tone, he repeated, "It's *good*."

They ate dinner, the candles lighting their smiling faces, and ate it all right down to the last delicious drop of gravy. They complimented Mom and Aunt Amy on the roast beef, and the peas and carrots, and the tender corn on the cob. The corn hadn't come from the Fremont's cornfield, naturally—everybody knew what was out there; and the field was going to weeds.

Then they polished off the dessert—homemade ice cream and cookies. And then they sat back, in the flickering light of the candles, and chatted, waiting for television.

There never was a lot of mumbling on television night—everybody came and had a good dinner at the Fremonts', and that was nice, and afterwards there was television and nobody really thought much about that—it just had to be put up with. So it was a pleasant enough get-together, aside from your having to watch what you said just as carefully as you always did everyplace. If a dangerous thought came into your mind, you just started mumbling, even right in the middle of a sentence. When you did that, the others just ignored you until you felt happier again and stopped.

Anthony liked television night. He had done only two or three awful things on television night in the whole past year.

Mom had put a bottle of brandy on the table, and they each had a tiny glass of it. Liquor was even more precious than tobacco. The villagers could make wine, but the grapes weren't right, and certainly the techniques weren't, and it wasn't very good wine. There were only a few bottles of real liquor left in the village—four rye, three Scotch, three brandy, nine real wine and half a bottle of Drambuie belonging to old McIntyre (only for marriages)—and when those were gone, that was it.

Afterward, everybody wished that the brandy hadn't been brought out. Because Dan Hollis drank more of it than he should have, and mixed it with a lot of the homemade wine. Nobody thought anything about it at first, because he didn't show it much outside, and it was his birthday party and a happy party, and Anthony liked these get-togethers and shouldn't see any reason to do anything even if he was listening.

But Dan Hollis got high, and did a fool thing. If they'd seen it coming, they'd have taken him outside and walked him around.

The first thing they knew, Dan stopped laughing right in the middle of the story about how Thelma Dunn had found the Perry Como record and dropped it and it hadn't broken because she'd moved faster than she ever had before in her life and caught it. He was fondling the record again, and looking longingly at the Fremonts' gramophone over in the corner, and suddenly he stopped laughing and his face got slack, and then it got ugly, and he said, "Oh, *Christ!*"

Immediately the room was still. So still they could hear the whirring movement of the grandfather's clock out in the hall. Pat Reilly had been playing the piano, softly. He stopped, his hands poised over the yellowed keys.

The candles on the dining-room table flickered in a cool breeze that blew through the lace curtains over the bay window.

"Keep playing, Pat," Anthony's father said softly.

Pat started again. He played *Night and Day,* but his eyes were sidewise on Dan Hollis, and he missed notes.

Dan stood in the middle of the room, holding the record. In his other hand he held a glass of brandy so hard his hand shook.

They were all looking at him.

"*Christ,*" he said again, and he made it sound like a dirty word.

Reverend Younger, who had been talking with Mom and Aunt Amy by the dining-room door, said "Christ" too—but he was using it in a prayer. His hands were clasped, and his eyes were closed.

John Sipich moved forward. "Now, Dan . . . it's *good* for you to talk that way. But you don't want to talk too much, you know."

Dan shook off the hand Sipich put on his arm.

"Can't even play my record," he said loudly. He looked down at the record, and then around at their faces. "Oh, my *God* . . ."

He threw the glassful of brandy against the wall. It splattered and ran down the wallpaper in streaks.

Some of the women gasped.

"Dan," Sipich said in a whisper. "Dan, cut it out——"

Pat Reilly was playing *Night and Day* louder, to cover up the sounds of the talk. It wouldn't do any good, though, if Anthony was listening.

Dan Hollis went over to the piano and stood by Pat's shoulder, swaying a little.

"Pat," he said. "Don't play *that*. Play *this*." And he began to sing. Softly, hoarsely, miserably: "Happy birthday to me . . . Happy birthday to me . . ."

"Dan!" Ethel Hollis screamed. She tried to run across the room to him. Mary Sipich grabbed his arm and held her back. "Dan," Ethel screamed again. "Stop——"

"My God, be quiet!" hissed Mary Sipich, and pushed her toward one of the men, who put his hand over her mouth and held her still.

"——Happy birthday, dear Danny," Dan sang. "Happy birthday to me!" He stopped and looked down at Pat Reilly. "Play it, Pat. Play it, so I can sing right . . . you know I can't carry a tune unless somebody plays it!"

Pat Reilly put his hand on the keys and began *Lover*—in a slow waltz tempo, the way Anthony liked it. Pat's face was white. His hands fumbled.

Dan Hollis stared over at the dining-room door. At Anthony's mother, and at Anthony's father who had gone to join her.

"You had him," he said. Tears gleamed on his cheeks as the candlelight caught them. *"You* had to go and *have* him . . ."

He closed his eyes, and the tears squeezed out. He sang loudly, "You are my sunshine . . . my only sunshine . . . you make me happy . . . when I am blue . . ."

Anthony *came* into the room.

Pat stopped playing. He froze. Everybody froze. The breeze rippled the curtains. Ethel Hollis couldn't even try to scream—she had fainted.

"Please don't take my sunshine . . . away . . ." Dan's voice faltered into silence. His eyes widened. He put both hands out in front of him, the empty glass in one, the record in the other. He hiccupped, and said, *"No——"*

"Bad man," Anthony said, and thought Dan Hollis into something like nothing anyone would have believed possible, and then he thought the thing into a grave deep, deep in the cornfield.

The glass and record thumped on the rug. Neither broke.

Anthony's purple gaze went around the room.

Some of the people began mumbling. They all tried to smile. The sound of mumbling filled the room like a far-off approval. Out of the murmuring came one or two clear voices:

"Oh, it's a very *good* thing," said John Sipich.

"A good thing," said Anthony's father, smiling. He'd had more practice in smiling than most of them. "A wonderful thing."

"It's swell . . . just swell," said Pat Reilly, tears leaking from eyes and nose, and he began to play the piano again, softly, his trembling hands feeling for *Night and Day.*

Anthony climbed up on top of the piano, and Pat played for two hours.

Afterward, they watched television. They all went into the front room, and lit just a few candles, and pulled up chairs around the set. It was a small-screen set, and they couldn't all sit close enough to it to see, but that didn't matter. They didn't even turn the set on. It wouldn't have worked anyway, there being no electricity in Peaksville.

They just sat silently, and watched the twisting, writhing shapes on the screen, and listened to the sounds that came out of the speaker, and none of them had any idea of what it was all about. They never did. It was always the same.

"It's real nice," Aunt Amy said once, her pale eyes on meaningless flickers and shadows. "But I liked it a little better when there were cities outside and we could get real——"

"Why, Amy!" said Mom. "It's good for you to say such a thing. Very good. But how can you mean it? Why, this television is *much* better than anything we ever used to get!"

"Yes," chimed in John Sipich. "It's fine. It's the best show we've ever seen!"

He sat on the couch, with two other men, holding Ethel Hollis flat against the cushions, holding her arms and legs and putting their hands over her mouth, so she couldn't start screaming again.

"It's really *good!*" he said again.

Mom looked out of the front window, across the darkened road, across Henderson's darkened wheat field to the vast, endless, gray nothingness in which the little village of Peaksville floated like a soul—the huge nothingness that was evident at night, when Anthony's brassy day had gone.

It did no good to wonder where they were . . . no good at all. Peaksville was just someplace. Someplace away from the world. It was wherever it had been since that day three years ago when Anthony had crept from her womb and old Doc Bates—God rest him—had screamed and dropped him and tried to kill him, and Anthony had whined and done the thing. He had taken the village someplace. Or had destroyed the world and left only the village, nobody knew which.

It did no good to wonder about it. Nothing at all did any good—except to live as they must live. Must always, always live, if Anthony would let them.

These thoughts were dangerous, she thought.

She began to mumble. The others started mumbling too. They had all been thinking, evidently.

The men on the couch whispered and whispered to Ethel Hollis, and when they took their hands away, she mumbled too.

While Anthony sat on top of the set and made television, they sat around and mumbled and watched the meaningless, flickering shapes far into the night.

Next day it snowed, and killed off half the crops—but it was a *good* day.

THE COLD EQUATIONS

by Tom Godwin

He was not alone.

There was nothing to indicate the fact but the white hand of the tiny gauge on the board before him. The control room was empty but for himself; there was no sound other than the murmur of the drives—but the white hand had moved. It had been on zero when the little ship was launched from the *Stardust;* now, an hour later, it had crept up. There was something in the supplies closet across the room, it was saying, some kind of a body that radiated heat.

It could be but one kind of a body—a living, human body.

He leaned back in the pilot's chair and drew a deep, slow breath, considering what he would have to do. He was an EDS pilot, inured to the sight of death, long since accustomed to it and to viewing the dying of another man with an objective lack of emotion, and he had no choice in what he must do. There could be no alternative—but it required a few moments of conditioning for even an EDS pilot to prepare himself to walk across the room and coldly, deliberately, take the life of a man he had yet to meet.

He would, of course, do it. It was the law, stated very bluntly and definitely in grim Paragraph L, Section 8, of Interstellar Regulations: *Any stowaway discovered in an EDS shall be jettisoned immediately following discovery.*

It was the law, and there could be no appeal.

First published in 1954

It was a law not of men's choosing but made imperative by the circumstances of the space frontier. Galactic expansion had followed the development of the hyperspace drive and as men scattered wide across the frontier there had come the problem of contact with the isolated first-colonies and exploration parties. The huge hyperspace cruisers were the product of the combined genius and effort of Earth and were long and expensive in the building. They were not available in such numbers that small colonies could possess them. The cruisers carried the colonists to their new worlds and made periodic visits, running on tight schedules, but they could not stop and turn aside to visit colonies scheduled to be visited at another time; such a delay would destroy their schedule and produce a confusion and uncertainty that would wreck the complex interdependence between old Earth and new worlds of the frontier.

Some method of delivering supplies or assistance when an emergency occurred on a world not scheduled for a visit had been needed and the Emergency Dispatch Ships had been the answer. Small and collapsible, they occupied little room in the hold of the cruiser; made of light metal and plastics, they were driven by a small rocket drive that consumed relatively little fuel. Each cruiser carried four EDS's and when a call for aid was received the nearest cruiser would drop into normal space long enough to launch an EDS with the needed supplies or personnel, then vanish again as it continued on its course.

The cruisers, powered by nuclear converters, did not use the liquid rocket fuel but nuclear converters were far too large and complex to permit their installation in the EDS's. The cruisers were forced by necessity to carry a limited amount of the bulky rocket fuel and the fuel was rationed with care; the cruiser's computers determining the exact amount of fuel each EDS would require for its mission. The computers considered the course coordinates, the mass of the EDS, the mass of pilot and cargo; they were very precise and accurate and omitted nothing from their calculations. They could not, however, foresee, and allow for, the added mass of a stowaway.

The *Stardust* had received the request from one of the exploration parties stationed on Woden; the six men of the party already being stricken with the fever carried by the green *kala* midges and their own supply of serum destroyed by the tornado that had torn through their camp. The *Stardust* had gone through the usual procedure; dropping into normal space to launch the EDS with the fever serum, then vanishing again in hyperspace. Now, an hour later, the gauge was saying there was something more than the small carton of serum in the supplies closet.

He let his eyes rest on the narrow white door of the closet. There, just inside, another man lived and breathed and was beginning to feel assured that discovery of his presence would now be too late for the pilot to alter the situation. It *was* too late—for the man behind the door it was far later than he thought and in a way he would find terrible to believe.

There could be no alternative. Additional fuel would be used during the hours of deceleration to compensate for the added mass of the stowaway; infinitesimal increments of fuel that would not be missed until the ship had almost reached its destination. Then, at some distance above the ground that might be as near as a thousand feet or as far as tens of thousands of feet, depending upon the mass of ship and cargo and the preceding period of deceleration, the unmissed increments of fuel would make their absence known; the EDS would expend its last drops of fuel with a sputter and go into whistling free fall. Ship and pilot and stowaway would merge together upon impact as a wreckage of metal and plastic, flesh and blood, driven deep into the soil. The stowaway had signed his own death warrant when he concealed himself on the ship; he could not be permitted to take seven others with him.

He looked again at the telltale white hand, then rose to his feet. What he must do would be unpleasant for both of them; the sooner it was over, the better. He stepped across the control room, to stand by the white door.

"Come out!" His command was harsh and abrupt above the murmur of the drive.

It seemed he could hear the whisper of a furtive movement inside the closet, then nothing. He visualized the stowaway cowering closer into one corner, suddenly wor-

ried by the possible consequences of his act and his self-
assurance evaporating.

"I said *out!*"

He heard the stowaway move to obey and he waited
with his eyes alert on the door and his hand near the
blaster at his side.

The door opened and the stowaway stepped through it,
smiling. "All right—I give up. Now what?"

It was a girl.

He stared without speaking, his hand dropping away
from the blaster and acceptance of what he saw coming
like a heavy and unexpected physical blow. The stowaway
was not a man—she was a girl in her teens, standing before
him in little white gypsy sandals with the top of her brown,
curly head hardly higher than his shoulder, with a faint,
sweet scent of perfume coming from her and her smiling
face tilted up so her eyes could look unknowing and unafraid into his as she waited for his answer.

Now what? Had it been asked in the deep, defiant voice
of a man he would have answered it with action, quick and
efficient. He would have taken the stowaway's identification disk and ordered him into the air lock. Had the stowaway refused to obey, he would have used the blaster. It
would not have taken long; within a minute the body
would have been ejected into space—had the stowaway
been a man.

He returned to the pilot's chair and motioned her to seat
herself on the boxlike bulk of the drive-control units that
set against the wall beside him. She obeyed, his silence
making the smile fade into the meek and guilty expression
of a pup that has been caught in mischief and knows it
must be punished.

"You still haven't told me," she said. "I'm guilty, so
what happens to me now? Do I pay a fine, or what?"

"What are you doing here?" he asked. "Why did you
stow away on this EDS?"

"I wanted to see my brother. He's with the government
survey crew on Woden and I haven't seen him for ten
years, not since he left Earth to go into government survey
work."

"What was your destination on the *Stardust?*"

"Mimir. I have a position waiting for me there. My brother has been sending money home all the time to us—my father and mother and I—and he paid for a special course in linguistics I was taking. I graduated sooner than expected and I was offered this job on Mimir. I knew it would be almost a year before Gerry's job was done on Woden so he could come on to Mimir and that's why I hid in the closet, there. There was plenty of room for me and I was willing to pay the fine. There were only the two of us kids—Gerry and I—and I haven't seen him for so long, and I didn't want to wait another year when I could see him now, even though I knew I would be breaking some kind of a regulation when I did it."

I knew I would be breaking some kind of a regulation— In a way, she could not be blamed for her ignorance of the law; she was of Earth and had not realized that the laws of the space frontier must, of necessity, be as hard and relentless as the environment that gave them birth. Yet, to protect such as her from the results of their own ignorance of the frontier, there had been a sign over the door that led to the section of the *Stardust* that housed EDS's; a sign that was plain for all to see and heed:

UNAUTHORIZED PERSONNEL
KEEP OUT!

"Does your brother know that you took passage on the *Stardust* for Mimir?"

"Oh, yes. I sent him a spacegram telling him about my graduation and about going to Mimir on the *Stardust* a month before I left Earth. I already knew Mimir was where he would be stationed in a little over a year. He gets a promotion then, and he'll be based on Mimir and not have to stay out a year at a time on field trips, like he does now."

There were two different survey groups on Woden, and he asked, "What is his name?"

"Cross—Gerry Cross. He's in Group Two—that was the way his address read. Do you know him?"

Group One had requested the serum; Group Two was eight thousand miles away, across the Western Sea.

"No, I've never met him," he said, then turned to the

control board and cut the deceleration to a fraction of a gravity; knowing as he did so that it could not avert the ultimate end, yet doing the only thing he could do to prolong that ultimate end. The sensation was like that of the ship suddenly dropping and the girl's involuntary movement of surprise half lifted her from the seat.

"We're going faster now, aren't we?" she asked. "Why are we doing that?"

He told her the truth. "To save fuel for a little while."

"You mean, we don't have very much?"

He delayed the answer he must give her so soon to ask: "How did you manage to stow away?"

"I just sort of walked in when no one was looking my way," she said. "I was practicing my Gelanese on the native girl who does the cleaning in the Ship's Supply office when someone came in with an order for supplies for the survey crew on Woden. I slipped into the closet there after the ship was ready to go and just before you came in. It was an impulse of the moment to stow away, so I could get to see Gerry—and from the way you keep looking at me so grim, I'm not sure it was a very wise impulse.

"But I'll be a model criminal—or do I mean prisoner?" She smiled at him again. "I intended to pay for my keep on top of paying the fine. I can cook and I can patch clothes for everyone and I know how to do all kinds of useful things, even a little bit about nursing."

There was one more question to ask:

"Did you know what the supplies were that the survey crew ordered?"

"Why, no. Equipment they needed in their work, I supposed."

Why couldn't she have been a man with some ulterior motive? A fugitive from justice, hoping to lose himself on a raw new world; an opportunist, seeking transportation to the new colonies where he might find golden fleece for the taking; a crackpot, with a mission—

Perhaps once in his lifetime an EDS pilot would find such a stowaway on his ship; warped men, mean and selfish men, brutal and dangerous men—but never, before, a smiling, blue-eyed girl who was willing to pay her fine and work for her keep that she might see her brother.

He turned to the board and turned the switch that would signal the *Stardust*. The call would be futile but he could not, until he had exhausted that one vain hope, seize her and thrust her into the air lock as he would an animal—or a man. The delay, in the meantime, would not be dangerous with the EDS decelerating at fractional gravity.

A voice spoke from the communicator. *"Stardust.* Identify yourself and proceed."

"Barton, EDS 34G11. Emergency. Give me Commander Delhart."

There was a faint confusion of noises as the request went through the proper channels. The girl was watching him, no longer smiling.

"Are you going to order them to come back after me?" she asked.

The communicator clicked and there was the sound of a distant voice saying, "Commander, the EDS requests—"

"Are they coming back after me?" she asked again. "Won't I get to see my brother, after all?"

"Barton?" The blunt, gruff voice of Commander Delhart came from the communicator. "What's this about an emergency?"

"A stowaway," he answered.

"A stowaway?" There was a slight surprise to the question. "That's rather unusual—but why the 'emergency' call? You discovered him in time so there should be no appreciable danger and I presume you've informed Ship's Records so his nearest relatives can be notified."

"That's why I had to call you, first. The stowaway is still aboard and the circumstances are so different—"

"Different?" the commander interrupted, impatience in his voice. "How can they be different? You know you have a limited supply of fuel; you also know the law, as well as I do: 'Any stowaway discovered in an EDS shall be jettisoned immediately following discovery.'"

There was the sound of a sharply indrawn breath from the girl. *"What does he mean?"*

"The stowaway is a girl."

"What?"

"She wanted to see her brother. She's only a kid and she didn't know what she was really doing."

"I see." All the curtness was gone from the commander's

voice. "So you called me in the hope I could do something?" Without waiting for an answer he went on. "I'm sorry—I can do nothing. This cruiser must maintain its schedule; the life of not one person but the lives of many depend on it. I know how you feel but I'm powerless to help you. You'll have to go through with it. I'll have you connected with Ship's Records."

The communicator faded to a faint rustle of sound and he turned back to the girl. She was leaning forward on the bench, almost rigid, her eyes fixed wide and frightened.

"What did he mean, to go through with it? To jettison me . . . to go through with it—what did he mean? Not the way it sounded . . . he couldn't have. What did he mean . . . what did he really mean?"

Her time was too short for the comfort of a lie to be more than a cruelly fleeting delusion.

"He meant it the way it sounded."

"*No!*" She recoiled from him as though he had struck her, one hand half upraised as though to fend him off and stark unwillingness to believe in her eyes.

"It will have to be."

"No! You're joking—you're insane! You can't mean it!"

"I'm sorry." He spoke slowly to her, gently. "I should have told you before—I should have, but I had to do what I could first; I had to call the *Stardust*. You heard what the commander said."

"But you can't—if you make me leave the ship, I'll *die*."

"I know." .

She searched his face and the unwillingness to believe left her eyes, giving way slowly to a look of dazed terror.

"You—know?" She spoke the words far apart, numb and wonderingly.

"I know. It has to be like that."

"You mean it—you really mean it." She sagged back against the wall, small and limp like a little rag doll and all the protesting and disbelief gone.

"You're going to do it—you're going to make me die?"

"I'm sorry," he said again. "You'll never know how sorry I am. It has to be that way and no human in the universe can change it."

"You're going to make me die and I didn't do anything

to die for—I didn't *do* anything—"

He sighed, deep and weary. "I know you didn't, child. I know you didn't—"

"EDS." The communicator rapped brisk and metallic. "This is Ship's Records. Give us all information on subject's identification disk."

He got out of his chair to stand over her. She clutched the edge of the seat, her upturned face white under the brown hair and the lipstick standing out like a blood-red cupid's bow.

"Now?"

"I want your identification disk," he said.

She released the edge of the seat and fumbled at the chain that suspended the plastic disk from her neck with fingers that were trembling and awkward. He reached down and unfastened the clasp for her, then returned with the disk to his chair.

"Here's your data, Records: Identification Number T837—"

"One moment," Records interrupted. "This is to be filed on the gray card, of course?"

"Yes."

"And the time of the execution?"

"I'll tell you later."

"Later? This is highly irregular; the time of the subject's death is required before—"

He kept the thickness out of his voice with an effort. "Then we'll do it in a highly irregular manner—you'll hear the disk read, first. The subject is a girl and she's listening to everything that's said. Are you capable of understanding that?"

There was a brief, almost shocked, silence, then Records said meekly: "Sorry. Go ahead."

He began to read the disk, reading it slowly to delay the inevitable for as long as possible, trying to help her by giving her what little time he could to recover from her first terror and let it resolve into the calm of acceptance and resignation.

"Number T8374 dash Y54. Name: Marilyn Lee Cross. Sex: Female. Born: July 7, 2160. *She was only eighteen.* Height: 5-3. Weight: 110. *Such a slight weight, yet enough to add fatally to the mass of the shell-thin bubble that was*

an EDS. Hair: Brown. Eyes: Blue. Complexion: Light.
Blood Type: O. *Irrelevant data.* Destination: Port City,
Mimir. *Invalid data—*"

He finished and said, "I'll call you later," then turned
once again to the girl. She was huddled back against the
wall, watching him with a look of numb and wondering
fascination.

"They're waiting for you to kill me, aren't they? They
want me dead, don't they? You and everybody on the
cruiser wants me dead, don't you?" Then the numbness
broke and her voice was that of a frightened and bewildered child. "Everybody wants me dead and I didn't *do*
anything. I didn't hurt anyone—I only wanted to see my
brother."

"It's not the way you think—it isn't that way, at all," he
said. "Nobody wants it this way; nobody would ever let it
be this way if it was humanly possible to change it."

"Then why is it! I don't understand. Why is it?"

"This ship is carrying *kala* fever serum to Group One
on Woden. Their own supply was destroyed by a tornado.
Group Two—the crew your brother is in—is eight thousand miles away across the Western Sea and their heli-
copters can't cross it to help Group One. The fever is invariably fatal unless the serum can be had in time, and the
six men in Group One will die unless this ship reaches
them on schedule. These little ships are always given barely
enough fuel to reach their destination and if you stay
aboard your added weight will cause it to use up all its
fuel before it reaches the ground. It will crash, then, and
you and I will die and so will the six men waiting for the
fever serum."

It was a full minute before she spoke, and as she considered his words the expression of numbness left her eyes.

"Is that it?" she asked at last. "Just that the ship doesn't
have enough fuel?"

"Yes."

"I can go alone or I can take seven others with me—is
that the way it is?"

"That's the way it is."

"And nobody wants me to have to die?"

"Nobody."

"Then maybe— Are you sure nothing can be done about it? Wouldn't people help me if they could?"

"Everyone would like to help you but there is nothing anyone can do. I did the only thing I could do when I called the *Stardust*."

"And it won't come back—but there might be other cruisers, mightn't there? Isn't there any hope at all that there might be someone, somewhere, who could do something to help me?"

She was leaning forward a little in her eagerness as she waited for his answer.

"No."

The word was like the drop of a cold stone and she again leaned back against the wall, the hope and eagerness leaving her face. "You're sure—you *know* you're sure?"

"I'm sure. There are no other cruisers within forty light-years; there is nothing and no one to change things."

She dropped her gaze to her lap and began twisting a pleat of her skirt between her fingers, saying no more as her mind began to adapt itself to the grim knowledge.

It was better so; with the going of all hope would go the fear; with the going of all hope would come resignation. She needed time and she could have so little of it. How much?

The EDS's were not equipped with hull-cooling units; their speed had to be reduced to a moderate level before entering the atmosphere. They were decelerating at .10 gravity; approaching their destination at a far higher speed than the computers had calculated on. The *Stardust* had been quite near Woden when she launched the EDS; their present velocity was putting them nearer by the second. There would be a critical point, soon to be reached, when he would have to resume deceleration. When he did so the girl's weight would be multiplied by the gravities of deceleration, would become, suddenly, a factor of paramount importance; the factor the computers had been ignorant of when they determined the amount of fuel the EDS should have. She would have to go when deceleration began; it could be no other way. When would that be— how long could he let her stay?

"How long can I stay?"

He winced involuntarily from the words that were so like an echo of his own thoughts. How long? He didn't know; he would have to ask the ship's computers. Each EDS was given a meager surplus of fuel to compensate for unfavorable conditions within the atmosphere and relatively little fuel was being consumed for the time being. The memory banks of the computers would still contain all data pertaining to the course set for the EDS; such data would not be erased until the EDS reached its destination. He had only to give the computers the new data; the girl's weight and the exact time at which he had reduced the deceleration to .10.

"Barton." Commander Delhart's voice came abruptly from the communicator, as he opened his mouth to call the *Stardust.* "A check with Records shows me you haven't completed your report. Did you reduce the deceleration?"

So the commander knew what he was trying to do.

"I'm decelerating at point ten," he answered. "I cut the deceleration at seventeen fifty and the weight is a hundred and ten. I would like to stay at point ten as long as the computers say I can. Will you give them the question?"

It was contrary to regulations for an EDS pilot to make any changes in the course or degree of deceleration the computers had set for him but the commander made no mention of the violation, neither did he ask the reason for it. It was not necessary for him to ask; he had not become commander of an interstellar cruiser without both intelligence and an understanding of human nature. He said only: "I'll have that given the computers."

The communicator fell silent and he and the girl waited, neither of them speaking. They would not have to wait long; the computers would give the answer within moments of the asking. The new factors would be fed into the steel maw of the first bank and the electrical impulses would go through the complex circuits. Here and there a relay might click, a tiny cog turn over, but it would be essentially the electrical impulses that found the answer; formless, mindless, invisible, determining with utter precision how long the pale girl beside him might live. Then five little segments of metal in the second bank would trip in rapid succession against an inked ribbon and a second steel maw would spit out the slip of paper that bore the answer.

The chronometer on the instrument board read 18:10 when the commander spoke again.

"You will resume deceleration at nineteen ten."

She looked toward the chronometer, then quickly away from it. "Is that when . . . when I go?" she asked. He nodded and she dropped her eyes to her lap again.

"I'll have the course corrections given you," the commander said. "Ordinarily I would never permit anything like this but I understand your position. There is nothing I can do, other than what I've just done, and you will not deviate from these new instructions. You will complete your report at nineteen ten. Now—here are the course corrections."

The voice of some unknown technician read them to him and he wrote them down on the pad clipped to the edge of the control board. There would, he saw, be periods of deceleration when he neared the atmosphere when the deceleration would be five gravities—and at five gravities, one hundred ten pounds would become five hundred fifty pounds.

The technician finished and he terminated the contact with a brief acknowledgment. Then, hesitating a moment, he reached out and shut off the communicator. It was 18:13 and he would have nothing to report until 19:10. In the meantime, it somehow seemed indecent to permit others to hear what she might say in her last hour.

He began to check the instrument readings, going over them with unnecessary slowness. She would have to accept the circumstances and there was nothing he could do to help her into acceptance; words of sympathy would only delay it.

It was 18:20 when she stirred from her motionlessness and spoke.

"So that's the way it has to be with me?"

He swung around to face her. "You understand now, don't you? No one would ever let it be like this if it could be changed."

"I understand," she said. Some of the color had returned to her face and the lipstick no longer stood out so vividly red. "There isn't enough fuel for me to stay; when I hid on this ship I got into something I didn't know anything about and now I have to pay for it."

She had violated a man-made law that said KEEP OUT but the penalty was not of men's making or desire and it was a penalty men could not revoke. A physical law had decreed: *h amount of fuel will power an EDS with a mass of m safely to its destination;* and a second physical law had decreed: *h amount of fuel will not power an EDS with a mass of m plus x safely to its destination.*

EDS's obeyed only physical laws and no amount of human sympathy for her could alter the second law.

"But I'm afraid. I don't want to die—not now. I want to live and nobody is doing anything to help me; everybody is letting me go ahead and acting just like nothing was going to happen to me. I'm going to die and nobody *cares.*"

"We all do," he said. "I do and the commander does and the clerk in Ship's Records; we all care and each of us did what little he could to help you. It wasn't enough—it was almost nothing—but it was all we could do."

"Not enough fuel—I can understand that," she said, as though she had not heard his own words. "But to have to die for it. *Me,* alone—"

How hard it must be for her to accept the fact. She had never known danger of death; had never known the environments where the lives of men could be as fragile and fleeting as sea foam tossed against a rocky shore. She belonged on gentle Earth, in that secure and peaceful society where she could be young and gay and laughing with the others of her kind; where life was precious and well-guarded and there was always the assurance that tomorrow would come. She belonged in that world of soft winds and warm suns, music and moonlight and gracious manners and not on the hard, bleak frontier.

"How did it happen to me, so terribly quickly? An hour ago I was on the *Stardust,* going to Mimir. Now the *Stardust* is going on without me and I'm going to die and I'll never see Gerry and Mama and Daddy again—I'll never see anything again."

He hesitated, wondering how he could explain it to her so she would really understand and not feel she had, somehow, been the victim of a reasonlessly cruel injustice. She did not know what the frontier was like; she thought in terms of safe-and-secure Earth. Pretty girls were not jettisoned on Earth; there was a law against it. On Earth her plight would have filled the newscasts and a fast black Patrol ship would have been racing to her rescue. Everyone, everywhere, would have known of Marilyn Lee Cross and no effort would have been spared to save her life. But this was not Earth and there were no Patrol ships; only the *Stardust,* leaving them behind at many times the speed of light. There was no one to help her, there would be no Marilyn Lee Cross smiling from the newscasts tomorrow. Marilyn Lee Cross would be but a poignant memory for an EDS pilot and a name on a gray card in Ship's Records.

"It's different here; it's not like back on Earth," he said. "It isn't that no one cares; it's that no one can do anything to help. The frontier is big and here along its rim the colonies and exploration parties are scattered so thin and far between. On Woden, for example, there are only sixteen men —sixteen men on an entire world. The exploration parties, the survey crews, the little first-colonies—they're all fighting alien environments, trying to make a way for those who will follow after. The environments fight back and those who go first usually make mistakes only once. There is no margin of safety along the rim of the frontier; there can't be until the way is made for the others who will come later, until the new worlds are tamed and settled. Until then men will have to pay the penalty for making mistakes with no one to help them because there is no one *to* help them."

"I was going to Mimir," she said. "I didn't know about the frontier; I was only going to Mimir and *it's* safe."

"Mimir is safe but you left the cruiser that was taking you there."

She was silent for a little while. "It was all so wonderful at first; there was plenty of room for me on this ship and I would be seeing Gerry so soon . . . I didn't know about the fuel, didn't know what would happen to me—"

Her words trailed away and he turned his attention to the viewscreen, not wanting to stare at her as she fought her way through the black horror of fear toward the calm gray of acceptance.

Woden was a ball, enshrouded in the blue haze of its atmosphere, swimming in space against the background of star-sprinkled dead blackness. The great mass of Manning's Continent sprawled like a gigantic hourglass in the Eastern Sea with the western half of the Eastern Continent still visible. There was a thin line of shadow along the right-hand edge of the globe and the Eastern Continent was disappearing into it as the planet turned on its axis. An hour before the entire continent had been in view, now a thousand miles of it had gone into the thin edge of shadow and around to the night that lay on the other side of the world. The dark blue spot that was Lotus Lake was approaching the shadow. It was somewhere near the southern edge of the lake that Group Two had their camp. It would be night there, soon, and quick behind the coming of night the rotation of Woden on its axis would put Group Two beyond the reach of the ship's radio.

He would have to tell her before it was too late for her to talk to her brother. In a way, it would be better for both of them should they not do so but it was not for him to decide. To each of them the last words would be something to hold and cherish, something that would cut like the blade of a knife yet would be infinitely precious to remember, she for her own brief moments to live and he for the rest of his life.

He held down the button that would flash the grid lines on the view-screen and used the known diameter of the planet to estimate the distance the southern tip of Lotus Lake had yet to go until it passed beyond radio range. It was approximately five hundred miles. Five hundred miles; thirty minutes—and the chronometer read 18:30. Allowing for error in estimating, it could not be later than 19:05 that the turning of Woden would cut off her brother's voice.

The first border of the Western Continent was already in sight along the left side of the world. Four thousand miles across it lay the shore of the Western Sea and the Camp of Group One. It had been in the Western Sea that the tornado had originated, to strike with such fury at the camp and destroy half their prefabricated buildings, including the one that housed the medical supplies. Two days before the tornado had not existed; it had been no more

than great gentle masses of air out over the calm Western
Sea. Group One had gone about their routine survey work,
unaware of the meeting of the air masses out at sea, unaware of the force the union was spawning. It had struck
their camp without warning; a thundering, roaring destruction that sought to annihilate all that lay before it. It had
passed on, leaving the wreckage in its wake. It had destroyed the labor of months and had doomed six men to
die and then, as though its task was accomplished, it once
more began to resolve into gentle masses of air. But for all
its deadliness, it had destroyed with neither malice nor
intent. It had been a blind and mindless force, obeying the
laws of nature, and it would have followed the same course
with the same fury had men never existed.

Existence required Order and there was order; the laws
of nature, irrevocable and immutable. Men could learn to
use them but men could not change them. The circumference of a circle was always pi times the diameter and
no science of Man would ever make it otherwise. The combination of chemical A with chemical B under condition C
invariably produced reaction D. The law of gravitation was
a rigid equation and it made no distincton between the fall
of a leaf and the ponderous circling of a binary star system.
The nuclear conversion process powered the cruisers that
carried men to the stars; the same process in the form of a
nova would destroy a world with equal efficiency. The laws
were, and the universe moved in obedience to them. Along
the frontier were arrayed all the forces of nature and sometimes they destroyed those who were fighting their way outward from Earth. The men of the frontier had long ago
learned the bitter futility of cursing the forces that would
destroy them for the forces were blind and deaf; the futility of looking to the heavens for mercy, for the stars of the
galaxy swung in their long, long sweep of two hundred
million years, as inexorably controlled as they by the laws
that knew neither hatred nor compassion.

The men of the frontier knew—but how was a girl from
Earth to fully understand? *H amount of fuel will not power
an EDS with a mass of m plus x safety to its destination.*
To himself and her brother and parents she was a sweet-
faced girl in her teens; to the laws of nature she was *x,*
the unwanted factor in a cold equation.

She stirred again on the seat. "Could I write a letter? I want to write to Mama and Daddy and I'd like to talk to Gerry. Could you let me talk to him over your radio there?"

"I'll try to get him," he said.

He switched on the normal-space transmitter and pressed the signal button. Someone answered the buzzer almost immediately.

"Hello. How's it going with you fellows now—is the EDS on its way?"

"This isn't Group One; this is the EDS," he said. "Is Gerry Cross there?"

"Gerry? He and two others went out in the helicopter this morning and aren't back yet. It's almost sundown, though, and he ought to be back right away—in less than an hour at the most."

"Can you connect me through to the radio in his 'copter?"

"Huh-uh. It's been out of commission for two months —some printed circuits went haywire and we can't get any more until the next cruiser stops by. Is it something important—bad news for him, or something?"

"Yes—it's very important. When he comes in get him to the transmitter as soon as you possibly can."

"I'll do that; I'll have one of the boys waiting at the field with a truck. Is there anything else I can do?"

"No, I guess that's all. Get him there as soon as you can and signal me."

He turned the volume to an inaudible minimum, an act that would not affect the functioning of the signal buzzer, and unclipped the pad of paper from the control board. He tore off the sheet containing his flight instructions and handed the pad to her, together with pencil.

"I'd better write to Gerry, too," she said as she took them. "He might not get back to camp in time."

She began to write, her fingers still clumsy and uncertain in the way they handled the pencil and the top of it trembling a little as she poised it between words. He turned back to the viewscreen, to stare at it without seeing it.

She was a lonely little child, trying to say her last good-by, and she would lay out her heart to them. She would tell them how much she loved them and she would tell them to not feel badly about it, that it was only something that must happen eventually to everyone and she was not afraid. The last would be a lie and it would be there to read between the sprawling, uneven lines; a valiant little lie that would make the hurt all the greater for them.

Her brother was of the frontier and he would understand. He would not hate the EDS pilot for doing nothing to prevent her going; he would know there had been nothing the pilot could do. He would understand, though the understanding would not soften the shock and pain when he learned his sister was gone. But the others, her father and mother—they would not understand. They were of Earth and they would think in the manner of those who had never lived where the safety margin of life was a thin, thin line—and sometimes not at all. What would they think of the faceless, unknown pilot who had sent her to her death?

They would hate him with cold and terrible intensity but it really didn't matter. He would never see them, never know them. He would have only the memories to remind him; only the nights to fear, when a blue-eyed girl in gypsy sandals would come in his dreams to die again—

He scowled at the viewscreen and tried to force his thoughts into less emotional channels. There was nothing he could do to help her. She had unknowingly subjected herself to the penalty of a law that recognized neither innocence nor youth nor beauty, that was incapable of sympathy or leniency. Regret was illogical—and yet, could knowing it to be illogical ever keep it away?

She stopped occasionally, as though trying to find the right words to tell them what she wanted them to know, then the pencil would resume its whispering to the paper. It was 18:37 when she folded the letter in a square and wrote a name on it. She began writing another, twice looking up at the chronometer as though she feared the black hand might reach its rendezvous before she had finished. It was 18:45 when she folded it as she had done the first letter and wrote a name and address on it.

She held the letters out to him. "Will you take care of these and see that they're enveloped and mailed?"

"Of course." He took them from her hand and placed them in a pocket of his gray uniform shirt.

"These can't be sent off until the next cruiser stops by and the *Stardust* will have long since told them about me, won't it?" she asked. He nodded and she went on, "That makes the letters not important in one way but in another way they're very important—to me, and to them."

"I know. I understand, and I'll take care of them."

She glanced at the chronometer, then back to him. "It seems to move faster all the time, doesn't it?"

He said nothing, unable to think of anything to say, and she asked, "Do you think Gerry will come back to camp in time?"

"I think so. They said he should be in right away."

She began to roll the pencil back and forth between her palms. "I hope he does. I feel sick and scared and I want to hear his voice again and maybe I won't feel so alone. I'm a coward and I can't help it."

"No," he said, "you're not a coward. You're afraid, but you're not a coward."

"Is there a difference?"

He nodded. "A lot of difference."

"I feel so alone. I never did feel like this before; like I was all by myself and there was nobody to care what happened to me. Always, before, there was Mama and Daddy there and my friends around me. I had lots of friends, and they had a going-away party for me the night before I left."

Friends and music and laughter for her to remember—and on the viewscreen Lotus Lake was going into the shadow.

"Is it the same with Gerry?" she asked. "I mean, if he should make a mistake, would he have to die for it, all alone and with no one to help him?"

"It's the same with all along the frontier; it will always be like that so long as there is a frontier."

"Gerry didn't tell us. He said the pay was good and he sent money home all the time because Daddy's little shop just brought in a bare living but he didn't tell us it was like this."

"He didn't tell you his work was dangerous?"

"Well—yes. He mentioned that, but we didn't understand. I always thought danger along the frontier was something that was a lot of fun; an exciting adventure, like in the three-D shows." A wan smile touched her face for a moment. "Only it's not, is it? It's not the same at all, because when it's real you can't go home after the show is over."

"No," he said. "No, you can't."

Her glance flicked from the chronometer to the door of the air lock then down to the pad and pencil she still held. She shifted her position slightly to lay them on the bench beside, moving one foot out a little. For the first time he saw that she was not wearing Vegan gypsy sandals but only cheap imitations; the expensive Vegan leather was some kind of grained plastic, the silver buckle was gilded iron, the jewels were colored glass. *Daddy's little shop just brought in a bare living*— She must have left college in her second year, to take the course in linguistics that would enable her to make her own way and help her brother provide for her parents, earning what she could by part-time work after classes were over. Her personal possessions on the *Stardust* would be taken back to her parents—they would neither be of much value nor occupy much storage space on the return voyage.

"Isn't it—" She stopped, and he looked at her questioningly. "Isn't it cold in here?" she asked, almost apologetically. "Doesn't it seem cold to you?"

"Why, yes," he said. He saw by the main temperature gauge that the room was at precisely normal temperature. "Yes, it's colder than it should be."

"I wish Gerry would get back before it's too late. Do you really think he will, and you didn't just say so to make me feel better?"

"I think he will—they said he would be in pretty soon." On the viewscreen Lotus Lake had gone into the shadow but for the thin blue line of its western edge and it was apparent he had overestimated the time she would have in which to talk to her brother. Reluctantly, he said to her, "His camp will be out of radio range in a few minutes; he's on that part of Woden that's in the shadow"—he indicated the viewscreen—"and the turning of Woden will put him beyond contact. There may not be much time left when he comes in—not much time to talk to him before he fades out. I wish I could do something about it—I would call him right now if I could."

"Not even as much time as I will have to stay?"

"I'm afraid not."

"Then—" She straightened and looked toward the air lock with pale resolution. "Then I'll go when Gerry passes beyond range. I won't wait any longer after that—I won't have anything to wait for."

Again there was nothing he could say.

"Maybe I shouldn't wait at all. Maybe I'm selfish—maybe it would be better for Gerry if you just told him about it afterward."

There was an unconscious pleading for denial in the way she spoke and he said, "He wouldn't want you to do that, to not wait for him."

"It's already coming dark where he is, isn't it? There will be all the long night before him, and Mama and Daddy don't know yet that I won't ever be coming back like I promised them I would. I've caused everyone I love to be hurt, haven't I? I didn't want to—I didn't intend to."

"It wasn't your fault," he said. "It wasn't your fault at all. They'll know that. They'll understand."

"At first I was so afraid to die that I was a coward and thought only of myself. Now, I see how selfish I was. The terrible thing about dying like this is not that I'll be gone but that I'll never see them again; never be able to tell them that I didn't take them for granted; never be able to tell them I knew of the sacrifices they made to make my life happier, that I knew all the things they did for me and that I loved them so much more than I ever told them. I've never told them any of those things. You don't tell them such things when you're young and your life is all before you—you're afraid of sounding sentimental and silly.

"But it's so different when you have to die—you wish you had told them while you could and you wish you could tell them you're sorry for all the little mean things you ever did or said to them. You wish you could tell them that you didn't really mean to ever hurt their feelings and for them to only remember that you always loved them far more than you ever let them know."

"You don't have to tell them that," he said. "They will know—they've always known it."

"Are you sure?" she asked. "How can you be sure? My people are strangers to you."

"Wherever you go, human nature and human hearts are the same."

"And they will know what I want them to know—that I love them?"

"They've always known it, in a way far better than you could ever put in words for them."

"I keep remembering the things they did for me, and it's the little things they did that seem to be the most important to me, now. Like Gerry—he sent me a bracelet of fire-rubies on my sixteenth birthday. It was beautiful—it must have cost him a month's pay. Yet, I remember him more for what he did the night my kitten got run over in the street. I was only six years old and he held me in his arms and wiped away my tears and told me not to cry, that Flossy was gone for just a little while, for just long enough to get herself a new fur coat and she would be on the foot of my bed the very next morning. I believed him and quit crying and went to sleep dreaming about my kitten coming back. When I woke up the next morning, there was Flossy on the foot of my bed in a brand-new white fur coat, just like he had said she would be.

"It wasn't until a long time later that Mama told me Gerry had got the pet-shop owner out of bed at four in the morning and, when the man got mad about it, Gerry told him he was either going to go down and sell him the white kitten right then or he'd break his neck."

"It's always the little things you remember people by; all the little things they did because they wanted to do them for you. You've done the same for Gerry and your father and mother; all kinds of things that you've forgotten about but that they will never forget."

"I hope I have. I would like for them to remember me like that."

"They will."

"I wish—" She swallowed. "The way I'll die—I wish they wouldn't ever think of that. I've read how people look who die in space—their insides all ruptured and exploded and their lungs out between their teeth and then, a few seconds later, they're all dry and shapeless and horribly ugly. I don't want them to ever think of me as something dead and horrible, like that."

"You're their own, their child and their sister. They could never think of you other than the way you would want them to; the way you looked the last time they saw you."

"I'm still afraid," she said. "I can't help it, but I don't want Gerry to know it. If he gets back in time, I'm going to act like I'm not afraid at all and—"

The signal buzzer interrupted her, quick and imperative.

"Gerry!" She came to her feet. "It's Gerry, now!"

He spun the volume control knob and asked: "Gerry Cross?"

"Yes," her brother answered, an undertone of tenseness to his reply. "The bad news—what is it?"

She answered for him, standing close behind him and leaning down a little toward the communicator, her hand resting small and cold on his shoulder.

"Hello, Gerry." There was only a faint quaver to betray the careful casualness of her voice. "I wanted to see you—"

"Marilyn!" There was sudden and terrible apprehension in the way he spoke her name. "What are you doing on that EDS?"

"I wanted to see you," she said again. "I wanted to see you, so I hid on this ship—"

"You *hid* on it?"

"I'm a stowaway . . . I didn't know what it would mean—"

Marilyn!" It was the cry of a man who calls hopeless and desperate to someone already and forever gone from him. "What have you done?"

"I . . . it's not—" Then her own composure broke and the cold little hand gripped his shoulder convulsively. "Don't, Gerry—I only wanted to see you; I didn't intend to hurt you. Please, Gerry, don't feel like that—"

Something warm and wet splashed on his wrist and he slid out of the chair, to help her into it and swing the microphone down to her own level.

"Don't feel like that—Don't let me go knowing you feel like that—"

The sob she had tried to hold back choked in her throat and her brother spoke to her. "Don't cry, Marilyn." His voice was suddenly deep and infinitely gentle, with all the pain held out of it. "Don't cry, Sis—you mustn't do that. It's all right, Honey—everything is all right."

"I—" Her lower lip quivered and she bit into it. "I didn't want you to feel that way—I just wanted us to say good-by because I have to go in a minute."

"Sure—sure. That's the way it will be, Sis. I didn't mean to sound the way I did." Then his voice changed to a tone of quick and urgent demand. "EDS—have you called the *Stardust?* Did you check with the computers?"

"I called tht *Stardust* almost an hour ago. It can't turn back, there are no other cruisers within forty light-years, and there isn't enough fuel."

"Are you sure that the computers had the correct data—sure of everything?"

"Yes—do you think I could ever let it happen if I wasn't sure? I did everything I could do. If there was anything at all I could do now, I would do it."

"He tried to help me, Gerry." Her lower lip was no longer trembling and the short sleeves of her blouse were wet where she had dried her tears. "No one can help me and I'm not going to cry any more and everything will be all right with you and Daddy and Mama, won't it?"

"Sure—sure it will. We'll make out fine."

Her brother's words were beginning to come in more faintly and he turned the volume control to maximum. "He's going out of range," he said to her. "He'll be gone within another minute."

"You're fading out, Gerry," she said. "You're going out of range. I wanted to tell you—but I can't, now. We must say good-by so soon—but maybe I'll see you again. Maybe I'll come to you in your dreams with my hair in braids and crying because the kitten in my arms is dead; maybe I'll be the touch of a breeze that whispers to you as it goes by; maybe I'll be one of those gold-winged larks you told me about, singing my silly head off to you; maybe, at times, I'll be nothing you can see but you will know I'm there beside you. Think of me like that, Gerry; always like that and not—the other way."

Dimmed to a whisper by the turning of Woden, the answer came back:

"Always like that, Marilyn—always like that and never any other way."

"Our time is up, Gerry—I have to go now. Good—" Her voice broke in mid-word and her mouth tried to twist into crying. She pressed her hand hard against it and when she spoke again the words came clear and true:

"Good-by, Gerry."

Faint and ineffably poignant and tender, the last words came from the cold metal of the communicator:

"Good-by, little sister—"

She sat motionless in the hush that followed, as though listening to the shadow-echoes of the words as they died away, then she turned away from the communicator, toward the air lock, and he pulled the black lever beside him. The inner door of the air lock slid swiftly open, to reveal the bare little cell that was waiting for her, and she walked to it.

She walked with her head up and the brown curls brushing her shoulders, with the white sandals stepping as sure and steady as the fractional gravity would permit and the gilded buckles twinkling with little lights of blue and red and crystal. He let her walk alone and made no move to help her, knowing she would not want it that way. She stepped into the air lock and turned to face him, only the pulse in her throat to betray the wild beating of her heart.

"I'm ready," she said.

He pushed the lever up and the door slid its quick barrier between them, inclosing her in black and utter darkness for her last moments of life. It clicked as it locked in place and he jerked down the red lever. There was a slight waver to the ship as the air gushed from the lock, a vibration to the wall as though something had bumped the outer door in passing, then there was nothing and the ship was dropping true and steady again. He shoved the red lever back to close the door on the empty air lock and turned away, to walk to the pilot's chair with the slow steps of a man old and weary.

Back in the pilot's chair he pressed the signal button of the normal-space transmitter. There was no response; he had expected none. Her brother would have to wait through the night until the turning of Woden permitted contact through Group One.

It was not yet time to resume deceleration and he waited while the ship dropped endlessly downward with him and the drives purred softly. He saw that the white hand of the supplies closet temperature gauge was on zero. A cold equation had been balanced and he was alone on the ship. Something shapeless and ugly was hurrying ahead of him, going to Woden where its brother was waiting through the night, but the empty ship still lived for a little while with the presence of the girl who had not known about the forces that killed with neither hatred nor malice. It seemed, almost, that she still sat small and bewildered and frightened on the metal box beside him, her words echoing hauntingly clear in the void she had left behind her:

I didn't do anything to die for—I didn't do anything—

FONDLY FAHRENHEIT

by Alfred Bester

He doesn't know which of us I am these days, but they know one truth. You must own nothing but yourself. You must make your own life, live your own life and die your own death . . . or else you will die another's.

The rice fields on Paragon III stretch for hundreds of miles like checkerboard tundras, a blue and brown mosaic under a burning sky of orange. In the evening, clouds whip like smoke, and the paddies rustle and murmur.

A long line of men marched across the paddies the evening we escaped from Paragon III. They were silent, armed, intent; a long rank of silhouetted statues looming against the smoking sky. Each man carried a gun. Each man wore a walkie-talkie belt pack, the speaker button in his ear, the microphone bug clipped to his throat, the glowing viewscreen strapped to his wrist like a green-eyed watch. The multitude of screens showed nothing but a multitude of individual paths through the paddies. The annunciators uttered no sound but the rustle and splash of steps. The men spoke infrequently, in heavy grunts, all speaking to all.

"Nothing here."

"Where's here?"

"Jenson's fields."

"You're drifting too far west."

"Close in the line there."

"Anybody covered the Grimson paddy?"

"Yeah. Nothing."

"She couldn't have walked this far."

First published in 1954

"Could have been carried."

"Think she's alive?"

"Why should she be dead?"

The slow refrain swept up and down the long line of beaters advancing towards the smoky sunset. The line of beaters wavered like a writhing snake, but never ceased its remorseless advance. One hundred men spaced fifty feet apart. Five thousand feet of ominous search. One mile of angry determination stretching from east to west across a compass of heat. Evening fell. Each man lit his search lamp. The writhing snake was transformed into a necklace of wavering diamonds.

"Clear here. Nothing."

"Nothing here."

"Nothing."

"What about the Allen paddies?"

"Covering them now."

"Think we missed her?"

"Maybe."

"We'll beat back and check."

"This'll be an all night job."

"Allen paddies clear."

"God damn! We've got to find her!"

"We'll find her."

"Here she is. Sector seven. Tune in."

The line stopped. The diamonds froze in the heat. There was silence. Each man gazed into the glowing screen on his wrist, tuning to sector seven. All tuned to one. All showed a small nude figure awash in the muddy water of a paddy. Alongside the figure an owner's stake of bronze read: VANDALEUR. The end of the line converged towards the Vandaleur field. The necklace turned into a cluster of stars. One hundred men gathered around a small nude body, a child dead in a rice paddy. There was no water in her mouth. There were fingerprints on her throat. Her innocent face was battered. Her body was torn. Clotted blood on her skin was crusted and hard.

"Dead three-four hours at least."

"Her mouth is dry."

"She wasn't drowned. Beaten to death."

In the dark evening heat the men swore softly. They picked up the body. One stopped the others and pointed to the child's fingernails. She had fought her murderer. Under the nails were particles of flesh and bright drops of scarlet blood, still liquid, still uncoagulated.

"That blood ought to be clotted too."

"Funny."

"Not so funny. What kind of blood don't clot?"

"Android."

"Looks like she was killed by one."

"Vandaleur owns an android."

"She couldn't be killed by an android."

"That's android blood under her nails."

"The police better check."

"The police'll prove I'm right."

"But androids can't kill."

"That's android blood, ain't it?"

"Androids can't kill. They're made that way."

"Looks like one android was made wrong."

"Jesus!"

And the thermometer that day registered 91.9° gloriously Fahrenheit.

So there we were aboard the Paragon Queen en route for Megaster V, James Vandaleur and his android. James Vandaleur counted his money and wept. In the second class cabin with him was his android, a magnificent creature with classic features and wide blue eyes. Raised on its forehead in a cameo of flesh were the letters MA, indicating that this was one of the rare multiple aptitude androids, worth $57,000 on the current exchange. There we were, weeping and counting and calmly watching.

"Twelve, fourteen, sixteen. Sixteen hundred dollars," Vandaleur wept. "That's all. Sixteen hundred dollars. My house was worth ten thousand. The land was worth five. There was furniture, cars, my paintings, etchings, my plane, my— And nothing to show for everything but sixteen hundred dollars. Christ!"

I leaped up from the table and turned on the android. I pulled a strap from one of the leather bags and beat the android. It didn't move.

"I must remind you," the android said, "that I am worth fifty-seven thousand dollars on the current exchange. I must warn you that you are endangering valuable property."

"You damned crazy machine," Vandaleur shouted.

"I am not a machine," the android answered. "The robot is a machine. The android is a chemical creation of synthetic tissue."

"What got into you?" Vandaleur cried. "Why did you do it? Damn you!" He beat the android savagely.

"I must remind you that I cannot be punished," I said. "The pleasure-pain syndrome is not incorporated in the android synthesis."

"Then why did you kill her?" Vandaleur shouted. "If it wasn't for kicks, why did you—"

"I must remind you," the android said, "that the second class cabins in these ships are not soundproofed."

Vandaleur dropped the strap and stood panting, staring at the creature he owned.

"Why did you do it? Why did you kill her?" I asked.

"I don't know," I answered.

"First it was malicious mischief. Small things. Petty destruction. I should have known there was something wrong with you then. Androids can't destroy. They can't harm. They—"

"There is no pleasure-pain syndrome incorporated in the android synthesis."

"Then it got to arson. Then serious destruction. Then assault . . . that engineer on Rigel. Each time worse. Each time we had to get out faster. Now it's murder. Christ! What's the matter with you? What's happened?"

"There are no self-check relays incorporated in the android brain."

"Each time we had to get out it was a step downhill. Look at me. In a second class cabin. Me. James Paleologue Vandaleur. There was a time when my father was the wealthiest— Now, sixteen hundred dollars in the world. That's all I've got. And you. Christ damn you!"

Vandaleur raised the strap to beat the android again, then dropped it and collapsed on a berth, sobbing. At last he pulled himself together.

"Instructions," he said.

The multiple aptitude android responded at once. It arose and awaited orders.

"My name is now Valentine. James Valentine. I stopped off on Paragon III for only one day to transfer to this ship for Megaster V. My occupation: Agent for one privately owned MA android which is for hire. Purpose of visit: To settle on Megaster V. Fix the papers."

The android removed Vandaleur's passport and papers from a bag, got pen and ink and sat down at the table. With an accurate flawless hand—an accomplished hand that could draw, write, paint, carve, engrave, etch, photograph, design, create and build—it meticulously forged new credentials for Vandaleur. Its owner watched me miserably.

"Create and build," I muttered. "And now destroy. Oh God! What am I going to do? Christ! If I could only get rid of you. If I didn't have to live off you. God! If only I'd inherited some guts instead of you."

Dallas Brady was Megaster's leading jewellery designer. She was short, stocky, amoral and a nymphomaniac. She hired Vandaleur's multiple aptitude android and put me to work in her shop. She seduced Vandaleur. In her bed one night, she asked abruptly: "Your name's Vandaleur, isn't it?"

"Yes," I murmured. Then: "No! No! It's Valentine. James Valentine."

"What happened on Paragon?" Dallas Brady asked. "I thought androids couldn't kill or destroy property. Prime Directives and Inhibitions set up for them when they're synthesized. Every company guarantees they can't."

"Valentine!" Vandaleur insisted.

"Oh, come off it," Dallas Brady said. "I've known for a week. I haven't hollered copper, have I?"

"The name is Valentine."

"You want to prove it? You want I should call the cops?" Dallas reached out and picked up the phone.

"For God's sake, Dallas!" Vandaleur leaped up and struggled to take the phone from her. She fended him off, laughing at him until he collapsed and wept in shame and helplessness.

"How did you find out?" he asked at last.

"The papers are full of it. And Valentine was a little too close to Vandaleur. That wasn't smart, was it?"

"I guess not. I'm not very smart."

"Your android's got quite a record, hasn't it? Assault. Arson. Destruction. What happened on Paragon?"

"It kidnapped a child. Took her into the rice fields and murdered her."

"Raped her?"

"I don't know."

"They're going to catch up with you."

"Don't I know it? Christ! We've been running for two years now. Seven planets in two years. I must have abandoned fifty thousand dollars worth of property in two years."

"You better find out what's wrong with it."

"How can I? Can I walk into a repair clinic and ask for an overhaul? What am I going to say? 'My android's just turned killer. Fix it.' They'd call the police right off." I began to shake. "They'd have that android dismantled inside one day. I'd probably be booked as accessory to murder."

"Why didn't you have it repaired before it got to murder?"

"I couldn't take the chance," Vandaleur explained angrily. "If they started fooling around with lobotomies and body chemistry and endocrine surgery, they might have destroyed its aptitudes. What would I have left to hire out? How would I live?"

"You could work yourself. People do."

"Work for what? You know I'm good for nothing. How could I compete with specialist androids and robots? Who can, unless he's got a terrific talent for a particular job?"

"Yeah. That's true."

"I lived off my old man all my life. Damn him! He had to go bust just before he died. Left me the android and that's all. The only way I can get along is living off what it earns."

"You better sell it before the cops catch up with you. You can live off fifty grand. Invest it."

"At 3 per cent? Fifteen hundred a year? When the android returns 15 per cent on its value? Eight thousand a year. That's what it earns. No, Dallas. I've got to go along with it."

"What are you going to do about its violence kick?"

"I can't do anything . . . except watch it and pray. What are you going to do about it?"

"Nothing. It's none of my business. Only one thing . . . I ought to get something for keeping my mouth shut."

"What?"

"The android works for me for free. Let somebody else pay you, but I get it for free."

The multiple aptitude android worked. Vandaleur collected its fees. His expenses were taken care of. His savings began to mount. As the warm spring of Megaster V turned to hot summer, I began investigating farms and properties. It would be possible, within a year or two, for us to settle down permanently, provided Dallas Brady's demands did not become rapacious.

On the first hot day of summer, the android began singing in Dallas Brady's workshop. It hovered over the electric furnace which, along with the weather, was broiling the shop, and sang an ancient tune that had been popular half a century before.

> *Oh, it's no feat to beat the heat.*
> *All reet! All reet!*
> *So jeet you seat*
> *Be fleet be fleet*
> *Cool and discreet*
> *Honey . . .*

It sang in a strange, halting voice, and its accomplished fingers were clasped behind its back, writhing in a strange rhumba all their own. Dallas Brady was surprised.

"You happy or something?" she asked.

"I must remind you that the pleasure-pain syndrome is not incorporated in the android synthesis," I answered. "All reet! All reet! Be fleet be fleet, cool and discreet, honey . . ."

Its fingers stopped their writhing and picked up a heavy pair of iron tongs. The android poked them into the glowing heart of the furnace, leaning far forward to peer into the lovely heat.

"Be careful, you damned fool!" Dallas Brady exclaimed. "You want to fall in?"

"I must remind you that I am worth fifty-seven thousand dollars on the current exchange," I said. "It is forbidden to endanger valuable property. All reet! All reet! Honey . . ."

It withdrew a crucible of glowing gold from the electric furnace, turned, capered hideously, sang crazily, and splashed a sluggish gobbet of molten gold over Dallas Brady's head. She screamed and collapsed, her hair and clothes flaming, her skin crackling. The android poured again while it capered and sang.

"Be fleet be fleet, cool and discreet, honey . . ." It sang and slowly poured and poured the molten gold. Then I left the workshop and rejoined James Vandaleur in his hotel suite. The android's charred clothes and squirming fingers warned its owner that something was very much wrong.

Vandaleur rushed to Dallas Brady's workshop, stared once, vomited and fled. I had enough time to pack one bag and raise nine hundred dollars on portable assets. He took a third class cabin on the Megaster Queen which left that morning for Lyra Alpha. He took me with him. He wept and counted his money and I beat the android again.

And the thermometer in Dallas Brady's workshop registered 98.1° beautifully Fahrenheit.

On Lyra Alpha we holed up in a small hotel near the university. There, Vandaleur carefully bruised my forehead until the letters MA were obliterated by the swelling and discoloration. The letters would reappear, but not for several months, and in the meantime Vandaleur hoped the hue and cry for an MA android would be forgotten. The android was hired out as a common laborer in the university power plant. Vandaleur, as James Valentine, eked out life on the android's small earnings.

I wasn't too unhappy. Most of the other residents in the hotel were university students, equally hard-up, but delightfully young and enthusiastic. There was one charming girl with sharp eyes and a quick mind. Her name was Wanda, and she and her beau, Ted Stark, took a tremendous interest in the killing android which was being mentioned in every paper in the galaxy.

"We've been studying the case," she and Jed said at one

of the casual student parties which happened to be held this night in Vandaleur's room. "We think we know what's causing it. We're going to do a paper." They were in a high state of excitement.

"Causing what?" somebody wanted to know.

"The android rampage."

"Obviously out of adjustment, isn't it? Body chemistry gone haywire. Maybe a kind of synthetic cancer, yes?"

"No." Wanda gave Jed a look of suppressed triumph.

"Well, what is it?"

"Something specific."

"What?"

"That would be telling."

"Oh, come on."

"Nothing doing."

"Won't you tell us?" I asked intently. "I . . . We're very much interested in what could go wrong with an android."

"No, Mr. Venice," Wanda said. "It's a unique idea and we've got to protect it. One thesis like this and we'll be set up for life. We can't take the chance of somebody stealing it."

"Can't you give us a hint?"

"No. Not a hint. Don't say a word, Jed. But I'll tell you this much, Mr. Venice. I'd hate to be the man who owns that android."

"You mean the police?" I asked.

"I mean projection, Mr. Venice. Projection! That's the danger . . . and I won't say any more. I've said too much as it is."

I heard steps outside, and a hoarse voice singing softly: "Be fleet be fleet, cool and discreet, honey . . ." My android entered the room, home from its tour of duty at the university power plant. It was not introduced. I motioned to it and I immediately responded to the command and went to the beer keg and took over Vandaleur's job of serving the guests. Its accomplished fingers writhed in a private rhumba of their own. Gradually they stopped their squirming, and the strange humming ended.

Androids were not unusual at the university. The wealthier students owned them along with cars and planes. Vandaleur's android provoked no comment, but young Wanda was sharp-eyed and quick-witted. She noted my bruised forehead and she was intent on the history-making thesis she and Jed Stark were going to write. After the party broke up, she consulted with Jed walking upstairs to her room.

"Jed, why'd that android have a bruised forehead?"

"Probably hurt itself, Wanda. It's working in the power plant. They fling a lot of heavy stuff around."

"That's all?"

"What else?"

"It could be a convenient bruise."

"Convenient for what?"

"Hiding what's stamped on its forehead."

"No point to that, Wanda. You don't have to see marks on a forehead to recognize an android. You don't have to see a trademark on a car to know it's a car."

"I don't mean it's trying to pass as a human. I mean it's trying to pass as a lower grade android."

"Why?"

"Suppose it had MA on its forehead."

"Multiple aptitude? Then why in hell would Venice waste it stoking furnaces if it could earn more—Oh. Oh! You mean it's—?"

Wanda nodded.

"Jesus!" Stark pursed his lips. "What do we do? Call the police?"

"No. We don't know if it's an MA for a fact. If it turns out to be an MA and the killing android, our paper comes first anyway. This is our big chance, Jed. If it's *that* android we can run a series of controlled tests and—"

"How do we find out for sure?"

"Easy. Infrared film. That'll show what's under the bruise. Borrow a camera. Buy some film. We'll sneak down to the power plant tomorrow afternoon and take some pictures. Then we'll know."

They stole down into the university power plant the following afternoon. It was a vast cellar, deep under the earth. It was dark, shadowy, luminous with burning light from the furnace doors. Above the roar of the fires they could hear a strange voice shouting and chanting the echoing vault: "All reet! All reet! So jeet your seat. Be fleet be fleet, cool and discreet, honey . . ." And they could see a capering figure dancing a lunatic rhumba in time to the music it shouted. The legs twisted. The arms waved. The fingers writhed.

Jed Stark raised the camera and began shooting his spool of infrared film, aiming the camera sights at that bobbing head. Then Wanda shrieked, for I saw them and came charging down on them, brandishing a polished steel shovel. It smashed the camera. It felled the girl and then the boy. Jed fought me for a desperate hissing moment before he was bludgeoned into helplessness. Then the android dragged them to the furnace and fed them to the flames, slowly, hideously. It capered and sang. Then it returned to my hotel.

The thermometer in the power plant registerd 100.9° murderously Fahrenheit. All reet! All reet!

We bought steerage on the Lyra Queen and Vandaleur and the android did odd jobs for their meals. During the night watches, Vandaleur would sit alone in the steerage head with a cardboard portfolio on his lap, puzzling over its contents. That portfolio was all he had managed to bring with him from Lyra Alpha. He had stolen it from Wanda's room. It was labelled ANDROID. It contained the secret of my sickness.

And it contained nothing but newspapers. Scores of newspapers from all over the galaxy, printed, microfilmed, engraved, offset, photostated . . . Rigel *Star-Banner* . . . Paragon *Picayune* . . . Megaster *Times-Leader* . . . Lalande *Journal* . . . Indi *Intelligencer* . . . Eridani *Telegram-News*. All reet! All reet!

Nothing but newspapers. Each paper contained an account of one crime in the android's ghastly career. Each paper also contained news, domestic and foreign, sports, society, weather, shipping news, stock exchange quotations, human interest stories, features, contents, puzzles. Somewhere in that mass of uncollated facts was the secret Wanda and Jed Sark had discovered. Vandaleur pored over the papers helplessly. It was beyond him. So jeet your seat!

"I'll sell you," I told the android. "Damn you. When we land on Terra, I'll sell you. I'll settle for 3 per cent on whatever you're worth."

"I am worth fifty-seven thousand dollars on the current exchange," I told him.

"If I can't sell you, I'll turn you in to the police," I said.

"I am valuable property," I answered. "It is forbidden to endanger valuable property. You won't have me destroyed."

"Christ damn you!" Vandaleur cried. "What? Are you arrogant? Do you know you can trust me to protect you? Is that the secret?"

The multiple aptitude android regarded him with calm accomplished eyes. "Sometimes," it said, "it is a good thing to be property."

It was 3 below zero when the Lyra Queen dropped at Croydon Field. A mixture of ice and snow swept across the field, fizzing and exploding into steam under the Queen's tail jets. The passengers trotted numbly across the blackened concrete to customs inspection, and thence to the airport bus that was to take them to London. Vandaleur and the android were broke. They walked.

By midnight they reached Piccadilly Circus. The December ice storm had not slackened and the statue of Eros was encrusted with ice. They turned right, walked down to Trafalgar Square and then along the Strand towards Soho, shaking with cold and wet. Just above Fleet Street, Vandaleur saw a solitary figure coming from the direction of St. Paul's. He drew the android into an alley.

"We've got to have money," he whispered. He pointed at the approaching figure. "He has money. Take it from him."

"The order cannot be obeyed," the android said.

"Take it from him," Vandaleur repeated. "By force. Do you understand? We're desperate."

"It is contrary to my prime directive," I said. "I cannot endanger life or property. The order cannot be obeyed."

"For God's sake!" Vandaleur burst out. "You've attacked, destroyed, murdered. Don't gibber about prime directives. You haven't any left. Get his money. Kill him if you have to. I tell you, we're desperate!"

"It is contrary to my prime directive," the android repeated. "The order cannot be obeyed."

I thrust the android back and leaped out at the stranger. He was tall, austere, competent. He had an air of hope curdled by cynicism. He carried a cane. I saw he was blind.

"Yes?" he said. "I hear you near me. What is it?"

"Sir . . ." Vandaleur hesitated. "I'm desperate."

"We are all desperate," the stranger replied. "Quietly desperate."

"Sir . . . I've got to have some money."

"Are you begging or stealing?" The sightless eyes passed over Vandaleur and the android.

"I'm prepared for either."

"Ah. So are we all. It is the history of our race." The stranger motioned over his shoulder. "I have been begging at St. Paul's, my friend. What I desire cannot be stolen. What is it you desire that you are lucky enough to be able to steal?"

"Money," Vandaleur said.

"Money for what? Come, my friend, let us exchange confidences. I will tell you why I beg, if you will tell me why you steal. My name is Blenheim."

"My name is . . . Vole."

"I was not begging for sight at St. Paul's, Mr. Vole. I was begging for a number."

"A number?"

"Ah, yes. Numbers rational, number irrational. Numbers imaginary. Positive integers. Negative integers. Fractions, positive and negative. Eh? You have never heard of Blenhem's immortal treatise on Twenty Zeros, or The Differences in Absence of Quantity?" Blenheim smiled bitterly. "I am a wizard of the Theory of Number, Mr. Vole, and I have exhausted the charm of number for myself. After fifty years of wizardry, senility approaches and the appetite vanishes. I have been praying in St. Paul's for inspiration. Dear God, I prayed, if You exist, send me a number."

Vandaleur slowly lifted the cardboard portfolio and touched Benheim's hand with it. "In here," he said, "is a number. A hidden number. A secret number. The number of a crime. Shall we exchange, Mr. Blenheim? Shelter for a number?"

"Neither begging nor stealing, eh?" Blenheim said. "But a bargain. So all life reduces to the banal." The sightless eyes again passed over Vandaleur and the android. "Perhaps the All-Mighty is not God but a merchant. Come home with me."

On the top floor of Blenheim's house we shared a room —two beds, two closets, two washstands, one bathroom. Vandaleur bruised my forehead again and sent me out to find work, and while the android worked, I consulted with Blenheim and read him the papers from the portfolio, one by one. All reet! All reet!

Vanadelur told him so much and no more. He was a student, I said, attempting a thesis on the murdering android. In these papers which he had collected were the facts that would explain the crimes of which Blenheim had heard nothing. There must be a correlation, a number, a statistic, something which would account for my derangement, I explained, and Blenheim was piqued by the mystery, the detective story, the human interest of number.

We examined the papers. As I read them aloud, he listed them and their contents in his blind, meticulous writing. And then I read his notes to him. He listed the papers by type, by type-face, by fact, by fancy, by article, spelling, words, theme, advertising, pictures, subject, politics, prejudices. He analyzed. He studied. He meditated. And we lived together on that top floor, always a little cold, always a little terrified, always a little closer . . . brought together by our fear of it, our hatred between us. Like a wedge driven into a living tree and splitting the trunk, only to be forever incorporated into the scar tissue, we grew together. Vandaleur and the android. Be fleet be fleet!

And one afternoon Blenheim called Vandaleur into his study and displayed his notes. "I think I've found it," he said, "but I can't understand it."

Vanadleur's heart leaped.

"Here are the correlations," Blenheim continued. "In fifty papers there are accounts of the criminal android. What is there, outside the depredations, that is also in fifty papers?"

"I don't know, Mr. Blenheim."

"It was a rhetorical question. Here is the answer. The weather."

"What?"

"The weather." Blenheim nodded. "Each crime was committed on a day when the temperature was above ninety degrees Fahrenheit."

"But that's impossible," Vandaleur exclaimed. "It was cool on Lyra Alpha."

"We have no record of any crime committed on Lyra Alpha. There is no paper."

"No. That's right. I—" Vandaleur was confused. Suddenly he exclaimed. "No. You're right. The furnace room. It was hot there. Hot! Of course. My God, yes! That's the answer. Dallas Brady's electric furance . . . The rice deltas on Paragon. So jeet your seat. Yes. But why? Why? My God, why?"

I came into the house at that moment, and passing the study, saw Vandaleur and Blenheim. I entered, awaiting commands, my multiple aptitudes devoted to service.

"That's the android, eh?" Blenheim said after a long moment.

"Yes," Vandaleur answered, still confused by the discovery. "And that explains why it refused to attack you that night on the Strand. It wasn't hot enough to break the prime directive. Only in the heat . . . The heat, all reet!" He looked at the android. A lunatic command passed from man to android. I refused. It is forbidden to endanger life. Vandaleur gestured furiously, then seized Blenheim's shoulders and yanked him back out of his desk chair. Blenheim shouted once. Vandaleur leaped on him like a tiger, pinning him to the floor and sealing his mouth with one hand.

"Find a weapon," he called to the android.

"It is forbidden to endanger life."

"This is a fight for self-preservation. Bring me a weapon!" He held the squirming mathematician with all his weight. I went at once to a cupboard where I knew a revolver was kept. I checked it. It was loaded with five cartridges. I handed it to Vandaleur. I took it, rammed the barrel against Blenheim's head and pulled the trigger. He shuddered once.

We had three hours before the cook returned from her day off. We looted the house. We took Blenheim's money and jewels. We packed a bag with clothes. We took Blenheim's notes, destroyed the newspapers; and we left, carefully locking the door behind us. In Blenheim's study we left a pile of crumpled papers under a half inch of burning candle. And we soaked the rug around it with kerosene. No, I did all that. The android refused. I am forbidden to endanger life or property.

All reet!

They took the tubes to Leicester Square, changed trains and rode to the British Museum. There they got off and went to a small Georgian house just off Russell Square. A shingle in the window read: NAN WEBB, PSYCHOMET-RIC CONSULTANT. Vandaleur had made a note of the address some weeks earlier. They went into the house. The android waited in the foyer with the bag. Vandaleur entered Nan Webb's office.

She was a tall women with grey shingled hair, very fine English complexion and very bad English legs. Her features were blunt, her expression acute. She nodded to Vandaleur, finished a letter, sealed it and looked up.

"My name," I said, "is Vanderbilt. James Vanderbilt."

"Quite."

"I'm an exchange student at London University."

"Quite."

"I've been researching on the killing android, and I think I've discovered something very interesting. I'd like your advice on it. What is your fee?"

"What is your college at the University?"

"Why?"

"There is a discount for students."

"Merton College."

"That will be two pounds, please."

Vandaleur placed two pounds in the desk and added to the fee Blenheim's notes. "There is a correlation," he said, "between the crimes of the android and the weather. You will note that each crime was committed when the temperature rose above ninety degrees Fahrenheit. Is there a psychometric answer for this?"

Nan Webb nodded, studied the notes for a moment, put down the sheets of paper and said: "Synesthesia, obviously."

"What?"

"Synesthesia," she repeated. "When a sensation, Mr. Vanderbilt, is interpreted immediately in terms of a sensation from a different sense organ from the one stimulated, it is called synesthesia. For example: A sound stimulus gives rise to a simultaneous sensation of definite color. Or color gives rise to a sensation of taste. Or a light stimulus gives rise to a sensation of sound. There can be confusion or short circuiting of any sensation of taste, smell, pain, pressure, temperature and so on. D'you understand?"

"I think so."

"Your research has uncovered the fact that the android most probably reacts to temperature stimulus above the ninety degree level synthesthetically. Most probably there is an endocrine response. Probably a temperature linkage with the android adrenal surrogate. High temperature brings about a response of fear, anger, excitement and violent physical activity . . . all within the province of the adrenal gland."

"Yes. I see. Then if the android were to be kept in cold climates . . ."

"There would be neither stimulus nor response. There would be no crimes. Quite."

"I see. What is projection?"

"How do you mean?"

"Is there any danger of projection with regard to the owner of the android?"

"Very interesting. Projection is a throwing forward. It is the process of throwing out upon another the ideas or impulses that belong to oneself. The paranoid, for example projects upon others his conflicts and disturbances in order to externalize them. He accuses, directly or by implication, other men of having the very sickness with which he is struggling himself."

"And the danger of projection?"

"It is the danger of believing what is implied. If you live with a psychotic who projects his sickness upon you, there is a danger of falling into his psychotic pattern and becoming virtually psychotic yourself. As, no doubt, is happening to you, Mr. Vandaleur."

Vandaleur leaped to his feet.

"You are an ass," Nan Webb went on crisply. She waved the sheets of notes. "This is no exchange student's writing. It's the unique cursive of the famous Blenheim. Every scholar in England knows this blind writing. There is no Merton College at London University. That was a miserable guess. Merton is one of the Oxford Colleges. And you, Mr. Vandaleur, are so obviously infected by association with your deranged android . . . by projection, if you will . . . that I hesitate between calling the Metropolitan Police and the Hospital for the Criminally Insane."

I took out the gun and shot her.

Reet!

"Antares II, Alpha Aurigae, Acrux IV, Pollux IX, Rigel Centaurus," Vandaleur said. "They're all cold. Cold as a witch's kiss. Mean temperature of 40° Fahrenheit. Never get hotter than 70. We're in business again. Watch that curve."

The multiple aptitude android swung the wheel with its accomplished hands. The car took the curve sweetly and sped on through the northern marshes, the reeds stretching for miles, brown and dry, under the cold English sky. The sun was sinking swiftly. Overhead, a lone flight of bustards flapped clumsily eastward. High above the flight, a lone helicopter drifted towards home and warmth.

"No more warmth for us," I said. "No more heat. We're safe when we're cold. We'll hole up in Scotland, make a little money, get across to Norway, build a bankroll and then slip out. We'll settle on Pollux. We're safe. We've licked it. We can live again."

There was a startling *bleep* from overhead, and then a ragged roar: "ATTENTION JAMES VANDALEUR AND ANDROID. ATTENTION JAMES VANDALEUR AND ANDROID!"

Vandaleur started and looked up. The lone helicopter was floating above them. From its belly came amplified commands: "YOU ARE SURROUNDED, THE ROAD IS BLOCKED. YOU ARE TO STOP YOUR CAR AT ONCE AND SUBMIT TO ARREST. STOP AT ONCE!"

I looked at Vandaleur for orders.

"Keep driving," Vandaleur snapped.

The helicopter dropped lower: "ATTENTION ANDROID. YOU ARE IN CONTROL OF THE VEHICLE. YOU ARE TO STOP AT ONCE. THIS IS A STATE DIRECTIVE SUPERSEDING ALL PRIVATE COMMANDS."

"What the hell are you doing?" I shouted.

"A state directive supersedes all private commands,"
the android answered. "I must point out to you that—"

"Get the hell away from the wheel," Vandaleur ordered.
I clubbed the android, yanked him sideways and squirmed
over him to the wheel. The car veered off the road in that
moment and went churning through the frozen mud and
dry reeds. Vandaleur regained control and continued westward through the marshes towards a parallel highway five
miles distant.

"We'll beat their God damned block," he grunted.

The car pounded and surged. The helicopter dropped
even lower. A searchlight blazed from the belly of the
plane.

"ATTENTION JAMES VANDALEUR AND AN-
DROID. SUBMIT TO ARREST. THIS IS A STATE
DIRECTIVE SUPERSEDING ALL PRIVATE COM-
MANDS."

"He can't submit," Vandaleur shouted wildly. "There's
no one to submit to. He can't and I won't."

"Christ!" I muttered. "We'll beat them yet. We'll beat
the block. We'll beat the heat. We'll—"

"I must point out to you," I said, "that I am required by
my prime directive to obey state directives which super-
sede all private commands. I must submit to arrest."

"Who says it's a state directive?" Vandaleur said. "Them?
Up in that plane? They've got to show credentials. They've
got to prove it's state authority before you submit. How
d'you know they're not crooks trying to trick us?"

Holding the wheel with one arm, he reached into his
side pocket to make sure the gun was still in place. The
car skidded. The tires squealed on frost and reeds. The
wheel was wrenched from his grasp and the car yawed
up a small hillock and overturned. The motor roared and
the wheels screamed. Vandaleur crawled out and dragged
the android with him. For the moment we were outside the
circle of light boring down from the helicopter. We
blundered off into the marsh, into the blackness, into
concealment . . . Vandaleur running with a pounding heart,
hauling the android along.

The helicopter circled and soared over the wrecked car,
searchlight peering, loudspeaker braying. On the highway
we had left, lights appeared as the pursuing and blocking

parties gathered and followed radio directions from the plane. Vandaleur and the android continued deeper and deeper into the marsh, working their way towards the parallel road and safety. It was night by now. The sky was a black matte. Not a star showed. The temperature was dropping. A southeast night wind knifed us to the bone.

Far behind there was a dull concussion. Vandaleur turned, gasping. The car's fuel had exploded. A geyser of flame shot up like a lurid fountain. It subsided into a low crater of burning reeds. Whipped by the wind, the distant hem of flame fanned up into a wall, ten feet high. The wall began marching down on us, crackling fiercely. Above it, a pall of oily smoke surged forward. Behind it, Vandaleur could make out the figures of men . . . a mass of beaters searching the marsh.

"Christ!" I cried and searched desperately for safety. He ran, dragging me with him, until their feet crunched through the surface ice of a pool. He trampled the ice furiously, then flung himself down in the numbing water, pulling the android with us.

The wall of flame approached. I could hear the crackle and feel the heat. He could see the searchers clearly. Vandaleur reached into his side pocket for the gun. The pocket was torn. The gun was gone. He groaned and shook with cold and terror. The light from the marsh fire was blinding. Overhead, the helicopter floated helplessly to one side, unable to fly through the smoke and flames and aid the searchers who were beating far to the right of us.

"They'll miss us," Vandaleur whispered. "Keep quiet. That's an order. They'll miss us. We'll beat them. We'll beat the fire. We'll—"

Three distinct shots sounded less than a hundred feet from the fugitives. *Blam! Blam! Blam!* They came from the last three cartridges in my gun as the marsh fire reached it where it had dropped, and exploded the shells. The searchers turned towards the sound and began working directly toward us. Vandaleur cursed hysterically and tried to submerge even deeper to escape the intolerable heat of the fire. The android began to twitch.

The wall of flame surged up to them. Vandaleur took a deep breath and prepared to submerge until the flame

passed over them. The android shuddered and burst into
an earsplitting scream.

"All reet! All reet!" it shouted. "Be fleet be fleet!"

"Damn you!" I shouted. I tried to drown it.

"Damn you!" I cursed him. I smashed his face.

The android battered Vandaleur, who fought it off until
it exploded out of the mud and staggered upright. Before
I could return to the attack, the live flames captured it
hypnotically. It danced and capered in a lunatic rhumba
before the wall of fire. Its legs twisted. Its arms waved. The
fingers writhed in a private rhumba of their own. It shrieked
and sang and ran in a crooked waltz before the embrace
of the heat, a muddy monster silhouetted against the brilliant sparkling flare.

The searchers shouted. There were shots. The android
spun around twice and then continued its horrid dance
before the face of the flames. There was a rising gust of
wind. The fire swept around the capering figure and enveloped it for a roaring moment. Then the fire swept on,
leaving behind it a sobbing mass of synthetic flesh oozing
scarlet blood that would never coagulate.

The thermometer would have registered 1200° won-
drously Fahrenheit.

Vandaleur didn't die. I got away. They missed him while
they watched the android caper and die. But I don't know
which of us he is these days. Projection, Wanda warned
me. Projection, Nan Webb told him. If you live with a
crazy man or a crazy machine long enough, I become crazy
too. Reet!

But we know one truth. We know they are wrong. The
new robot and Vandaleur know that because the new robot's started twitching too. Reet! Here on cold Pollux, the
robot is twitching and singing. No heat, but my fingers
writhe. No heat, but it's taken the little Talley girl off for
a solitary walk. A cheap labor robot. A servo-mechanism
. . . all I could afford . . . but it's twitching and humming
and walking alone with the child somewhere and I can't
find them. Christ! Vandaleur can't find me before it's too
late. Cool and discreet, honey, in the dancing frost while
the thermometer registers 10° fondly Fahrenheit.

THE COUNTRY OF THE KIND

by Damon Knight

The attendant at the car lot was daydreaming when I pulled up—a big, lazy-looking man in black satin chequered down the front. I was wearing scarlet, myself; it suited my mood. I got out, almost on his toes.

"Park or storage?" he asked automatically, turning around. Then he realized who I was, and ducked his head away.

"Neither," I told him.

There was a hand torch on a shelf in the repair shed right behind him. I got it and came back. I knelt down to where I could reach behind the front wheel, and ignited the torch. I turned it on the axle and suspension. They glowed cherry red, then white, and fused together. Then I got up and turned the flame on both tires until the rubberoid stank and sizzled and melted down to the pavement. The attendant didn't say anything.

I left him there, looking at the mess on his nice clean concrete.

It had been a nice car, too; but I could get another any time. And I felt like walking. I went down the winding road, sleepy in the afternoon sunlight, dappled with shade and smelling of cool leaves. You couldn't see the houses; they were all sunken or hidden by shrubbery, or a little of both. That was the fad I'd heard about; it was what I'd come here to see. Not that anything the dulls did would be worth looking at.

I turned off at random and crossed a rolling lawn, went

First published in 1955

591

through a second hedge of hawthorn in blossom, and came out next to a big sunken games court.

The tennis net was up, and two couples were going at it, just working up a little sweat—young, about half my age, all four of them. Three dark-haired, one blonde. They were evenly matched, and both couples played well together; they were enjoying themselves.

I watched for a minute. But by then the nearest two were beginning to sense I was there, anyhow. I walked down onto the court, just as the blonde was about to serve. She looked at me frozen across the net, poised on tiptoe. The others stood.

"Off," I told them. "Game's over."

I watched the blonde. She was not especially pretty, as they go, but compactly and gracefully put together. She came down slowly, flat-footed without awkwardness, and tucked the racket under her arm; then the surprise was over and she was trotting off the court after the other three.

I followed their voices around the curve of the path, between towering masses of lilacs, inhaling the sweetness, until I came to what looked like a little sunning spot. There was a sundial, and a birdbath, and towels lying around on the grass. One couple, the dark-haired pair, was still in sight farther down the path, heads bobbing along. The other couple had disappeared.

I found the handle in the grass without any trouble. The mechanism responded, and an oblong section of turf rose up. It was the stair I had, not the elevator, but that was all right. I ran down the steps and into the first door I saw, and was in the top-floor lounge, an oval room lit with diffused simulated sunlight from above. The furniture was all comfortably bloated, sprawling and ugly; the carpet was deep, and there was a fresh flower scent in the air.

The blonde was over at the near end with her back to me, studying the autochef keyboard. She was half out of her playsuit. She pushed it the rest of the way down and stepped out of it, then turned and saw me.

She was surprised again; she hadn't thought I might follow her down.

I got up close before it occurred to her to move; then

it was too late. She knew she couldn't get away from me; she closed her eyes and leaned back against the paneling, turning a little pale. Her lips and her golden brows went up in the middle.

I looked her over and told her a few uncomplimentary things about herself. She trembled, but didn't answer. On an impulse, I leaned over and dialed the autochef to hot cheese sauce. I cut the safety out of circuit and put the quantity dial all the way up. I dialed *soup tureen* and then *punch bowl*.

The stuff began to come out in about a minute, steaming hot. I took the tureens and splashed them up and down the wall on either side of her. Then when the first punch bowl came out I used the empty bowls as scoops. I clotted the carpet with the stuff; I made streamers of it all along the walls, and dumped puddles into what furniture I could reach. Where it cooled it would harden, and where it hardened it would cling.

I wanted to splash it across her body, but it would've hurt, and we couldn't have that. The punch bowls of hot sauce were still coming out of the autochef, crowding each other around the vent. I punched *cancel*, and then *sauterne* (*swt., Calif.*).

It came out well chilled in open bottles. I took the first one and had my arm back just about to throw a nice line of the stuff right across her midriff, when a voice said behind me:

"Watch out for cold wine."

My arm twitched and a little stream of the wine splashed across her thighs. She was ready for it; her eyes had opened at the voice, and she barely jumped.

I whirled around, fighting mad. The man was standing there where he had come out of the stair well. He was thinner in the face than most, bronzed, wide-chested, with alert blue eyes. If it hadn't been for him, I knew it would have worked—the blonde would have mistaken the chill splash for a scalding one.

I could hear the scream in my mind, and I wanted it.

I took a step toward him, and my foot slipped. I went down clumsily, wrenching one knee. I got up shaking and tight all over. I wasn't in control of myself. I screamed, "You—you—" I turned and got one of the punch bowls and lifted it in both hands, heedless of how the hot sauce was slopping over onto my wrists, and I had it almost in the air toward him when the sickness took me—that damned buzzing in my head, louder, louder, drowning everything out.

When I came to, they were both gone. I got up off the floor, weak as death, and staggered over to the nearest chair. My clothes were slimed and sticky. I wanted to die. I wanted to drop into that dark furry hole that was yawning for me and never come up; but made myself stay awake and get out of the chair.

Going down in the elevator, I almost blacked out again. The blonde and the thin man weren't in any of the second-floor bedrooms. I made sure of that, and then I emptied the closets and bureau drawers onto the floor, dragged the whole mess into one of the bedrooms and stuffed the tub with it, then turned on the water.

I tried the third floor: maintenance and storage. It was empty. I turned the furnace on and set the thermostat up as high as it would go. I disconnected all the safety circuits and alarms. I opened the freezer doors and dialed them to defrost. I propped the stair well door open and went back up in the elevator.

On the second floor I stopped long enough to open the stairway door there—the water was halfway toward it, creeping across the floor—and then searched the top floor. No one was there. I opened book reels and threw them unwinding across the room; I would have done more, but I could hardly stand. I got up to the surface and collapsed on the lawn: that furry pit swallowed me up, dead and drowned.

While I slept, water poured down the open stair well and filled the third level. Thawing food packages floated out into the rooms. Water seeped into wall panels and machine housings; circuits shorted and fuses blew. The air conditioning stopped, but the pile kept heating. The water rose.

Spoiled food, floating supplies, grimy water surged up the stair well. The second and first levels were bigger and would take longer to fill, but they'd fill. Rugs, furnishings, clothing, all the things in the house would be waterlogged and ruined. Probably the weight of so much water would shift the house, rupture water pipes and other fluid intakes. It would take a repair crew more than a day just to clean up the mess. The house itself was done for, not repairable. The blonde and the thin man would never live in it again.

Serve them right.

The dulls could build another house; they built like beavers. There was only one of me in the world.

The earliest memory I have is of some woman, probably the cresh-mother, staring at me with a expression of shock and horror. Just that. I've tried to remember what happened directly before or after, but I can't. Before, there's nothing but the dark formless shaft of no-memory that runs back to birth. Afterward, the big calm.

From my fifth year, it must have been, to my fifteenth, everything I can remember floats in a pleasant dim sea. Nothing was terribly important. I was languid and soft; I drifted. Walking merged into sleep.

In my fifteenth year it was the fashion in love-play for the young people to pair off for months or longer. "Loving steady," we called it. I remember how the older people protested that it was unhealthy; but we were all normal juniors, and nearly as free as adults under the law.

All but me.

The first steady girl I had was named Elen. She had blonde hair, almost white, worn long; her lashes were dark and her eyes pale green. Startling eyes: they didn't look as if they were looking at you. They looked blind.

Several times she gave me strange startled glances, something between fright and anger. Once it was because I held her too tightly, and hurt her; other times, it seemed to be for nothing at all.

In our group, a pairing that broke up sooner than four weeks was a little suspect—there must be something wrong with one partner or both, or the pairing would have lasted longer.

Four weeks and a day after Elen and I made our pairing, she told me she was breaking it.

I'd thought I was ready. But I felt the room spin half around me till the wall came against my palm and stopped.

The room had been in use as a hobby chamber; there was a rack of plasticraft knives under my hand. I took one without thinking, and when I saw it I thought, *I'll frighten her*.

And I saw the startled, half-angry look in her pale eyes as I went toward her; but this is curious: she wasn't looking at the knife. She was looking at my face.

The elders found me later with the blood on me, and put me into a locked room. Then it was my turn to be frightened, because I realized for the first time that it was possible for a human being to do what I had done.

And if I could do it to Elen, I thought, surely they could do it to me.

But they couldn't. They set me free: they had to.

And it was then I understood that I was the king of the world. . . .

The sky was turning clear violet when I woke up, and shadow was spilling out from the hedges. I went down the hill until I saw the ghostly blue of photon tubes glowing in a big oblong, just outside the commerce area. I went that way, by habit.

Other people were lining up at the entrance to show their books and be admitted. I brushed by them, seeing the shocked faces and feeling their bodies flinch away, and went on into the robing chamber.

Straps, aqualungs, masks and flippers were all for the taking. I stripped, dropping the clothes where I stood, and put the underwater equipment on. I strode out to the poolside, monstrous, like a being from another world. I adjusted the lung and the flippers, and slipped into the water.

Underneath, it was all crystal blue, with the forms of swimmers sliding through it like pale angels. Schools of small fish scattered as I went down. My heart was beating with a painful joy.

Down, far down, I saw a girl slowly undulating through the motions of sinuous underwater dance, writhing around and around a ribbed column of imitation coral. She had a suction-tipped fish lance in her hand, but she was not using it; she was only dancing, all by herself, down at the bottom of the water.

I swam after her. She was young and delicately made, and when she saw the deliberately clumsy motions I made in imitation of hers, her eyes glinted with amusement behind her mask. She bowed to me in mockery, and slowly glided off with simple, exaggerated movements, like a child's ballet.

I followed. Around her and around I swam, stiff-legged, first more child-like and awkward than she, then subtly parodying her motions; then improving on them until I was dancing an intricate, mocking dance around her.

I saw her eyes widen. She matched her rhythm to mine, then, and together, apart, together again we coiled the wake of our dancing. At last, exhausted, we clung together where a bridge of plastic coral arched over us. Her cool body was in the bend of my arm; behind two thicknesses of vitrin—a world away!—her eyes were friendly and kind.

There was a moment when, two strangers yet one flesh, we felt our souls speak to one another across the abyss of matter. It was a truncated embrace—we could not kiss, we could not speak—but her hands lay confidingly on my shoulders, and her eyes looked into mine.

That moment had to end. She gestured toward the surface, and left me. I followed her up. I was feeling drowsy and almost at peace, after my sickness. I thought . . . I don't know what I thought.

We rose together at the side of the pool. She turned to me, removing her mask: and her smile stopped, and melted away. She stared at me with horrified disgust, wrinkling her nose.

"Pyah!" she said, and turned, awkward in her flippers. Watching her, I saw her fall into the arms of a white-haired man, and heard her hysterical voice tumbling over itself.

"But don't you remember?" the man's voice rumbled. "You should know it by heart." He turned. "Hal, is there a copy of it in the clubhouse?"

A murmur answered him, and in a few moments a young man came out holding a slender brown pamphlet.

I knew that pamphlet. I could even have told you what page the white-haired man opened it to; what sentences the girl was reading as I watched.

I waited. I don't know why.

I heard her voice rising: "To think that I let him *touch* me!" And the white-haired man reassured her, the words rumbling, too low to hear. I saw her back straighten. She looked across at me . . . only a few yards in that scented, blue-lit air; a world away . . . and folded up the pamphlet into a hard wad, threw it, and turned on her heel.

The pamphlet landed almost at my feet. I touched it with my toe, and it opened to the page I had been thinking of:

> . . . sedation until his 15th year, when for sexual reasons it became no longer practicable. While the advisors and medical staff hesitated, he killed a girl of the group by violence.

And farther down:

> The solution finally adopted was three-fold.
> 1. *A sanction*—the only sanction possible to our humane, permissive society. Excommunication: not to speak to him, touch him willingly, or acknowledge his existence.
> 2. *A precaution*. Taking advantage of a mild predisposition to epilepsy, a variant of the so-called Kusko analog technique was employed, to prevent by an epileptic seizure any future act of violence.
> 3. *A warning*. A careful alteration of his body chemistry was effected to make his exhaled and exuded wastes emit a strongly pungent and offensive odor. In mercy, he himself was rendered unable to detect this smell.
> Fortunately, the genetic and environmental accidents which combined to produce this atavism have been fully explained and can never again . . .

The words stopped meaning anything, as they always did at that point. I didn't want to read any farther; it was all nonsense, anyway. I was the king of the world.

I got up and went away, out into the night, blind to the dulls who thronged the rooms I passed.

Two squares away was the commerce area. I found a clothing outlet and went in. All the free clothes in the display cases were drab: those were for worthless floaters, not for me. I went past them to the specials, and found a combination I could stand—silver and blue, with a severe black piping down the tunic. A dull would have said it was "nice." I punched for it. The automatic looked me over with its dull glassy eye, and croaked, "Your contribution book, please."

I could have had a contribution book, for the trouble of stepping out into the street and taking it away from the first passer-by; but I didn't have the patience. I picked up the one-legged table from the refreshment nook, hefted it, and swung it at the cabinet door. The metal shrieked and dented, opposite the catch. I swung once more to the same place, and the door sprang open. I pulled out clothing in handfuls till I got a set that would fit me.

I bathed and changed, and then went prowling in the big multi-outlet down the avenue. All those places are arranged pretty much alike, no matter what the local managers do to them. I went straight to the knives, and picked out three in graduated sizes, down to the size of my fingernail. Then I had to take my chances. I tried the furniture department, where I had had good luck once in a while, but this year all they were using was metal. I had to have seasoned wood.

I knew where there was a big cache of cherry wood, in good-sized blocks, in a forgotten warehouse up north at a place called Kootenay. I could have carried some around with me—enough for years—but what for, when the world belonged to me?

It didn't take me long. Down in the workshop section, of all places, I found some antiques—tables and benches, all with wooden tops. While the dulls collected down at the other end of the room, pretending not to notice, I sawed off a good oblong chunk of the smallest bench, and made a base for it out of another.

As long as I was there, it was a good place to work, and I could eat and sleep upstairs, so I stayed.

I knew what I wanted to do. It was going to be a man, sitting, with his legs crossed and his forearms resting down along his calves. His head was going to be tilted back, and his eyes closed, as if he were turning his face up at the sun.

In three days it was finished. The trunk and limbs had a shape that was not man and not wood, but something in between: something that hadn't existed before I made it.

Beauty. That was the old word.

I had carved one of the figure's hands hanging loosely, and the other one curled shut. There had to be a time to stop and say it was finished. I took the smallest knife, the one I had been using to scrape the wood smooth, and cut away the handle and ground down what was left of the shaft to a thin spike. Then I drilled a hole into the wood of the figurine's hand, in the hollow between thumb and curled finger. I fitted the knife blade in there; in the small hand it was a sword.

I cemented it in place. Then I took the sharp blade and stabbed my thumb, and smeared the blade.

I hunted most of that day, and finally found the right place—a niche in an outcropping of striated brown rock, in a little triangular half-wild patch that had been left where two roads forked. Nothing was permanent, of course, in a community like this one that might change its houses every five years or so, to follow the fashion; but this spot had been left to itself for a long time. It was the best I could do.

I had the paper ready: it was one of a batch I had printed up a year ago. The paper was treated, and I knew it would stay legible a long time. I hid a little photo capsule in the back of the niche, and ran the control wire to a staple in the base of the figurine. I put the figurine down on top of the paper, and anchored it lightly to the rock with two spots of all-cement. I had done it so often that it came naturally; I knew just how much cement would hold the figurine steady against a casual hand, but yield to one that really wanted to pull it down.

Then I stepped back to look: and the power and the pity of it made my breath come short, and tears start to my eyes.

Reflected light gleamed fitfully on the dark-stained blade that hung from his hand. He was sitting alone in that niche that closed him in like a coffin. His eyes were shut, and his head tilted back, as if he were turning his face up to the sun.

But only rock was over his head. There was no sun for him.

Hunched on the cool bare ground under a pepper tree, I was looking down across the road at the shadowed niche where my figurine sat.

I was all finished here. There was nothing more to keep me, and yet I couldn't leave.

People walked past now and then—not often. The community seemed half deserted, as if most of the people had flocked off to a surf party somewhere, or a contribution meeting, or to watch a new house being dug to replace the one I had wrecked. . . . There was a little wind blowing toward me, cool and lonesome in the leaves.

Up the other side of the hollow there was a terrace, and on that terrace, half an hour ago, I had seen a brief flash of color—a boy's head, with a red cap on it, moving past and out of sight.

That was why I had to stay. I was thinking how that boy might come down from his terrace and into my road, and passing the little wild triangle of land, see my figurine. I was thinking he might not pass by indifferently, but stop: and go closer to look: and pick up the wooden man: and read what was written on the paper underneath.

I believed that sometime it had to happen. I wanted it so hard that I ached.

My carvings were all over the world, wherever I had wandered. There was one in Congo City, carved of ebony, dusty-black; one on Cyprus, of bone; one in New Bombay, of shell; one in Chang-teh, of jade.

They were like signs printed in red and green, in a color-blind world. Only the one I was looking for would ever pick one of them up, and read the message I knew by heart.

TO YOU WHO CAN SEE, the first sentence said, I OFFER YOU A WORLD. . . .

There was a flash of color up on the terrace. I stiffened. A minute later, here it came again, from a different direction: it was the boy, clambering down the slope, brilliant against the green, with his red sharp-billed cap like a woodpecker's head.

I held my breath.

He came toward me through the fluttering leaves, ticked off by pencils of sunlight as he passed. He was a brown boy, I could see at this distance, with a serious thin face.

His ears stuck out, flickering pink with the sun behind them, and his elbow and knee pads made him look knobby.

He reached the fork in the road, and chose the path on my side. I huddled into myself as he came nearer. *Let him see it, let him not see me,* I thought fiercely.

My fingers closed around a stone.

He was nearer, walking jerkily with his hands in his pockets, watching his feet mostly.

When he was almost opposite me, I threw the stone.

It rustled through the leaves below the niche in the rock. The boy's head turned. He stopped, staring. I think he saw the figurine then. I'm sure he saw it.

He took one step.

"Risha!" came floating down from the terrace.

And he looked up. "Here," he piped.

I saw the woman's head, tiny at the top of the terrace. She called something I didn't hear; I was standing up, tight with anger.

Then the wind shifted. It blew from me to the boy. He whirled around, his eyes big, and clapped a hand to his nose.

"Oh, what a stench!" he said.

He turned to shout, "Coming!" and then he was gone, hurrying back up the road, into the unstable blur of green.

My own chance, ruined. He would have been the image, I knew, if it hadn't been for that damned woman, and the wind shifting. . . . They were all against me, people, wind and all.

And the figurine still sat, blind eyes turned up to the rocky sky.

There was something inside me that told me to take my disappointment and go away from there, and not come back.

I knew I would be sorry. I did it anyway: took the image out of the niche, and the paper with it, and climbed the slope. At the top I heard his clear voice laughing.

There was a thing that might have been an ornamental mound, or the camouflaged top of a buried house. I went around it, tripping over my own feet, and came upon the boy kneeling on the turf. He was playing with a brown and white puppy.

He looked up with the laughter going out of his face. There was no wind, and he could smell me. I knew it was bad. No wind, and the puppy to distract him—everything about it was wrong. But I went to him blindly anyhow, and fell on one knee, and shoved the figurine at his face.

"Look—" I said.

He went over backwards in his hurry: he couldn't even have seen the image, except as a brown blur coming at him. He scrambled up, with the puppy whining and yapping around his heels, and ran for the mound.

I was up after him, clawing up moist earth and grass as I rose. In the other hand I still had the image clutched, and the paper with it.

A door popped open and swallowed him and popped shut again in my face. With the flat of my hand I beat the vines around it until I hit the doorplate by accident and the door opened. I dived in, shouting, "Wait," and was in a spiral passage, lit pearl-gray, winding downward. Down I went headlong, and came out at the wrong door—an underground conservatory, humid and hot under the yellow lights, with dripping rank leaves in long rows. I went down the aisle raging, overturning the tanks, until I came to a vestibule and an elevator.

Down I went again to the third level and a labyrinth of guest rooms, all echoing, all empty. At last I found a ramp leading upward, past the conservatory, and at the end of it voices.

The door was clear vitrin, and I paused on the near side of it looking and listening. There was the boy, and a woman old enough to be his mother, just—sister or cousin, more likely—and an elderly woman in a hard chair holding the puppy. The room was comfortable and tasteless, like other rooms.

I saw the shock grow on their faces as I burst in: it was always the same, they knew I would like to kill them, but they never expected that I would come uninvited into a house. It was not done.

There was that boy, so close I could touch him, but the shock of all of them was quivering in the air, smothering, like a blanket that would deaden my voice. I felt I had to shout.

"Everything they tell you is lies!" I said. "See here— here, this is the truth!" I had the figurine in front of his eyes, but he didn't see.

"Risha, go below," said the young woman quietly. He turned to obey, quick as a ferret. I got in front of him again. "Stay," I said, breathing hard. "Look—"

"Remember, Risha, don't speak," said the woman.

I couldn't stand any more. Where the boy went I don't know; I ceased to see him. With the image in one hand and the paper with it, I leaped at the woman. I was almost quick enough; I almost reached her; but the buzzing took me in the middle of a step, louder, louder, like the end of the world.

It was the second time that week. When I came to, I was sick and too faint to move for a long time.

The house was silent. They had gone, of course . . . the house had been defiled, having me in it. They wouldn't live here again, but would build elsewhere.

My eyes blurred. After a while I stood up and looked around at the room. The walls were hung with a gray close-woven cloth that looked as if it would tear, and I thought of ripping it down in strips, breaking furniture, stuffing carpets and bedding into the oubliette. . . . But I didn't have the heart for it. I was too tired. Thirty years. . . . They had given me all the kingdoms of the world, and the glory thereof, thirty years ago. It was more than one man alone could bear, for thirty years.

At last I stooped and picked up the figurine, and the paper that was supposed to go under it—crumpled now, with the forlorn look of a message that someone has thrown away unread.

I sighed bitterly.

I smoothed it out and read the last part.

YOU CAN SHARE THE WORLD WITH ME. THEY CAN'T STOP YOU. STRIKE NOW—PICK UP A SHARP THING AND STAB, OR A HEAVY THING AND CRUSH. THAT'S ALL. THAT WILL MAKE YOU FREE. ANYONE CAN DO IT.

Anyone. Someone. Anyone.

FLOWERS FOR ALGERNON

by Daniel Keyes

progris riport 1—martch 5, 1965

Dr. Strauss says I shud rite down what I think and evrey thing that happins to me from now on. I dont know why but he says its importint so they will see if they will use me. I hope they use me. Miss Kinnian says maybe they can make me smart. I want to be smart. My name is Charlie Gordon. I am 37 years old and 2 weeks ago was my birthday. I have nuthing more to rite now so I will close for today.

progris riport 2—martch 6

I had a test today. I think I faled it. and I think that maybe now they wont use me. What happind is a nice young man was in the room and he had some white cards with ink spilled all over them. He sed Charlie what do you see on this card. I was very skared even tho I had my rabits foot in my pockit because when I was a kid I always faled tests in school and I spilled ink to.

I told him I saw a inkblot. He said yes and it made me feel good. I thot that was all but when I got up he stopped me. He said now sit down Charlie we are not thru yet. Then I don't remember so good but he wantid me to say what was in the ink. I dint see nuthing in the ink but he said there was picturs there other pepul saw some picturs. I couldn't see any picturs. I reely tryed to see. I held the card close up and then far away. Then I said if I had my

First published in 1959

glases I could see better I usally only ware my glases in the movies or TV but I said they are in the closit in the hall. I got them. Then I said let me see that card agen I bet Ill find it now.

I tryed hard but I still couldnt find the pictures I only saw the ink. I told him maybe I need new glases. He rote somthing down on a paper and I got skared of faling the test. I told him it was a very nice inkblot with little points all around the edges. He looked very sad so that wasnt it. I said please let me try agen. Ill get it in a few minits becaus Im not so fast somtimes. Im a slow reeder too in Miss Kinnians class for slow adults but Im trying very hard.

He gave me a chance with another card that had 2 kinds of ink spilled on it red and blue.

He was very nice and talked slow like Miss Kinnian does and he explaned it to me that it was a *raw shok*. He said pepul see things in the ink. I said show me where. He said think. I told him I think a inkblot but that wasnt rite eather. He said what does it remind you—pretend something. I closd my eyes for a long time to pretend. I told him I pretned a fowntan pen with ink leeking all over a table cloth. Then he got up and went out.

I dont think I passd the *raw shok* test.

progris report 3—martch 7

Dr Strauss and Dr Nemur say it dont matter about the inkblots. I told them I dint spill the ink on the cards and I couldnt see anything in the ink. They said that maybe they will still use me. I said Miss Kinnian never gave me tests like that one only spelling and reading. They said Miss Kinnian told that I was her bestist pupil in the adult nite scool becaus I tryed the hardist and I reely wantid to lern. They said how come you went to the adult nite scool all by yourself Charlie. How did you find it. I said I askd pepul and sumbody told me where I shud go to lern to read and spell good. They said why did you want to. I told them becaus all my life I wantid to be smart and not dumb. But its very hard to be smart. They said you know it will probly be tempirery. I said yes. Miss Kinnian told me. I dont care if it herts.

Later I had more crazy tests today. The nice lady who gave it me told me the name and I asked her how do you spellit so I can rite it in my progris riport. THEMATIC APPERCEPTION TEST. I don't know the frist 2 words but I know what *test* means. You got to pass it or you get bad marks. This test lookd easy becaus I coud see the picturs. Only this time she dint want me to tell her the picturs. That mixd me up. I said the man yesterday said I shoud tell him what I saw in the ink she said that dont make no difrence. She said make up storys about the pepul in the picturs.

I told her how can you tell storys about pepul you never met. I said why shud I make up lies. I never tell lies any more becaus I always get caut.

She told me this test and the other one the raw-shok was for getting personalty. I laffed so hard. I said how can you get that thing from ink-blots and fotos. She got sore and put her picturs away. I don't care. It was sily. I gess I faled that test too.

Later some men in white coats took me to a difernt part of the hospitil and gave me a game to play. It was like a race with a white mouse. They called the mouse Algernon. Algernon was in a box with a lot of twists and turns like all kinds of walls and they gave me a pencil and a paper with lines and lots of boxes. On one side it said START and on the other end it said FINISH. They said it was *amazed* and that Algernon and me had the same *amazed* to do. I dint see howe we could have the same *amazed* if Algernon had a box and I had a paper but I dint say nothing. Anyway there wasnt time because the race started.

One of the men had a watch he was trying to hide so I woudnt see it so I tryed not to look and that made me nervus.

Anyway that test made me feel worser than all the others because they did it over 10 times with difernt *amazeds* and Algernon won every time. I dint know that mice were so smart. Maybe thats because Algernon is a white mouse. Maybe white mice are smarter than other mice.

progris riport 4—Mar 8

Their going to use me! Im so exited I can hardly write. Dr Nemur and Dr Strauss had a argament about it first. Dr Nemur was in the office when Dr Strauss brot me in. Dr Nemur was worryed about using me but Dr Strauss told him Miss Kinnian rekemmended me the best from all the people who was teaching. I like Miss Kinnian becaus shes a very smart teacher. And she said Charlie your going to have a second chance. If you volenteer for this experament you mite get smart. They dont know if it will be perminint but theirs a chance. Thats why I said ok even when I was scared because she said it was an operashun. She said dont be scared Charlie you done so much with so little I think you deserv it most of all.

So I got scaird when Dr Nemur and Dr Strauss argud about it. Dr Strauss said I had something that was very good. He said I had a good *motor-vation*. I never even knew I had that. I felt proud when he said that not every body with an eye-q of 68 had that thing. I dont know what it is or where I got it but he said Algernon had it too. Algernons *motor-vation* is the cheese they put in his box. But it cant be that because I didnt eat any cheese this week.

Then he told Dr Nemur something I dint understand so while they were talking I wrote down some of the words.

He said Dr Nemur I know Charlie is not what you had in mind as the first of your new brede of intelek** (couldnt get the word) superman. But most people of his low ment** are host** and uncoop** they are usualy dull apath** and hard to reach. He has a good natcher hes intristed and eager to please.

Dr Nemur said remember he will be the first human beeng ever to have his intelijence trippled by surgicle meens.

Dr Strauss said exakly. Look at how well hes lerned to read and write for his low mentel age its as grate an acheve** as you and I lerning einstines therey of **vity without help. That shows the intenss motor-vation. Its comparat** a tremen** achev** I say we use Charlie.

I dint get all the words and they were talking to fast

but it sounded like Dr Strauss was on my side and like the other one wasnt.

Then Dr Nemur nodded he said all right maybe your right. We will use Charlie. When he said that I got so exited I jumped up and shook his hand for being so good to me. I told him thank you doc you wont be sorry for giving me a second chance. And I mean it like I told him. After the operashun Im gonna try to be smart. Im gonna try awful hard.

progris ript 5—Mar 10

Im skared. Lots of people who work here and the nurses and the people who gave me the tests came to bring me candy and wish me luck. I hope I have luck. I got my rabits foot and my lucky penny and my horse shoe. Only a black cat crossed me when I was comming to the hospitil. Dr Strauss says dont be supersitis Charlie this is sience. Anyway Im keeping my rabits foot with me.

I asked Dr Strauss if Ill beat Algernon in the race after the operashun and he said maybe. If the operashun works Ill show that mouse I can be as smart as he is. Maybe smarter. Then Ill be abel to read better and spell the words good and know lots of things and be like other people. I want to be smart like other people. If it works perminint they will make everybody smart all over the wurld.

They dint give me anything to eat this morning. I dont know what that eating has to do with getting smart. Im very hungry and Dr Nemur took away my box of candy. That Dr Nemur is a grouch. Dr Strauss says I can have it back after the operashun. You cant eat befor a operashun . . .

Progress Report 6—Mar 15

The operashun dint hurt. He did it while I was sleeping. They took off the bandijis from my eyes and my head today so I can make a PROGRESS REPORT. Dr Nemur who looked at some of my other ones said I spell PROGRESS wrong and he told me how to spell it and REPORT too. I got to try and remember that.

I have a very bad memary for spelling. Dr Strauss says

its ok to tell about all the things that happin to me but he says I should tell more about what I feel and what I think. When I told him I dont know how to think he said try. All the time when the bandijis were on my eyes I tryed to think. Nothing happened. I dont know what to think about. Maybe if I ask him he will tell me how I can think now that Im suppose to get smart. What do smart people think about. Fancy things I suppose. I wish I knew some fancy things alredy.

Progress Report 7—mar 19

Nothing is happining. I had lots of tests and different kinds of races with Algernon. I hate that mouse. He always beats me. Dr Strauss said I got to play those games. And he said some time I got to take those tests over again. Thse inkblots are stupid. And those pictures are stupid too. I like to draw a picture of a man and a woman but I wont make up lies about people.

I got a headache from trying to think so much. I thot Dr Strauss was my frend but he dont help me. He dont tell me what to think or when Ill get smart. Miss Kinnian dint come to see me. I think writing these progress reports are stupid too.

Progress Report 8—Mar 23

Im going back to work at the factery. They said it was better I shud go back to work but I cant tell anyone what the operashun was for and I have to come to the hospitil for an hour evry night after work. They are gonna pay me mony every month for lerning to be smart.

Im glad Im going back to work because I miss my job and all my frends and all the fun we have there.

Dr Strauss says I shud keep writing things down but I dont have to do it every day just when I think of something or something speshul happins. He says dont get dis- coridged because it takes time and it happins slow. He says it took a long time with Algernon before he got 3 times smarter then he was before. Thats why Algernon beats me all the time because he had that operashun too. That makes me feel better. I could probly do that *amazed* faster than a reglar mouse. Maybe some day Ill beat Algernon. Boy that would be something. So far Algernon looks like he mite be smart perminent.

Mar 25 (I dont have to write PROGRESS REPORT on top any more just when I hand it in once a week for Dr Nemur to read. I just have to put the date on. That saves time)

We had a lot of fun at the factery today. Joe Carp said hey look where Charlie had his operashun what did they do Charlie put some brains in. I was going to tell him but I remembered Dr Strauss said no. Then Frank Reilly said what did you do Charlie forget your key and open your door the hard way. That made me laff. Their really my friends and they like me.

Sometimes somebody will say hey look at Joe or Frank or George he really pulled a Charlie Gordon. I dont know why they say that but they always laff. This morning Amos Borg who is the 4 man at Donnegans used my name when he shouted at Ernie the office boy. Ernie lost a packige. He said Ernie for godsake what are you trying to be a Charlie Gordon. I dont understand why he said that. I never lost any packiges.

Mar 28 Dr Strauss came to my room tonight to see why I dint come in like I was suppose to. I told him I dont like to race with Algernon any more. He said I dont have to for a while but I shud come in. He had a present for me only it wasnt a present but just for lend. I thot it was a little television but it wasnt. He said I got to turn it on when I go to sleep. I said your kidding why shud I turn it on when Im going to sleep. Who ever herd of a thing like that. But he said if I want to get smart I got to do what he says. I told him I dont think I was going to get smart and he put his hand on my sholder and said Charlie you dont know it yet but your getting smarter all the time. You wont notice for a while. I think he was just being nice to make me feel good because I dont look any smarter.

Oh yes I almost forgot. I asked him when I can go back to the class at Miss Kinnians school. He said I wont go their. He said that soon Miss Kinnian will come to the hospitil to start and teach me speshul. I was mad at her for not comming to see me when I got the operashun but I like her so maybe we will be frends again.

Mar 29 That crazy TV kept me up all night. How can I sleep with something yelling crazy things all night in my ears. And the nutty pictures. Wow. I dont know what it says when Im up so how am I going to know when Im sleeping.

Dr Strauss says its ok. He says my brains are lerning when I sleep and that will help me when Miss Kinnian starts my lessons in the hospitl (only I found out it isnt a hospitil its a labatory). I think its all crazy. If you can get smart when your sleeping why do people go to school. That thing I dont think will work. I use to watch the late show and the late late show on TV all the time and it never made me smart. Maybe you have to sleep while you watch it.

PROGRESS REPORT 9—April 3

Dr Strauss showed me how to keep the TV turned low so now I can sleep. I dont hear a thing. And I still dont understand what it says. A few times I play it over in the morning to find out what I lerned when I was sleeping and I dont think so. Miss Kinnian says Maybe its another langwidge or something. But most times it sounds american. It talks so fast faster then even Miss Gold who was my teacher in 6 grade and I remember she talked so fast I couldnt understand her.

I told Dr Strauss what good is it to get smart in my sleep. I want to be smart when Im awake. He says its the same thing and I have two minds. Theres the *subconscious* and the *conscious* (that's how you spell it). And one dont tell the other one what its doing. They dont even talk to each other. Thats why I dream. And boy have I been having crazy dreams. Wow. Ever since that night TV. The late late late late late show.

I forgot to ask him if it was only me or if everybody had those two minds.

(I just looked up the word in the dictionary Dr Strauss gave me. The word is *subconscious. adj. Of the nature of mental operations yet not present in consciousness; as, sub-*

conscious conflict of desires.) Theres more but I still don't
know what it means. This isnt a very good dictionary for
dumb people like me.

Anyway the headache is from the party. My frends from
the factery Jos Carp and Frank Reilly invited me to go
with them to Muggsys Saloon for some drinks. I dont like
to drink but they said we will have lots of fun. I had a
good time.

Joe Carp said I shoud show the girls how I mop out the
toilet in the factery and he got me a mop. I showed them
and everyone laffed when I told that Mr Donnegan said
I was the best janiter he ever had because I like my job
and do it good and never come late or miss a day except
for my operashun.

I said Miss Kinnian always said Charlie be proud of
your job because you do it good.

Everybody laffed and we had a good time and they gave
me lots of drinks and Joe said Charlie is a card when hes
potted. I dont know what that means but everybody likes
me and we have fun. I cant wait to be smart like my best
frends Joe Carp and Frank Reilly.

I dont remember how the party was over but I think
I went out to buy a newspaper and coffe for Joe and Frank
and when I came back there was no one their. I looked for
them all over till late. Then I dont remember so good but
I think I got sleepy or sick. A nice cop brot me back home.
Thats what my landlady Mrs Flynn says.

But I got a headache and a big lump on my head and
black and blue all over. I think maybe I fell but Joe Carp
says it was the cop they beat up drunks some times. I don't
think so. Miss Kinnian says cops are to help people. Anyway I got a bad headache and Im sick and hurt all over.
I dont think Ill drink anymore.

April 6 I beat Algernon! I dint even know I beat him until
Burt the tester told me. Then the second time I lost because I got so excited I fell off the chair before I finished.
But after that I beat him 8 more times. I must be getting
smart to beat a smart mouse like Algernon. But I dont *feel*
smarter.

I wanted to race Algernon some more but Bert said thats
enough for one day. They let me hold him for a minit. Hes

not so bad. Hes soft like a ball of cotton. He blinks and when he opens his eyes their black and pink on the eges.

I said can I feed him because I felt bad to beat him and I wanted to be nice and make frends. Burt said no Algernon is a very specshul mouse with an operashun like mine, and he was the first of all the animals to stay smart so long. He told me Algernon is so smart that every day he has to solve a test to get his food. Its a thing like a lock on a door that changes every time Algernon goes in to eat so he has to lern something new to get his food. That made me sad because if he couldnt lern he would be hungry.

I dont think its right to make you pass a test to eat. How woud Dr Nemur like it to have to pass a test every time he wants to eat. I think Ill be frends with Algernon.

April 9 Tonight after work Miss Kinnian was at the laboratory. She looked like she was glad to see me but scared. I told her dont worry Miss Kinnian Im not smart yet and she laffed. She said I have confidence in you Charlie the way you struggled so hard to read and write better than all the others. At werst you will have it for a littel wile and your doing somthing for sience.

We are reading a very hard book. I never read such a hard book before. Its called *Robinson Crusoe* about a man who gets merooned on a dessert Iland. Hes smart and figers out all kinds of things so he can have a house and food and hes a good swimmer. Only I feel sorry because hes all alone and has no frends. But I think their must be somebody else on the iland because theres a picture with his funny umbrella looking at footprints. I hope he gets a frend and not be lonly.

April 10 Miss Kinnian teaches me to spell better. She says look at a word and close your eyes and say it over and over until you remember. I have lots of truble with *through* that you say *threw* and *enough* and *tough* that you dont say *new* and *tew*. You got to say *enuff* and *tuff*. Thats how I use to write it before I started to get smart. Im confused but Miss Kinnian says theres no reason in spelling.

Apr 14 Finished *Robinson Crusoe.* I want to find out more about what happens to him but Miss Kinnian says thats all there is. *Why*

April 15 Miss Kinnian says Im lerning fast. She read some of the Progress Reports and she looked at me kind of funny. She says Im a fine person and Ill show them all. I asked her why. She said never mind but I shouldnt feel bad if I find out that everybody isnt nice like I think. She said for a person who god gave so little to you done more then a lot of people with brains they never even used. I said all my frends are smart people but there good. They like me and they never did anything that wasn't nice. Then she got something in her eye and she had to run out to the ladys room.

Apr 16 Today, I lerned, the *comma*, this is a comma (,) a period, with a tail, Miss Kinnian, says its importent, because, it makes writng, better, she said, somebody, coud lose, a lot of money, if a comma, isnt, in the, right place, I dont have, any money, and I dont see, how a comma, keeps you, from losing it.

But she says, everybody, uses commas, so Ill use, them too,

Apr 17 I used the comma wrong. Its punctuation. Miss Kinnian told me to look up long words in the dictionary to lern to spell them. I said whats the difference if you can read it anyway. She said its part of your education so now on Ill look up all the words Im not sure how to spell. It takes a long time to write that way but I think Im remembering. I only have to look up once and after that I get it right. Anyway thats how come I got the word *punctuation* right. (Its that way in the dictionary). Miss Kinnian says a period is punctuation too, and there are lots of other marks to lern. I told her I thot all the periods had to have tails but she said no.

You got to mix them up, she showed? me" how. to mix! them (up,. and now; I can! mix up all kinds" of punctuation, in! my writing? There, are lots! of rules? to lern; but I'm gettin'g them in my head.

One thing I? like about, Dear Miss Kinnian: (thats the way it goes in a business letter if I ever go into business)

616   Daniel Keyes

is she, always gives me' a reason" when—I ask. She's a
gen'ius! I wish! I cou'd be smart" like, her;
    (Punctuation, is; fun!)

April 18 What a dope I am! I didn't even understand what
she was talking about. I read the grammar book last night
and it explanes the whole thing. Then I saw it was the
same way as Miss Kinnian was trying to tell me, but I
didn't get it. I got up in the middle of the night, and the
whole thing straightened out in my mind.

Miss Kinnian said that the TV working in my sleep
helped out. She said I reached a plateau. Thats like the
flat top of a hill.

After I figgered out how punctuation worked, I read
over all my old Progress Reports from the beginning. Boy,
did I have crazy spelling and punctuation! I told Miss
Kinnian I ought to go over the pages and fix all the mistakes but she said, "No, Charlie, Dr. Nemur wants them
just as they are. That's why he let you keep them after
they were photostated, to see your own progress. You're
coming along fast, Charlie."

That made me feel good. After the lesson I went down
and played with Algernon. We don't race any more.

April 20 I feel sick inside. Not sick like for a doctor, but
inside my chest it feels empty like gettng punched and a
heartburn at the same time.

I wasn't going to write about it, but I guess I got to,
because it's important. Today was the first time I ever
stayed home from work.

Last night Joe Carp and Frank Reilly invited me to a
party. There were lots of girls and some men from the
factory. I remembered how sick I got last time I drank too
much, so I told Joe I didn't want anything to drink. He
gave me a plain Coke instead. It tasted funny, but I
thought it was just a bad taste in my mouth.

We had a lot of fun for a while. Joe said I should dance
with Ellen and she would teach me the steps. I fell a few
times and I couldn't understand why because no one else
was dancing besides Ellen and me. And all the time I was
tripping because somebody's foot was always sticking out.

Then when I got up I saw the look on Joe's face and it

gave me a funny feeling in my stomack. "He's a scream," one of the girls said. Everybody was laughing.

Frank said, "I ain't laughed so much since we sent him off for the newspaper that night at Muggsy's and ditched him."

"Look at him. His face is red."

"He's blushing. Charlie is blushing."

"Hey, Ellen, what'd you do to Charlie? I never saw him act like that before."

I didn't know what to do or where to turn. Everyone was looking at me and laughing and I felt naked. I wanted to hide myself. I ran out into the street and I threw up. Then I walked home. It's a funny thing I never knew that Joe and Frank and the others liked to have me around all the time to make fun of me.

Now I know what it means when they say "to pull a Charlie Gordon."

I'm ashamed.

PROGRESS REPORT 11

April 21 Still didn't go into the factory. I told Mrs. Flynn my landlady to call and tell Mr. Donnegan I was sick. Mrs. Flynn looks at me very funny lately like she's scared of me.

I think it's a good thing about finding out how everybody laughs at me. I thought about it a lot. It's because I'm so dumb and I don't even know when I'm doing something dumb. People think it's funny when a dumb person can't do things the same way they can.

Anyway, now I know I'm getting smarter every day. I know punctuation and I can spell good. I like to look up all the hard words in the dictionary and I remember them. I'm reading a lot now, and Miss Kinnian says I read very fast. Sometimes I even understand what I'm reading about, and it stays in my mind. There are times when I can close my eyes and think of a page and it all comes back like a picture.

Besides history, geography, and arithmetic, Miss Kinnian said I should start to learn a few foreign languages. Dr. Strauss gave me some more tapes to play while I sleep. I still don't understand how that conscious and unconscious mind works, but Dr. Strauss says not to worry yet. He asked me to promise that when I start learning college subjects next week I wouldn't read any books on psychology —that is, until he gives me permission.

I feel a lot better today, but I guess I'm still a little angry that all the time people were laughing and making fun of me because I wasn't so smart. When I become intelligent like Dr. Strauss says, with three times my I.Q. of 68, then maybe I'll be like everyone else and people will like me and be friendly.

I'm not sure what an I.Q. is. Dr. Nemur said it was something that measured how intelligent you were—like a scale in the drugstore weighs pounds. But Dr. Strauss had a big argument with him and said an I.Q. didn't weigh intelligence at all. He said an I.Q. showed how much intelligence you could get, like the numbers on the outside of a measuring cup. You still had to fill the cup up with stuff.

Then when I asked Burt, who gives me my intelligence tests and works with Algernon, he said that both of them were wrong (only I had to promise not to tell them he said so). Burt says that the I.Q. measures a lot of different things including some of the things you learned already, and it really isn't any good at all.

So I still don't know what I.Q. is except that mine is going to be over 200 soon. I didn't want to say anything, but I don't see how if they don't know *what* it is, or *where* it is—I don't see how they know *how much* of it you've got.

Dr. Nemur says I have to take a *Rorshach Test* tomorrow. I wonder what *that* is.

April 22 I found out what a *Rorshach* is. It's the test I took before the operation—the one with the inkblots on the pieces of cardboard. The man who gave me the test was the same one.

I was scared to death of those inkblots. I knew he was going to ask me to find the pictures and I knew I wouldn't be able to. I was thinking to myself, if only there was some way of knowing what kind of pictures were hidden there. Maybe there weren't any pictures at all. Maybe it was just a trick to see if I was dumb enough to look for something that wasn't there. Just thinking about that made me sore at him.

"All right, Charlie," he said, "you've seen these cards before, remember?"

"Of course I remember."

The way I said it, he knew I was angry, and he looked surprised. "Yes, of course. Now I want you to look at this one. What might this be? What do you see on this card? People see all sorts of things in these inkblots. Tell me what it might be for you—what it makes you think of?"

I was shocked. That wasn't what I had expected him to say at all. "You mean there are no pictures hidden in those inkblots?"

He frowned and took off his glasses. "What?"

"Pictures. Hidden in the inkblots. Last time you told me that everyone could see them and you wanted me to find them too."

He explained to me that the last time he had used almost the exact same words he was using now. I didn't believe it, and I still have the suspicion that he misled me at the time just for the fun of it. Unless—I don't know any more—could I have been *that* feeble-minded?

We went through the cards slowly. One of them looked like a pair of bats tugging at something. Another one looked like two men fencing with swords. I imagined all sorts of things. I guess I got carried away. But I didn't trust him any more, and I kept turning them around and even looking on the back to see if there was anything there I was supposed to catch. While he was making notes, I peeked out of the corner of my eye to read it. But it was all in code that looked like this:

WF+A DdF-Ad orig. WF-A SF+obj

The test still doesn't make sense to me. It seems to me that anyone could make up lies about things that they didn't really see. How could he know I wasn't making a fool of him by mentioning things that I didn't really imagine? Maybe I'll understand it when Dr. Strauss lets me read up on psychology.

April 25 I figured out a new way to line up the machines in the factory, and Mr. Donnegan says it will save him ten thousand dollars a year in labor and increased production. He gave me a twenty-five dollar bonus.

I wanted to take Joe Carp and Frank Reilly out to lunch to celebrate, but Joe said he had to buy some things for his wife, and Frank said he was meeting his cousin for lunch. I guess it'll take a little time for them to get used to the changes in me. Everybody seems to be frightened of me. When I went over to Amos Borg and tapped him on the shoulder, he jumped up in the air.

People don't talk to me much any more or kid around the way they used to. It makes the job kind of lonely.

April 27 I got up the nerve today to ask Miss Kinnian to have dinner with me tomorrow night to celebrate my bonus.

At first she wasn't sure it was right, but I asked Dr. Strauss and he said it was okay. Dr. Strauss and Dr. Nemur don't seem to be getting along so well. They're arguing all the time. This evening when I came in to ask Dr. Strauss about having dinner with Miss Kinnian, I heard hm shouting. Dr. Nemur was saying that it was *his* experiment and *his* research, and Dr. Strauss was shouting back that he contributed just as much, because he found me through Miss Kinnian and he performed the operation. Dr. Strauss said that someday thousands of neurosurgeons might be using his technique all over the world.

Dr. Nemur wanted to publish the results of the experiment at the end of this month. Dr. Strauss wanted to wait a while longer to be sure. Dr. Strauss said that Dr. Nemur was more interested in the Chair of Psychology at Princeton than he was in the experiment. Dr. Nemur said that Dr. Strauss was nothing but an opportunist who was trying to ride to glory on *his* coattails.

When I left afterwards, I found myself trembling. I don't know why for sure, but it was as if I'd seen both men clearly for the first time. I remember hearing Burt say that Dr. Nemur had a shrew of a wife who was pushing him all the time to get things published so that he could become famous. Burt said that the dream of her life was to have a big-shot husband.

Was Dr. Strauss really trying to ride on his coattails?

April 28 I don't understand why I never noticed how beautiful Miss Kinnian really is. She has brown eyes and feathery brown hair that comes to the top of her neck. She's only thirty-four! I think from the beginning I had the feeling that she was an unreachable genius—and very, very old. Now, every time I see her she grows younger and more lovely.

We had dinner and a long talk. When she said that I was coming along so fast that soon I'd be leaving her behind, I laughed.

"It's true, Charlie. You're already a better reader than I am. You can read a whole page at a glance while I can take in only a few lines at a time. And you remember every single thing you read. I'm lucky if I can recall the main thoughts and the general meaning."

"I don't feel intelligent. There are so many things I don't understand."

She took out a cigarette and I lit it for her. "You've got to be a *little* patient. You're accomplishing in days and weeks what it takes normal people to do in half a lifetime. That's what makes it so amazing. You're like a giant sponge, soaking things in. Facts, figures, general knowledge. And soon you'll begin to connect them, too. You'll see how the different branches of learning are related. There are many levels, Charlie, like steps on a giant ladder that take you up higher and higher to see more and more of the world around you.

"I can see only a little bit of that, Charlie, and I won't go much higher than I am now, but you'll keep climbing up and up, and see more and more, and each step will open new worlds that you never even knew existed." She frowned. "I hope . . . I just hope to God—"

"What?"

"Never mind, Charles. I just hope I wasn't wrong to advise you to go into this in the first place."

I laughed. "How could that be? It worked, didn't it? Even Algernon is still smart."

We sat there silently for a while and I knew what she was thinking about as she watched me toying with the chain of my rabbit's foot and my keys. I didn't want to think of that possibility any more than elderly people want to think of death. I *knew* that this was only the beginning.

I knew what she meant about levels because I'd seen some of them already. The thought of leaving her behind made me sad.

I'm in love with Miss Kinnian.

PROGRESS REPORT 12

April 30 I've quit my job with Donnegan's Plastic Box Company. Mr. Donnegan insisted that it would be better for all concerned if I left. What did I do to make them hate me so?

The first I knew of it was when Mr. Donnegan showed me the petition. Eight hundred and forty names, everyone connected with the factory, except Fanny Girden. Scanning the list quickly, I saw at once that hers was the only missing name. All the rest demanded that I be fired.

Joe Carp and Frank Reilly wouldn't talk to me about it. No one else would either, except Fanny. She was one of the few people I'd known who set her mind to something and believed it no matter what the rest of the world proved, said, or did—and Fanny did not believe that I should have been fired. She had been against the petition on principle and despite the pressure and threats she'd held out.

"Which don't mean to say," she remarked, "that I don't think there's something mighty strange about you, Charlie. Them changes. I don't know. You used to be a good, dependable, ordinary man—not too bright maybe, but honest. Who knows what you done to yourself to get so smart all of a sudden. Like everybody around here's been saying, Charlie, it's not right."

"But how can you say that, Fanny? What's wrong with a man becoming intelligent and wanting to acquire knowledge and understanding of the world around him?"

She stared down at her work and I turned to leave. Without looking at me, she said: "It was evil when Eve listened to the snake and ate from the tree of knowledge. It was evil when she saw that she was naked. If not for that none of us would ever have to grow old and sick and die."

Once again now I have the feeling of shame burning inside me. This intelligence has driven a wedge between me and all the people I once knew and loved. Before, they laughed at me and despised me for my ignorance and dull-ness; now, they hate me for my knowledge and under-standing. What in God's name do they want of me?

They've driven me out of the factory. Now I'm more alone than ever before . . .

May 15 Dr. Strauss is very angry at me for not having written my progress reports in two weeks. He's justified be-cause the lab is now paying me a regular salary. I told him I was too busy thinking and reading. When I pointed out that writing was such a slow process that it made me im-patient with my poor handwriting, he suggested that I learn to type. It's much easier to write now because I can type nearly seventy-five words a minute. Dr. Strauss continually reminds me of the need to speak and write simply so that people will be able to understand me.

I'll try to review all the things that happened to me during the last two weeks. Algernon and I were presented to the American Psychological Association sitting in con-vention with the World Psychological Association last Tuesday. We created quite a sensation. Dr. Nemur and Dr. Strauss were proud of us.

I suspect that Dr. Nemur, who is sixty—ten years older than Dr. Strauss—finds it necessary to see tangible results of his work. Undoubtedly the result of pressure by Mrs. Nemur.

Contrary to my earlier impressions of him, I realize that Dr. Nemur is not at all a genius. He has a very good mind, but it struggles under the spectre of self-doubt. He wants people to take him for a genius. Therefore, it is important for him to feel that his work is accepted by the world. I believe that Dr. Nemur was afraid of further delay be-cause he worried that someone else might make a discovery along these lines and take the credit from him.

Dr. Strauss on the other hand might be called a genius, although I feel that his areas of knowledge are too limited. He was educated in the tradition of narrow specialization; the broader aspects of background were neglected far more than necessary—even for a neurosurgeon.

I was shocked to learn that the only ancient languages he could read were Latin, Greek, and Hebrew, and that he knows almost nothing of mathematics beyond the elemen-

tary levels of the calculus of variations. When he admitted
this to me, I found myself almost annoyed. It was as if
he'd hidden this part of himself in order to deceive me,
pretending—as do many people I've discovered—to be
what he is not. No one I've ever known is what he appears
to be on the surface.

Dr. Nemur appears to be uncomfortable around me.
Sometimes when I try to talk to him, he just looks at me
strangely and turns away. I was angry at first when Dr.
Strauss told me I was giving Dr. Nemur an inferiority
complex. I thought he was mocking me and I'm over-
sensitive at being made fun of.

How was I to know that a highly respected psycho-
experimentalist like Nemur was unacquainted with Hindustani and Chinese? It's absurd when you consider the work
that is being done in India and China today in the very
field of his study.

I asked Dr. Strauss how Nemur could refute Raha-
jamati's attack on his method and results if Nemur couldn't
even read them in the first place. That strange look on Dr.
Strauss' face can only mean one of two things. Either he
doesn't want to tell Nemur what they're saying in India,
or else—and this worries me—Dr. Strauss doesn't know
either. I must be careful to speak and write clearly and
simply so that people won't laugh.

May 18 I am very disturbed. I saw Miss Kinnian last night
for the first time in over a week. I tried to avoid all discussions of intellectual concepts and to keep the conversation on a simple, everyday level, but she just stared at me
blankly and asked me what I meant about the mathematical variance equivalent in Dorbermann's *Fifth Concerto*.

When I tried to explain she stopped me and laughed. I
guess I got angry, but I suspect I'm approaching her on
the wrong level. No matter what I try to discuss with her,
I am unable to communicate. I must review Vrostadt's
equations on *Levels of Semantic Progression*. I find that
I don't communicate with people much any more. Thank
God for books and music and things I can think about. I
am alone in my apartment at Mrs. Flynn's boardinghouse
most of the time and seldom speak to anyone.

May 20 I would not have noticed the new dishwasher, a boy of about sixteen, at the corner diner where I take my evening meals if not for the incident of the broken dishes.

They crashed to the floor, shattering and sending bits of white china under the tables. The boy stood there, dazed and frightened, holding the empty tray in his hand. The whistles and catcalls from the customers (the cries of "hey, there go the profits!" . . . *"Mazeltov!"* . . . and "well, *he* didn't work here very long . . ." which invariably seem to follow the breaking of glass or dishware in a public restaurant) all seemed to confuse him.

When the owner came to see what the excitement was about, the boy cowered as if he expected to be struck and threw up his arms as if to ward off the blow.

"All right! All right, you dope," shouted the owner, "don't just stand there! Get the broom and sweep that mess up. A broom . . . a broom, you idiot! It's in the kitchen. Sweep up all the pieces."

The boy saw that he was not going to be punished. His frightened expression disappeared and he smiled and hummed as he came back with the broom to sweep the floor. A few of the rowdier customers kept up the remarks, amusing themselves at his expense.

"Here, sonny, over here there's a nice piece behind you . . ."

"C'mon, do it again . . ."

"He's not so dumb. It's easier to break 'em than to wash 'em . . ."

As his vacant eyes moved across the crowd of amused onlookers, he slowly mirrored their smiles and finally broke into an uncertain grin at the joke which he obviously did not understand.

I felt sick inside as I looked at his dull, vacuous smile, the wide, bright eyes of a child, uncertain but eager to please. They were laughing at him because he was mentally retarded.

And I had been laughing at him too.

Suddenly, I was furious at myself and all those who were smirking at him. I jumped up and shouted, "Shut up! Leave him alone! It's not his fault he can't understand! He can't help what he is! But for God's sake . . . he's still a human being!"

The room grew silent. I cursed myself for losing control and creating a scene. I tried not to look at the boy as I paid my check and walked out without touching my food. I felt ashamed for both of us.

How strange it is that people of honest feelings and sensibility, who would not take advantage of a man born without arms or legs or eyes—how such people think nothing of abusing a man born with low intelligence. It infuriated me to think that not too long ago I, like this boy, had foolishly played the clown.

And I had almost forgotten.

I'd hidden the picture of the old Charlie Gordon from myself because now that I was intelligent it was something that had to be pushed out of my mind. But today in looking at that boy, for the first time I saw what I had been. *I was just like him!*

Only a short time ago, I learned that people laughed at me. Now I can see that unknowingly I joined with them in laughing at myself. That hurts most of all.

I have often reread my progress reports and seen the illiteracy, the childish naïveté, the mind of low intelligence peering from a dark room, through the keyhole, at the dazzling light outside. I see that even in my dullness I knew that I was inferior, and that other people had something I lacked—something denied me. In my mental blindness, I thought that it was somehow connected with the ability to read and write, and I was sure that if I could get those skills I would automatically have intelligence too.

Even a feeble-minded man wants to be like other men.

A child may not know how to feed itself, or what to eat, yet it knows of hunger.

This then is what I was like, I never knew. Even with my gift of intellectual awareness, I never really knew.

This day was good for me. Seeing the past more clearly, I have decided to use my knowledge and skills to work in the field of increasing human intelligence levels. Who is better equipped for this work? Who else has lived in both worlds? These are my people. Let me use my gift to do something for them.

Tomorrow, I will discuss with Dr. Strauss the manner in which I can work in this area. I may be able to help him work out the problems of widespread use of the technique which was used on me. I have several good ideas of my own.

There is so much that might be done with this technique. If I could be made into a genius, what about thousands of others like myself? What fantastic levels might be achieved by using this technique on normal people? On *geniuses?*

There are so many doors to open. I am impatient to begin.

PROGRESS REPORT 13

May 23 It happened today. Algernon bit me. I visited the lab to see him as I do occasionally, and when I took him out of his cage, he snapped at my hand. I put him back and watched him for a while. He was unusually disturbed and vicious.

May 24 Burt, who is in charge of the experimental animals, tells me that Algernon is changing. He is less co-operative; he refuses to run the maze any more; general motivation has decreased. And he hasn't been eating. Everyone is upset about what this may mean.

May 25 They've been feeding Algernon, who now refuses to work the shifting-lock problem. Everyone identifies me with Algernon. In a way we're both the first of our kind. They're all pretending that Algernon's behavior is not necessarily significant for me. But it's hard to hide the fact that some of the other animals who were used in this experiment are showing strange behavior.

Dr. Strauss and Dr. Nemur have asked me not to come to the lab any more. I know what they're thinking but I can't accept it. I am going ahead with my plans to carry their research forward. With all due respect to both of these fine scientists, I am well aware of their limitations. If there is an answer, I'll have to find it out for myself. Suddenly, time has become very important to me.

May 29 I have been given a lab of my own and permission to go ahead with the research. I'm on to something. Working day and night. I've had a cot moved into the lab. Most of my writing time is spent on the notes which I keep in a separate folder, but from time to time I feel it necessary to put down my moods and my thoughts out of sheer habit.

I find the *calculus of intelligence* to be a fascinating study. Here is the place for the application of all the knowledge I have acquired. In a sense it's the problem I've been concerned with all my life.

May 31 Dr. Strauss thinks I'm working too hard. Dr. Nemur says I'm trying to cram a lifetime of research and thought into a few weeks. I know I should rest, but I'm driven on by something inside that won't let me stop. I've got to find the reason for the sharp regression in Algernon. I've got to know *if* and *when* it will happen to me.

June 4

LETTER TO DR. STRAUSS: *(Copy)*
Dear Dr. Strauss:

Under separate cover I am sending you a copy of my report entitled, "The Algernon-Gordon Effect: A Study of Structure and Function of Increased Intelligence," which I would like to have you read and have published.

As you see, my experiments are completed. I have included in my report all of my formulae, as well as mathematical analysis in the appendix. Of course, these should be verified.

Because of its importance to both you and Dr. Nemur (and need I say to myself, too?) I have checked and rechecked my results a dozen times in the hope of finding an error. I am sorry to say the results must stand. Yet for the sake of science, I am grateful for the little bit that I here add to the knowledge of the function of the human mind and of the laws governing the artificial increase of human intelligence.

I recall your once saying to me that an experimental *failure* or the *disproving* of a theory was as important to the advancement of learning as a success would be. I know now that this is true. I am sorry, however, that my own contribution to the field must rest upon the ashes of the work of two men I regard so highly.

Yours truly,
Charles Gordon

encl.: rept.

June 5 I must not become emotional. The facts and the results of my experiments are clear, and the more sensational aspects of my own rapid climb cannot obscure the fact that the tripling of intelligence by the surgical technique developed by Drs. Strauss and Nemur must be viewed as having little or no practical applicability (at the present time) to the increase of human intelligence.

As I review the records and data on Alernon, I see that although he is still in his physical infancy, he has regressed mentally. Motor activity is impaired; there is a general reduction of glandular activity; there is an accelerated loss of co-ordination.

There are also strong indications of progressive amnesia.

As will be seen by my report, these and other physical and mental deterioration syndromes can be predicted with statistically significant results by the application of my formula.

The surgical stimulus to which we were both subjected has resulted in an intensification and acceleration of all mental processes. The unforeseen development, which I have taken the liberty of calling the *Algernon-Gordon Effect*, is the logical extention of the entire intelligence speed-up. The hypothesis here proven may be described simply in the following terms: Artificially increased intelligence deteriorates at a rate of time directly proportional to the quantity of the increase.

I feel that this, in itself, is an important discovery.

As long as I am able to write, I will continue to record my thoughts in these progress reports. It is one of my few pleasures. However, by all indications, my own mental deterioration will be very rapid.

I have already begun to notice signs of emotional instability and forgetfulness, the first symptoms of the burn-out.

June 10 Deterioration progressing. I have become absent-minded. Algernon died two days ago. Dissection shows my predictions were right. His brain had decreased in weight and there was a general smoothing out of cerebral convolutions as well as a deepening and broadening of brain fissures.

I guess the same thing is or will soon be happening to me. Now that it's definite, I don't want it to happen.

I put Algernon's body in a cheese box and buried him in the back yard. I cried.

June 15 Dr. Strauss came to see me again. I wouldn't open the door and I told him to go away. I want to be left to myself. I have become touchy and irritable. I feel the darkness closing in. It's hard to throw off thoughts of suicide. I keep telling myself how important this introspective journal will be.

It's a strange sensation to pick up a book that you've read and enjoyed just a few months ago and discover that you don't remember it. I remembered how great I thought John Milton was, but when I picked up *Paradise Lost* I couldn't understand it at all. I got so angry I threw the book across the room.

I've got to try to hold on to some of it. Some of the things I've learned. Oh, God, please don't take it all away.

June 19 Sometimes, at night, I go out for a walk. Last night I couldn't remember where I lived. A policeman took me home. I have the strange feeling that this has all happened to me before—a long time ago. I keep telling myself I'm the only person in the world who can describe what's happening to me.

June 21 Why can't I remember? I've got to fight. I lie in bed for days and I don't know who or where I am. Then it all comes back to me in a flash. Fugues of amnesia. Symptoms of senility—second childhood. I can watch them coming on. It's so cruelly logical. I learned so much and so fast. Now my mind is deteriorating rapidly. I won't let it happen. I'll fight it. I can't help thinking of the boy in the restaurant, the blank expression, the silly smile, the people laughing at him. No—please—not that again . . .

June 22 I'm forgetting things that I learned recently. It seems to be following the classic pattern—the last things learned are the first things forgotten. Or is that the pattern? I'd better look it up again. . . .

I reread my paper on the *Algernon-Gordon Effect* and

I get the strange feeling that it was written by someone else. There are parts I don't even understand.

Motor activity impaired. I keep tripping over things, and it becomes increasingly difficult to type.

June 23 I've given up using the typewriter completely. My co-ordination is bad. I feel that I'm moving slower and slower. Had a terrible shock today. I picked up a copy of an article I used in my research, Krueger's *Uber psychische Ganzheit,* to see if it would help me understand what I had done. First I thought there was something wrong with my eyes. Then I realized I could no longer read German. I tested myself in other languages. All gone.

June 30 A week since I dared to write again. It's slipping away like sand through my fingers. Most of the books I have are too hard for me now. I get angry with them because I know I read and understood them just a few weeks ago.

I keep telling myself I must keep writing these reports so that somebody will know what is happening to me. But it gets harder to form the words and remember spellings. I have to look up even simple words in the dictionary now and it makes me impatient with myself.

Dr. Strauss comes around almost every day, but I told him I wouldn't see or speak to anybody. He feels guilty. They all do. But I don't blame anyone. I knew what might happen. But how it hurts.

July 7 I don't know where the week went. Todays Sunday I know because I can see through my window people going to church. I think I stayed in bed all week but I remember Mrs. Flynn bringing food to me a few times. I keep saying over and over Ive got to do something but then I forget or maybe its just easier not to do what I say Im going to do.

I think of my mother and father a lot these days. I found a picture of them with me taken at a beach. My father has a big ball under his arm and my mother is holding me by the hand. I dont remember them the way they are in the picture. All I remember is my father drunk most of the time and arguing with mom about money.

He never shaved much and he used to scratch my face

when he hugged me. My mother said he died but Cousin
Miltie said he heard his mom and dad say that my father
ran away with another woman. When I asked my mother
she slapped my face and said my father was dead. I don't
think I ever found out which was true but I don't care
much. (He said he was going to take me to see cows on
a farm once but he never did. He never kept his
promises . . .)

July 10 My landlady Mrs Flynn is very worried about me.
She says the way I lay around all day and dont do anything I remind her of her son before she threw him out of
the house. She said she doesnt like loafers. If Im sick its
one thing, but if Im a loafer thats another thing and she
wont have it. I told her I think Im sick.

I try to read a little bit every day, mostly stories, but
sometimes I have to read the same thing over and over
again because I dont know what it means. And its hard to
write. I know I should look up all the words in the dictionary but its so hard and Im so tired all the time.

Then I got the idea that I would only use the easy words
instead of the long hard ones. That saves time. I put flowers
on Algernons grave about once a week. Mrs. Flynn thinks
Im crazy to put flowers on a mouses grave but I told her
that Algernon was special.

July 14 Its sunday again. I dont have anything to do to
keep me busy now because my television set is broke and
I dont have any money to get it fixed. (I think I lost this
months check from the lab. I dont remember)

I get awful headaches and asperin doesnt help me much.
Mrs Flynn knows Im really sick and she feels very sorry
for me. Shes a wonderful woman whenever someone is
sick.

July 22 Mrs. Flynn called a strange doctor to see me. She
was afraid I was going to die. I told the doctor I wasnt too
sick and that I only forget sometimes. He asked me did
I have any friends or relatives and I said no I dont have
any. I told him I had a friend called Algernon once but
he was a mouse and we used to run races together. He
looked at me kind of funny like he thought I was crazy.

He smiled when I told him I used to be a genius. He talked to me like I was a baby and he winked at Mrs Flynn. I got mad and chased him out because he was making fun of me the way they all used to.

July 24 I have no more money and Mrs. Flynn says I got to go to work somewhere and pay the rent because I havent paid for over two months. I dont know any work but the job I used to have at Donnegans Plastic Box Company. I dont want to go back there because they all knew me when I was smart and maybe theyll laugh at me. But I dont know what else to do to get money.

July 25 I was looking at some of my old progress reports and its very funny but I cant read what I wrote. I can make out some of the words but they dont make sense.

Miss Kinnian came to the door but I said go away I dont want to see you. She cried and I cried too but I wouldn't let her in because I didn't want her to laugh at me. I told her I didn't like her any more. I told her I didn't want to be smart any more. Thats not true. I still love her and I still want to be smart but I had to say that so shed go away. She gave Mrs Flynn money to pay the rent. I dont want that. I got to get a job.

Please . . . please let me not forget how to read and write . . .

July 27 Mr Donnegan was very nice when I came back and asked him for my old job of janitor. First he was very suspicious but I told him what happened to me then he looked very sad and put his hand on my shoulder and said Charlie Gordon you got guts.

Everybody looked at me when I came downstairs and started working in the toilet sweeping it out like I used to. I told myself Charlie if they make fun of you dont get sore because you remember their not so smart as you once thot they were. And besides they were once your friends and if they laughed at you that doesnt mean anything because they liked you too.

One of the new men who came to work there after I went away made a nasty crack he said hey Charlie I hear your a very smart fella a real quiz kid. Say something intelligent. I felt bad but Joe Carp came over and grabbed him by the shirt and said leave him alone you lousy cracker or Ill break your neck. I didn't expect Joe to take my part so I guess hes really my friend.

Later Frank Reilly came over and said Charlie if anybody bothers you or trys to take advantage you call me or Joe and we will set em straight. I said thanks Frank and I got choked up so I had to turn around and go into the supply room so he wouldnt see me cry. Its good to have friends.

July 28 I did a dumb thing today I forgot I wasnt in Miss Kinnians class at the adult center any more like I use to be. I went in and sat down in my old seat in the back of the room and she looked at me funny and she said Charles. I dint remember she ever called me that before only Charlie so I said hello Miss Kinnian Im redy for my lesin today only I lost my reader that we was using. She startid to cry and run out of the room and everybody looked at me and I saw they wasnt the same pepul who used to be in my class.

Then all of a sudden I remember some things about the operashun and me getting smart and I said holy smoke I reely pulled a Charlie Gordon that time. I went away before she come back to the room.

Thats why Im going away from New York for good. I dont want to do nothing like that agen. I dont want Miss Kinnian to feel sorry for me. Evry body feels sorry at the factery and I dont want that eather so Im going someplace where nobody knows that Charlie Gordon was once a genus and now he cant even reed a book or rite good.

Im taking a cuple of books along and even if I cant reed them Ill practise hard and maybe I wont forget every thing I lerned. If I try reel hard maybe Ill be a littel bit smarter then I was before the operashun. I got my rabits foot and my luky penny and maybe they will help me.

If you ever reed this Miss Kinnian dont be sorry for me Im glad I got a second chanse to be smart becaus I lerned a lot of things that I never even new were in this world and Im grateful that I saw it all for a little bit. I dont know why Im dumb agen or what I did wrong maybe its becaus I dint try hard enuff. But if I try and practis very hard maybe Ill get a little smarter and know what all the words are. I remember a littel bit how nice I had a feeling with the blue book that has the torn cover when I red it. Thats why Im gonna keep trying to get smart so I can have that feeling agen. Its a good feeling to know things and be smart. I wish I had it rite now if I did I would sit down and reed all the time. Anyway I bet Im the first dumb person in the world who ever found out something importent for sience. I remember I did somthing but I dont remember what. So I gess its like I did it for all the dumb pepul like me.

Good-by Miss Kinnian and Dr Strauss and evrybody. And P.S. please tell Dr Nemur not to be such a grouch when pepul laff at him and he would have more friends. Its easy to make frends if you let pepul laff at you. Im going to have lots of frends where I go.

P.P.S. Please if you get a chanse put some flowrs on Algernons grave in the bak yard . . .

A ROSE FOR ECCLESIASTES

by Roger Zelazny

I was busy translating one of my *Madrigals Macabre* into Martian on the morning I was found acceptable. The intercom had buzzed briefly, and I dropped my pencil and flipped on the toggle in a single motion.

"Mister G," piped Morton's youthful contralto, "the old man says I should 'get hold of that damned conceited rhymer' right away, and send him to his cabin. Since there's only one damned conceited rhymer . . ."

"Let not ambition mock thy useful toil." I cut him off.

So, the Martians had finally made up their minds! I knocked an inch and a half of ash from a smoldering butt, and took my first drag since I had lit it. The entire month's anticipation tried hard to crowd itself into the moment, but could not quite make it. I was frightened to walk those forty feet and hear Emory say the words I already knew he would say; and that feeling elbowed the other one into the background.

So I finished the stanza I was translating before I got up.

It took only a moment to reach Emory's door. I knocked twice and opened it, just as he growled, "Come in."

"You wanted to see me?" I sat down quickly to save him the trouble of offering me a seat.

"That was fast. What did you do, run?"

I regarded his paternal discontent:

Little fatty flecks beneath pale eyes, thinning hair, and an Irish nose; a voice a decibel louder than anyone else's. . . .

Hamlet to Claudius: "I was working."

First published in 1963

"Hah!" he snorted. "Come off it. No one's ever seen you do any of that stuff."

I shrugged my shoulders and started to rise.

"If that's what you called me down here—"

"Sit down!"

He stood up. He walked around his desk. He hovered above me and glared down. (A hard trick, even when I'm in a low chair.)

"You are undoubtedly the most antagonistic bastard I've ever had to work with!" he bellowed, like a belly-stung buffalo. "Why the hell don't you act like a human being sometime and surprise everybody? I'm willing to admit you're smart, maybe even a genius, but—oh, hell!" He made a heaving gesture with both hands and walked back to his chair.

"Betty has finally talked them into letting you go in." His voice was normal again. "They receive you this afternoon. Draw one of the jeepsters after lunch, and get down there."

"Okay," I said.

"That's all, then."

I nodded, got to my feet. My hand was on the doorknob when he said:

"I don't have to tell you how important this is. Don't treat them the way you treat us."

I closed the door behind me.

I don't remember what I had for lunch. I was nervous, but I knew instinctively that I wouldn't muff it. My Boston publishers expected a Martian Idyll, or at least a Saint-Exupéry job on space flight. The National Science Association wanted a complete report on the Rise and Fall of the Martian Empire.

They would both be pleased. I knew.

That's the reason everyone is jealous—why they hate me. I always come through, and I can come through better than anyone else.

I shoveled in a final anthill of slop, and made my way to our car barn. I drew one jeepster and headed it toward Tirellian.

Flames of sand, lousy with iron oxide, set fire to the buggy. They swarmed over the open top and bit through my scarf; they set to work pitting my goggles.

The jeepster, swaying and panting like a little donkey I once rode through the Himalayas, kept kicking me in the seat of the pants. The Mountains of Tirellian shuffled their feet and moved toward me at a cockeyed angle.

Suddenly I was heading uphill, and I shifted gears to accommodate the engine's braying. Not like Gobi, not like the Great Southwestern Desert, I mused. Just red, just dead . . . without even a cactus.

I reached the crest of the hill, but I had raised too much dust to see what was ahead. It didn't matter, though; I have a head full of maps. I bore to the left and downhill, adjusting the throttle. A cross-wind and solid ground beat down the fires. I felt like Ulysses in Melebolge—with a terza-rima speech in one hand and an eye out for Dante.

I rounded a rock pagoda and arrived.

Betty waved as I crunched to a halt, then jumped down.

"Hi," I choked, unwinding my scarf and shaking out a pound and a half of grit. "Like, where do I go and who do I see?"

She permitted herself a brief Germanic giggle—more at my starting a sentence with "like" than at my discomfort —then she started talking. (She is a top linguist, so a word from the Village Idiom still tickles her!)

I appreciate her precise, furry talk; informational, and all that. I had enough in the way of social pleasantries before me to last at least the rest of my life. I looked at her chocolate-bar eyes and perfect teeth, at her sun-bleached hair, close-cropped to the head (I hate blondes!), and decided that she was in love with me.

"Mr. Gallinger, the Matriarch is waiting inside to be introduced. She has consented to open the Temple records for your study." She paused here to pat her hair and squirm a little. Did my gaze make her nervous?

"They are religious documents, as well as their only history," she continued, "sort of like the Mahabharata. She expects you to observe certain rituals in handling them, like repeating the sacred words when you turn pages—she will teach you the system."

I nodded quickly, several times.

"Fine, let's go in."

"Uh—" She paused. "Do not forget their Eleven Forms of Politeness and Degree. They take matters of form quite seriously—and do not get into any discussions over the equality of the sexes—"

"I know all about their taboos," I broke in. "Don't worry. I've lived in the Orient, remember?"

She dropped her eyes and seized my hand. I almost jerked it away.

"It will look better if I enter leading you."

I swallowed my comments, and followed her, like Samson in Gaza.

Inside, my last thought met with a strange correspondence. The Matriarch's quarters were a rather abstract version of what I imagine the tents of the tribes of Israel to have been like. Abstract, I say, because it was all frescoed brick, peaked like a huge tent, with animal-skin representations like gray-blue scars, that looked as if they had been laid on the walls with a palette knife.

The Matriarch, M'Cwyie, was short, white-haired, fifty-ish, and dressed like a Gypsy queen. With her rainbow of voluminous skirts she looked like an inverted punch bowl set atop a cushion.

Accepting my obeisances, she regarded me as an owl might a rabbit. The lids of those black, black eyes jumped upwards as she discovered my perfect accent. —The tape recorder Betty had carried on her interviews had done its part, and I knew the language reports from the first two expeditions, verbatim. I'm all hell when it comes to picking up accents.

"You are the poet?"

"Yes," I replied.

"Recite one of your poems, please."

"I'm sorry, but nothing short of a thorough translating job would do justice to your language and my poetry, and I don't know enough of your language yet."

"Oh?"

"But I've been making such translations for my own amusement, as an exercise in grammar," I continued. "I'd be honored to bring a few of them along one of the times that I come here."

"Yes. Do so."

Score one for me!

She turned to Betty.

"You may go now."

Betty muttered the parting formalities, gave me a strange
sidewise look, and was gone. She apparently had expected
to stay and "assist" me. She wanted a piece of the glory,
like everyone else. But I was the Schliemann at this Troy,
and there would be only one name on the Association
report!

M'Cwyie rose, and I noticed that she gained very
little height by standing. But then I'm six-six and look
like a poplar in October: thin, bright red on top, and
towering above everyone else.

"Our records are very, very old," she began. "Betty says
that your word for their age is 'millennia.' "

I nodded appreciatively.

"I'm very eager to see them."

"They are not here. We will have to go into the Temple
—they may not be removed."

I was suddenly wary.

"You have no objections to my copying them, do you?"

"No. I see that you respect them, or your desire would
not be so great."

"Excellent."

She seemed amused. I asked her what was funny.

"The High Tongue may not be so easy for a foreigner
to learn."

It came through fast.

No one on the first expedition had gotten this close. I
had had no way of knowing that this was a double-lan-
guage deal—a classical as well as a vulgar. I knew some of
the Prakrit, now I had to learn all their Sanskrit.

"Ouch! and damn!"

"Pardon, please?"

"It's non-translatable, M'Cwyie. But imagine yourself
having to learn the High Tongue in a hurry, and you
can guess at the sentiment."

She seemed amused again, and told me to remove my
shoes.

She guided me through an alcove . . .

. . . and into a burst of Byzantine brilliance!

No Earthman had ever been in this room before,
or I would have heard about it. Carter, the first expedition's linguist, with the help of one Mary Allen,
M.D., had learned all the grammar and vocabulary

that I knew while sitting cross-legged in the antechamber.

We had had no idea this existed. Greedily, I cast my eyes about. A highly sophisticated system of esthetics lay behind the decor. We would have to revise our entire estimation of Martian culture.

For one thing, the ceiling was vaulted and corbeled; for another, there were side-columns with reverse flutings; for another—oh hell! The place was big. Posh. You could never have guessed it from the shaggy outsides.

I bent forward to study the gilt filigree on a ceremonial table. M'Cwyie semed a bit smug at my intentness, but I'd still have hated to play poker with her.

The table was loaded with books.

With my toe, I traced a mosaic on the floor.

"Is your entire city within this one building?"

"Yes, it goes far back into the mountain."

"I see," I said, seeing nothing.

I couldn't ask her for a conducted tour, yet.

She moved to a small stool by the table.

"Shall we begin your friendship with the High Tongue?"

I was trying to photograph the hall with my eyes, knowing I would have to get a camera in here, somehow, sooner or later. I tore my gaze from a statuette and nodded, hard.

"Yes, introduce me."

I sat down.

For the next three weeks alphabet-bugs chased each other behind my eyelids whenever I tried to sleep. The sky was an unclouded pool of turquoise that rippled calligraphies whenever I swept my eyes across it. I drank quarts of coffee while I worked and mixed cocktails of Benzedrine and champagne for my coffee breaks.

M'Cwyie tutored me two hours every morning, and occasionally for another two in the evening. I spent an additional fourteen hours a day on my own, once I had gotten up sufficient momentum to go ahead alone.

And at night the elevator of time dropped me to its bottom floors. . . .

I was six again, learning my Hebrew, Greek, Latin, and Aramaic. I was ten, sneaking peeks at the *Iliad*. When Daddy wasn't spreading hellfire brimstone, and brotherly love, he was teaching me to dig the Word, like in the original.

Lord! There are so many originals and so *many* words!
When I was twelve I started pointing out the little differences between what he was preaching and what I was
reading.

The fundamentalist vigor of his reply brooked no debate. It was worse than any beating. I kept my mouth shut
after that and learned to appreciate Old Testament poetry.

*—Lord, I am sorry! Daddy—Sir—I am sorry! —It
couldn't be! It couldn't be. . . .*

On the day the boy graduated from high school, with
the French, German, Spanish, and Latin awards, Dad
Gallinger had told his fourteen-year-old, six-foot scarecrow
of a son that he wanted him to enter the ministry. I remember how his son was evasive:

"Sir," he had said, "I'd sort of like to study on my
own for a year or so, and then take pre-theology courses
at some liberal arts university. I feel I'm still sort of young
to try a seminary, straight off."

The Voice of God: "But you have the gift of tongues,
my son. You can preach the Gospel in all the lands of
Babel. You were born to be a missionary. You say you are
young, but time is rushing by you like a whirlwind. Start
early, and you will enjoy added years of service."

The added years of service were so many added tails to
the cat repeatedly laid on my back. I can't see his face
now; I never can. Maybe it is because I was always afraid
to look at it then.

And years later, when he was dead, and laid out, in
black, amidst bouquets, amidst weeping congregationalists,
amidst prayers, red faces, handkerchiefs, hands patting
your shoulders, solemn faced comforters . . . I looked at
him and did not recognize him.

We had met nine months before my birth, this stranger
and I. He had never been cruel—stern, demanding, with
contempt for everyone's shortcomings—but never cruel.
He was also all that I had had of a mother. And brothers.
And sisters. He had tolerated my three years at St. John's,
possibly because of its name, never knowing how liberal
and delightful a place it really was.

But I never knew him, the man atop the catafalque demanded nothing now; I was free not to preach the Word.
But now I wanted to, in a different way. I wanted to preach
a word that I could never have voiced while he lived.

I did not return for my senior year in the fall. I had a small inheritance coming, and a bit of trouble getting control of it, since I was still under eighteen. But I managed.

It was Greenwich Village I finally settled upon.

Not telling any well-meaning parishioners my new address, I entered into a daily routine of writing poetry and teaching myself Japanese and Hindustani. I grew a fiery beard, drank espresso, and learned to play chess. I wanted to try a couple of the other paths to salvation.

After that, it was two years in India with the Old Peace Corps—which broke me of my Buddhism, and gave me my *Pipes of Krishna* lyrics and the Pulitzer they deserved.

Then back to the States for my degree, grad work in linguistics, and more prizes.

Then one day a ship went to Mars. The vessel settling in its New Mexico nest of fires contained a new language. —It was fantastic, exotic, and esthetically overpowering. After I had learned all there was to know about it, and written my book, I was famous in new circles:

"Go, Gallinger. Dip your bucket in the well, and bring us a drink of Mars. Go, learn another world—but remain aloof, rail at it gently like Auden—and hand us its soul in iambics."

And I came to the land where the sun is a tarnished penny, where the wind is a whip, where two moons play at hot rod games, and a hell of sand gives you the incendiary itches whenever you look at it.

I rose from my twistings on the bunk and crossed the darkened cabin to a port. The desert was a carpet of endless orange, bulging from the sweepings of centuries beneath it.

"I a stranger, unafraid— This is the land— I've got it made!"

I laughed.

I had the High Tongue by the tail already—or the roots, if you want your puns anatomical, as well as correct.

The High and Low Tongues were not so dissimilar as they had first seemed. I had enough of the one to get me through the murkier parts of the other. I had the grammar and all the commoner irregular verbs down cold; the dictionary I was constructing grew by the day, like a tulip, and would bloom shortly. Every time I played the tapes the stem lengthened.

Now was the time to tax my ingenuity, to really drive the lessons home. I had purposely refrained from plunging into the major texts until I could do justice to them. I had been reading minor commentaries, bits of verse, fragments of history. And one thing had impressed me strongly in all that I read.

They wrote about concrete things: rock, sand, water, winds; and the tenor couched within these elemental symbols was fiercely pessimistic. It reminded me of some Buddhist texts, but even more so, I realized from my recent *recherches*, it was like parts of the Old Testament. Specifically, it reminded me of the Book of Ecclesiastes.

That, then, would be it. The sentiment, as well as the vocabulary, was so similar that it would be a perfect exercise. Like putting Poe into French. I would never be a convert to the Way of Malann, but I would show them that an Earthman had once thought the same thoughts, felt similarly.

I switched on my desk lamp and sought King James amidst my books.

Vanity of vanities, saith the Preacher, vanity of vanities; all is vanity. What profit hath a man . . .

My progress seemed to startle M'Cwyie. She peered at me, like Sartre's Other, across the tabletop. I ran through a chapter in the Book of Locar. I didn't look up, but I could feel the tight net her eyes were working about my head, shoulders, and rabid hands. I turned another page.

Was she weighing the net, judging the size of the catch? And what for? The books said nothing of fishers on Mars. Especially of men. They said that some god named Malann had spat, or had done something disgusting (depending on the version you read), and that life had gotten underway as a disease in inorganic matter. They said that movement was its first law, its first law, and that the dance was the only legitimate reply to the inorganic . . . the dance's quality its justification,—fication . . . and love is a disease in organic matter—Inorganic matter?

I shook my head. I had almost been asleep.

"M'narra."

I stood and stretched. Her eyes outlined me greedily now. So I met them, and they dropped.

"I grow tired. I want to rest awhile. I didn't sleep much last night."

She nodded, Earth's shorthand for "yes," as she had learned from me.

"You wish to relax, and see the explicitness of the doctrine of Locar in its fullness?"

"Pardon me?"

"You wish to se a Dance of Locar?"

"Oh." Their damned circuits of form and periphrasis here ran worse than the Korean! "Yes. Surely. Any time it's going to be done I'd be happy to watch."

I continued, "In the meantime, I've been meaning to ask you whether I might take some pictures—"

"Now is the time. Sit down. Rest. I will call the musicians."

She bustled out through a door I had never been past.

Well, now, the dance was the highest art, according to Locar, not to mention Havelock Ellis, and I was about to see how their centuries-dead philosopher felt it should be conducted. I rubbed my eyes and snapped over, touching my toes a few times.

The blood began pounding in my head, and I sucked in a couple deep breaths. I bent again and there was a flurry of motion at the door.

To the trio who entered with M'Cwyie I must have looked as if I were searching for the marbles I had just lost, bent over like that.

I grinned weakly and straightened up, my face red from more than exertion. I hadn't expected them *that* quickly.

Suddenly I thought of Havelock Ellis again in his area of greatest popularity.

The little redheaded doll, wearing, sari-like, a diaphanous piece of the Martian sky, looked up in wonder—as a child at some colorful flag on a high pole.

"Hello," I said, or its equivalent.

She bowed before replying. Evidently I had been promoted in status.

"I shall dance," said the red wound in that pale, pale cameo, her face. Eyes, the color of dream and her dress, pulled away from mine.

She drifted to the center of the room.

Standing there, like a figure in an Etruscan frieze, she was either meditating or regarding the design on the floor.

Was the mosaic symbolic of something? I studied it. If it was, it eluded me; it would make an attractive bathroom floor or patio, but I couldn't see much in it beyond that.

The other two were paint-spattered sparrows like M'Cwyie, in their middle years. One settled to the floor with a triple-stringed instrument faintly resembling a *samisen*. The other held a simple woodblock and two drumsticks.

M'Cwyie disdained her stool and was seated upon the floor before I realized it. I followed suit.

The *samisen* player was still tuning it up, so I leaned toward M'Cwyie.

"What is the dancer's name?"

"Braxa," she replied, without looking at me, and raised her left hand, slowly, which meant yes, and go ahead, and let it begin.

The stringed-thing throbbed like a toothache, and a tick-tocking, like ghosts of all the clocks they had never invented, sprang from the block.

Braxa was a statue, both hands raised to her face, elbows high and outspread.

The music became a metaphor for fire.

Crackle, purr, snap . . .

She did not move.

The hissing altered to splashes. The cadence slowed. It was water now, the most precious thing in the world, gurgling clear then green over mossy rocks.

Still she did not move.

Glissandos. A pause.

Then, so faint I could hardly be sure at first, the tremble of the winds began. Softly, gently, sighing and halting, uncertain. A pause, a sob, then a repetition of the first statement, only louder.

Were my eyes completely bugged from my reading, or was Braxa actually trembling, all over, head to foot.

She was.

She began a microscopic swaying. A fraction of an inch

right, then left. Her fingers opened like the petals of a flower, and I could see that her eyes were closed.

Her eyes opened. They were distant, glassy, looking through me and the walls. Her swaying became more pronounced, merged with the beat.

The wind was sweeping in from the desert now, falling against Tirellian like waves on a dike. Her fingers moved, they were the gusts. Her arms, slow pendulums, descended, began a counter-movement.

The gale was coming now. She began an axial movement and her hands caught up with the rest of her body, only now her shoulders commenced to writhe out a figure-eight.

The wind! The wind, I say. O wild, enigmatic! O muse of St. John Perse!

The cyclone was twisting around those eyes, its still center. Her head was thrown back, but I knew there was no ceiling between her gaze, passive as Buddha's, and the unchanging skies. Only the two moons, perhaps, interrupted their slumber in that elemental Nirvana of uninhabited turquoise.

Years ago, I had seen the Devadais in India, the streetdancers, spinning their colorful webs, drawing in the male insect. But Braxa was more than this: she was a Ramadjany, like those votaries of Rama, incarnation of Vishnu, who had given the dance to man: the sacred dancers.

The clicking was monotonously steady now; the whine of the strings made me think of the stinging rays of the sun, their heat stolen by the wind's halations; the blue was Sarasvati and Mary, and a girl named Laura. I heard a sitàr from somewhere, watched this statue come to life, and inhaled a divine afflatus.

I was again Rimbaud with his hashish, Baudelaire with his laudanum, Poe, De Quincy, Wilde, Mallarme and Aleister Crowley. I was, for a fleeting second, my father in his dark pulpit and darker suit, the hymns and the organ's wheeze transmuted to bright wind.

She was a spun weather vane, a feathered crucifix hovering in the air, a clothes-line holding one bright garment lashed parallel to the ground. Her shoulder was bare now, and her right breast moved up and down like a moon in the sky, its red nipple appearing momently above a fold and vanishing again. The music was as formal as Job's argument with God. Her dance was God's reply.

The music slowed, settled; it had been met, matched, answered. Her garment, as if alive, crept back into the more sedate folds it originally held.

She dropped low, lower, to the floor. Her head fell upon her raised knees. She did not move.

There was silence.

I realized, from the ache across my shoulders, how tensely I had been sitting. My armpits were wet. Rivulets had been running down my sides. What did one do now? Applaud?

I sought M'Cwyie from the corner of my eye. She raised her right hand.

As if by telepathy the girl shuddered all over and stood. The musicians also rose. So did M'Cwyie.

I got to my feet, with a Charley Horse in my left leg, and said, "It was beautiful," inane as that sounds.

I received three different High Forms of "thank you."

There was a flurry of color and I was alone again with M'Cwyie.

"That is the one hundred-seventeenth of the two thousand, two hundred-twenty-four dances of Locar."

I looked down at her.

"Whether Locar was right or wrong, he worked out a fine reply to the inorganic."

She smiled.

"Are the dances of your world like this?"

"Some of them are similar. I was reminded of them as I watched Braxa—but I've never seen anything exactly like hers."

"She is good," M'Cwyie said. "She knows all the dances."

A hint of her earlier expression which had troubled me . . .

It was gone in an instant.

"I must tend my duties now." She moved to the table and closed the books. "M'narra."

"Good-bye." I slipped into my boots.

"Good-bye, Gallinger."

I walked out the door, mounted the jeepster, and roared across the evening into night, my wings of risen desert flapping slowly behind me.

II

I had just closed the door behind Betty, after a brief grammar session, when I heard the voices in the hall. My vent was opened a fraction, so I stood there and eavesdropped:

Morton's fruity treble: "Guess what? He said 'hello' to me awhile ago."

"Hmmph!" Emory's elephant lungs exploded. "Either he's slipping, or you were standing in his way and he wanted you to move."

"Probably didn't recognize me. I don't think he sleeps any more, now he has that language to play with. I had night watch last week, and every night I passed his door at 0300—I always heard that recorder going. At 0500 when I got off, he was still at it."

"The guy *is* working hard," Emory admitted, grudgingly. "In fact, I think he's taking some kind of dope to keep awake. He looks sort of glassy-eyed these days. Maybe that's natural for a poet, though."

Betty had been standing there, because she broke in then:

"Regardless of what you think of him, it's going to take me at least a year to learn what he's picked up in three weeks. And I'm just a linguist, not a poet."

Morton must have been nursing a crush on her bovine charms. It's the only reason I can think of for his dropping his guns to say what he did.

"I took a course in modern poetry when I was back at the university," he began. "We read six authors—Yeats, Pound, Eliot, Crane, Stevens, and Gallinger—and on the last day of the semester, when the prof was feeling a little rhetorical, he said, 'These six names are written on the century, and all the gates of criticism and hell shall not prevail against them.'

"Myself," he continued, "I thought his *Pipes of Krishna* and his *Madrigals* were great. I was honored to be chosen for an expedition he was going on.

"I think he's spoken two dozen words to me since I met him," he finished.

The Defense: "Did it ever occur to you," Betty said, "that he might be tremendously self-conscious about his appearance? He was also a precocious child, and probably never even had school friends. He's sensitive and very introverted."

"Sensitive? Self-conscious?" Emory choked and gagged. "The man is as proud as Lucifer, and he's a walking insult machine. You press a button like 'Hello' or 'Nice day' and he thumbs his nose at you. He's got it down to a reflex."

They muttered a few other pleasantries and drifted away.

Well bless you, Morton boy. You little pimple-faced, ivy-bred connoisseur! I've never taken a course in my poetry, but I'm glad someone said that. The Gates of Hell. Well now! Maybe Daddy's prayers got heard somewhere, and I am a missionary, after all!

Only . . .

. . . Only a missionary needs something to convert people *to*. I have my private system of esthetics, and I suppose it oozes an ethical by-product somewhere. But if I ever had anything to preach, really, even in my poems, I wouldn't care to preach it to such lowlifes as you. If you think I'm a slob, I'm also a snob, and there's no room for you in my Heaven—it's a private place, where Swift, Shaw, and Petronius Arbiter come to dinner.

And oh, the feasts we have! The Trimalchio's, the Emory's we dissect!

We finish you with the soup, Morton!

I turned and settled at my desk. I wanted to write something. Ecclesiastes could take a night off. I wanted to write a poem, a poem about the one hundred-seventeenth dance of Locar; about a rose following the light, traced by the wind, sick, like Blake's rose, dying. . . .

I found a pencil and began.

When I had finished I was pleased. It wasn't great—at least, it was no greater than it needed to be—High Martian not being my strongest tongue. I groped, and put it into English, with partial rhymes. Maybe I'd stick it in my next book. I called it *Braxa:*

In a land of wind and red, where the icy evening of Time freezes milk in the breasts of Life, as two moons overhead—cat and dog in alleyways of dream—scratch and scramble agelessly my flight . . .

This final flower turns a burning head.

I put it away and found some phenobarbital. I was suddenly tired.

When I showed my poem to M'Cwyie the next day, she read it through several times, very slowly.

"It is lovely," she said. "But you used three words from your own language. 'Cat' and 'dog,' I assume, are two small animals with a hereditary hatred for one another. But what is 'flower'?"

"Oh," I said. "I've never come across your word for 'flower,' but I was actually thinking of an Earth flower, the rose."

"What is it like?"

"Well, its petals are generally bright red. That's what I meant, on one level, by 'burning heads.' I also wanted it to imply fever, though, and red hair, and the fire of life. The rose, itself, has a thorny stem, green leaves, and a distinct, pleasing aroma."

"I wish I could see one."

"I suppose it could be arranged. I'll check."

"Do it, please. You are a—" She used the word for "prophet," or religious poet, like Isaiah or Locar. "—and your poem is inspired. I shall tell Braxa of it."

I declined the nomination, but felt flattered.

This, then, I decided, was the strategic day, the day on which to ask whether I might bring in the microfilm machine and the camera. I wanted to copy all their texts, I explained, and I couldn't write fast enough to do it.

She surprised me by agreeing immediately. But she bowled me over with her invitation.

"Would you like to come and stay here while you do this thing? Then you can work night and day, any time you want—except when the Temple is being used, of course."

I bowed.

"I should be honored."

"Good. Bring your machines when you want, and I will show you a room."

"Will this afternoon be all right?"

"Certainly."

"Then I will go now and get things ready. Until this afternoon . . ."

"Good-bye."

I anticipated a little trouble from Emory, but not much. Everyone back at the ship was anxious to see the Martians, poke needles in the Martians, ask them about Martian climate, diseases, soil chemistry, politics, and mushrooms (our botanist was a fungus nut, but a reasonably good guy)—and only four or five had actually gotten to see them. The crew had been spending most of its time excavating dead cities and their acropolises. We played the game by strict rules, and the natives were as fiercely insular as the nineteenth-century Japanese. I figured I would meet with little resistance, and I figured right.

In fact, I got the distinct impression that everyone was happy to see me move out.

I stopped in the hydroponics room to speak with our mushroom master.

"Hi, Kane. Grow any toadstools in the sand yet?"

He sniffed. He always sniffs. Maybe he's allergic to plants.

"Hello, Gallinger. No, I haven't had any success with toadstools, but look behind the car barn next time you're out there. I've got a few cacti going."

"Great," I observed. Doc Kane was about my only friend aboard, not counting Betty.

"Say, I came down to ask you a favor."

"Name it."

"I want a rose."

"A what?"

"A rose. You know, a nice red American Beauty job— thorns, pretty smelling—"

"I don't think it will take in this soil. *Sniff, sniff.*"

"No, you don't understand. I don't want to plant it, I just want the flowers."

"I'd have to use the tanks." He scratched his hairless dome. "It would take at least three months to get you flowers, even under forced growth."

"Will you do it?"

"Sure, if you don't mind the wait."

"Not at all. In fact, three months will just make it before we leave." I looked about at the pools of crawling slime, at the trays of shoots. "—I'm moving up to Tirellian today, but I'll be in and out all the time. I'll be here when it blooms."

"Moving up there, eh? Moore said they're an in-group."

"I guess I'm 'in' then."

"Looks that way—I still don't see how you learned their language, though. Of course, I had trouble with French and German for my Ph. D., but last week I heard Betty demonstrate it at lunch. It sounds like a lot of weird noises. She says speaking it is like working a *Times* crossword and trying to imitate birdcalls at the same time."

I laughed, and took the cigarette he offered me.

"It's complicated," I acknowledged. "But, well, it's as if you suddenly came across a whole new class of mycetae here—you'd dream about it at night."

His eyes were gleaming.

"Wouldn't that be something! I might, yet, you know."

"Maybe you will."

He chuckled as we walked to the door.

"I'll start your roses tonight. Take it easy down there."

"You bet. Thanks."

Like I said, a fungus nut, but a fairly good guy.

My quarters in the Citadel of Tirellian were directly adjacent to the Temple, on the inward side and slightly to the left. They were a considerable improvement over my cramped cabin, and I was pleased that Martian culture had progressed sufficiently to discover the desirability of the mattress over the pallet. Also, the bed was long enough to accommodate me, which was surprising.

So I unpacked and took sixteen 35 mm. shots of the Temple, before starting on the books.

I took 'stats until I was sick of turning pages without knowing what they said. So I started translating a work of history.

"Lo. In the thirty-seventh year of the Process of Cillen the rains came, which gave rise to rejoicing, for it was a rare and untoward occurrence, and commonly construed a blessing.

"But it was not the life-giving semen of Malann which fell from the heavens. It was the blood of the universe, spurting from an artery. And the last days were upon us. The final dance was to begin.

"The rains brought the plague that does not kill, and the last passes of Locar began with their drumming. . . ."

I asked myself what the hell Tamur meant, for he was

an historian and supposedly committed to fact. This was
not their Apocalypse.

Unless they could be one and the same . . .?

Why not? I mused. Tirellian's handful of people were
the remnant of what had obviously been a highly developed
culture. They had had wars, but no holocausts; science,
but little technology. A plague, a plague that did not kill
. . . ? Could that have done it? How, if it wasn't fatal?

I read on, but the nature of the plague was not dis-
cussed. I turned pages, skipped around, and drew a blank.

*M'Cwyie! M'Cwyie! When I want to question you most,
you are not around!*

Would it be a *faux* to go looking for her? Yes, I decided.
I was restricted to the rooms I had been shown, that had
been an implicit understanding. I would have to wait to
find out.

So I cursed long and loud, in many languages, doubtless
burning Malann's sacred ears, there in his Temple.

He did not see fit to strike me dead, so I decided to call
it a day and hit the sack.

I must have been asleep for several hours when Braxa
entered my room with a tiny lamp. She dragged me awake
by tugging at my pajama sleeve.

I said hello. Thinking back, there is not much else I
could have said.

"Hello."

"I have come," she said, "to hear the poem."

"What poem?"

"Yours."

"Oh."

I yawned, sat up, and did things people usually do when
awakened in the middle of the night to read poetry.

"That is very kind of you, but isn't the hour a trifle
awkward?"

"I don't mind," she said.

Someday I am going to write an article for the *Journal
of Semantics*, called "Tone of Voice: An Insufficient Vehicle for Irony."

However, I was awake, so I grabbed my robe.

"What sort of animal is that?" she asked, pointing at
the silk dragon on my lapel.

"Mythical," I replied. "Now look, it's late. I am tired.

I have much to do in the morning. And M'Cwyie just might get the wrong idea if she learns you were here."

"Wrong idea?"

"You know damned well what I mean!" It was the first time I had had an opportunity to use Martian profanity, and it failed.

"No," she said, "I do not know."

She seemed frightened, like a puppy being scolded without knowing what it has done wrong.

I softened. Her red cloak matched her hair and lips so perfectly, and those lips were trembling.

"Here now, I didn't mean to upset you. On my world there are certain, uh, mores, concerning people of different sex alone together in bedrooms, and not allied by marriage. . . . Um, I mean, you see what I mean?"

"No."

They were jade, her eyes.

"Well, it's sort of . . . Well, it's sex, that's what it is."

A light was switched on in those jade lamps.

"Oh, you mean having children!"

"Yes. That's it! Exactly."

She laughed. It was the first time I had heard laughter in Tirellian. It sounded like a violinist striking his high strings with the bow, in short little chops. It was not an altogether pleasant thing to hear, especially because she laughed too long.

When she had finished she moved closer.

"I remember, now," she said. "We used to have such rules. Half a Process ago, when I was a child, we had such rules. But"—she looked as if she were ready to laugh again —"there is no need for them now."

My mind moved like a tape recorder played at triple speed.

Half a Process! HalfaProcessa-ProcessaProcess! No! Yes! Half a Process was two hundred-forty-three years, roughly speaking!

—Time enough to learn the 2224 dances of Locar.

—Time enough to grow old, if you were human.

—Earth-style human, I mean.

I looked at her again, pale as the white queen in an ivory chess set. She was human, I'd stake my soul—alive, normal, healthy. I'd stake my life—woman, my body . . .

But she was two and a half centuries old, which made

M'Cwyie Methuselah's grandma. It flattered me to think of their repeated complimenting of my skills, as linguist, as poet. These superior beings!

But what did she mean "there is no such need for them now?" Why the near-hysteria? Why all those funny looks I'd been getting from M'Cwyie?

I suddenly knew I was close to something important, besides a beautiful girl.

"Tell me," I said, in my Casual Voice, "did it have anything to do with 'the plague that does not kill,' of which Tamur wrote."

"Yes," she replied, "the children born after the Rains could have no children of their own, and—"

"And what?" I was leaning forward, memory set at "record."

"—and the men had no desire to get any."

I sagged backward against the bedpost. Racial sterility, masculine impotence, following phenomenal weather. Had some vagabond cloud of radioactive junk from God knows where penetrated their weak atmosphere one day? One day long before Shiaparelli saw the canals, mythical as my dragon, before those "canals" had given rise to some correct guesses for all the wrong reasons, had Braxa been alive, dancing, here—damned in the womb since blind Milton had written of another paradise, equally lost?

I found a cigarette. Good thing I had thought to bring ashtrays. Mars had never had a tobacco industry either. Or booze. The ascetics I had met in India had been Dionysiac compared to this.

"What is that tube of fire?"

"A cigarette. Want one?"

"Yes, please."

She sat beside me, and I lighted it for her.

"It irritates the nose."

"Yes. Draw some into your lungs, hold it there, and exhale."

A moment passed.

"Ooh," she said.

A pause, then, "Is it sacred?"

"No, it's nicotine," I answered, "a very *ersatz* form of divinity."

Another pause.

"Please don't ask me to translate 'ersatz.' "

"I won't. I get this feeling sometimes when I dance."

"It will pass in a moment."

"Tell me your poem now."

An idea hit me.

"Wait a minute," I said; "I may have something better."

I got up and rummaged through my notebooks, then I returned and sat beside her.

"These are the first three chapters of the Book of Ecclesiastes," I explained. "It is very similar to your own sacred books."

I started reading.

I got through eleven verses before she cried out, "Please don't read that! Tell me one of yours!"

I stopped and tossed the notebook onto a nearby table. She was shaking, not as she had quivered that day she danced as the wind, but with the jitter of unshed tears. She held her cigarette awkwardly, like a pencil. Clumsily, I put my arm about her shoulders.

"He is so sad," she said, "like all the others."

So I twisted my mind like a bright ribbon, folded it, and tied the crazy Christmas knots I love so well. From German to Martian, with love, I did an impromptu paraphrasal of a poem about a Spanish dancer. I thought it would please her. I was right.

"Ooh," she said again. "Did you write that?"

"No, it's by a better man than I."

"I don't believe you. You wrote it."

"No, a man named Rilke did."

"But you brought it across to my language. Light another match, so I can see how she danced."

I did.

"The fires of forever," she mused, "and she stamped them out, 'with small, firm feet.' I wish I could dance like that."

"You're better than any Gypsy," I laughed, blowing it out.

"No, I'm not. I couldn't do that."

Her cigarette was burning down, so I removed it from her fingers and put it out, along with my own.

"Do you want me to dance for you?"

"No," I said. "Go to bed."

She smiled, and before I realized it, had unclasped the fold of red at her shoulder.

And everything fell away.
And I swallowed, with some difficulty.
"All right," she said.
So I kissed her, as the breath of fallen cloth extinguished the lamp.

III

The days were like Shelley's leaves: yellow, red, brown, whipped in bright gusts by the west wind. They swirled past me with the rattle of microfilm. Almost all the books were recorded now. It would take scholars years to get through them, to properly assess their value. Mars was locked in my desk.

Ecclesiastes, abandoned and returned to a dozen times, was almost ready to speak in the High Tongue.

I whistled when I wasn't in the Temple. I wrote reams of poetry I would have been ashamed of before. Evenings I would walk with Braxa, across the dunes or up into the mountains. Sometimes she would dance for me; and I would read something long, and in dactylic hexameter. She still thought I was Rilke, and I almost kidded myself into believing it. Here I was, staying at the Castle Duino, writing his *Elegies*.

. . . It is strange to inhabit the Earth no more,
to use no longer customs scarce acquired,
nor interpret roses . . .

No! Never interpret roses! Don't. Smell them (sniff, Kane!), pick them, enjoy them. Live in the moment. Hold to it tightly. But charge not the gods to explain. So fast the leaves go by, are blown . . .

And no one ever noticed us. Or cared.

Laura. Laura and Braxa. They rhyme, you know, with a bit of a clash. Tall, cool, and blonde was she (I hate blondes!), and Daddy had turned me inside out, like a pocket, and I thought she could fill me again. But the big, beat word-slinger, with Judas-beard and dog-trust in his eyes, oh, he had been a fine decoration at her parties. And that was all.

How the machine cursed me in the Temple! It blasphemed Malann and Gallinger. And the wild west wind went by and something was not far behind.

The last days were upon us.

A day went by and I did not see Braxa, and a night.

And a second. A third.

I was half-mad. I hadn't realized how close we had become, how important she had been. With the dumb assurance of presence, I had fought against questioning roses.

I had to ask. I didn't want to, but I had no choice.

"Where is she, M'Cwyie? Where is Braxa?"

"She is gone," she said.

"Where?"

"I do not know."

I looked at those devil-bird eyes. Anathema maranatha rose to my lips.

"I must know."

She looked through me.

"She has left us. She is gone. Up in the hills, I suppose. Or the desert. It does not matter. What does anything matter? The dance draws to a close. The Temple will soon be empty."

"Why? Why did she leave?"

"I do not know."

"I must see her again. We lift off in a matter of days."

"I am sorry, Gallinger."

"So am I," I said, and slammed shut a book without saying "m'narra."

I stood up.

"I will find her."

I left the Temple. M'Cwyie was a seated statue. My boots were still where I had left them.

All day I roared up and down the dunes, going nowhere. To the crew of the *Aspic* I must ahve looked like a sandstorm, all by myself. Finally, I had to return for more fuel.

Emory came stalking out.

"Okay, make it good. You look like the abominable dust man. Why the rodeo?"

"Why, I, uh, lost something."

"In the middle of the desert? Was it one of your sonnets? They're the only thing I can think of that you'd make such a fuss over."

"No, dammit! It was something personal."

George had finished filling the tank. I started to mount the jeepster again.

"Hold on there!" he grabbed my arm.

"You're not going back until you tell me what this is all about."

I could have broken his grip, but then he could order me dragged back by the heels, and quite a few people would enjoy doing the dragging. So I forced myself to speak slowly, softly:

"It's simply that I lost my watch. My mother gave it to me and it's a family heirloom. I want to find it before we leave."

"You sure it's not in your cabin, or down in Tirellian?"

"I've already checked."

"Maybe somebody hid it to irritate you. You know you're not the most popular guy around."

I shook my head.

"I thought of that. But I always carry it in my right pocket. I think it might have bounced out going over the dunes."

He narrowed his eyes.

"I remember reading on a book jacket that your mother died when you were born."

"That's right," I said, biting my tongue. "The watch belonged to her father and she wanted me to have it. My father kept it for me."

"Hmph!" he snorted. "That's a pretty strange way to look for a watch, riding up and down in a jeepster."

"I could see the light shining off it that way," I offered, lamely.

"Well, it's starting to get dark," he observed. "No sense looking any more today.

"Throw a dust sheet over the jeepster," he directed a mechanic.

He patted my arm.

"Come on in and get a shower, and something to eat. You look as if you could use both."

Little fatty flecks beneath pale eyes, thinning hair, and an Irish nose; a voice a decibel louder than anyone else's.

. . .

His only qualification for leadership!

I stood there, hating him. Claudius! If only this were the fifth act!

But suddenly the idea of a shower, and food, came through to me. I could use both badly. If I insisted on hurrying back immediately I might arouse more suspicion.

So I brushed some sand from my sleeve.

"You're right. That sounds like a good idea."

"Come on, we'll eat in my cabin."

The shower was a blessing, clean khakis were the grace of God, and the food smelled like Heaven.

"Smells pretty good," I said.

We hacked up our steaks in silence. When we got to the dessert and coffee he suggested:

"Why don't you take the night off? Stay here and get some sleep."

I shook my head.

"I'm pretty busy. Finishing up. There's not much time left."

"A couple of days ago you said you were almost finished."

"Almost, but not quite."

"You also said they'll be holding a service in the Temple tonight."

"That's right. I'm going to work in my room."

He shrugged his shoulders.

Finally, he said, "Gallinger," and I looked up because my name means trouble.

"It shouldn't be any of my business," he said, "but it is. Betty says you have a girl down there."

There was no question mark. It was a statement hanging in the air. Waiting.

Betty, you're a bitch. You're a cow and a bitch. And a jealous one, at that. Why didn't you keep your nose where it belonged, shut your eyes? Your mouth?

"So?" I said, a statement with question mark.

"So," he answered it, "it is my duty, as head of this expedition, to see that relations with the natives are carried on in a friendly, and diplomatic manner."

"You speak of them," I said, "as though they are aborigines. Nothing could be further from the truth."

I rose.

"When my papers are published everyone on Earth will know that truth. I'll tell them things Doctor Moore never even guessed at. I'll tell the tragedy of a doomed race, waiting for death, resigned and disinterested. I'll tell why, and it will break hard, scholarly hearts. I'll write about it, and they will give me more prizes, and this time I won't want them.

"My God!" I exclaimed. "They had a culture when our ancestors were clubbing the saber-tooth and finding out how fire works!"

"*Do* you have a girl down there?"

"Yes!" I said. Yes, *Claudius! Yes, Daddy! Yes, Emory!* "I do. But I'm going to let you in on a scholarly scoop now. They're already dead. They're sterile. In one more generation there won't be any Martians."

I paused, then added, "Except in my papers, except on a few pieces of microfilm and tape. And in some poems, about a girl who did give a damn and could only bitch about the unfairness of it all by dancing."

"Oh," he said.

After awhile:

"You *have* been behaving differently these past couple months. You've even been downright civil on occasion. I couldn't help wondering what was happening. I didn't know anything mattered that strongly to you."

I bowed my head.

"Is she the reason you were racing around the desert?"

I nodded.

"Why?"

I looked up.

"Because she's out there, somewhere. I don't know where, or why. And I've got to find her before we go."

"Oh," he said again.

Then he leaned back, opened a drawer, and took out something wrapped in a towel. He unwound it. A framed photo of a woman lay on the table.

"My wife," he said.

It was an attractive face, with big, almond eyes.

"I'm a Navy man, you know," he begun. "Young officer once. Met her in Japan.

"Where I come from it wasn't considered right to marry into another race, so we never did. But she was my wife. When she died I was on the other side of the world. They took my children, and I've never seen them since. I couldn't learn what orphanage, what home, they were put into. That was long ago. Very few people know about it."

"I'm sorry," I said.

"Don't be. Forget it. But"—he shifted in his chair and looked at me—"if you do want to take her back with you —do it. It'll mean my neck, but I'm too old to ever head another expedition like this one. So go ahead."

He gulped his cold coffee.

"Get your jeepster."

He swiveled the chair around.

I tried to say "thank you" twice, but I couldn't. So I got up and walked out.

"Sayonara, and all that," he muttered behind me.

"Here it is, Gallinger!" I heard a shout.

I turned on my heel and looked back up the ramp. "Kane!"

He was limned in the port, shadow against light, but I had heard him sniff.

I returned the few steps.

"Here what is?"

"Your rose."

He produced a plastic container, divided internally. The lower half was filled with liquid. The stem ran down into it. The other half, a glass of claret in this horrible night, was a large, newly opened rose.

"Thank you," I said, tucking it into my jacket.

"Going back to Tirellian, eh?"

"Yes."

"I saw you come aboard, so I got it ready. Just missed you at the Captain's cabin. He was busy. Hollered out that I could catch you at the barns."

"Thanks aagin."

"It's chemically treated. It will stay in bloom for weeks."

I nodded. I was gone.

Up into the mountains now. Far. Far. The sky was a bucket of ice in which no moons floated. The going became steeper, and the little donkey protested. I whipped him with the throttle and went on. Up. Up. I spotted a green, unwinking star, and felt a lump in my throat. The encased rose beat against my chest like an extra heart. The donkey brayed, long and loudly, then began to cough. I lashed him some more and he died.

I threw the emergency brake on and got out. I began to walk.

So cold, so cold it grows. Up here. At night? Why? Why did she do it? Why flee the campfire when night comes on?

And I was up, down, around, and through every chasm, gorge, and pass, with my long-legged strides and an ease of movement never known on Earth.

Barely two days remain, my love, and thou hast forsaken me. Why?

I crawled under overhangs. I leaped over ridges. I scraped my knees, an elbow. I heard my jacket tear.

No answer, Malann? Do you really hate your people this much? Then I'll try someone else. Vishnu, you're the Preserver. Preserve her, please! Let me find her.

Jehovah?

Adonis? Osiris? Thammuz? Manitou? Legba? Where is she?

I ranged far and high, and slipped.

Stones ground underfoot and I dangled over an edge. My fingers so cold. It was hard to grip the rock.

I looked down.

Twelve feet or so. I let go and dropped, landed rolling. Then I heard her scream.

I lay there, not moving, looking up. Against the night, above, she called.

"Gallinger!"

I lay still.

"Gallinger!"

And she was gone.

I heard stones rattle and knew she was coming down some path to the right of me.

I jumped up and ducked into the shadow of a boulder.

She rounded a cut-off, and picked her way, uncertainly, through the stones.

"Gallinger?"

I stepped out and seized her shoulders.

"Braxa."

She screamed again, then began to cry, crowding against me. It was the first time I had ever heard her cry.

"Why?" I asked. "Why?"

But she only clung to me and sobbed.

Finally, "I thought you had killed yourself."

"Maybe I would have," I said. "Why did you leave Tirellian? And me?"

"Didn't M'Cwyie tell you? Didn't you guess?"

"I didn't guess, and M'Cwyie said she didn't know."

"Then she lied. She knows."

"What? What is it she knows?"

She shook all over, then was silent for a long time. I realized suddenly that she was wearing only her flimsy dancer's costume. I pushed her from me, took off my jacket, and put it about her shoulders.

"Great Malann!" I cried. "You'll freeze to death!"

"No," she said, "I won't.'

I was transferring the rose-case to my pocket.

"What is that?" she asked.

"A rose," I answered. "You can't make it out much in the dark. I once compared you to one. Remember?"

"Ye-Yes. May I carry it?"

"Sure." I stuck it in the jacket pocket.

"Well? I'm still waiting for an explanation."

"You really do not know?" she asked.

"No!"

"When the Rains came," she said, "apparently only our men were affected, which was enough. . . . Because I—wasn't—affected—apparently—"

"Oh," I said. "Oh."

We stood there, and I thought.

"Well, why did you run? What's wrong with being pregnant on Mars? Tamur was mistaken. Your people can live again."

She laughed, again that wild violin played by a Paginini gone mad. I stopped her before it went too far.

"How?" she finally asked, rubbing her cheek.

"Your people live longer than ours. If our child is normal it will mean our races can intermarry. There must still be other fertile women of your race. Why not?"

"You have read the Book of Locar," she said, "and yet you ask me that? Death was decided, voted upon, and passed, shortly after it appeared in this form. But long before, the followers of Locar knew. They decided it long ago. 'We have done all things,' they said, 'we have seen all things, we have heard and felt all things. The dance was good. Now let it end.' "

"You can't believe that."

"What I believe does not matter," she replied. "M'Cwyie

and the Mothers have decided we must die. Their very title is now a mockery, but their decisions will be upheld. There is only one prophecy left, and it is mistaken. We will die."

"No," I said.

"What, then?"

"Come back with me, to Earth."

"No."

"All right, then. Come with me now."

"Where?"

"Back to Tirellian. I'm going to talk to the Mothers."

"You can't! There is a Ceremony tonight!"

I laughed.

"A ceremony for a god who knocks you down, and then kicks you in the teeth?"

"He is still Malann," she answered. "We are still his people."

"You and my father would have gotten along fine," I snarled. "But I am going, and you are coming with me, even if I have to carry you—and I'm bigger than you are."

"But you are not bigger than Ontro."

"Who the hell is Ontro?"

"He will stop you, Gallinger. He is the Fist of Malann."

IV

I scudded the jeepster to a halt in front of the only entrance I knew, M'Cwyie's. Braxa, who had seen the rose in a headlamp, now cradled it in her lap, like our child, and said nothing. There was a passive, lovely look on her face.

"Are they in the Temple now?" I wanted to know.

The Madonna-expression did not change. I repeated the question. She stirred.

"Yes," she said, from a distance, "but you cannot go in."

"We'll see."

I circled and helped her down.

I led her by the hand, and she moved as if in a trance. In the light of the new-risen moon, her eyes looked as they had the day I met her, when she had danced. I snapped my fingers. Nothing happened.

So I pushed the door open and led her in. The room was half-lighted.

And she screamed for the third time that evening:
"Do not harm him, Ontro! It is Gallinger!"

I had never seen a Martian man before, only women.
So I had no way of knowing whether he was a freak,
thought I suspected it strongly.

I looked up at him.

His half-naked body was covered with moles and swell-
ings. Gland trouble, I guessed.

I had thought I was the tallest man on the planet, but
he was seven feet tall and overweight. Now I knew where
my giant bed had come from!

"Go back," he said. "She may enter. You may not."

"I must get my books and things."

He raised a huge left arm. I followed it. All my be-
longings lay neatly stacked in the corner.

"I must go in. I must talk with M'Cwyie and the
Mothers."

"You may not."

"The lives of your people depend on it."

"Go back," he boomed. "Go home to *your* people,
Gallinger. Leave *us!*"

My name sounded so different on his lips, like someone
else's. How old was he? I wondered. Three hundred?
Four? Had he been a Temple guardian all his life? Why?
Who was there to guard against it? I didn't like the way
he moved. I had seen men who moved like that before.

"Go back," he repeated.

If they had refined their martial arts as far as they had
their dances, or, worse yet, if their fighting arts were a
part of the dance, I was in for trouble.

"Go on in," I said to Braxa. "Give the rose to M'Cwyie.
Tell her that I sent it. Tell her I'll be there shortly."

"I will do as you ask. Remember me on Earth, Gallinger.
Good-bye."

I did not answer her, and she walked past Ontro and
into the next room, bearing her rose.

"Now will you leave?" he asked. "If you like, I will
tell her that we fought and you almost beat me, but I
knocked you unconscious and carried you back to your
ship."

"No," I said, "either I go around you or go over
you, but I am going through."

He dropped into a crouch, arms extended.

"It is a sin to lay hands on a holy man," he rumbled, "but I will stop you, Gallinger."

My memory was a fogged window, suddenly exposed to fresh air. Things cleared. I looked back six years.

I was a student of Oriental Languages at the University of Tokyo. It was my twice-weekly night of recreation. I stood in a thirty-foot circle in the Kodokan, the *judogi* lashed about my high hips by a brown belt. I was *Ik-kyu*, one notch below the lowest degree of expert. A brown diamond above my right breast said "Jiu-Jitsu" in Japanese, and it meant *atemiwaza*, really, because of the one striking-technique I had worked out, found unbelievably suitable to my size, and won matches with.

But I had never used it on a man, and it was five years since I had practiced. I was out of shape, I knew, but I tried hard to force my mind *tsuki no kokoro*, like the moon, reflecting the all of Ontro.

Somewhere out of the past, a voice said, "*Hajime,* let it begin."

I snapped into my *neko-ashi-dachi* cat-stance, and his eyes burned strangely. He hurried to correct his own position—and I threw it at him!

My one trick!

My long leg lashed up like a broken spring. Seven feet off the ground my foot connected with his jaw as he tried to leap backward.

His head snapped back and he fell. A soft moan escaped his lips. *That's all there is to it,* I thought. *Sorry, old fellow.*

And as I stepped over him, somehow, groggily, he tripped me, and I fell across his body. I couldn't believe he had strength enough to remain conscious after that blow, let alone move. I hated to punish him any more.

But he found my throat and slipped a forearm across it before I realized there was a purpose to his action.

No! Don't let it end like this!

It was a bar of steel across my windpipe, my carotids. Then I realized that he was still unconscious, and that this was a reflex instilled by countless years of training. I had seen it happen once, in *shiai*. The man had died because he had been choked unconscious and still fought on, and his opponent thought he had not been applying the choke properly. He tried harder.

But it was rare, so very rare!

I jammed my elbows into his ribs and threw my head back in his face. The grip eased, but not enough. I hated to do it, but I reached up and broke his little finger.

The arm went loose and I twisted free.

He lay there panting, face contorted. My heart went out to the fallen giant, defending his people, his religion, following his orders. I cursed myself as I had never cursed before, for walking over him, instead of around.

I staggered across the room to my little heap of possessions. I sat on the projector case and lit a cigarette.

I couldn't go into the Temple until I got my breath back, until I thought of something to say.

How do you talk a race out of killing itself?

Suddenly—

—Could it happen? Would it work that way? If I read them the Book of Ecclesiastes—if I read them a greater piece of literature than any Locar ever wrote—and as somber—and as pessimistic—and showed them that our race had gone on despite one man's condemning all of life in the highest poetry—showed them that the vanity he had mocked had borne us to the Heavens—would they believe it—would they change their minds?

I ground out my cigarette on the beautiful floor, and found my notebook. A strange fury rose within me as I stood.

And I walked into the Temple to preach the Black Gospel according to Gallinger, from the Book of Life.

There was silence all about me.

M'Cwyie had been reading Locar, the rose set at her right hand, target of all eyes.

Until I entered.

Hundreds of people were seated on the floor, barefoot. The few men were as small as the women, I noted.

I had my boots on.

Go all the way, I figured. *You either lose or you win —everything!*

A dozen crones sat in a semicircle behind M'Cwyie. The Mothers.

The barren earth, the dry wombs, the fire-touched.

I moved to the table.

"Dying yourselves, you would condemn your people,"

I addressed them, "that they may not know the life you have known—the joys, the sorrows, the fullness. —But it is not true that you all must die." I addressed the multitude now. "Those who say this lie. Braxa knows, for she will bear a child—"

They sat there, like rows of Buddhas. M'Cwyie drew back into the semicircle.

"—my child!" I continued, wondering what my father would have thought of this sermon.

". . . And all the women young enough may bear children. It is only your men who are sterile. —And if you permit the doctors of the next expedition to examine you, perhaps even the men may be helped. But if they cannot, you can mate with men of Earth.

"And ours is not an insignificant people, an insignificant place," I went on. "Thousands of years ago, the Locar of our world wrote a book saying that it was. He spoke as Locar did, but we did not lie down, despite plagues, wars, and famines. We did not die. One by one we beat down the diseases, we fed the hungry, we fought the wars, and, recently, have gone a long time without them. We may finally have conquered them. I do not know.

"But we have crossed millions of miles of nothingness. We have visited another world. And our Locar had said, 'Why bother? What is the worth of it? It is all vanity, anyhow.'

"And the secret is," I lowered my voice, as at a poetry reading, "he was right! It *is* vanity! it *is* pride! It is the hybris of rationalism to always attack the prophet, the mystic, the god. It is our blasphemy which has made us great, and will sustain us, and which the gods secretly admire in us. —All the truly sacred names of God are blasphemous things to speak!"

I was working up a sweat. I paused dizzily.

"Here is the Book of Ecclesiastes," I announced, and began:

" 'Vanity of vanities, saith the Preacher, vanity of vanities; all is vanity. What profit hath a man . . .' "

I spotted Braxa in the back, mute, rapt.

I wondered what she was thinking.

And I wound the hours of night about me, like black thread on a spool.

Oh it was late! I had spoken till day came, and still I spoke. I finished Ecclesiastes and continued Gallinger.

And when I finished there was still only a silence.

The Buddhas, all in a row, had not stirred through the night. And after a long while M'Cwyie raised her right hand. One by one the Mothers did the same.

And I knew what that meant.

It meant no, do not, cease, and stop.

It meant that I had failed.

I walked slowly from the room and slumped beside my baggage.

Ontro was gone. Good that I had not killed him. . . .

After a thousand years M'Cwyie entered.

She said, "Your job is finished."

I did not move.

"The prophecy is fulfilled," she said. "My people are rejoicing. You have won, holy man. Now leave us quickly."

My mind was a deflated balloon. I pumped a little air back into it.

"I'm not a holy man," I said, "just a second-rate poet with a bad case of hybris."

I lit my last cigarette.

Finally, "All right, what prophecy?"

"The Promise of Locar," she replied, as though the explaining were unnecessary, "that a holy man would come from the Heavens to save us in our last hours, if all the dances of Locar were completed. He would defeat the Fist of Malann and bring us life."

"How?"

"As with Braxa, and as the example in the Temple."

"Example?"

"You read us his words, as great as Locar's. You read to us how there is 'nothing new under the sun.' And you mocked his words as you read them—showing us a new thing.

"There has never been a flower on Mars," she said, "but we will learn to grow them.

"You are the Sacred Scoffer," she finished. "He-Who-Must-Mock-in-the-Temple—you go shod on holy ground."

"But you voted 'no,' " I said.

"I voted not to carry out our original plan, and to let Braxa's child live instead."

"Oh." The cigarette fell from my fingers. How close it had been! How little I had known!

"And Braxa?"

"She was chosen half a Process ago to do the dances—to wait for you."

"But she said that Ontro would stop me."

M'Cwyie stood there for a long time.

"She had never believed the prophecy herself. Things are not well with her now. She ran away, fearing it was true. When you completed it and we voted, she knew."

"Then she does not love me? Never did?"

"I am sorry, Gallinger. It was the one part of her duty she never managed."

"Duty," I said flatly. . . . Dutydutyduty! Tra-la!

"She has said good-bye; she does not wish to see you again.

". . . and we will never forget your teachings," she added.

"Don't," I said, automatically, suddenly knowing the great paradox which lies at the heart of all miracles. I did not believe a word of my own gospel, never had.

I stood, like a drunken man, and muttered "M'narra."

I went outside, into my last day on Mars.

I have conquered thee, Malann—and the victory is thine! Rest easy on thy starry bed. God damned!

I left the jeepster there and walked back to the *Aspic*, leaving the burden of life so many footsteps behind me. I went to my cabin, locked the door, and took forty-four sleeping pills.

But when I awakened I was in the dispensary, and alive.

I felt the throb of engines as I slowly stood up and somehow made it to the port.

Blurred Mars hung like a swollen belly above me, until it dissolved, brimmed over, and streamed down my face.